green stains on page edge 06/12 BG

DATE DUE		
DEC 18 2011		
	MAR 0 2012	
MAR 3 0 2012	DEC 17 2011	
OCT 2 0 2012	JUN 2 9 2012	
FEB 0 2013	FEB 1 7 2013	
MAY 2 1 2013		

The Urbana Free Library

To renew: call 217-367-4057
or go to "*urbanafreelibrary.org*"
and select "Renew/Request Items"

Adventures in Oz

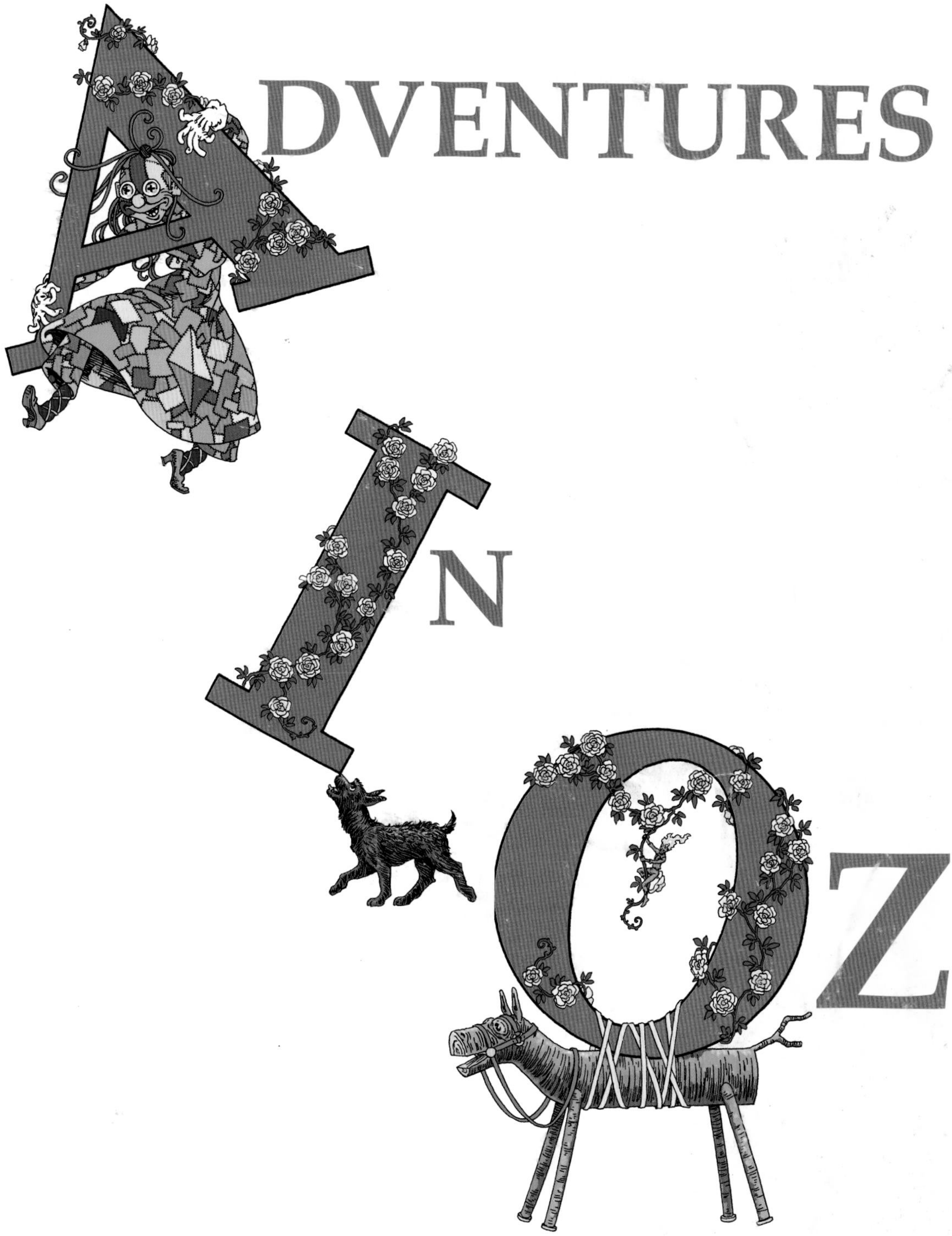

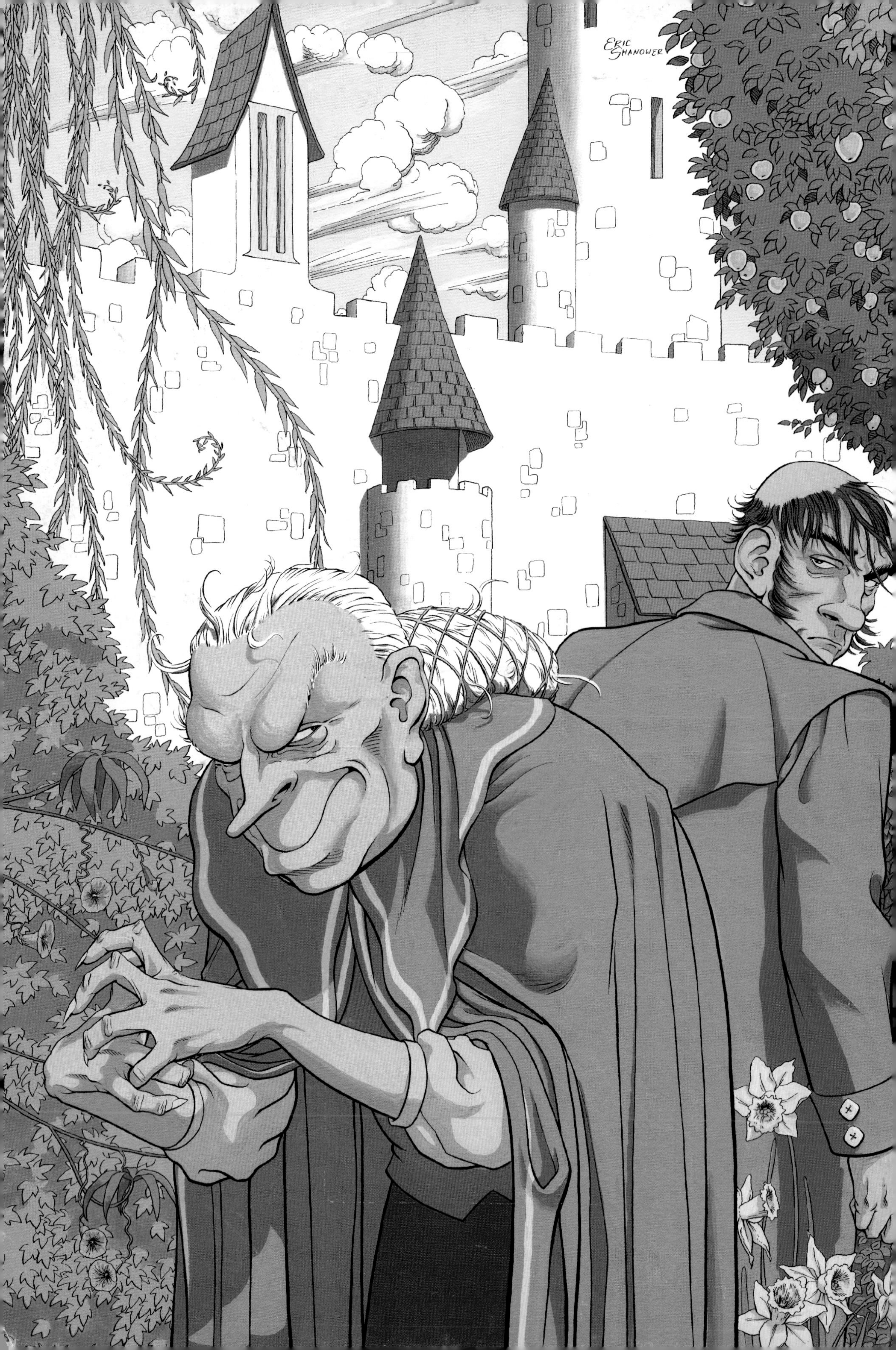
ERIC
SHANOWER

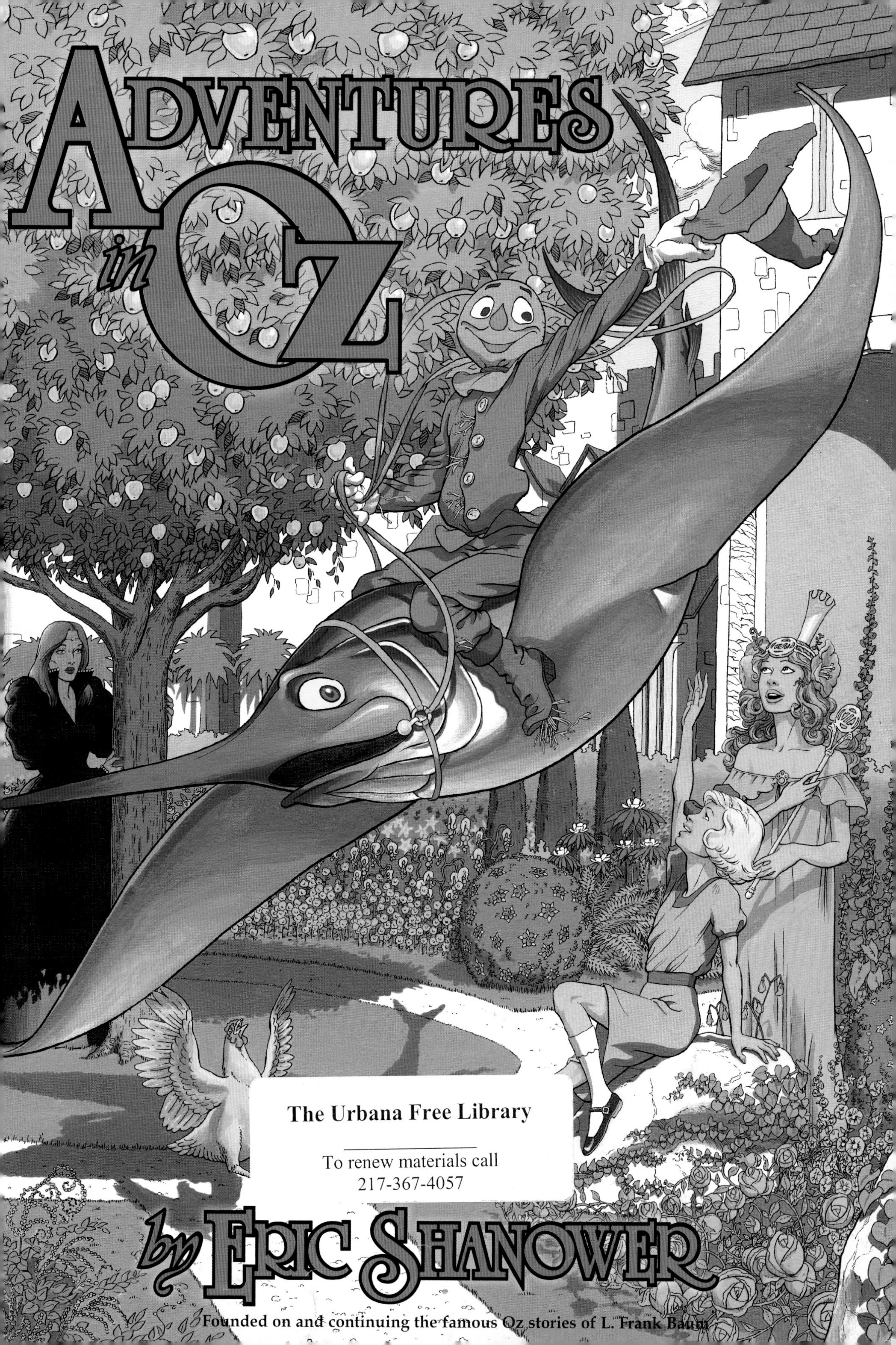
ADVENTURES in OZ
by ERIC SHANOWER
Founded on and continuing the famous Oz stories of L. Frank Baum

Eric Shanower
Writer and Illustrator

John Uhrich
Production Artist

Neil Uyetake
Design Production Director

Rick Oliver
Original editor for *The Enchanted Apples of Oz, The Secret
Island of Oz, The Ice King of Oz,* and *The Forgotten Forest of Oz*

Byron Erickson and Anina Bennett
Original editors for *The Blue Witch of Oz*

Willie Schubert
Calligrapher for *The Secret Island of Oz*

Tom McCraw
Painting Assistant for *The Secret Island of Oz*

www.IDWPUBLISHING.com

Published by:
IDW Publishing
4411 Morena Blvd., Suite 106
San Diego, CA 92117

ISBN: 978-1-60010-003-1

10 09 08 07   6 5 4 3 2

IDW Publishing is:
Ted Adams, Co-President • Robbie Robbins, Co-President
Chris Ryall, Publisher/Editor-in-Chief • Kris Oprisko, Vice President
Alan Payne, Vice President of Sales • Neil Uyetake, Art Director
Dan Taylor, Editor • Justin Eisinger, Editorial Assistant
Chris Mowry, Graphic Artist • Matthew Ruzicka, CPA, Controller
Alonzo Simon, Shipping Manager • Alex Garner, Creative Director
Yumiko Miyano, Business Development • Rick Privman, Business Development

TABLE OF CONTENTS

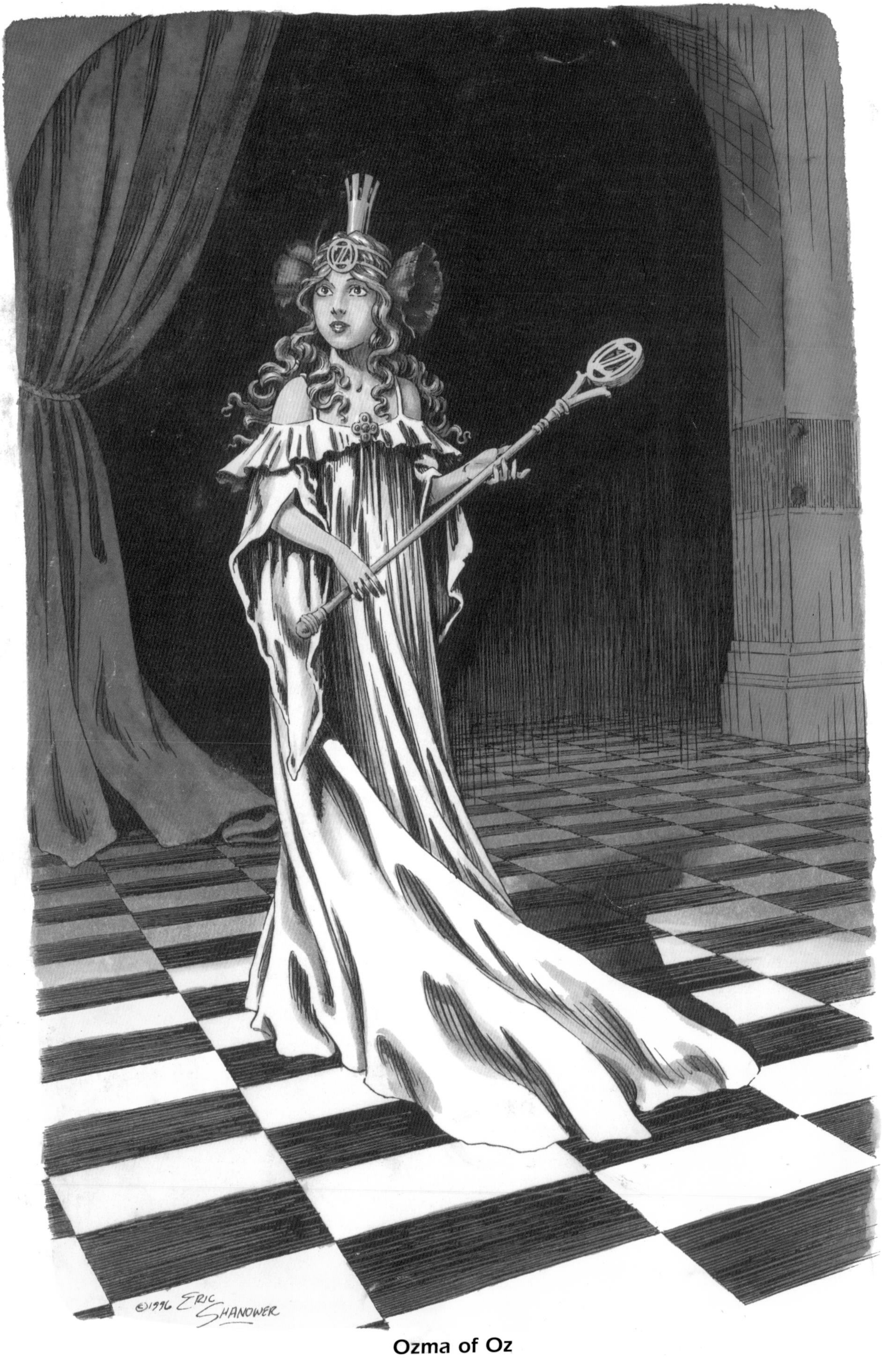
©1996 ERIC SHANOWER

Ozma of Oz

Just a Word Before You Start

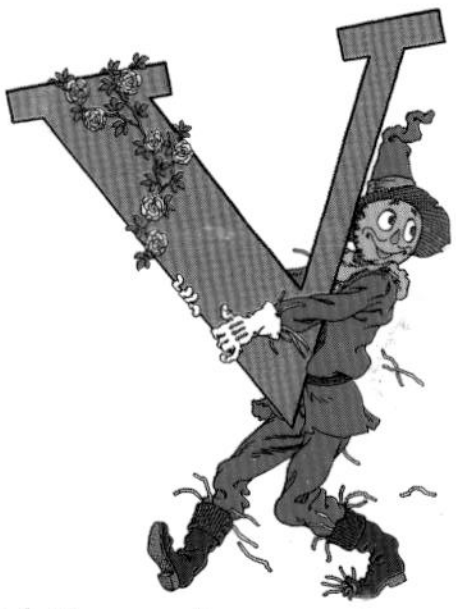

VISIT THE MARVELOUS LAND OF OZ! You don't need a cyclone or an earthquake or a whirlpool to reach Oz. Just turn a few pages and you're there.

First, however, you might like to know a few things about the place you'll be visiting. A lot has happened in the Land of Oz since that day years ago when Dorothy Gale first arrived.

Long, long ago, the fairy queen Lurline and her band were flying over Oz. They were so charmed by the lovely country that they decided to enchant it. They turned it into a magical place where no one ever gets sick, people only grow older if they choose to, and no one ever dies. To protect Oz from the rest of the world, Lurline surrounded it with a desert. One touch of the desert's sands turns flesh to dust, so Oz sometimes isn't an easy place to reach.

One day, a man riding in a large balloon sailed down from the clouds above Oz. The people hailed him as a great Wizard and made him their ruler. The Wizard had them build the Emerald City for his capital in the center of the country. From there, he ruled in seclusion until Dorothy Gale exposed him as a simple circus performer from Nebraska.

The rightful ruler of Oz was actually a girl named Ozma. She was descended from a long line of fairy rulers that the fairy queen Lurline appointed to rule Oz. A witch imprisoned Ozma under an enchantment for many years. At last the enchantment was broken, and today, Ozma rules the Land of Oz with sweetness and charm.

Oz is divided into four major countries: the Munchkin Country lies in the east where the favorite color is blue; the Winkie Country lies in the west where the favorite color is yellow; the Quadling Country lies in the south where the favorite color is red; the Gillikin Country lies in the north where the favorite color is purple; and in the center of Oz lies the Emerald City, where the favorite color is green.

Turn the page and you'll see a map of Oz. Notice that the compass directions are different from ours here in the Great Outside World. Oz is a magical place full of mystery and the strange case of Oz's compass directions is merely another of those mysteries.

Each of the four countries of Oz has its own ruler. Nick Chopper is a man made all out of tin who used to be a simple woodman, but now he's the Emperor of the Winkies in the west. In the south, the Quadlings are ruled by one of the most powerful sorceresses ever known, Glinda the Good. The Munchkins and Gillikins have their ruling families as well, but all are subject to the supreme ruler of Oz, Ozma, who lives in a beautiful, emerald-studded marble palace in the Emerald City.

Ozma has gathered many friends and advisors to help her rule her marvelous country. Among them are:

- Dorothy Gale from Kansas, who is Ozma's best friend—Ozma made Dorothy a princess of Oz, but Dorothy is too normal and everyday to let such an exalted title make her conceited
- A living Scarecrow whose brains supplied by the Wizard have made him the most popular man in Oz
- The wonderful Wizard of Oz, who has learned to perform real magic
- The Cowardly Lion and the Hungry Tiger, who are Ozma's bodyguards
- The Soldier with the Green Whiskers, Oz's sole army—he keeps his gun unloaded so that he's in no danger of hurting anyone

You'll meet many other delightful and amusing personalities in this book too. So what are you waiting for? Let's go to Oz!

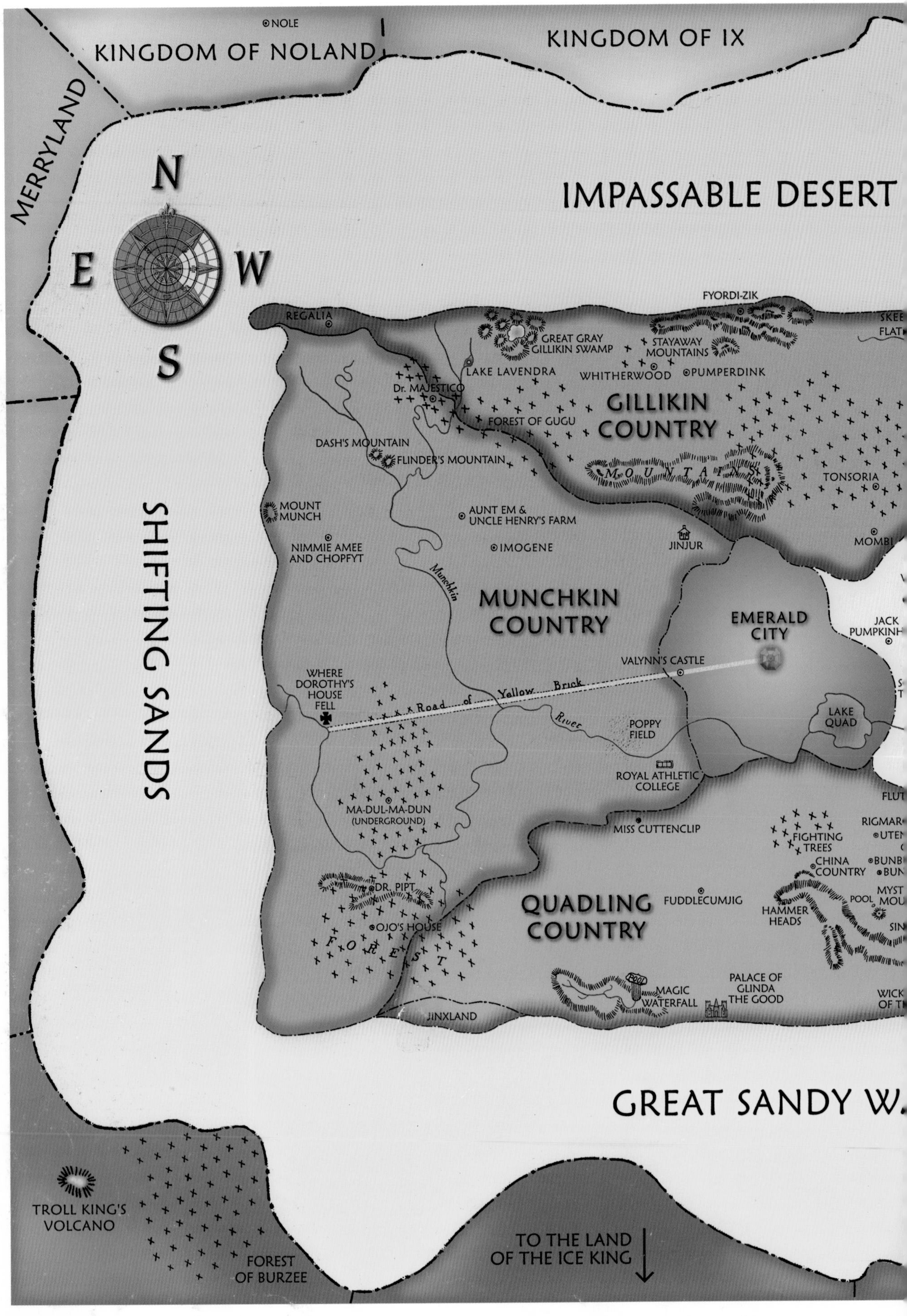

NOLE
KINGDOM OF NOLAND
KINGDOM OF IX
MERRYLAND
IMPASSABLE DESERT
N
E
W
S
SHIFTING SANDS
FYORDI-ZIK
REGALIA
GREAT GRAY GILLIKIN SWAMP
STAYAWAY MOUNTAINS
LAKE LAVENDRA
WHITHERWOOD
PUMPERDINK
Dr. MAJESTICO
GILLIKIN COUNTRY
FOREST OF GUGU
DASH'S MOUNTAIN
FLINDER'S MOUNTAIN
MOUNTAINS
TONSORIA
MOUNT MUNCH
AUNT EM & UNCLE HENRY'S FARM
IMOGENE
JINJUR
NIMMIE AMEE AND CHOPFYT
Munchkin
MUNCHKIN COUNTRY
EMERALD CITY
VALYNN'S CASTLE
WHERE DOROTHY'S HOUSE FELL
Road of Yellow Brick
River
POPPY FIELD
LAKE QUAD
ROYAL ATHLETIC COLLEGE
MA-DUL-MA-DUN (UNDERGROUND)
MISS CUTTENCLIP
FIGHTING TREES
CHINA COUNTRY
DR. PIPT
QUADLING COUNTRY
FUDDLECUMJIG
HAMMER HEADS
POOL
OJO'S HOUSE
FOREST
POOL
MAGIC WATERFALL
PALACE OF GLINDA THE GOOD
JINXLAND
TROLL KING'S VOLCANO
FOREST OF BURZEE
TO THE LAND OF THE ICE KING

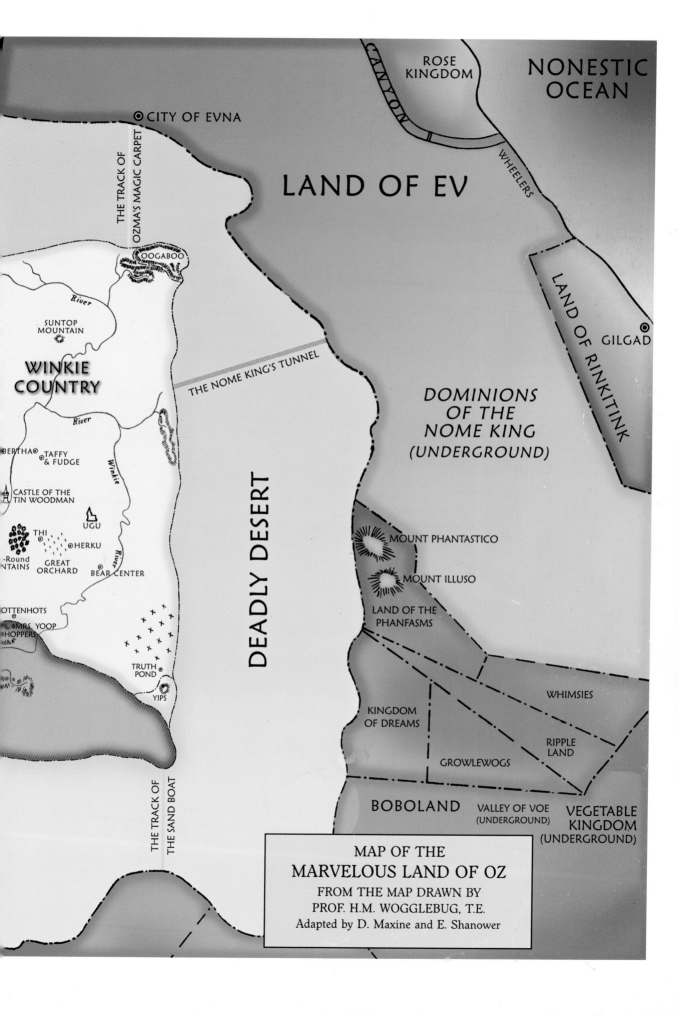

ROSE KINGDOM

NONESTIC OCEAN

CANYON

WHEELERS

LAND OF EV

◎ CITY OF EVNA

THE TRACK OF OZMA'S MAGIC CARPET

OOGABOO

River

SUNTOP MOUNTAIN

WINKIE COUNTRY

LAND OF RINKITINK

GILGAD ◎

THE NOME KING'S TUNNEL

DOMINIONS OF THE NOME KING (UNDERGROUND)

River

BERTHA ◎ ◎ TAFFY & FUDGE

CASTLE OF THE TIN WOODMAN

Winkie

UGU

THI ◎

◎ HERKU

-Round NTAINS

GREAT ORCHARD

BEAR CENTER

River

MOUNT PHANTASTICO

MOUNT ILLUSO

LAND OF THE PHANFASMS

DEADLY DESERT

OTTENHOTS

◎ MRS. YOOP

HOPPERS

WHIMSIES

TRUTH POND ◎

KINGDOM OF DREAMS

RIPPLE LAND

YIPS

GROWLEWOGS

THE TRACK OF THE SAND BOAT

BOBOLAND

VALLEY OF VOE (UNDERGROUND)

VEGETABLE KINGDOM (UNDERGROUND)

MAP OF THE
MARVELOUS LAND OF OZ
FROM THE MAP DRAWN BY
PROF. H.M. WOGGLEBUG, T.E.
Adapted by D. Maxine and E. Shanower

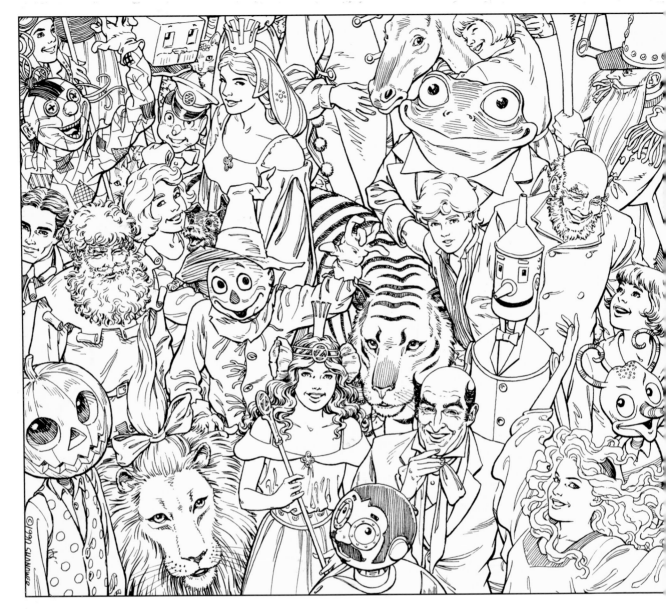

ACKNOWLEDGEMENTS

I'd like to thank all the people associated with the original printings of the Oz graphic novels: tho: at First Comics and Dark Horse Comics, particularly my editors Rick Oliver, Byron Erickson, and Anir Bennett; First Comics publisher Rick Obadiah; and my agent at the time, Mike Friedrich.

I'd like to thank Jay Geldhof, Dan Seitler, those of my instructors at the Joe Kubert School of Cartoc and Graphic Art, particularly Joe Kubert, who contributed to my original Oz comic book propos: Glenn Ingersoll for comments on my plot for *The Enchanted Apples of Oz*, Karen Shanower for her vit last-minute assistance with *Enchanted Apples*, Willie Schubert for lettering *The Secret Island of Oz*, and I Brubaker and David Maxine for comments on *The Forgotten Forest of Oz*.

In particular, I thank Tom McCraw for help during *Secret Island*, not only for his assistance wi painting, but for it all.

I'd like to thank everyone associated with this new edition as well: Ed Brubaker again for helpir IDW and me to get together; everyone at IDW, particularly Ted Adams, Chris Ryall, Robbie Robbins, ar Neil Uyetake; and both Tom McCraw and David Maxine again for loaning artwork for reproduction.

I extend my greatest appreciation to John Uhrich for his attention to detail and painstaking effor to make the present volume the definitive printing of my Oz graphic novels.

The Enchanted Apples of Oz

To Margaret and Chris
for enchantment created.

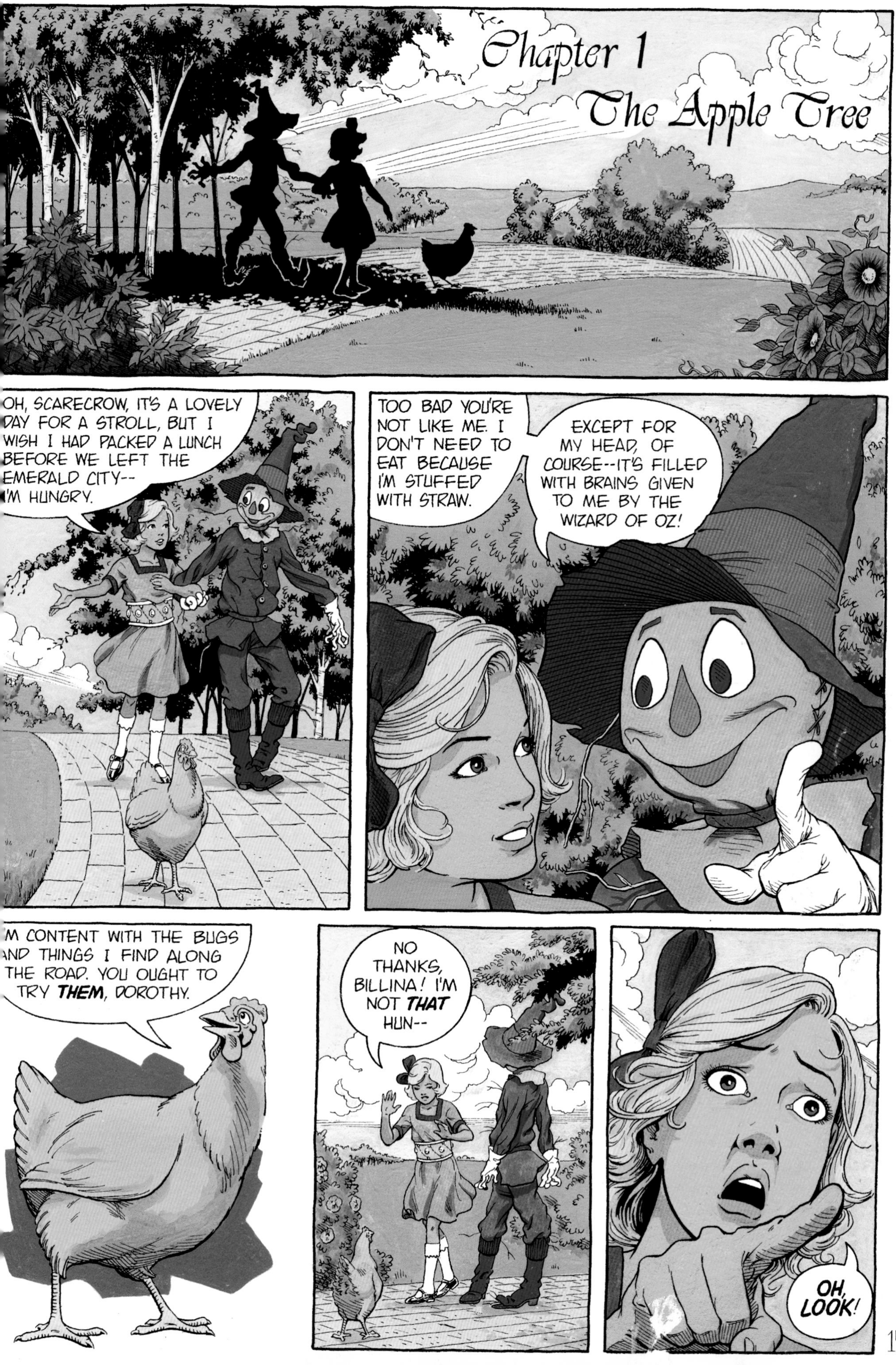
Chapter 1
The Apple Tree
OH, SCARECROW, IT'S A LOVELY DAY FOR A STROLL, BUT I WISH I HAD PACKED A LUNCH BEFORE WE LEFT THE EMERALD CITY-- I'M HUNGRY.
TOO BAD YOU'RE NOT LIKE ME. I DON'T NEED TO EAT BECAUSE I'M STUFFED WITH STRAW.
EXCEPT FOR MY HEAD, OF COURSE--IT'S FILLED WITH BRAINS GIVEN TO ME BY THE WIZARD OF OZ!
I'M CONTENT WITH THE BUGS AND THINGS I FIND ALONG THE ROAD. YOU OUGHT TO TRY **THEM**, DOROTHY.
NO THANKS, BILLINA! I'M NOT **THAT** HUN--
OH, LOOK!

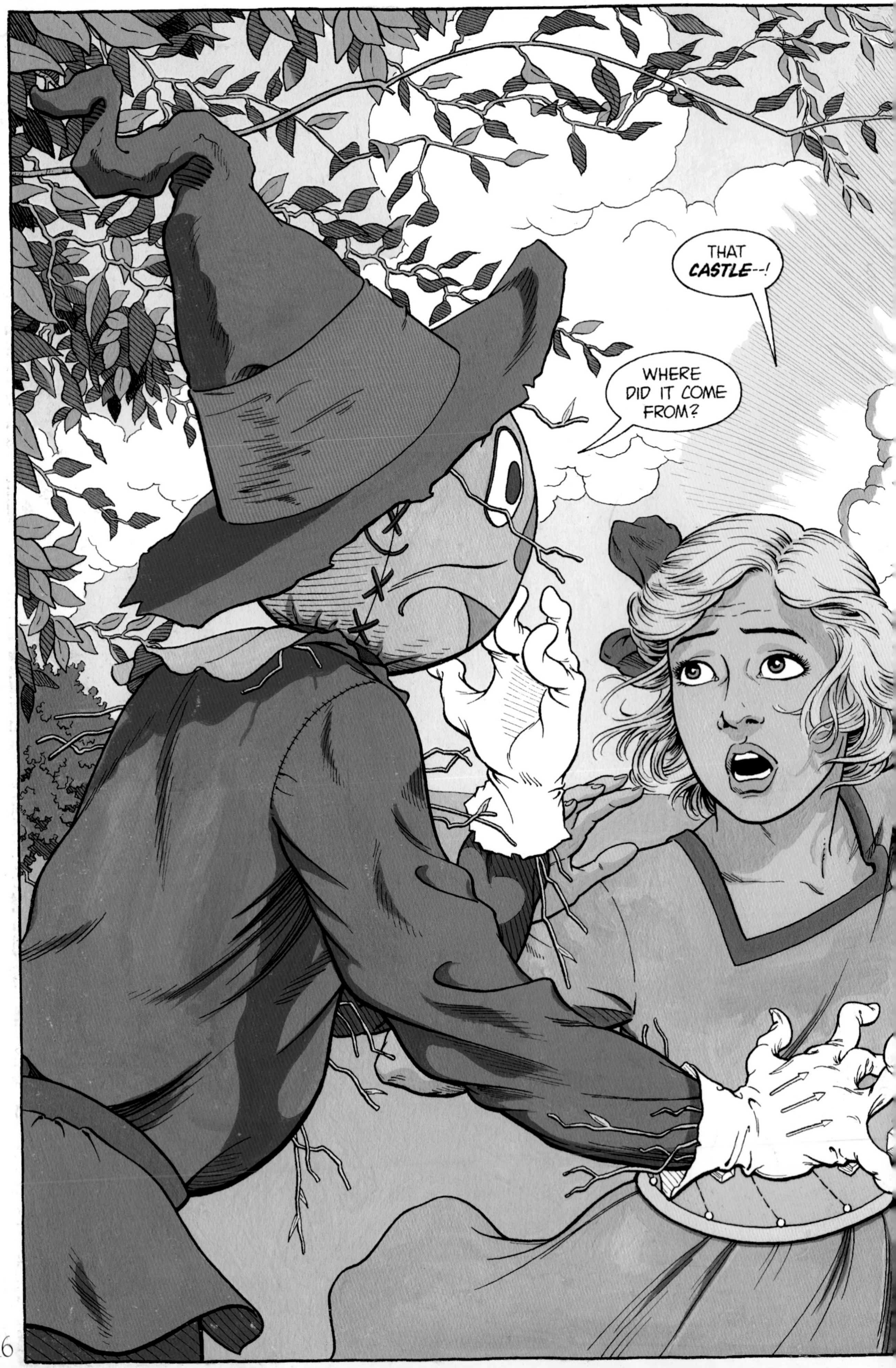
THAT CASTLE--!
WHERE DID IT COME FROM?

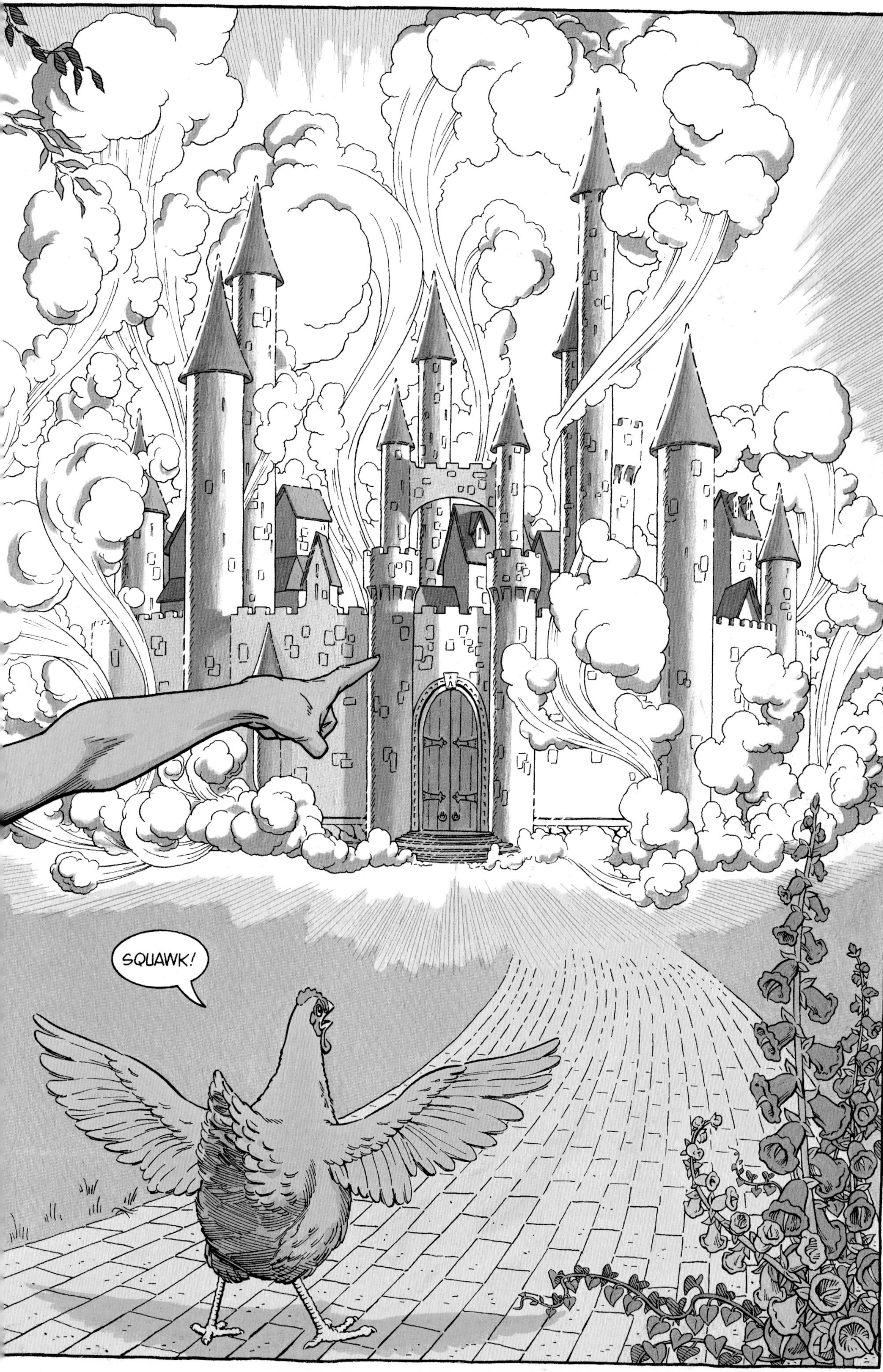
SQUAWK!

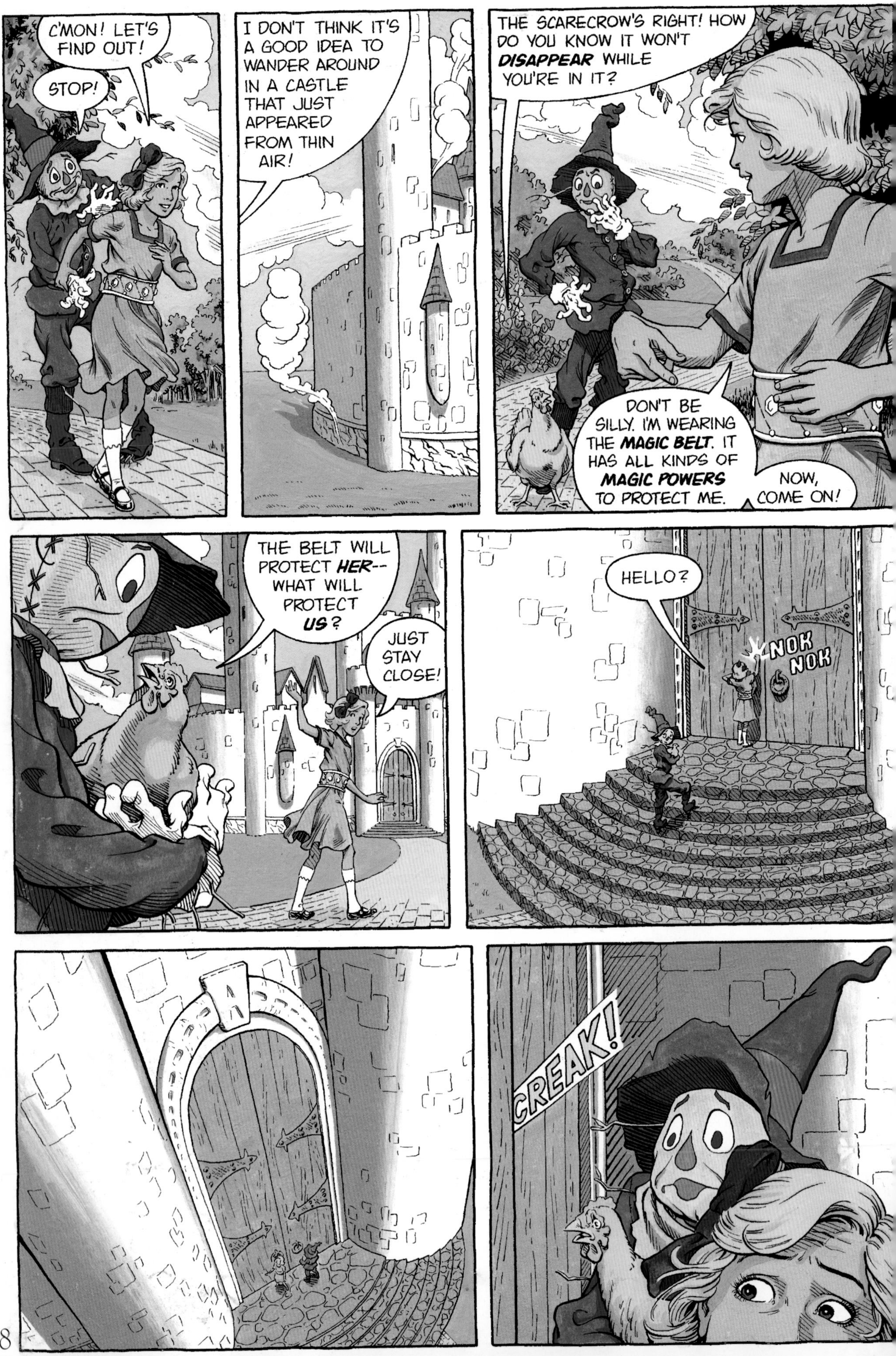
C'MON! LET'S FIND OUT!
STOP!
I DON'T THINK IT'S A GOOD IDEA TO WANDER AROUND IN A CASTLE THAT JUST APPEARED FROM THIN AIR!
THE SCARECROW'S RIGHT! HOW DO YOU KNOW IT WON'T DISAPPEAR WHILE YOU'RE IN IT?
DON'T BE SILLY. I'M WEARING THE MAGIC BELT. IT HAS ALL KINDS OF MAGIC POWERS TO PROTECT ME.
NOW, COME ON!
THE BELT WILL PROTECT HER--WHAT WILL PROTECT US?
JUST STAY CLOSE!
HELLO?
NOK NOK
CREAK!

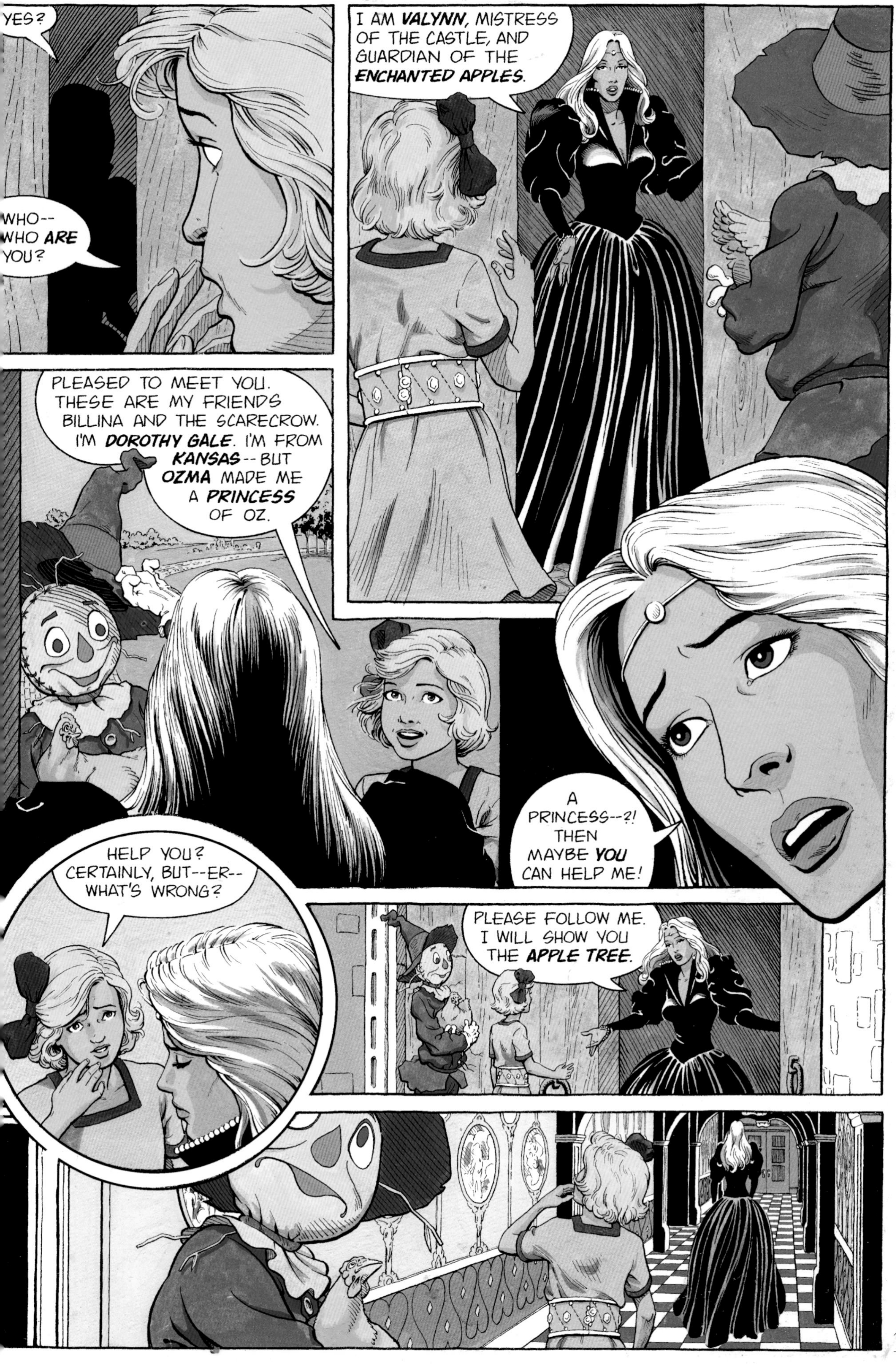
YES?
WHO-- WHO **ARE** YOU?
I AM **VALYNN**, MISTRESS OF THE CASTLE, AND GUARDIAN OF THE **ENCHANTED APPLES**.
PLEASED TO MEET YOU. THESE ARE MY FRIENDS BILLINA AND THE SCARECROW. I'M **DOROTHY GALE**. I'M FROM **KANSAS**--BUT **OZMA** MADE ME A **PRINCESS** OF OZ.
A PRINCESS--?! THEN MAYBE **YOU** CAN HELP ME!
HELP YOU? CERTAINLY, BUT--ER-- WHAT'S WRONG?
PLEASE FOLLOW ME. I WILL SHOW YOU THE **APPLE TREE**.

THIS IS THE ENCHANTED APPLE TREE. IT IS MY DUTY TO **GUARD** THE TREE AND PREVENT ANYONE FROM **PICKING** THE APPLES.

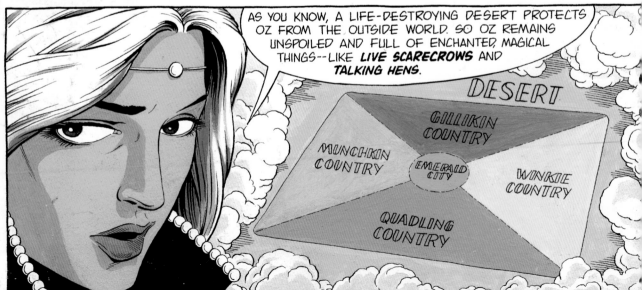

AS YOU KNOW, A LIFE-DESTROYING DESERT PROTECTS OZ FROM THE OUTSIDE WORLD. SO OZ REMAINS UNSPOILED AND FULL OF ENCHANTED, MAGICAL THINGS--LIKE **LIVE SCARECROWS** AND **TALKING HENS**.

DESERT

GILLIKIN COUNTRY

MUNCHKIN COUNTRY

EMERALD CITY

WINKIE COUNTRY

QUADLING COUNTRY

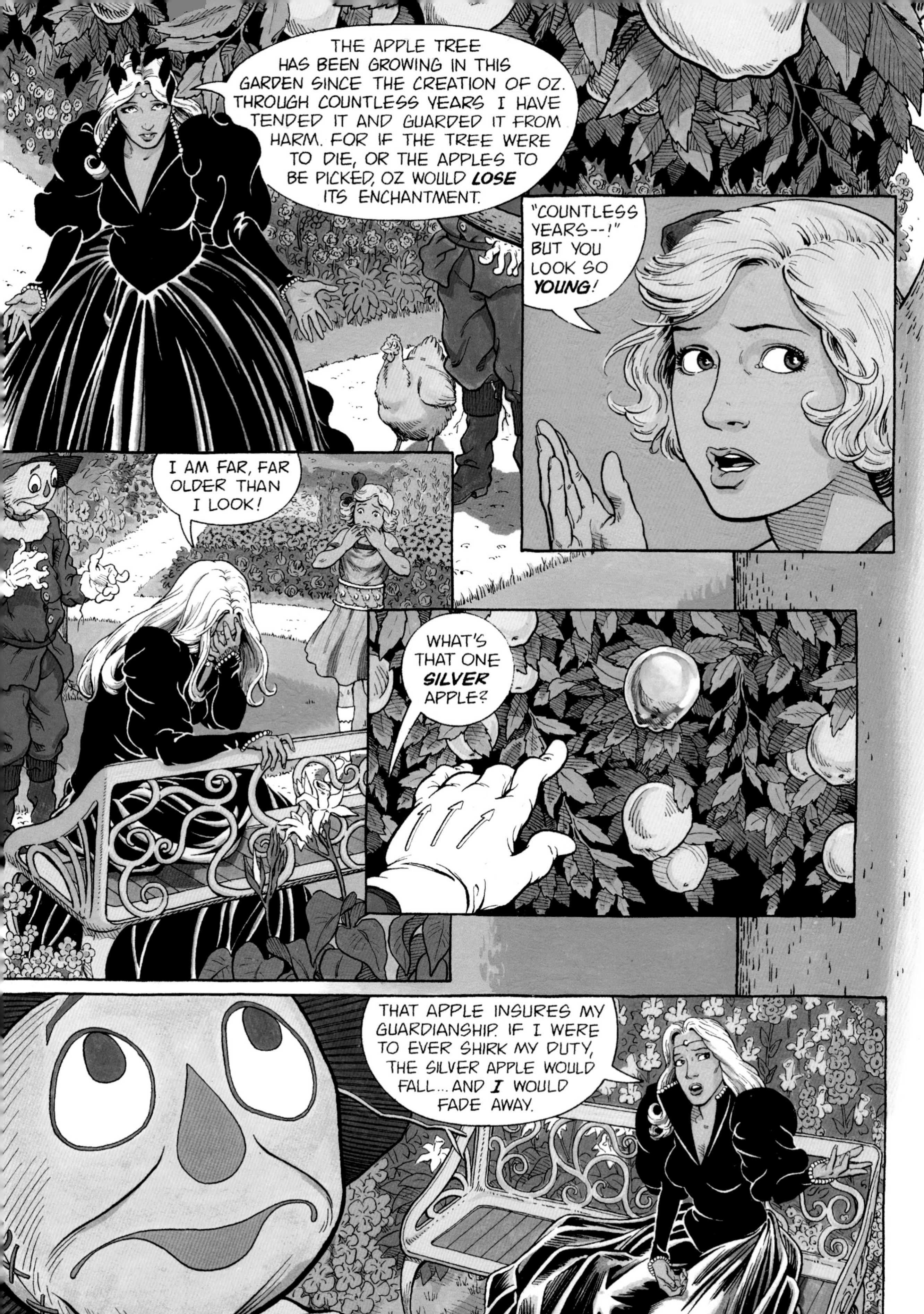
THE APPLE TREE HAS BEEN GROWING IN THIS GARDEN SINCE THE CREATION OF OZ. THROUGH COUNTLESS YEARS I HAVE TENDED IT AND GUARDED IT FROM HARM. FOR IF THE TREE WERE TO DIE, OR THE APPLES TO BE PICKED, OZ WOULD LOSE ITS ENCHANTMENT.
"COUNTLESS YEARS--!" BUT YOU LOOK SO YOUNG!
I AM FAR, FAR OLDER THAN I LOOK!
WHAT'S THAT ONE SILVER APPLE?
THAT APPLE INSURES MY GUARDIANSHIP. IF I WERE TO EVER SHIRK MY DUTY, THE SILVER APPLE WOULD FALL... AND I WOULD FADE AWAY.

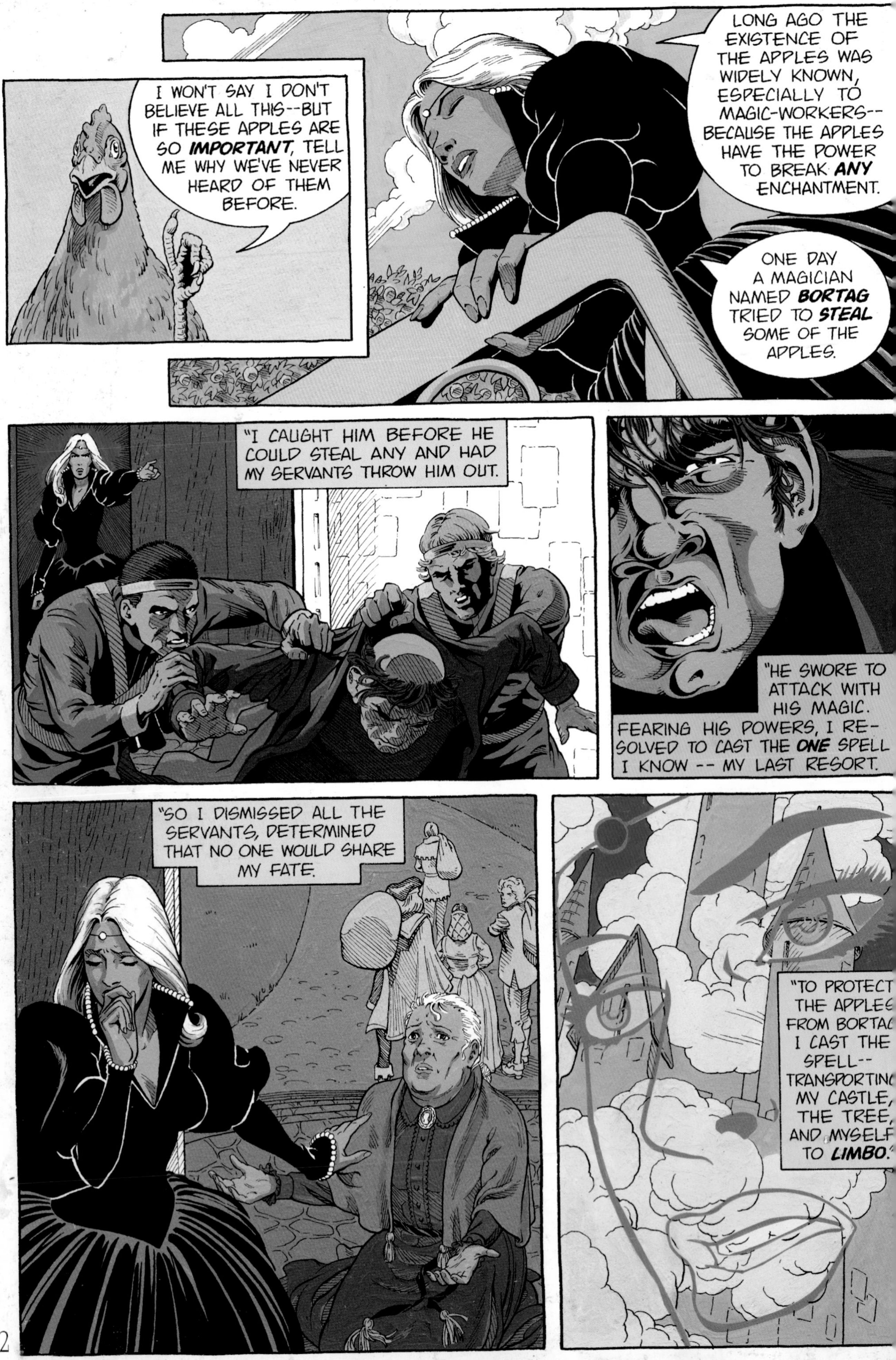
I WON'T SAY I DON'T BELIEVE ALL THIS--BUT IF THESE APPLES ARE SO **IMPORTANT**, TELL ME WHY WE'VE NEVER HEARD OF THEM BEFORE.
LONG AGO THE EXISTENCE OF THE APPLES WAS WIDELY KNOWN, ESPECIALLY TO MAGIC-WORKERS--BECAUSE THE APPLES HAVE THE POWER TO BREAK **ANY** ENCHANTMENT.
ONE DAY A MAGICIAN NAMED **BORTAG** TRIED TO **STEAL** SOME OF THE APPLES.
"I CAUGHT HIM BEFORE HE COULD STEAL ANY AND HAD MY SERVANTS THROW HIM OUT.
"HE SWORE TO ATTACK WITH HIS MAGIC. FEARING HIS POWERS, I RESOLVED TO CAST THE **ONE** SPELL I KNOW -- MY LAST RESORT.
"SO I DISMISSED ALL THE SERVANTS, DETERMINED THAT NO ONE WOULD SHARE MY FATE.
"TO PROTECT THE APPLES FROM BORTAG I CAST THE SPELL-- TRANSPORTING MY CASTLE, THE TREE, AND MYSELF TO **LIMBO**."

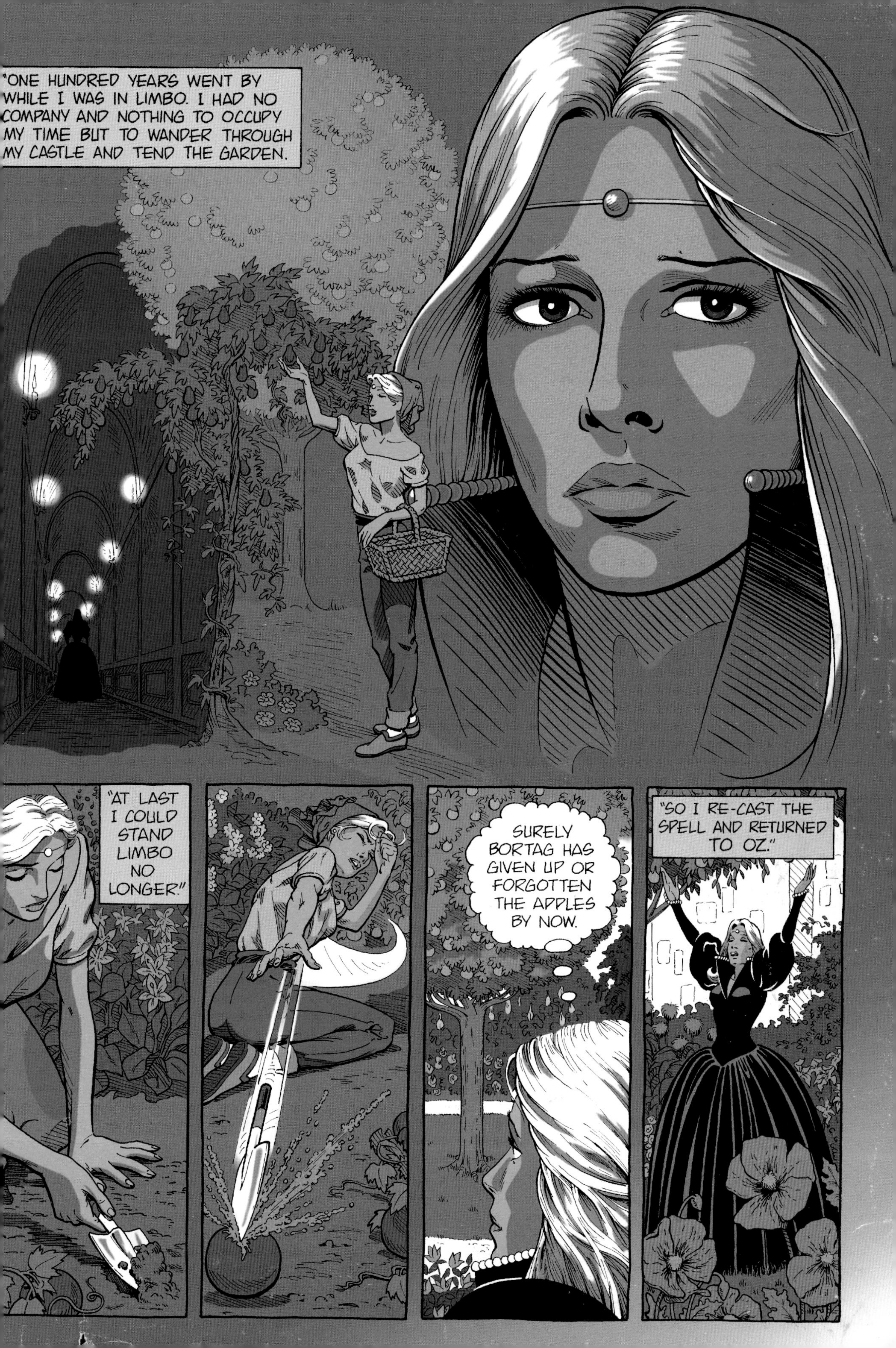
"ONE HUNDRED YEARS WENT BY WHILE I WAS IN LIMBO. I HAD NO COMPANY AND NOTHING TO OCCUPY MY TIME BUT TO WANDER THROUGH MY CASTLE AND TEND THE GARDEN.
"AT LAST I COULD STAND LIMBO NO LONGER."
SURELY BORTAG HAS GIVEN UP OR FORGOTTEN THE APPLES BY NOW.
"SO I RE-CAST THE SPELL AND RETURNED TO OZ."

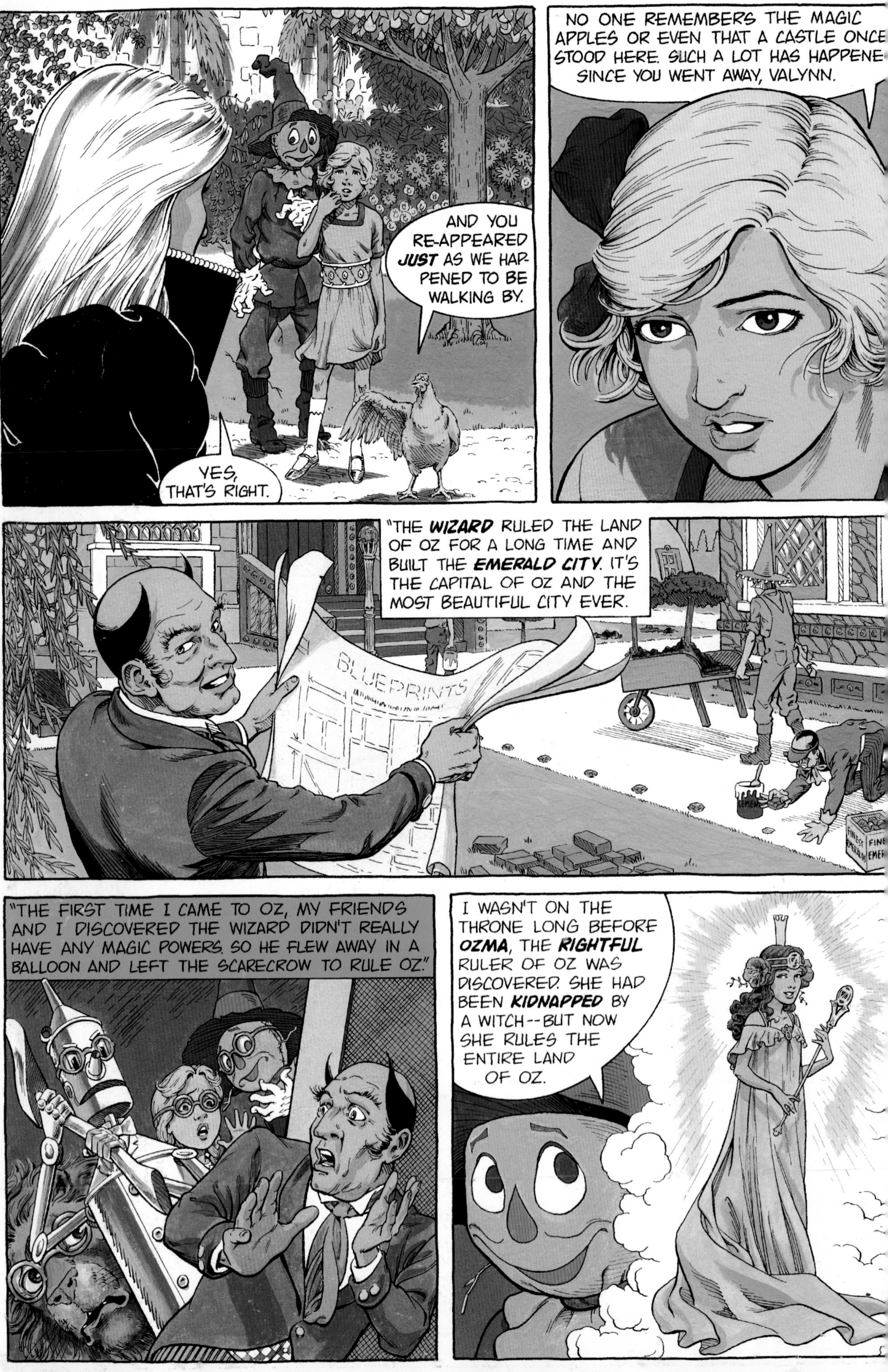
AND YOU RE-APPEARED JUST AS WE HAPPENED TO BE WALKING BY.
YES, THAT'S RIGHT.
NO ONE REMEMBERS THE MAGIC APPLES OR EVEN THAT A CASTLE ONCE STOOD HERE. SUCH A LOT HAS HAPPENE SINCE YOU WENT AWAY, VALYNN.
"THE WIZARD RULED THE LAND OF OZ FOR A LONG TIME AND BUILT THE EMERALD CITY. IT'S THE CAPITAL OF OZ AND THE MOST BEAUTIFUL CITY EVER.
BLUEPRINTS
"THE FIRST TIME I CAME TO OZ, MY FRIENDS AND I DISCOVERED THE WIZARD DIDN'T REALLY HAVE ANY MAGIC POWERS. SO HE FLEW AWAY IN A BALLOON AND LEFT THE SCARECROW TO RULE OZ."
I WASN'T ON THE THRONE LONG BEFORE OZMA, THE RIGHTFUL RULER OF OZ WAS DISCOVERED. SHE HAD BEEN KIDNAPPED BY A WITCH--BUT NOW SHE RULES THE ENTIRE LAND OF OZ.

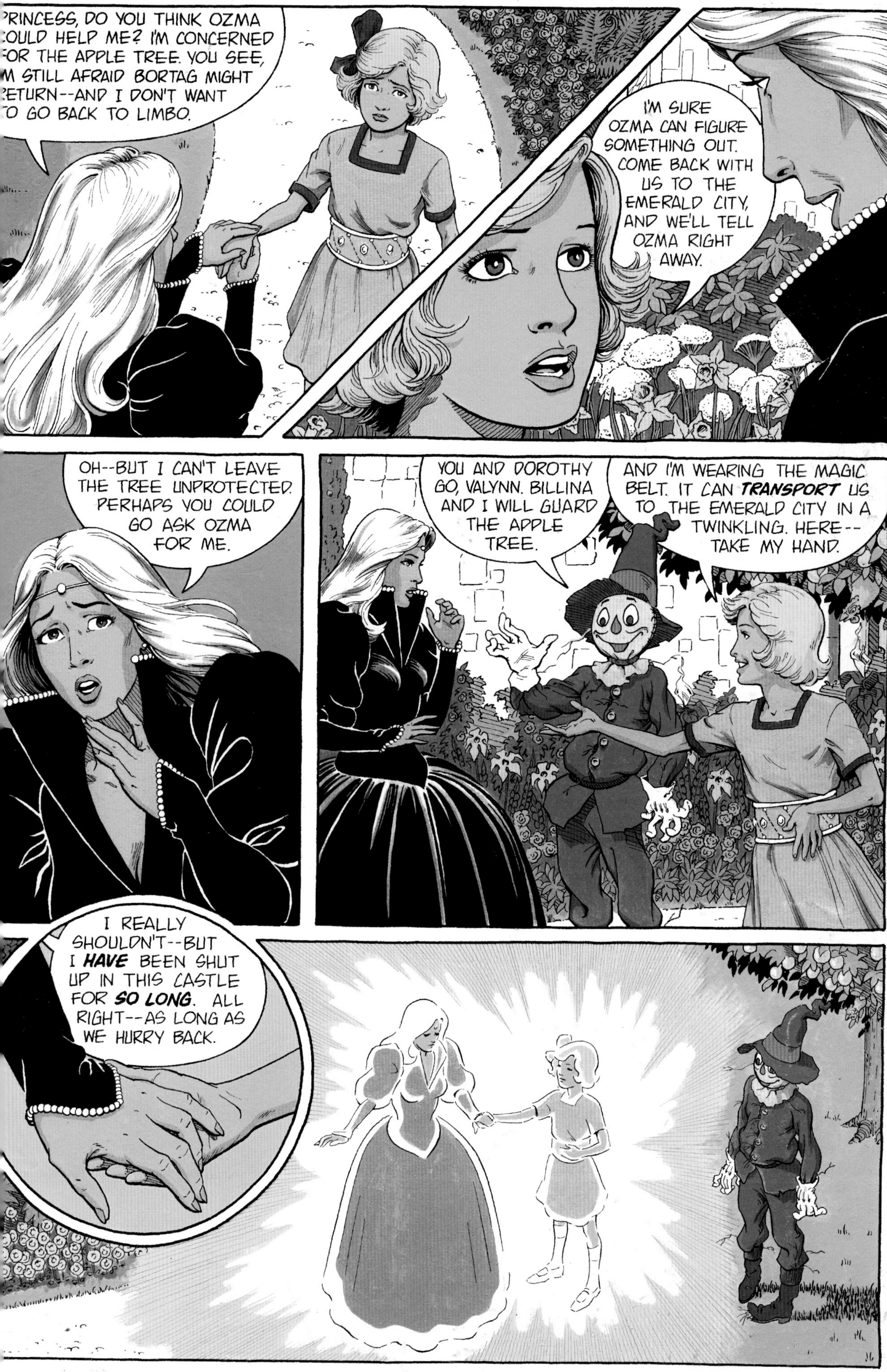
PRINCESS, DO YOU THINK OZMA COULD HELP ME? I'M CONCERNED FOR THE APPLE TREE. YOU SEE, I'M STILL AFRAID BORTAG MIGHT RETURN--AND I DON'T WANT TO GO BACK TO LIMBO.
I'M SURE OZMA CAN FIGURE SOMETHING OUT. COME BACK WITH US TO THE EMERALD CITY, AND WE'LL TELL OZMA RIGHT AWAY.
OH--BUT I CAN'T LEAVE THE TREE UNPROTECTED. PERHAPS YOU COULD GO ASK OZMA FOR ME.
YOU AND DOROTHY GO, VALYNN. BILLINA AND I WILL GUARD THE APPLE TREE.
AND I'M WEARING THE MAGIC BELT. IT CAN TRANSPORT US TO THE EMERALD CITY IN A TWINKLING. HERE--TAKE MY HAND.
I REALLY SHOULDN'T--BUT I HAVE BEEN SHUT UP IN THIS CASTLE FOR SO LONG. ALL RIGHT--AS LONG AS WE HURRY BACK.

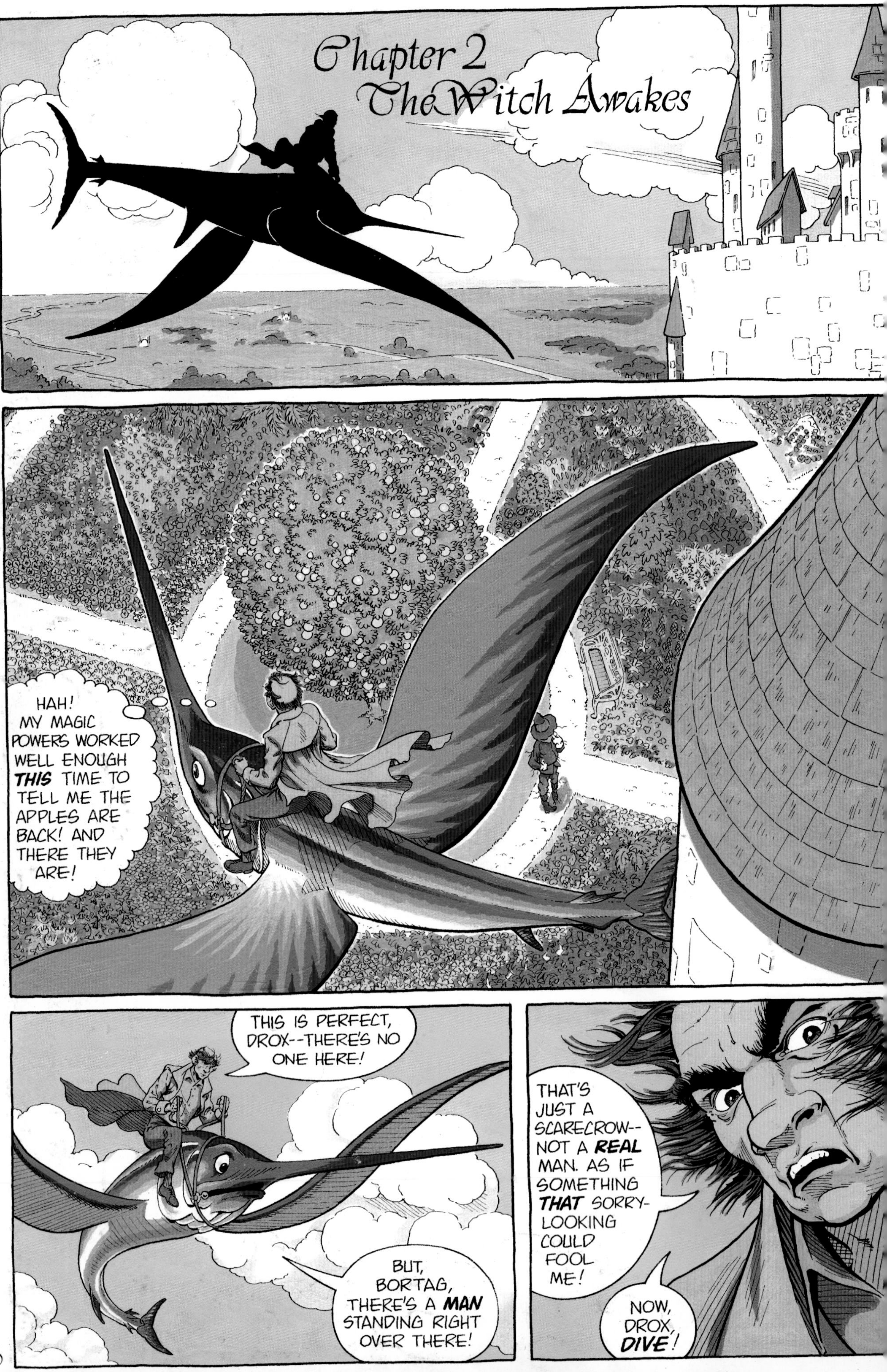
Chapter 2
The Witch Awakes
HAH! MY MAGIC POWERS WORKED WELL ENOUGH THIS TIME TO TELL ME THE APPLES ARE BACK! AND THERE THEY ARE!
THIS IS PERFECT, DROX--THERE'S NO ONE HERE!
BUT, BORTAG, THERE'S A MAN STANDING RIGHT OVER THERE!
THAT'S JUST A SCARECROW--NOT A REAL MAN. AS IF SOMETHING THAT SORRY-LOOKING COULD FOOL ME!
NOW, DROX, DIVE!

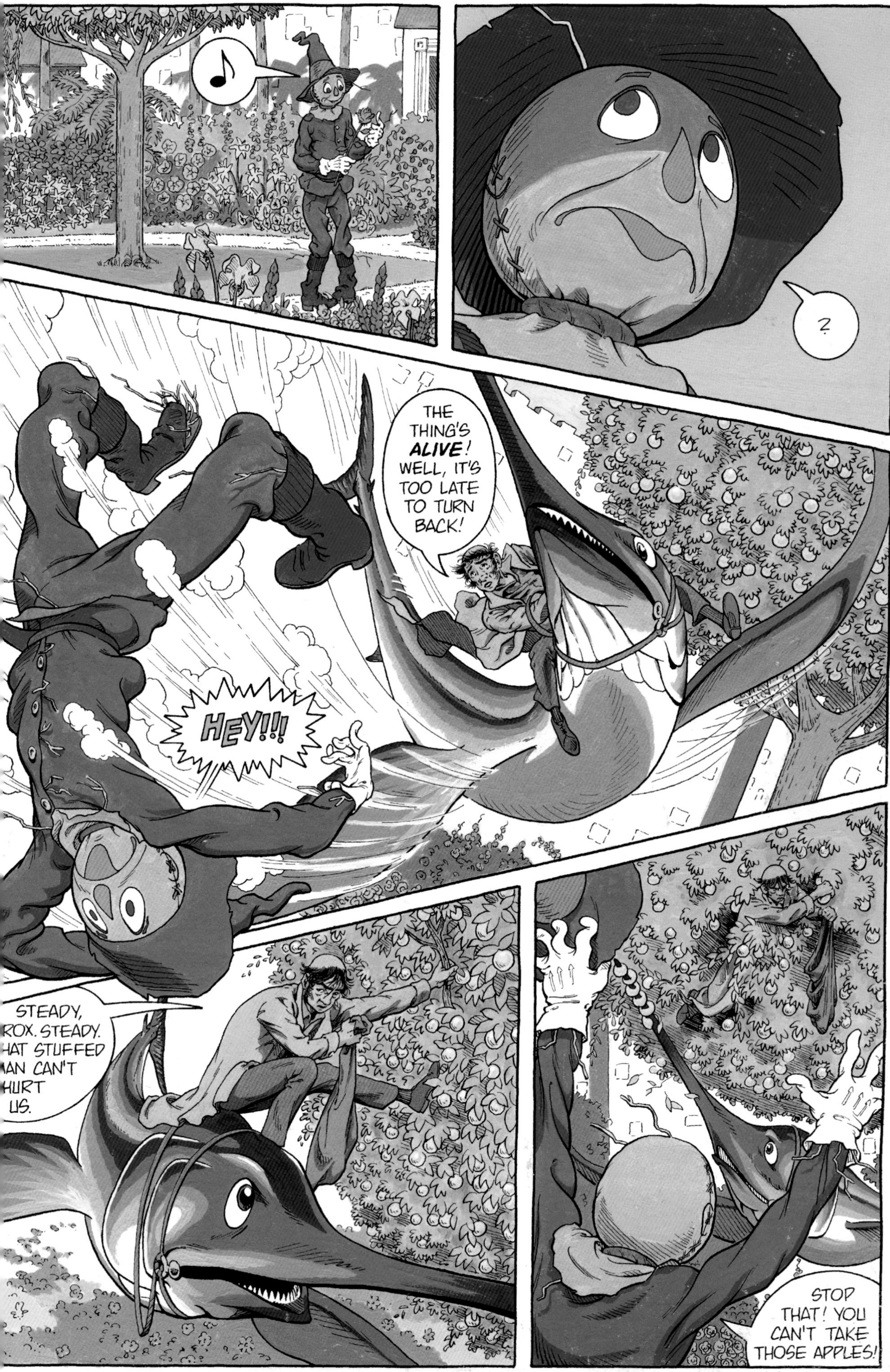
♪
?
THE THING'S **ALIVE**! WELL, IT'S TOO LATE TO TURN BACK!
HEY!!!
STEADY, ROX. STEADY. HAT STUFFED AN CAN'T URT US.
STOP THAT! YOU CAN'T TAKE THOSE APPLES!

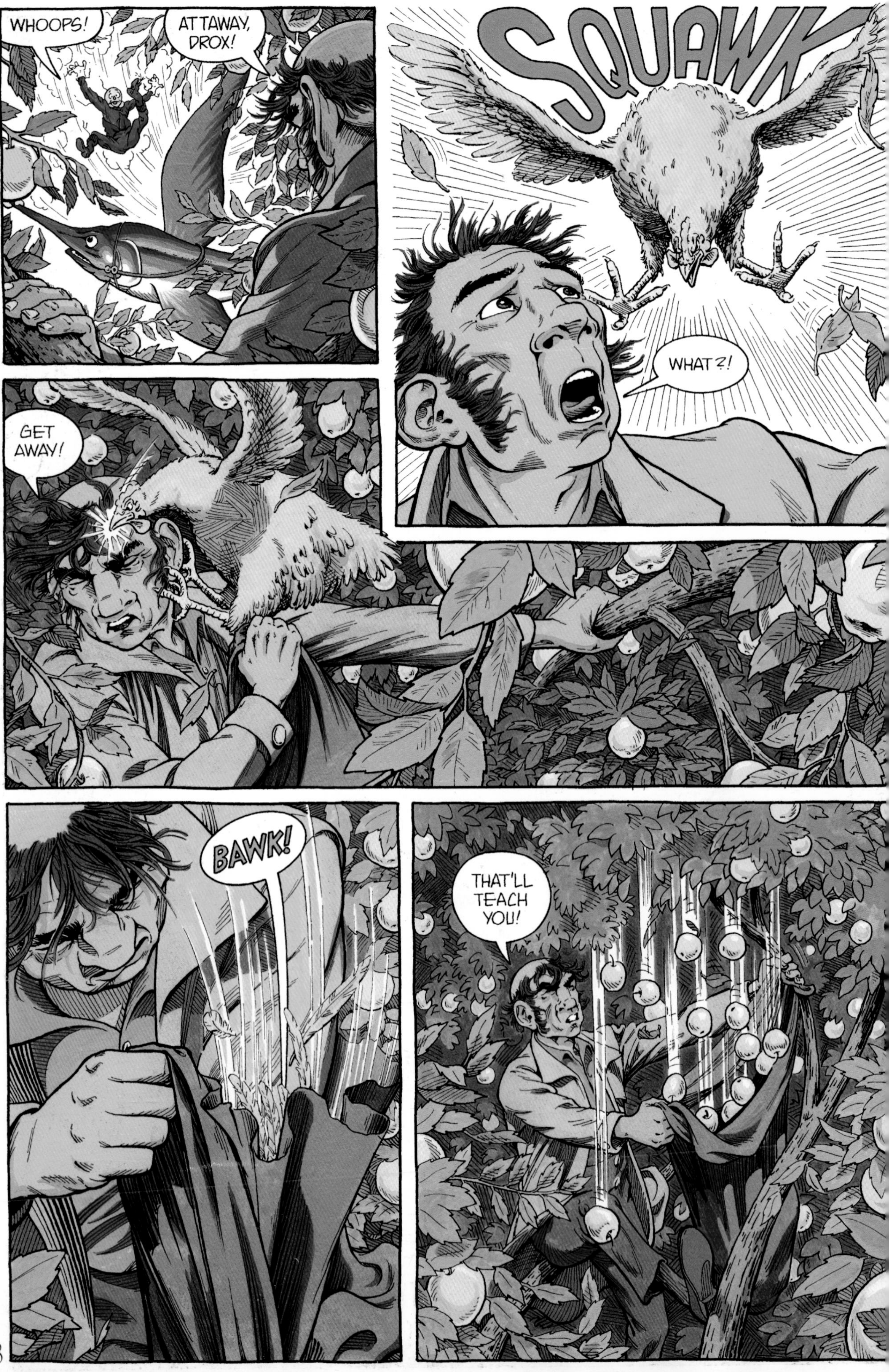
WHOOPS!
ATTAWAY, DROX!
SQUAWK
WHAT?!
GET AWAY!
BAWK!
THAT'LL TEACH YOU!

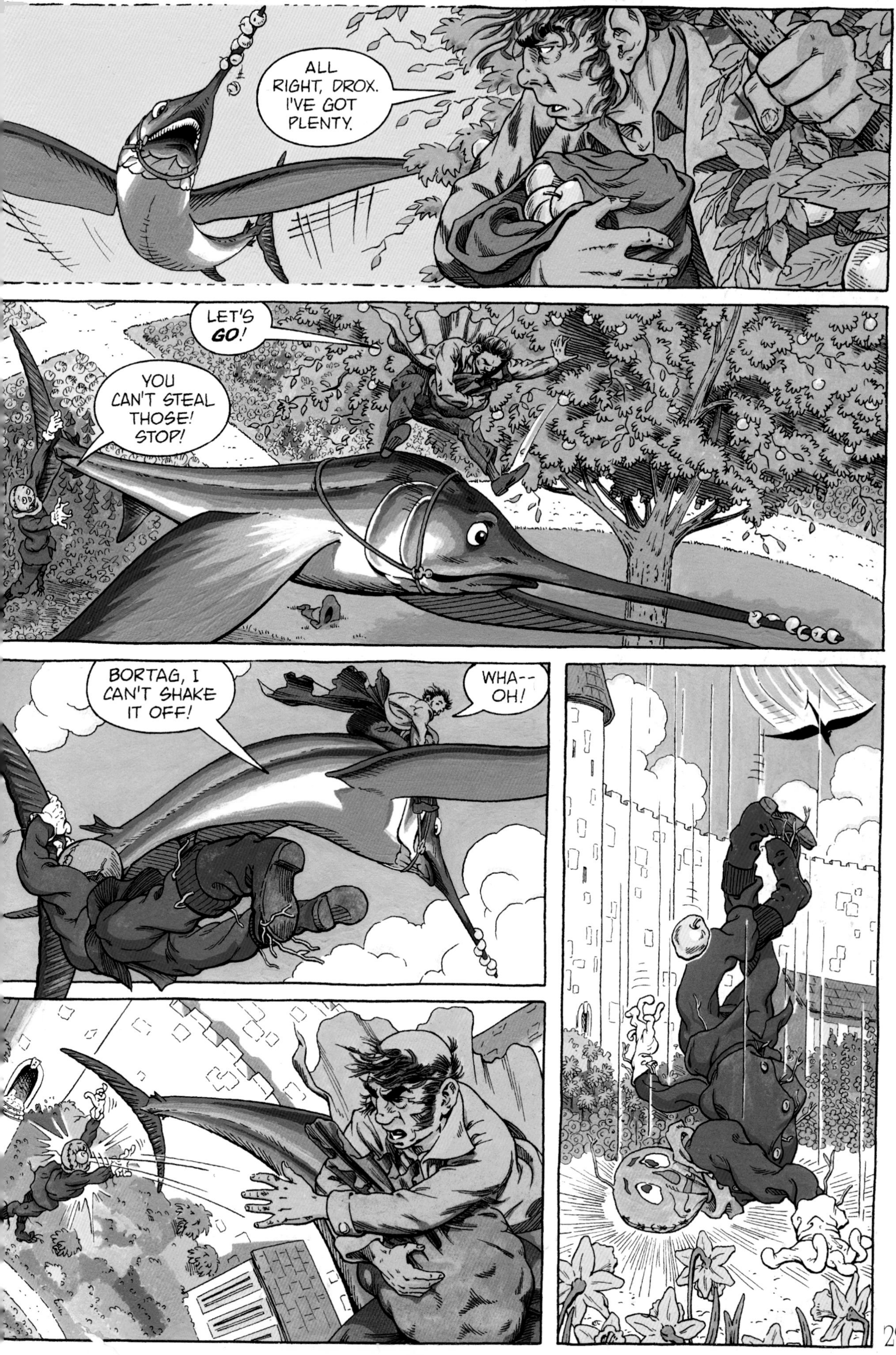
ALL RIGHT, DROX. I'VE GOT PLENTY.
LET'S GO!
YOU CAN'T STEAL THOSE! STOP!
BORTAG, I CAN'T SHAKE IT OFF!
WHA-- OH!

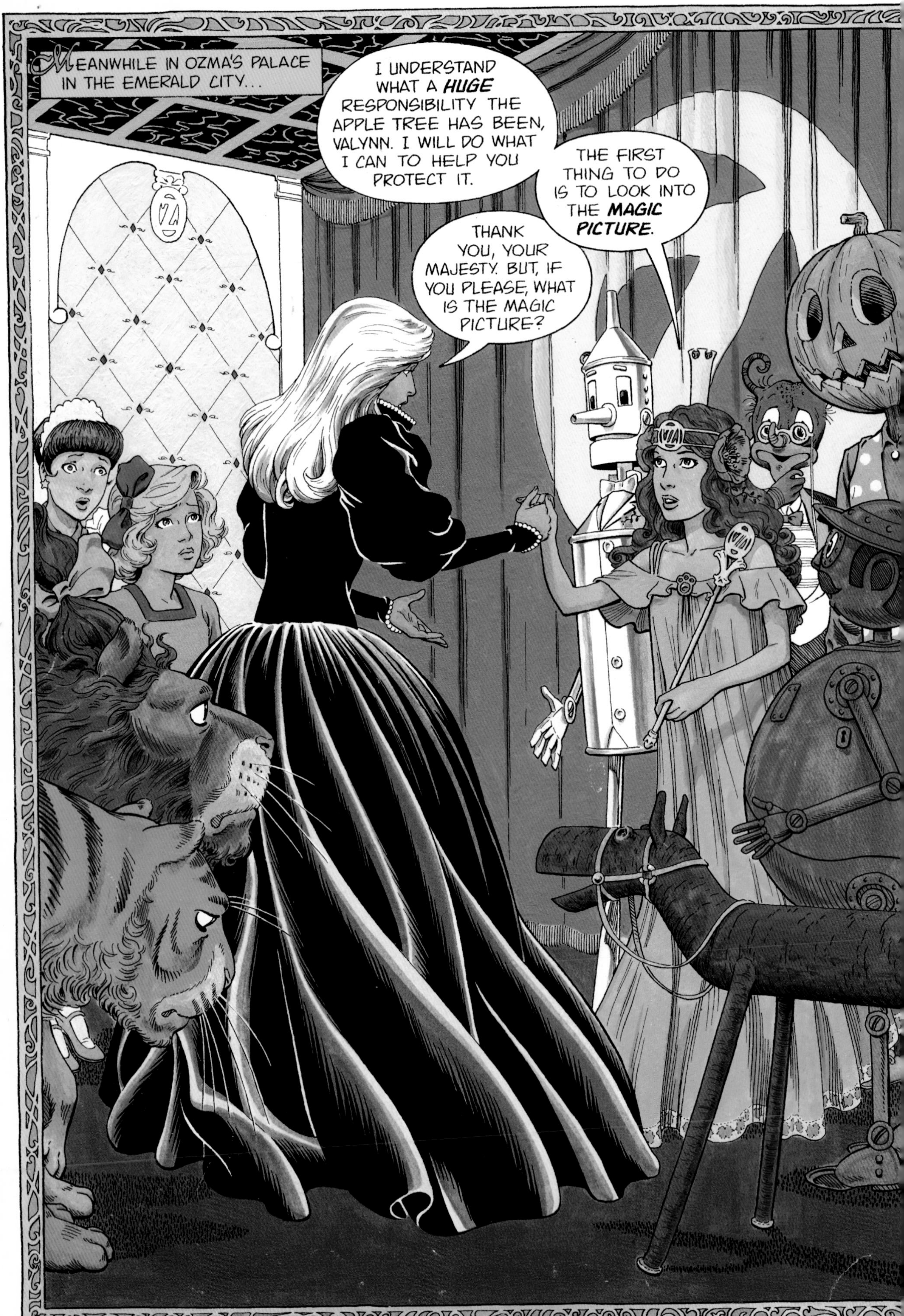
MEANWHILE IN OZMA'S PALACE IN THE EMERALD CITY...
I UNDERSTAND WHAT A **HUGE** RESPONSIBILITY THE APPLE TREE HAS BEEN, VALYNN. I WILL DO WHAT I CAN TO HELP YOU PROTECT IT.
THE FIRST THING TO DO IS TO LOOK INTO THE **MAGIC PICTURE**.
THANK YOU, YOUR MAJESTY. BUT, IF YOU PLEASE, WHAT IS THE MAGIC PICTURE?

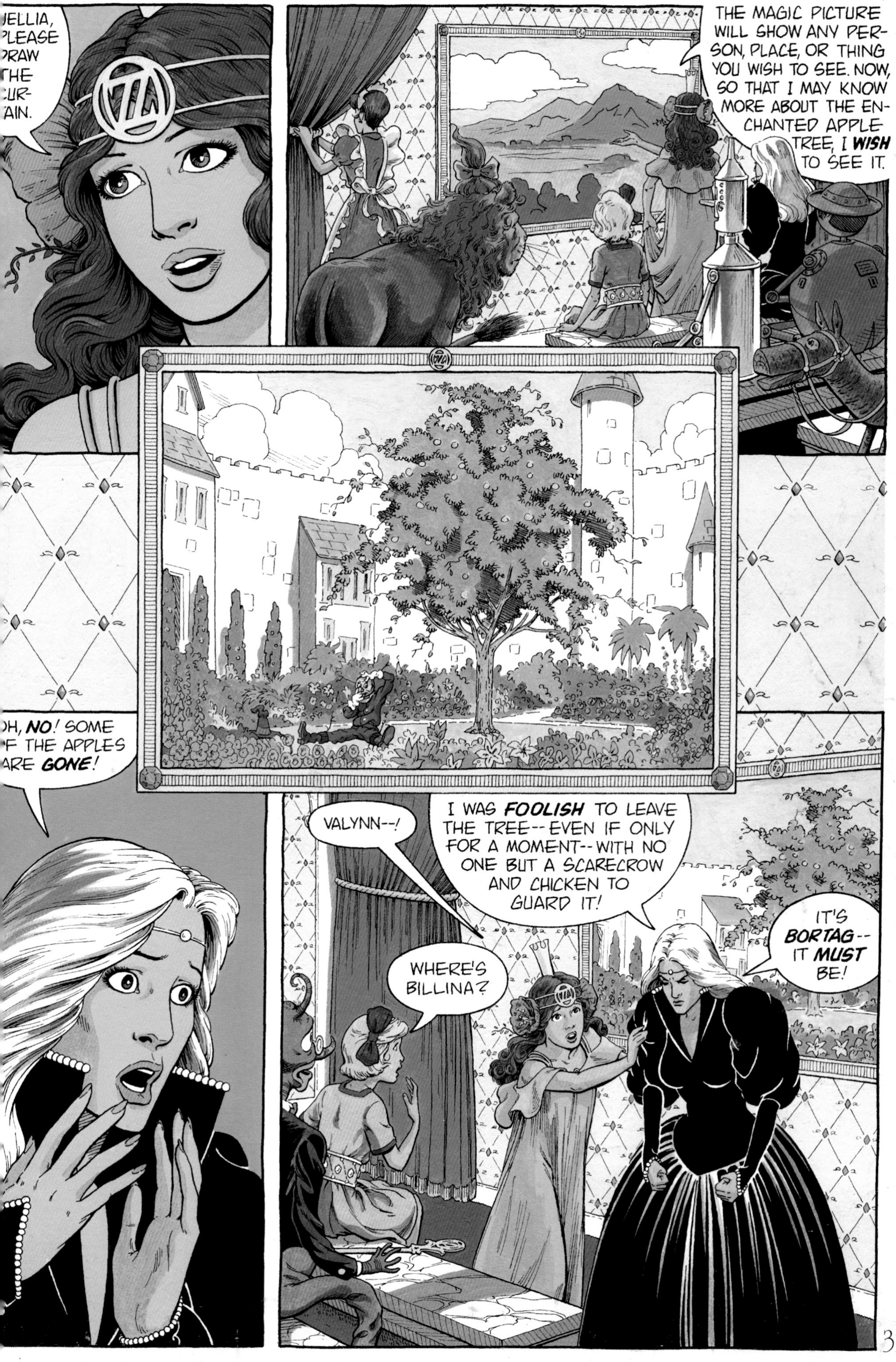
JELLIA, PLEASE DRAW THE CUR-TAIN.
THE MAGIC PICTURE WILL SHOW ANY PER-SON, PLACE, OR THING YOU WISH TO SEE. NOW, SO THAT I MAY KNOW MORE ABOUT THE EN-CHANTED APPLE TREE, I **WISH** TO SEE IT.
OH, **NO**! SOME OF THE APPLES ARE **GONE**!
VALYNN--!
I WAS **FOOLISH** TO LEAVE THE TREE--EVEN IF ONLY FOR A MOMENT--WITH NO ONE BUT A SCARECROW AND CHICKEN TO GUARD IT!
WHERE'S BILLINA?
IT'S **BORTAG**--IT **MUST** BE!

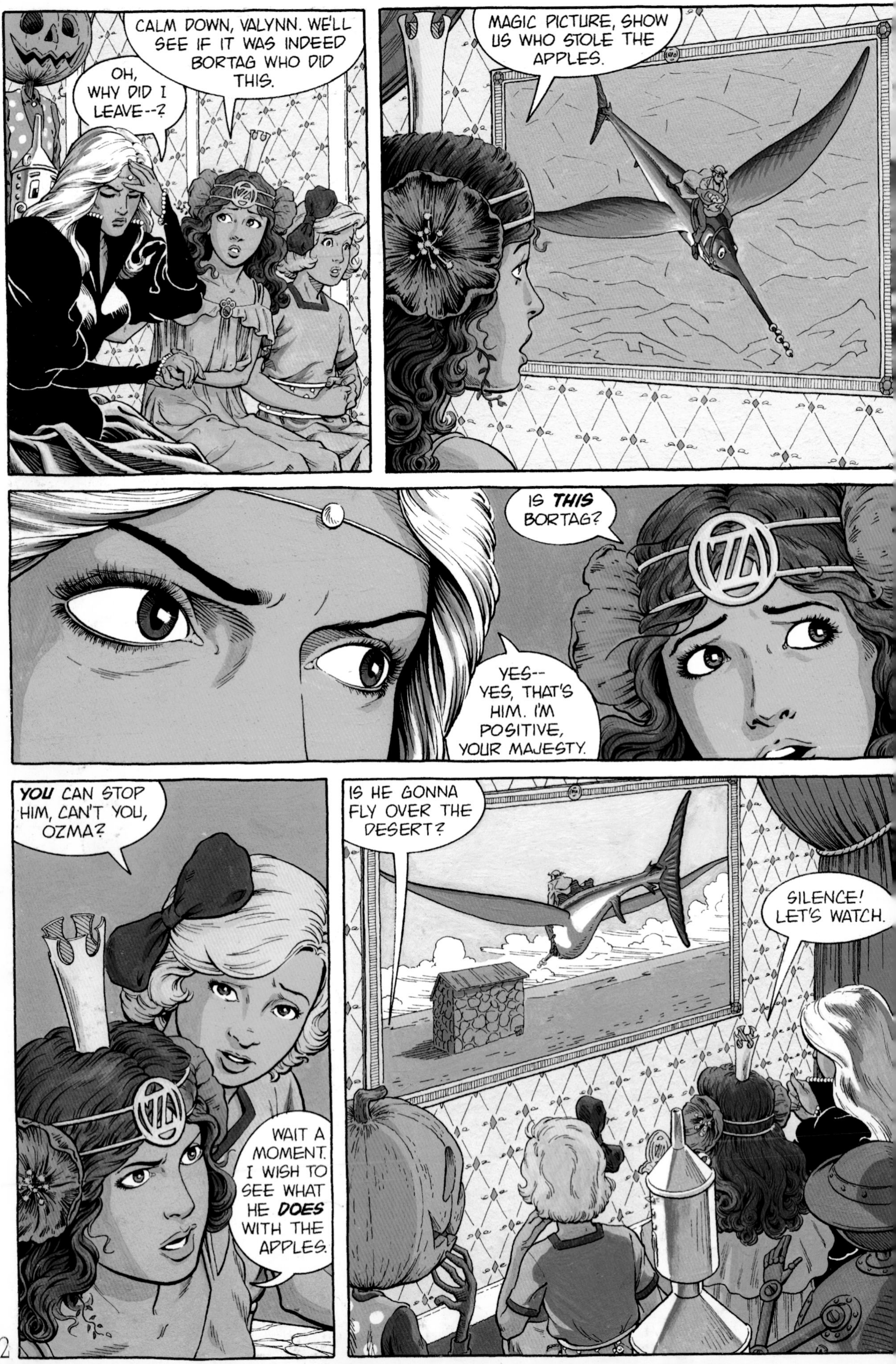
OH, WHY DID I LEAVE--?
CALM DOWN, VALYNN. WE'LL SEE IF IT WAS INDEED BORTAG WHO DID THIS.
MAGIC PICTURE, SHOW US WHO STOLE THE APPLES.
IS **THIS** BORTAG?
YES-- YES, THAT'S HIM. I'M POSITIVE, YOUR MAJESTY.
YOU CAN STOP HIM, CAN'T YOU, OZMA?
WAIT A MOMENT. I WISH TO SEE WHAT HE **DOES** WITH THE APPLES.
IS HE GONNA FLY OVER THE DESERT?
SILENCE! LET'S WATCH.

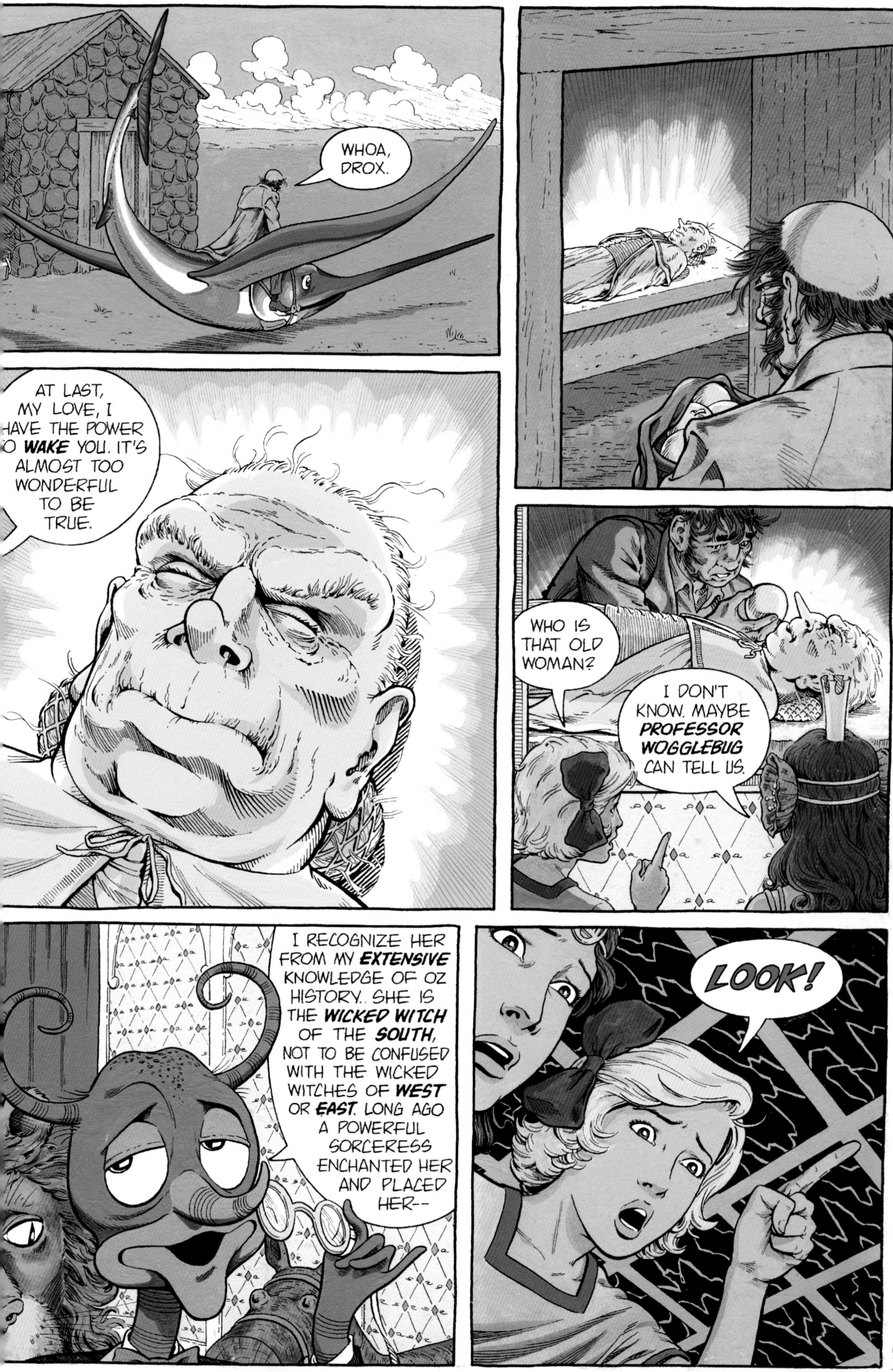
WHOA, DROX.
AT LAST, MY LOVE, I HAVE THE POWER TO WAKE YOU. IT'S ALMOST TOO WONDERFUL TO BE TRUE.
WHO IS THAT OLD WOMAN?
I DON'T KNOW. MAYBE PROFESSOR WOGGLEBUG CAN TELL US.
I RECOGNIZE HER FROM MY EXTENSIVE KNOWLEDGE OF OZ HISTORY. SHE IS THE WICKED WITCH OF THE SOUTH, NOT TO BE CONFUSED WITH THE WICKED WITCHES OF WEST OR EAST. LONG AGO A POWERFUL SORCERESS ENCHANTED HER AND PLACED HER--
LOOK!

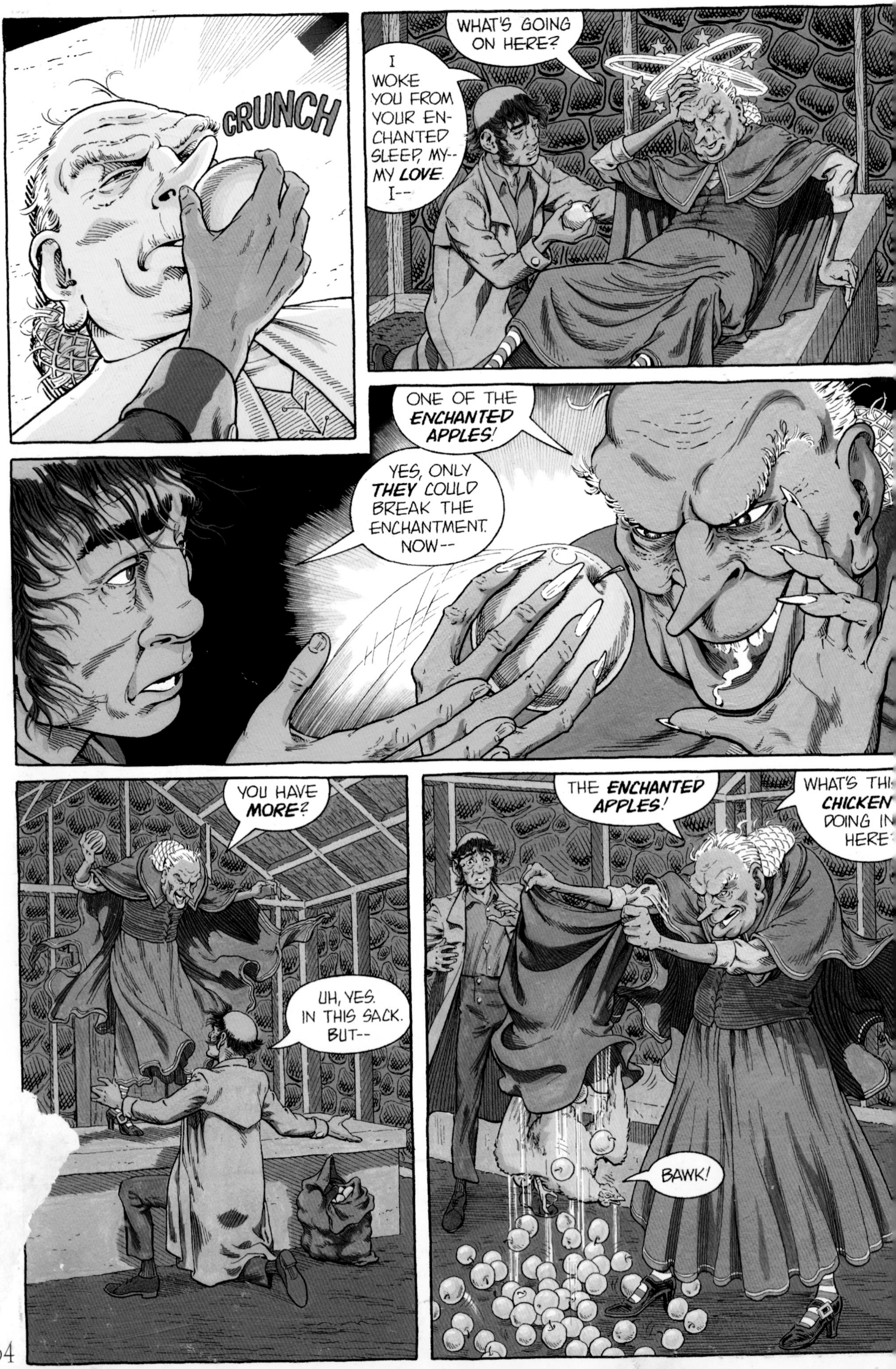
CRUNCH
WHAT'S GOING ON HERE?
I WOKE YOU FROM YOUR EN-CHANTED SLEEP, MY-- MY LOVE. I--
ONE OF THE ENCHANTED APPLES!
YES, ONLY THEY COULD BREAK THE ENCHANTMENT. NOW--
YOU HAVE MORE?
UH, YES. IN THIS SACK. BUT--
THE ENCHANTED APPLES!
WHAT'S THI CHICKEN DOING IN HERE
BAWK!

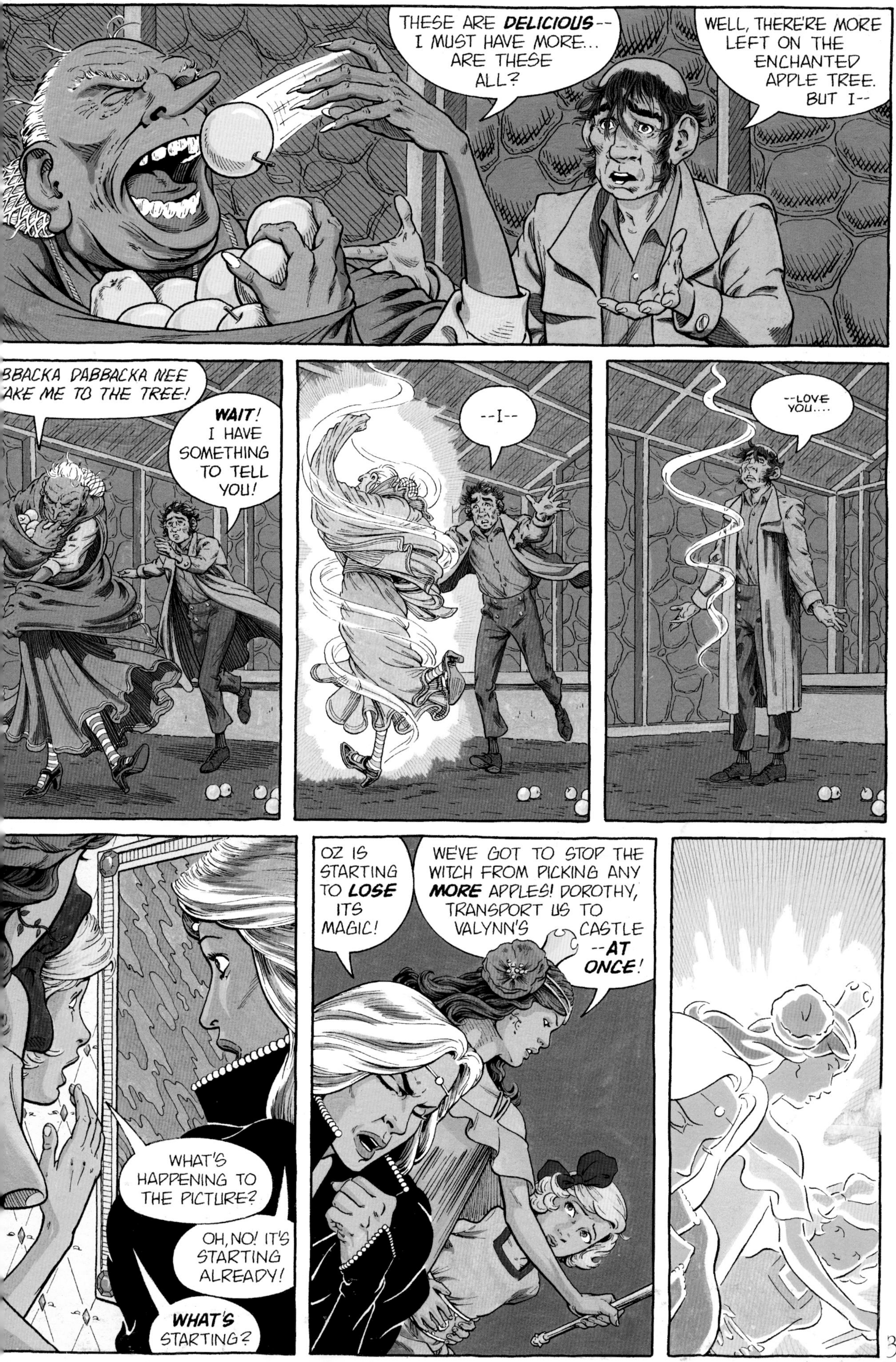
THESE ARE DELICIOUS-- I MUST HAVE MORE... ARE THESE ALL?
WELL, THERE'RE MORE LEFT ON THE ENCHANTED APPLE TREE. BUT I--
BBACKA DABBACKA NEE AKE ME TO THE TREE!
WAIT! I HAVE SOMETHING TO TELL YOU!
--I--
--LOVE YOU....
WHAT'S HAPPENING TO THE PICTURE?
OH, NO! IT'S STARTING ALREADY!
WHAT'S STARTING?
OZ IS STARTING TO LOSE ITS MAGIC!
WE'VE GOT TO STOP THE WITCH FROM PICKING ANY MORE APPLES! DOROTHY, TRANSPORT US TO VALYNN'S CASTLE --AT ONCE!

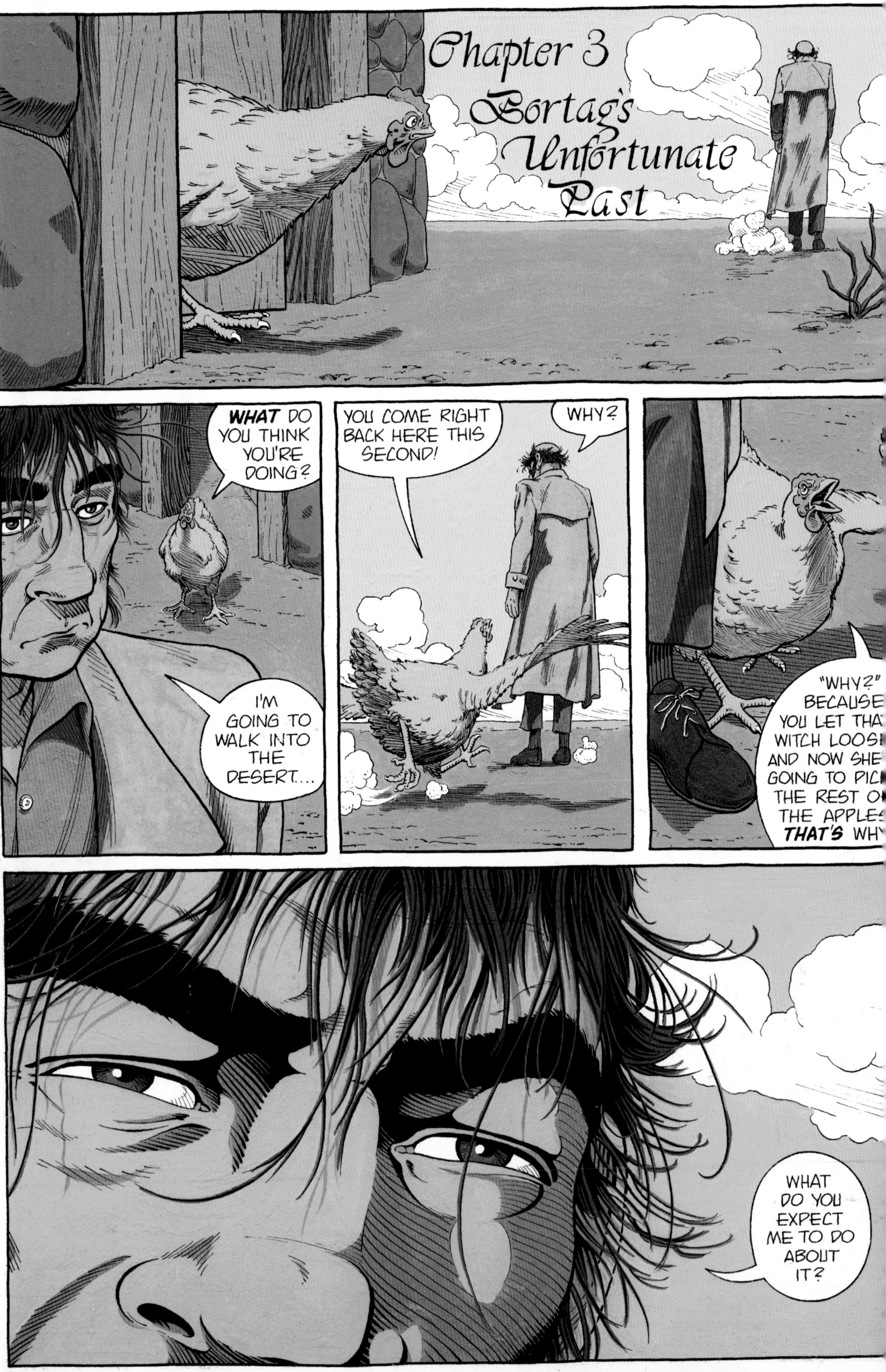
Chapter 3
Bortag's Unfortunate Past
WHAT DO YOU THINK YOU'RE DOING?
I'M GOING TO WALK INTO THE DESERT...
YOU COME RIGHT BACK HERE THIS SECOND!
WHY?
"WHY?" BECAUSE YOU LET THA WITCH LOOS AND NOW SHE GOING TO PIC THE REST O THE APPLE THAT'S WH
WHAT DO YOU EXPECT ME TO DO ABOUT IT?

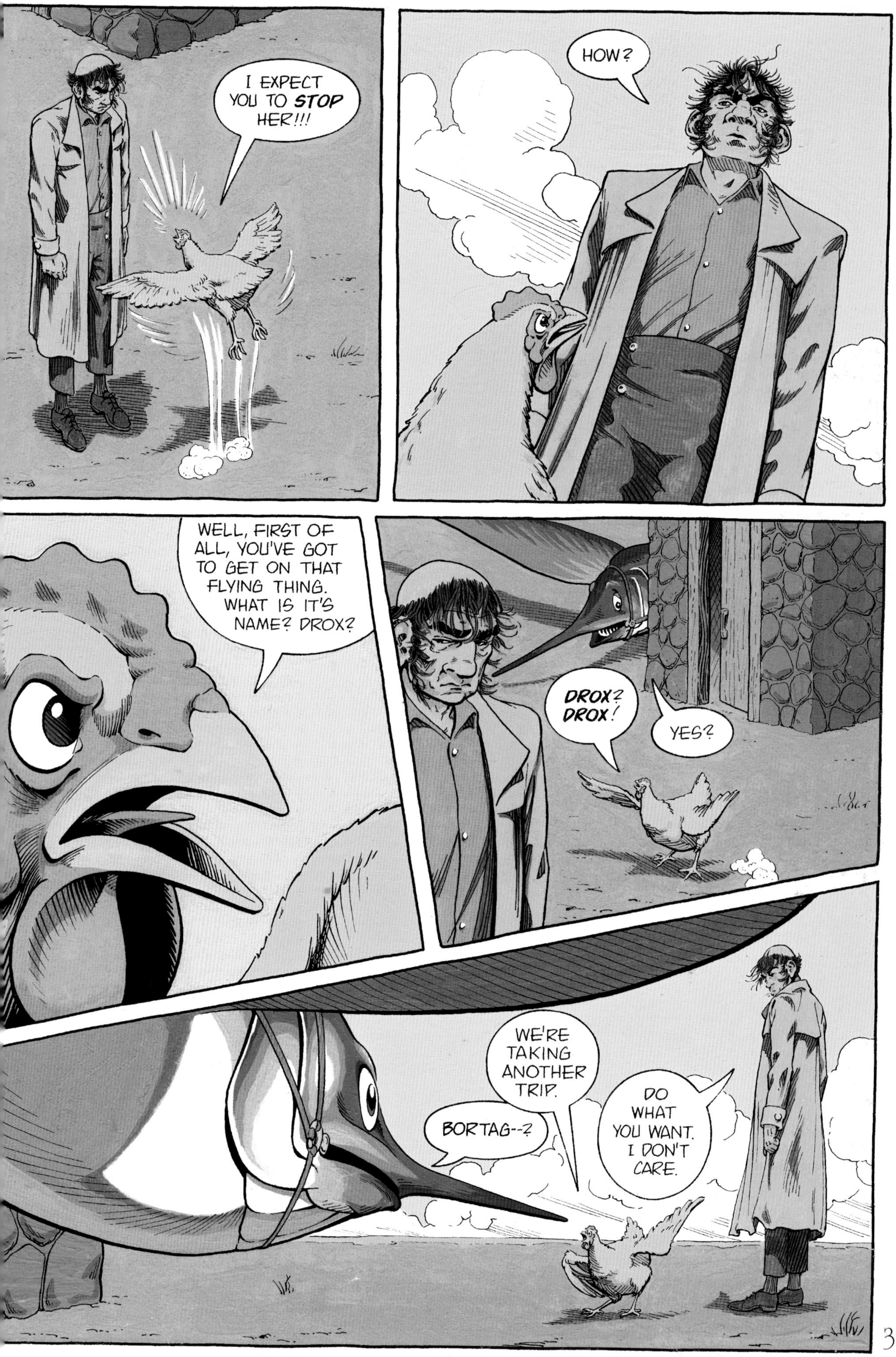
I EXPECT YOU TO STOP HER!!!
HOW?
WELL, FIRST OF ALL, YOU'VE GOT TO GET ON THAT FLYING THING. WHAT IS IT'S NAME? DROX?
DROX? DROX!
YES?
WE'RE TAKING ANOTHER TRIP.
BORTAG--?
DO WHAT YOU WANT. I DON'T CARE.

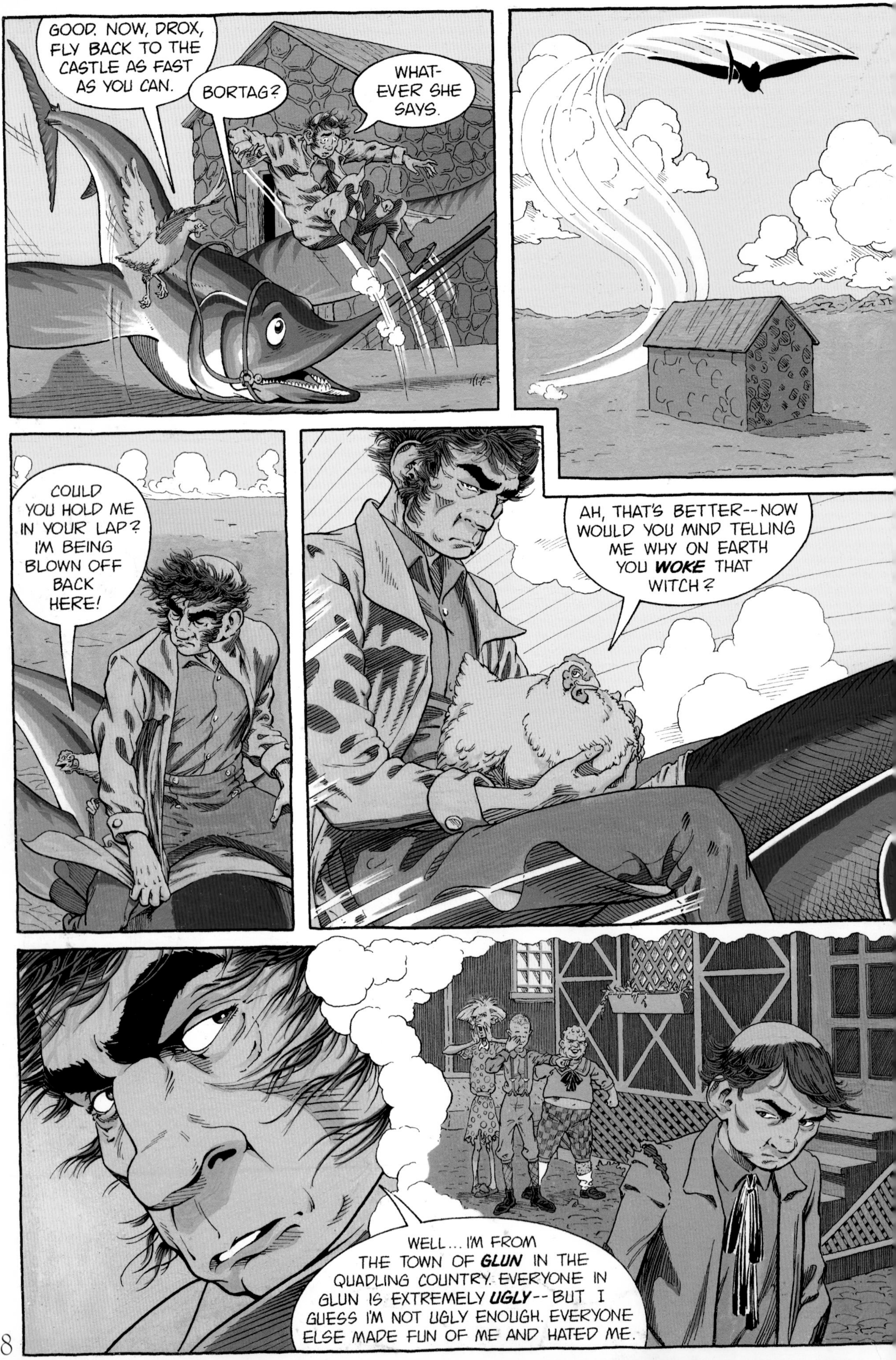
GOOD. NOW, DROX, FLY BACK TO THE CASTLE AS FAST AS YOU CAN.
BORTAG?
WHAT-EVER SHE SAYS.
COULD YOU HOLD ME IN YOUR LAP? I'M BEING BLOWN OFF BACK HERE!
AH, THAT'S BETTER--NOW WOULD YOU MIND TELLING ME WHY ON EARTH YOU WOKE THAT WITCH?
WELL... I'M FROM THE TOWN OF GLUN IN THE QUADLING COUNTRY. EVERYONE IN GLUN IS EXTREMELY UGLY--BUT I GUESS I'M NOT UGLY ENOUGH. EVERYONE ELSE MADE FUN OF ME AND HATED ME.

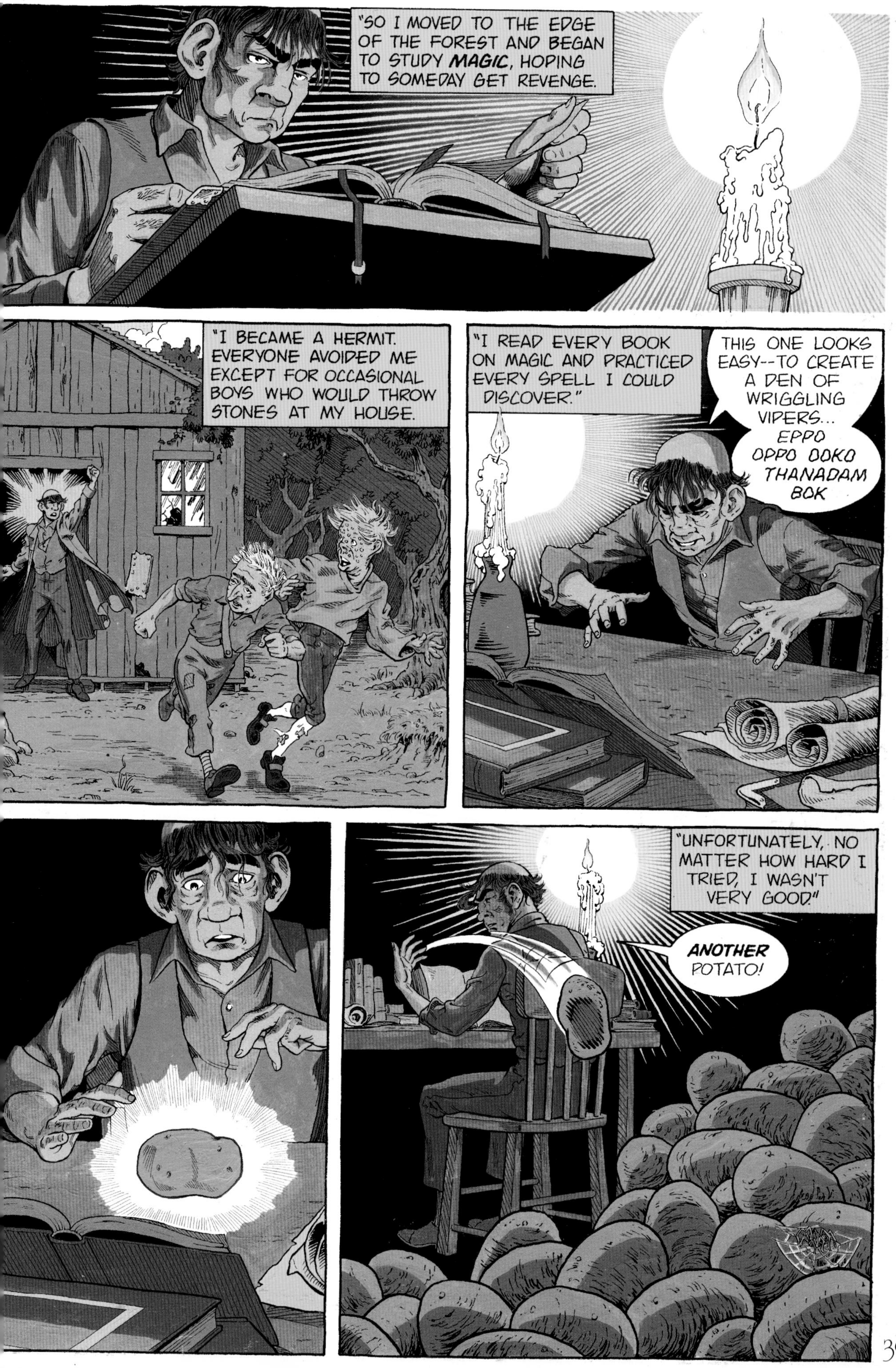
"SO I MOVED TO THE EDGE OF THE FOREST AND BEGAN TO STUDY MAGIC, HOPING TO SOMEDAY GET REVENGE.
"I BECAME A HERMIT. EVERYONE AVOIDED ME EXCEPT FOR OCCASIONAL BOYS WHO WOULD THROW STONES AT MY HOUSE.
"I READ EVERY BOOK ON MAGIC AND PRACTICED EVERY SPELL I COULD DISCOVER."
THIS ONE LOOKS EASY--TO CREATE A DEN OF WRIGGLING VIPERS... EPPO OPPO OOKO THANADAM BOK
"UNFORTUNATELY, NO MATTER HOW HARD I TRIED, I WASN'T VERY GOOD."
ANOTHER POTATO!

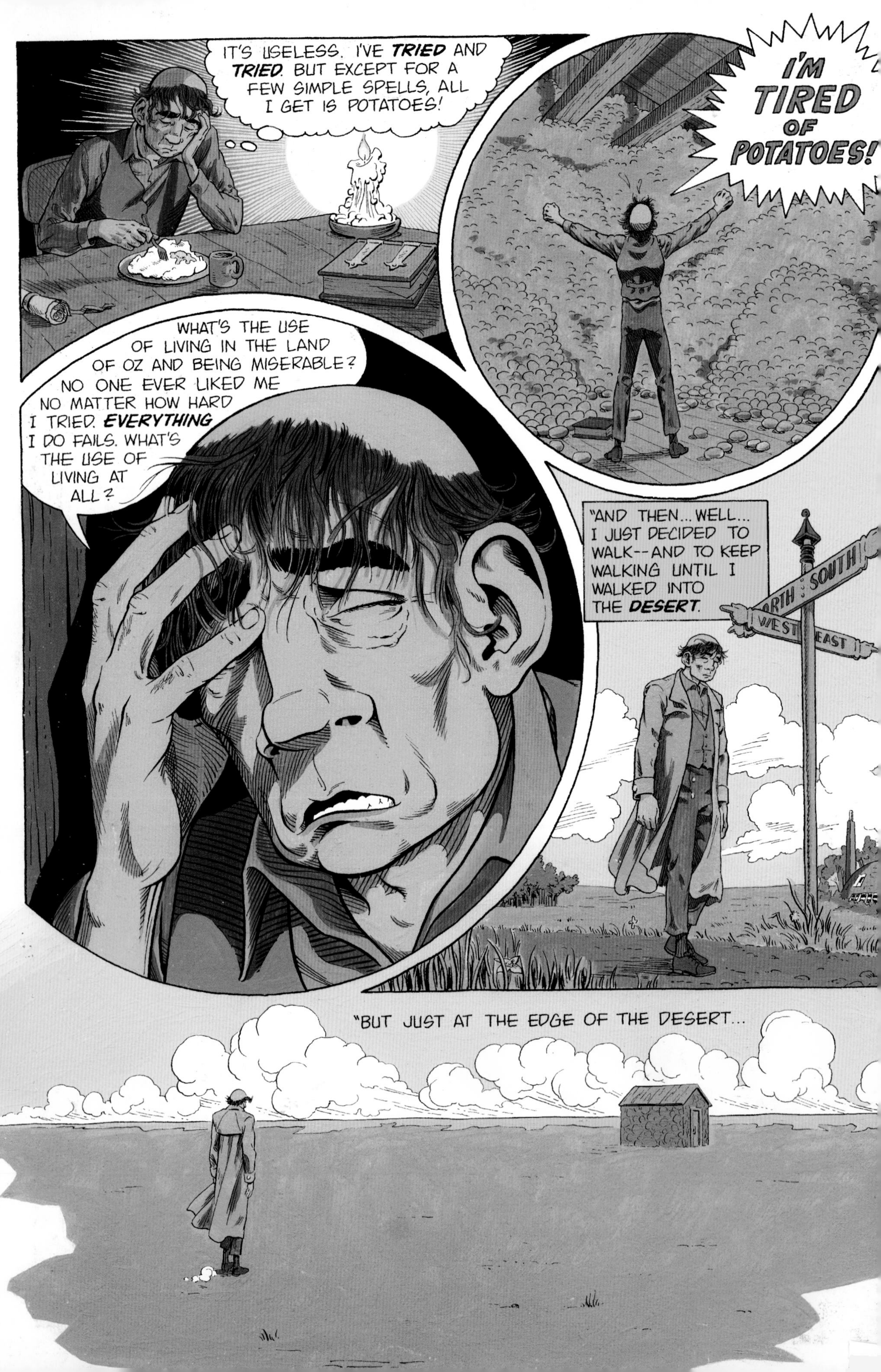
IT'S USELESS. I'VE TRIED AND TRIED. BUT EXCEPT FOR A FEW SIMPLE SPELLS, ALL I GET IS POTATOES!
I'M TIRED OF POTATOES!
WHAT'S THE USE OF LIVING IN THE LAND OF OZ AND BEING MISERABLE? NO ONE EVER LIKED ME NO MATTER HOW HARD I TRIED. EVERYTHING I DO FAILS. WHAT'S THE USE OF LIVING AT ALL?
"AND THEN... WELL... I JUST DECIDED TO WALK--AND TO KEEP WALKING UNTIL I WALKED INTO THE DESERT.
SOUTH
ORTH
WEST
EAST
"BUT JUST AT THE EDGE OF THE DESERT...

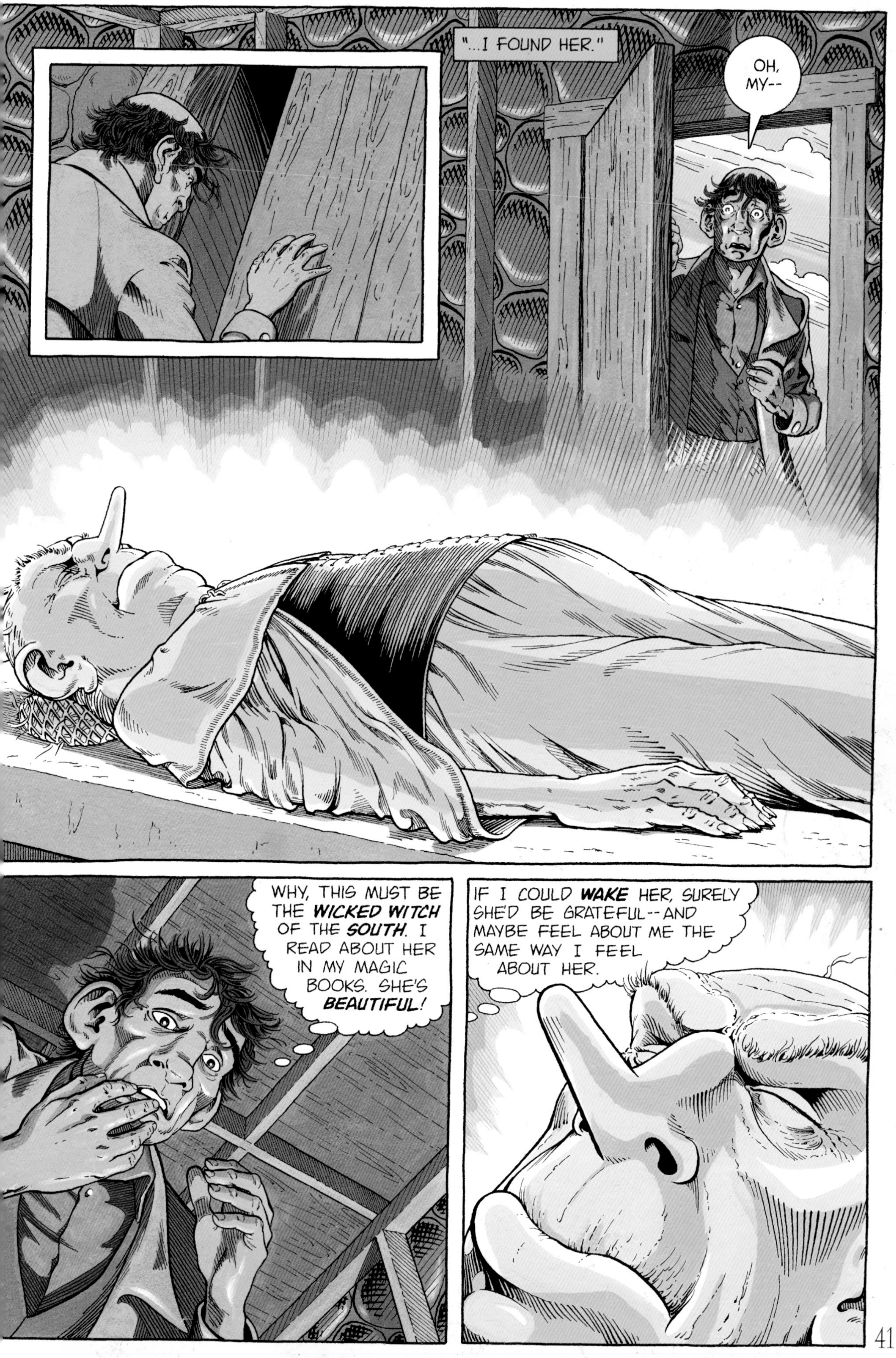
"...I FOUND HER."
OH, MY--
WHY, THIS MUST BE THE WICKED WITCH OF THE SOUTH. I READ ABOUT HER IN MY MAGIC BOOKS. SHE'S BEAUTIFUL!
IF I COULD WAKE HER, SURELY SHE'D BE GRATEFUL--AND MAYBE FEEL ABOUT ME THE SAME WAY I FEEL ABOUT HER.

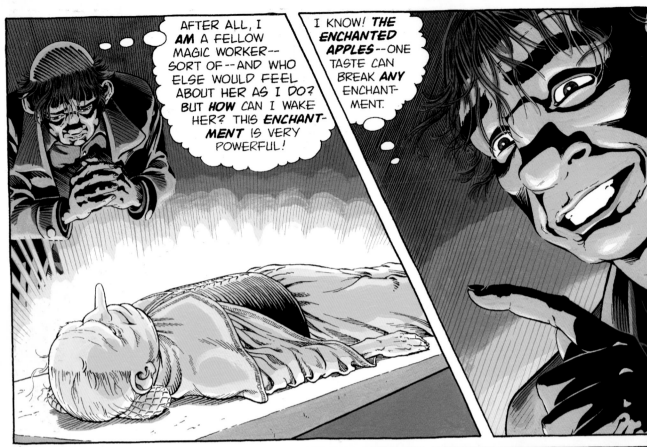

AFTER ALL, I **AM** A FELLOW MAGIC WORKER-- SORT OF --AND WHO ELSE WOULD FEEL ABOUT HER AS I DO? BUT **HOW** CAN I WAKE HER? THIS **ENCHANTMENT** IS VERY POWERFUL!

I KNOW! **THE ENCHANTED APPLES**--ONE TASTE CAN BREAK **ANY** ENCHANTMENT.

"SO AGAIN I SET OUT, BUT THIS TIME I WAS **DETERMINED** NOT TO FAIL. I HAD TO GET AN APPLE, THOUGH I KNEW THEY WERE FORBIDDEN.

"I GOT INTO THE CASTLE WITHOUT MUCH TROUBLE...

"...BUT I DIDN'T GET AN APPLE.

HOPING TO **SCARE** THEM INTO GIVING ME AN APPLE, I THREATENED TO USE MY MAGIC AGAINST THEM. I DIDN'T HAVE MUCH HOPE--A MAGICAL ATTACK WAS BEYOND MY NEW ABILITIES. WHAT COULD I DO, THROW **POTATOES** AT THEM?

"I SCARED THEM, ALL RIGHT, BUT NOT AS I HAD INTENDED."

"SO I WENT BACK TO THE WITCH."

SOMEDAY THE APPLES WILL COME BACK. I DON'T KNOW WHEN, BUT I'LL WAIT--AND WHEN THEY DO, **NOTHING** WILL STOP ME FROM TAKING ONE.

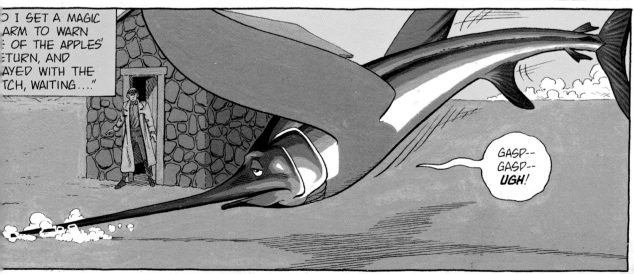

"SO I SET A MAGIC ALARM TO WARN ME OF THE APPLES' RETURN, AND STAYED WITH THE WITCH, WAITING...."

GASP-- GASP-- **UGH!**

43

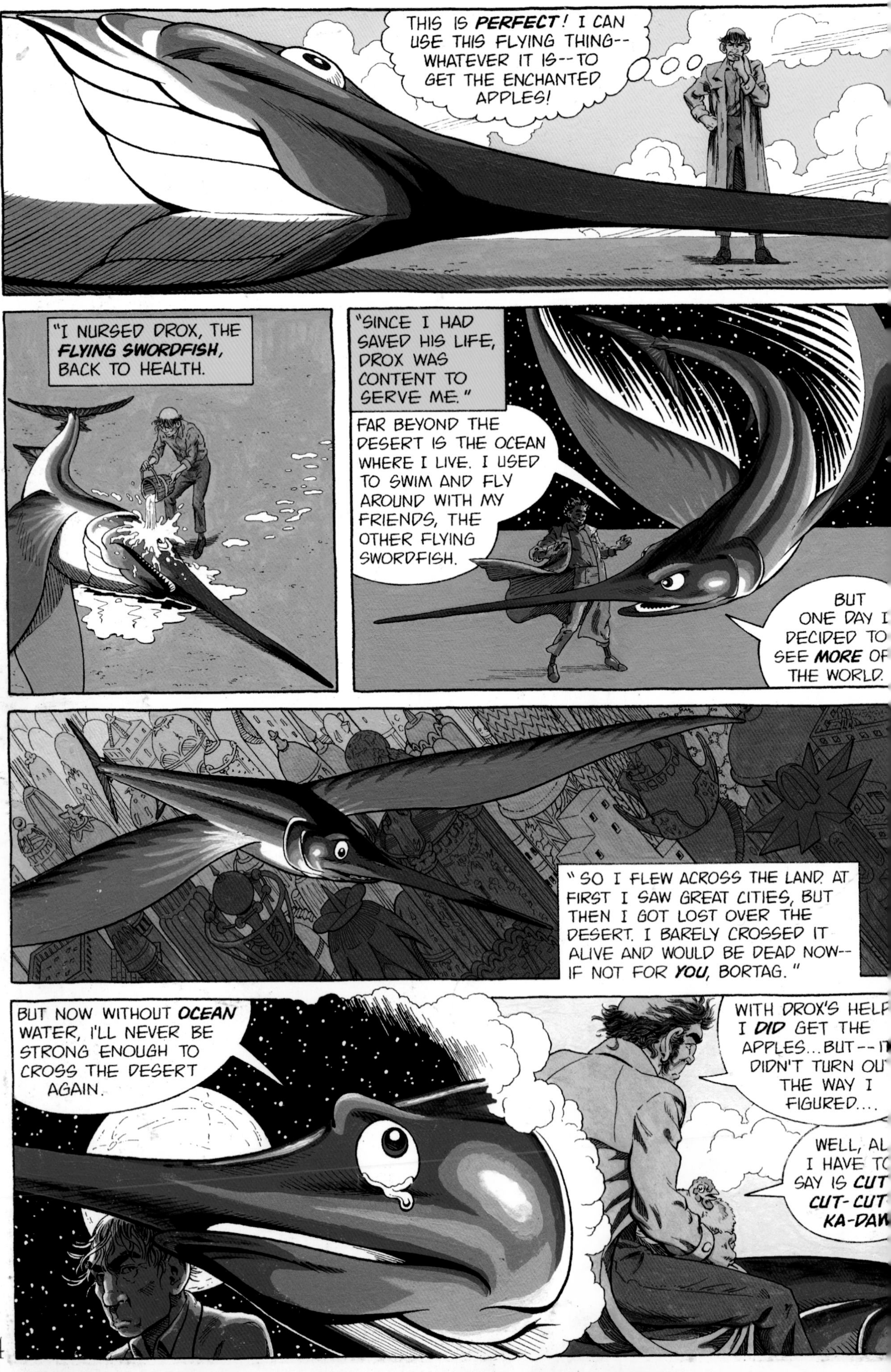

THIS IS PERFECT! I CAN USE THIS FLYING THING-- WHATEVER IT IS--TO GET THE ENCHANTED APPLES!
"I NURSED DROX, THE FLYING SWORDFISH, BACK TO HEALTH.
"SINCE I HAD SAVED HIS LIFE, DROX WAS CONTENT TO SERVE ME."
FAR BEYOND THE DESERT IS THE OCEAN WHERE I LIVE. I USED TO SWIM AND FLY AROUND WITH MY FRIENDS, THE OTHER FLYING SWORDFISH.
BUT ONE DAY I DECIDED TO SEE MORE OF THE WORLD.
"SO I FLEW ACROSS THE LAND. AT FIRST I SAW GREAT CITIES, BUT THEN I GOT LOST OVER THE DESERT. I BARELY CROSSED IT ALIVE AND WOULD BE DEAD NOW-- IF NOT FOR YOU, BORTAG."
BUT NOW WITHOUT OCEAN WATER, I'LL NEVER BE STRONG ENOUGH TO CROSS THE DESERT AGAIN.
WITH DROX'S HELP I DID GET THE APPLES...BUT--IT DIDN'T TURN OUT THE WAY I FIGURED....
WELL, ALL I HAVE TO SAY IS CUT CUT-CUT KA-DAW

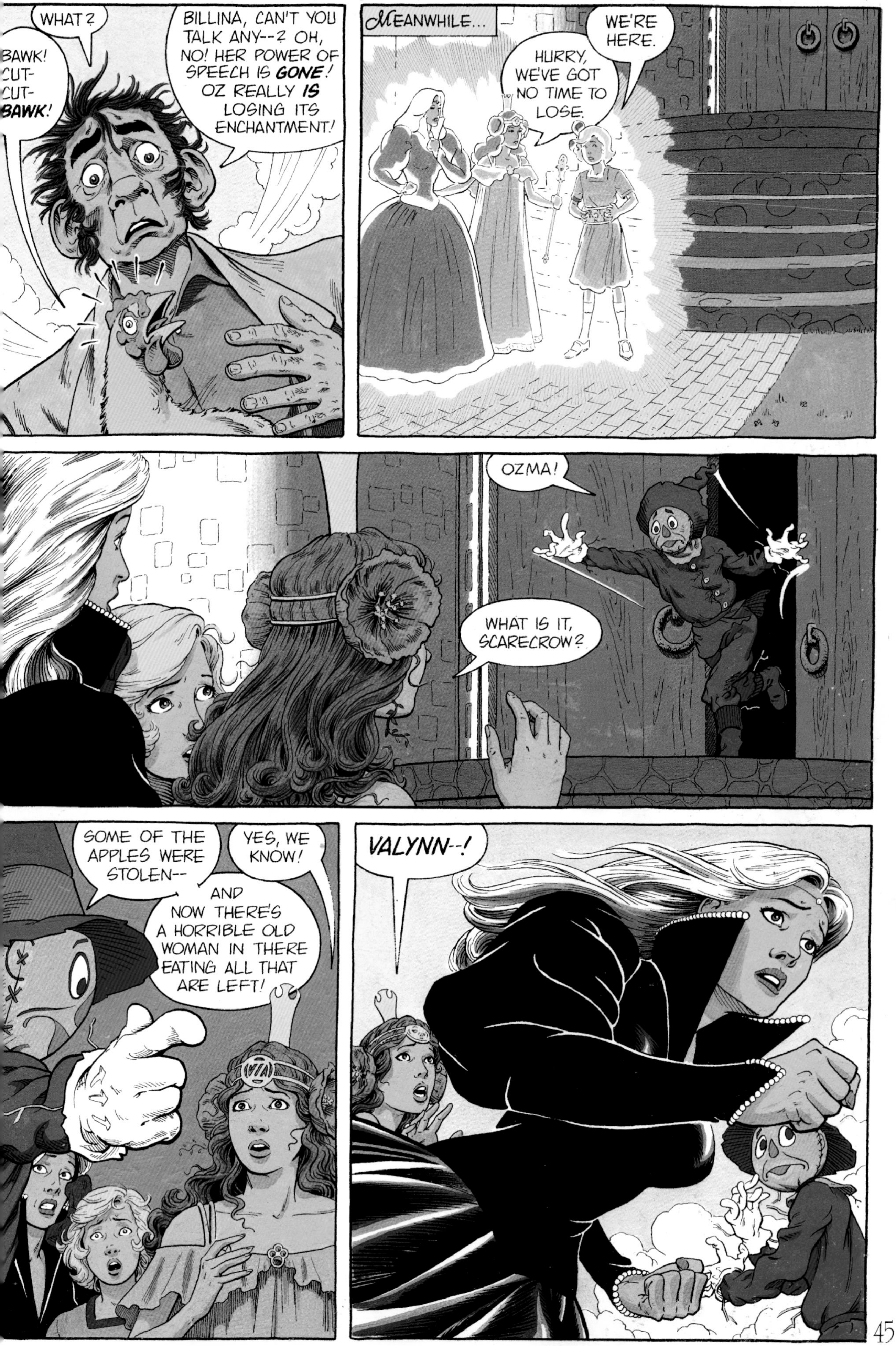
WHAT?
BAWK! CUT-CUT-BAWK!
BILLINA, CAN'T YOU TALK ANY--? OH, NO! HER POWER OF SPEECH IS GONE! OZ REALLY IS LOSING ITS ENCHANTMENT!
MEANWHILE...
WE'RE HERE.
HURRY, WE'VE GOT NO TIME TO LOSE.
OZMA!
WHAT IS IT, SCARECROW?
SOME OF THE APPLES WERE STOLEN--
YES, WE KNOW!
AND NOW THERE'S A HORRIBLE OLD WOMAN IN THERE EATING ALL THAT ARE LEFT!
VALYNN--!

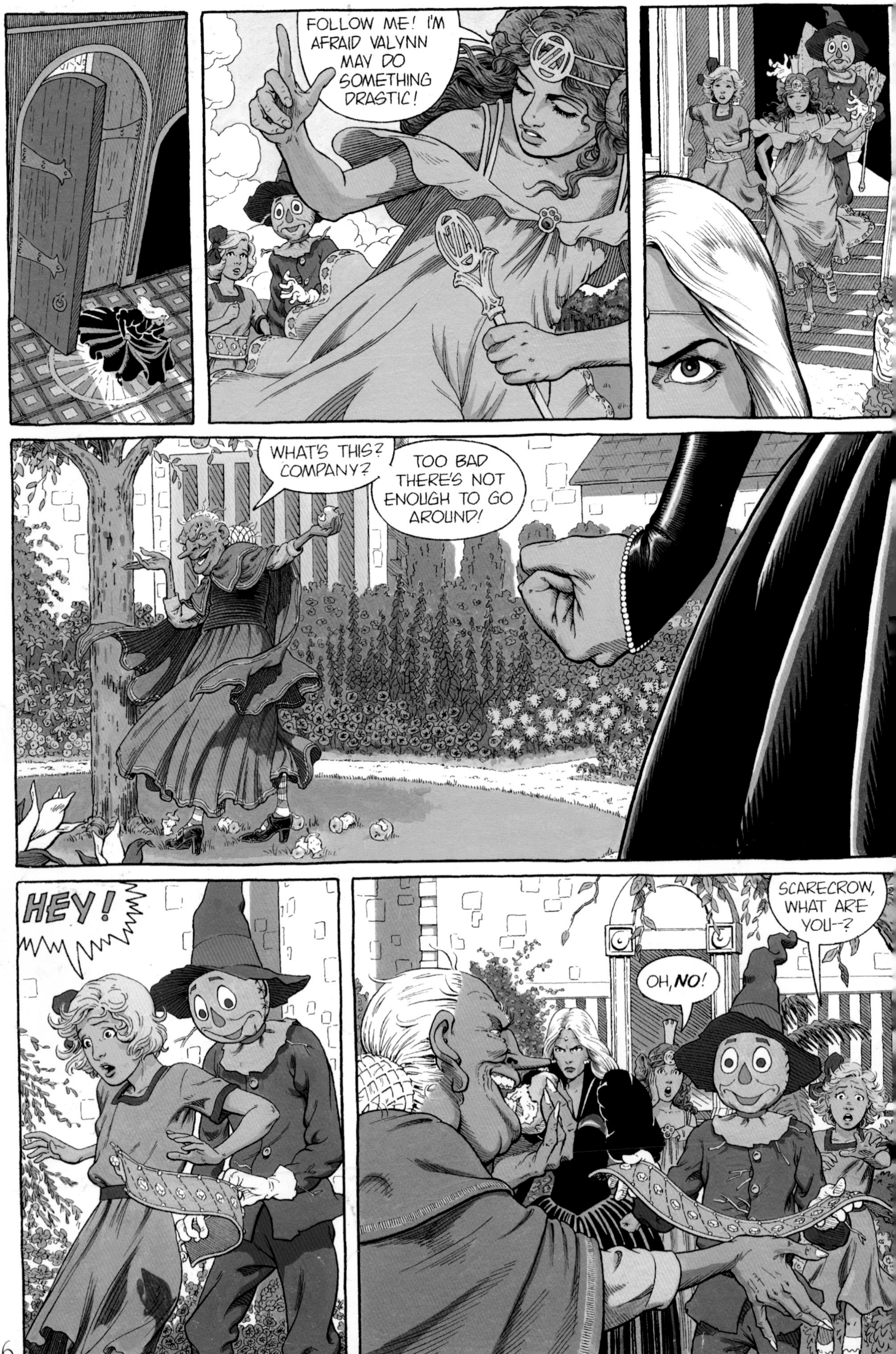
FOLLOW ME! I'M AFRAID VALYNN MAY DO SOMETHING DRASTIC!
WHAT'S THIS? COMPANY?
TOO BAD THERE'S NOT ENOUGH TO GO AROUND!
HEY!
SCARECROW, WHAT ARE YOU--?
OH, NO!

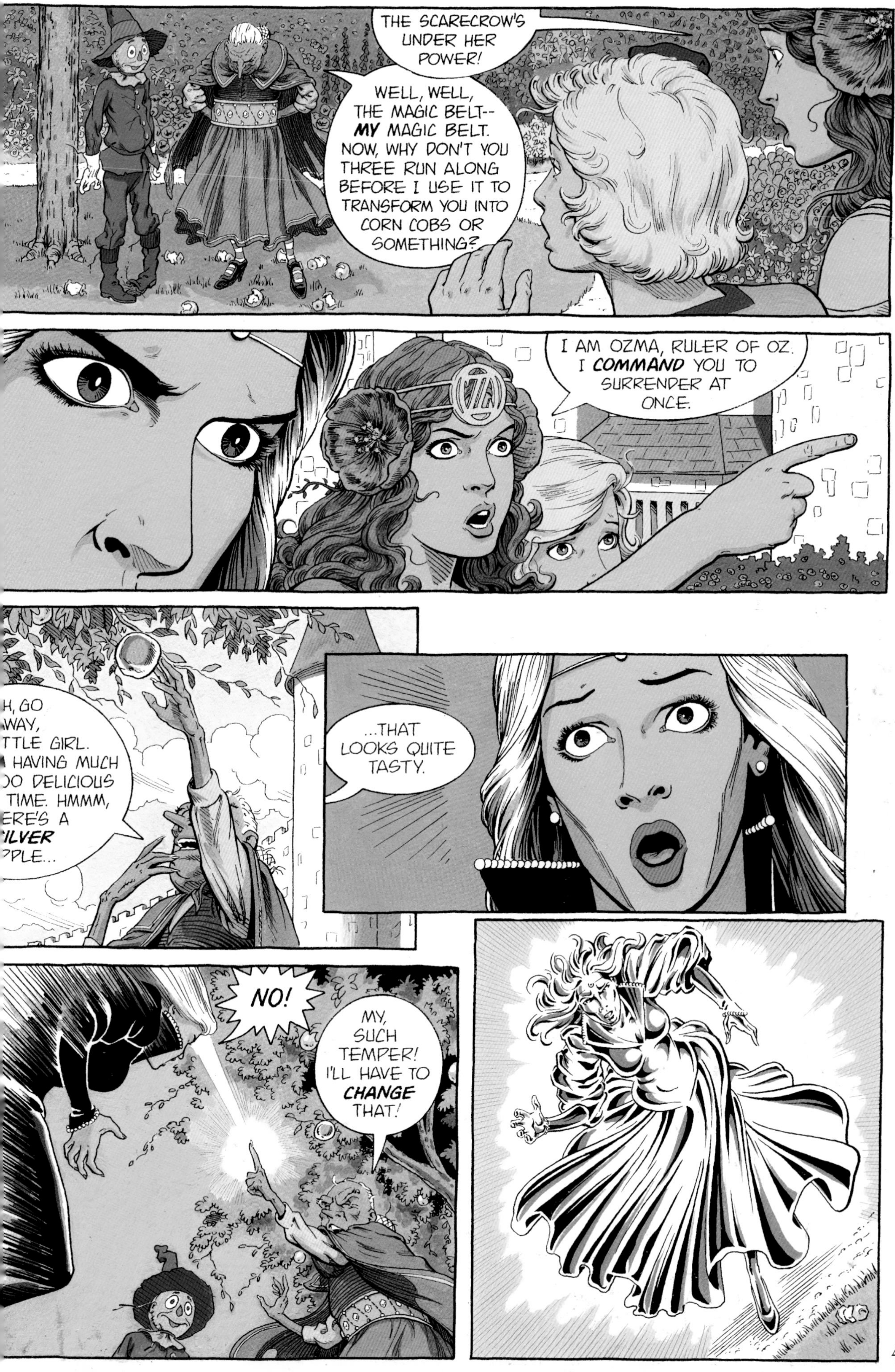
THE SCARECROW'S UNDER HER POWER!
WELL, WELL, THE MAGIC BELT-- MY MAGIC BELT. NOW, WHY DON'T YOU THREE RUN ALONG BEFORE I USE IT TO TRANSFORM YOU INTO CORN COBS OR SOMETHING?
I AM OZMA, RULER OF OZ. I COMMAND YOU TO SURRENDER AT ONCE.
H, GO WAY, TTLE GIRL. HAVING MUCH OO DELICIOUS TIME. HMMM, ERE'S A ILVER PPLE...
...THAT LOOKS QUITE TASTY.
NO!
MY, SUCH TEMPER! I'LL HAVE TO CHANGE THAT!

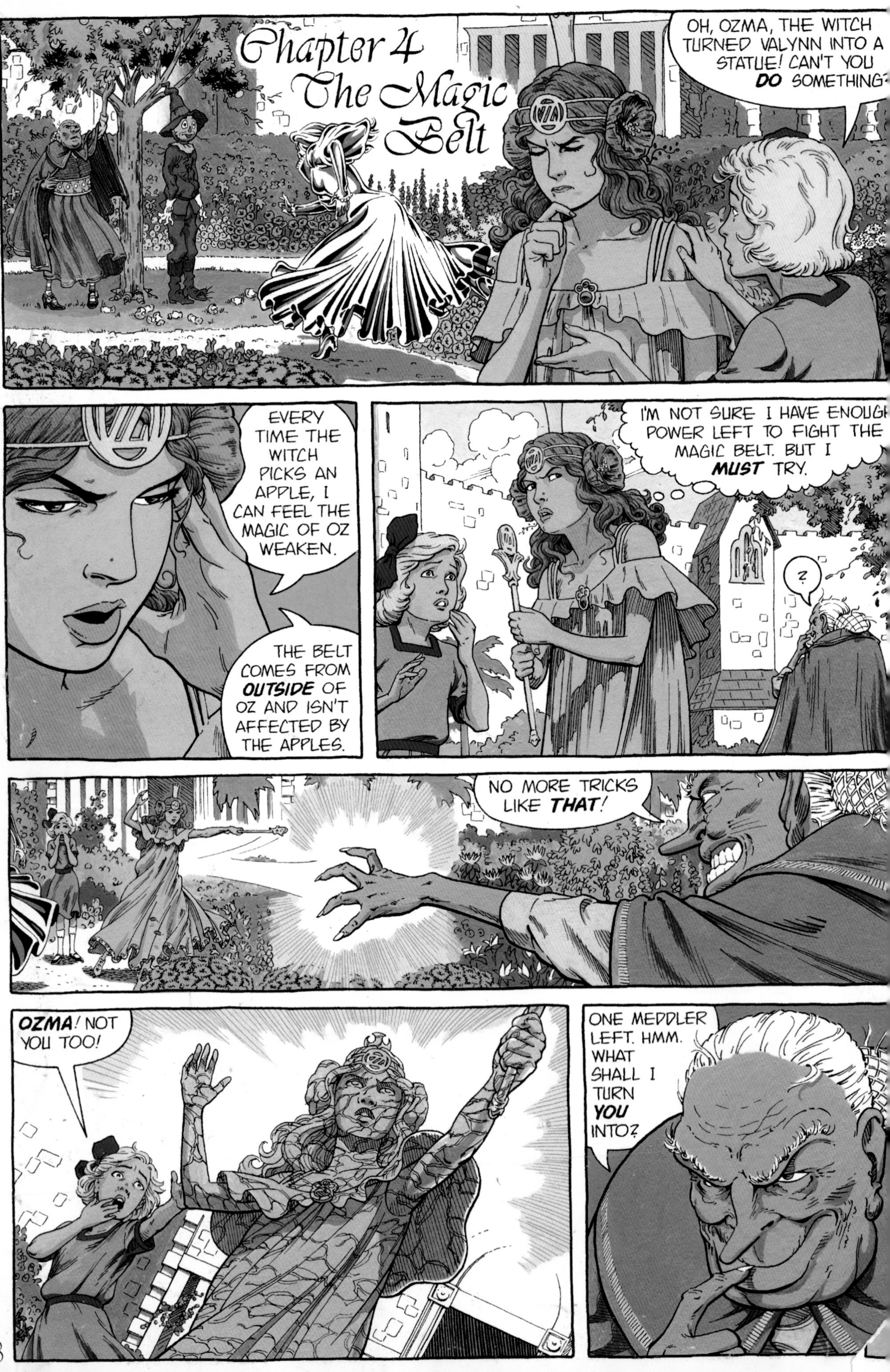

Chapter 4
The Magic Belt
OH, OZMA, THE WITCH TURNED VALYNN INTO A STATUE! CAN'T YOU DO SOMETHING?
EVERY TIME THE WITCH PICKS AN APPLE, I CAN FEEL THE MAGIC OF OZ WEAKEN.
THE BELT COMES FROM OUTSIDE OF OZ AND ISN'T AFFECTED BY THE APPLES.
I'M NOT SURE I HAVE ENOUGH POWER LEFT TO FIGHT THE MAGIC BELT. BUT I MUST TRY.
?
NO MORE TRICKS LIKE THAT!
OZMA! NOT YOU TOO!
ONE MEDDLER LEFT. HMM. WHAT SHALL I TURN YOU INTO?

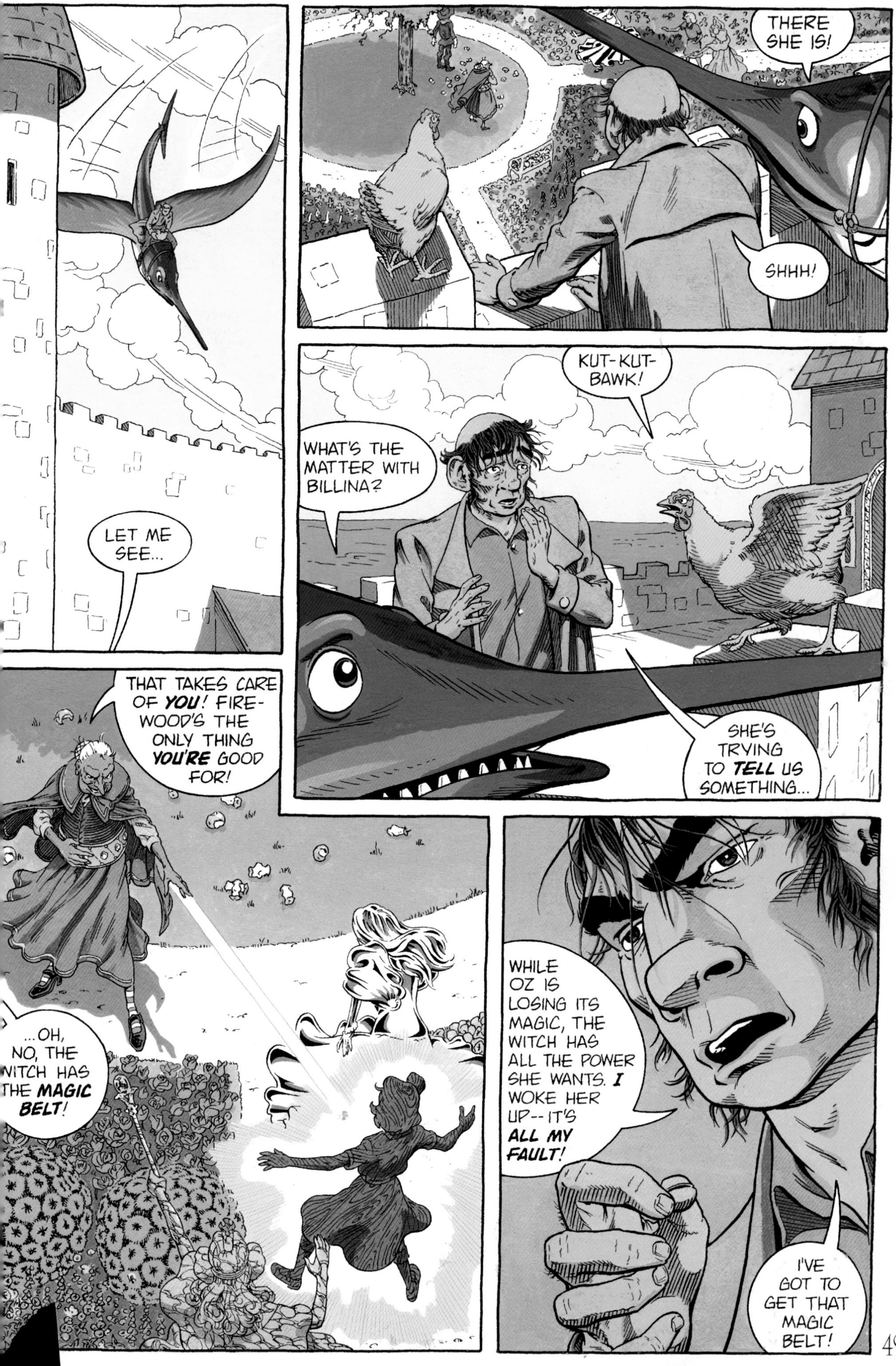

LET ME SEE...
THERE SHE IS!
SHHH!
KUT-KUT-BAWK!
WHAT'S THE MATTER WITH BILLINA?
SHE'S TRYING TO **TELL** US SOMETHING...
THAT TAKES CARE OF **YOU**! FIRE-WOOD'S THE ONLY THING **YOU'RE** GOOD FOR!
...OH, NO, THE WITCH HAS THE **MAGIC BELT**!
WHILE OZ IS LOSING ITS MAGIC, THE WITCH HAS ALL THE POWER SHE WANTS. **I** WOKE HER UP-- IT'S **ALL MY FAULT**!
I'VE GOT TO GET THAT MAGIC BELT!

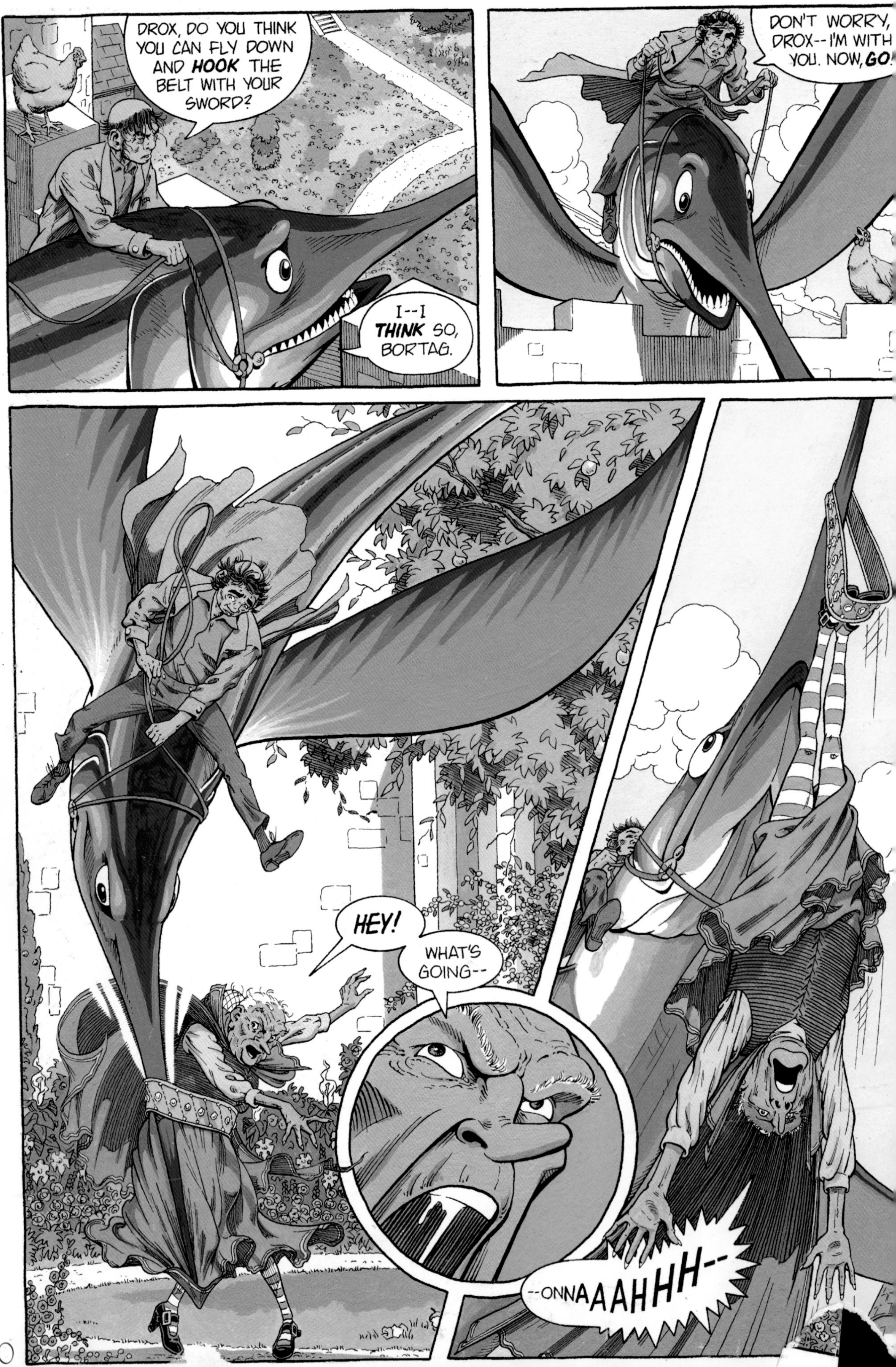
DROX, DO YOU THINK YOU CAN FLY DOWN AND **HOOK** THE BELT WITH YOUR SWORD?
I--I **THINK** SO, BORTAG.
DON'T WORRY, DROX--I'M WITH YOU. NOW, **GO**!
HEY!
WHAT'S GOING--
--ONNAAAHHH--

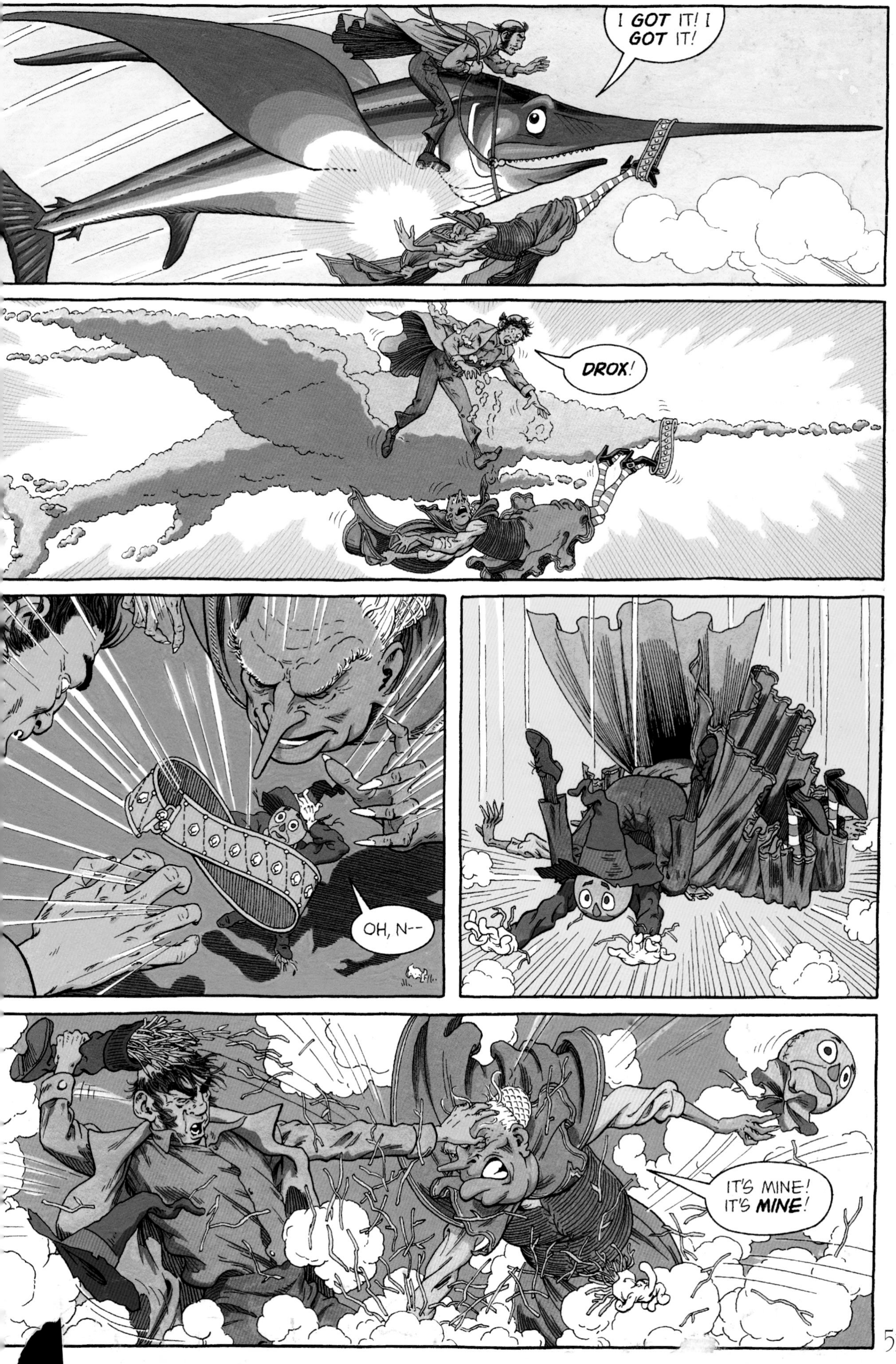
I GOT IT! I GOT IT!
DROX!
OH, N--
IT'S MINE! IT'S MINE!

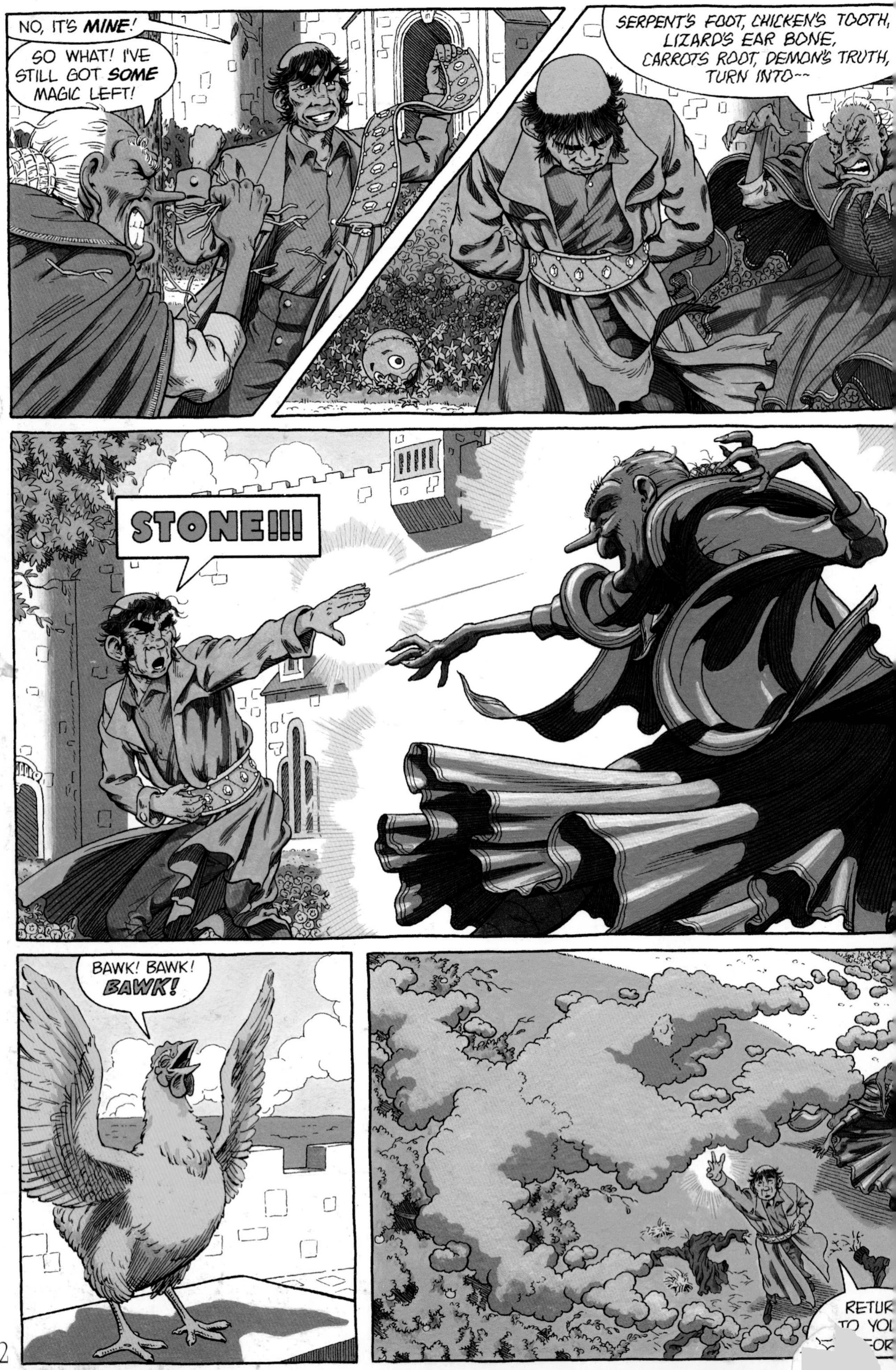
NO, IT'S MINE!
SO WHAT! I'VE STILL GOT SOME MAGIC LEFT!
SERPENT'S FOOT, CHICKEN'S TOOTH, LIZARD'S EAR BONE, CARROTS ROOT, DEMON'S TRUTH, TURN INTO~~
STONE!!!
BAWK! BAWK! BAWK!
RETUR
TO YO
FOR

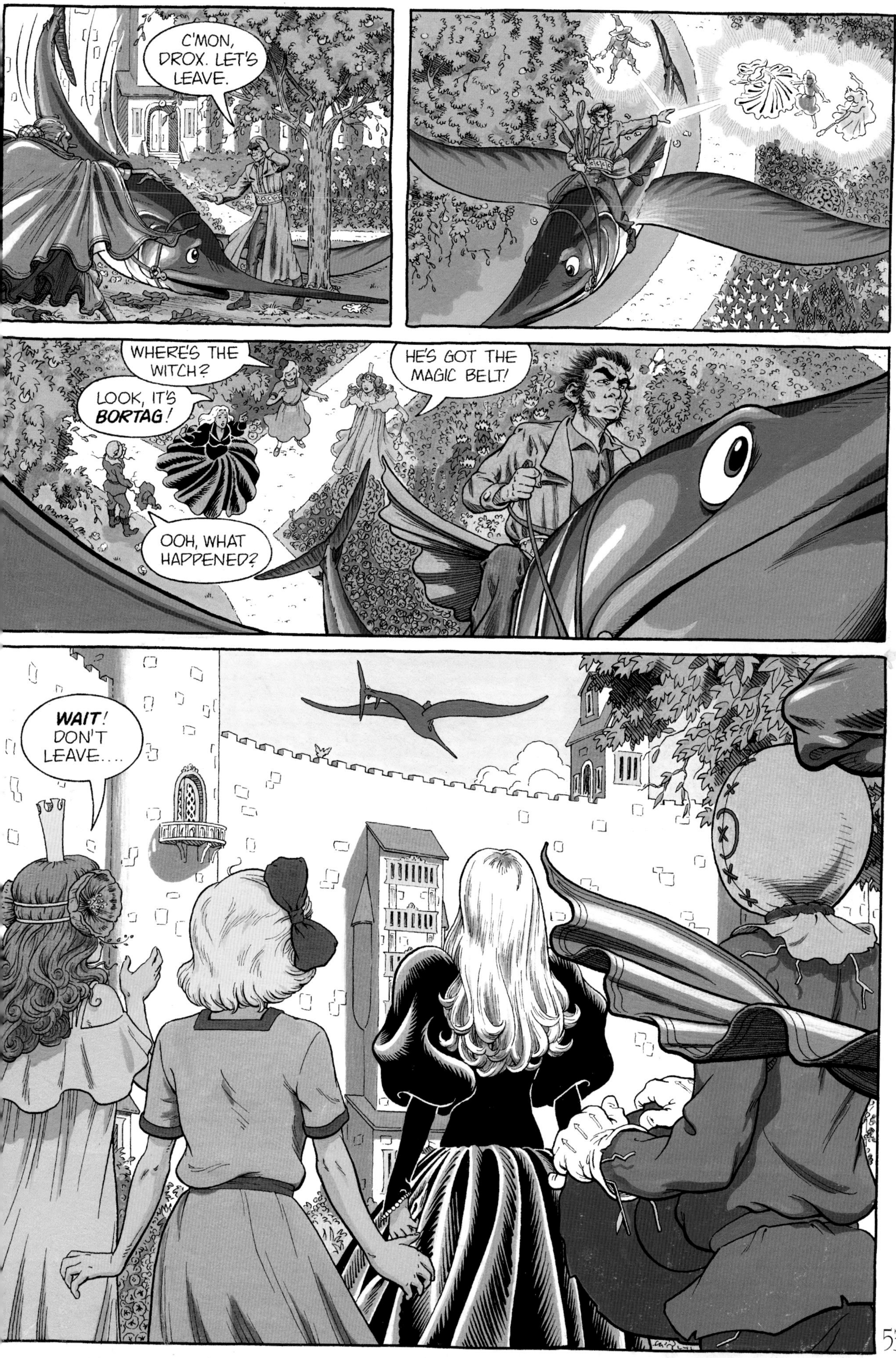
C'MON, DROX. LET'S LEAVE.
WHERE'S THE WITCH?
LOOK, IT'S **BORTAG**!
HE'S GOT THE MAGIC BELT!
OOH, WHAT HAPPENED?
WAIT! DON'T LEAVE....

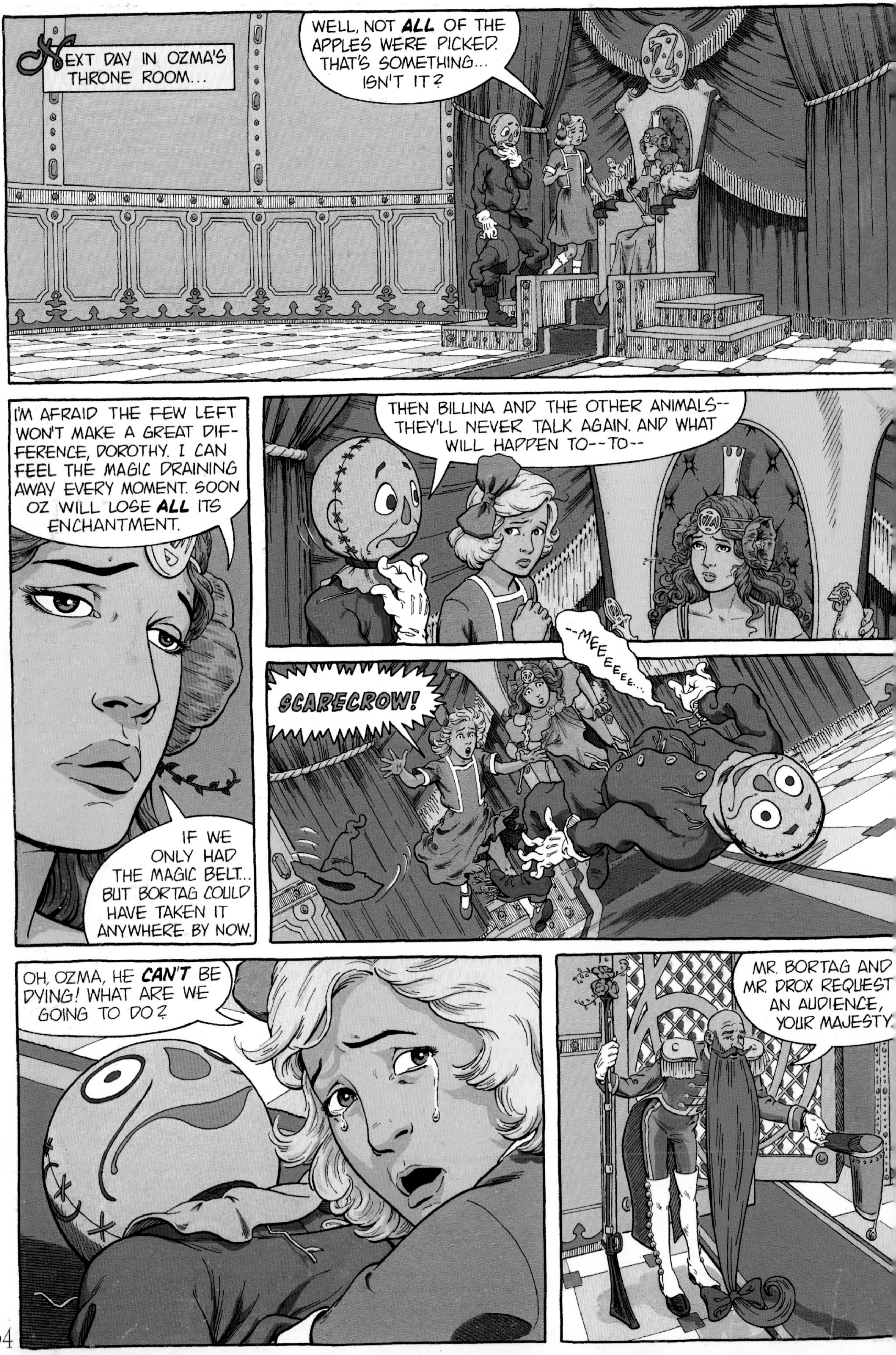
NEXT DAY IN OZMA'S THRONE ROOM...
WELL, NOT ALL OF THE APPLES WERE PICKED. THAT'S SOMETHING... ISN'T IT?
I'M AFRAID THE FEW LEFT WON'T MAKE A GREAT DIFFERENCE, DOROTHY. I CAN FEEL THE MAGIC DRAINING AWAY EVERY MOMENT. SOON OZ WILL LOSE ALL ITS ENCHANTMENT.
IF WE ONLY HAD THE MAGIC BELT... BUT BORTAG COULD HAVE TAKEN IT ANYWHERE BY NOW.
THEN BILLINA AND THE OTHER ANIMALS-- THEY'LL NEVER TALK AGAIN. AND WHAT WILL HAPPEN TO--TO--
--MEEEEEE...
SCARECROW!
OH, OZMA, HE CAN'T BE DYING! WHAT ARE WE GOING TO DO?
MR. BORTAG AND MR. DROX REQUEST AN AUDIENCE, YOUR MAJESTY.

SHOW THEM IN *AT ONCE!*

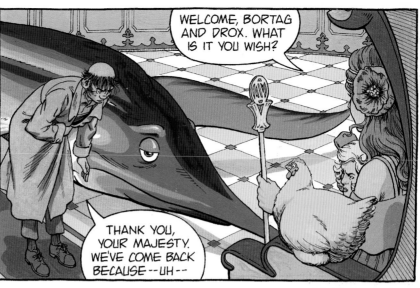

WELCOME, BORTAG AND DROX. WHAT IS IT YOU WISH?

THANK YOU, YOUR MAJESTY. WE'VE COME BACK BECAUSE--UH--

WELL...ER... WE'VE COME TO RETURN *THIS*.

UM, Y'SEE, I THOUGHT THE MAGIC BELT COULD GIVE ME EVERYTHING I EVER WANTED--THAT'S WHY I KEPT IT.

BUT AS SOON AS I HAD IT, I REALIZED THAT ALL I EVER REALLY WANTED WAS FOR SOMEONE TO *LIKE* ME. AND I FOUND THAT I ALREADY HAD WHAT I WANTED--

--A *TRUE FRIEND*--DROX. SO PLEASE, YOUR MAJESTY, I'VE NO RIGHT TO ASK, BUT COULD YOU TRANSPORT HIM BACK TO THE OCEAN AND SEND ME WITH HIM?

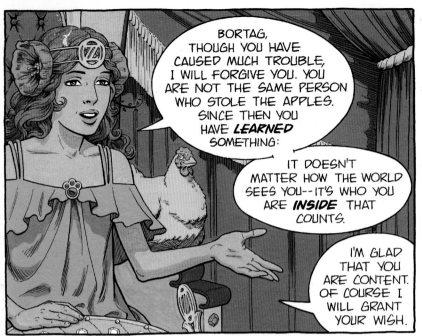

BORTAG, THOUGH YOU HAVE CAUSED MUCH TROUBLE, I WILL FORGIVE YOU. YOU ARE NOT THE SAME PERSON WHO STOLE THE APPLES. SINCE THEN YOU HAVE **LEARNED** SOMETHING:

IT DOESN'T MATTER HOW THE WORLD SEES YOU--IT'S WHO YOU ARE **INSIDE** THAT COUNTS.

I'M GLAD THAT YOU ARE CONTENT. OF COURSE I WILL GRANT YOUR WISH.

BUT THERE IS SOMETHING ELSE I **MUST** DO FIRST.

56

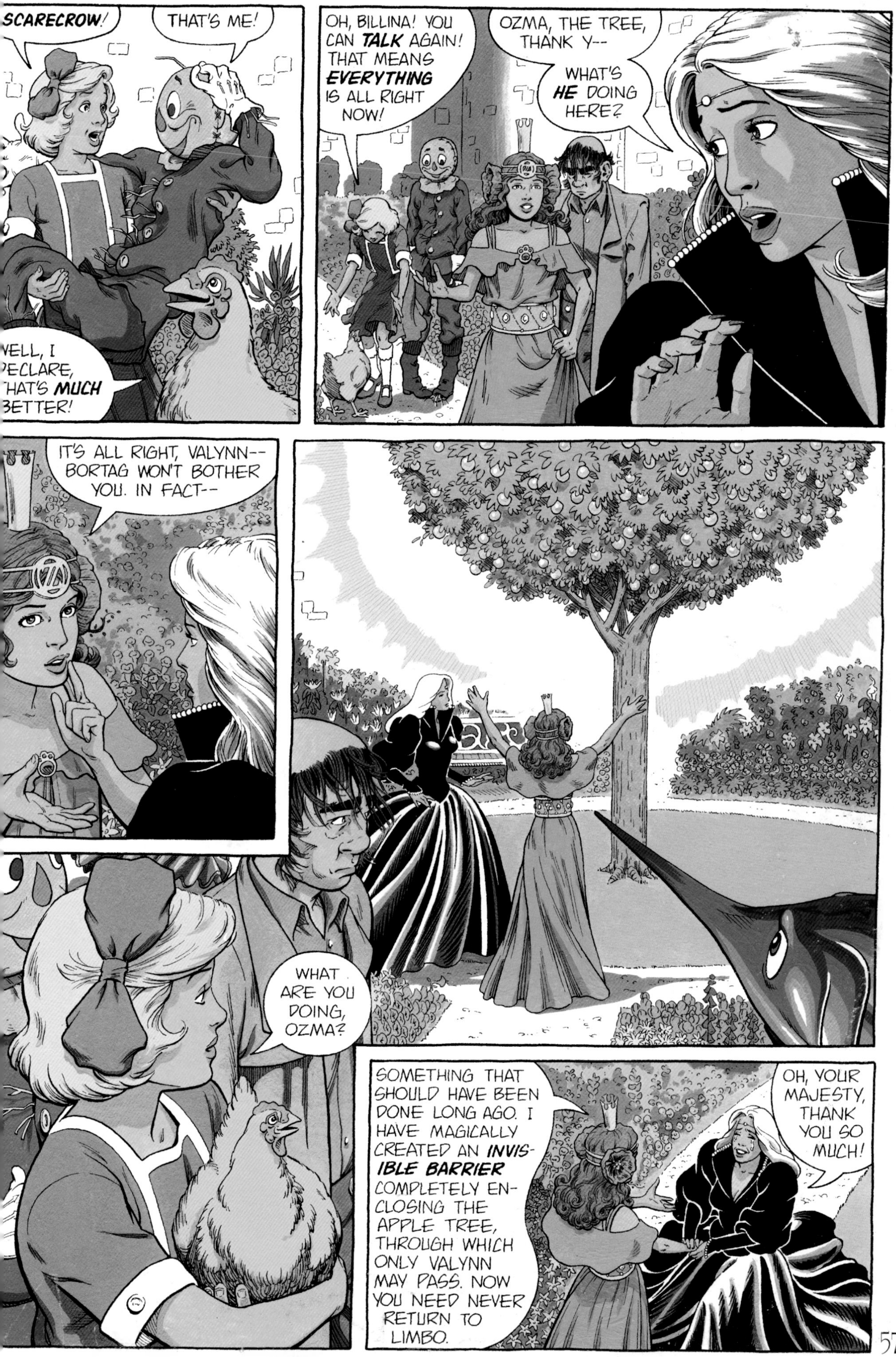
SCARECROW!
THAT'S ME!
WELL, I DECLARE, THAT'S MUCH BETTER!
OH, BILLINA! YOU CAN TALK AGAIN! THAT MEANS EVERYTHING IS ALL RIGHT NOW!
OZMA, THE TREE, THANK Y--
WHAT'S HE DOING HERE?
IT'S ALL RIGHT, VALYNN-- BORTAG WON'T BOTHER YOU. IN FACT--
WHAT ARE YOU DOING, OZMA?
SOMETHING THAT SHOULD HAVE BEEN DONE LONG AGO. I HAVE MAGICALLY CREATED AN INVISIBLE BARRIER COMPLETELY ENCLOSING THE APPLE TREE, THROUGH WHICH ONLY VALYNN MAY PASS. NOW YOU NEED NEVER RETURN TO LIMBO.
OH, YOUR MAJESTY, THANK YOU SO MUCH!

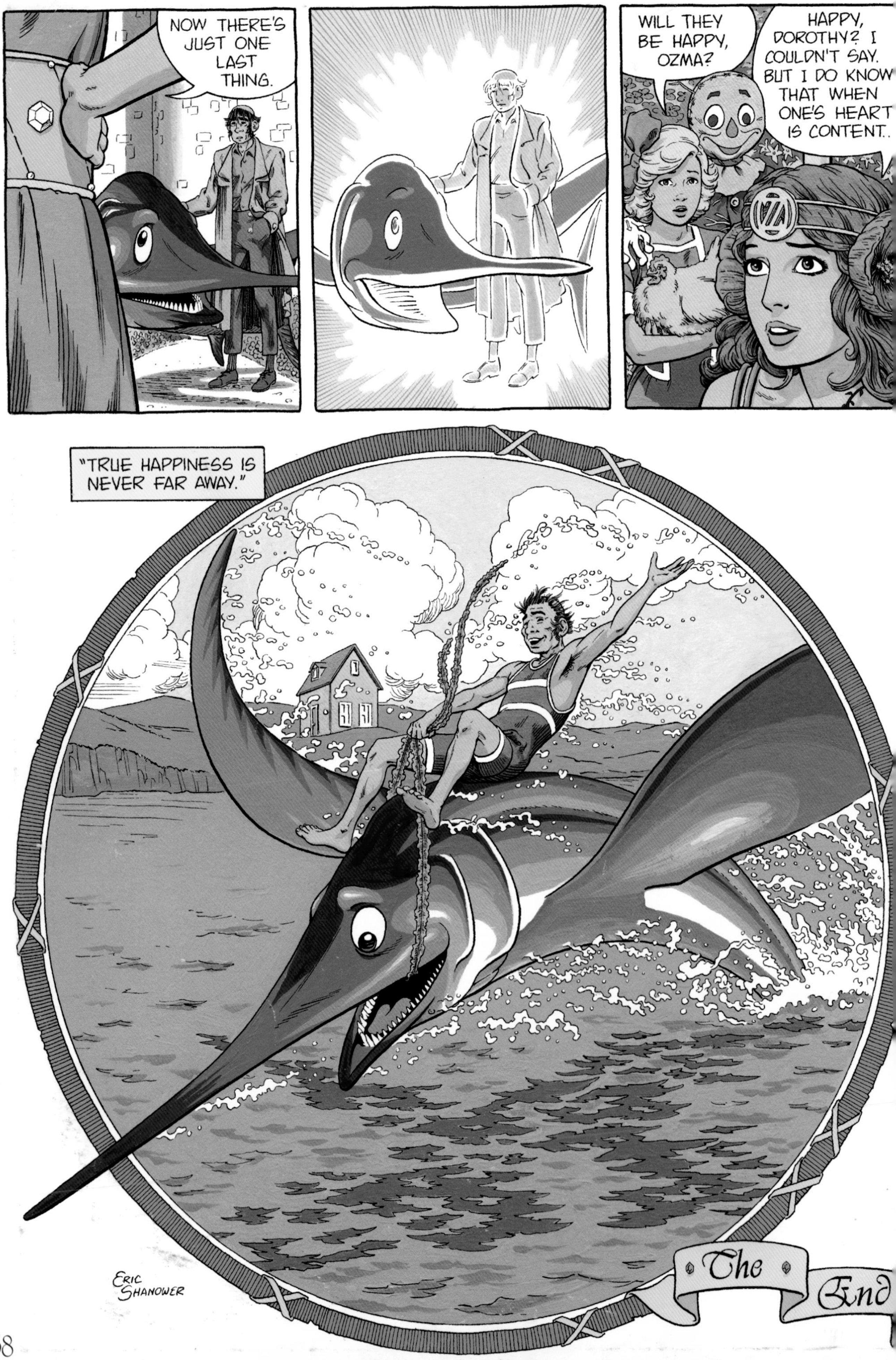
NOW THERE'S JUST ONE LAST THING.
WILL THEY BE HAPPY, OZMA?
HAPPY, DOROTHY? I COULDN'T SAY. BUT I DO KNOW THAT WHEN ONE'S HEART IS CONTENT...
"TRUE HAPPINESS IS NEVER FAR AWAY."
ERIC SHANOWER
The End

The SECRET ISLAND of Oz

Dedicated
with love
to my parents

Chapter 1 The Crimson-tailed Quipperug

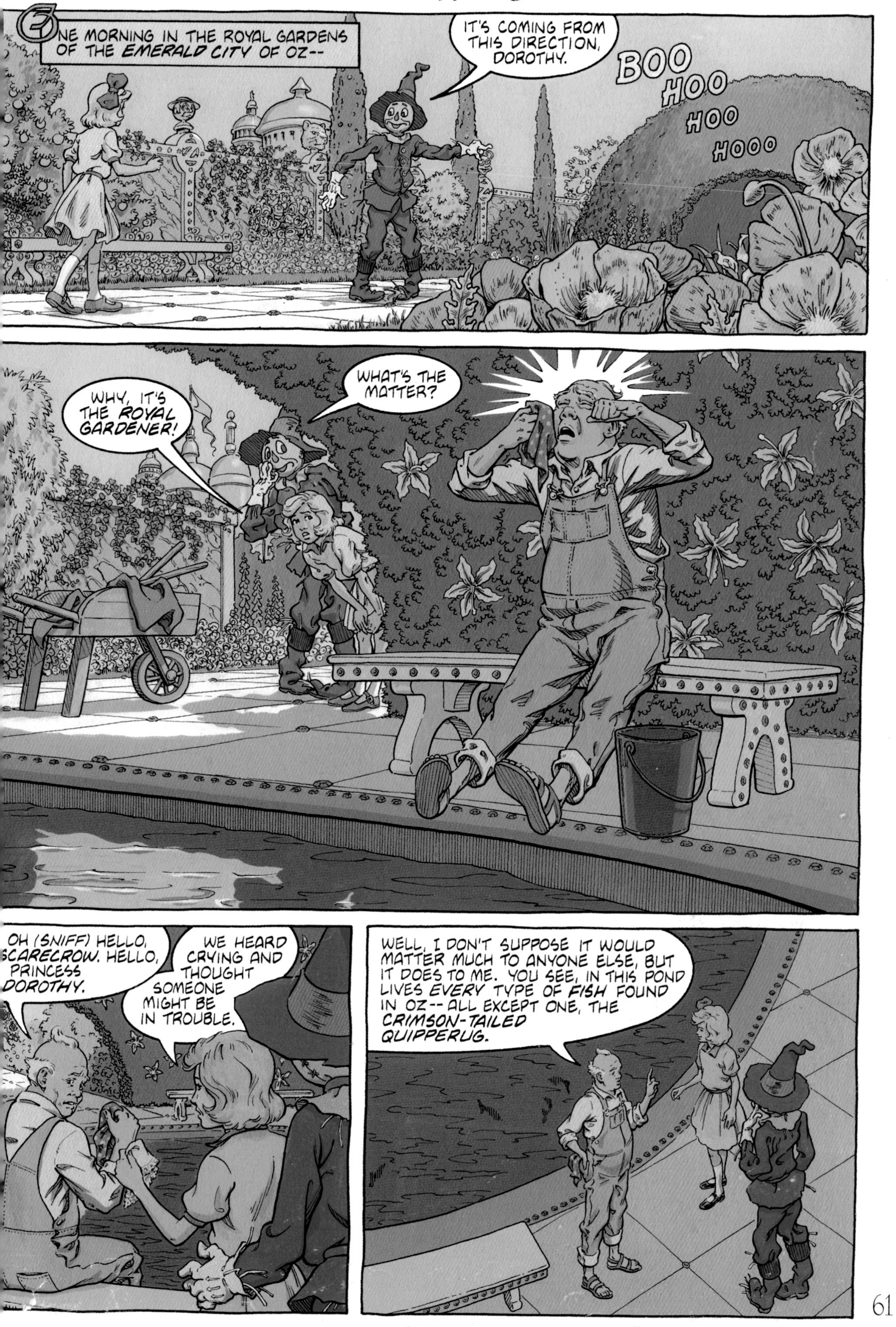
ONE MORNING IN THE ROYAL GARDENS OF THE EMERALD CITY OF OZ--
IT'S COMING FROM THIS DIRECTION, DOROTHY.
BOO HOO HOO HOOO
WHY, IT'S THE ROYAL GARDENER!
WHAT'S THE MATTER?
OH (SNIFF) HELLO, SCARECROW. HELLO, PRINCESS DOROTHY.
WE HEARD CRYING AND THOUGHT SOMEONE MIGHT BE IN TROUBLE.
WELL, I DON'T SUPPOSE IT WOULD MATTER MUCH TO ANYONE ELSE, BUT IT DOES TO ME. YOU SEE, IN THIS POND LIVES EVERY TYPE OF FISH FOUND IN OZ-- ALL EXCEPT ONE, THE CRIMSON-TAILED QUIPPERUG.

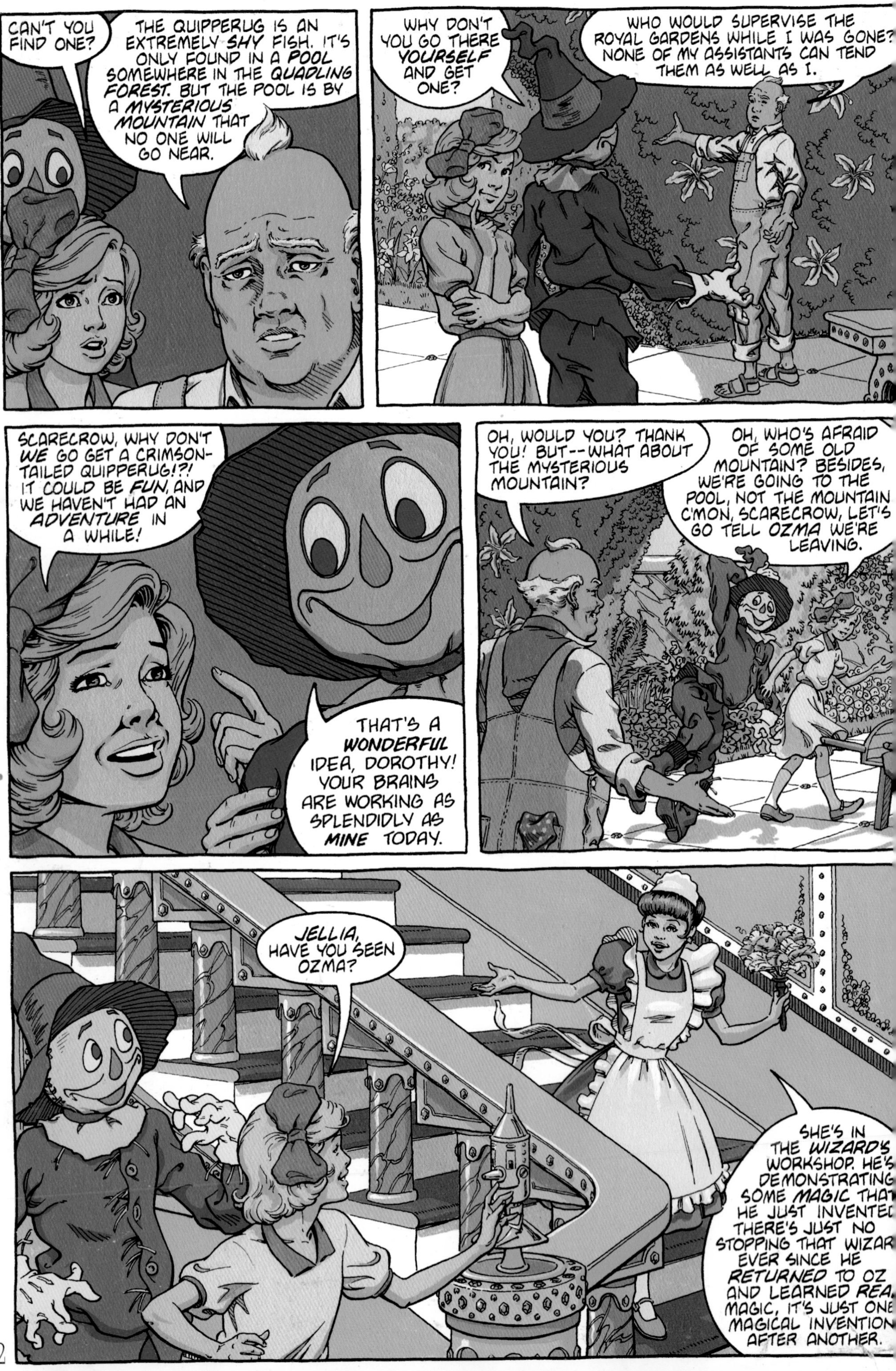
CAN'T YOU FIND ONE?
THE QUIPPERUG IS AN EXTREMELY SHY FISH. IT'S ONLY FOUND IN A POOL SOMEWHERE IN THE QUADLING FOREST. BUT THE POOL IS BY A MYSTERIOUS MOUNTAIN THAT NO ONE WILL GO NEAR.
WHY DON'T YOU GO THERE YOURSELF AND GET ONE?
WHO WOULD SUPERVISE THE ROYAL GARDENS WHILE I WAS GONE? NONE OF MY ASSISTANTS CAN TEND THEM AS WELL AS I.
SCARECROW, WHY DON'T WE GO GET A CRIMSON-TAILED QUIPPERUG!?! IT COULD BE FUN, AND WE HAVEN'T HAD AN ADVENTURE IN A WHILE!
THAT'S A WONDERFUL IDEA, DOROTHY! YOUR BRAINS ARE WORKING AS SPLENDIDLY AS MINE TODAY.
OH, WOULD YOU? THANK YOU! BUT--WHAT ABOUT THE MYSTERIOUS MOUNTAIN?
OH, WHO'S AFRAID OF SOME OLD MOUNTAIN? BESIDES, WE'RE GOING TO THE POOL, NOT THE MOUNTAIN. C'MON, SCARECROW, LET'S GO TELL OZMA WE'RE LEAVING.
JELLIA, HAVE YOU SEEN OZMA?
SHE'S IN THE WIZARD'S WORKSHOP. HE'S DEMONSTRATING SOME MAGIC THAT HE JUST INVENTED. THERE'S JUST NO STOPPING THAT WIZARD EVER SINCE HE RETURNED TO OZ AND LEARNED REAL MAGIC. IT'S JUST ONE MAGICAL INVENTION AFTER ANOTHER.

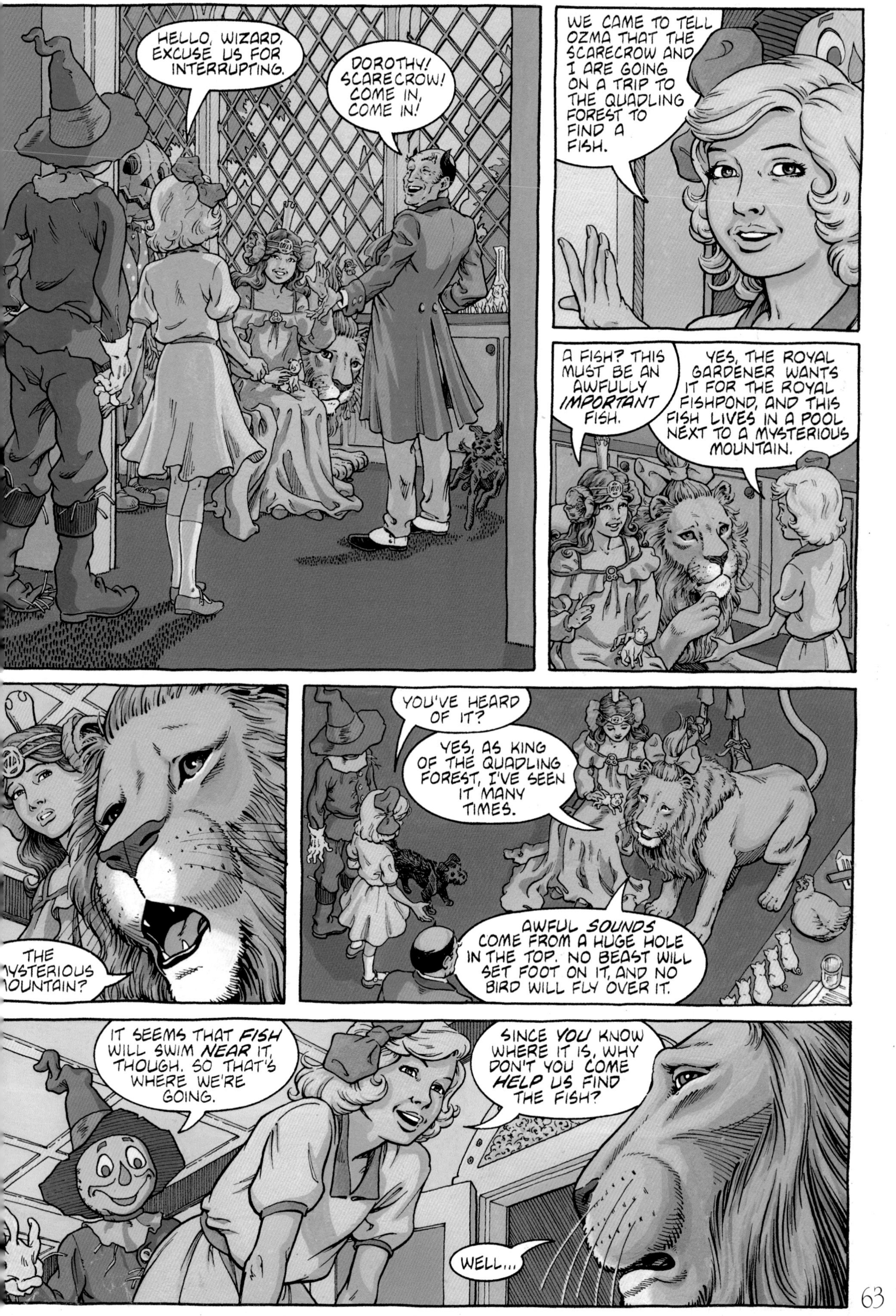
HELLO, WIZARD, EXCUSE US FOR INTERRUPTING.
DOROTHY! SCARECROW! COME IN, COME IN!
WE CAME TO TELL OZMA THAT THE SCARECROW AND I ARE GOING ON A TRIP TO THE QUADLING FOREST TO FIND A FISH.
A FISH? THIS MUST BE AN AWFULLY IMPORTANT FISH.
YES, THE ROYAL GARDENER WANTS IT FOR THE ROYAL FISHPOND, AND THIS FISH LIVES IN A POOL NEXT TO A MYSTERIOUS MOUNTAIN.
THE MYSTERIOUS MOUNTAIN?
YOU'VE HEARD OF IT?
YES, AS KING OF THE QUADLING FOREST, I'VE SEEN IT MANY TIMES.
AWFUL SOUNDS COME FROM A HUGE HOLE IN THE TOP. NO BEAST WILL SET FOOT ON IT, AND NO BIRD WILL FLY OVER IT.
IT SEEMS THAT FISH WILL SWIM NEAR IT, THOUGH. SO THAT'S WHERE WE'RE GOING.
SINCE YOU KNOW WHERE IT IS, WHY DON'T YOU COME HELP US FIND THE FISH?
WELL...

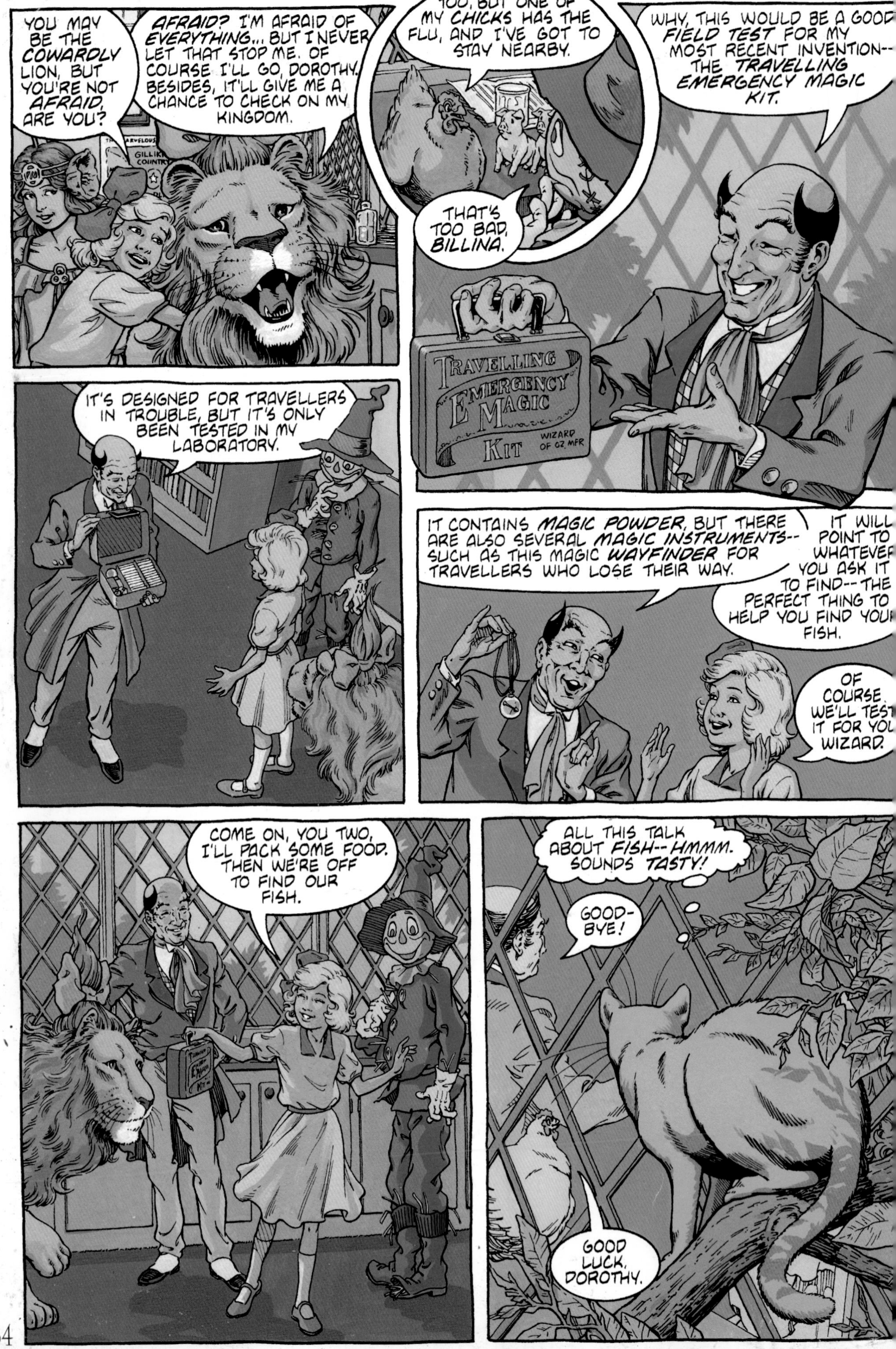

YOU MAY BE THE COWARDLY LION, BUT YOU'RE NOT AFRAID, ARE YOU?
AFRAID? I'M AFRAID OF EVERYTHING... BUT I NEVER LET THAT STOP ME. OF COURSE I'LL GO, DOROTHY. BESIDES, IT'LL GIVE ME A CHANCE TO CHECK ON MY KINGDOM.
I'D GO TOO, BUT ONE OF MY CHICKS HAS THE FLU, AND I'VE GOT TO STAY NEARBY.
THAT'S TOO BAD, BILLINA.
WHY, THIS WOULD BE A GOOD FIELD TEST FOR MY MOST RECENT INVENTION-- THE TRAVELLING EMERGENCY MAGIC KIT.
TRAVELLING EMERGENCY MAGIC KIT
WIZARD OF OZ MFR
IT'S DESIGNED FOR TRAVELLERS IN TROUBLE, BUT IT'S ONLY BEEN TESTED IN MY LABORATORY.
IT CONTAINS MAGIC POWDER, BUT THERE ARE ALSO SEVERAL MAGIC INSTRUMENTS-- SUCH AS THIS MAGIC WAYFINDER FOR TRAVELLERS WHO LOSE THEIR WAY.
IT WILL POINT TO WHATEVER YOU ASK IT TO FIND-- THE PERFECT THING TO HELP YOU FIND YOUR FISH.
OF COURSE. WE'LL TEST IT FOR YOU WIZARD.
COME ON, YOU TWO, I'LL PACK SOME FOOD. THEN WE'RE OFF TO FIND OUR FISH.
ALL THIS TALK ABOUT FISH-- HMMM. SOUNDS TASTY!
GOOD-BYE!
GOOD LUCK, DOROTHY.

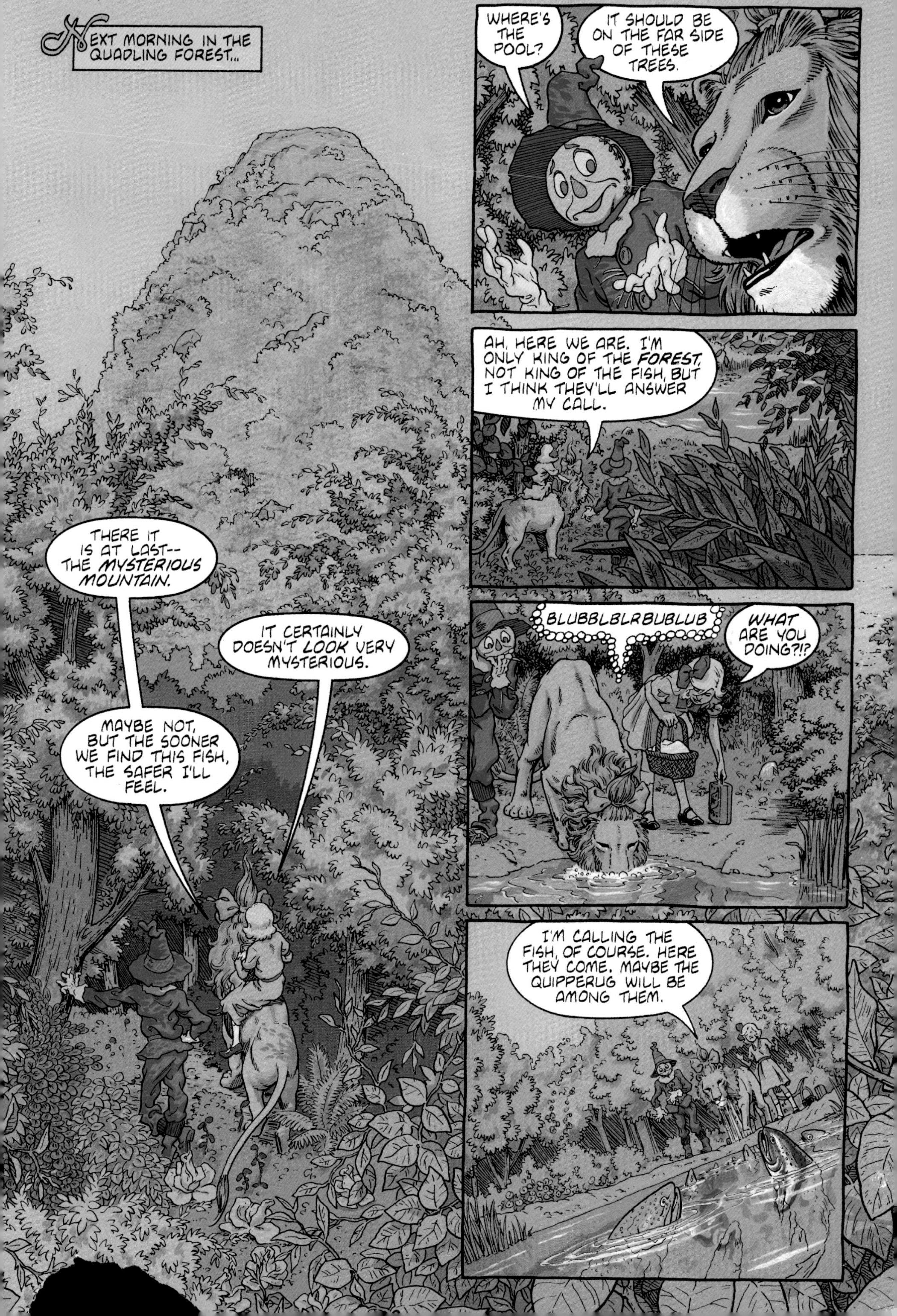

NEXT MORNING IN THE QUADLING FOREST...
THERE IT IS AT LAST-- THE MYSTERIOUS MOUNTAIN.
IT CERTAINLY DOESN'T LOOK VERY MYSTERIOUS.
MAYBE NOT, BUT THE SOONER WE FIND THIS FISH, THE SAFER I'LL FEEL.
WHERE'S THE POOL?
IT SHOULD BE ON THE FAR SIDE OF THESE TREES.
AH, HERE WE ARE. I'M ONLY KING OF THE FOREST, NOT KING OF THE FISH, BUT I THINK THEY'LL ANSWER MY CALL.
BLUBBLBLRBUBLUB
WHAT ARE YOU DOING?!?
I'M CALLING THE FISH, OF COURSE. HERE THEY COME. MAYBE THE QUIPPERUG WILL BE AMONG THEM.

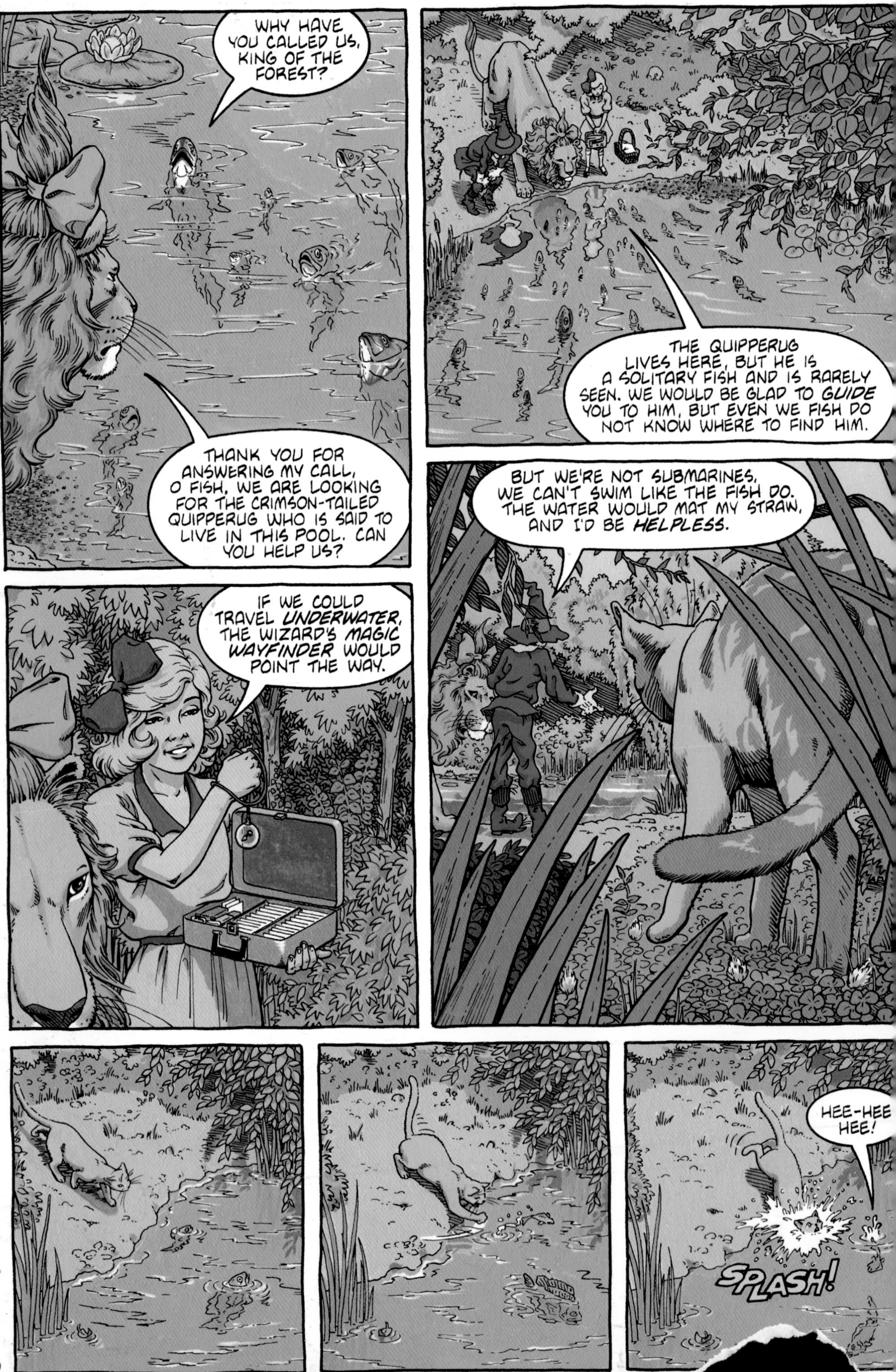

WHY HAVE YOU CALLED US, KING OF THE FOREST?
THANK YOU FOR ANSWERING MY CALL, O FISH. WE ARE LOOKING FOR THE CRIMSON-TAILED QUIPPERUG WHO IS SAID TO LIVE IN THIS POOL. CAN YOU HELP US?
THE QUIPPERUG LIVES HERE, BUT HE IS A SOLITARY FISH AND IS RARELY SEEN. WE WOULD BE GLAD TO GUIDE YOU TO HIM, BUT EVEN WE FISH DO NOT KNOW WHERE TO FIND HIM.
IF WE COULD TRAVEL UNDERWATER, THE WIZARD'S MAGIC WAYFINDER WOULD POINT THE WAY.
BUT WE'RE NOT SUBMARINES. WE CAN'T SWIM LIKE THE FISH DO. THE WATER WOULD MAT MY STRAW, AND I'D BE HELPLESS.
HEE-HEE HEE!
SPLASH!

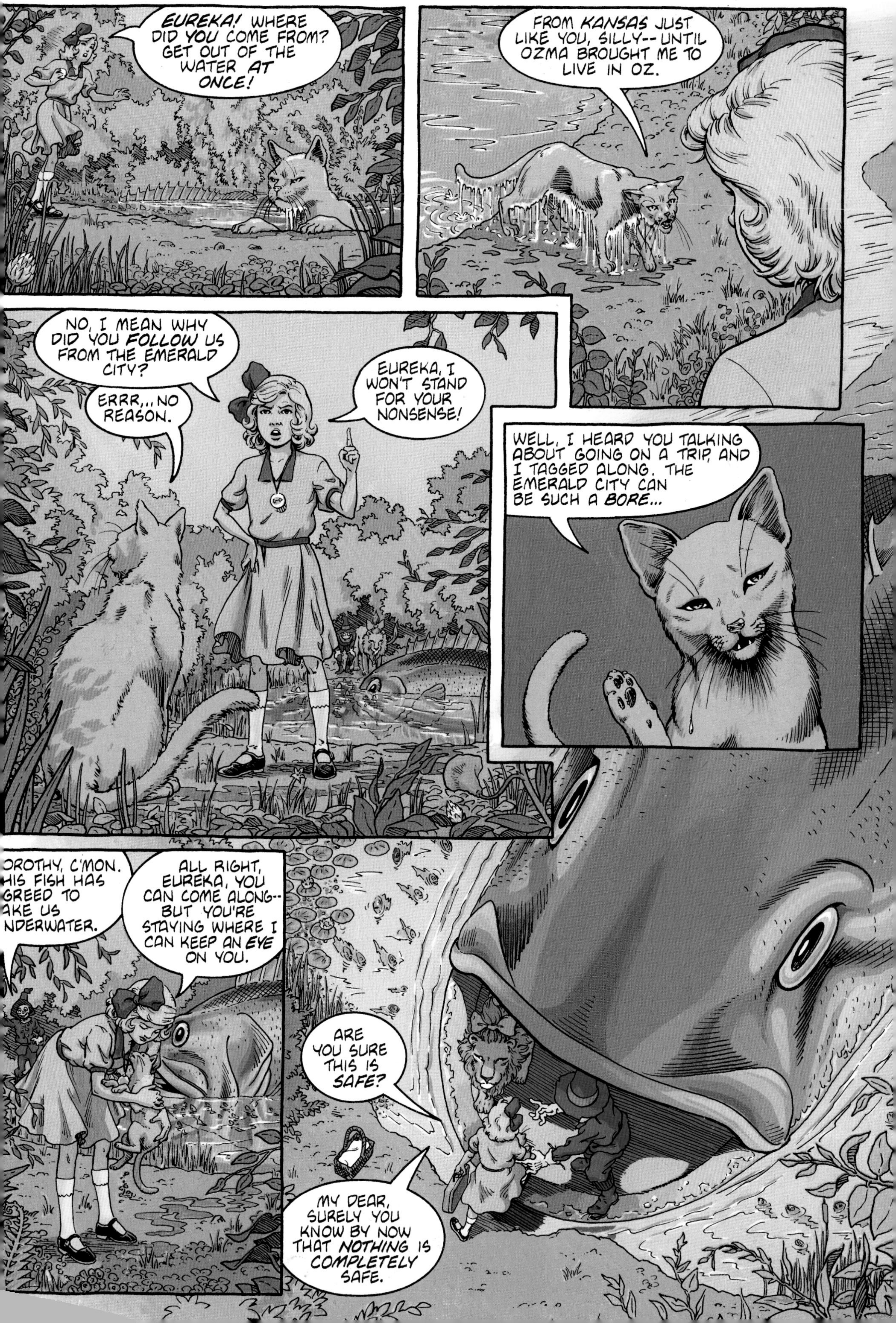
EUREKA! WHERE DID YOU COME FROM? GET OUT OF THE WATER AT ONCE!
FROM KANSAS JUST LIKE YOU, SILLY-- UNTIL OZMA BROUGHT ME TO LIVE IN OZ.
NO, I MEAN WHY DID YOU FOLLOW US FROM THE EMERALD CITY?
ERRR,.. NO REASON.
EUREKA, I WON'T STAND FOR YOUR NONSENSE!
WELL, I HEARD YOU TALKING ABOUT GOING ON A TRIP, AND I TAGGED ALONG. THE EMERALD CITY CAN BE SUCH A BORE...
OROTHY, C'MON. HIS FISH HAS GREED TO AKE US NDERWATER.
ALL RIGHT, EUREKA, YOU CAN COME ALONG-- BUT YOU'RE STAYING WHERE I CAN KEEP AN EYE ON YOU.
ARE YOU SURE THIS IS SAFE?
MY DEAR, SURELY YOU KNOW BY NOW THAT NOTHING IS COMPLETELY SAFE.

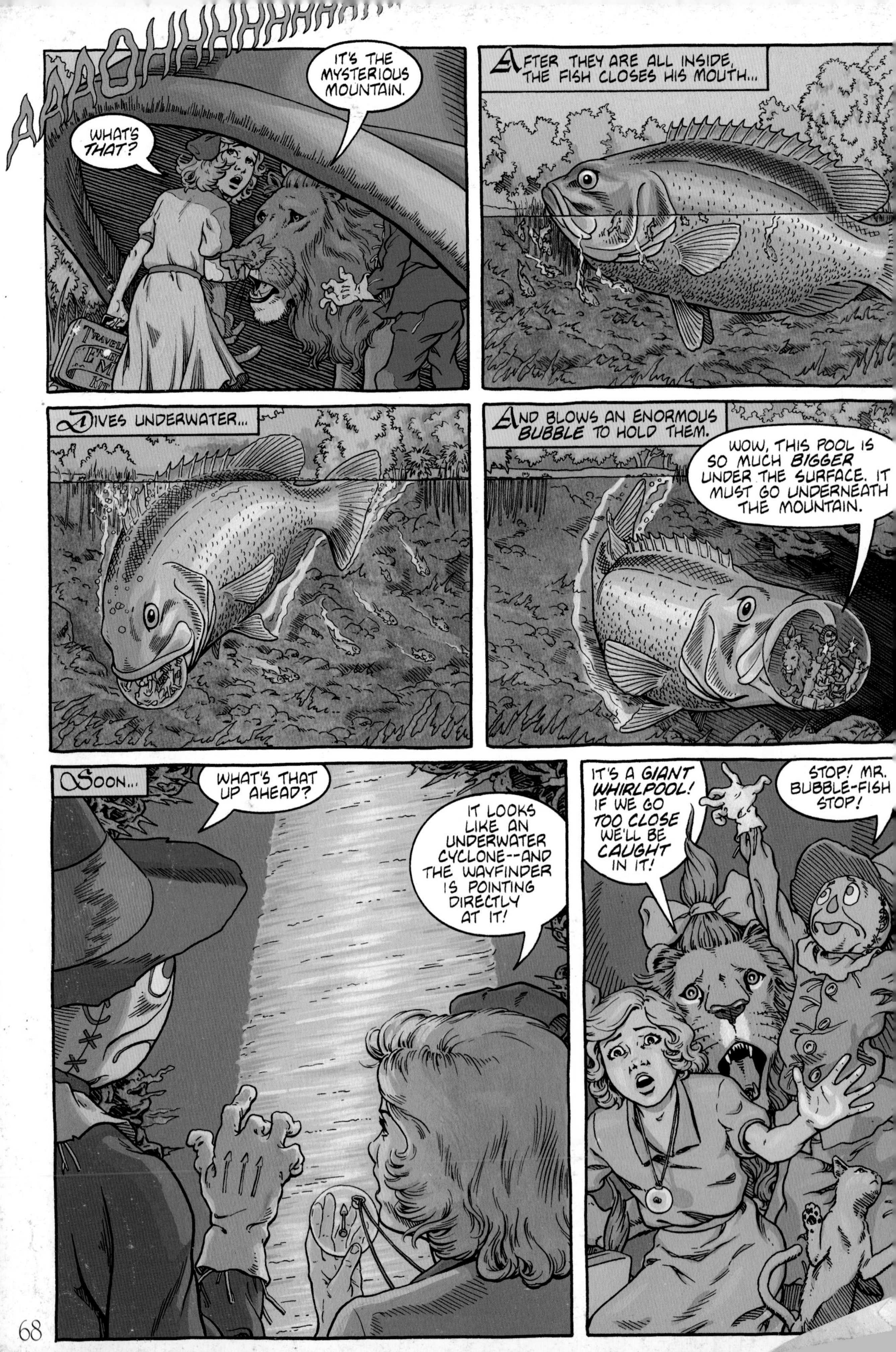
AAAOHHHHHHHH...
WHAT'S THAT?
IT'S THE MYSTERIOUS MOUNTAIN.
AFTER THEY ARE ALL INSIDE, THE FISH CLOSES HIS MOUTH...
DIVES UNDERWATER...
AND BLOWS AN ENORMOUS BUBBLE TO HOLD THEM.
WOW, THIS POOL IS SO MUCH BIGGER UNDER THE SURFACE. IT MUST GO UNDERNEATH THE MOUNTAIN.
SOON...
WHAT'S THAT UP AHEAD?
IT LOOKS LIKE AN UNDERWATER CYCLONE--AND THE WAYFINDER IS POINTING DIRECTLY AT IT!
IT'S A GIANT WHIRLPOOL! IF WE GO TOO CLOSE WE'LL BE CAUGHT IN IT!
STOP! MR. BUBBLE-FISH STOP!

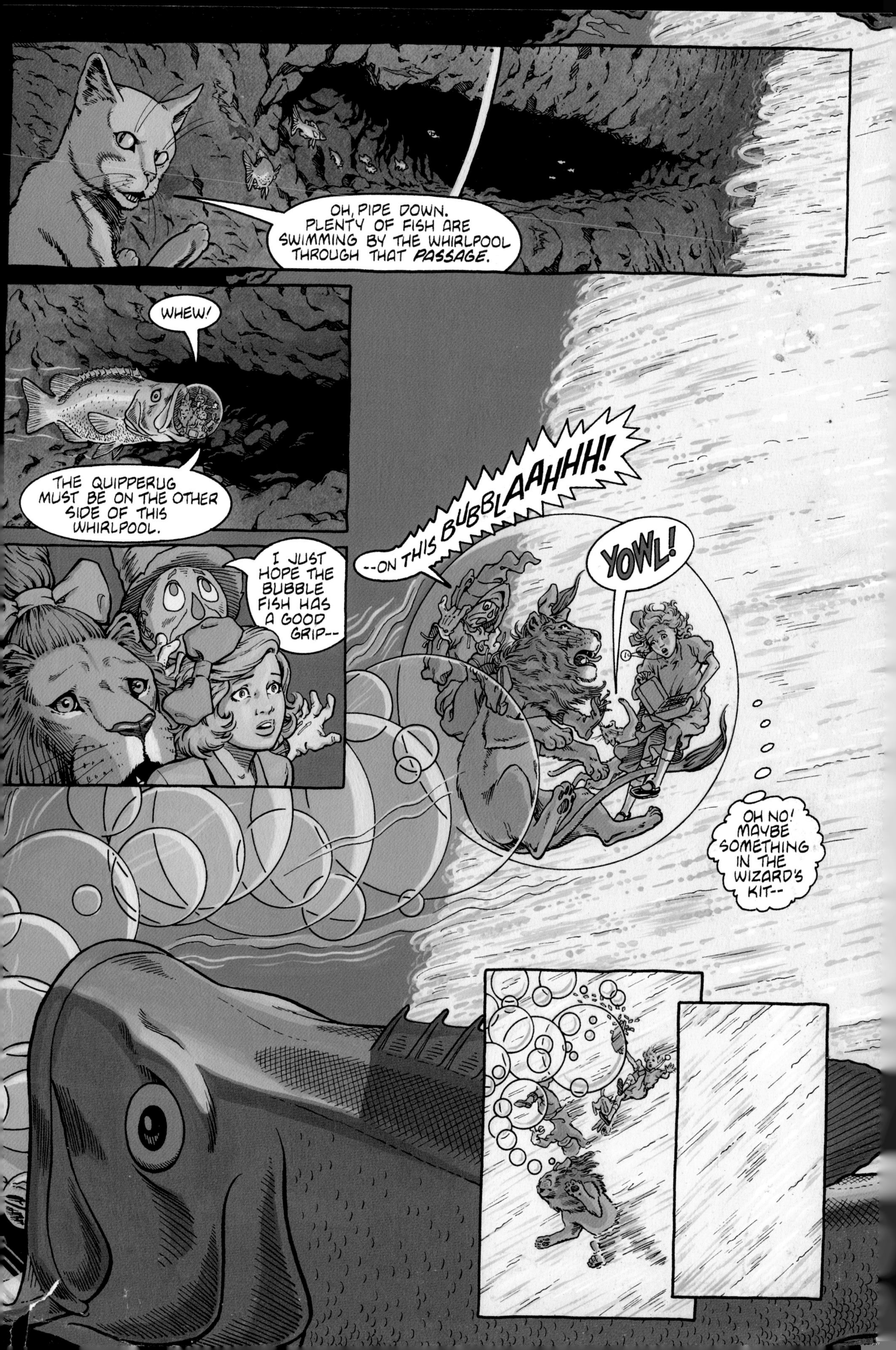
OH, PIPE DOWN. PLENTY OF FISH ARE SWIMMING BY THE WHIRLPOOL THROUGH THAT PASSAGE.
WHEW!
THE QUIPPERUG MUST BE ON THE OTHER SIDE OF THIS WHIRLPOOL.
I JUST HOPE THE BUBBLE FISH HAS A GOOD GRIP--
--ON THIS BUBBLAAHHHH!
YOWL!
OH NO! MAYBE SOMETHING IN THE WIZARD'S KIT--

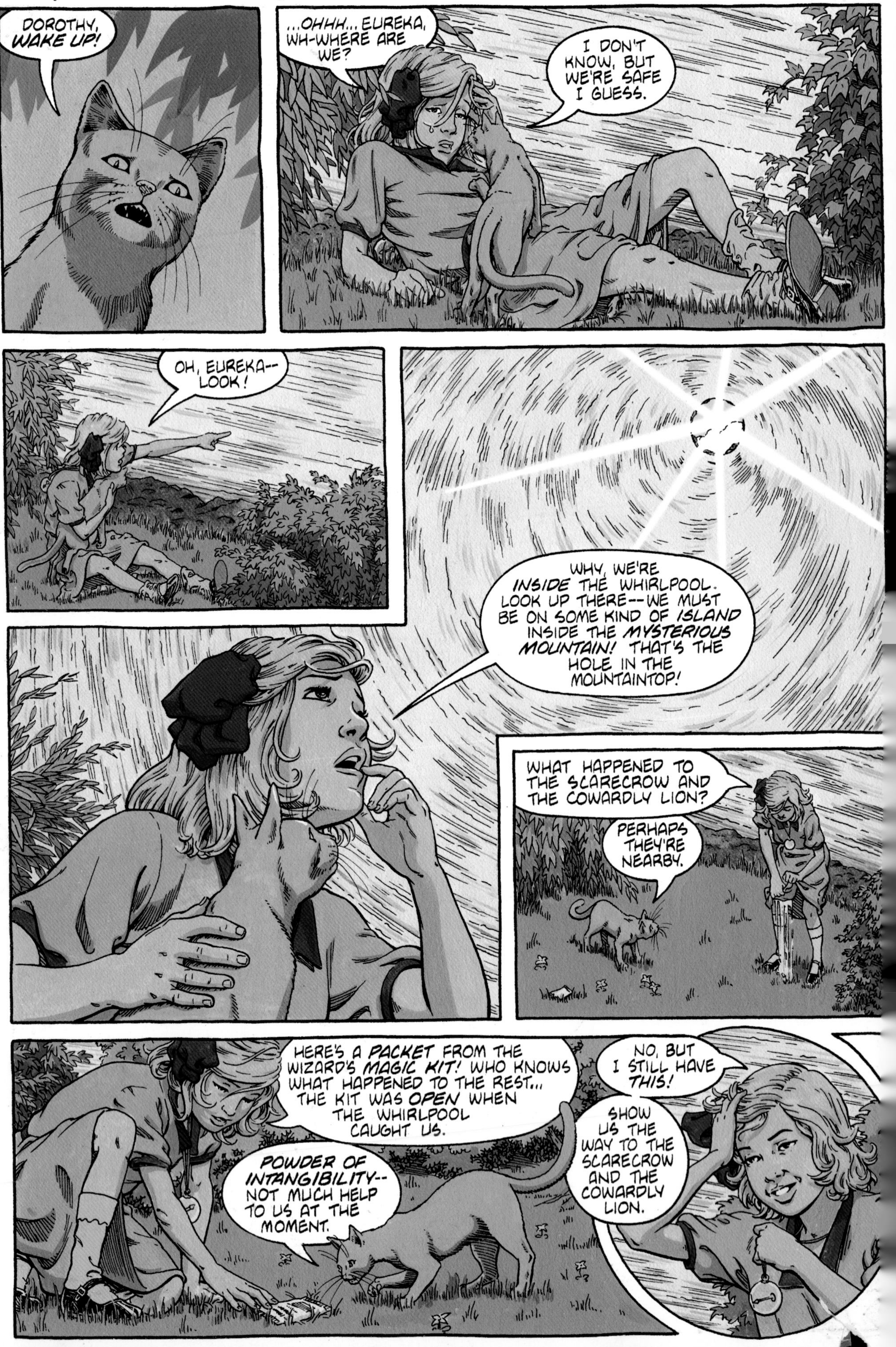
DOROTHY, WAKE UP!
...OHHH... EUREKA, WH-WHERE ARE WE?
I DON'T KNOW, BUT WE'RE SAFE I GUESS.
OH, EUREKA-- LOOK!
WHY, WE'RE INSIDE THE WHIRLPOOL. LOOK UP THERE--WE MUST BE ON SOME KIND OF ISLAND INSIDE THE MYSTERIOUS MOUNTAIN! THAT'S THE HOLE IN THE MOUNTAINTOP!
WHAT HAPPENED TO THE SCARECROW AND THE COWARDLY LION?
PERHAPS THEY'RE NEARBY.
HERE'S A PACKET FROM THE WIZARD'S MAGIC KIT! WHO KNOWS WHAT HAPPENED TO THE REST... THE KIT WAS OPEN WHEN THE WHIRLPOOL CAUGHT US.
POWDER OF INTANGIBILITY-- NOT MUCH HELP TO US AT THE MOMENT.
NO, BUT I STILL HAVE THIS!
SHOW US THE WAY TO THE SCARECROW AND THE COWARDLY LION.

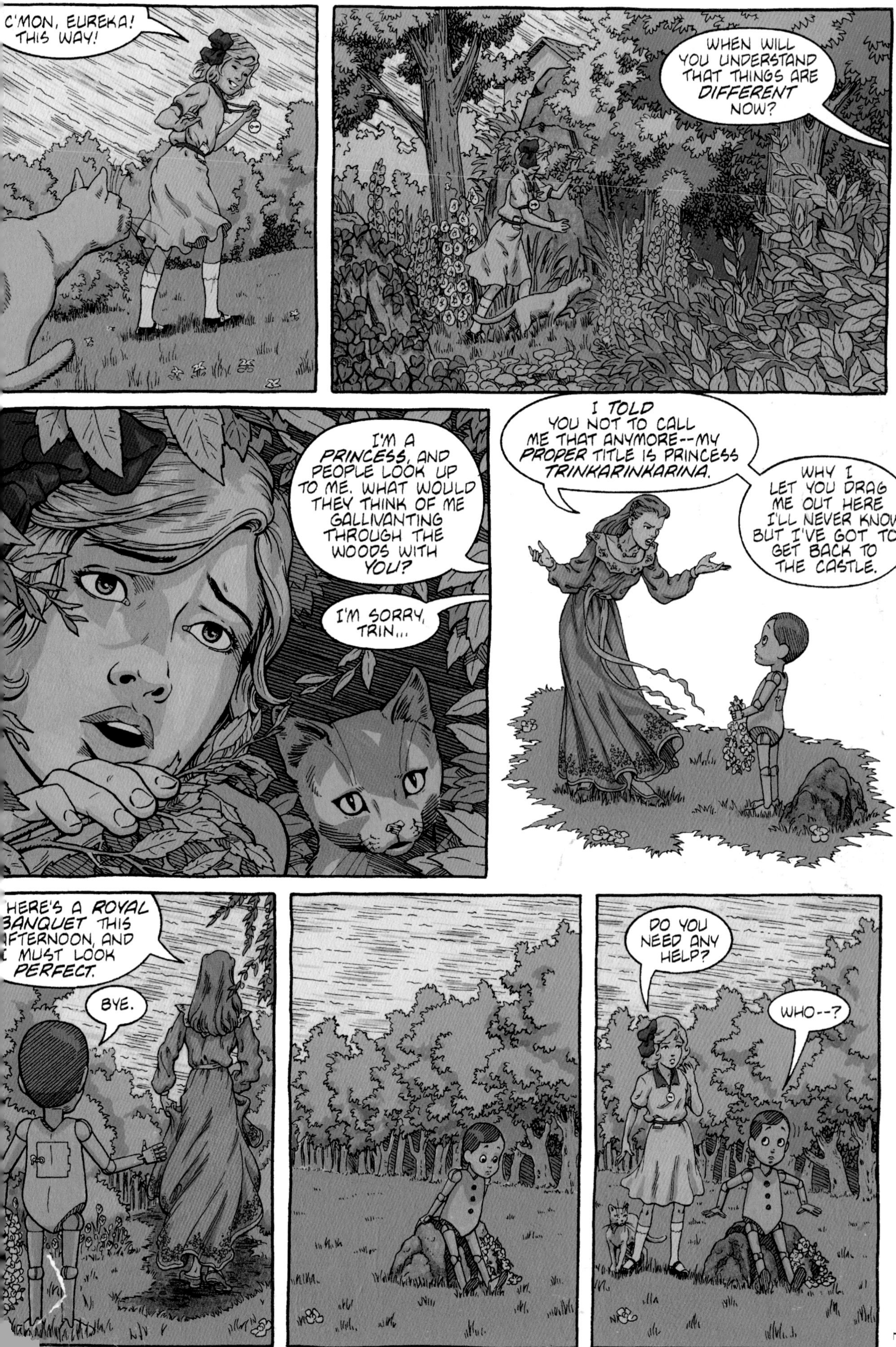

C'MON, EUREKA! THIS WAY!
WHEN WILL YOU UNDERSTAND THAT THINGS ARE DIFFERENT NOW?
I'M A PRINCESS, AND PEOPLE LOOK UP TO ME. WHAT WOULD THEY THINK OF ME GALLIVANTING THROUGH THE WOODS WITH YOU?
I'M SORRY, TRIN...
I TOLD YOU NOT TO CALL ME THAT ANYMORE--MY PROPER TITLE IS PRINCESS TRINKARINKARINA.
WHY I LET YOU DRAG ME OUT HERE I'LL NEVER KNOW, BUT I'VE GOT TO GET BACK TO THE CASTLE.
HERE'S A ROYAL BANQUET THIS AFTERNOON, AND MUST LOOK PERFECT.
BYE.
DO YOU NEED ANY HELP?
WHO--?

HELLO, I'M DOROTHY GALE, AND THIS IS EUREKA. WE HEARD THAT PRINCESS YELLING AT YOU AND THOUGHT MAYBE YOU NEEDED HELP.

OH NO, YOU CAN'T DO ANYTHING ABOUT *THAT*. BUT I'M PLEASED TO MEET YOU. I'M *KNOTBOY*.

KNOTBOY! THAT'S YOUR *NAME*?

EUREKA! DON'T BE RUDE!

WHAT A FUNNY CREATURE. I'VE NEVER SEEN ANYTHING LIKE YOU BEFORE.

LOOK WHO'S TALKING.

EUREKA, WILL YOU STOP?!

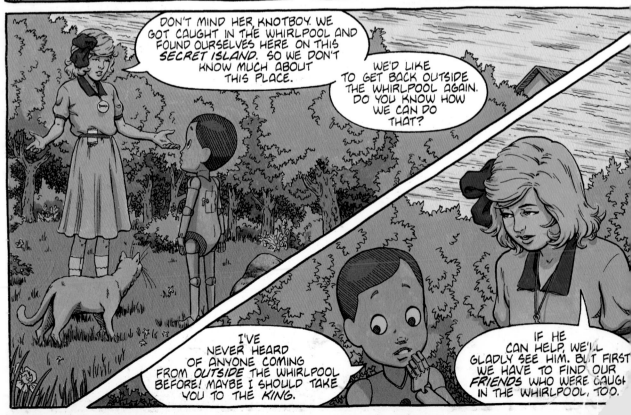

DON'T MIND HER, KNOTBOY. WE GOT CAUGHT IN THE WHIRLPOOL AND FOUND OURSELVES HERE ON THIS *SECRET ISLAND*. SO WE DON'T KNOW MUCH ABOUT THIS PLACE.

WE'D LIKE TO GET BACK OUTSIDE THE WHIRLPOOL AGAIN. DO YOU KNOW HOW WE CAN DO THAT?

I'VE NEVER HEARD OF ANYONE COMING FROM *OUTSIDE* THE WHIRLPOOL BEFORE! MAYBE I SHOULD TAKE YOU TO THE *KING*.

IF HE CAN HELP, WE'LL GLADLY SEE HIM. BUT FIRST WE HAVE TO FIND OUR *FRIENDS* WHO WERE CAUGH IN THE WHIRLPOOL, TOO.

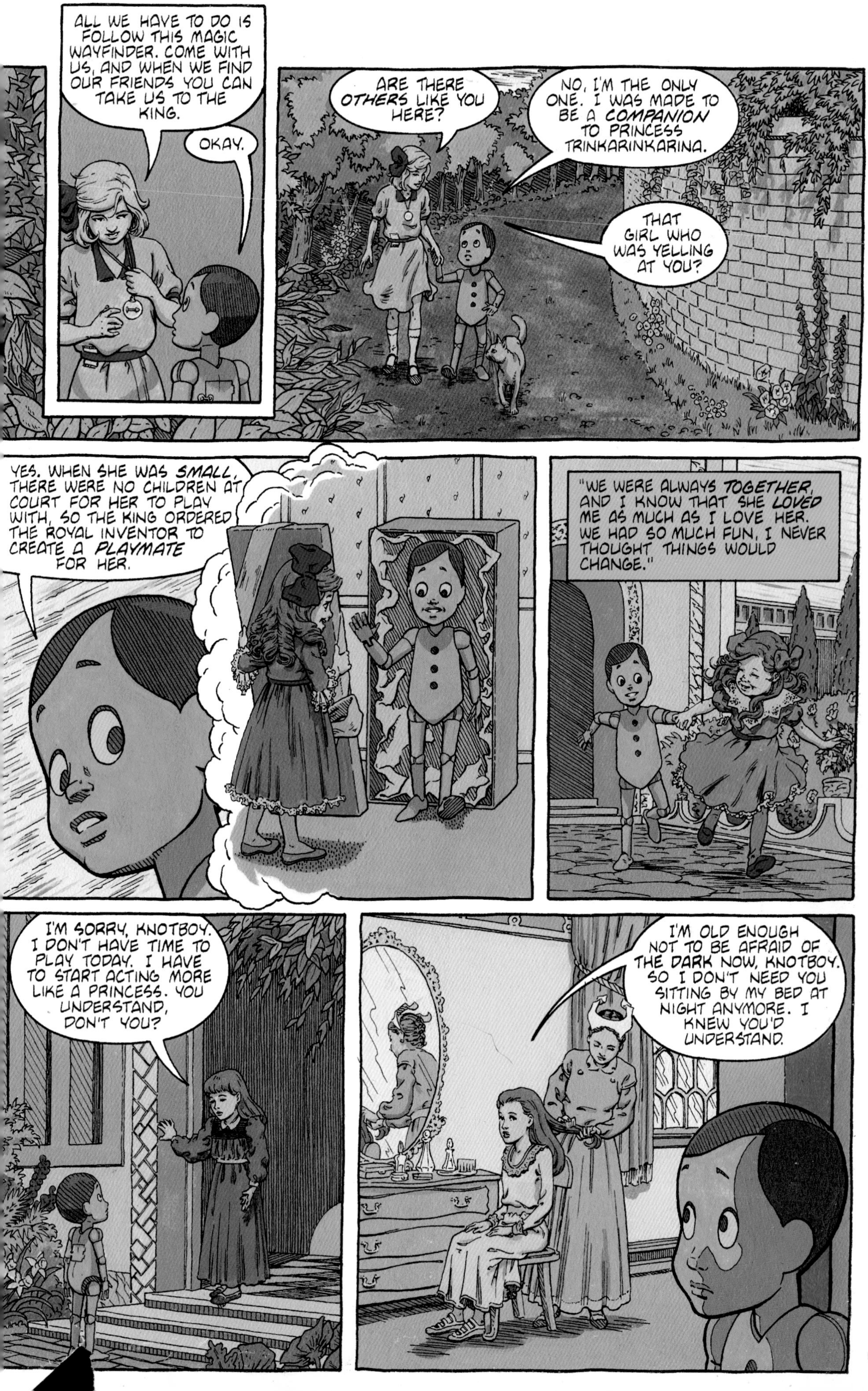

ALL WE HAVE TO DO IS FOLLOW THIS MAGIC WAYFINDER. COME WITH US, AND WHEN WE FIND OUR FRIENDS YOU CAN TAKE US TO THE KING.
OKAY.
ARE THERE OTHERS LIKE YOU HERE?
NO, I'M THE ONLY ONE. I WAS MADE TO BE A COMPANION TO PRINCESS TRINKARINKARINA.
THAT GIRL WHO WAS YELLING AT YOU?
YES. WHEN SHE WAS SMALL, THERE WERE NO CHILDREN AT COURT FOR HER TO PLAY WITH, SO THE KING ORDERED THE ROYAL INVENTOR TO CREATE A PLAYMATE FOR HER.
"WE WERE ALWAYS TOGETHER, AND I KNOW THAT SHE LOVED ME AS MUCH AS I LOVE HER. WE HAD SO MUCH FUN, I NEVER THOUGHT THINGS WOULD CHANGE."
I'M SORRY, KNOTBOY. I DON'T HAVE TIME TO PLAY TODAY. I HAVE TO START ACTING MORE LIKE A PRINCESS. YOU UNDERSTAND, DON'T YOU?
I'M OLD ENOUGH NOT TO BE AFRAID OF THE DARK NOW, KNOTBOY. SO I DON'T NEED YOU SITTING BY MY BED AT NIGHT ANYMORE. I KNEW YOU'D UNDERSTAND.

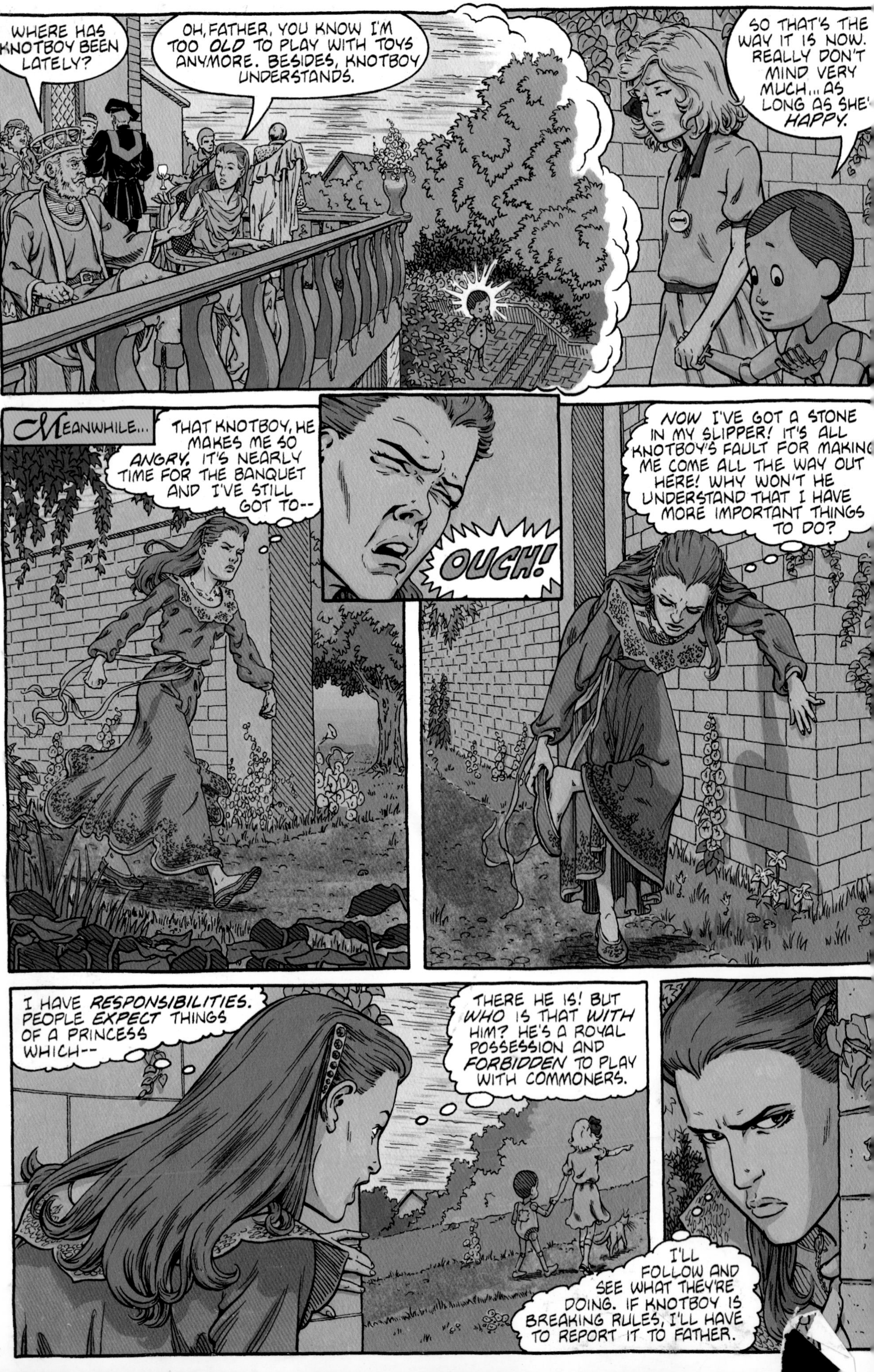
WHERE HAS KNOTBOY BEEN LATELY?
OH, FATHER, YOU KNOW I'M TOO OLD TO PLAY WITH TOYS ANYMORE. BESIDES, KNOTBOY UNDERSTANDS.
SO THAT'S THE WAY IT IS NOW. REALLY DON'T MIND VERY MUCH... AS LONG AS SHE'S HAPPY.
MEANWHILE...
THAT KNOTBOY, HE MAKES ME SO ANGRY. IT'S NEARLY TIME FOR THE BANQUET AND I'VE STILL GOT TO--
OUCH!
NOW I'VE GOT A STONE IN MY SLIPPER! IT'S ALL KNOTBOY'S FAULT FOR MAKING ME COME ALL THE WAY OUT HERE! WHY WON'T HE UNDERSTAND THAT I HAVE MORE IMPORTANT THINGS TO DO?
I HAVE RESPONSIBILITIES. PEOPLE EXPECT THINGS OF A PRINCESS WHICH--
THERE HE IS! BUT WHO IS THAT WITH HIM? HE'S A ROYAL POSSESSION AND FORBIDDEN TO PLAY WITH COMMONERS.
I'LL FOLLOW AND SEE WHAT THEY'RE DOING. IF KNOTBOY IS BREAKING RULES, I'LL HAVE TO REPORT IT TO FATHER.

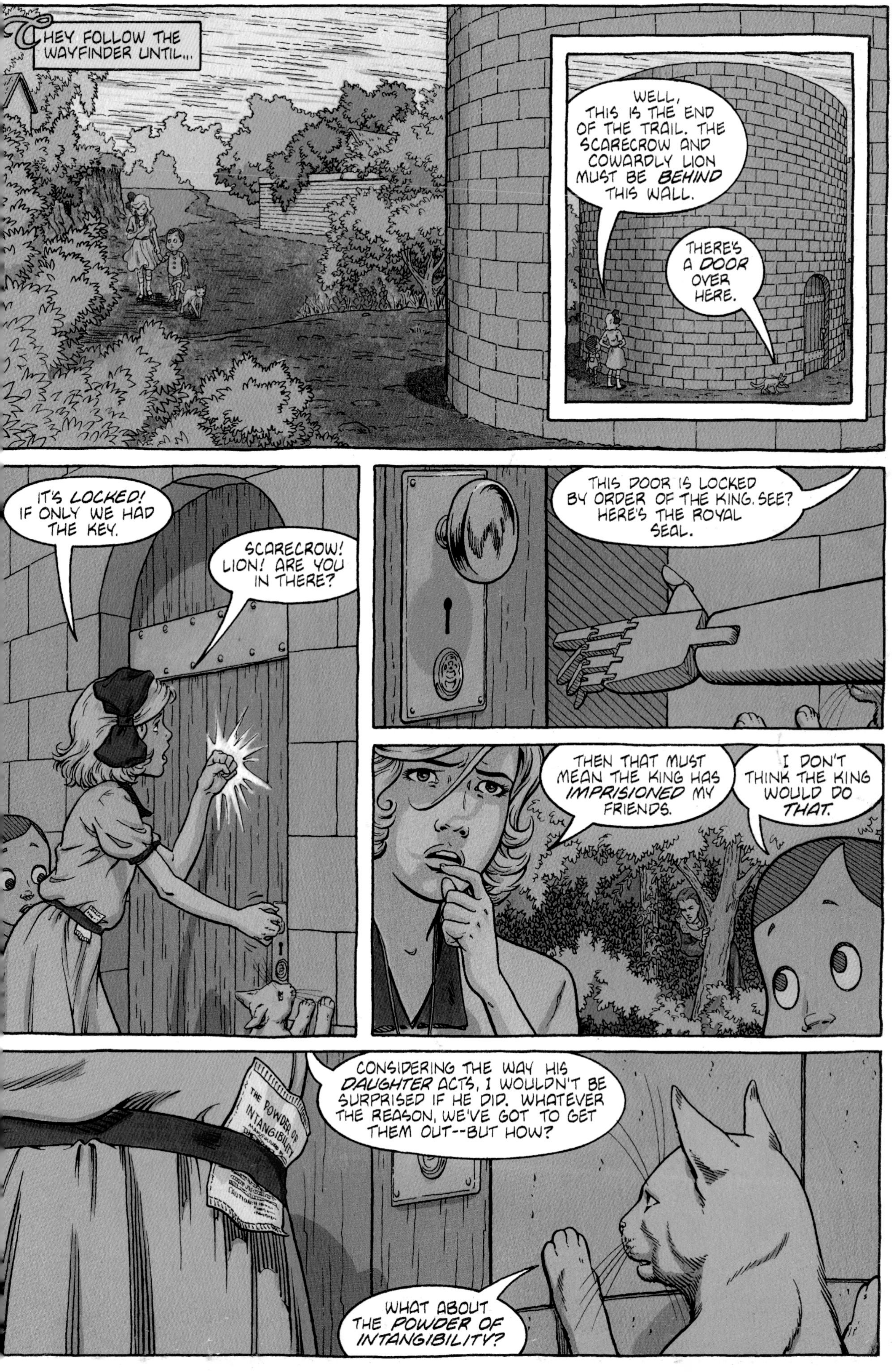
THEY FOLLOW THE WAYFINDER UNTIL...
WELL, THIS IS THE END OF THE TRAIL. THE SCARECROW AND COWARDLY LION MUST BE *BEHIND* THIS WALL.
THERE'S A *DOOR* OVER HERE.
IT'S *LOCKED!* IF ONLY WE HAD THE KEY.
SCARECROW! LION! ARE YOU IN THERE?
THIS DOOR IS LOCKED BY ORDER OF THE KING. SEE? HERE'S THE ROYAL SEAL.
THEN THAT MUST MEAN THE KING HAS *IMPRISIONED* MY FRIENDS.
I DON'T THINK THE KING WOULD DO *THAT.*
CONSIDERING THE WAY HIS *DAUGHTER* ACTS, I WOULDN'T BE SURPRISED IF HE DID. WHATEVER THE REASON, WE'VE GOT TO GET THEM OUT--BUT HOW?
THE POWDER OF INTANGIBILITY
WHAT ABOUT THE *POWDER OF INTANGIBILITY?*

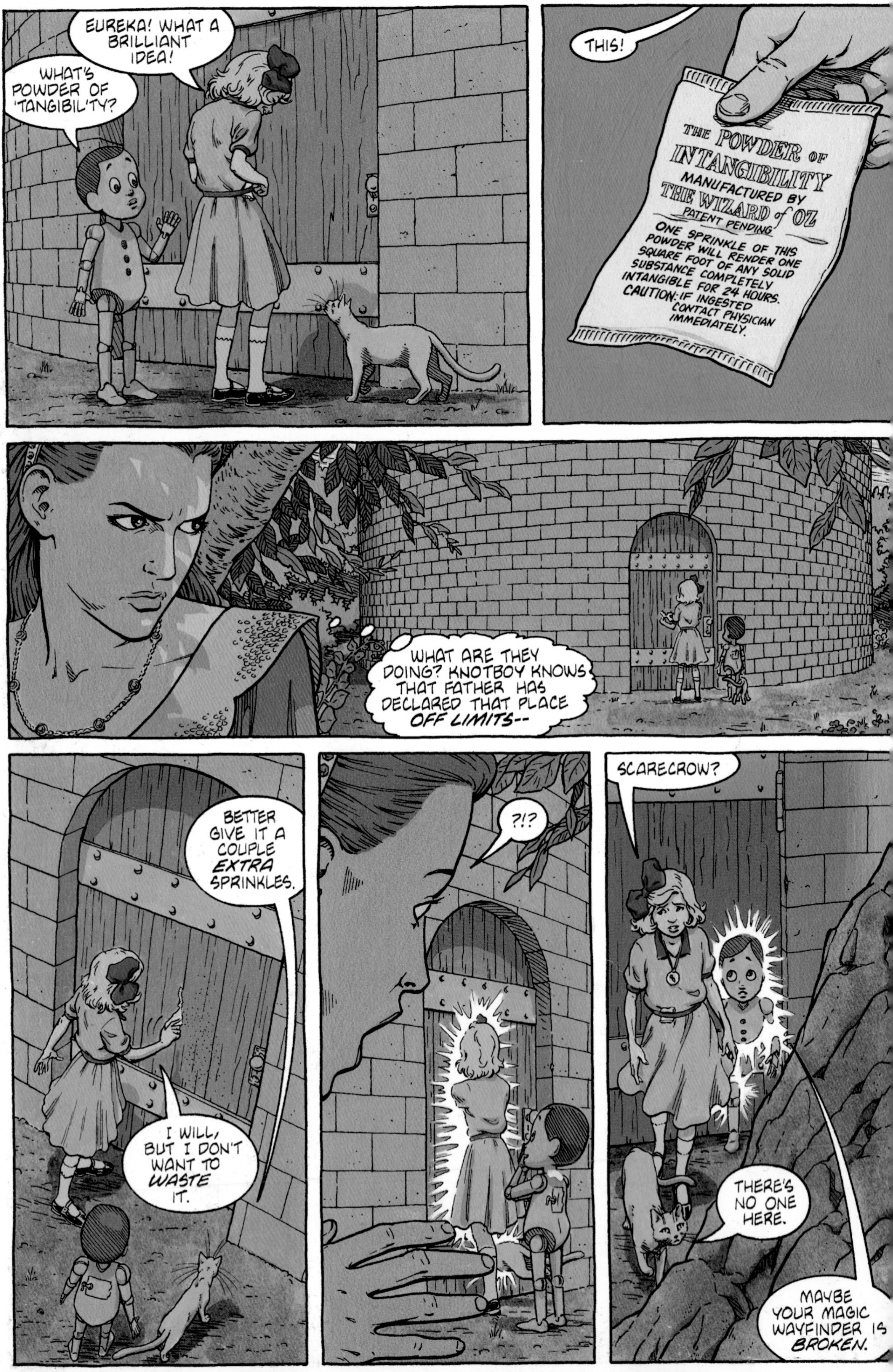
WHAT'S POWDER OF 'TANGIBIL'TY?
EUREKA! WHAT A BRILLIANT IDEA!
THIS!
THE POWDER OF INTANGIBILITY
MANUFACTURED BY THE WIZARD of OZ
PATENT PENDING
ONE SPRINKLE OF THIS POWDER WILL RENDER ONE SQUARE FOOT OF ANY SOLID SUBSTANCE COMPLETELY INTANGIBLE FOR 24 HOURS.
CAUTION: IF INGESTED CONTACT PHYSICIAN IMMEDIATELY.
WHAT ARE THEY DOING? KNOTBOY KNOWS THAT FATHER HAS DECLARED THAT PLACE OFF LIMITS--
BETTER GIVE IT A COUPLE EXTRA SPRINKLES.
I WILL, BUT I DON'T WANT TO WASTE IT.
?!?
SCARECROW?
THERE'S NO ONE HERE.
MAYBE YOUR MAGIC WAYFINDER IS BROKEN.

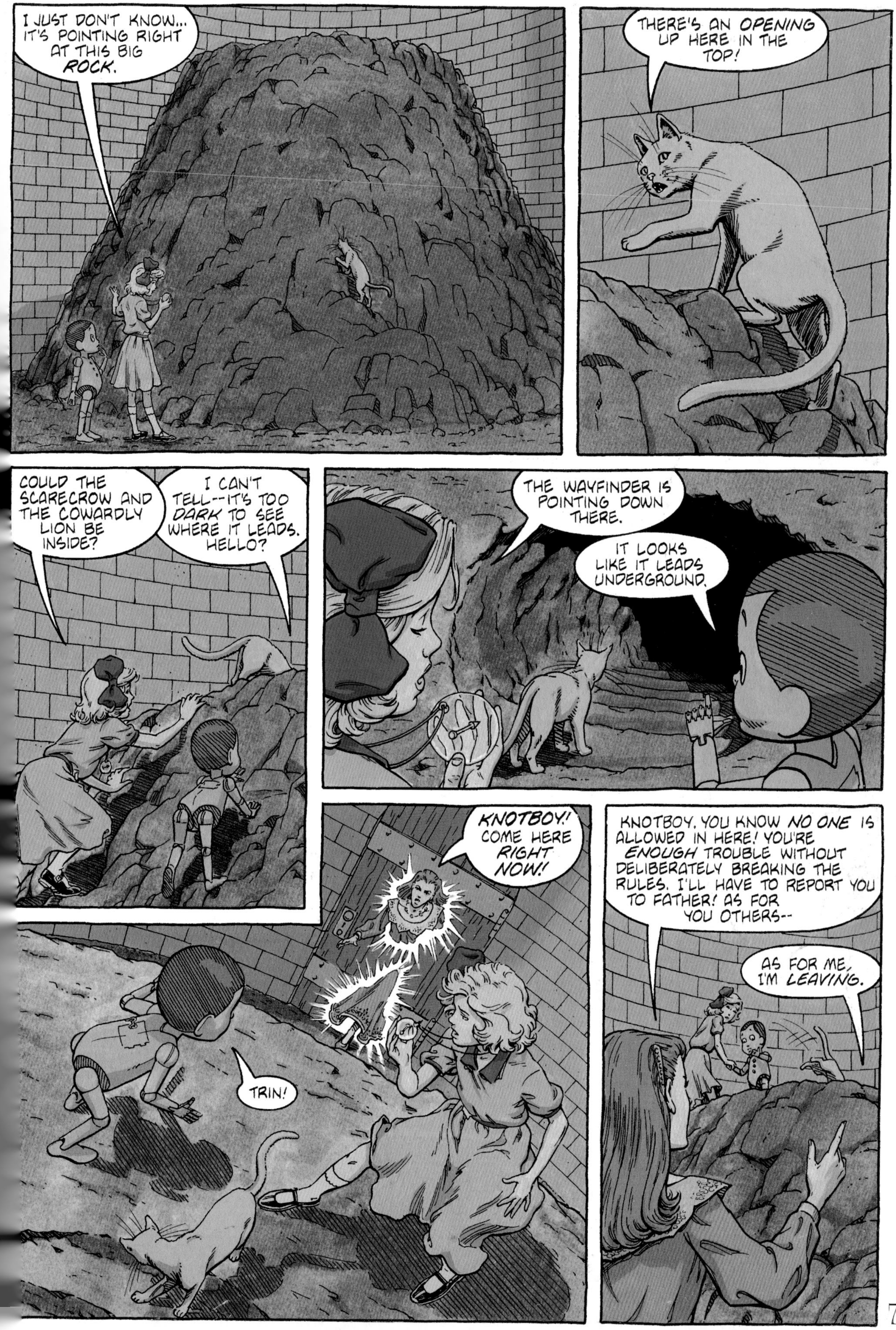
I JUST DON'T KNOW... IT'S POINTING RIGHT AT THIS BIG *ROCK*.
THERE'S AN *OPENING* UP HERE IN THE TOP!
COULD THE SCARECROW AND THE COWARDLY LION BE INSIDE?
I CAN'T TELL--IT'S TOO *DARK* TO SEE WHERE IT LEADS. HELLO?
THE WAYFINDER IS POINTING DOWN THERE.
IT LOOKS LIKE IT LEADS UNDERGROUND.
KNOTBOY! COME HERE *RIGHT NOW!*
TRIN!
KNOTBOY, YOU KNOW *NO ONE* IS ALLOWED IN HERE! YOU'RE *ENOUGH* TROUBLE WITHOUT DELIBERATELY BREAKING THE RULES. I'LL HAVE TO REPORT YOU TO FATHER! AS FOR YOU OTHERS--
AS FOR ME, I'M *LEAVING*.

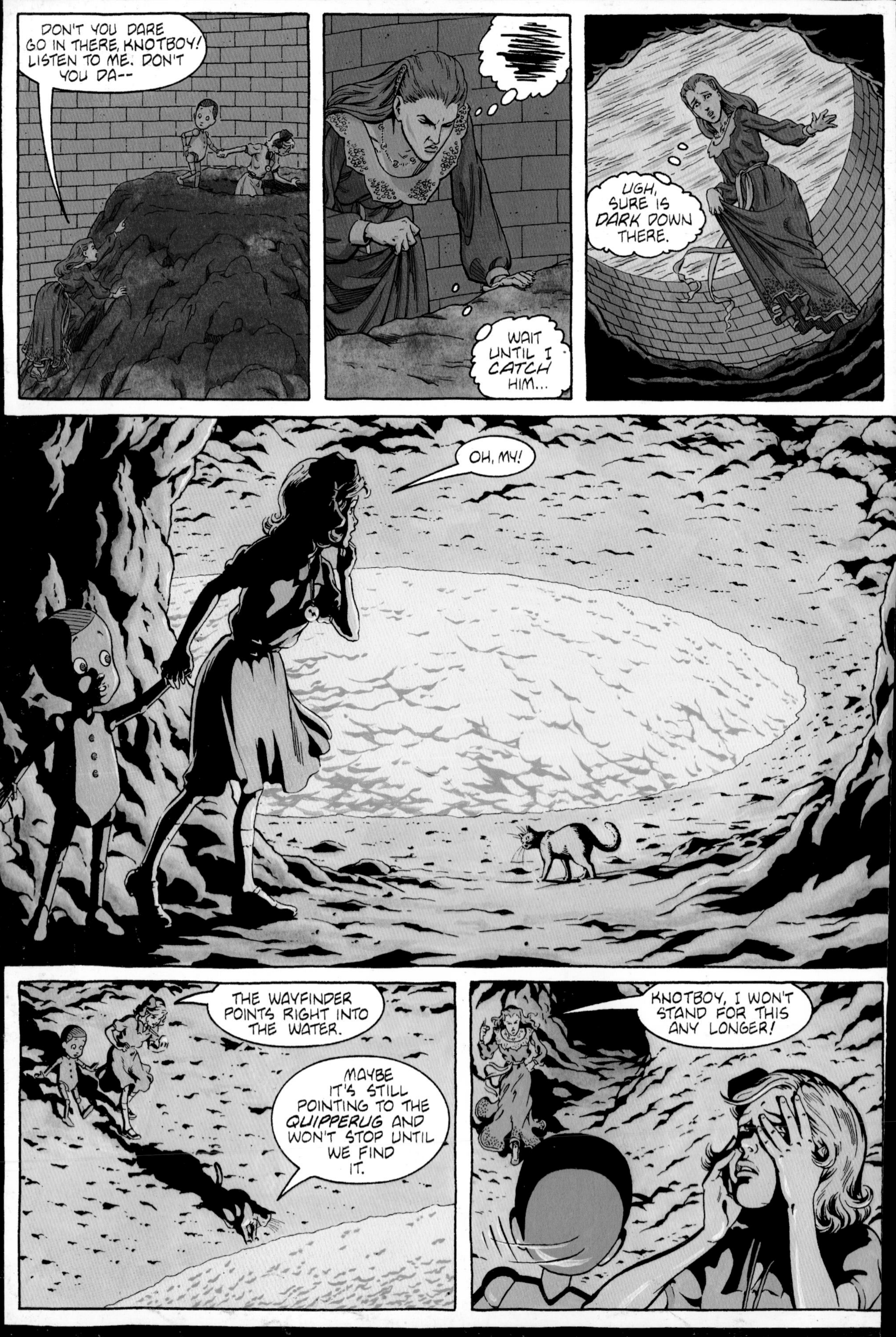
DON'T YOU DARE GO IN THERE, KNOTBOY! LISTEN TO ME. DON'T YOU DA--
WAIT UNTIL I CATCH HIM...
UGH, SURE IS DARK DOWN THERE.
OH, MY!
THE WAYFINDER POINTS RIGHT INTO THE WATER.
MAYBE IT'S STILL POINTING TO THE QUIPPERUG AND WON'T STOP UNTIL WE FIND IT.
KNOTBOY, I WON'T STAND FOR THIS ANY LONGER!

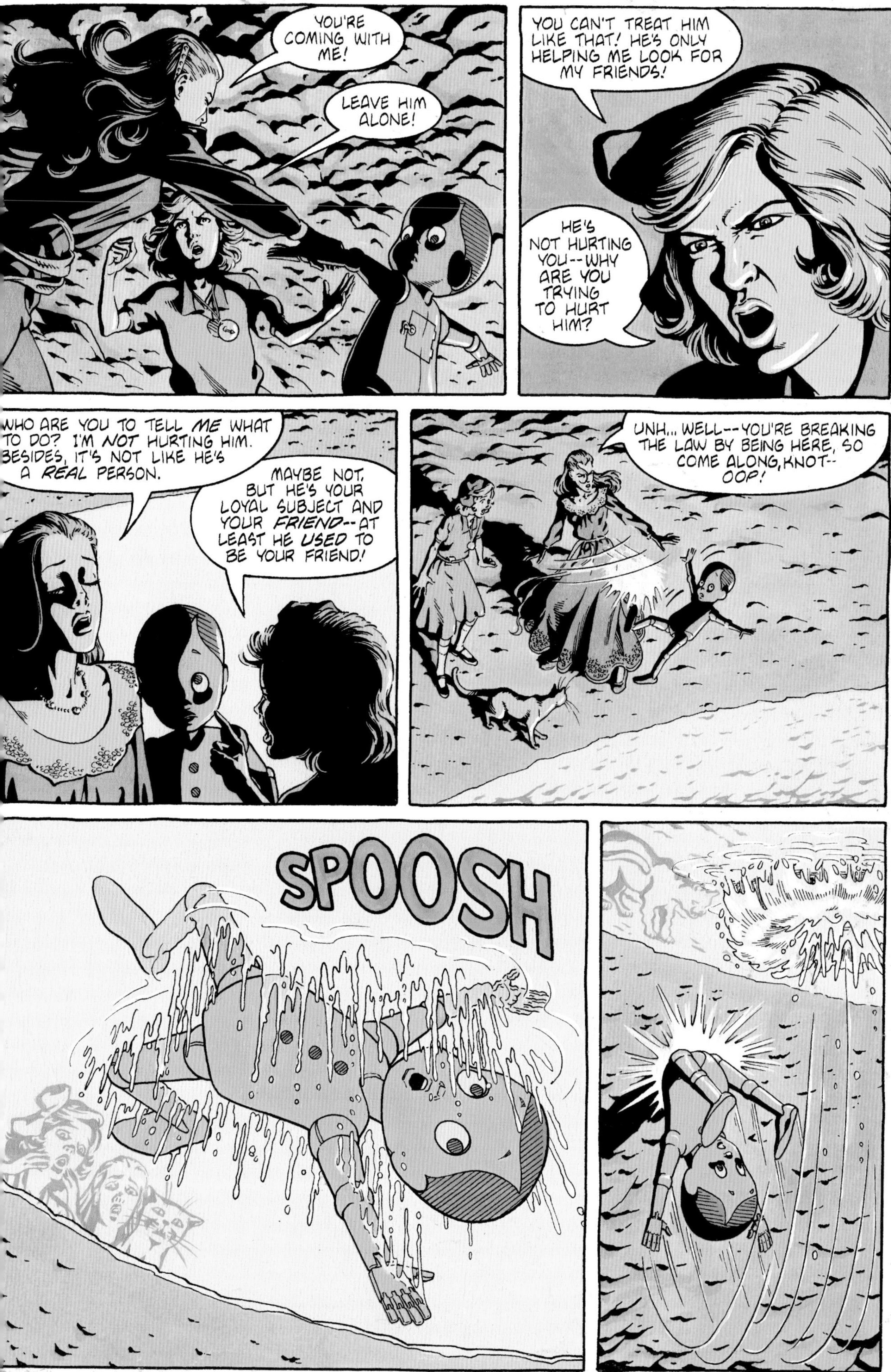
YOU'RE COMING WITH ME!
LEAVE HIM ALONE!
YOU CAN'T TREAT HIM LIKE THAT! HE'S ONLY HELPING ME LOOK FOR MY FRIENDS!
HE'S NOT HURTING YOU--WHY ARE YOU TRYING TO HURT HIM?
WHO ARE YOU TO TELL *ME* WHAT TO DO? I'M *NOT* HURTING HIM. BESIDES, IT'S NOT LIKE HE'S A *REAL* PERSON.
MAYBE NOT, BUT HE'S YOUR LOYAL SUBJECT AND YOUR *FRIEND*--AT LEAST HE *USED* TO BE YOUR FRIEND!
UNH... WELL--YOU'RE BREAKING THE LAW BY BEING HERE, SO COME ALONG, KNOT--OOP!
SPOOSH

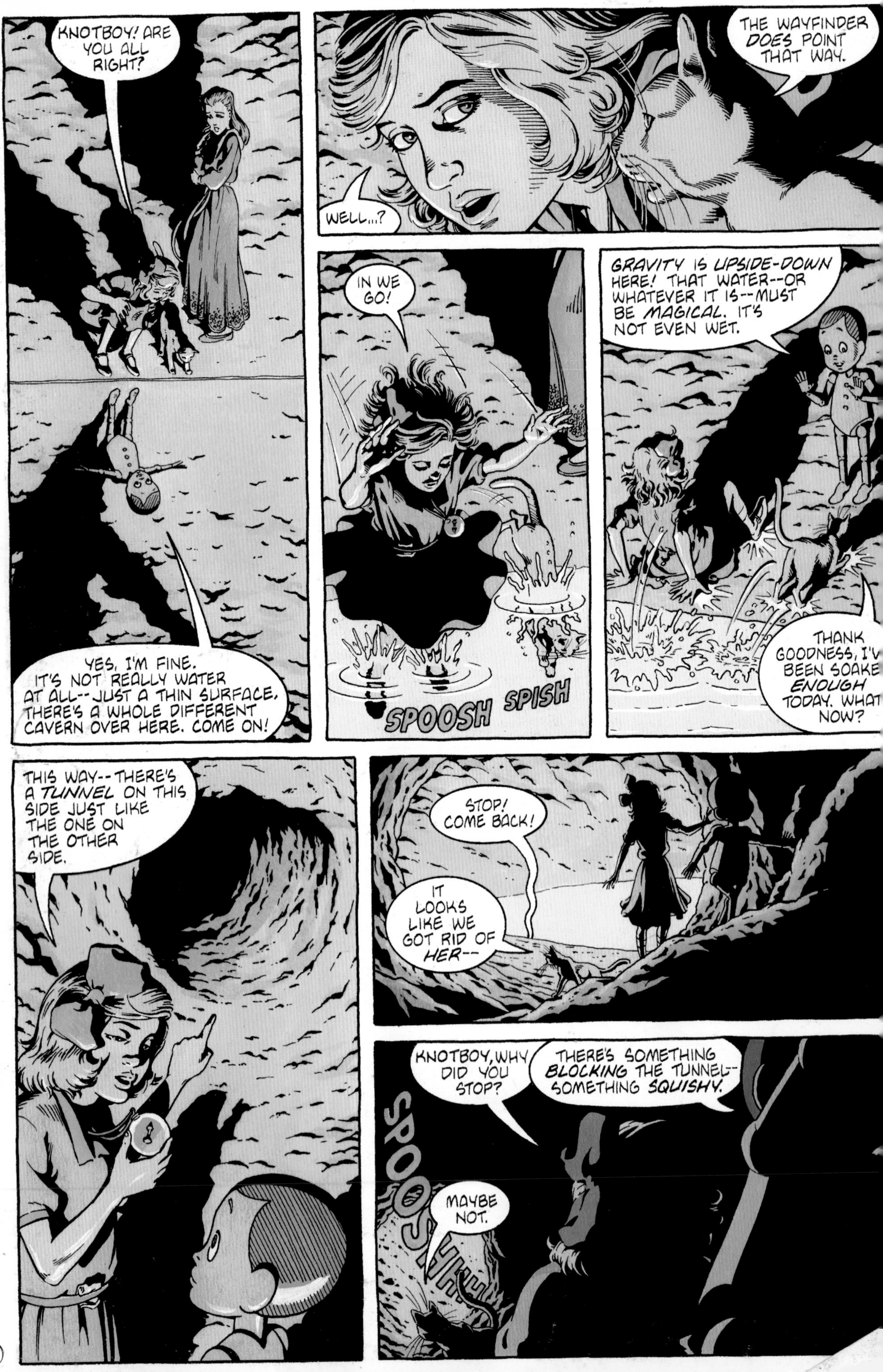

KNOTBOY! ARE YOU ALL RIGHT?
YES, I'M FINE. IT'S NOT REALLY WATER AT ALL-- JUST A THIN SURFACE. THERE'S A WHOLE DIFFERENT CAVERN OVER HERE. COME ON!
WELL...?
THE WAYFINDER *DOES* POINT THAT WAY.
IN WE GO!
SPOOSH
SPISH
GRAVITY IS UPSIDE-DOWN HERE! THAT WATER--OR WHATEVER IT IS--MUST BE *MAGICAL*. IT'S NOT EVEN WET.
THANK GOODNESS, I'V BEEN SOAKE *ENOUGH* TODAY. WHAT NOW?
THIS WAY--THERE'S A *TUNNEL* ON THIS SIDE JUST LIKE THE ONE ON THE OTHER SIDE.
STOP! COME BACK!
IT LOOKS LIKE WE GOT RID OF *HER*--
KNOTBOY, WHY DID YOU STOP?
THERE'S SOMETHING *BLOCKING* THE TUNNEL-- SOMETHING *SQUISHY*.
SPOOSHHH
MAYBE NOT.

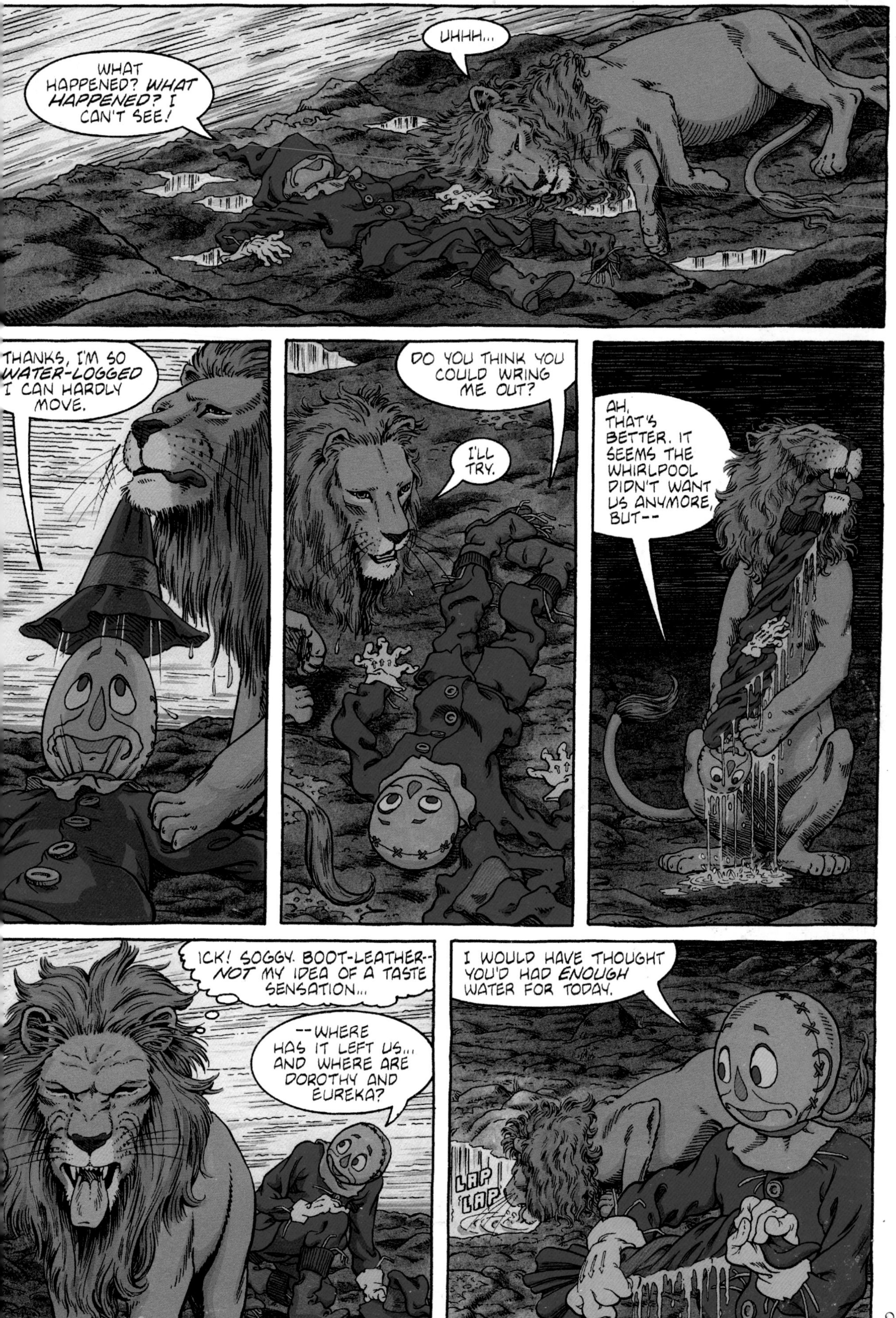
WHAT HAPPENED? WHAT HAPPENED? I CAN'T SEE!
UHHH...
THANKS, I'M SO WATER-LOGGED I CAN HARDLY MOVE.
DO YOU THINK YOU COULD WRING ME OUT?
I'LL TRY.
AH, THAT'S BETTER. IT SEEMS THE WHIRLPOOL DIDN'T WANT US ANYMORE, BUT--
ICK! SOGGY. BOOT-LEATHER-- NOT MY IDEA OF A TASTE SENSATION...
--WHERE HAS IT LEFT US... AND WHERE ARE DOROTHY AND EUREKA?
I WOULD HAVE THOUGHT YOU'D HAD ENOUGH WATER FOR TODAY.
LAP LAP

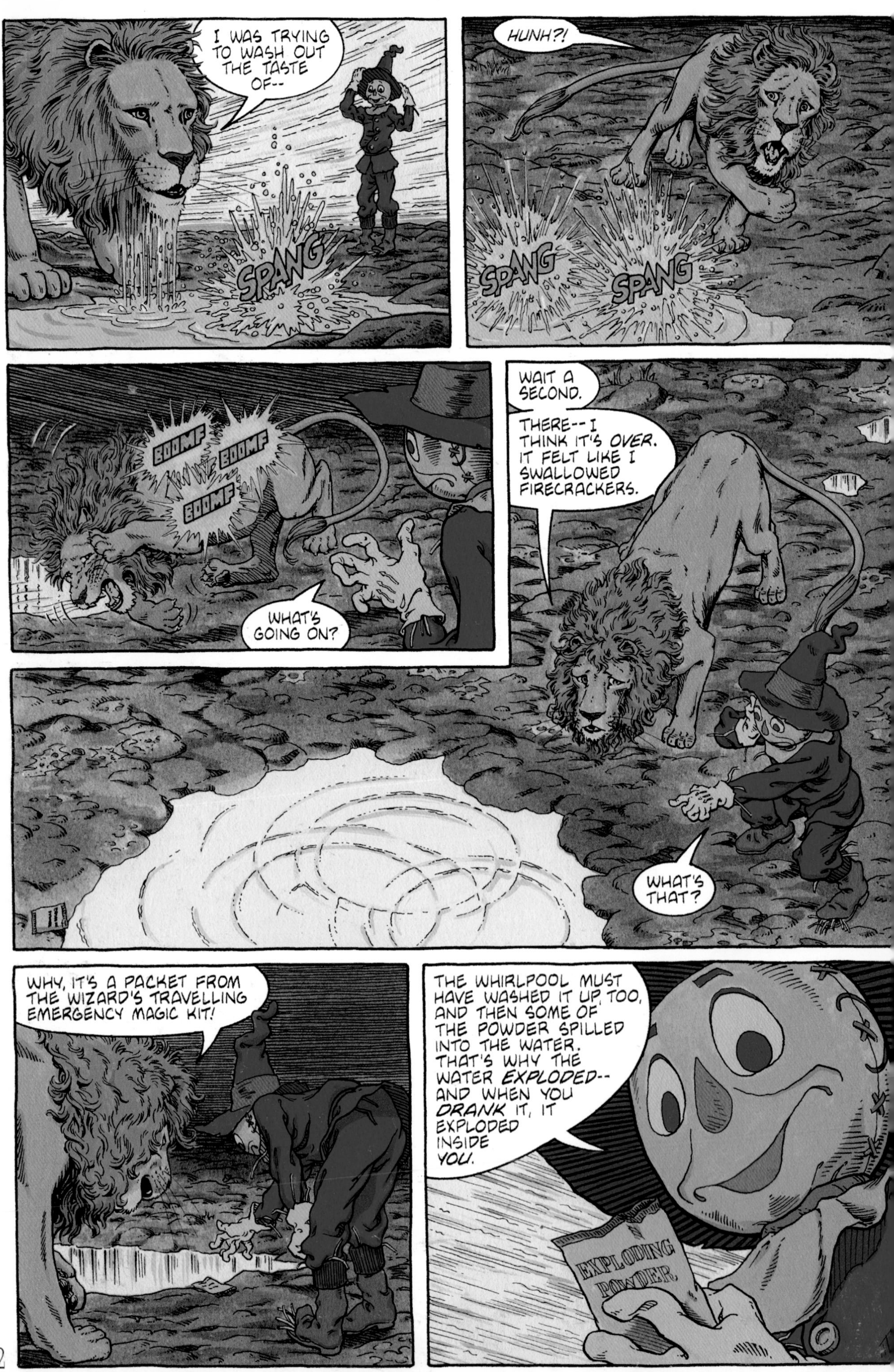
I WAS TRYING TO WASH OUT THE TASTE OF--
SPANG
HUNH?!
SPANG
SPANG
BOOMF
BOOMF
BOOMF
WHAT'S GOING ON?
WAIT A SECOND.
THERE-- I THINK IT'S OVER. IT FELT LIKE I SWALLOWED FIRECRACKERS.
WHAT'S THAT?
WHY, IT'S A PACKET FROM THE WIZARD'S TRAVELLING EMERGENCY MAGIC KIT!
THE WHIRLPOOL MUST HAVE WASHED IT UP, TOO, AND THEN SOME OF THE POWDER SPILLED INTO THE WATER. THAT'S WHY THE WATER EXPLODED-- AND WHEN YOU DRANK IT, IT EXPLODED INSIDE YOU.
EXPLODING POWDER

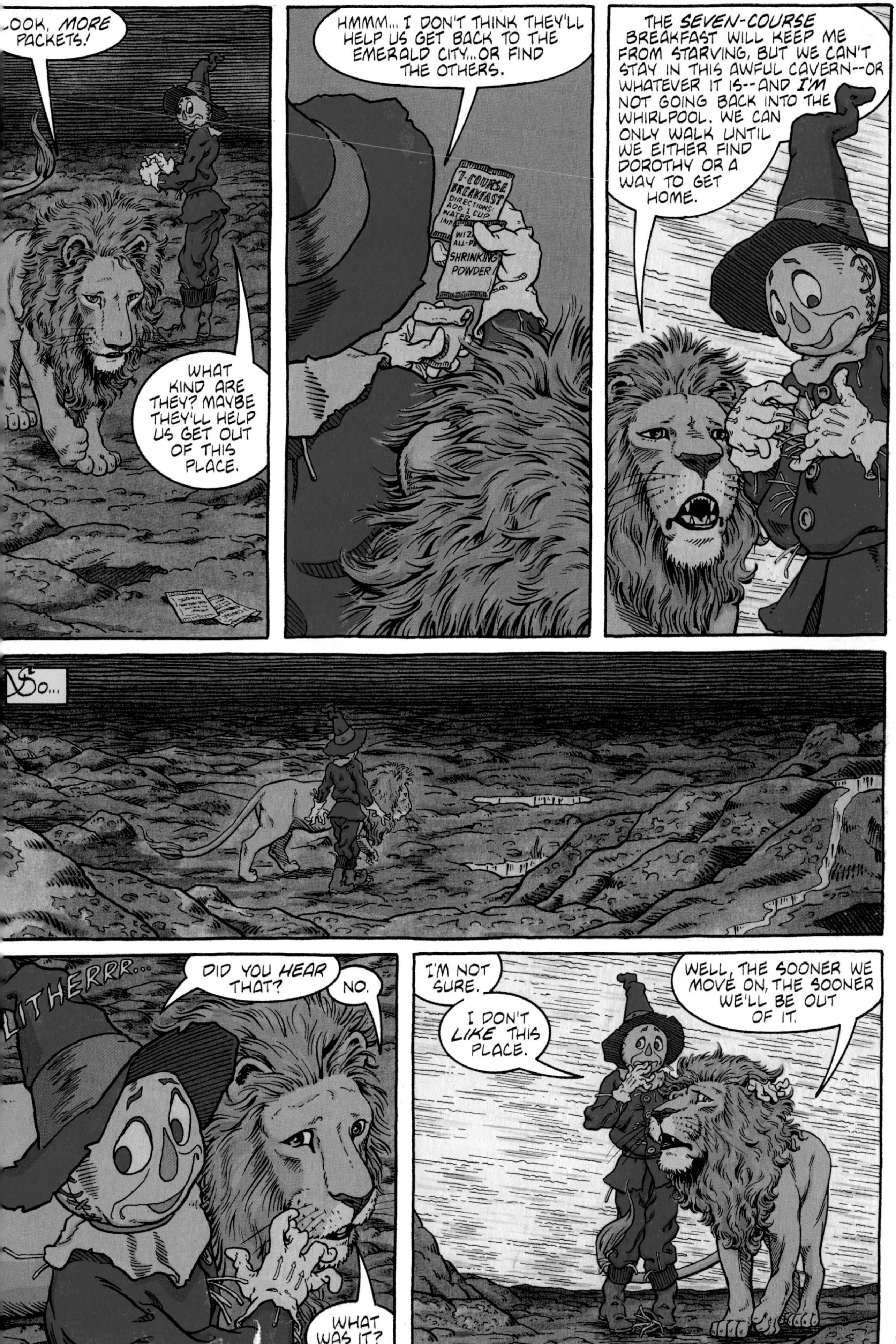
LOOK, MORE PACKETS!
WHAT KIND ARE THEY? MAYBE THEY'LL HELP US GET OUT OF THIS PLACE.
HMMM... I DON'T THINK THEY'LL HELP US GET BACK TO THE EMERALD CITY...OR FIND THE OTHERS.
7-COURSE BREAKFAST DIRECTIONS: ADD 1 CUP WATER
SHRINKING POWDER
THE SEVEN-COURSE BREAKFAST WILL KEEP ME FROM STARVING, BUT WE CAN'T STAY IN THIS AWFUL CAVERN--OR WHATEVER IT IS--AND I'M NOT GOING BACK INTO THE WHIRLPOOL. WE CAN ONLY WALK UNTIL WE EITHER FIND DOROTHY OR A WAY TO GET HOME.
SO...
LITHERRR...
DID YOU HEAR THAT?
NO.
WHAT WAS IT?
I'M NOT SURE.
I DON'T LIKE THIS PLACE.
WELL, THE SOONER WE MOVE ON, THE SOONER WE'LL BE OUT OF IT.

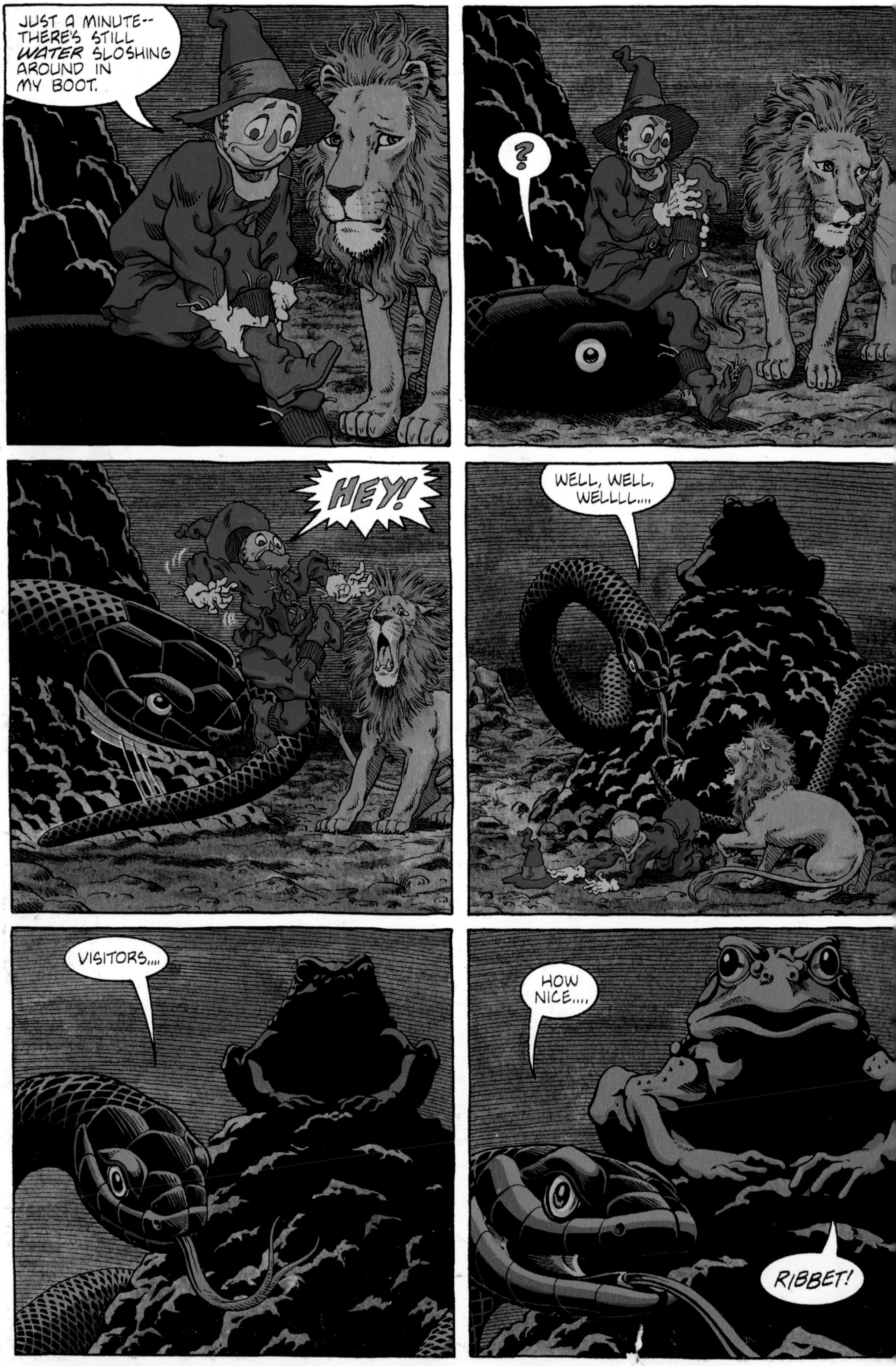
JUST A MINUTE--
THERE'S STILL WATER SLOSHING AROUND IN MY BOOT.
?
HEY!
WELL, WELL, WELLLL....
VISITORS....
HOW NICE....
RIBBET!

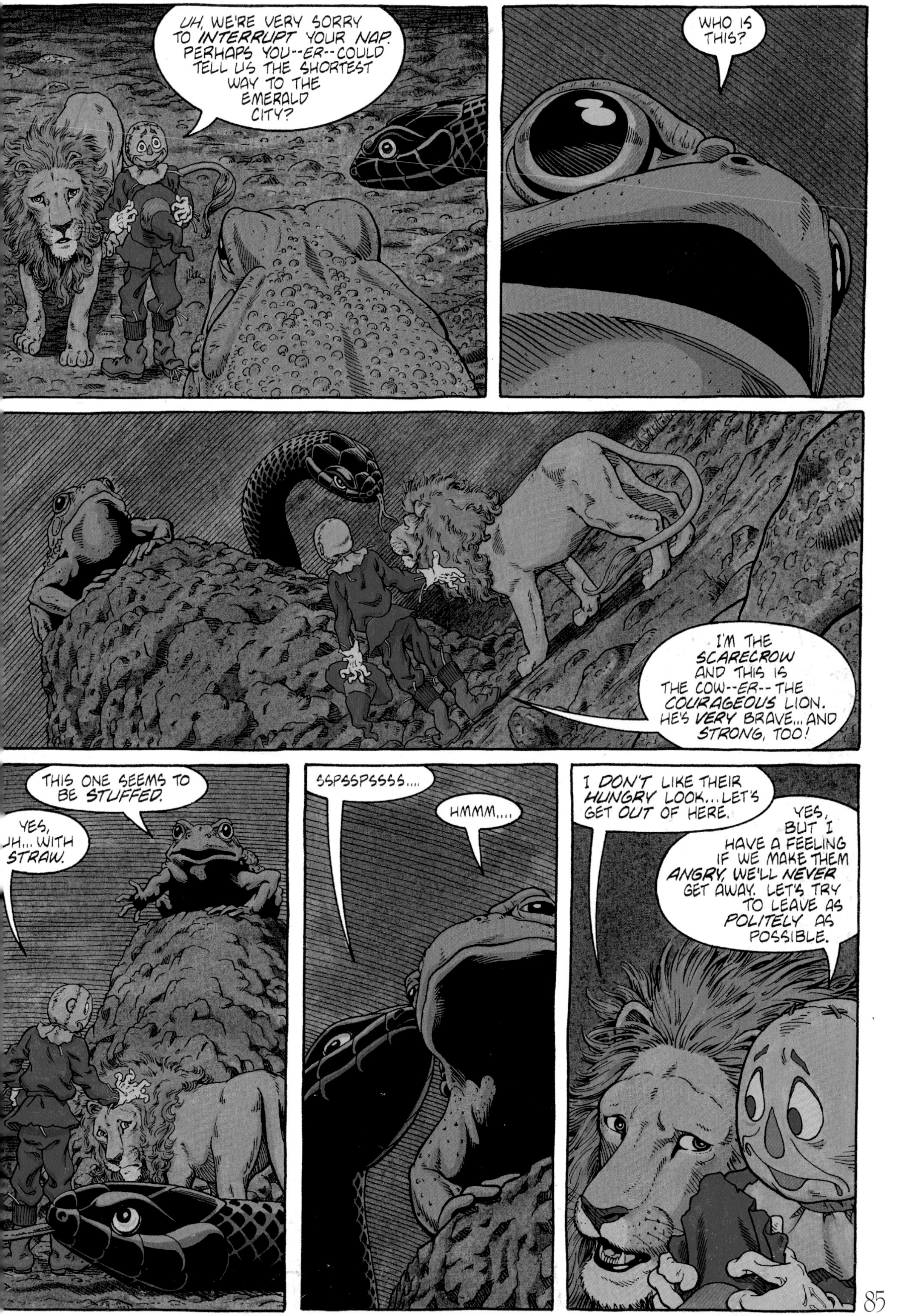
UH, WE'RE VERY SORRY TO INTERRUPT YOUR NAP. PERHAPS YOU--ER--COULD TELL US THE SHORTEST WAY TO THE EMERALD CITY?
WHO IS THIS?
I'M THE SCARECROW AND THIS IS THE COW--ER-- THE COURAGEOUS LION. HE'S VERY BRAVE... AND STRONG, TOO!
THIS ONE SEEMS TO BE STUFFED.
YES, UH... WITH STRAW.
SSPSSPSSSS....
HMMM....
I DON'T LIKE THEIR HUNGRY LOOK... LET'S GET OUT OF HERE.
YES, BUT I HAVE A FEELING IF WE MAKE THEM ANGRY, WE'LL NEVER GET AWAY. LET'S TRY TO LEAVE AS POLITELY AS POSSIBLE.

WE ARE *DELIGHTED* THAT YOU'RE HERE; WE GET SO LITTLE *AMUSEMENT*, YOU SEE.

YOU SIMPLY *MUST* STAY TO DINNER.

I DON'T THINK *I'LL* APPRECIATE WHAT'S ON THE MENU.

THANK YOU *VERY* MUCH. THAT'S *VERY* KIND; BUT WE REALLY MUST BE GOING--SO IF YOU COULD DIRECT US--

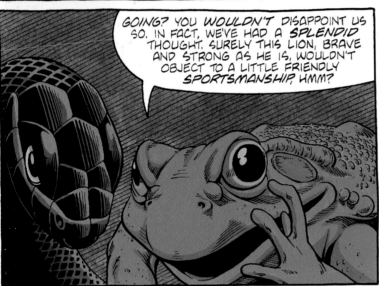

GOING? YOU *WOULDN'T* DISAPPOINT US SO. IN FACT, WE'VE HAD A *SPLENDID* THOUGHT. SURELY THIS LION, BRAVE AND STRONG AS HE IS, WOULDN'T OBJECT TO A LITTLE FRIENDLY *SPORTSMANSHIP*, HMM?

WHAT EXACTLY DO YOU MEAN?

OH, JUST A BIT OF A *CONTEST* BETWEEN YOU AND OUR FRIEND, THE *SNAKE*, TO PROVIDE A LITTLE ENTERTAINMENT IN OUR EMPTY LIVES. *SURELY* YOU'LL BE SO KIND.

IN FACT, IF YOU *WIN*, WE'LL SEND YOU ON YOUR WAY *IMMEDIATELY*. AND IF YOU *LOSE*, YOU'LL DO NOTHING MORE DIFFICULT THAN TO ACCEPT OUR INVITATION TO-- RIBBET-- *DINNER*.

SSSSSSS....

I *DEFINITELY* DON'T LIKE THIS. HOW DO WE *BACK OUT* WITHOUT MAKING THEM ANGRY?

WE CAN'T BESIDES THIS CONTEST SOUNDS LIKE OUR CHANCE TO *ESCAPE*; SO YOU BETTER WIN.

WELL?

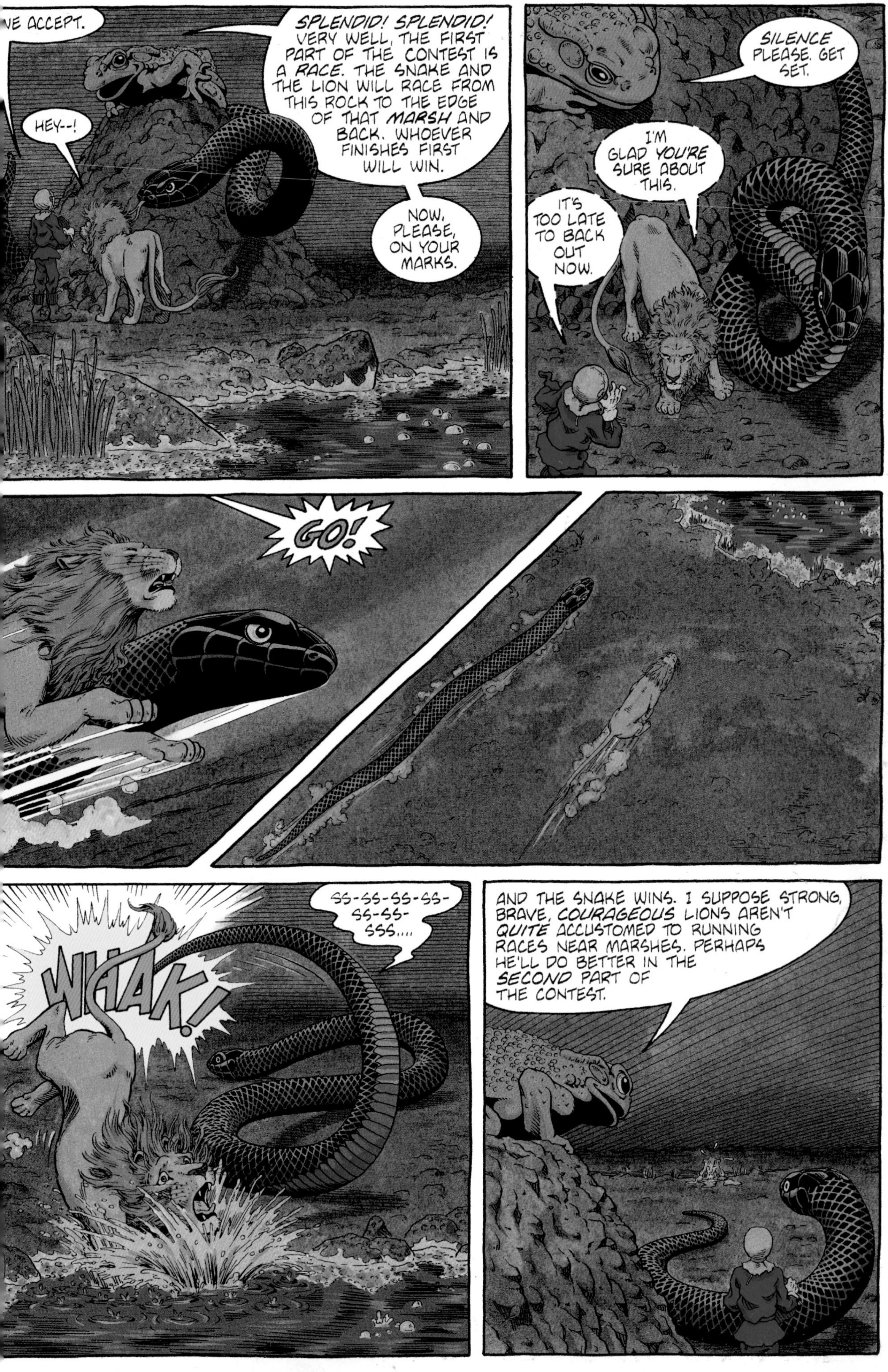

...WE ACCEPT.
SPLENDID! SPLENDID! VERY WELL, THE FIRST PART OF THE CONTEST IS A RACE. THE SNAKE AND THE LION WILL RACE FROM THIS ROCK TO THE EDGE OF THAT MARSH AND BACK. WHOEVER FINISHES FIRST WILL WIN.
HEY--!
NOW, PLEASE, ON YOUR MARKS.
SILENCE PLEASE. GET SET.
I'M GLAD YOU'RE SURE ABOUT THIS.
IT'S TOO LATE TO BACK OUT NOW.
GO!
SS-SS-SS-SS-SS-SS-SSS....
WHAK!
AND THE SNAKE WINS. I SUPPOSE STRONG, BRAVE, COURAGEOUS LIONS AREN'T QUITE ACCUSTOMED TO RUNNING RACES NEAR MARSHES. PERHAPS HE'LL DO BETTER IN THE SECOND PART OF THE CONTEST.

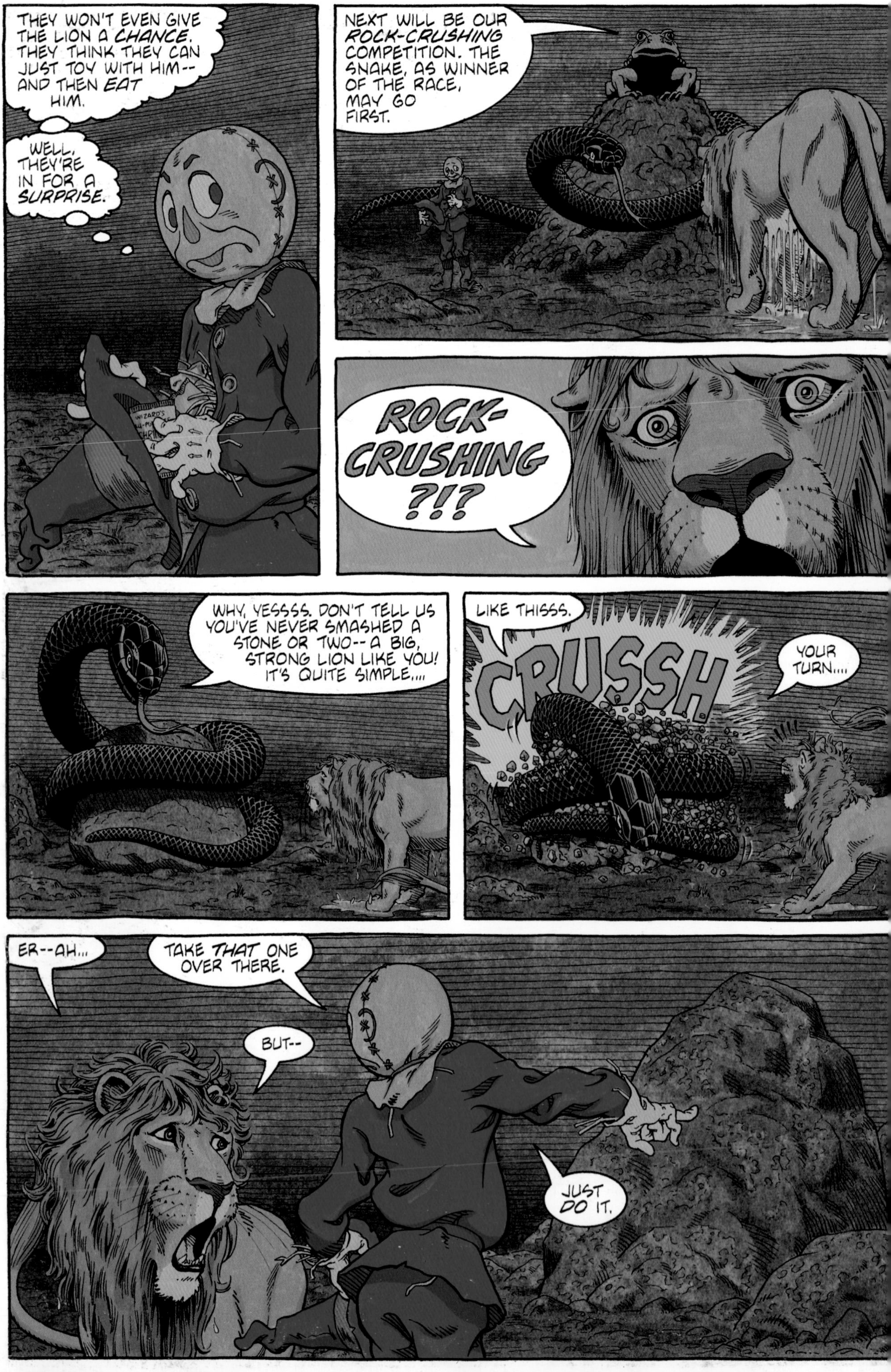
THEY WON'T EVEN GIVE THE LION A CHANCE. THEY THINK THEY CAN JUST TOY WITH HIM-- AND THEN EAT HIM.
WELL, THEY'RE IN FOR A SURPRISE.
NEXT WILL BE OUR ROCK-CRUSHING COMPETITION. THE SNAKE, AS WINNER OF THE RACE, MAY GO FIRST.
ROCK-CRUSHING ?!?
WHY, YESSSS. DON'T TELL US YOU'VE NEVER SMASHED A STONE OR TWO-- A BIG, STRONG LION LIKE YOU! IT'S QUITE SIMPLE....
LIKE THISSS.
CRUSSH
YOUR TURN....
ER--AH...
TAKE THAT ONE OVER THERE.
BUT--
JUST DO IT.

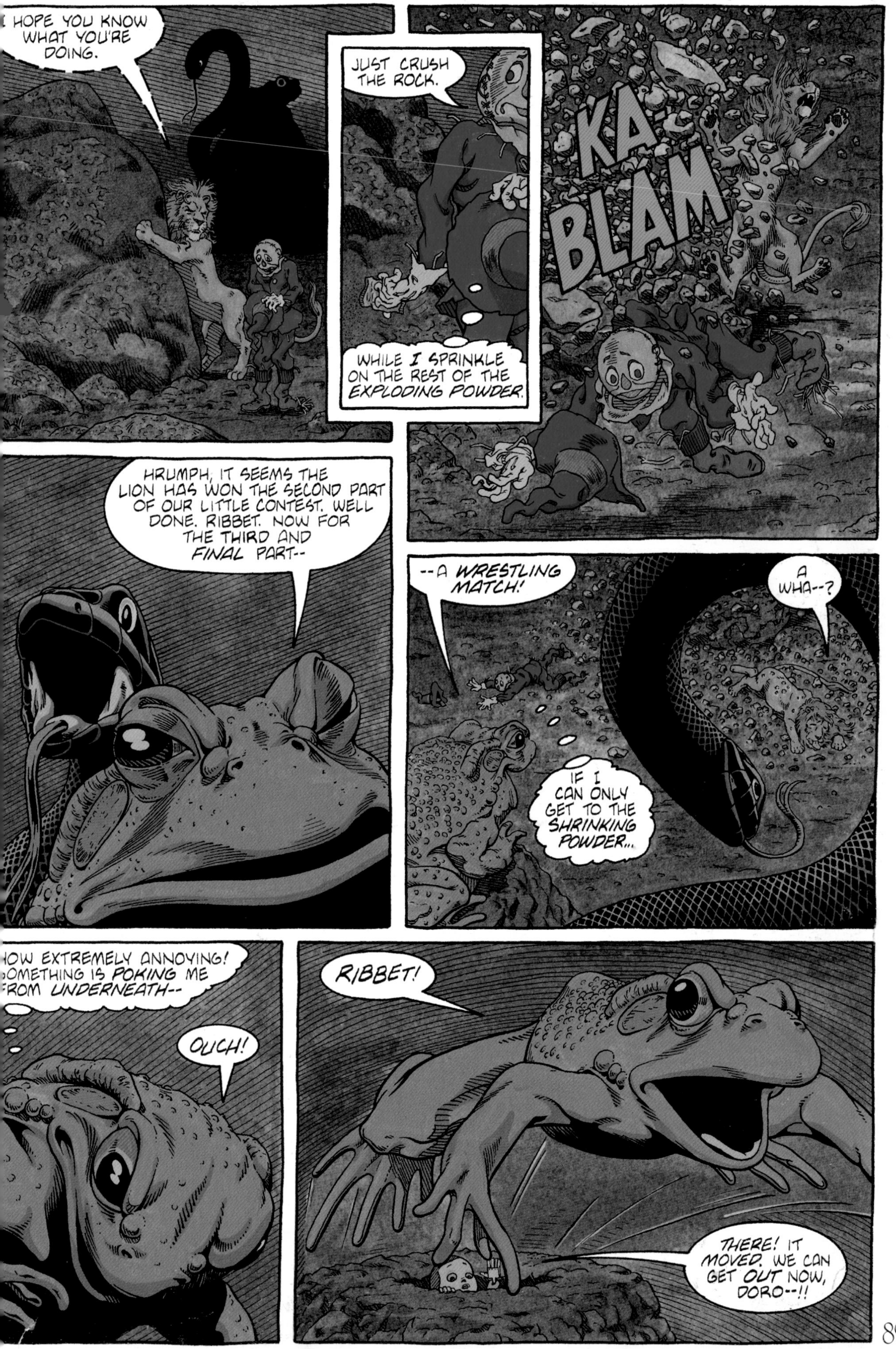

I HOPE YOU KNOW WHAT YOU'RE DOING.
JUST CRUSH THE ROCK.
WHILE I SPRINKLE ON THE REST OF THE EXPLODING POWDER.
KA-BLAM
HRUMPH, IT SEEMS THE LION HAS WON THE SECOND PART OF OUR LITTLE CONTEST. WELL DONE. RIBBET. NOW FOR THE THIRD AND FINAL PART--
--A WRESTLING MATCH!
A WHA--?
IF I CAN ONLY GET TO THE SHRINKING POWDER...
HOW EXTREMELY ANNOYING! SOMETHING IS POKING ME FROM UNDERNEATH--
OUCH!
RIBBET!
THERE! IT MOVED. WE CAN GET OUT NOW, DORO--!!

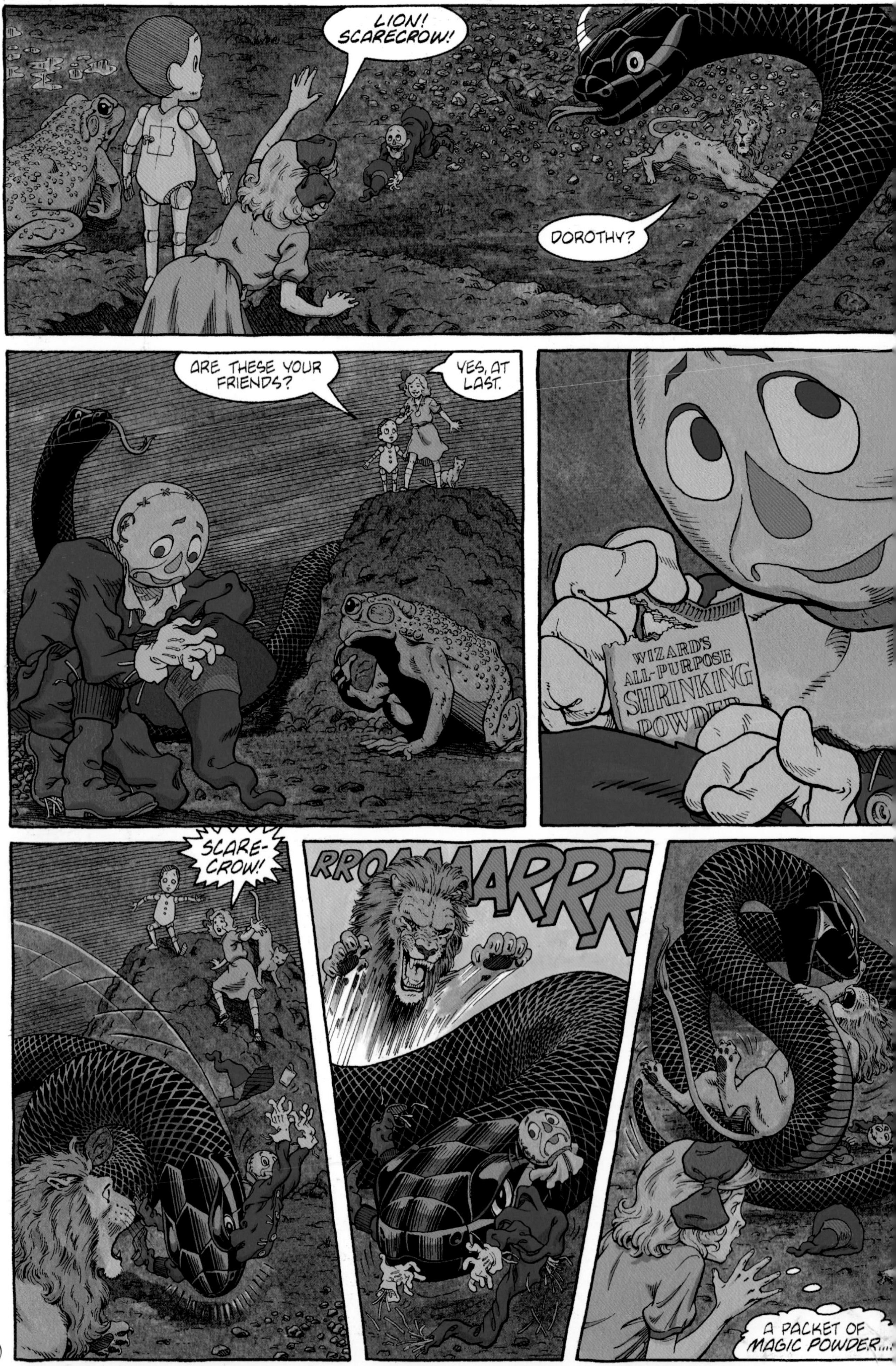
LION! SCARECROW!
DOROTHY?
ARE THESE YOUR FRIENDS?
YES, AT LAST.
WIZARD'S ALL-PURPOSE SHRINKING POWDER
SCARE-CROW!
RROAAARRR
A PACKET OF MAGIC POWDER...

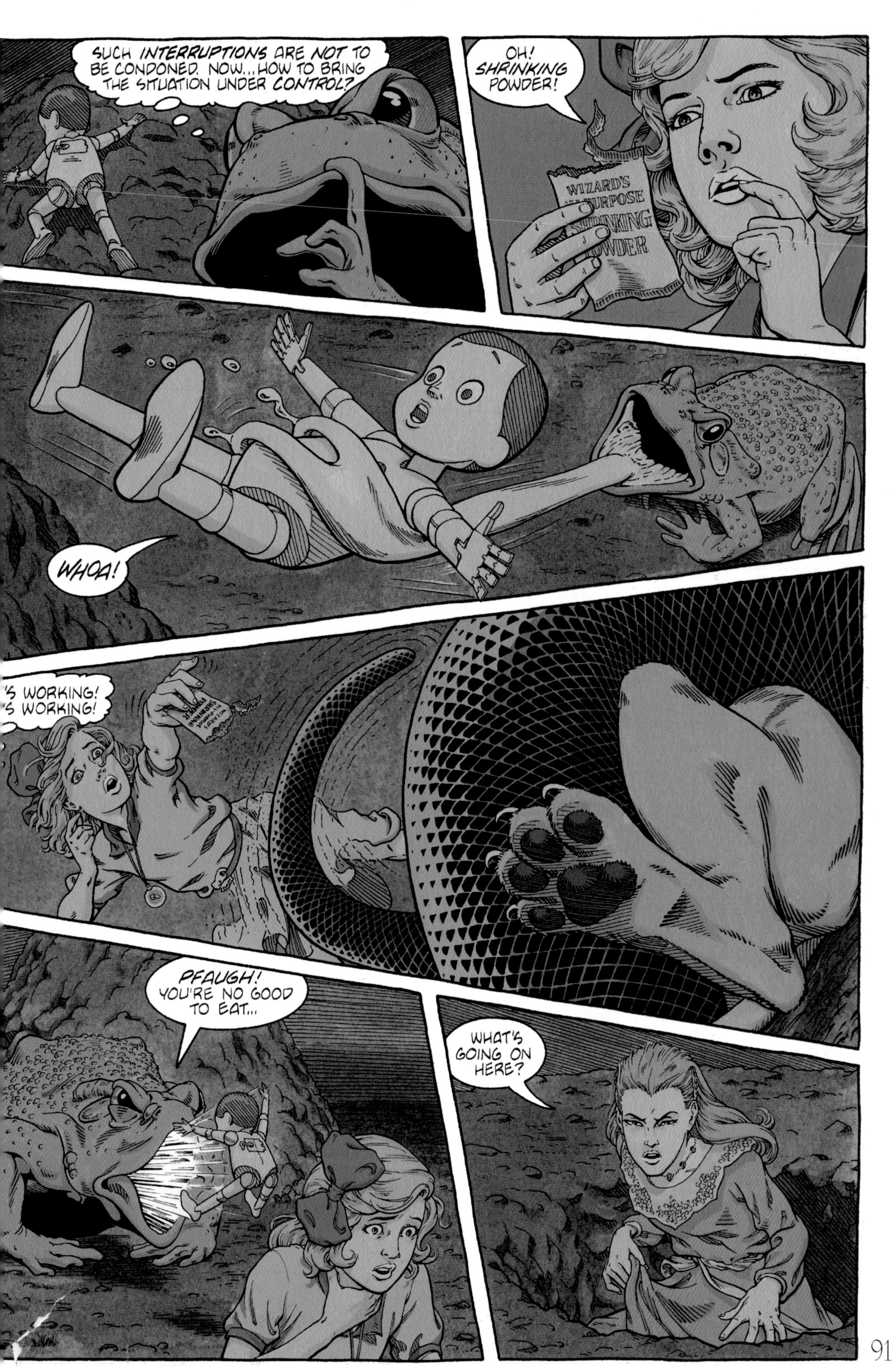
SUCH INTERRUPTIONS ARE NOT TO BE CONDONED. NOW... HOW TO BRING THE SITUATION UNDER CONTROL?
OH! SHRINKING POWDER!
WIZARD'S ALL-PURPOSE SHRINKING POWDER
WHOA!
'S WORKING! 'S WORKING!
PFAUGH! YOU'RE NO GOOD TO EAT...
WHAT'S GOING ON HERE?

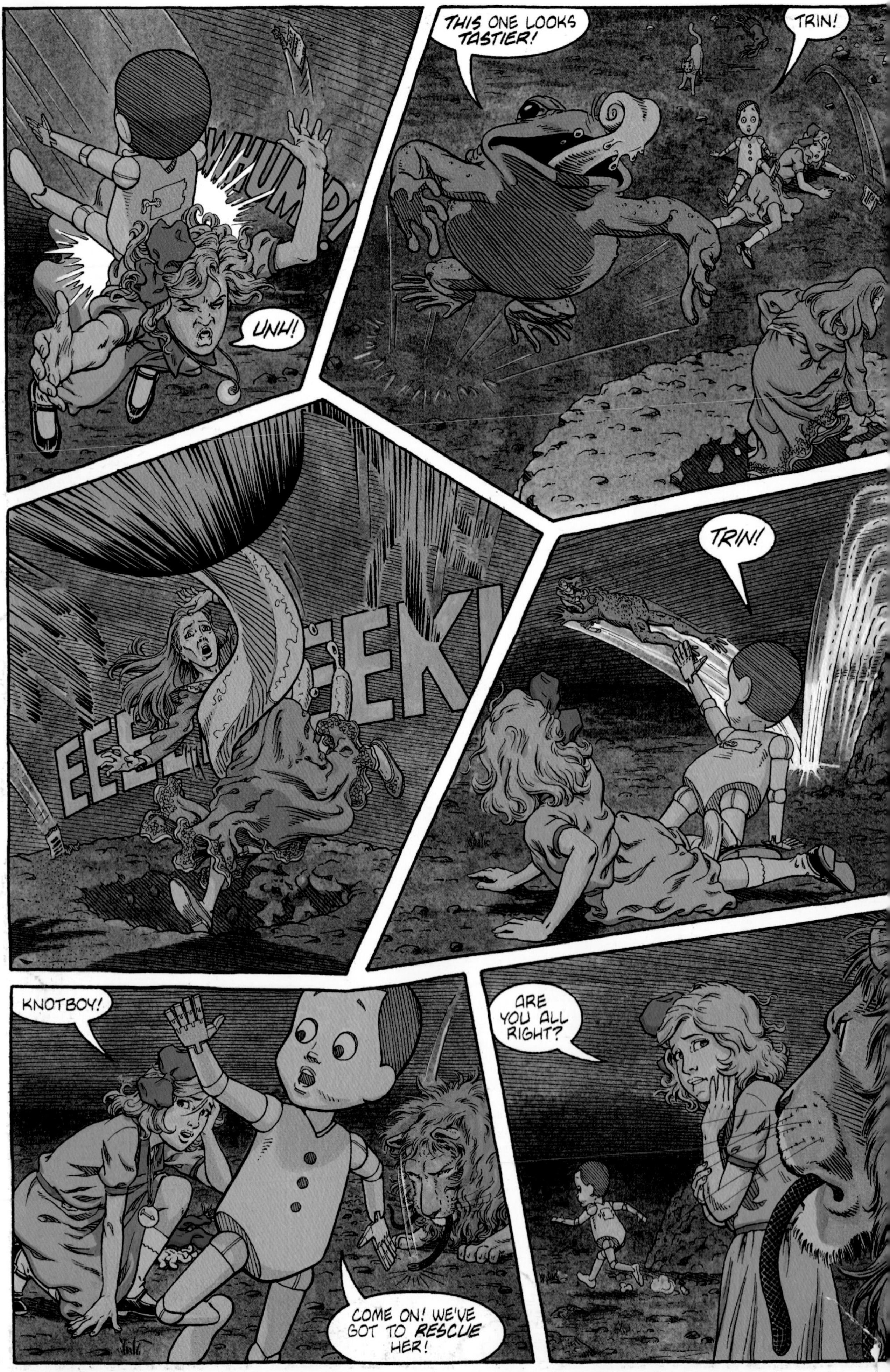
WHUMP!
UNH!
THIS ONE LOOKS TASTIER!
TRIN!
EEEEEEK!
TRIN!
KNOTBOY!
COME ON! WE'VE GOT TO RESCUE HER!
ARE YOU ALL RIGHT?

YES, I'M FINE.
THEN THROW THAT THING AWAY. WE'VE GOT TO HELP KNOTBOY!
OH! SCARECROW--
DON'T WORRY ABOUT ME--GO HELP YOUR FRIENDS.
THE SCARECROW'S RIGHT. LET'S GO!
OH, NO! I'LL NEVER FIND THEM IN THERE!
STOP! LET ME GO!
YOU CAN'T DO THIS TO ME!
IF TRIN JUST KEEPS SHOUTING...
...I'M A PRINCESS...

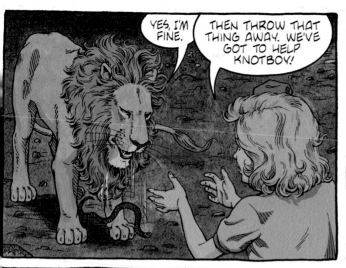

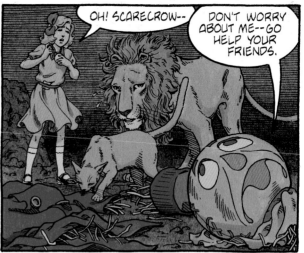

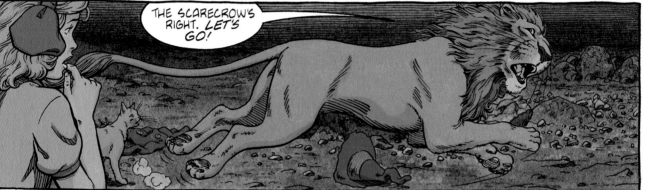

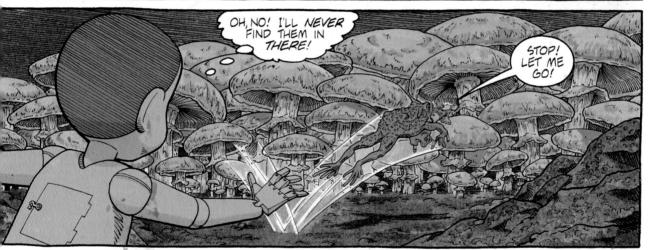

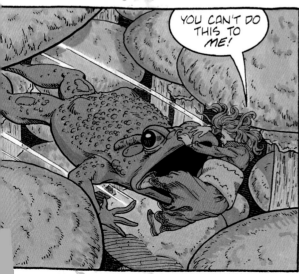

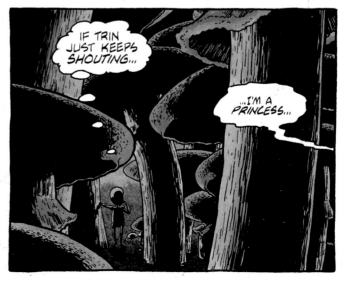

I DON'T HEAR HER ANYMORE-- HOW WILL I *EVER* FIND HER NOW?

I JUST *HAVE* TO!

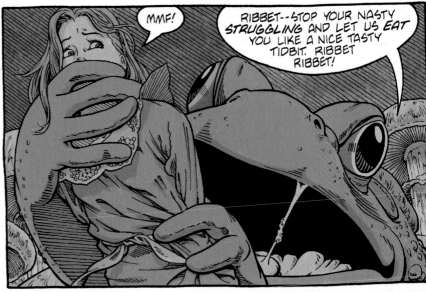

MMF!

RIBBET--STOP YOUR NASTY *STRUGGLING* AND LET US *EAT* YOU LIKE A NICE TASTY TIDBIT. RIBBET RIBBET!

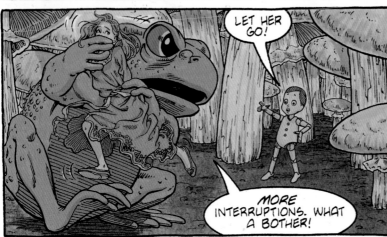

LET HER GO!

MORE INTERRUPTIONS. WHAT A BOTHER!

SPLORP

THINKS IT'S *SMART*, THE LITTLE PIPSQUEAK...

PLIP

94

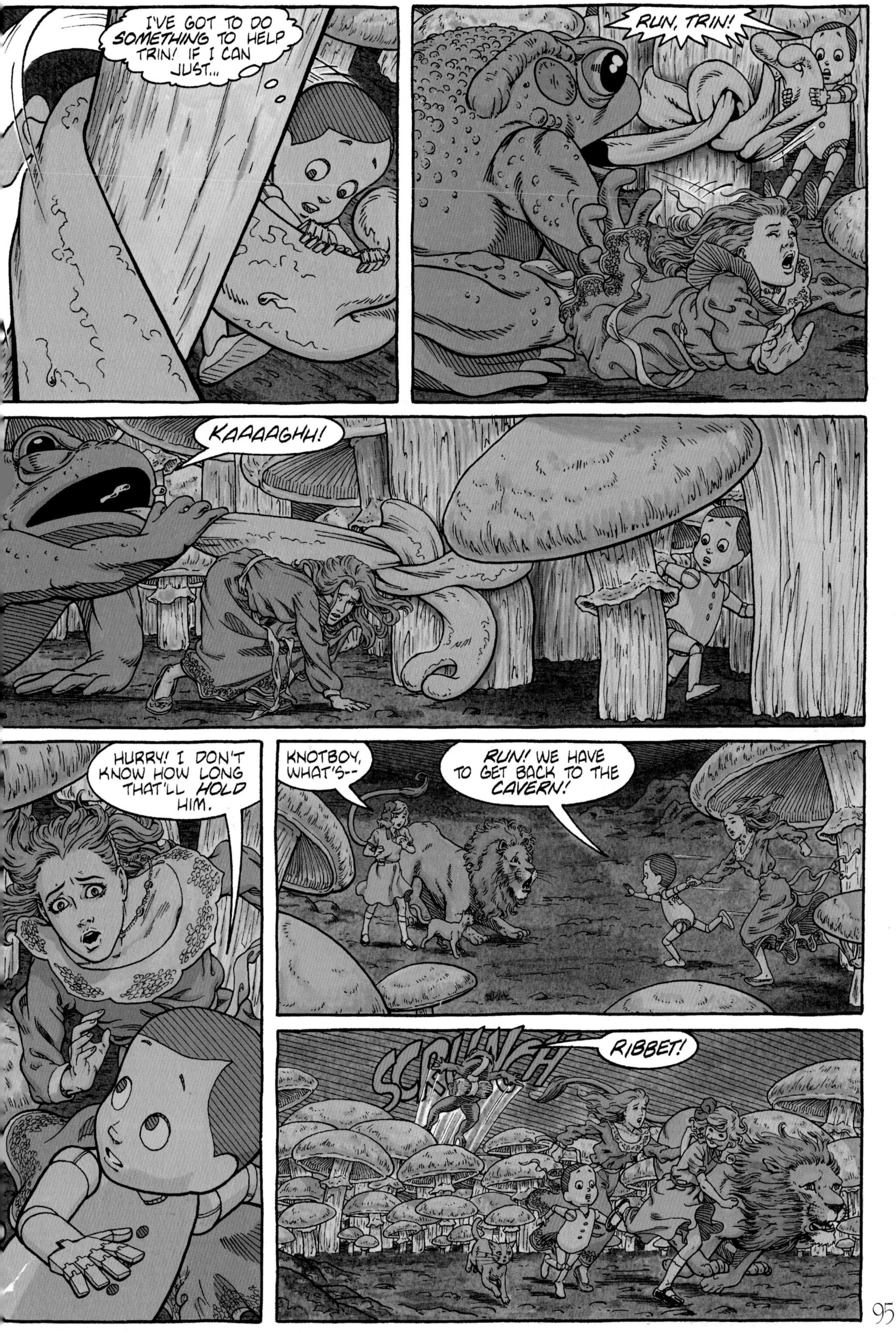
I'VE GOT TO DO SOMETHING TO HELP TRIN! IF I CAN JUST...
RUN, TRIN!
KAAAAGHH!
HURRY! I DON'T KNOW HOW LONG THAT'LL HOLD HIM.
KNOTBOY, WHAT'S--
RUN! WE HAVE TO GET BACK TO THE CAVERN!
SCRUNCH
RIBBET!

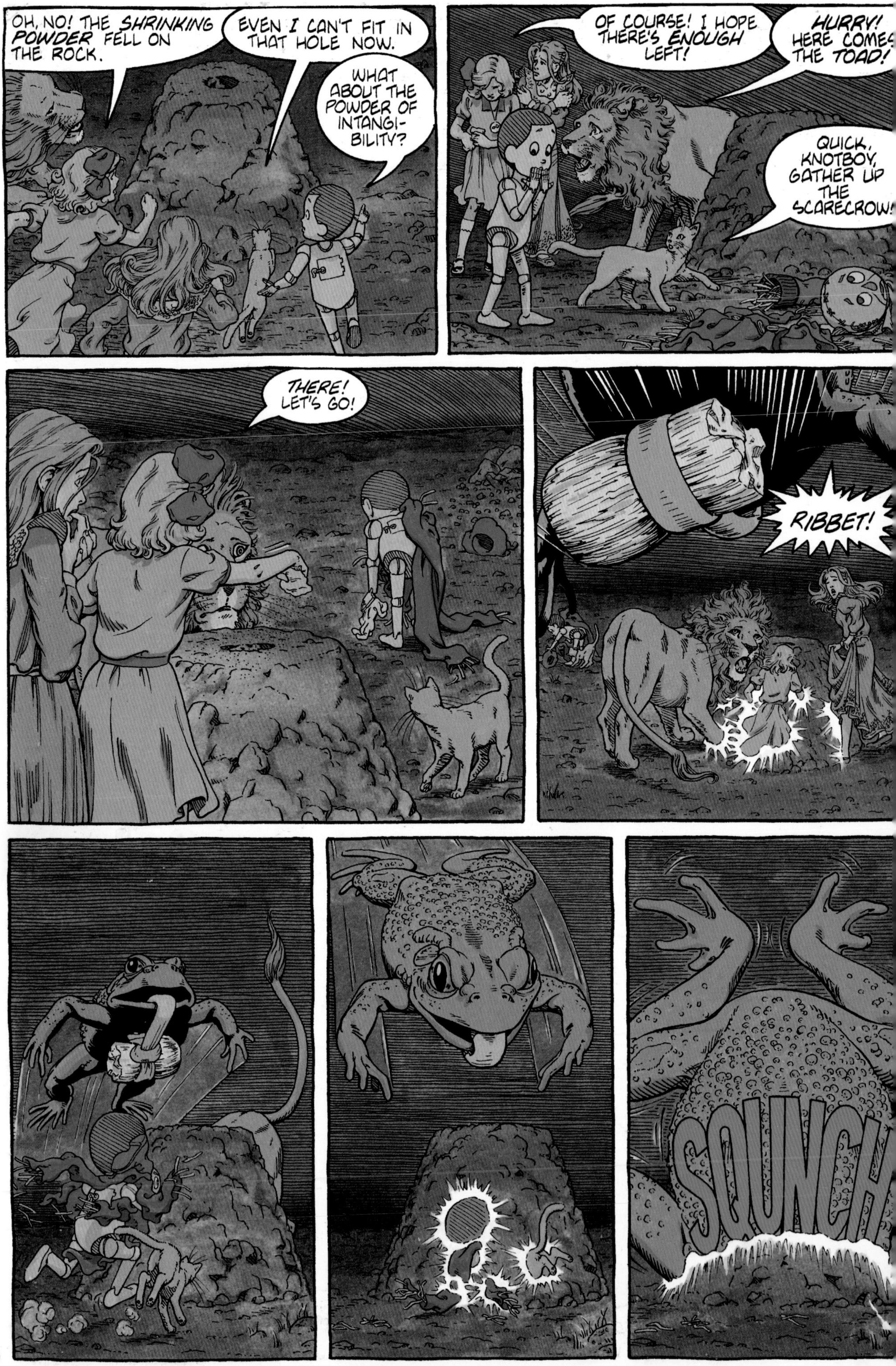

OH, NO! THE SHRINKING POWDER FELL ON THE ROCK.
EVEN I CAN'T FIT IN THAT HOLE NOW.
WHAT ABOUT THE POWDER OF INTANGI-BILITY?
OF COURSE! I HOPE THERE'S ENOUGH LEFT!
HURRY! HERE COMES THE TOAD!
QUICK, KNOTBOY, GATHER UP THE SCARECROW!
THERE! LET'S GO!
RIBBET!
SQUNCH

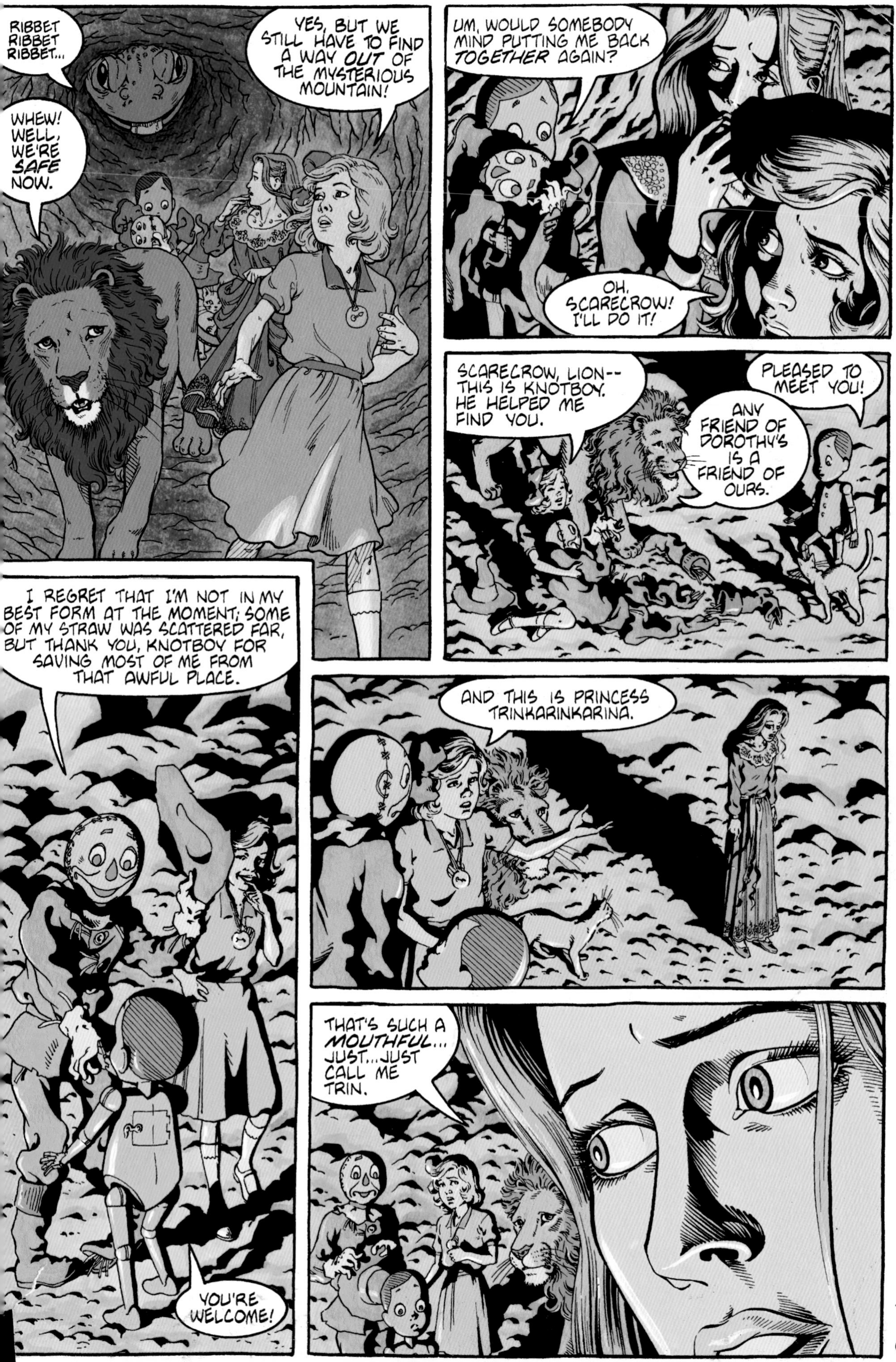
RIBBET RIBBET RIBBET...
YES, BUT WE STILL HAVE TO FIND A WAY *OUT* OF THE MYSTERIOUS MOUNTAIN!
WHEW! WELL, WE'RE *SAFE* NOW.
UM, WOULD SOMEBODY MIND PUTTING ME BACK *TOGETHER* AGAIN?
OH, SCARECROW! I'LL DO IT!
SCARECROW, LION-- THIS IS KNOTBOY. HE HELPED ME FIND YOU.
PLEASED TO MEET YOU!
ANY FRIEND OF DOROTHY'S IS A FRIEND OF OURS.
I REGRET THAT I'M NOT IN MY BEST FORM AT THE MOMENT; SOME OF MY STRAW WAS SCATTERED FAR, BUT THANK YOU, KNOTBOY FOR SAVING MOST OF ME FROM THAT AWFUL PLACE.
YOU'RE WELCOME!
AND THIS IS PRINCESS TRINKARINKARINA.
THAT'S SUCH A *MOUTHFUL*... JUST...JUST CALL ME TRIN.

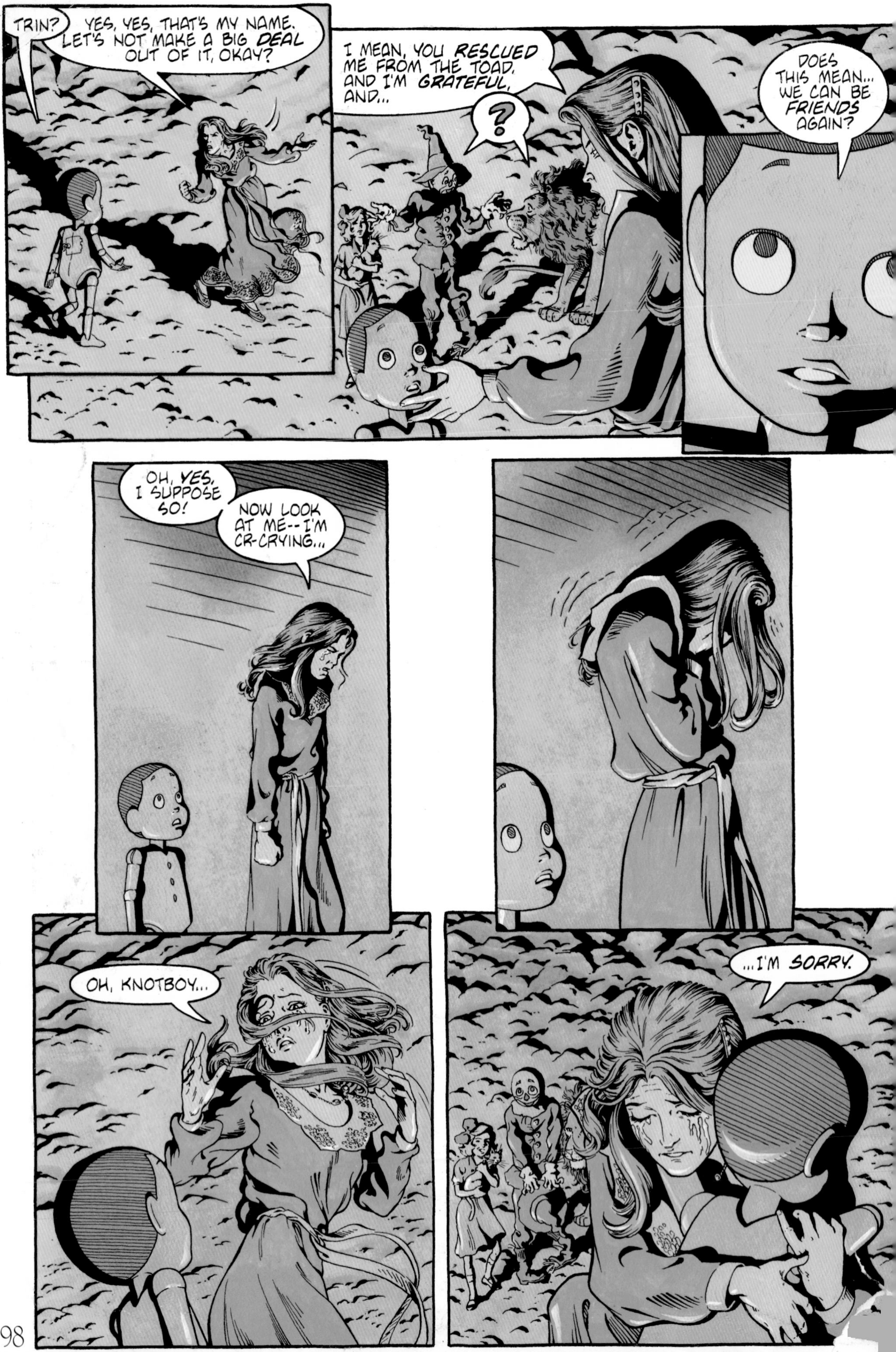

TRIN?
YES, YES, THAT'S MY NAME. LET'S NOT MAKE A BIG DEAL OUT OF IT, OKAY?
I MEAN, YOU RESCUED ME FROM THE TOAD, AND I'M GRATEFUL, AND...
?
DOES THIS MEAN... WE CAN BE FRIENDS AGAIN?
OH, YES, I SUPPOSE SO!
NOW LOOK AT ME-- I'M CR-CRYING...
OH, KNOTBOY...
...I'M SORRY.

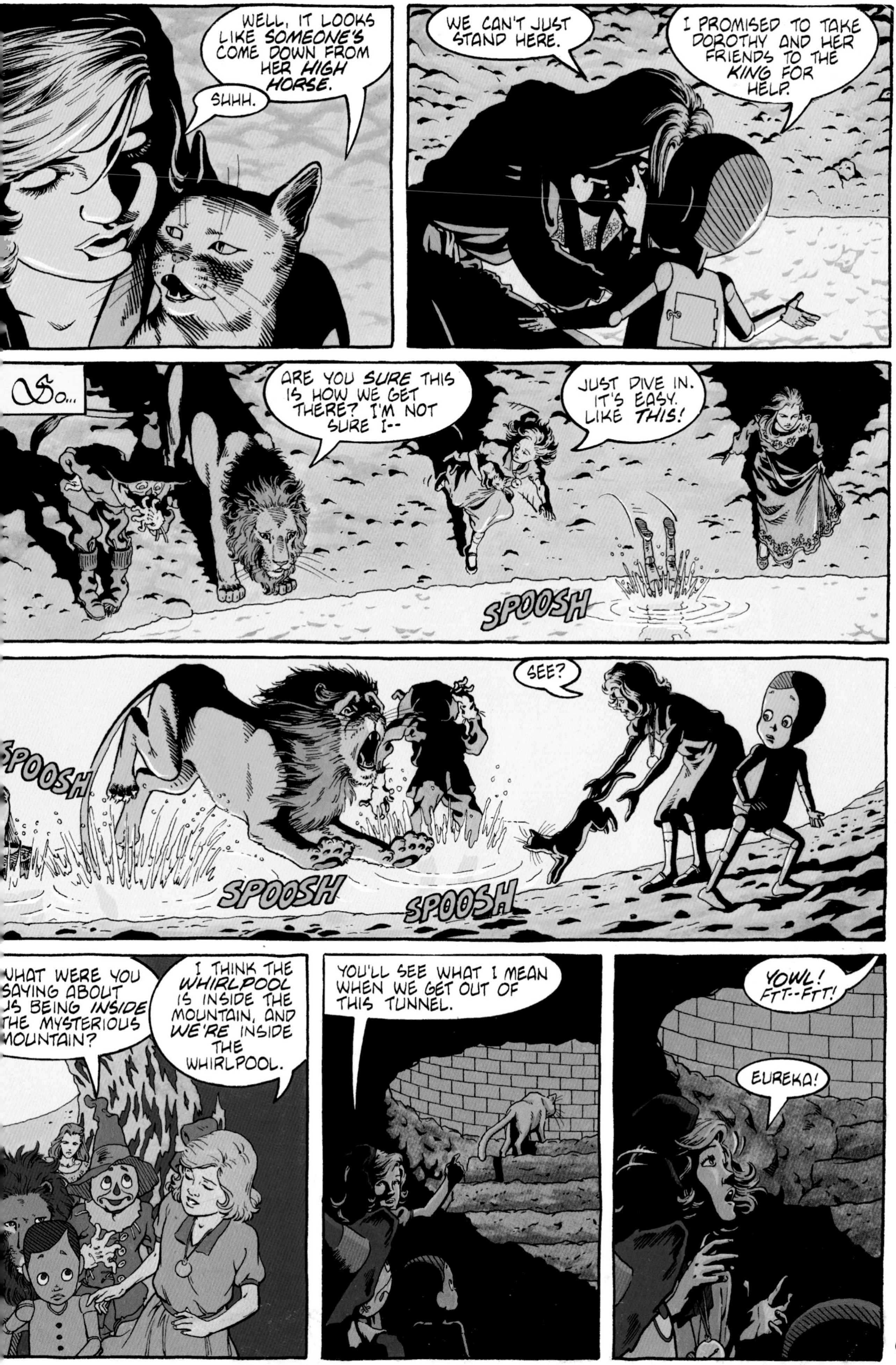

WELL, IT LOOKS LIKE SOMEONE'S COME DOWN FROM HER HIGH HORSE.
SHHH.
WE CAN'T JUST STAND HERE.
I PROMISED TO TAKE DOROTHY AND HER FRIENDS TO THE KING FOR HELP.
So...
ARE YOU SURE THIS IS HOW WE GET THERE? I'M NOT SURE I--
JUST DIVE IN. IT'S EASY. LIKE THIS!
SPOOSH
SEE?
SPOOSH
SPOOSH
SPOOSH
WHAT WERE YOU SAYING ABOUT US BEING INSIDE THE MYSTERIOUS MOUNTAIN?
I THINK THE WHIRLPOOL IS INSIDE THE MOUNTAIN, AND WE'RE INSIDE THE WHIRLPOOL.
YOU'LL SEE WHAT I MEAN WHEN WE GET OUT OF THIS TUNNEL.
YOWL! FTT--FTT!
EUREKA!

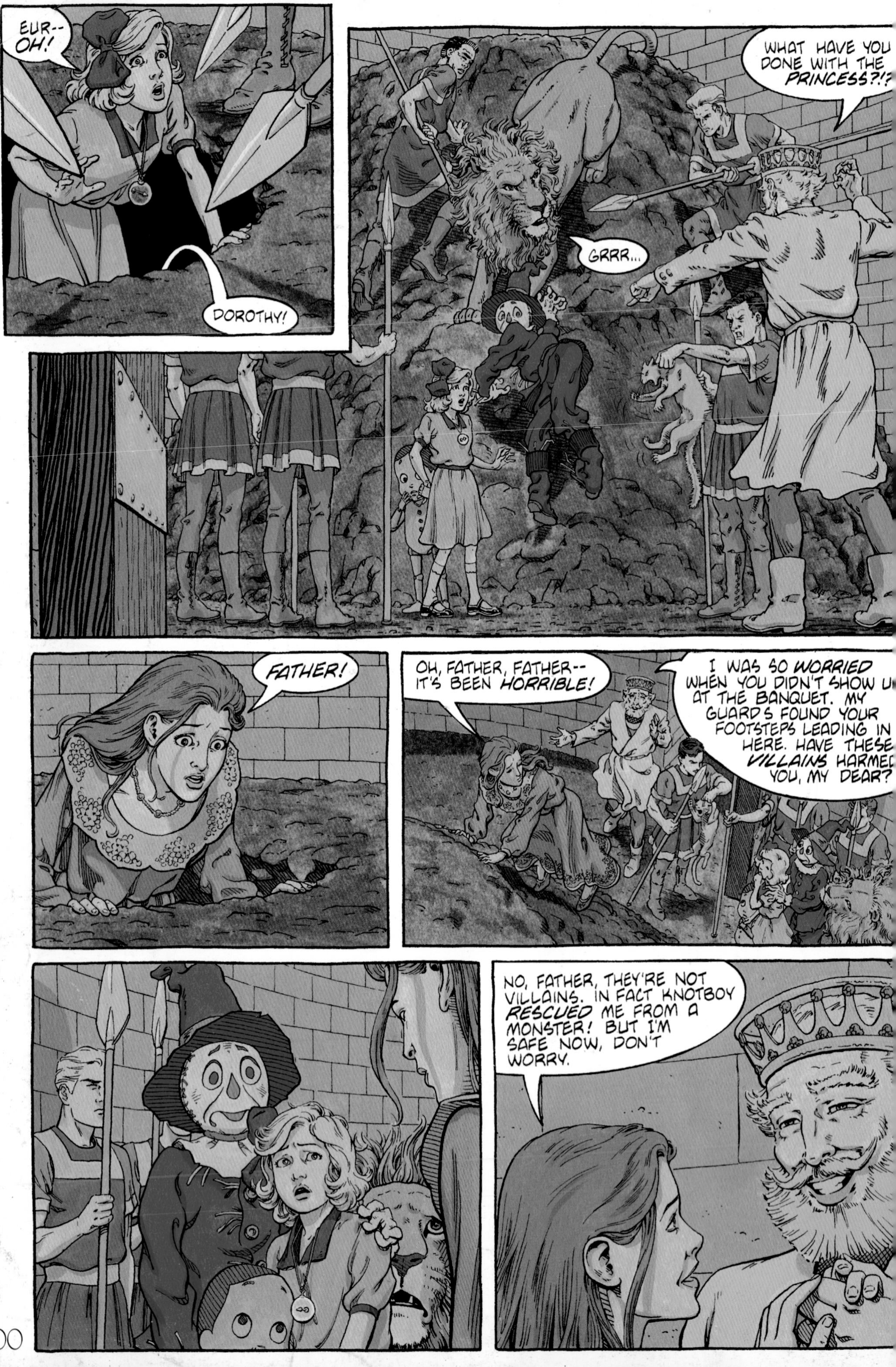
EUR--
OH!
DOROTHY!
WHAT HAVE YOU DONE WITH THE PRINCESS?!?
GRRR...
FATHER!
OH, FATHER, FATHER-- IT'S BEEN HORRIBLE!
I WAS SO WORRIED WHEN YOU DIDN'T SHOW U AT THE BANQUET. MY GUARDS FOUND YOUR FOOTSTEPS LEADING IN HERE. HAVE THESE VILLAINS HARMED YOU, MY DEAR?
NO, FATHER, THEY'RE NOT VILLAINS. IN FACT KNOTBOY RESCUED ME FROM A MONSTER! BUT I'M SAFE NOW, DON'T WORRY.

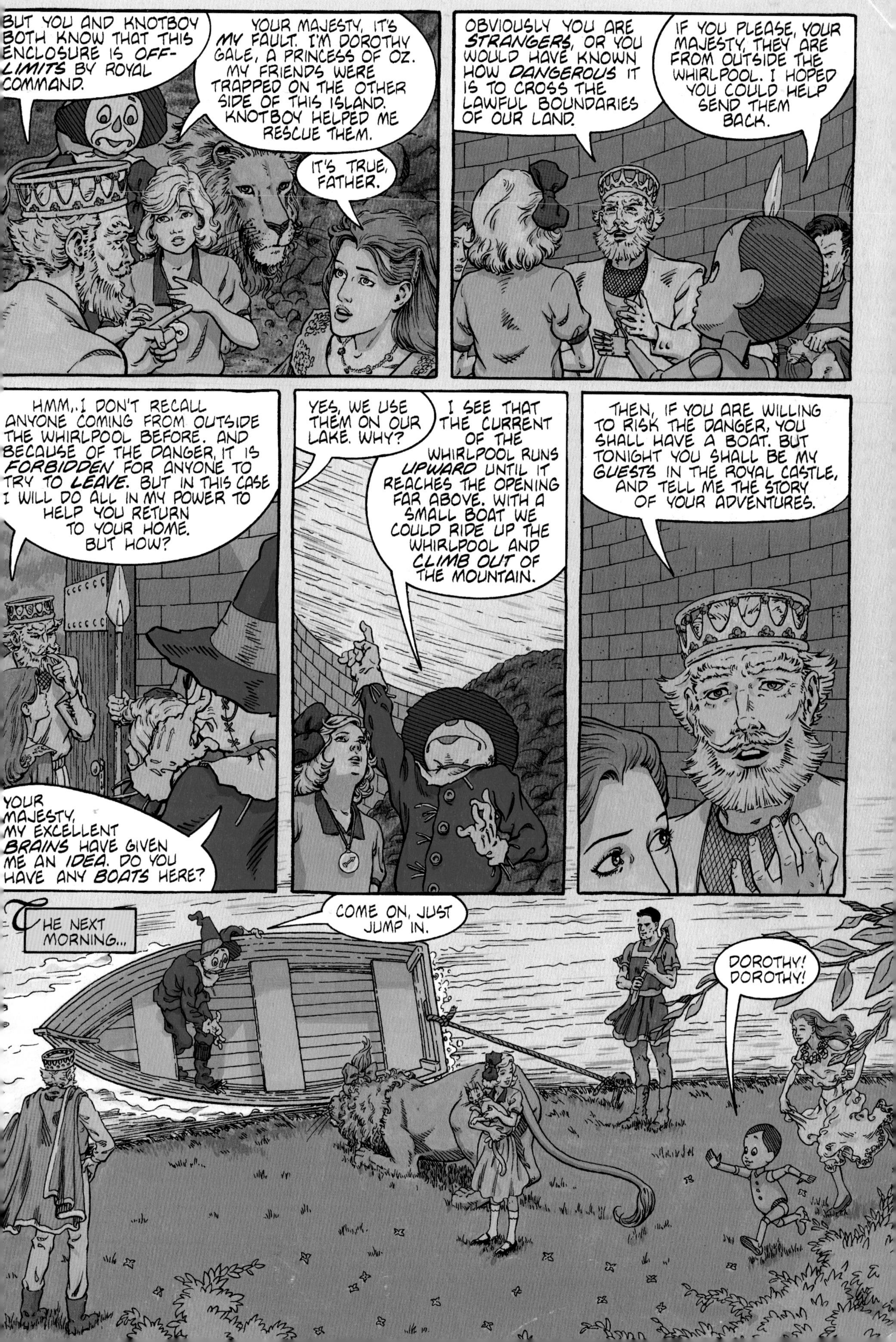

BUT YOU AND KNOTBOY BOTH KNOW THAT THIS ENCLOSURE IS OFF-LIMITS BY ROYAL COMMAND.
YOUR MAJESTY, IT'S MY FAULT. I'M DOROTHY GALE, A PRINCESS OF OZ. MY FRIENDS WERE TRAPPED ON THE OTHER SIDE OF THIS ISLAND. KNOTBOY HELPED ME RESCUE THEM.
IT'S TRUE, FATHER.
OBVIOUSLY YOU ARE STRANGERS, OR YOU WOULD HAVE KNOWN HOW DANGEROUS IT IS TO CROSS THE LAWFUL BOUNDARIES OF OUR LAND.
IF YOU PLEASE, YOUR MAJESTY, THEY ARE FROM OUTSIDE THE WHIRLPOOL. I HOPED YOU COULD HELP SEND THEM BACK.
HMM.. I DON'T RECALL ANYONE COMING FROM OUTSIDE THE WHIRLPOOL BEFORE. AND BECAUSE OF THE DANGER, IT IS FORBIDDEN FOR ANYONE TO TRY TO LEAVE. BUT IN THIS CASE I WILL DO ALL IN MY POWER TO HELP YOU RETURN TO YOUR HOME. BUT HOW?
YOUR MAJESTY, MY EXCELLENT BRAINS HAVE GIVEN ME AN IDEA. DO YOU HAVE ANY BOATS HERE?
YES, WE USE THEM ON OUR LAKE. WHY?
I SEE THAT THE CURRENT OF THE WHIRLPOOL RUNS UPWARD UNTIL IT REACHES THE OPENING FAR ABOVE. WITH A SMALL BOAT WE COULD RIDE UP THE WHIRLPOOL AND CLIMB OUT OF THE MOUNTAIN.
THEN, IF YOU ARE WILLING TO RISK THE DANGER, YOU SHALL HAVE A BOAT. BUT TONIGHT YOU SHALL BE MY GUESTS IN THE ROYAL CASTLE, AND TELL ME THE STORY OF YOUR ADVENTURES.
THE NEXT MORNING...
COME ON, JUST JUMP IN.
DOROTHY! DOROTHY!

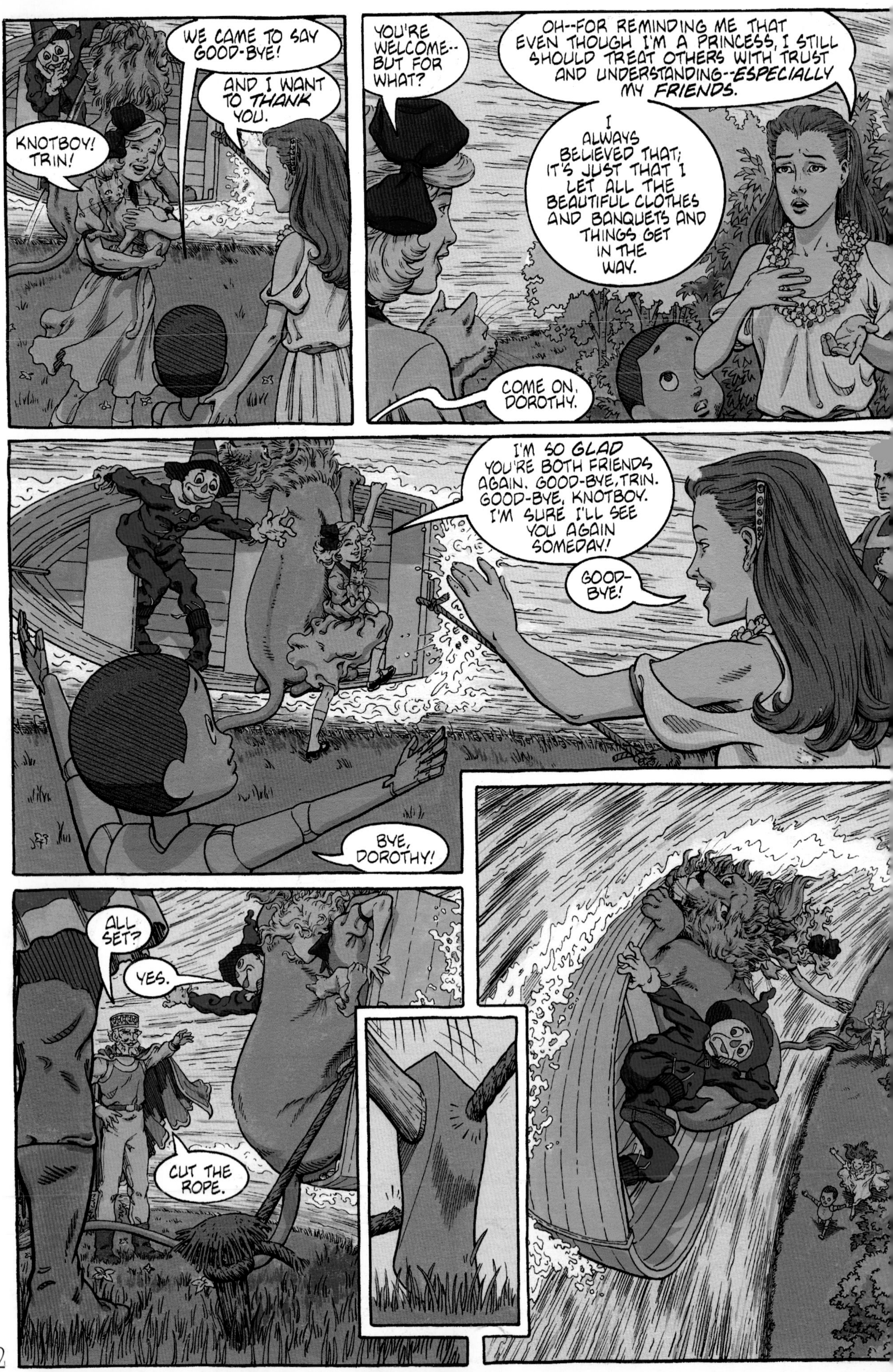
WE CAME TO SAY GOOD-BYE!
KNOTBOY! TRIN!
AND I WANT TO THANK YOU.
YOU'RE WELCOME-- BUT FOR WHAT?
OH--FOR REMINDING ME THAT EVEN THOUGH I'M A PRINCESS, I STILL SHOULD TREAT OTHERS WITH TRUST AND UNDERSTANDING--ESPECIALLY MY FRIENDS.
I ALWAYS BELIEVED THAT; IT'S JUST THAT I LET ALL THE BEAUTIFUL CLOTHES AND BANQUETS AND THINGS GET IN THE WAY.
COME ON, DOROTHY.
I'M SO GLAD YOU'RE BOTH FRIENDS AGAIN. GOOD-BYE, TRIN. GOOD-BYE, KNOTBOY. I'M SURE I'LL SEE YOU AGAIN SOMEDAY!
GOOD-BYE!
BYE, DOROTHY!
ALL SET?
YES.
CUT THE ROPE.

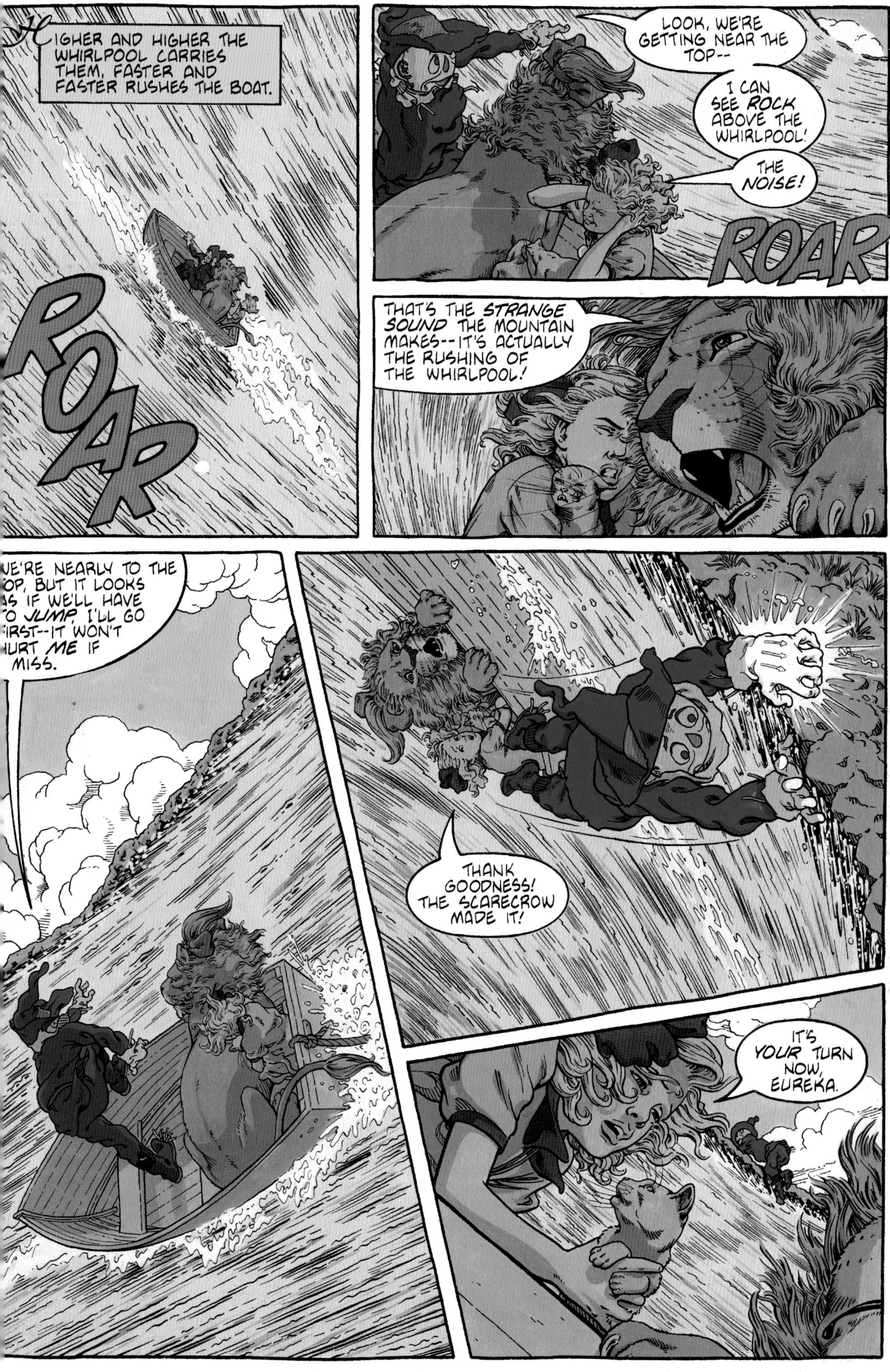
HIGHER AND HIGHER THE WHIRLPOOL CARRIES THEM, FASTER AND FASTER RUSHES THE BOAT.
ROAR
LOOK, WE'RE GETTING NEAR THE TOP--
I CAN SEE ROCK ABOVE THE WHIRLPOOL!
THE NOISE!
ROAR
THAT'S THE STRANGE SOUND THE MOUNTAIN MAKES--IT'S ACTUALLY THE RUSHING OF THE WHIRLPOOL!
WE'RE NEARLY TO THE TOP, BUT IT LOOKS AS IF WE'LL HAVE TO JUMP. I'LL GO FIRST--IT WON'T HURT ME IF I MISS.
THANK GOODNESS! THE SCARECROW MADE IT!
IT'S YOUR TURN NOW, EUREKA.

QUICK, LION, BEFORE THE BOAT GOES *OVER* THE *EDGE* OF THE WHIRLPOOL!

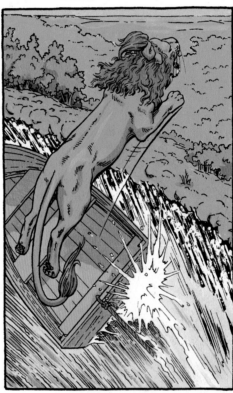

CRASH

SPLINTER

YIKES!

YOU DON'T HAVE TO BE *SCARED* ANYMORE, WE'RE SAFE!

LET'S START FOR *HOME.*

BUT I *DO* HAVE TO BE SCARED NOW-- I DIDN'T HAVE A *CHANCE* BEFORE.

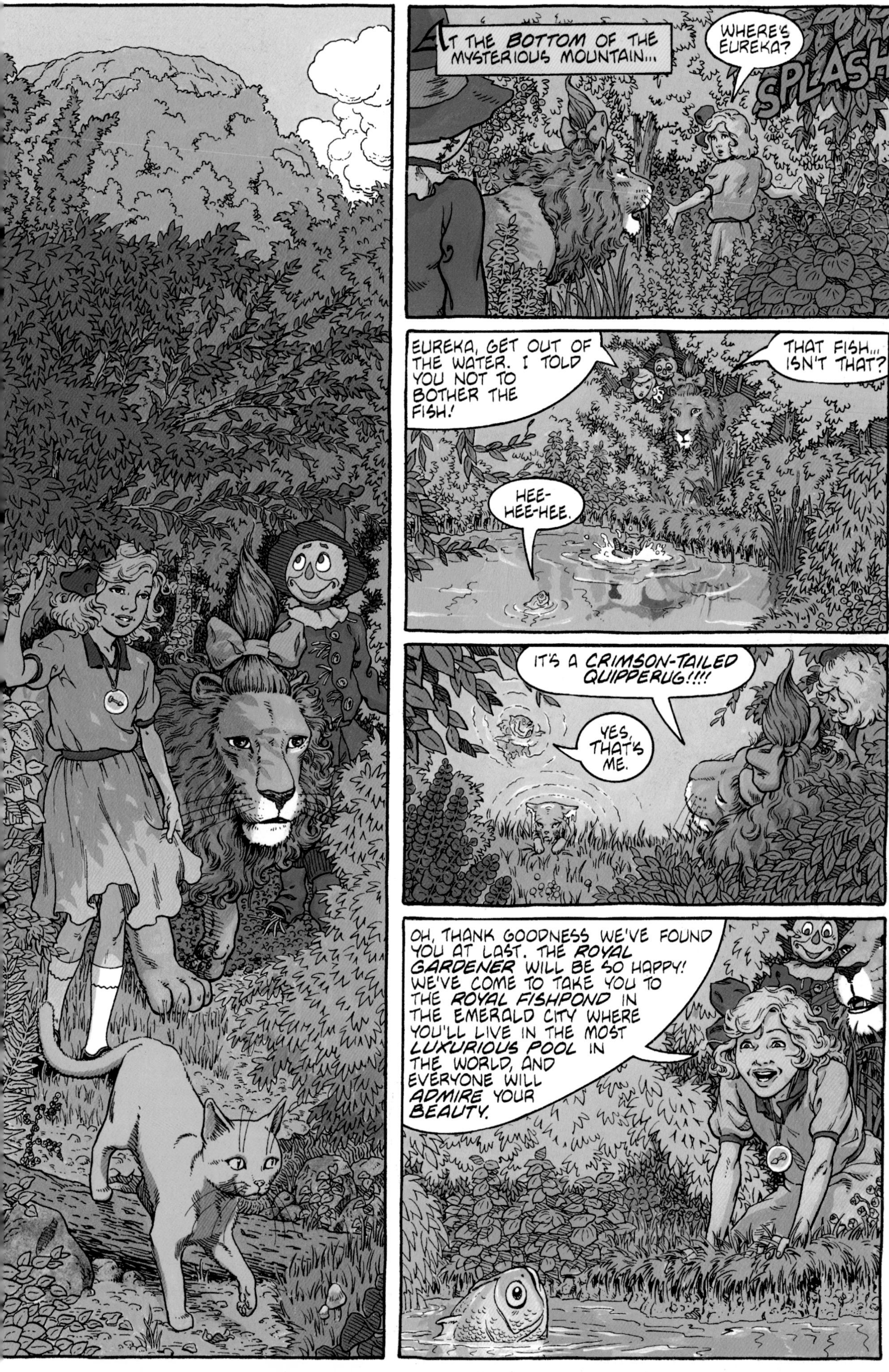
AT THE BOTTOM OF THE MYSTERIOUS MOUNTAIN...
WHERE'S EUREKA?
SPLASH
EUREKA, GET OUT OF THE WATER. I TOLD YOU NOT TO BOTHER THE FISH!
THAT FISH... ISN'T THAT?
HEE-HEE-HEE.
IT'S A CRIMSON-TAILED QUIPPERUG!!!!
YES, THAT'S ME.
OH, THANK GOODNESS WE'VE FOUND YOU AT LAST. THE ROYAL GARDENER WILL BE SO HAPPY! WE'VE COME TO TAKE YOU TO THE ROYAL FISHPOND IN THE EMERALD CITY WHERE YOU'LL LIVE IN THE MOST LUXURIOUS POOL IN THE WORLD, AND EVERYONE WILL ADMIRE YOUR BEAUTY.

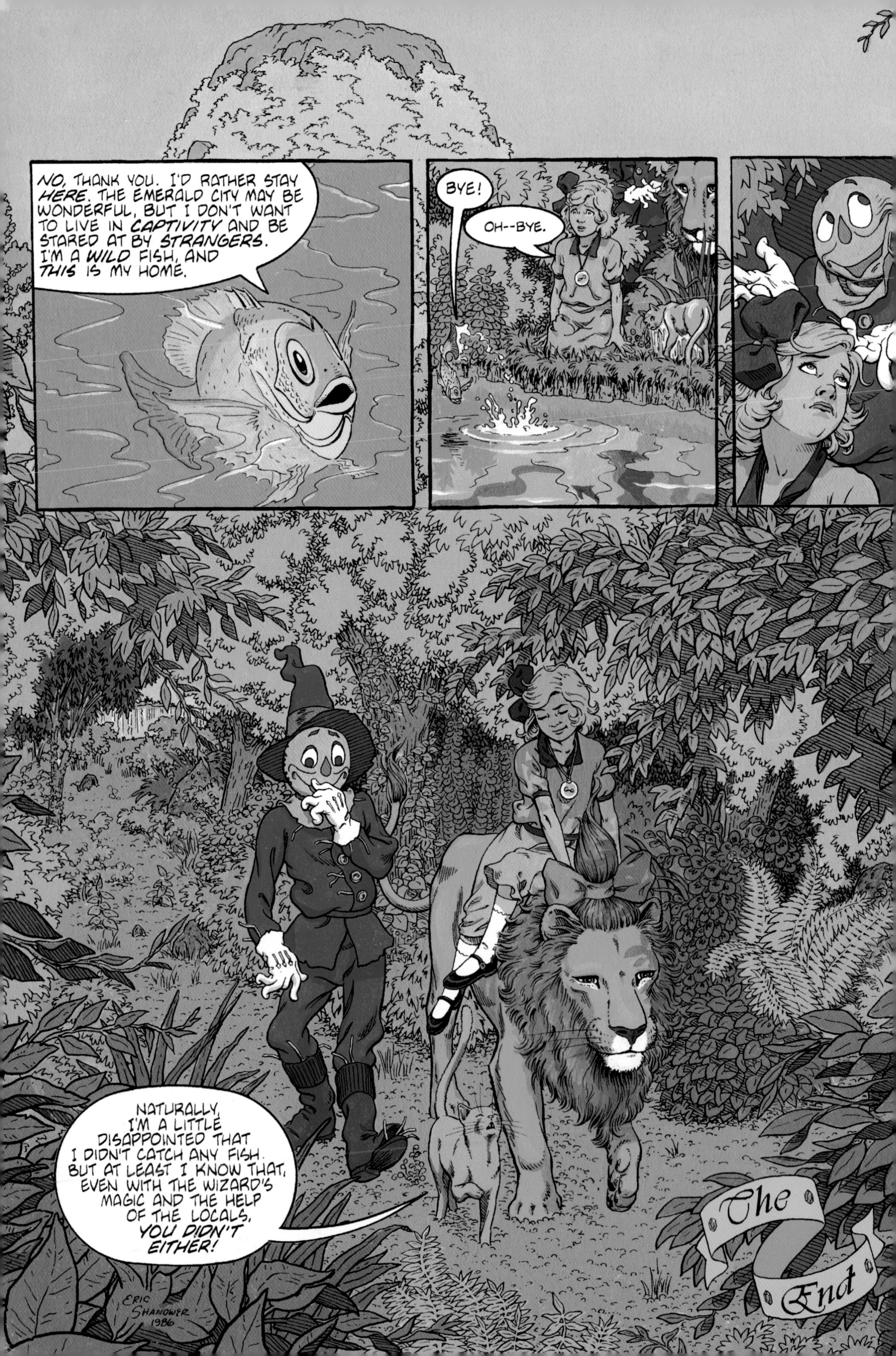

NO, THANK YOU. I'D RATHER STAY HERE. THE EMERALD CITY MAY BE WONDERFUL, BUT I DON'T WANT TO LIVE IN CAPTIVITY AND BE STARED AT BY STRANGERS. I'M A WILD FISH, AND THIS IS MY HOME.
BYE!
OH--BYE.
NATURALLY, I'M A LITTLE DISAPPOINTED THAT I DIDN'T CATCH ANY FISH. BUT AT LEAST I KNOW THAT, EVEN WITH THE WIZARD'S MAGIC AND THE HELP OF THE LOCALS, YOU DIDN'T EITHER!
ERIC SHANOWER 1986
The End

The ICE KING of OZ

To the Olsons:
Mary, Rick, Jimmy, and Amy
with gratitude

Chapter One The Proposal

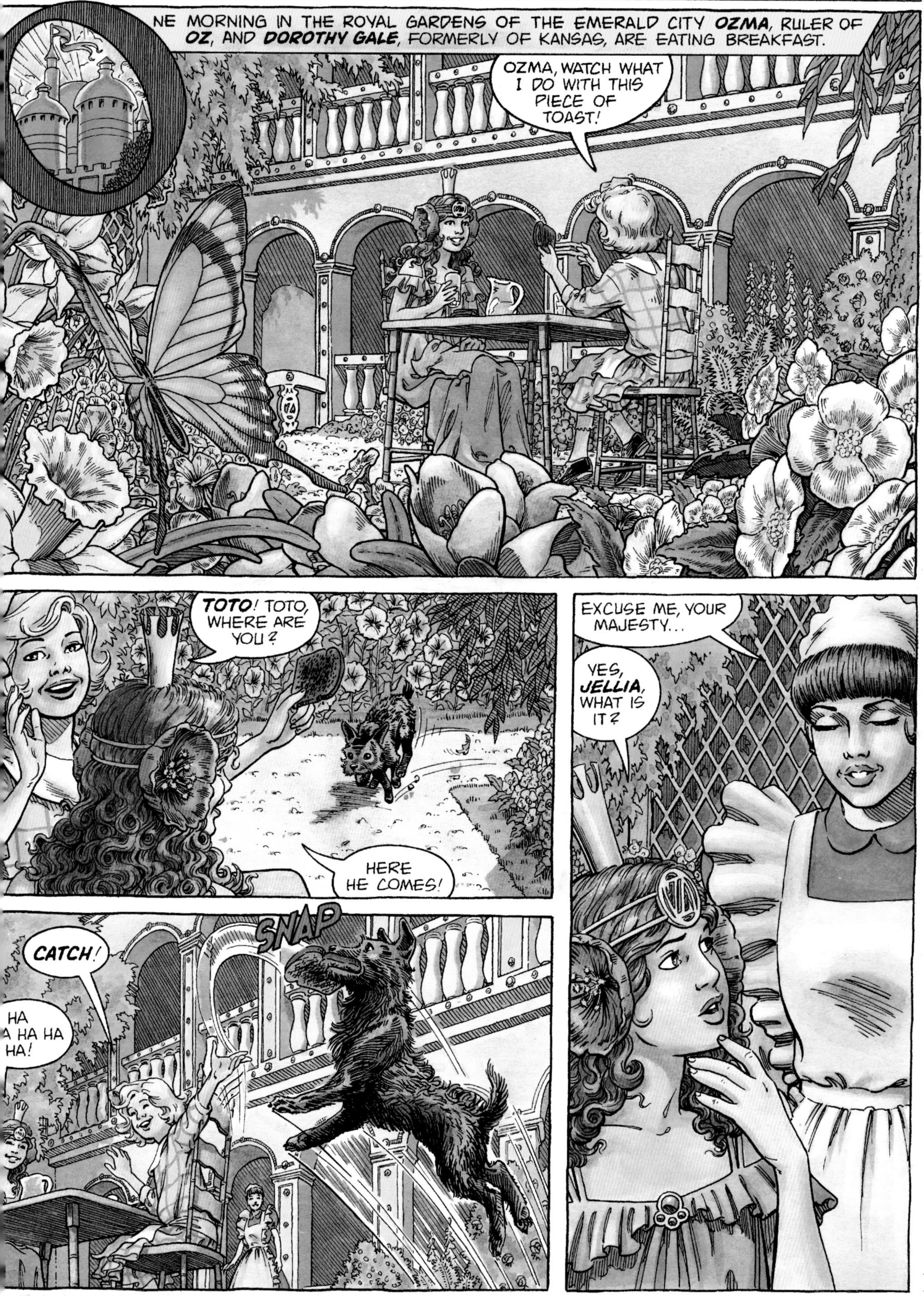

ONE MORNING IN THE ROYAL GARDENS OF THE EMERALD CITY OZMA, RULER OF OZ, AND DOROTHY GALE, FORMERLY OF KANSAS, ARE EATING BREAKFAST.
OZMA, WATCH WHAT I DO WITH THIS PIECE OF TOAST!
TOTO! TOTO, WHERE ARE YOU?
HERE HE COMES!
CATCH!
SNAP
HA A HA HA HA!
EXCUSE ME, YOUR MAJESTY...
YES, JELLIA, WHAT IS IT?

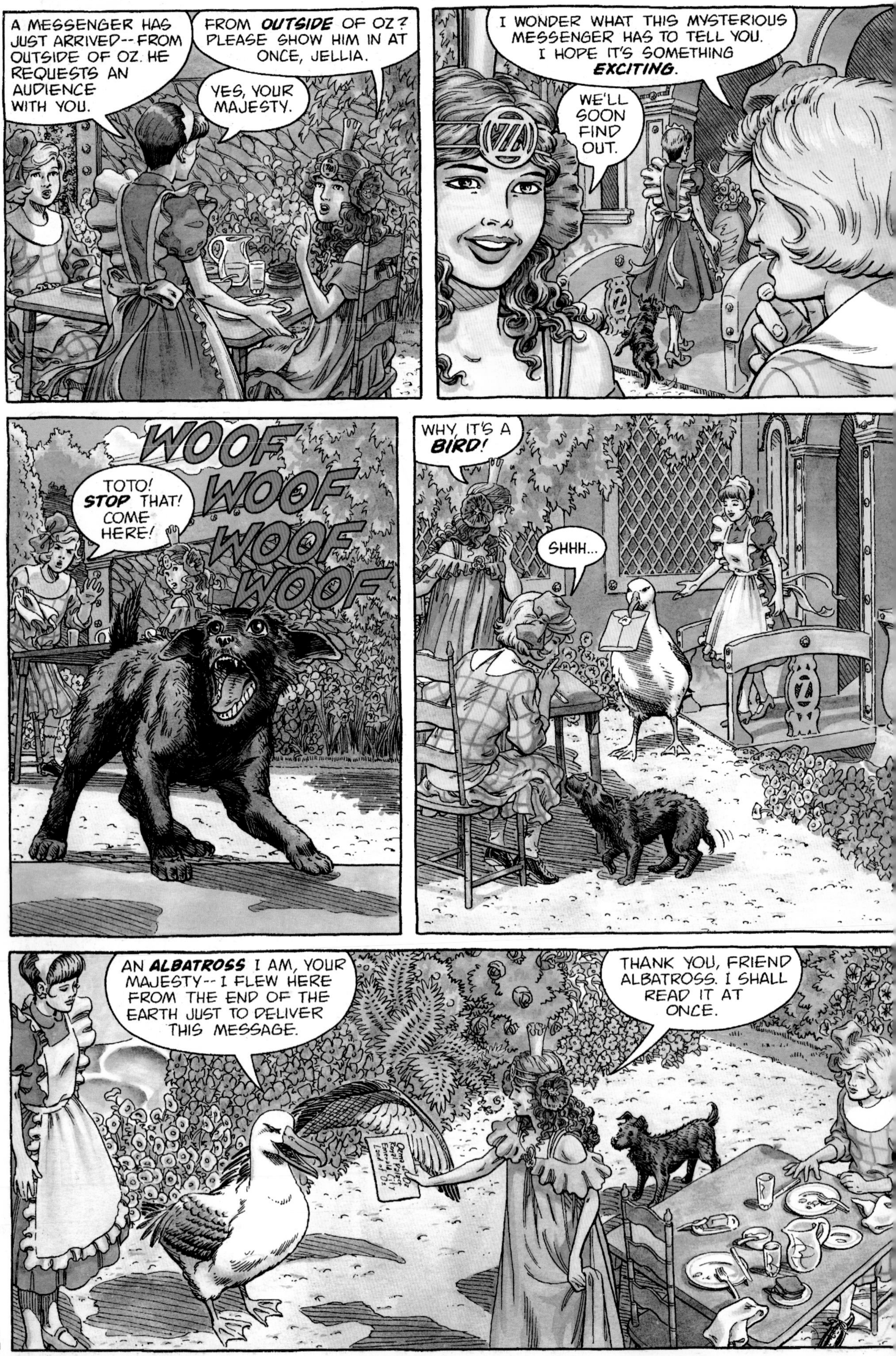
A MESSENGER HAS JUST ARRIVED--FROM OUTSIDE OF OZ. HE REQUESTS AN AUDIENCE WITH YOU.
FROM **OUTSIDE** OF OZ? PLEASE SHOW HIM IN AT ONCE, JELLIA.
YES, YOUR MAJESTY.
I WONDER WHAT THIS MYSTERIOUS MESSENGER HAS TO TELL YOU. I HOPE IT'S SOMETHING **EXCITING**.
WE'LL SOON FIND OUT.
WOOF WOOF WOOF WOOF
TOTO! **STOP** THAT! COME HERE!
WHY, IT'S A **BIRD**!
SHHH...
AN **ALBATROSS** I AM, YOUR MAJESTY-- I FLEW HERE FROM THE END OF THE EARTH JUST TO DELIVER THIS MESSAGE.
THANK YOU, FRIEND ALBATROSS. I SHALL READ IT AT ONCE.

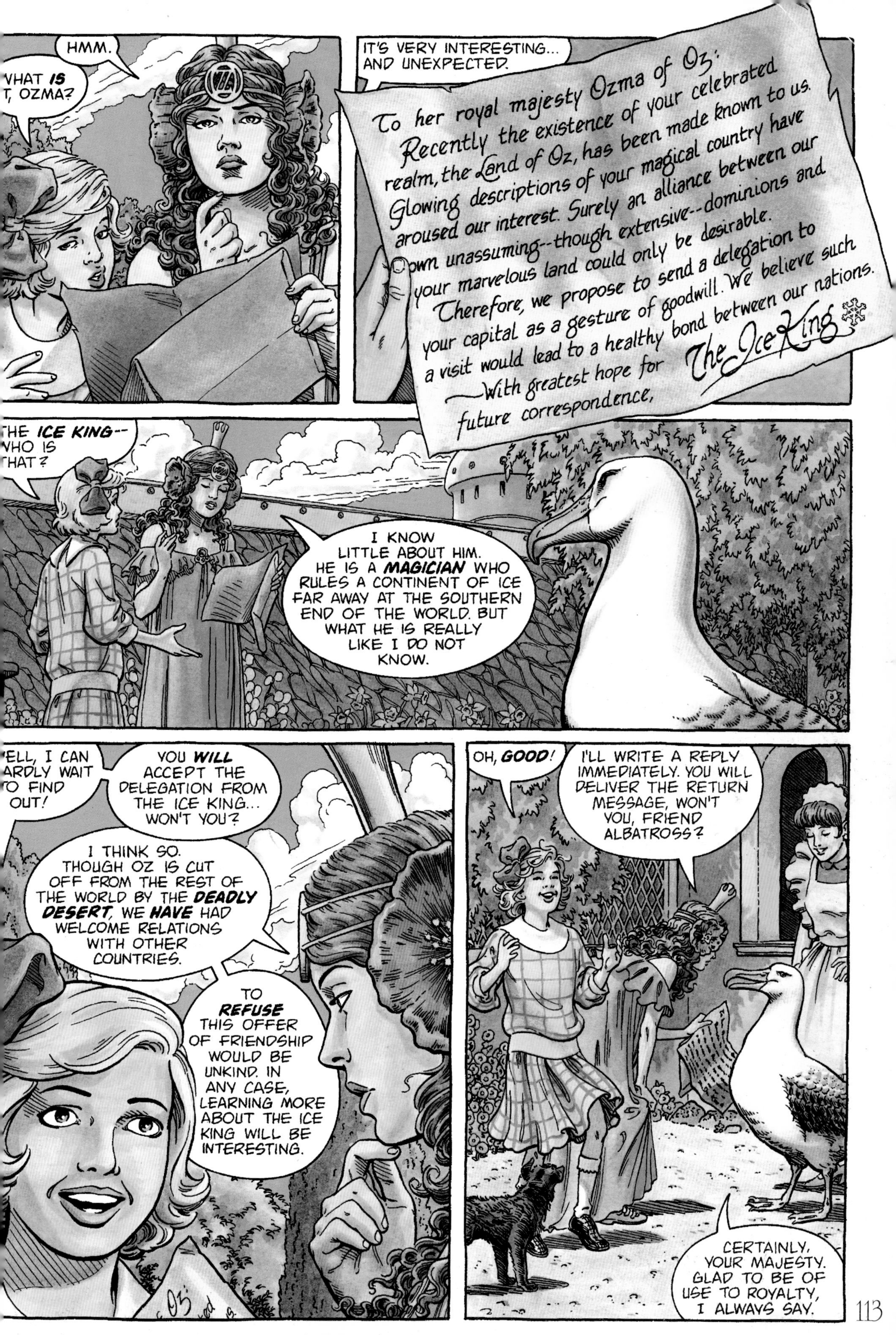
HMM.
VHAT *IS* T, OZMA?
IT'S VERY INTERESTING... AND UNEXPECTED.
To her royal majesty Ozma of Oz:
Recently the existence of your celebrated realm, the Land of Oz, has been made known to us. Glowing descriptions of your magical country have aroused our interest. Surely an alliance between our own unassuming--though extensive--dominions and your marvelous land could only be desirable.
Therefore, we propose to send a delegation to your capital as a gesture of goodwill. We believe such a visit would lead to a healthy bond between our nations.
—With greatest hope for future correspondence,
The Ice King
THE *ICE KING*-- VHO IS THAT?
I KNOW LITTLE ABOUT HIM. HE IS A *MAGICIAN* WHO RULES A CONTINENT OF ICE FAR AWAY AT THE SOUTHERN END OF THE WORLD. BUT WHAT HE IS REALLY LIKE I DO NOT KNOW.
ELL, I CAN ARDLY WAIT TO FIND OUT!
YOU *WILL* ACCEPT THE DELEGATION FROM THE ICE KING... WON'T YOU?
I THINK SO. THOUGH OZ IS CUT OFF FROM THE REST OF THE WORLD BY THE *DEADLY DESERT*, WE *HAVE* HAD WELCOME RELATIONS WITH OTHER COUNTRIES.
TO *REFUSE* THIS OFFER OF FRIENDSHIP WOULD BE UNKIND. IN ANY CASE, LEARNING MORE ABOUT THE ICE KING WILL BE INTERESTING.
OH, *GOOD*!
I'LL WRITE A REPLY IMMEDIATELY. YOU WILL DELIVER THE RETURN MESSAGE, WON'T YOU, FRIEND ALBATROSS?
CERTAINLY, YOUR MAJESTY. GLAD TO BE OF USE TO ROYALTY, I ALWAYS SAY.

FOR SEVERAL WEEKS THE EMERALD CITY BUSTLES WITH ACTIVITY.

EVERYONE IS GETTING READY FOR THE IMPORTANT VISITORS...

THE SHIPMENT OF NEW CURTAINS JUST CAME IN. WHERE DO YOU WANT THEM?

THEY EAT ICE CREAM, RIGHT? I'VE ORDERED **500 GALLONS** FOR THE BANQUET.

JELLIA, JELLIA!

EVERYONE.

NOT TOO MUCH OFF THE TOP NOW.

AT LAST, ON A THURSDAY MORNING AT TEN O'CLOCK, THE DELEGATION MAGICALLY ARRIVES.

POOF

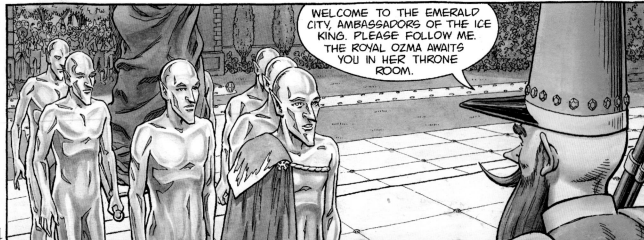

WELCOME TO THE EMERALD CITY, AMBASSADORS OF THE ICE KING. PLEASE FOLLOW ME. THE ROYAL OZMA AWAITS YOU IN HER THRONE ROOM.

114

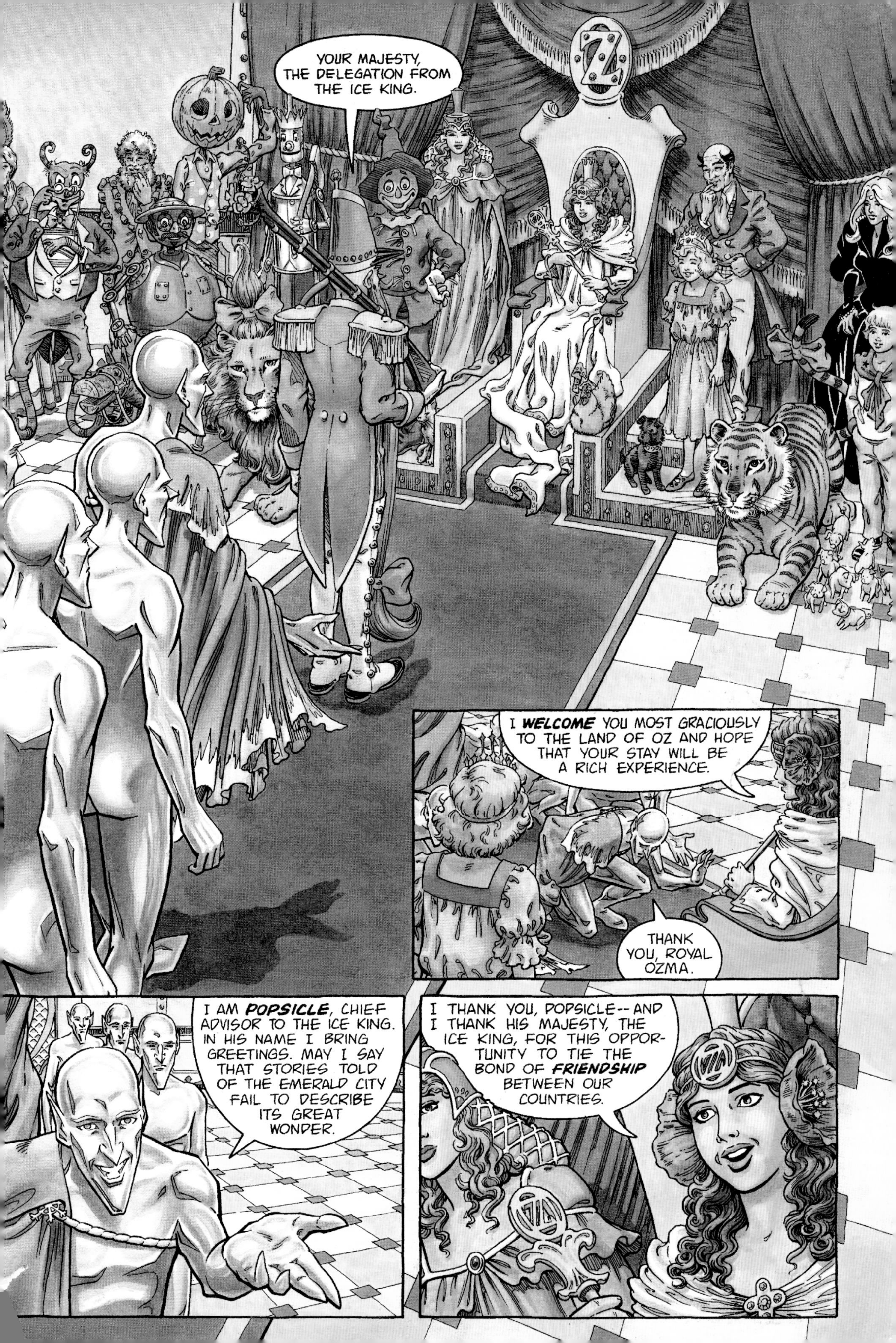
YOUR MAJESTY, THE DELEGATION FROM THE ICE KING.
I **WELCOME** YOU MOST GRACIOUSLY TO THE LAND OF OZ AND HOPE THAT YOUR STAY WILL BE A RICH EXPERIENCE.
THANK YOU, ROYAL OZMA.
I AM **POPSICLE**, CHIEF ADVISOR TO THE ICE KING. IN HIS NAME I BRING GREETINGS. MAY I SAY THAT STORIES TOLD OF THE EMERALD CITY FAIL TO DESCRIBE ITS GREAT WONDER.
I THANK YOU, POPSICLE-- AND I THANK HIS MAJESTY, THE ICE KING, FOR THIS OPPORTUNITY TO TIE THE BOND OF **FRIENDSHIP** BETWEEN OUR COUNTRIES.

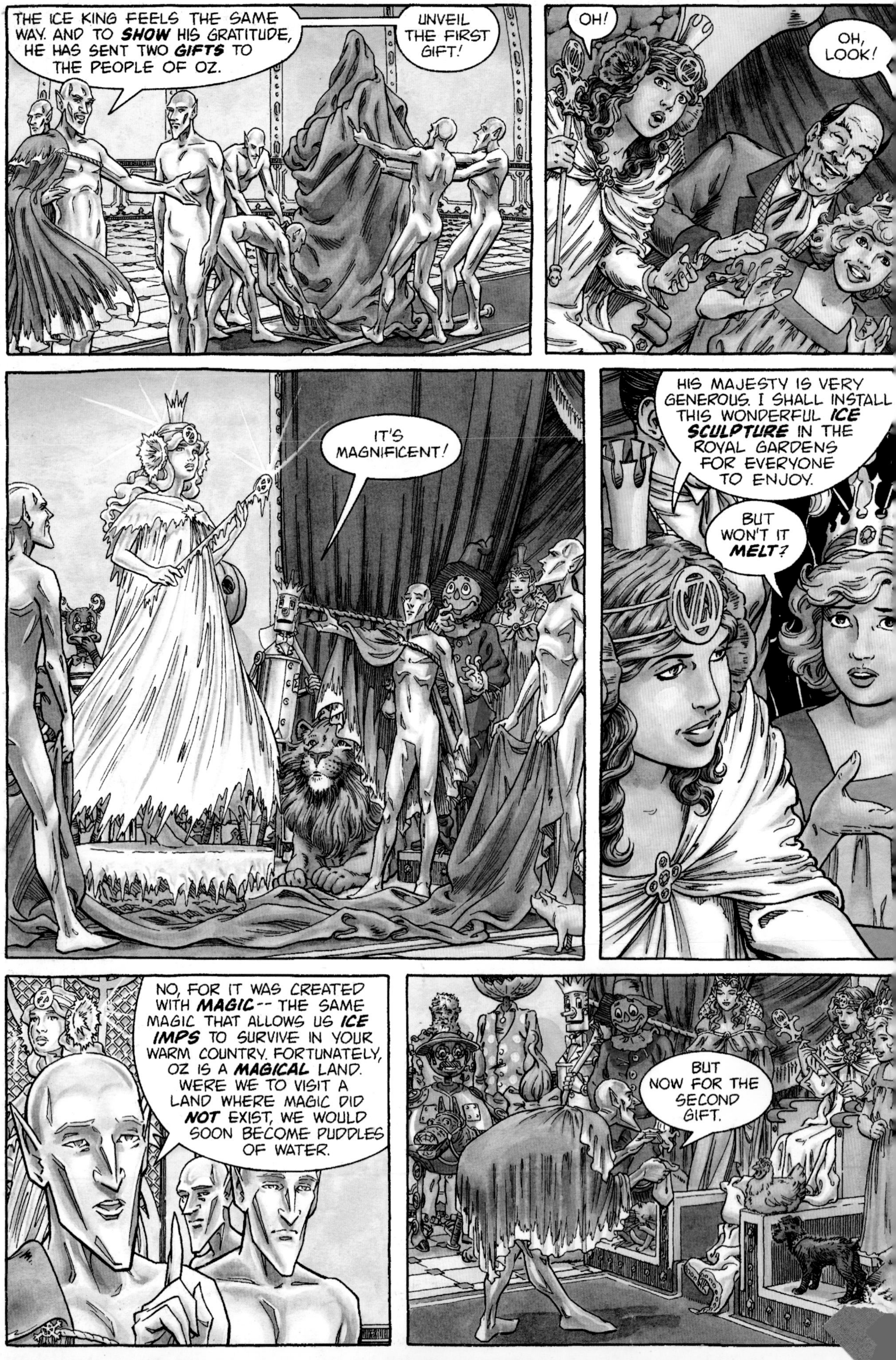
THE ICE KING FEELS THE SAME WAY. AND TO SHOW HIS GRATITUDE, HE HAS SENT TWO GIFTS TO THE PEOPLE OF OZ.
UNVEIL THE FIRST GIFT!
OH!
OH, LOOK!
IT'S MAGNIFICENT!
HIS MAJESTY IS VERY GENEROUS. I SHALL INSTALL THIS WONDERFUL ICE SCULPTURE IN THE ROYAL GARDENS FOR EVERYONE TO ENJOY.
BUT WON'T IT MELT?
NO, FOR IT WAS CREATED WITH MAGIC-- THE SAME MAGIC THAT ALLOWS US ICE IMPS TO SURVIVE IN YOUR WARM COUNTRY. FORTUNATELY, OZ IS A MAGICAL LAND. WERE WE TO VISIT A LAND WHERE MAGIC DID NOT EXIST, WE WOULD SOON BECOME PUDDLES OF WATER.
BUT NOW FOR THE SECOND GIFT.

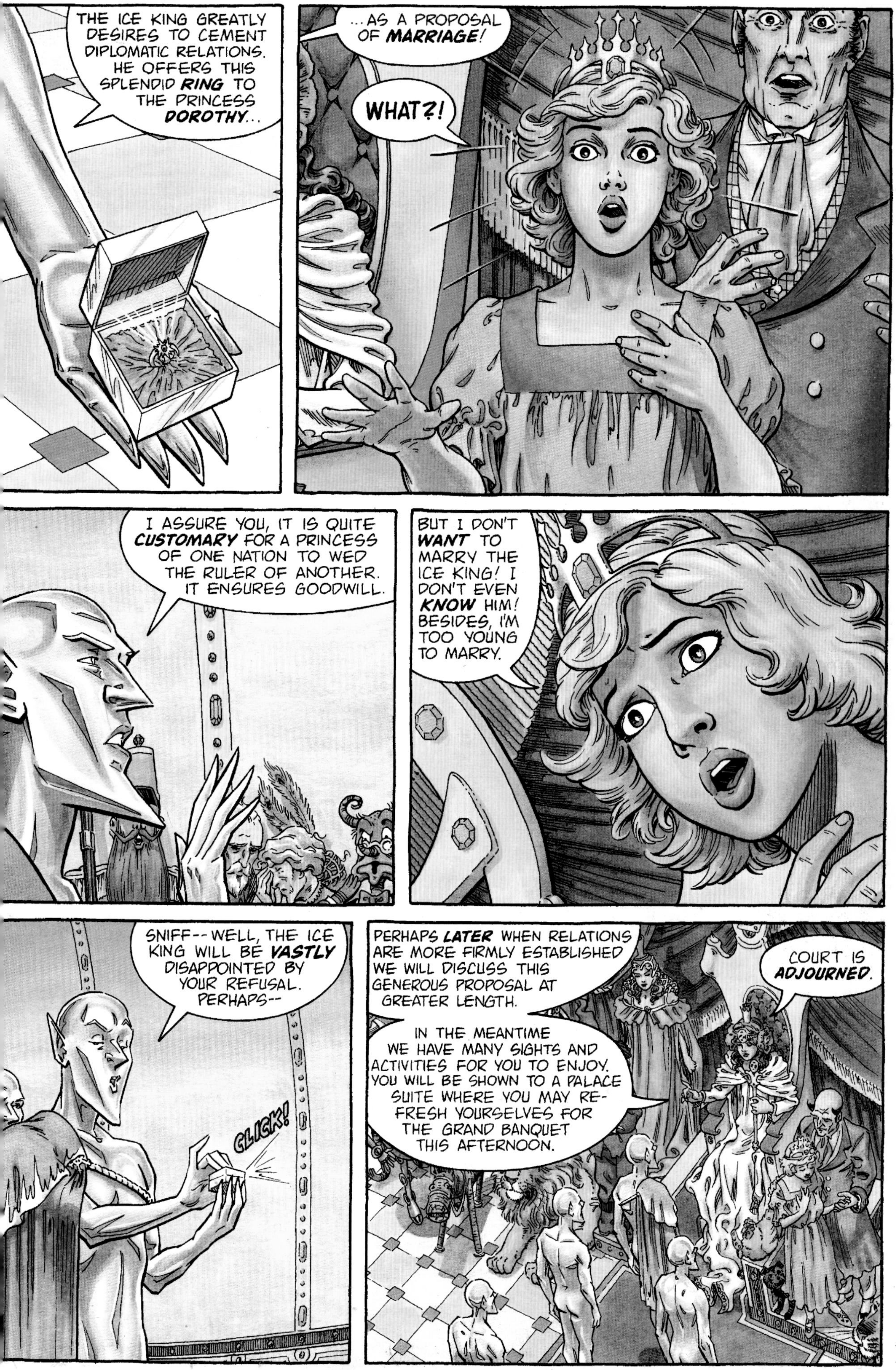
THE ICE KING GREATLY DESIRES TO CEMENT DIPLOMATIC RELATIONS. HE OFFERS THIS SPLENDID RING TO THE PRINCESS DOROTHY...
...AS A PROPOSAL OF MARRIAGE!
WHAT?!
I ASSURE YOU, IT IS QUITE CUSTOMARY FOR A PRINCESS OF ONE NATION TO WED THE RULER OF ANOTHER. IT ENSURES GOODWILL.
BUT I DON'T WANT TO MARRY THE ICE KING! I DON'T EVEN KNOW HIM! BESIDES, I'M TOO YOUNG TO MARRY.
SNIFF-- WELL, THE ICE KING WILL BE VASTLY DISAPPOINTED BY YOUR REFUSAL. PERHAPS--
CLICK!
PERHAPS LATER WHEN RELATIONS ARE MORE FIRMLY ESTABLISHED WE WILL DISCUSS THIS GENEROUS PROPOSAL AT GREATER LENGTH.
IN THE MEANTIME WE HAVE MANY SIGHTS AND ACTIVITIES FOR YOU TO ENJOY. YOU WILL BE SHOWN TO A PALACE SUITE WHERE YOU MAY RE-FRESH YOURSELVES FOR THE GRAND BANQUET THIS AFTERNOON.
COURT IS ADJOURNED.

Chapter Two Treachery

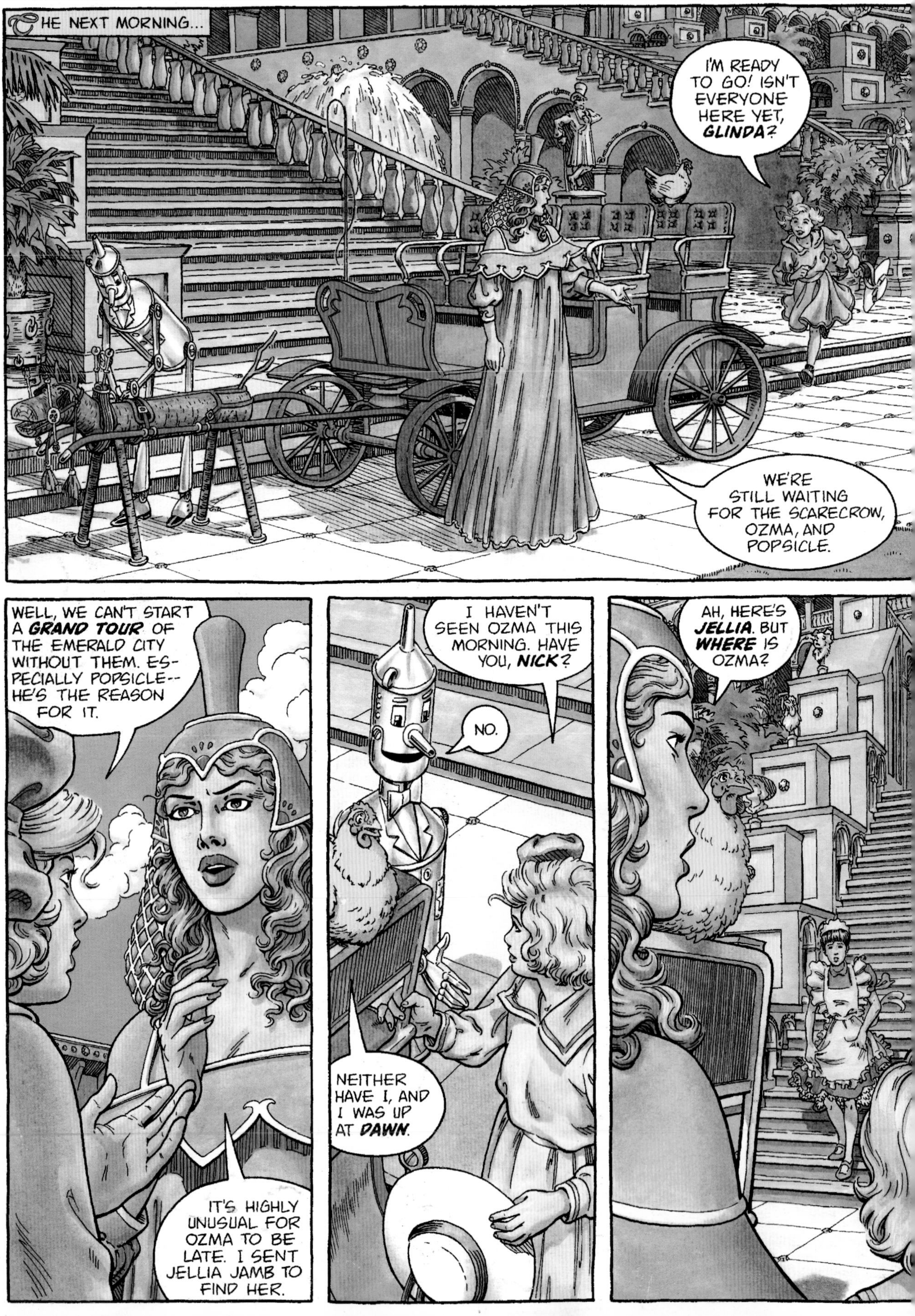
THE NEXT MORNING...
I'M READY TO GO! ISN'T EVERYONE HERE YET, GLINDA?
WE'RE STILL WAITING FOR THE SCARECROW, OZMA, AND POPSICLE.
WELL, WE CAN'T START A GRAND TOUR OF THE EMERALD CITY WITHOUT THEM. ESPECIALLY POPSICLE-- HE'S THE REASON FOR IT.
IT'S HIGHLY UNUSUAL FOR OZMA TO BE LATE. I SENT JELLIA JAMB TO FIND HER.
I HAVEN'T SEEN OZMA THIS MORNING. HAVE YOU, NICK?
NO.
NEITHER HAVE I, AND I WAS UP AT DAWN.
AH, HERE'S JELLIA. BUT WHERE IS OZMA?

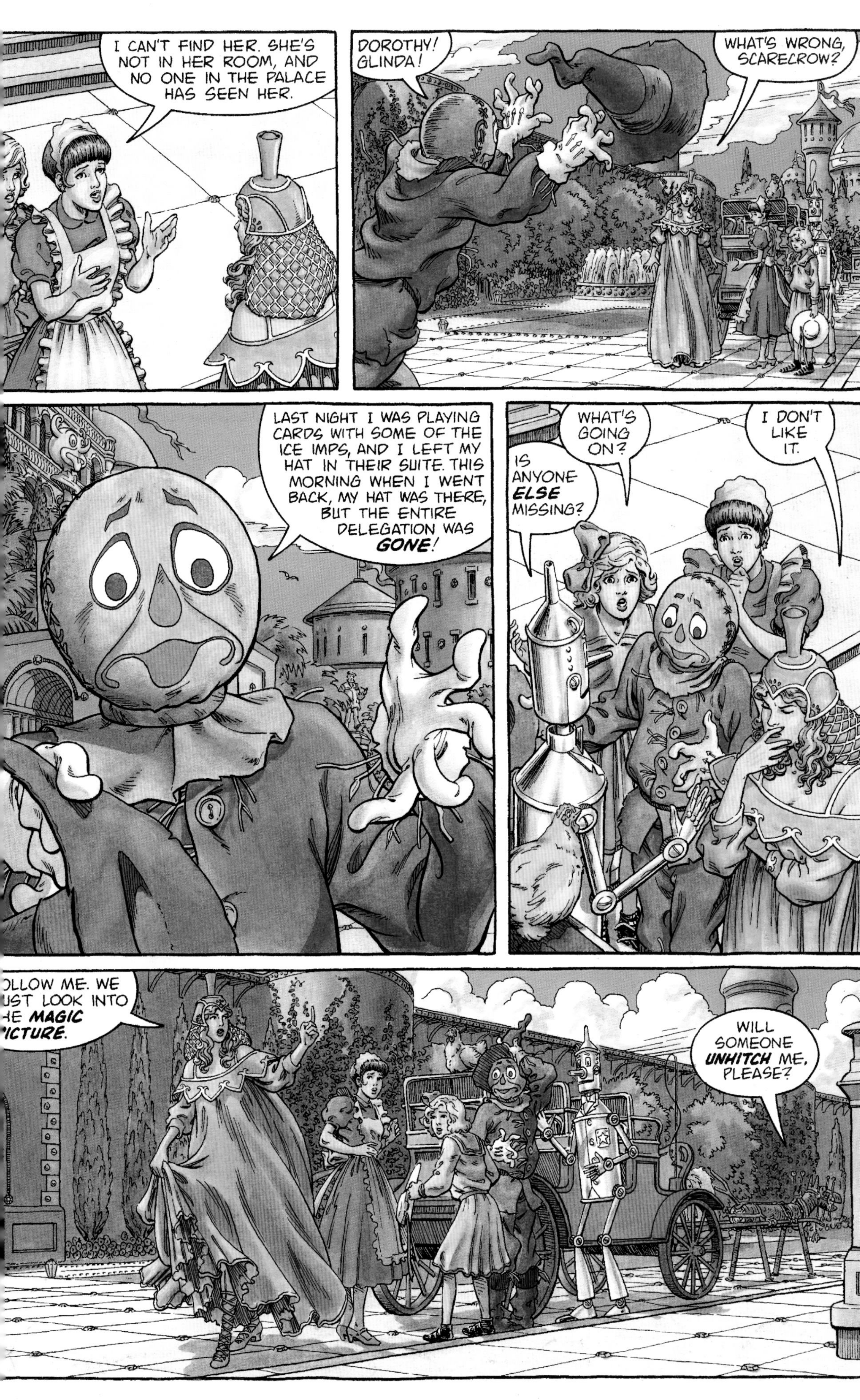

I CAN'T FIND HER. SHE'S NOT IN HER ROOM, AND NO ONE IN THE PALACE HAS SEEN HER.
DOROTHY! GLINDA!
WHAT'S WRONG, SCARECROW?
LAST NIGHT I WAS PLAYING CARDS WITH SOME OF THE ICE IMPS, AND I LEFT MY HAT IN THEIR SUITE. THIS MORNING WHEN I WENT BACK, MY HAT WAS THERE, BUT THE ENTIRE DELEGATION WAS **GONE**!
WHAT'S GOING ON?
I DON'T LIKE IT.
IS ANYONE **ELSE** MISSING?
OLLOW ME. WE UST LOOK INTO HE **MAGIC** ICTURE.
WILL SOMEONE **UNHITCH** ME, PLEASE?

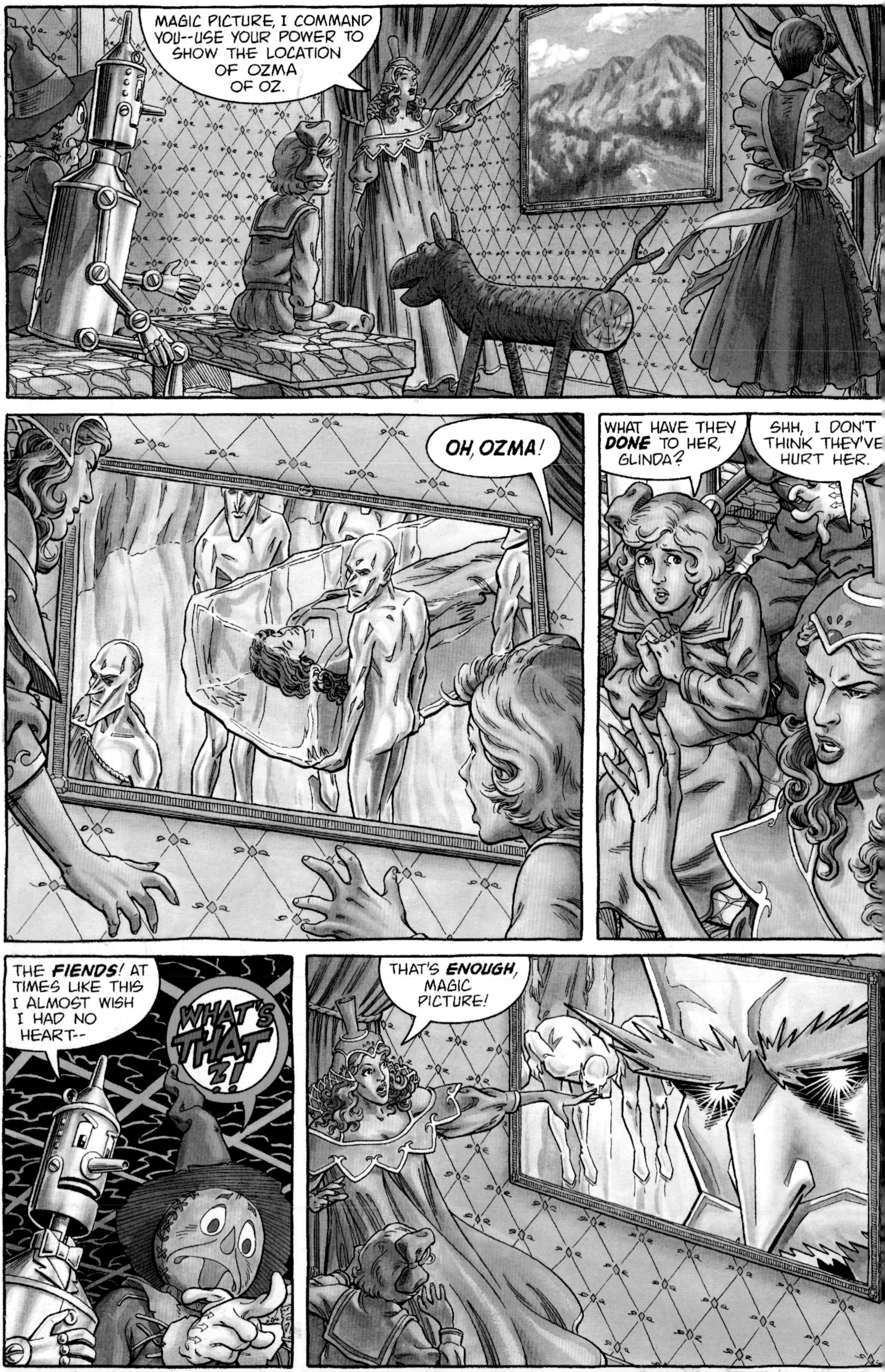
MAGIC PICTURE, I COMMAND YOU--USE YOUR POWER TO SHOW THE LOCATION OF OZMA OF OZ.
OH, OZMA!
WHAT HAVE THEY **DONE** TO HER, GLINDA?
SHH, I DON'T THINK THEY'VE HURT HER.
THE **FIENDS**! AT TIMES LIKE THIS I ALMOST WISH I HAD NO HEART--
WHAT'S THAT ?!
THAT'S **ENOUGH**, MAGIC PICTURE!

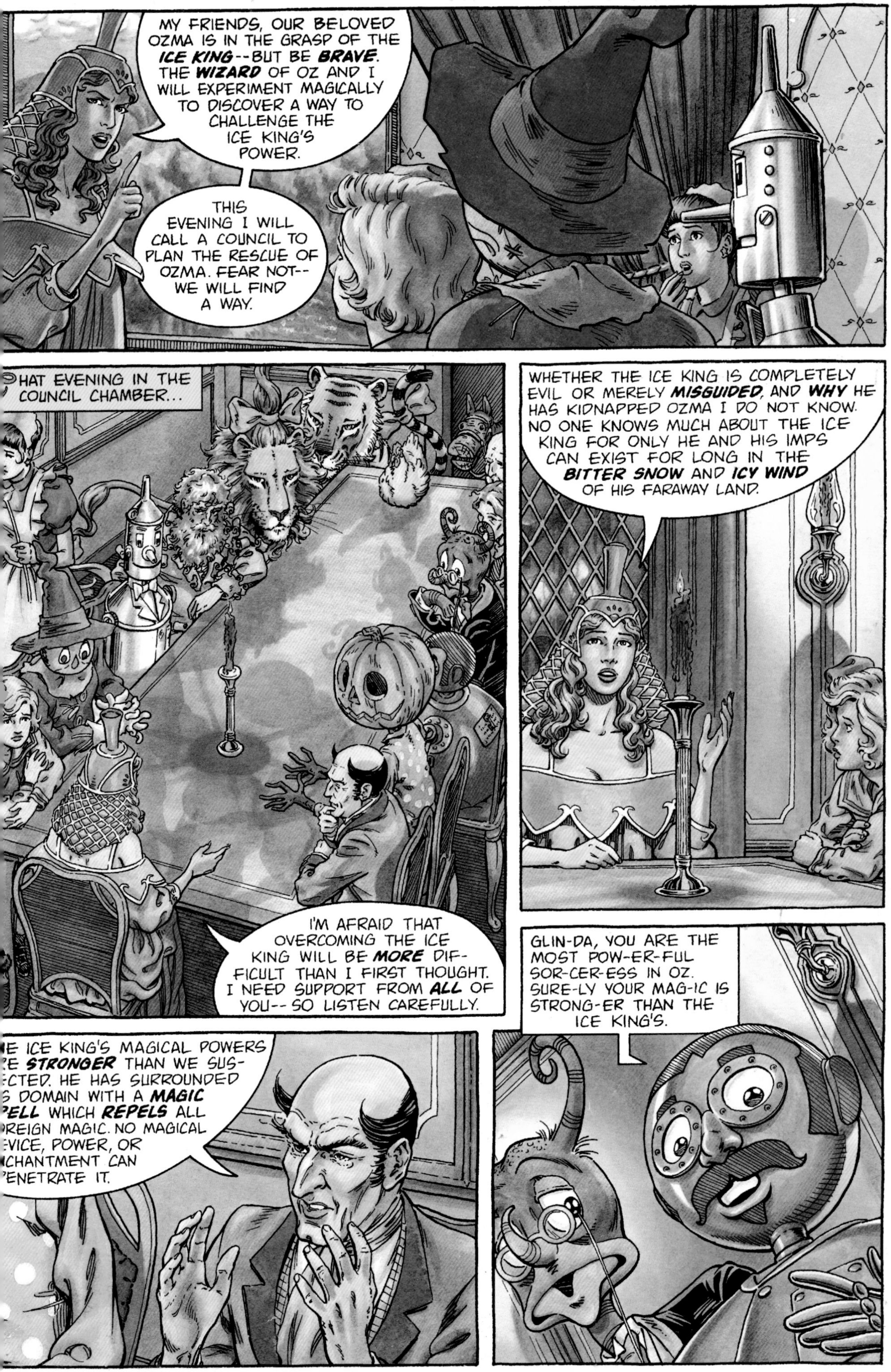
MY FRIENDS, OUR BELOVED OZMA IS IN THE GRASP OF THE ICE KING--BUT BE BRAVE. THE WIZARD OF OZ AND I WILL EXPERIMENT MAGICALLY TO DISCOVER A WAY TO CHALLENGE THE ICE KING'S POWER.
THIS EVENING I WILL CALL A COUNCIL TO PLAN THE RESCUE OF OZMA. FEAR NOT--WE WILL FIND A WAY.
HAT EVENING IN THE COUNCIL CHAMBER...
I'M AFRAID THAT OVERCOMING THE ICE KING WILL BE MORE DIF-FICULT THAN I FIRST THOUGHT. I NEED SUPPORT FROM ALL OF YOU-- SO LISTEN CAREFULLY.
WHETHER THE ICE KING IS COMPLETELY EVIL OR MERELY MISGUIDED, AND WHY HE HAS KIDNAPPED OZMA I DO NOT KNOW. NO ONE KNOWS MUCH ABOUT THE ICE KING FOR ONLY HE AND HIS IMPS CAN EXIST FOR LONG IN THE BITTER SNOW AND ICY WIND OF HIS FARAWAY LAND.
E ICE KING'S MAGICAL POWERS E STRONGER THAN WE SUS-ECTED. HE HAS SURROUNDED S DOMAIN WITH A MAGIC ELL WHICH REPELS ALL REIGN MAGIC. NO MAGICAL EVICE, POWER, OR CHANTMENT CAN ENETRATE IT.
GLIN-DA, YOU ARE THE MOST POW-ER-FUL SOR-CER-ESS IN OZ. SURE-LY YOUR MAG-IC IS STRONG-ER THAN THE ICE KING'S.

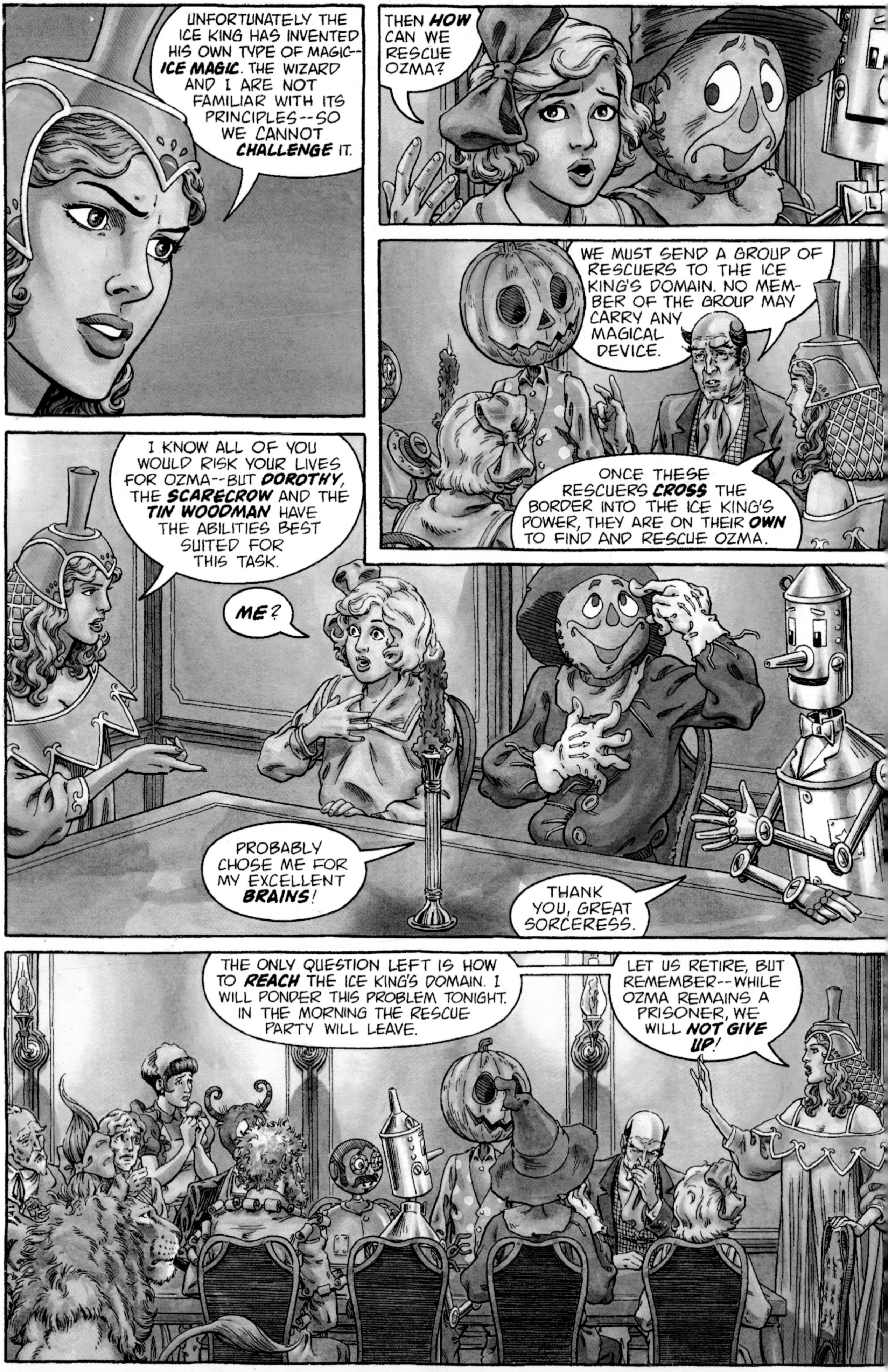
UNFORTUNATELY THE ICE KING HAS INVENTED HIS OWN TYPE OF MAGIC--ICE MAGIC. THE WIZARD AND I ARE NOT FAMILIAR WITH ITS PRINCIPLES--SO WE CANNOT CHALLENGE IT.
THEN HOW CAN WE RESCUE OZMA?
WE MUST SEND A GROUP OF RESCUERS TO THE ICE KING'S DOMAIN. NO MEMBER OF THE GROUP MAY CARRY ANY MAGICAL DEVICE.
ONCE THESE RESCUERS CROSS THE BORDER INTO THE ICE KING'S POWER, THEY ARE ON THEIR OWN TO FIND AND RESCUE OZMA.
I KNOW ALL OF YOU WOULD RISK YOUR LIVES FOR OZMA--BUT DOROTHY, THE SCARECROW AND THE TIN WOODMAN HAVE THE ABILITIES BEST SUITED FOR THIS TASK.
ME?
PROBABLY CHOSE ME FOR MY EXCELLENT BRAINS!
THANK YOU, GREAT SORCERESS.
THE ONLY QUESTION LEFT IS HOW TO REACH THE ICE KING'S DOMAIN. I WILL PONDER THIS PROBLEM TONIGHT. IN THE MORNING THE RESCUE PARTY WILL LEAVE.
LET US RETIRE, BUT REMEMBER--WHILE OZMA REMAINS A PRISONER, WE WILL NOT GIVE UP!

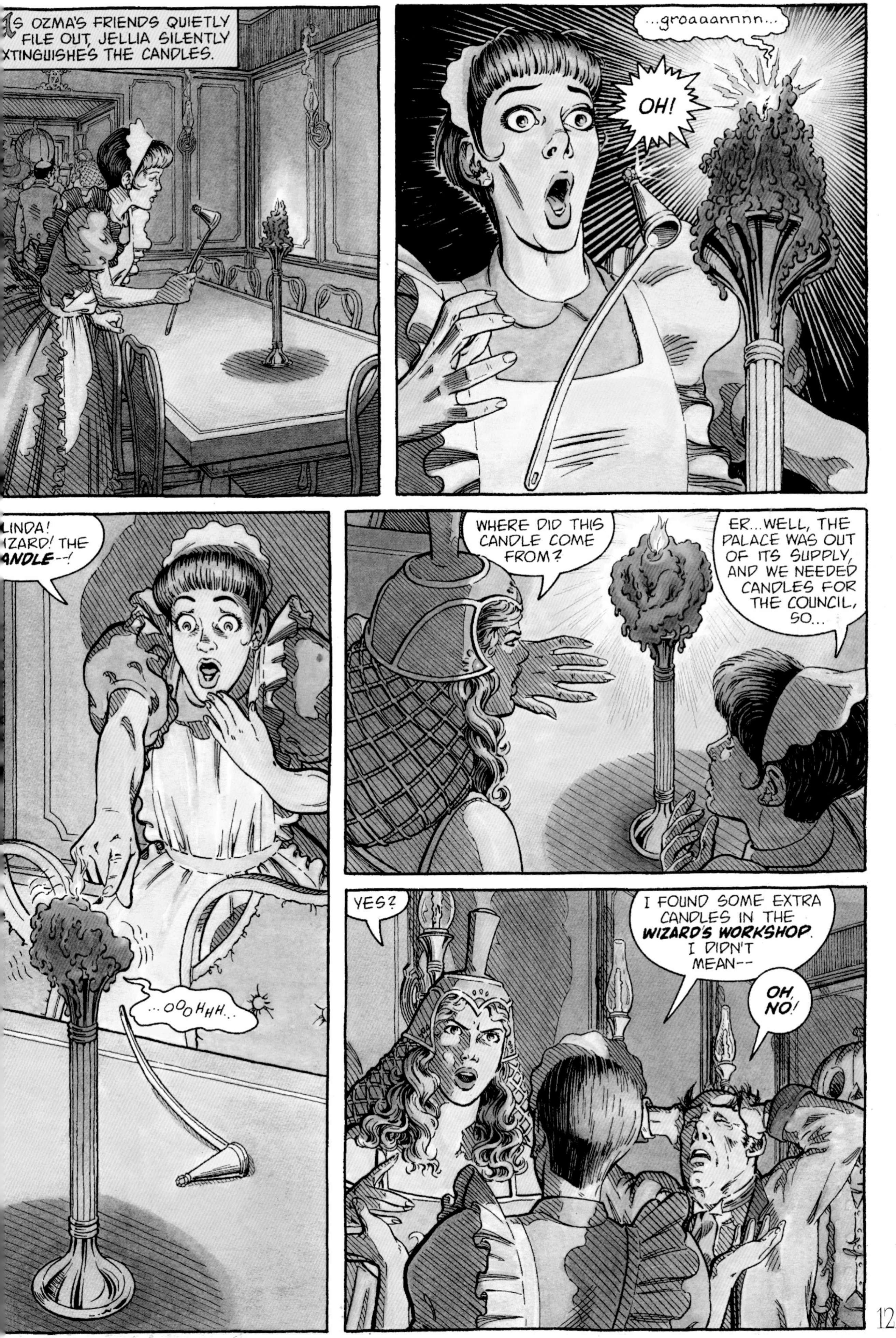
S OZMA'S FRIENDS QUIETLY
FILE OUT, JELLIA SILENTLY
XTINGUISHES THE CANDLES.
...groaaannnn...
OH!
LINDA! IZARD! THE **ANDLE**--!
...OOOHHH...
WHERE DID THIS CANDLE COME FROM?
ER...WELL, THE PALACE WAS OUT OF ITS SUPPLY, AND WE NEEDED CANDLES FOR THE COUNCIL, SO...
YES?
I FOUND SOME EXTRA CANDLES IN THE **WIZARD'S WORKSHOP**. I DIDN'T MEAN--
OH, NO!

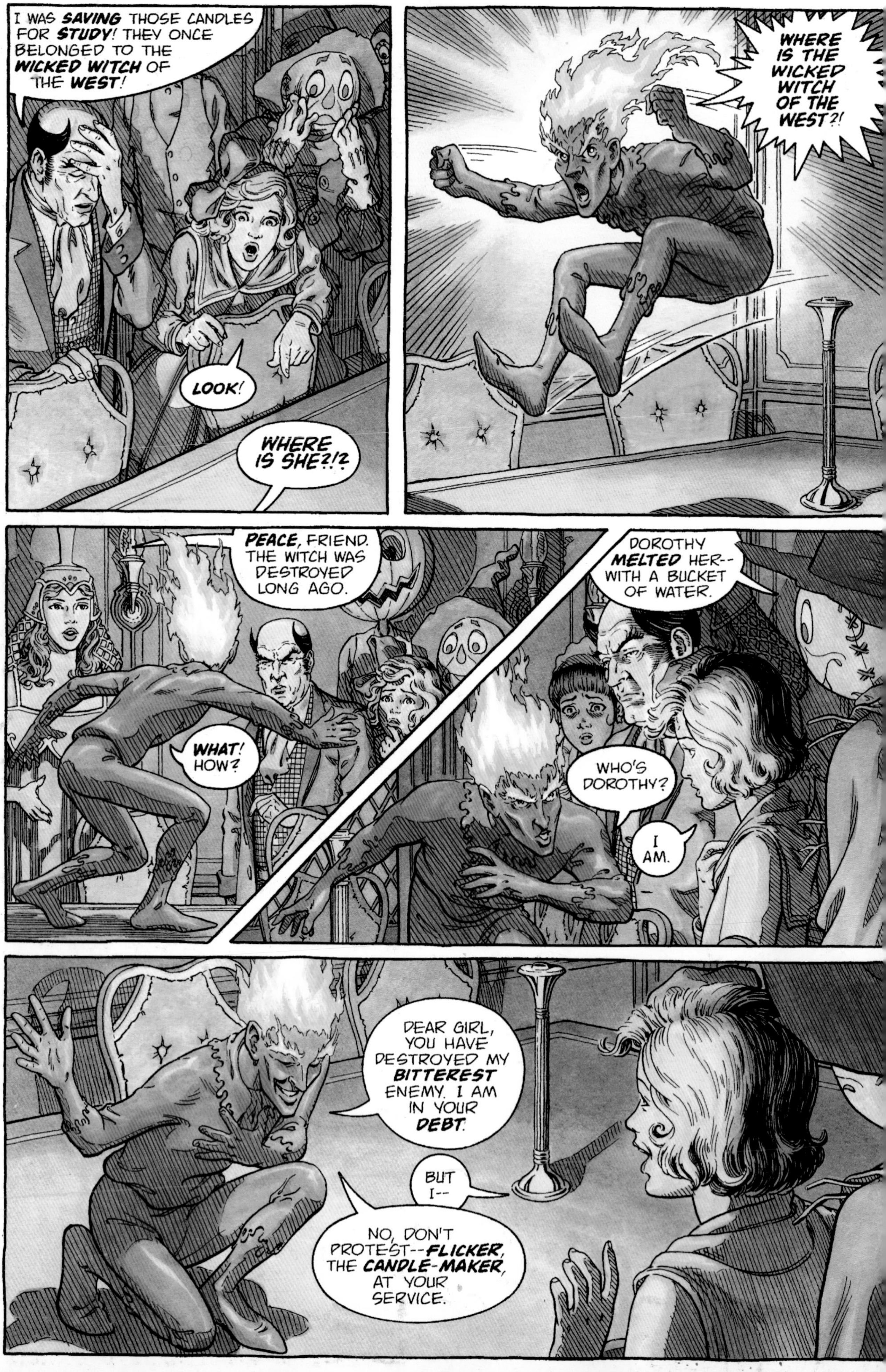
I WAS SAVING THOSE CANDLES FOR STUDY! THEY ONCE BELONGED TO THE WICKED WITCH OF THE WEST!
LOOK!
WHERE IS SHE?!?
WHERE IS THE WICKED WITCH OF THE WEST?!
PEACE, FRIEND. THE WITCH WAS DESTROYED LONG AGO.
WHAT! HOW?
DOROTHY MELTED HER-- WITH A BUCKET OF WATER.
WHO'S DOROTHY?
I AM.
DEAR GIRL, YOU HAVE DESTROYED MY BITTEREST ENEMY. I AM IN YOUR DEBT.
BUT I--
NO, DON'T PROTEST--FLICKER, THE CANDLE-MAKER, AT YOUR SERVICE.

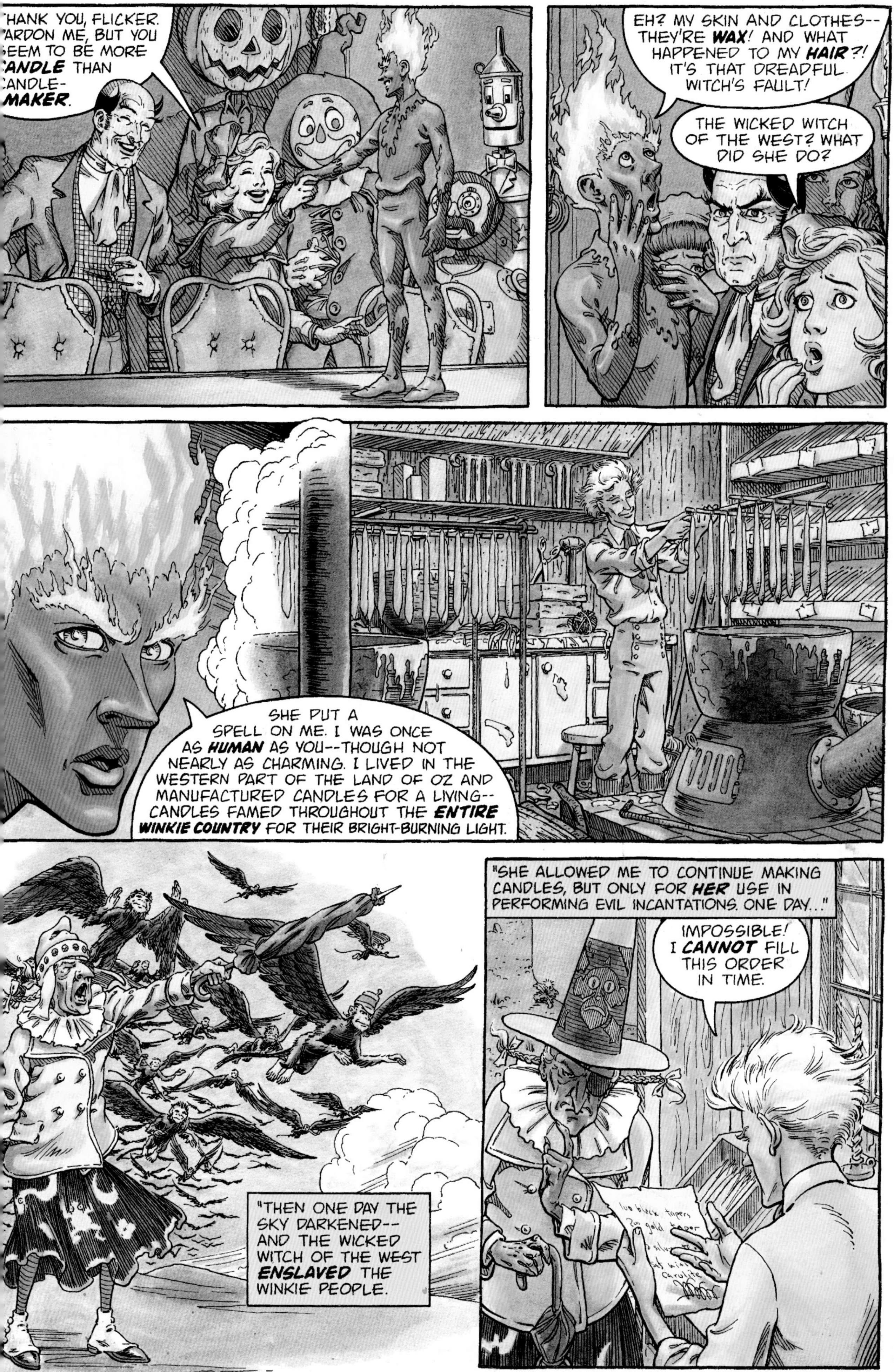
THANK YOU, FLICKER. PARDON ME, BUT YOU SEEM TO BE MORE CANDLE THAN CANDLE-MAKER.
EH? MY SKIN AND CLOTHES-- THEY'RE WAX! AND WHAT HAPPENED TO MY HAIR?! IT'S THAT DREADFUL WITCH'S FAULT!
THE WICKED WITCH OF THE WEST? WHAT DID SHE DO?
SHE PUT A SPELL ON ME. I WAS ONCE AS HUMAN AS YOU--THOUGH NOT NEARLY AS CHARMING. I LIVED IN THE WESTERN PART OF THE LAND OF OZ AND MANUFACTURED CANDLES FOR A LIVING-- CANDLES FAMED THROUGHOUT THE ENTIRE WINKIE COUNTRY FOR THEIR BRIGHT-BURNING LIGHT.
"THEN ONE DAY THE SKY DARKENED-- AND THE WICKED WITCH OF THE WEST ENSLAVED THE WINKIE PEOPLE.
"SHE ALLOWED ME TO CONTINUE MAKING CANDLES, BUT ONLY FOR HER USE IN PERFORMING EVIL INCANTATIONS. ONE DAY..."
IMPOSSIBLE! I CANNOT FILL THIS ORDER IN TIME.

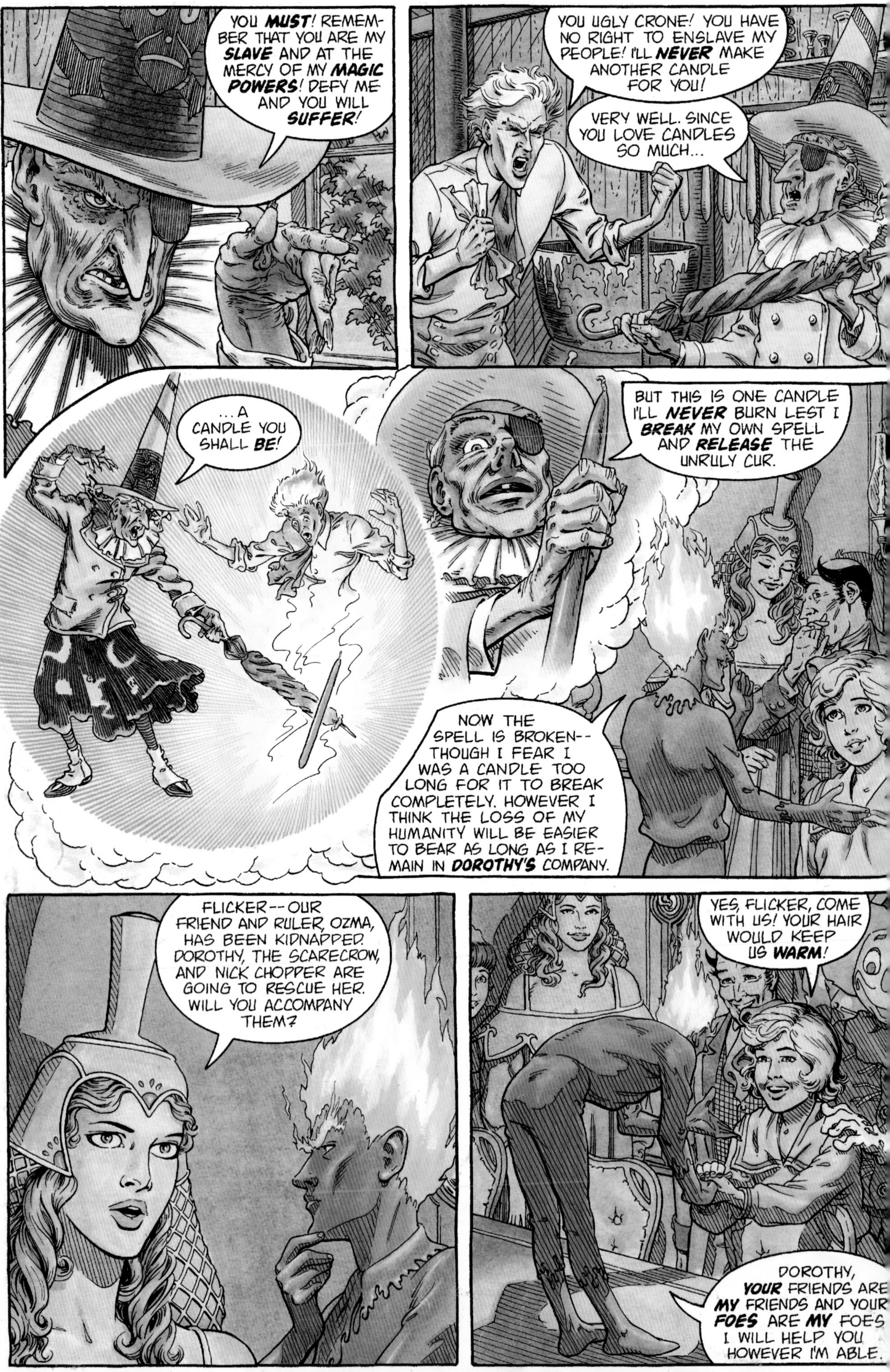
YOU MUST! REMEMBER THAT YOU ARE MY SLAVE AND AT THE MERCY OF MY MAGIC POWERS! DEFY ME AND YOU WILL SUFFER!
YOU UGLY CRONE! YOU HAVE NO RIGHT TO ENSLAVE MY PEOPLE! I'LL NEVER MAKE ANOTHER CANDLE FOR YOU!
VERY WELL. SINCE YOU LOVE CANDLES SO MUCH...
...A CANDLE YOU SHALL BE!
BUT THIS IS ONE CANDLE I'LL NEVER BURN LEST I BREAK MY OWN SPELL AND RELEASE THE UNRULY CUR.
NOW THE SPELL IS BROKEN--THOUGH I FEAR I WAS A CANDLE TOO LONG FOR IT TO BREAK COMPLETELY. HOWEVER I THINK THE LOSS OF MY HUMANITY WILL BE EASIER TO BEAR AS LONG AS I REMAIN IN DOROTHY'S COMPANY.
FLICKER--OUR FRIEND AND RULER, OZMA, HAS BEEN KIDNAPPED. DOROTHY, THE SCARECROW, AND NICK CHOPPER ARE GOING TO RESCUE HER. WILL YOU ACCOMPANY THEM?
YES, FLICKER, COME WITH US! YOUR HAIR WOULD KEEP US WARM!
DOROTHY, YOUR FRIENDS ARE MY FRIENDS AND YOUR FOES ARE MY FOES I WILL HELP YOU HOWEVER I'M ABLE.

Chapter Three — The Land of Ice

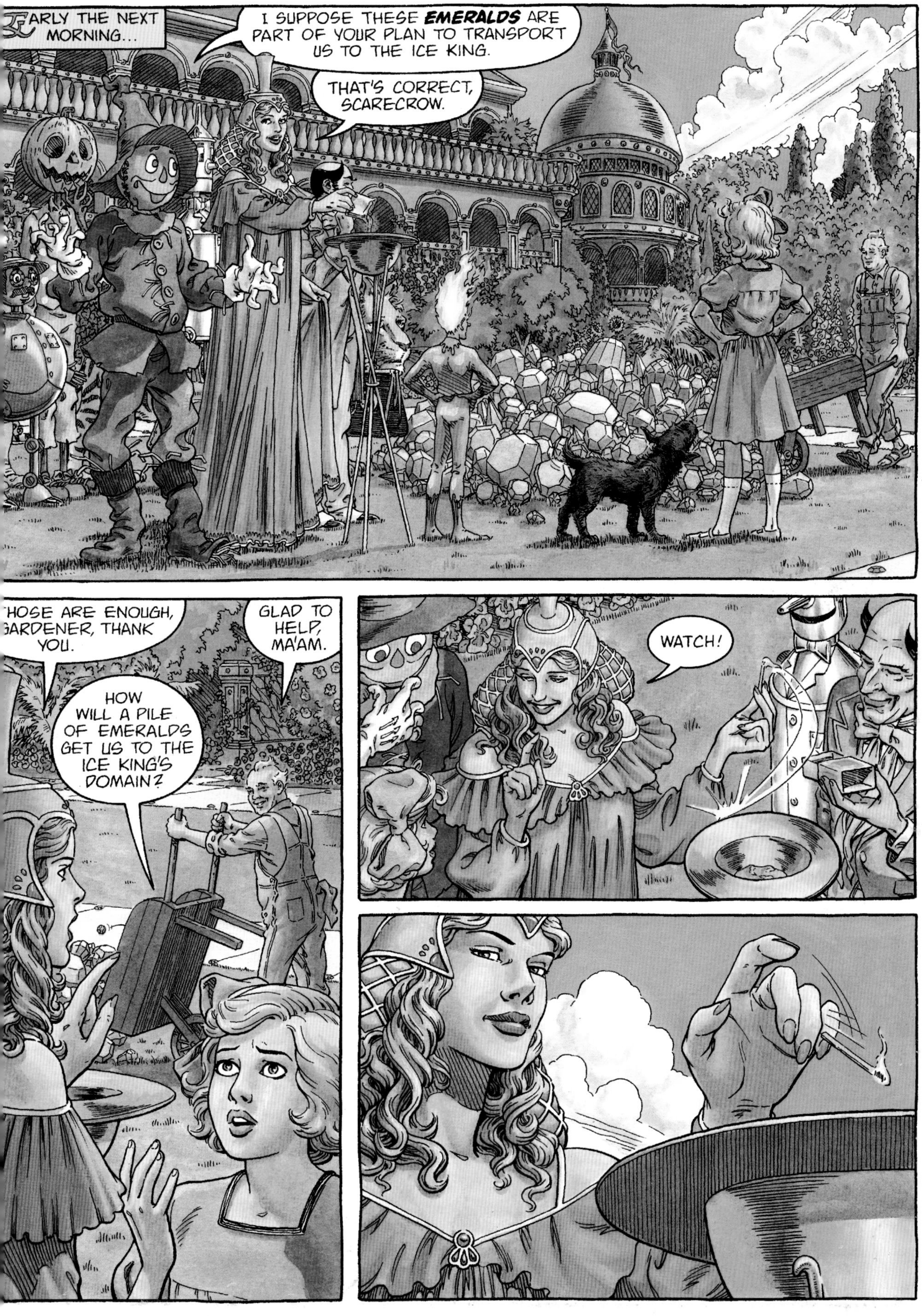

EARLY THE NEXT MORNING...
I SUPPOSE THESE EMERALDS ARE PART OF YOUR PLAN TO TRANSPORT US TO THE ICE KING.
THAT'S CORRECT, SCARECROW.
THOSE ARE ENOUGH, GARDENER, THANK YOU.
GLAD TO HELP, MA'AM.
HOW WILL A PILE OF EMERALDS GET US TO THE ICE KING'S DOMAIN?
WATCH!

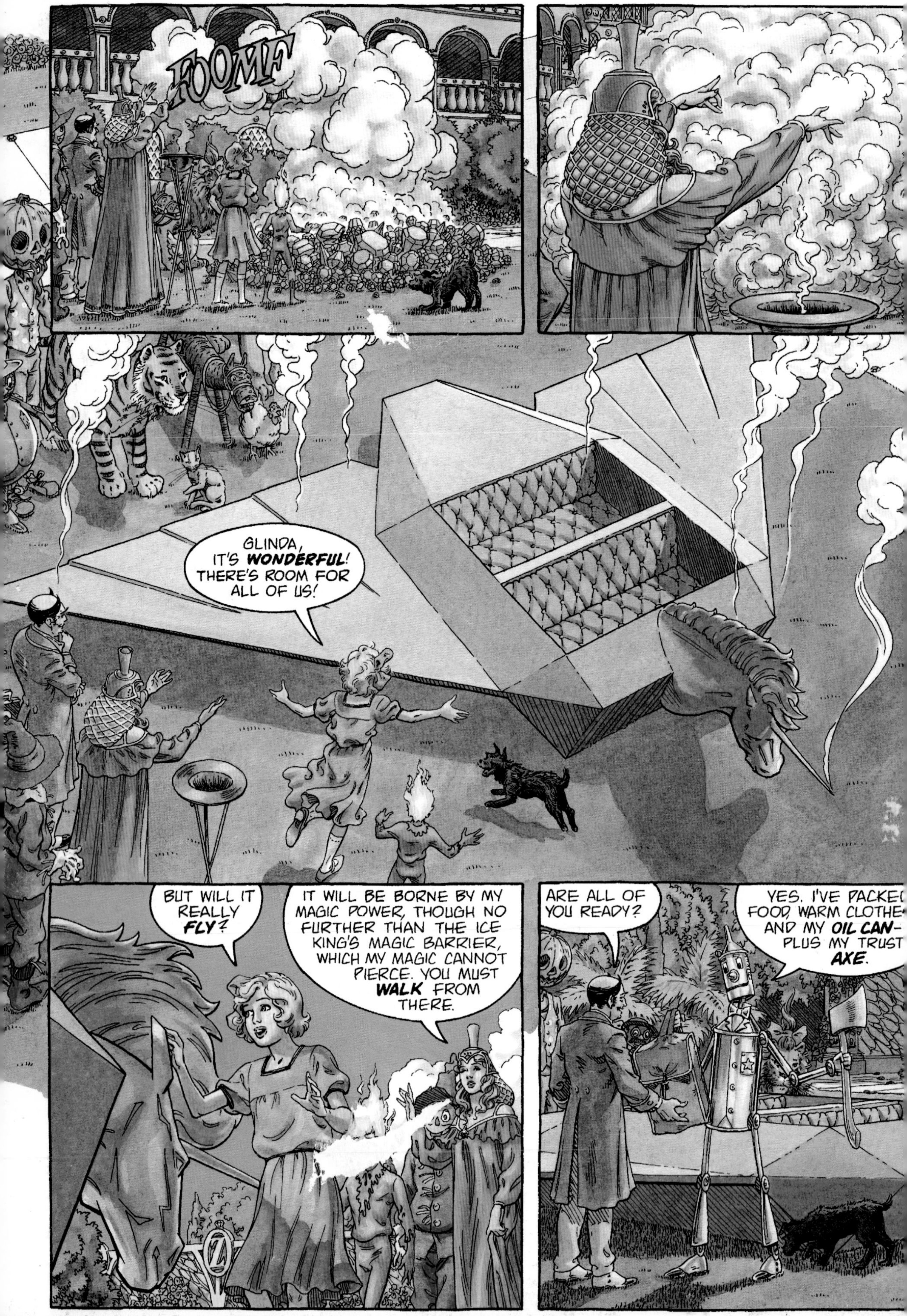
FOOMF
GLINDA, IT'S **WONDERFUL**! THERE'S ROOM FOR ALL OF US!
BUT WILL IT REALLY **FLY**?
IT WILL BE BORNE BY MY MAGIC POWER, THOUGH NO FURTHER THAN THE ICE KING'S MAGIC BARRIER, WHICH MY MAGIC CANNOT PIERCE. YOU MUST **WALK** FROM THERE.
ARE ALL OF YOU READY?
YES. I'VE PACKE FOOD, WARM CLOTHE AND MY **OIL CAN**— PLUS MY TRUST **AXE**.

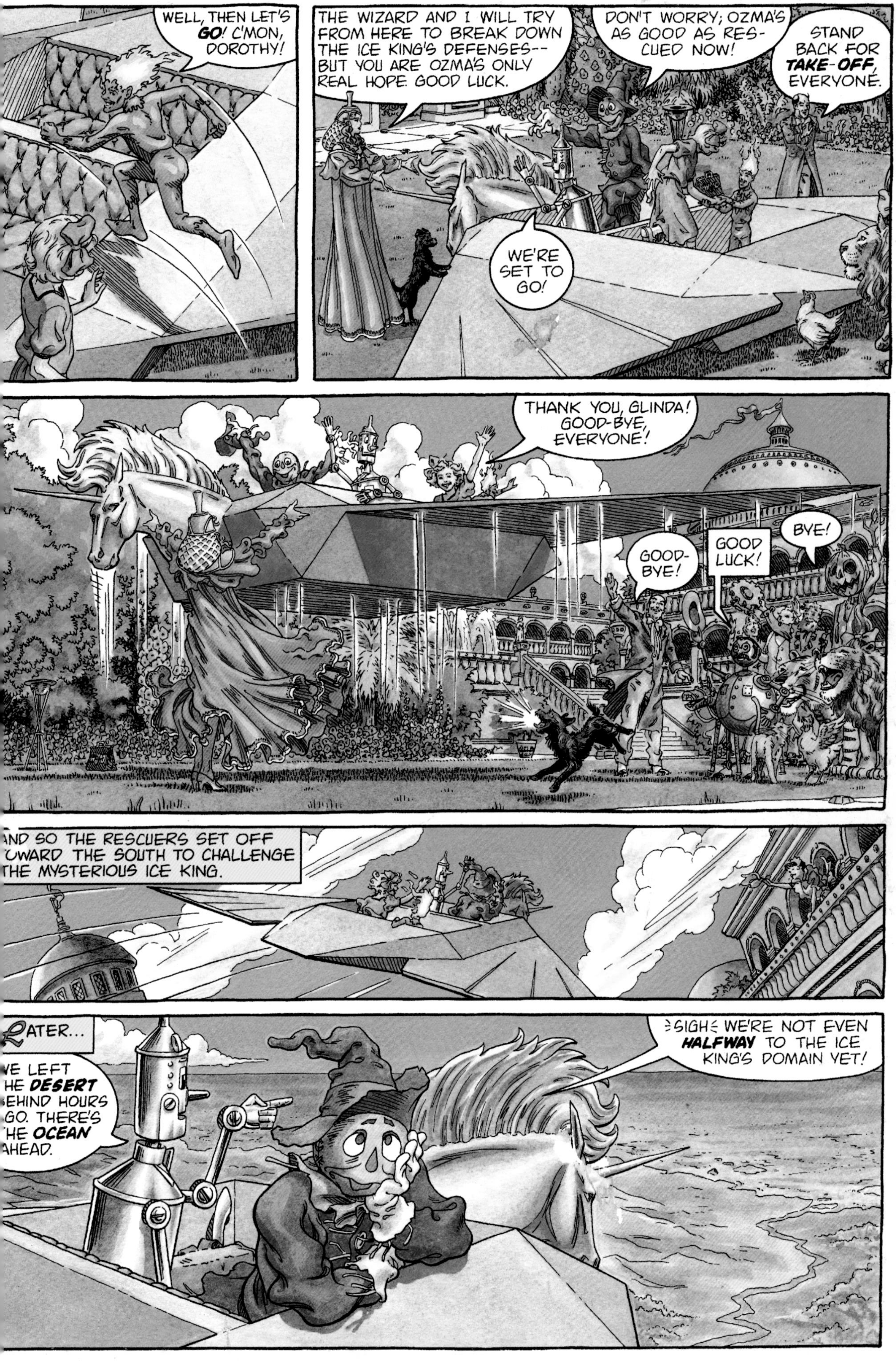
WELL, THEN LET'S **GO**! C'MON, DOROTHY!
THE WIZARD AND I WILL TRY FROM HERE TO BREAK DOWN THE ICE KING'S DEFENSES-- BUT YOU ARE OZMA'S ONLY REAL HOPE. GOOD LUCK.
DON'T WORRY; OZMA'S AS GOOD AS RES-CUED NOW!
STAND BACK FOR **TAKE-OFF**, EVERYONE.
WE'RE SET TO GO!
THANK YOU, GLINDA! GOOD-BYE, EVERYONE!
GOOD-BYE!
GOOD LUCK!
BYE!
AND SO THE RESCUERS SET OFF TOWARD THE SOUTH TO CHALLENGE THE MYSTERIOUS ICE KING.
LATER...
WE LEFT THE **DESERT** BEHIND HOURS AGO. THERE'S THE **OCEAN** AHEAD.
SIGH WE'RE NOT EVEN **HALFWAY** TO THE ICE KING'S DOMAIN YET!

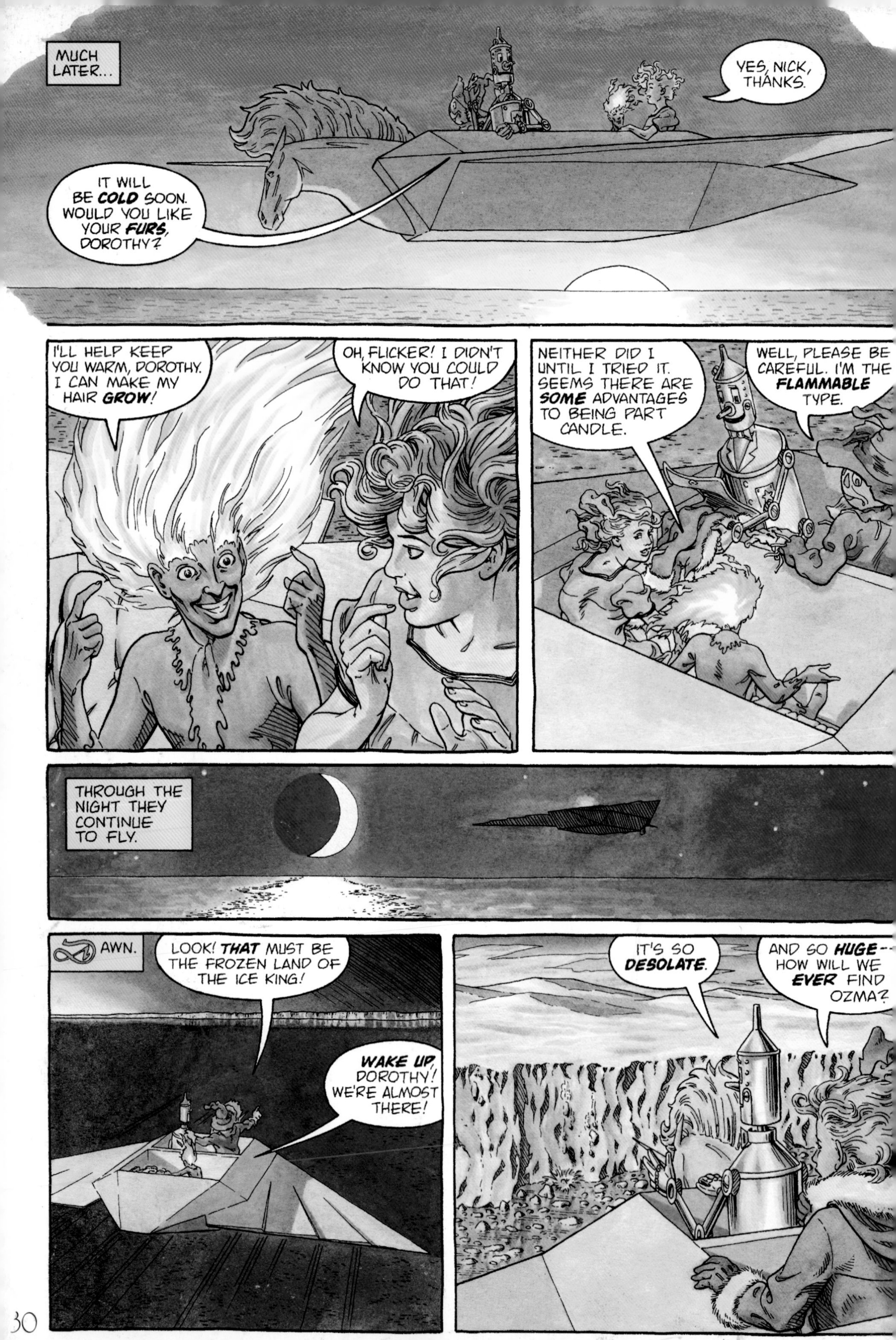
MUCH LATER...
YES, NICK, THANKS.
IT WILL BE COLD SOON. WOULD YOU LIKE YOUR FURS, DOROTHY?
I'LL HELP KEEP YOU WARM, DOROTHY. I CAN MAKE MY HAIR GROW!
OH, FLICKER! I DIDN'T KNOW YOU COULD DO THAT!
NEITHER DID I UNTIL I TRIED IT. SEEMS THERE ARE SOME ADVANTAGES TO BEING PART CANDLE.
WELL, PLEASE BE CAREFUL. I'M THE FLAMMABLE TYPE.
THROUGH THE NIGHT THEY CONTINUE TO FLY.
DAWN.
LOOK! THAT MUST BE THE FROZEN LAND OF THE ICE KING!
WAKE UP, DOROTHY! WE'RE ALMOST THERE!
IT'S SO DESOLATE.
AND SO HUGE-- HOW WILL WE EVER FIND OZMA?

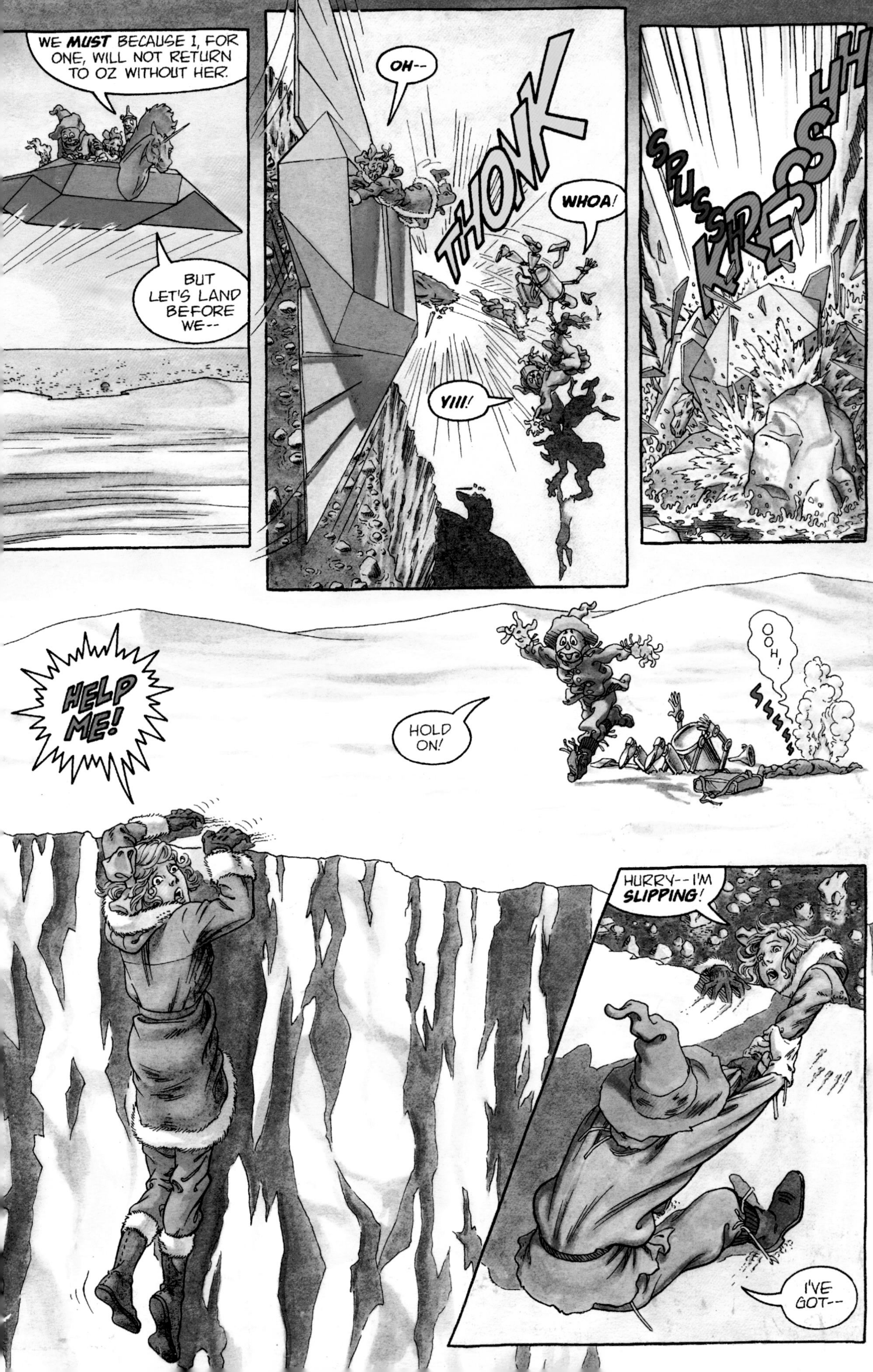

WE **MUST** BECAUSE I, FOR ONE, WILL NOT RETURN TO OZ WITHOUT HER.
BUT LET'S LAND BEFORE WE--
OH--
THONK
WHOA!
YIII!
SPLUSSSH
KRESSHH
HELP ME!
HOLD ON!
OOH!
HURRY--I'M **SLIPPING**!
I'VE GOT--

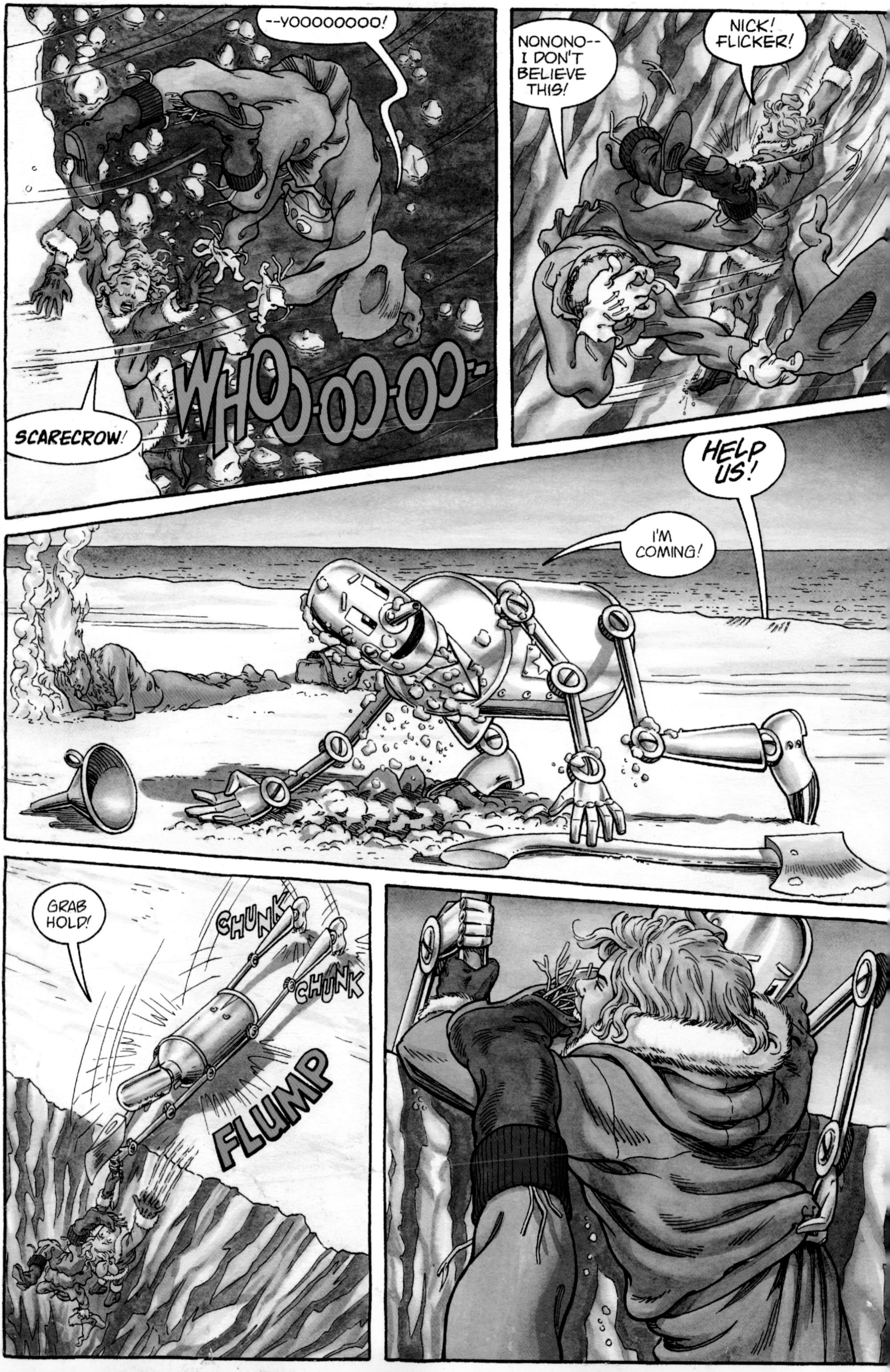
--YOOOOOOOO!
SCARECROW!
WHOOO-OO-OO-
NICK! FLICKER!
NONONO-- I DON'T BELIEVE THIS!
HELP US!
I'M COMING!
GRAB HOLD!
CHUNK
CHUNK
FLUMP

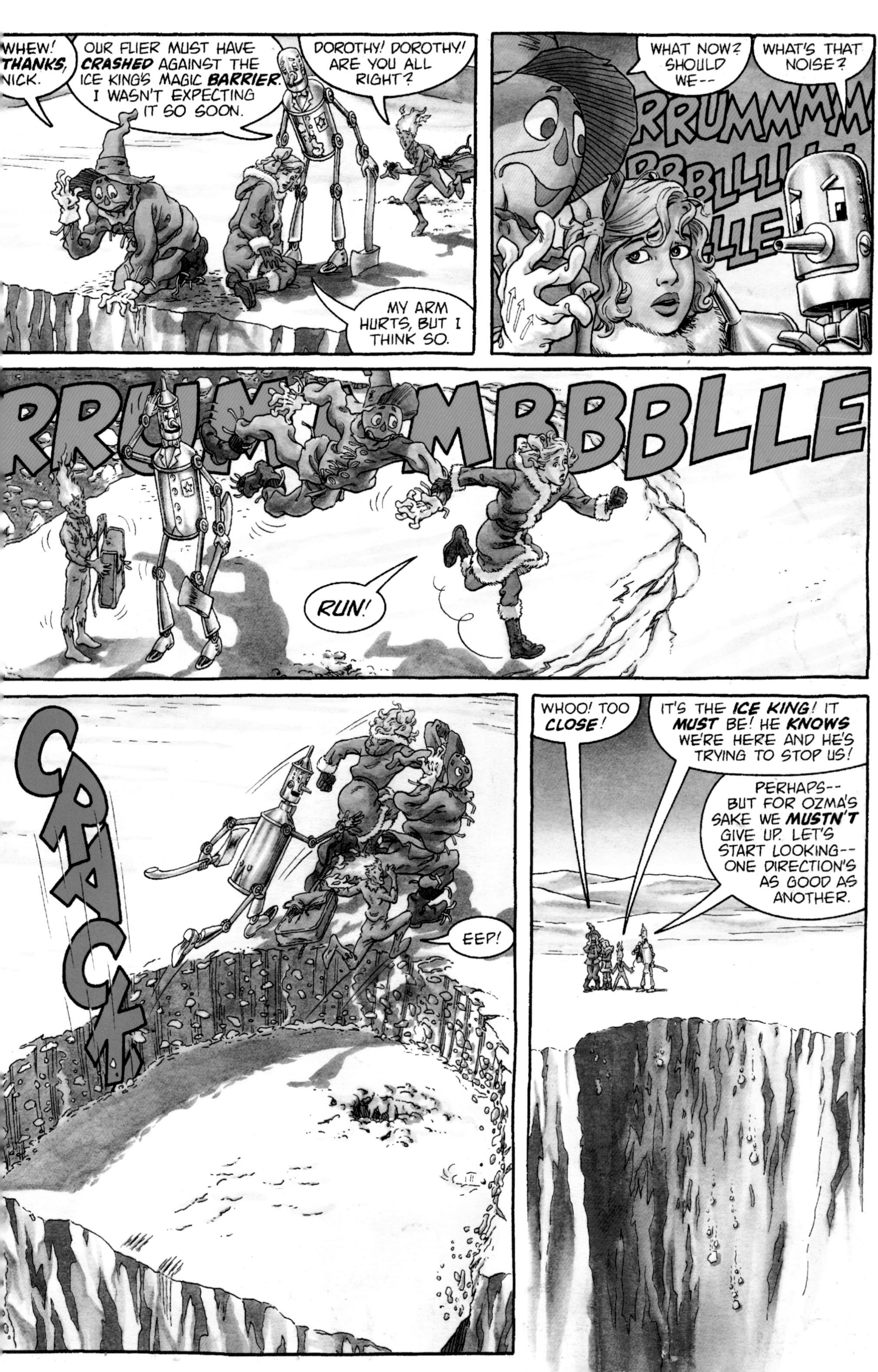
WHEW! THANKS, NICK.
OUR FLIER MUST HAVE CRASHED AGAINST THE ICE KING'S MAGIC BARRIER. I WASN'T EXPECTING IT SO SOON.
DOROTHY! DOROTHY! ARE YOU ALL RIGHT?
MY ARM HURTS, BUT I THINK SO.
WHAT NOW? SHOULD WE--
WHAT'S THAT NOISE?
RRUMMMM
BBLLLL
LLE
RRUMMMBBLLE
RUN!
CRACK
EEP!
WHOO! TOO CLOSE!
IT'S THE ICE KING! IT MUST BE! HE KNOWS WE'RE HERE AND HE'S TRYING TO STOP US!
PERHAPS-- BUT FOR OZMA'S SAKE WE MUSTN'T GIVE UP. LET'S START LOOKING-- ONE DIRECTION'S AS GOOD AS ANOTHER.

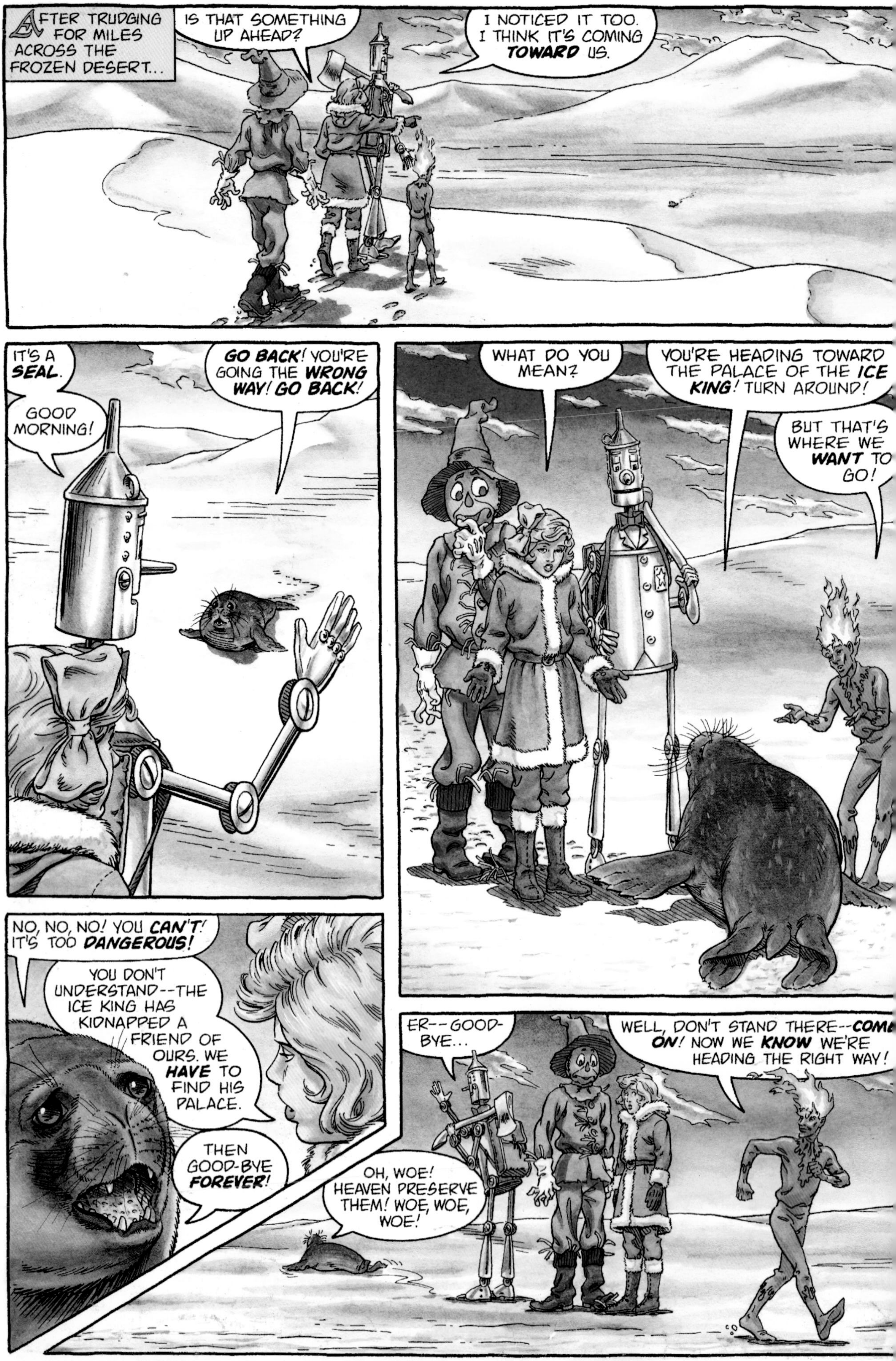
AFTER TRUDGING FOR MILES ACROSS THE FROZEN DESERT...
IS THAT SOMETHING UP AHEAD?
I NOTICED IT TOO. I THINK IT'S COMING TOWARD US.
IT'S A SEAL.
GOOD MORNING!
GO BACK! YOU'RE GOING THE WRONG WAY! GO BACK!
WHAT DO YOU MEAN?
YOU'RE HEADING TOWARD THE PALACE OF THE ICE KING! TURN AROUND!
BUT THAT'S WHERE WE WANT TO GO!
NO, NO, NO! YOU CAN'T! IT'S TOO DANGEROUS!
YOU DON'T UNDERSTAND--THE ICE KING HAS KIDNAPPED A FRIEND OF OURS. WE HAVE TO FIND HIS PALACE.
THEN GOOD-BYE FOREVER!
ER--GOOD-BYE...
WELL, DON'T STAND THERE--COME ON! NOW WE KNOW WE'RE HEADING THE RIGHT WAY!
OH, WOE! HEAVEN PRESERVE THEM! WOE, WOE, WOE!

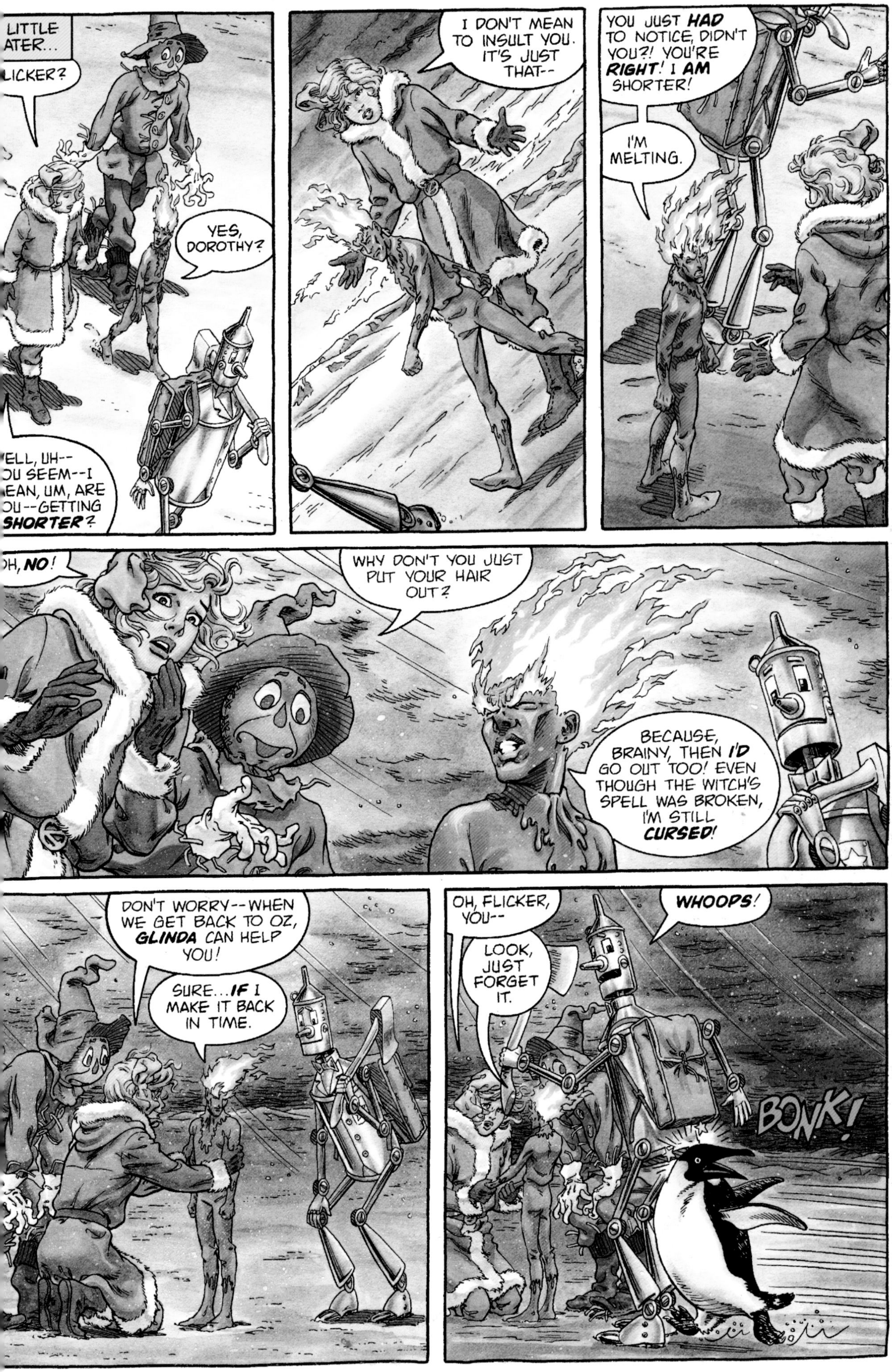
LITTLE
ATER...
LICKER?
YES, DOROTHY?
ELL, UH-- OU SEEM--I EAN, UM, ARE OU--GETTING **SHORTER**?
I DON'T MEAN TO INSULT YOU. IT'S JUST THAT--
YOU JUST **HAD** TO NOTICE, DIDN'T YOU?! YOU'RE **RIGHT**! I **AM** SHORTER!
I'M MELTING.
H, **NO**!
WHY DON'T YOU JUST PUT YOUR HAIR OUT?
BECAUSE, BRAINY, THEN **I'D** GO OUT TOO! EVEN THOUGH THE WITCH'S SPELL WAS BROKEN, I'M STILL **CURSED**!
DON'T WORRY--WHEN WE GET BACK TO OZ, **GLINDA** CAN HELP YOU!
SURE... **IF** I MAKE IT BACK IN TIME.
OH, FLICKER, YOU--
LOOK, JUST FORGET IT.
WHOOPS!
BONK!

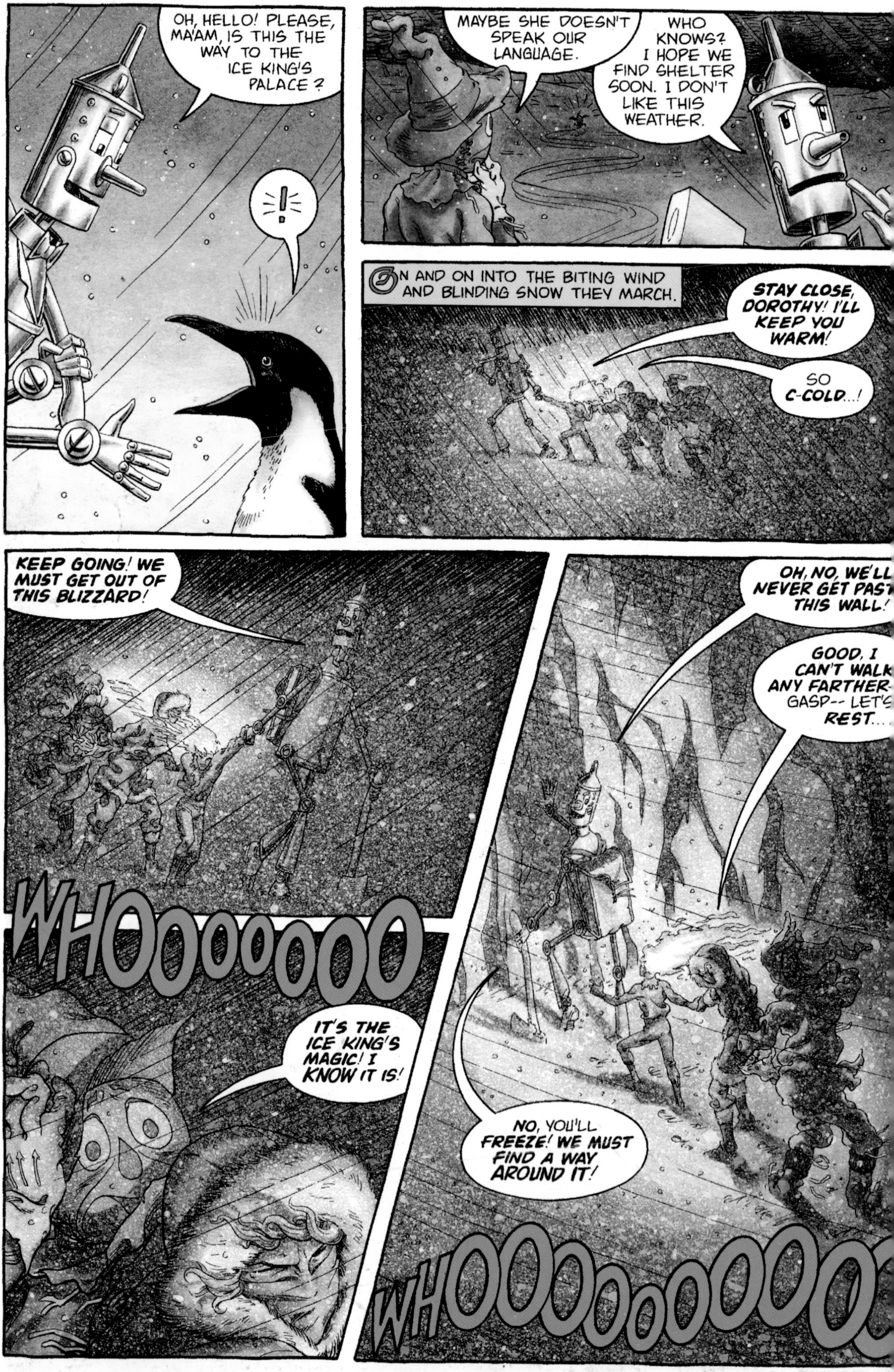
OH, HELLO! PLEASE, MA'AM, IS THIS THE WAY TO THE ICE KING'S PALACE?
!
MAYBE SHE DOESN'T SPEAK OUR LANGUAGE.
WHO KNOWS? I HOPE WE FIND SHELTER SOON. I DON'T LIKE THIS WEATHER.
ON AND ON INTO THE BITING WIND AND BLINDING SNOW THEY MARCH.
STAY CLOSE, DOROTHY! I'LL KEEP YOU WARM!
SO C-COLD...!
KEEP GOING! WE MUST GET OUT OF THIS BLIZZARD!
WHOOOOOOO
IT'S THE ICE KING'S MAGIC! I KNOW IT IS!
OH, NO, WE'LL NEVER GET PAST THIS WALL!
GOOD, I CAN'T WALK ANY FARTHER-- GASP-- LET'S REST...
NO, YOU'LL FREEZE! WE MUST FIND A WAY AROUND IT!
WHOOOOOOOOOOOO

Chapter Four In the Ice Palace

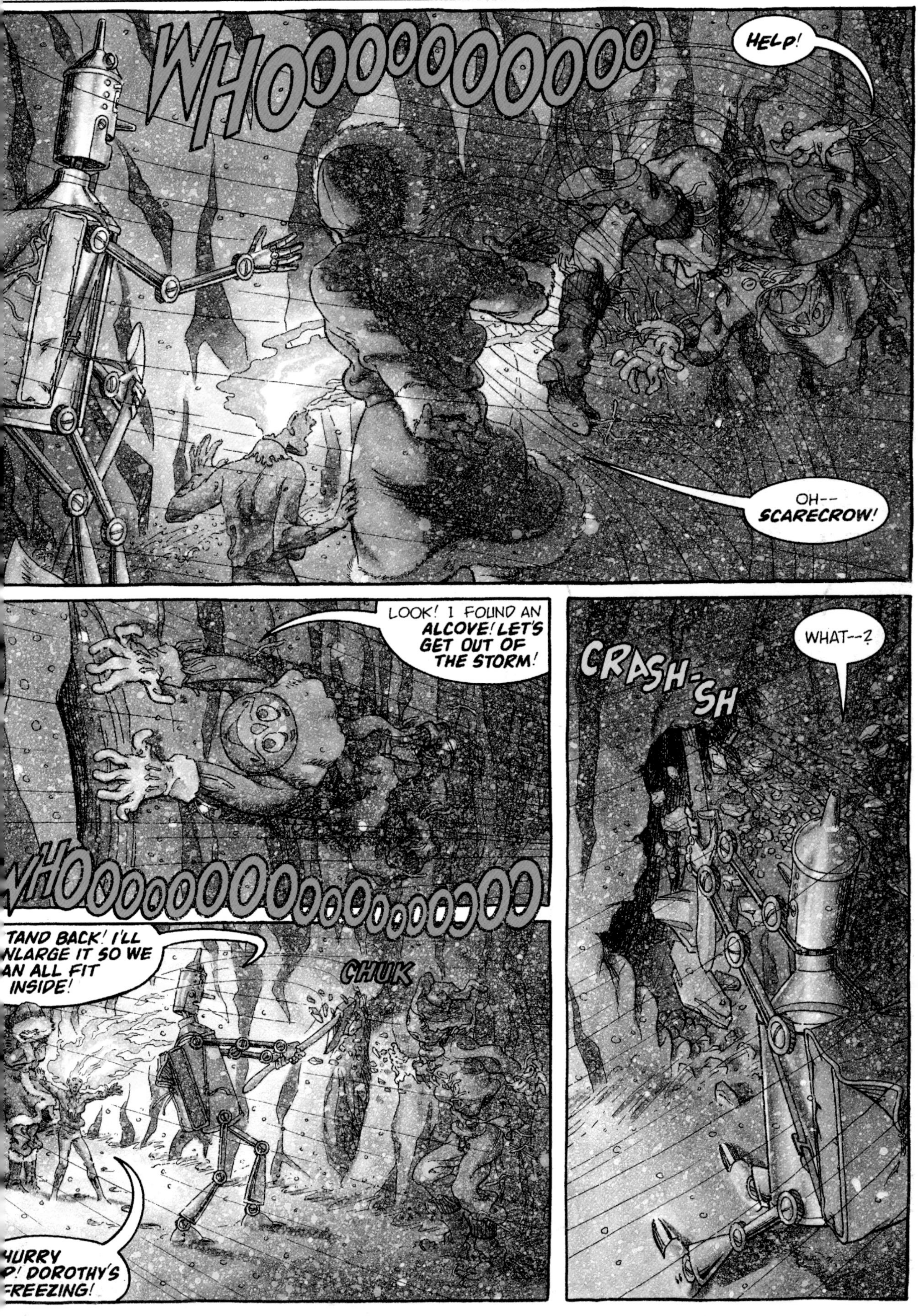
WHOOOOOOOOOO
HELP!
OH-- SCARECROW!
LOOK! I FOUND AN ALCOVE! LET'S GET OUT OF THE STORM!
WHOOOOOOOOOOOOOOOO
TAND BACK! I'LL NLARGE IT SO WE AN ALL FIT INSIDE!
CHUK
HURRY P! DOROTHY'S FREEZING!
CRASH-SH
WHAT--?

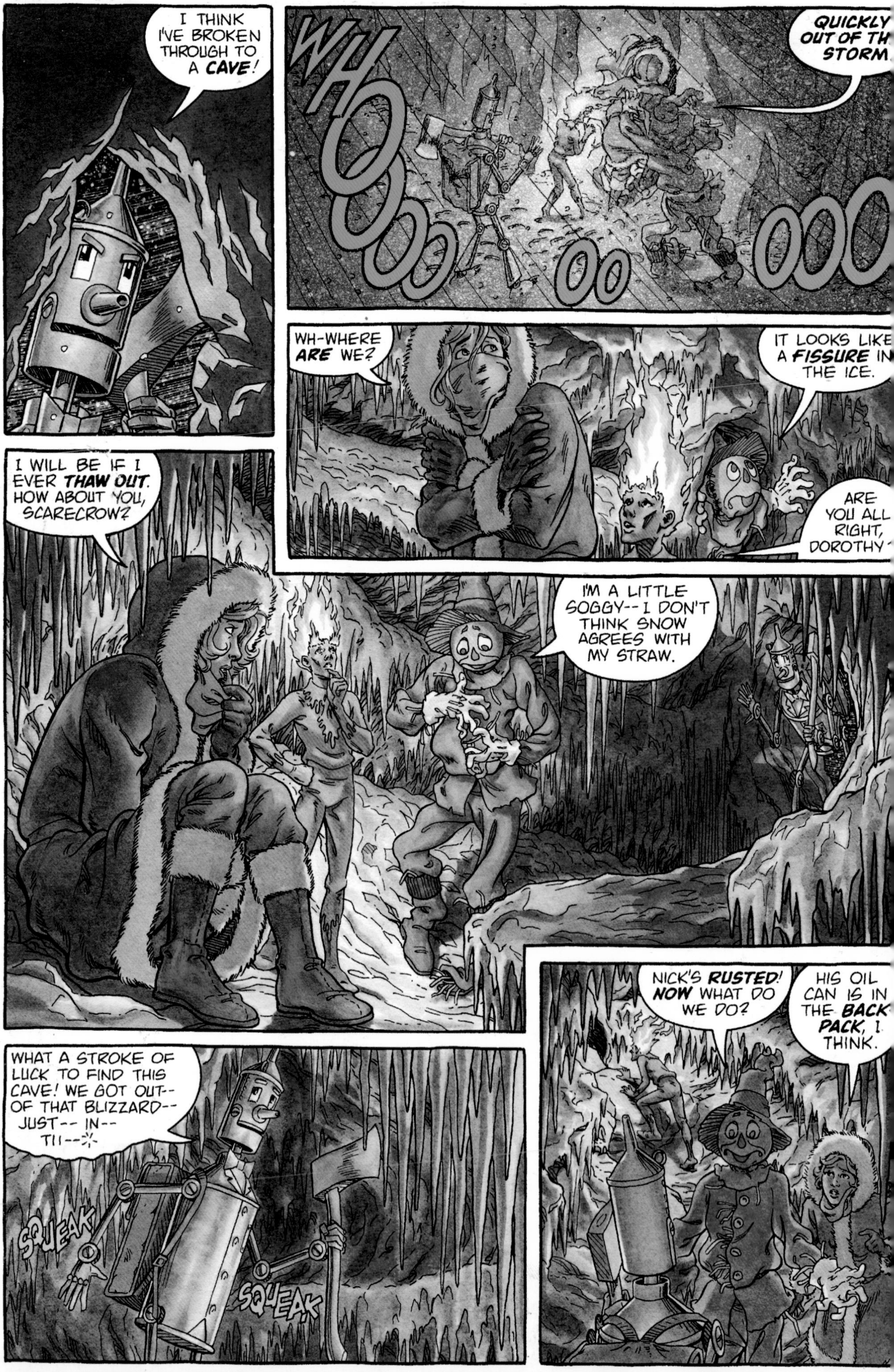
I THINK I'VE BROKEN THROUGH TO A CAVE!
WHOOOOOOOOOO
QUICKLY OUT OF TH STORM
WH-WHERE ARE WE?
IT LOOKS LIKE A FISSURE IN THE ICE.
ARE YOU ALL RIGHT, DOROTHY
I WILL BE IF I EVER THAW OUT. HOW ABOUT YOU, SCARECROW?
I'M A LITTLE SOGGY-- I DON'T THINK SNOW AGREES WITH MY STRAW.
WHAT A STROKE OF LUCK TO FIND THIS CAVE! WE GOT OUT-- OF THAT BLIZZARD-- JUST-- IN-- TI--
SQUEAK
SQUEAK
NICK'S RUSTED! NOW WHAT DO WE DO?
HIS OIL CAN IS IN THE BACK PACK, I THINK.

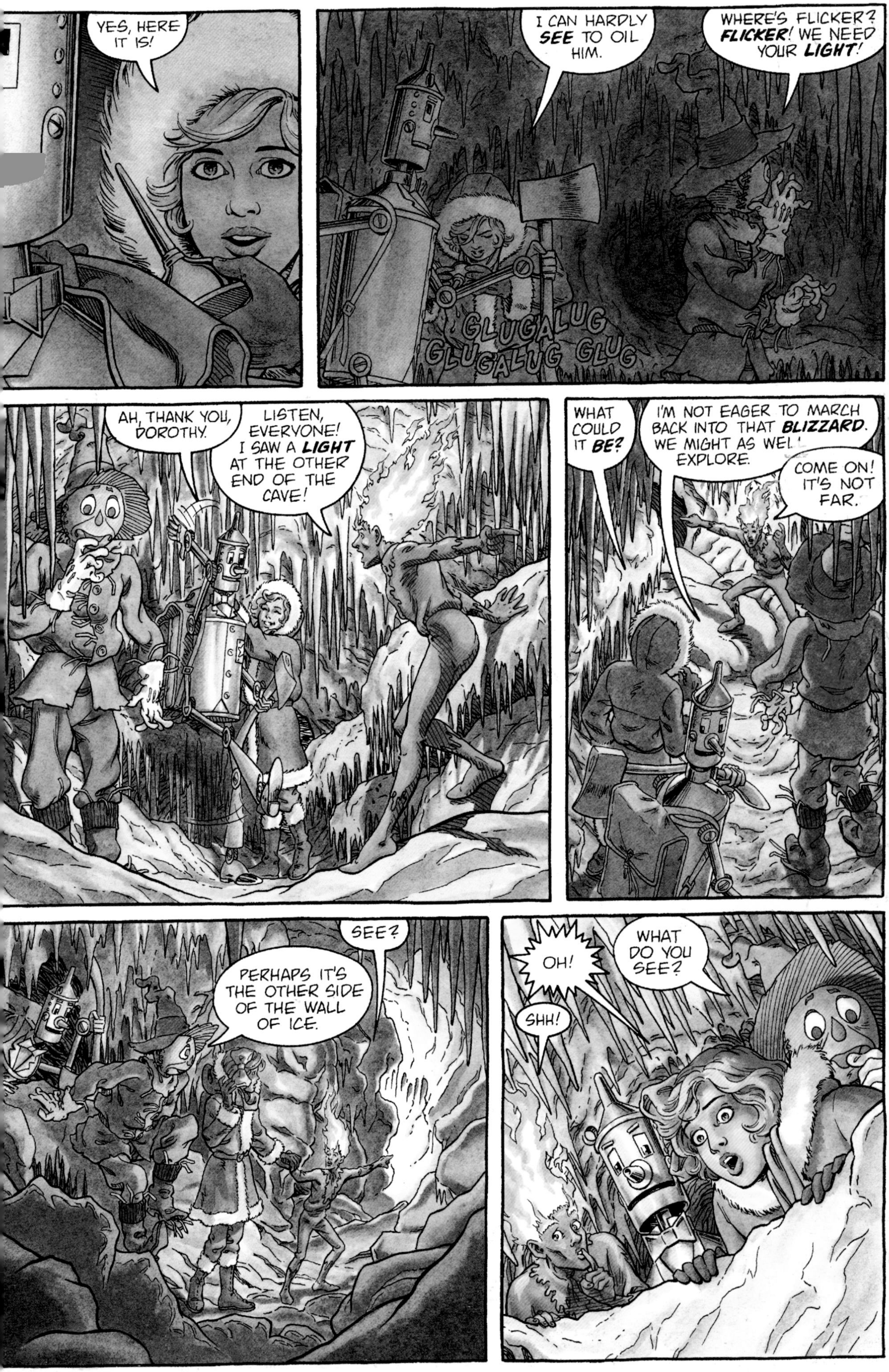

YES, HERE IT IS!
I CAN HARDLY SEE TO OIL HIM.
WHERE'S FLICKER? FLICKER! WE NEED YOUR LIGHT!
GLUGALUG GLUGALUG GLUG
AH, THANK YOU, DOROTHY.
LISTEN, EVERYONE! I SAW A LIGHT AT THE OTHER END OF THE CAVE!
WHAT COULD IT BE?
I'M NOT EAGER TO MARCH BACK INTO THAT BLIZZARD. WE MIGHT AS WELL EXPLORE.
COME ON! IT'S NOT FAR.
SEE?
PERHAPS IT'S THE OTHER SIDE OF THE WALL OF ICE.
OH!
WHAT DO YOU SEE?
SHH!

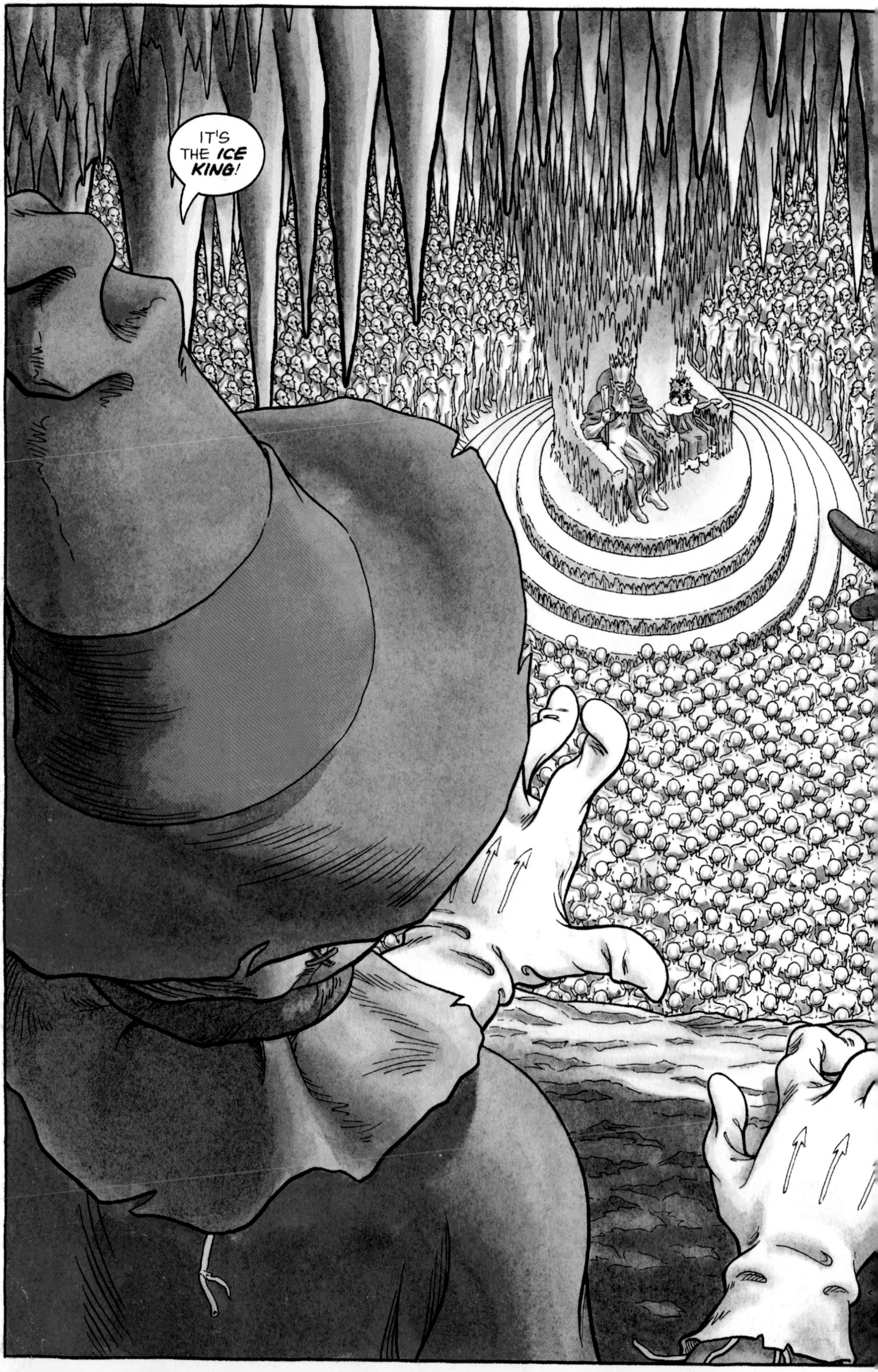
IT'S THE ICE KING!

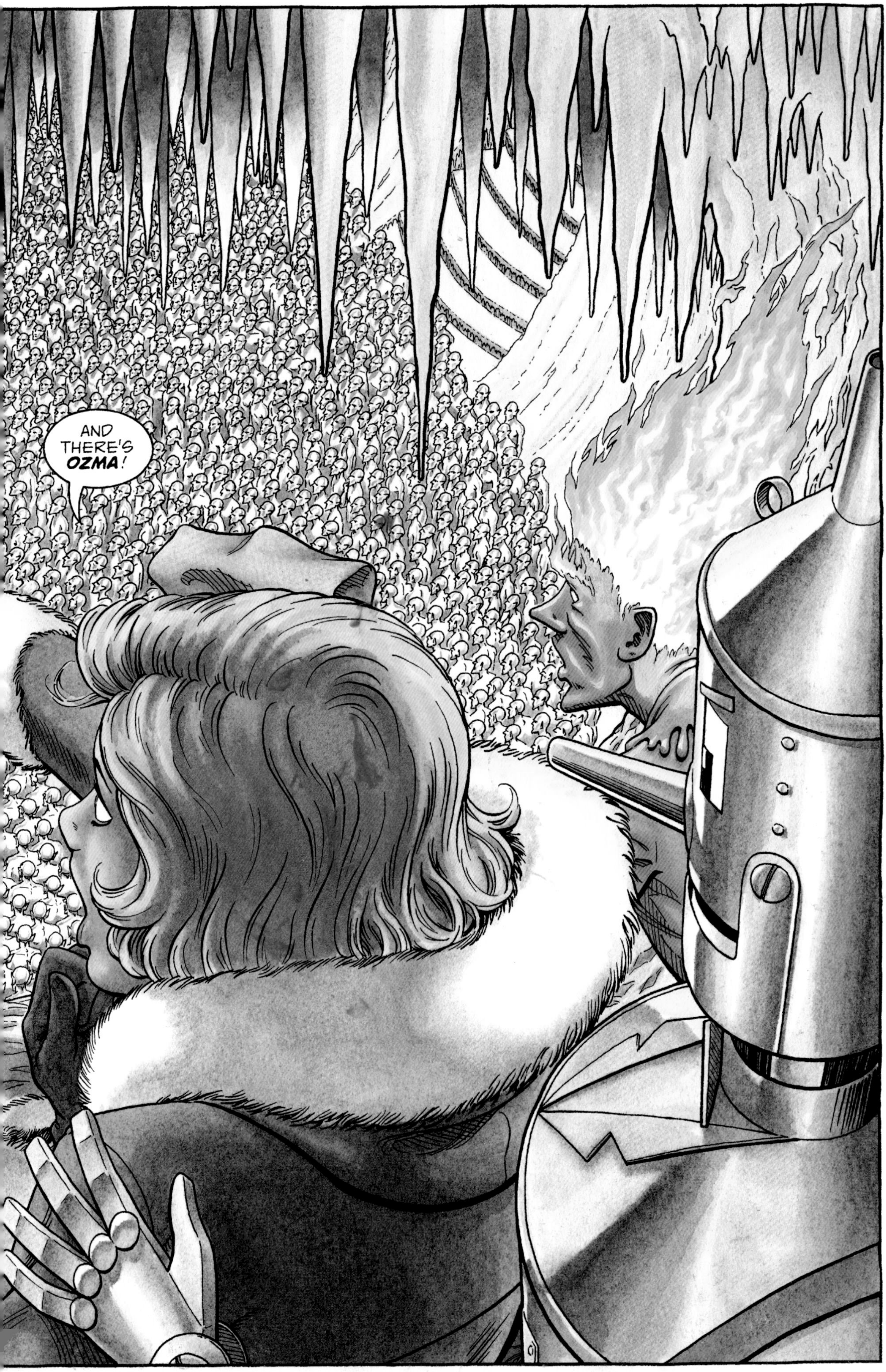
AND THERE'S OZMA!

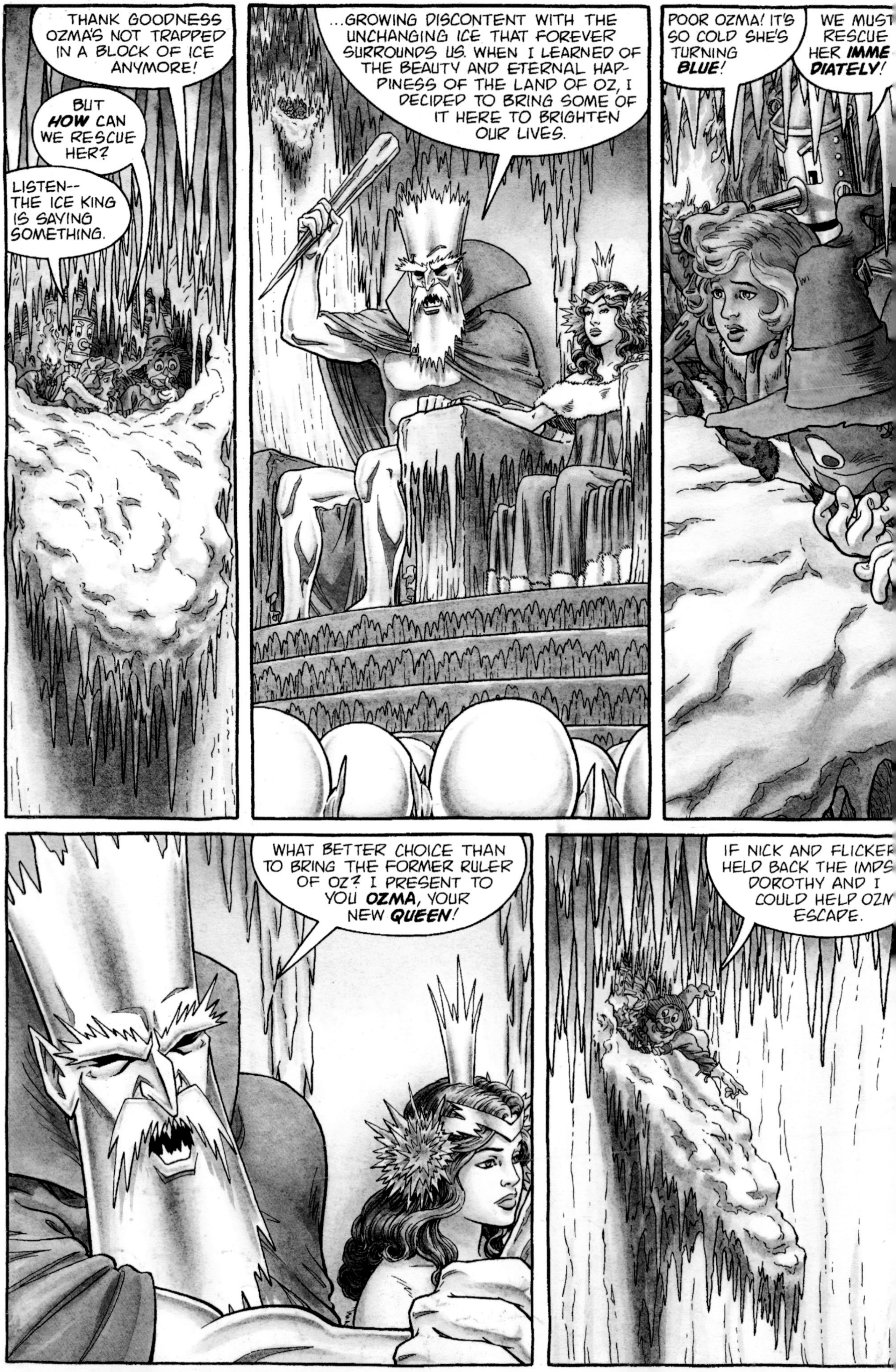
THANK GOODNESS OZMA'S NOT TRAPPED IN A BLOCK OF ICE ANYMORE!
BUT **HOW** CAN WE RESCUE HER?
LISTEN-- THE ICE KING IS SAYING SOMETHING.
...GROWING DISCONTENT WITH THE UNCHANGING ICE THAT FOREVER SURROUNDS US. WHEN I LEARNED OF THE BEAUTY AND ETERNAL HAPPINESS OF THE LAND OF OZ, I DECIDED TO BRING SOME OF IT HERE TO BRIGHTEN OUR LIVES.
POOR OZMA! IT'S SO COLD SHE'S TURNING **BLUE**!
WE MUST RESCUE HER **IMMEDIATELY**!
WHAT BETTER CHOICE THAN TO BRING THE FORMER RULER OF OZ? I PRESENT TO YOU **OZMA**, YOUR NEW **QUEEN**!
IF NICK AND FLICKER HELD BACK THE IMPS DOROTHY AND I COULD HELP OZM ESCAPE.

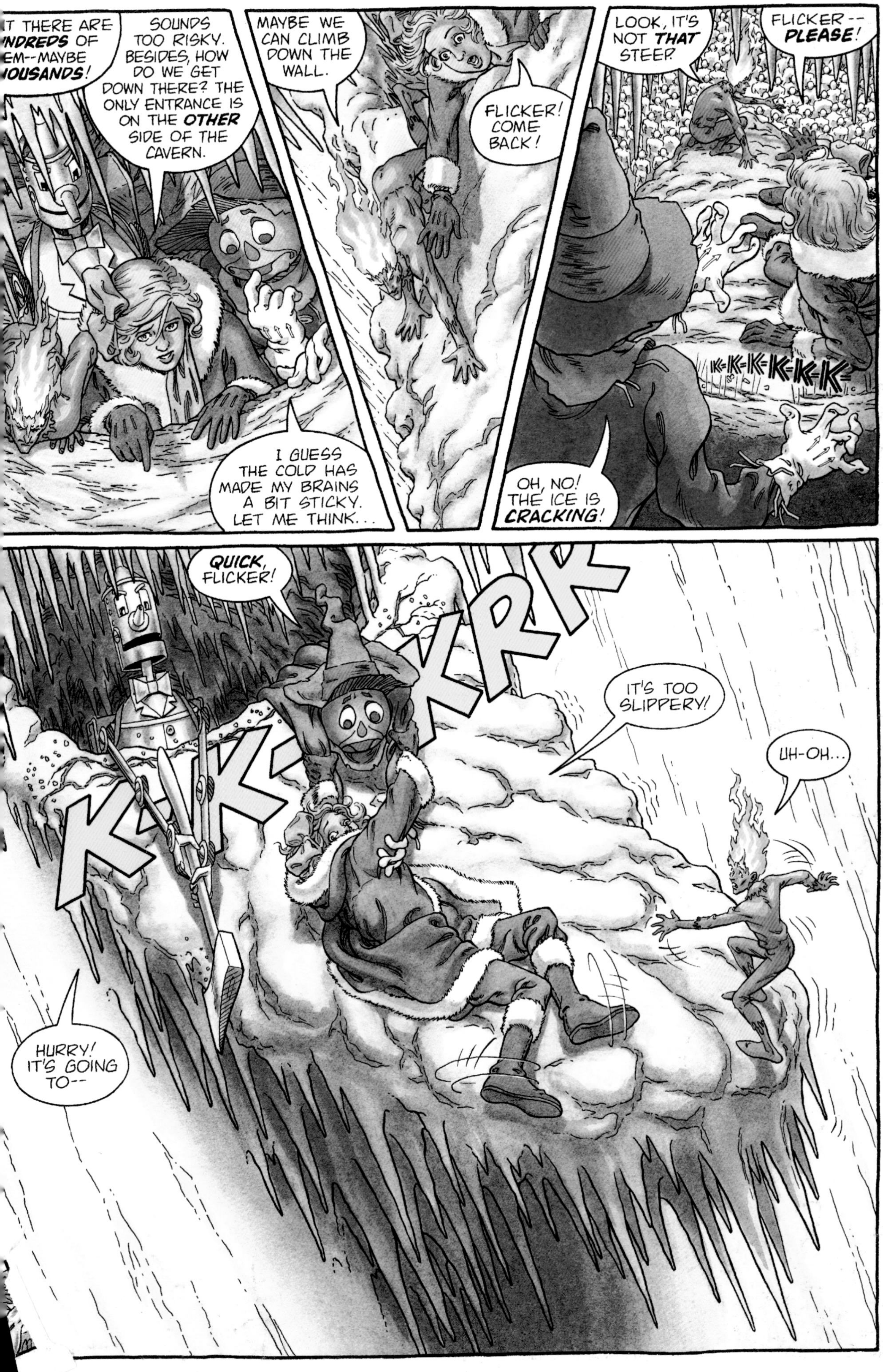

T THERE ARE UNDREDS OF EM--MAYBE HOUSANDS!
SOUNDS TOO RISKY. BESIDES, HOW DO WE GET DOWN THERE? THE ONLY ENTRANCE IS ON THE OTHER SIDE OF THE CAVERN.
I GUESS THE COLD HAS MADE MY BRAINS A BIT STICKY. LET ME THINK...
MAYBE WE CAN CLIMB DOWN THE WALL.
FLICKER! COME BACK!
LOOK, IT'S NOT THAT STEEP.
FLICKER-- PLEASE!
KKKKKKKK
OH, NO! THE ICE IS CRACKING!
QUICK, FLICKER!
K-K-KRRR
IT'S TOO SLIPPERY!
UH-OH...
HURRY! IT'S GOING TO--

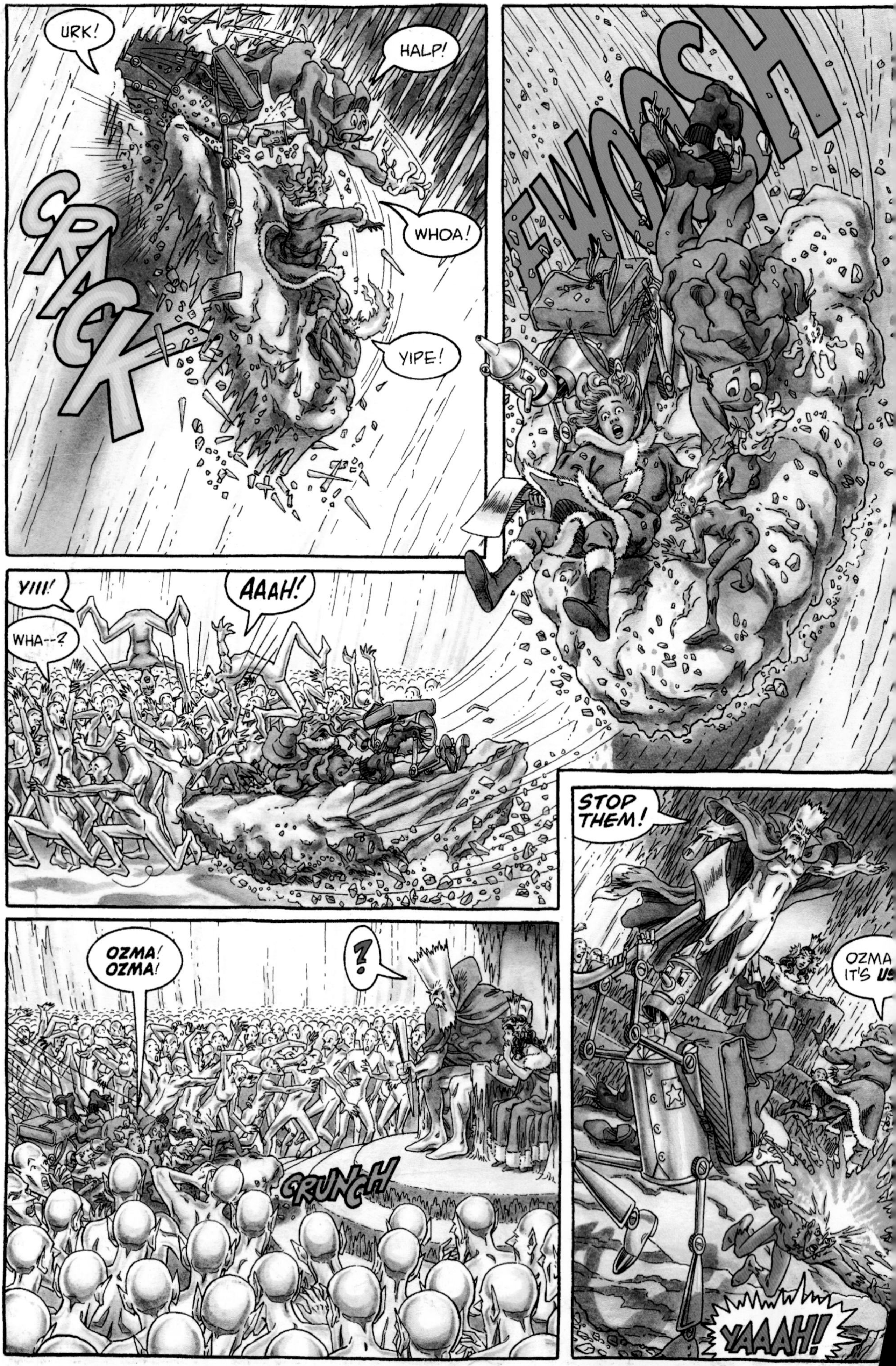
URK!
HALP!
CRACK
WHOA!
YIPE!
FWOOSH
YIII!
WHA--?
AAAH!
STOP THEM!
OZMA! OZMA!
?
CRUNCH
OZMA IT'S US
YAAAH!

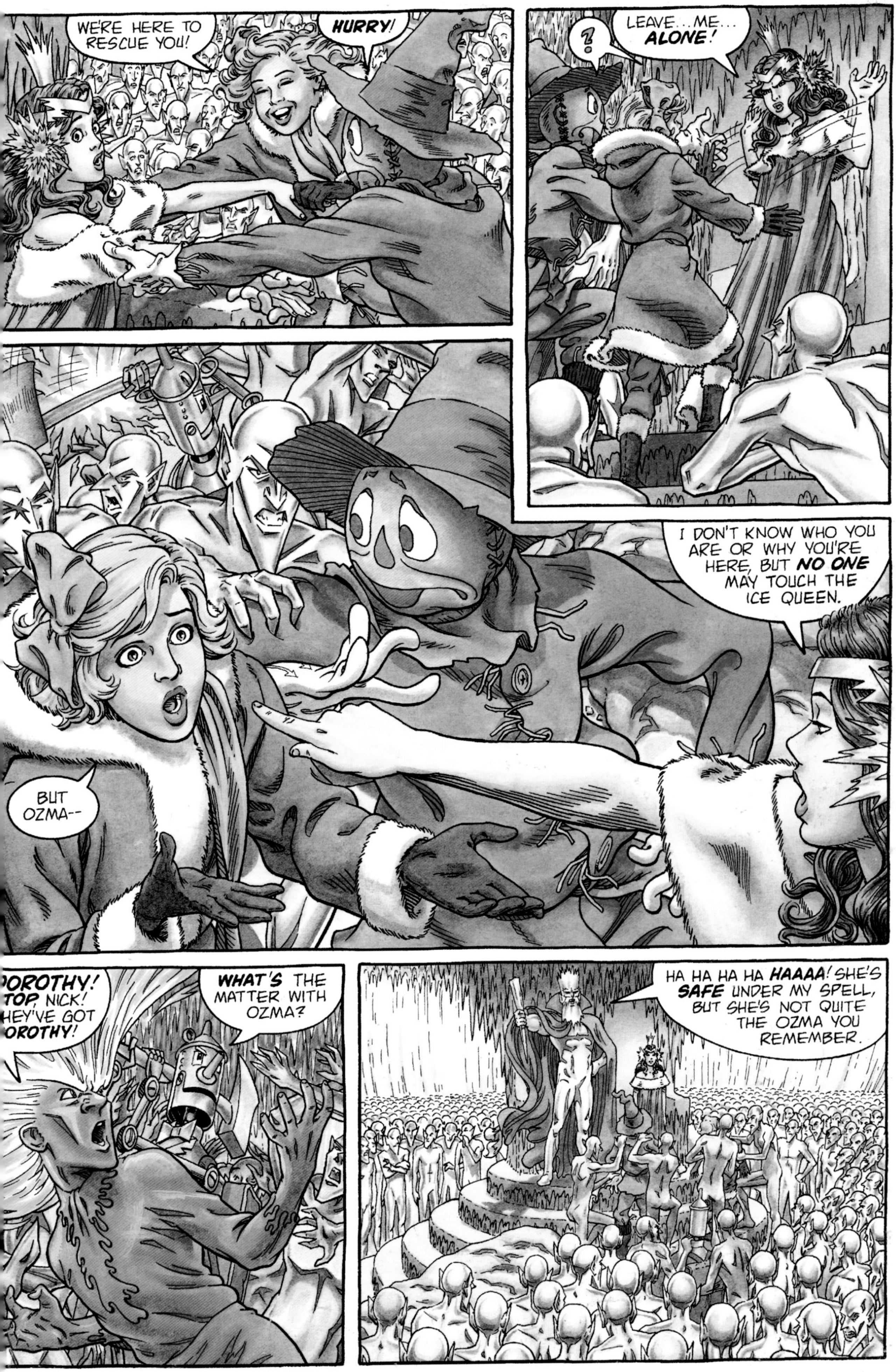
WE'RE HERE TO RESCUE YOU!
HURRY!
?
LEAVE... ME... ALONE!
I DON'T KNOW WHO YOU ARE OR WHY YOU'RE HERE, BUT NO ONE MAY TOUCH THE ICE QUEEN.
BUT OZMA--
OROTHY! TOP, NICK! HEY'VE GOT OROTHY!
WHAT'S THE MATTER WITH OZMA?
HA HA HA HA HAAAA! SHE'S SAFE UNDER MY SPELL, BUT SHE'S NOT QUITE THE OZMA YOU REMEMBER.

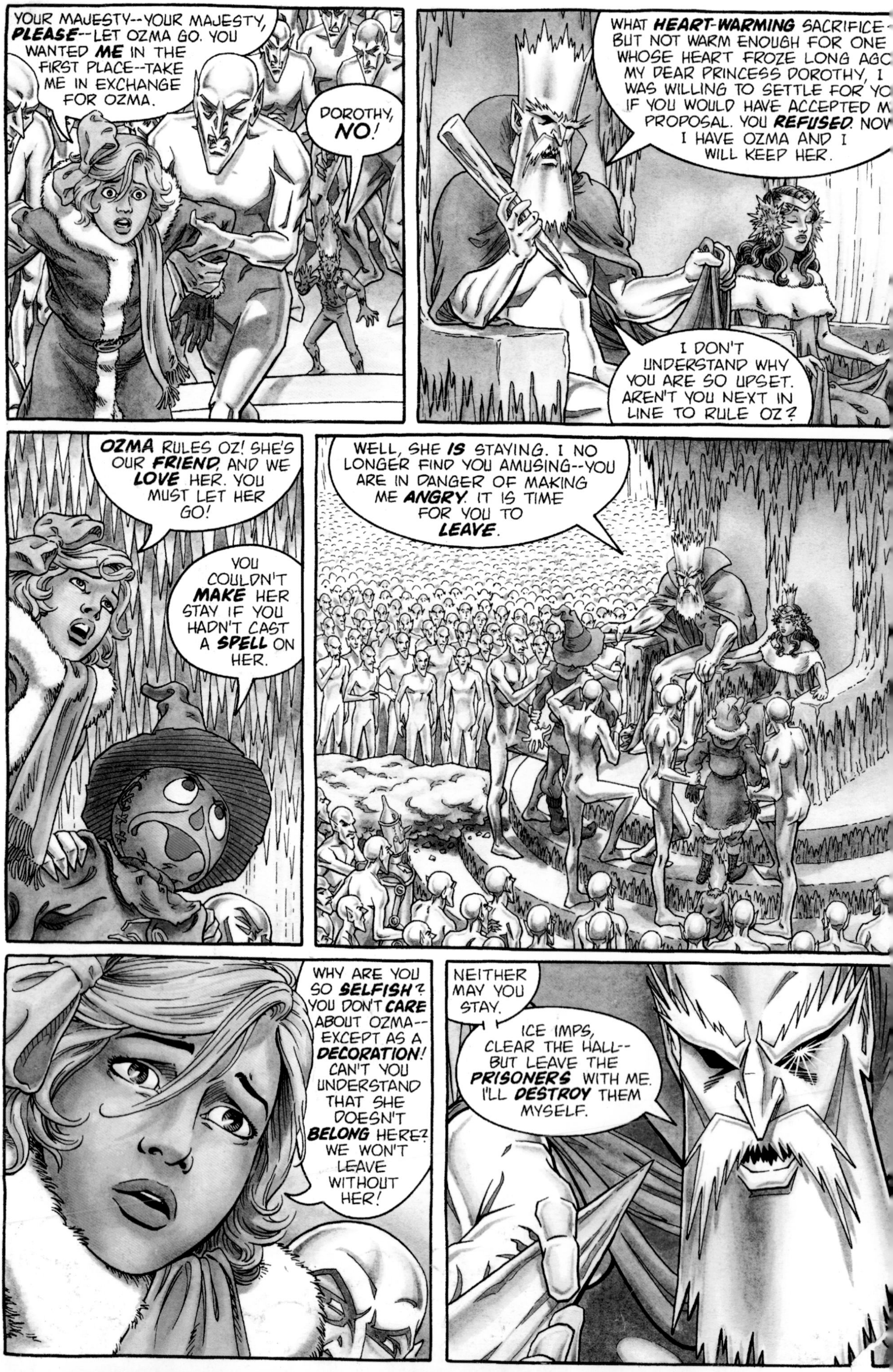
YOUR MAJESTY--YOUR MAJESTY, PLEASE--LET OZMA GO. YOU WANTED ME IN THE FIRST PLACE--TAKE ME IN EXCHANGE FOR OZMA.
DOROTHY, NO!
WHAT HEART-WARMING SACRIFICE-- BUT NOT WARM ENOUGH FOR ONE WHOSE HEART FROZE LONG AG MY DEAR PRINCESS DOROTHY, I WAS WILLING TO SETTLE FOR YO IF YOU WOULD HAVE ACCEPTED M PROPOSAL. YOU REFUSED. NO I HAVE OZMA AND I WILL KEEP HER.
I DON'T UNDERSTAND WHY YOU ARE SO UPSET. AREN'T YOU NEXT IN LINE TO RULE OZ?
OZMA RULES OZ! SHE'S OUR FRIEND, AND WE LOVE HER. YOU MUST LET HER GO!
YOU COULDN'T MAKE HER STAY IF YOU HADN'T CAST A SPELL ON HER.
WELL, SHE IS STAYING. I NO LONGER FIND YOU AMUSING--YOU ARE IN DANGER OF MAKING ME ANGRY. IT IS TIME FOR YOU TO LEAVE.
WHY ARE YOU SO SELFISH? YOU DON'T CARE ABOUT OZMA-- EXCEPT AS A DECORATION! CAN'T YOU UNDERSTAND THAT SHE DOESN'T BELONG HERE? WE WON'T LEAVE WITHOUT HER!
NEITHER MAY YOU STAY.
ICE IMPS, CLEAR THE HALL-- BUT LEAVE THE PRISONERS WITH ME. I'LL DESTROY THEM MYSELF.

Chapter Five The Ice King's Power

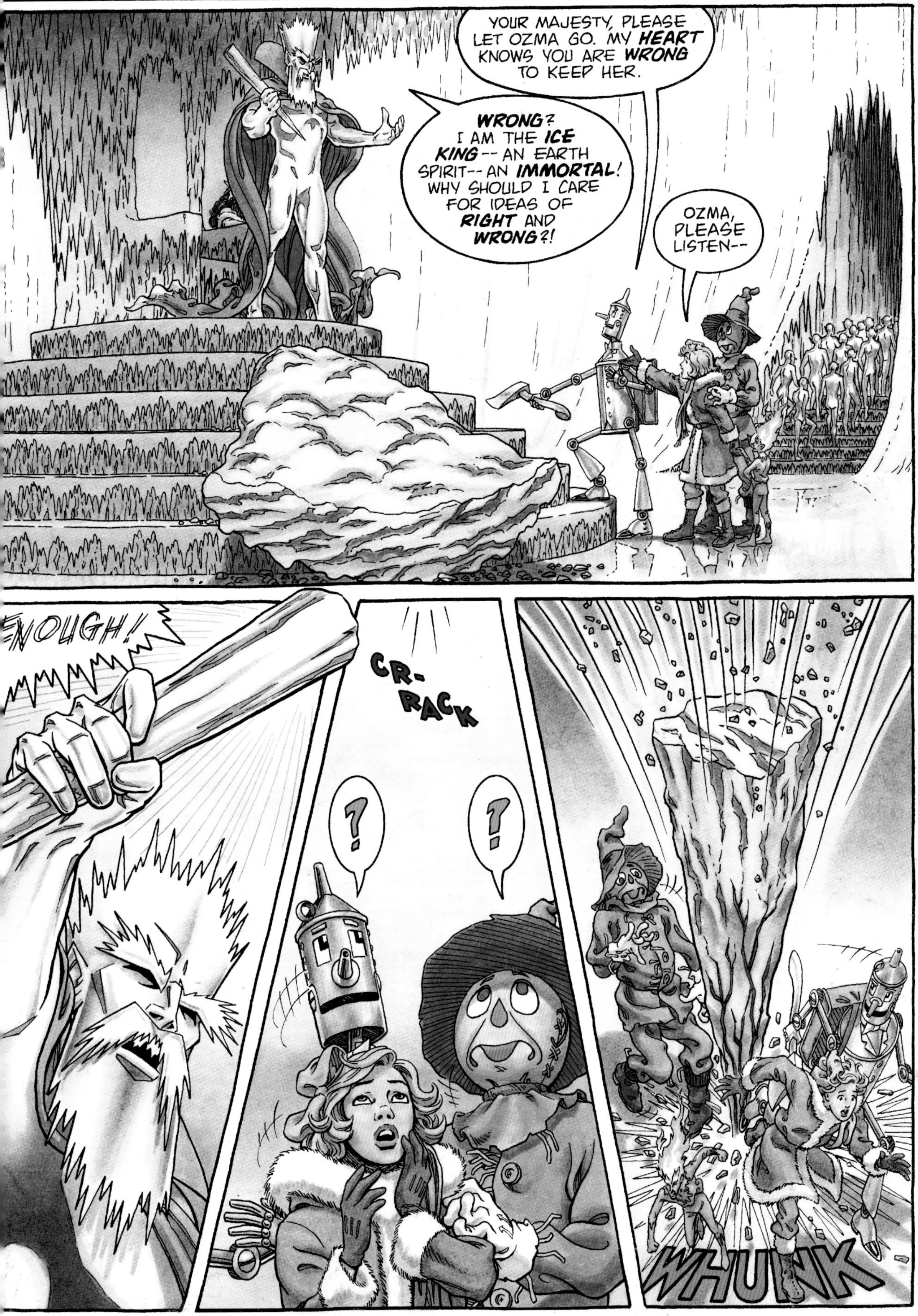
YOUR MAJESTY, PLEASE LET OZMA GO. MY HEART KNOWS YOU ARE WRONG TO KEEP HER.
WRONG? I AM THE ICE KING-- AN EARTH SPIRIT-- AN IMMORTAL! WHY SHOULD I CARE FOR IDEAS OF RIGHT AND WRONG?!
OZMA, PLEASE LISTEN--
ENOUGH!
CR-RACK
?
?
WHUNK

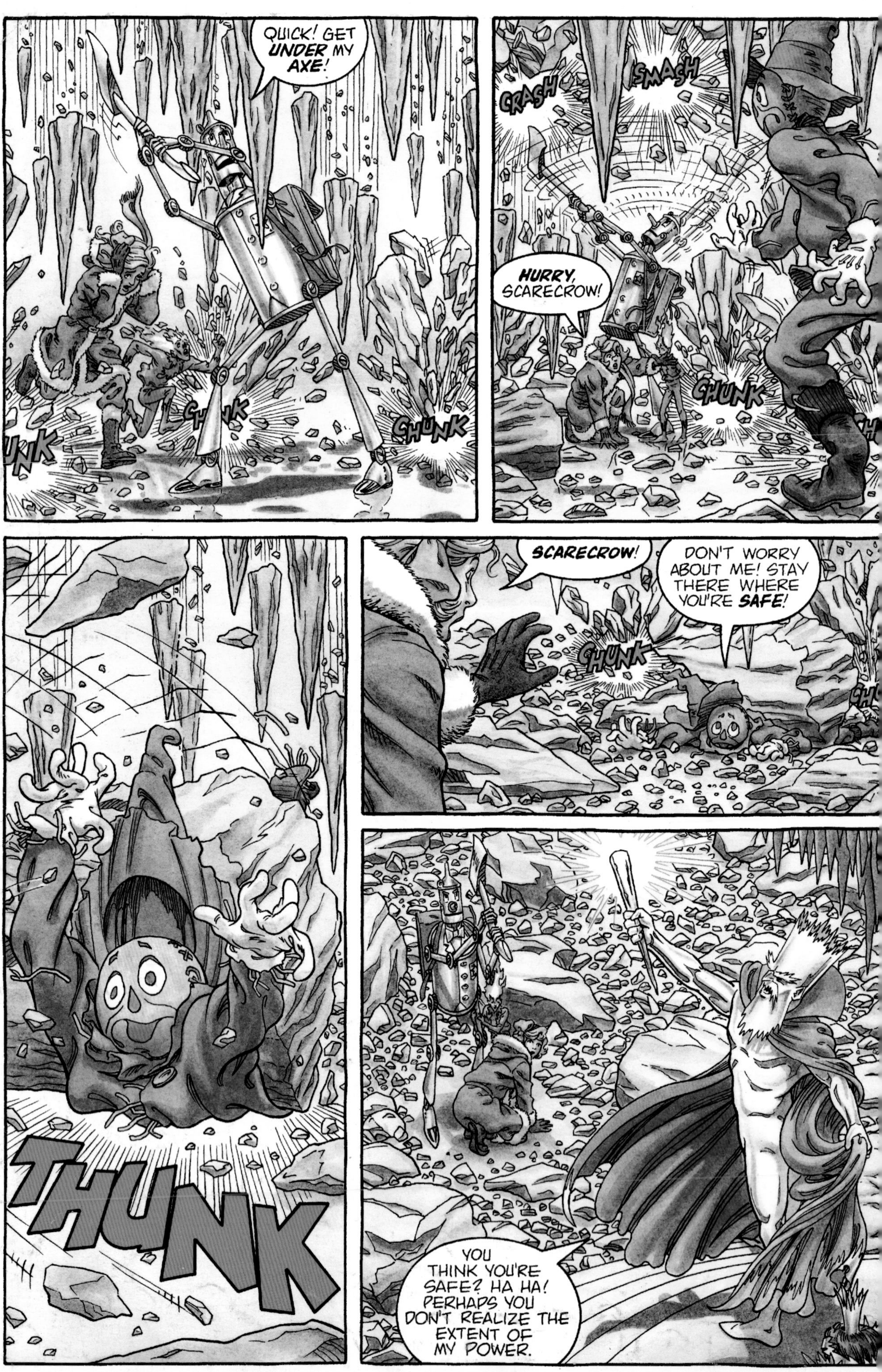
QUICK! GET **UNDER** MY **AXE**!
CHUNK
CHUNK
CHUNK
CRASH
SMASH
HURRY, SCARECROW!
CHUNK
THUNK
SCARECROW!
DON'T WORRY ABOUT ME! STAY THERE WHERE YOU'RE **SAFE**!
CHUNK
YOU THINK YOU'RE SAFE? HA HA! PERHAPS YOU DON'T REALIZE THE EXTENT OF MY POWER.

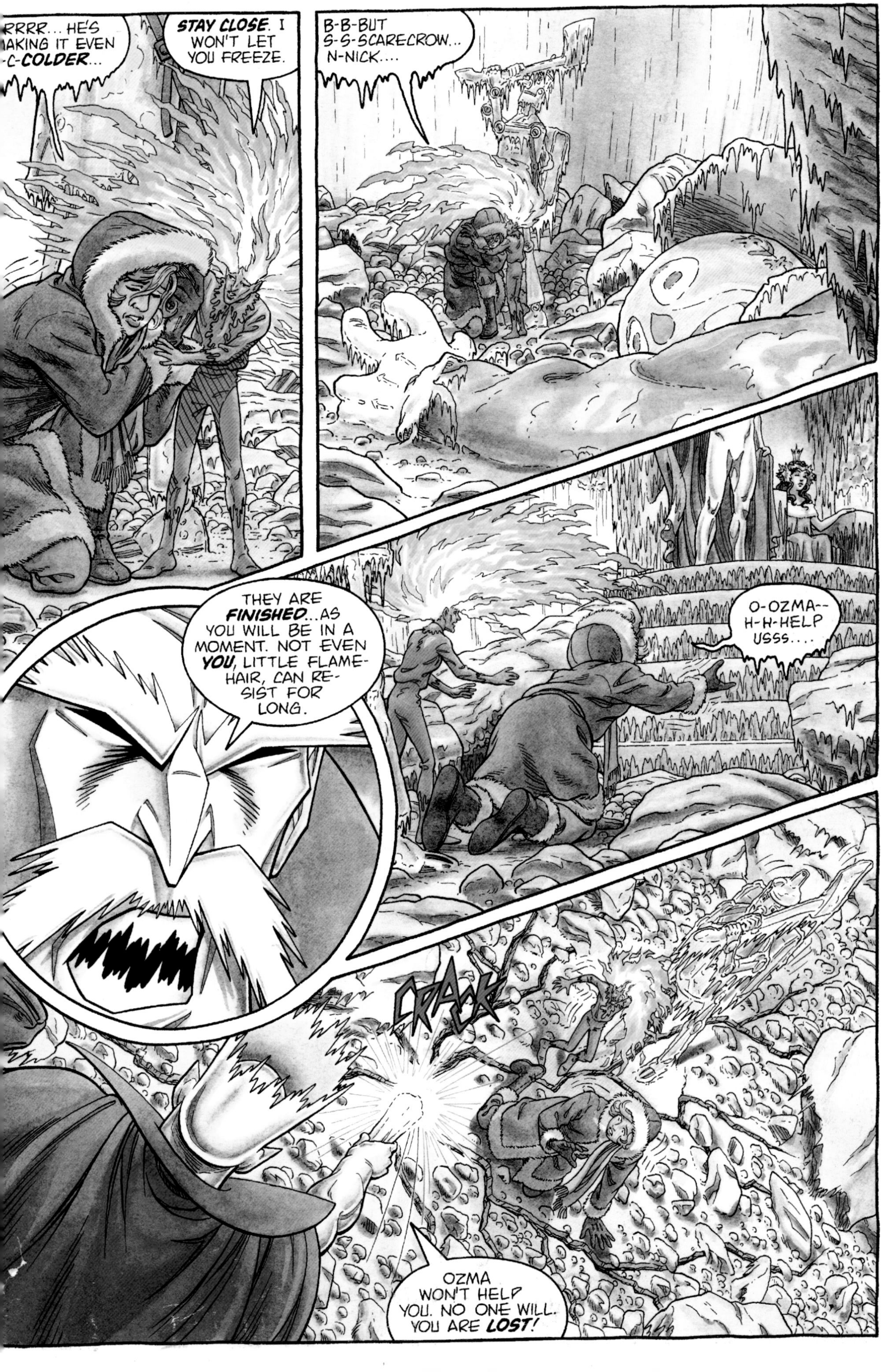
RRRR... HE'S MAKING IT EVEN C-C-COLDER...
STAY CLOSE. I WON'T LET YOU FREEZE.
B-B-BUT S-S-SCARECROW... N-NICK....
THEY ARE FINISHED...AS YOU WILL BE IN A MOMENT. NOT EVEN YOU, LITTLE FLAME-HAIR, CAN RESIST FOR LONG.
O-OZMA-- H-H-HELP USSS....
CRACK
OZMA WON'T HELP YOU. NO ONE WILL. YOU ARE LOST!

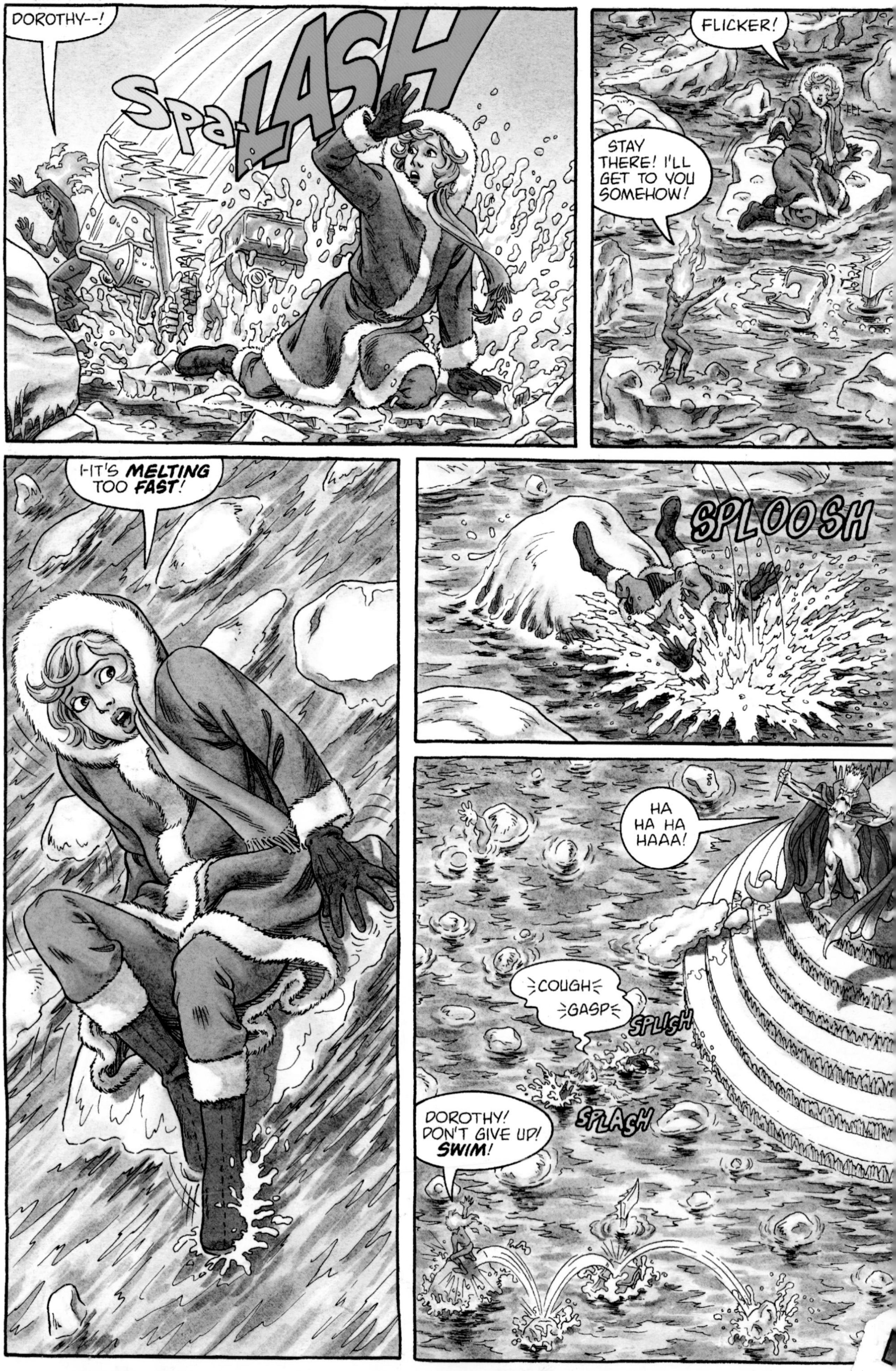
DOROTHY--!
Spa-LASH
FLICKER!
STAY THERE! I'LL GET TO YOU SOMEHOW!
I-IT'S **MELTING** TOO **FAST**!
SPLOOSH
HA HA HA HAAA!
COUGH
GASP
SPLISH
SPLASH
DOROTHY! DON'T GIVE UP! **SWIM**!

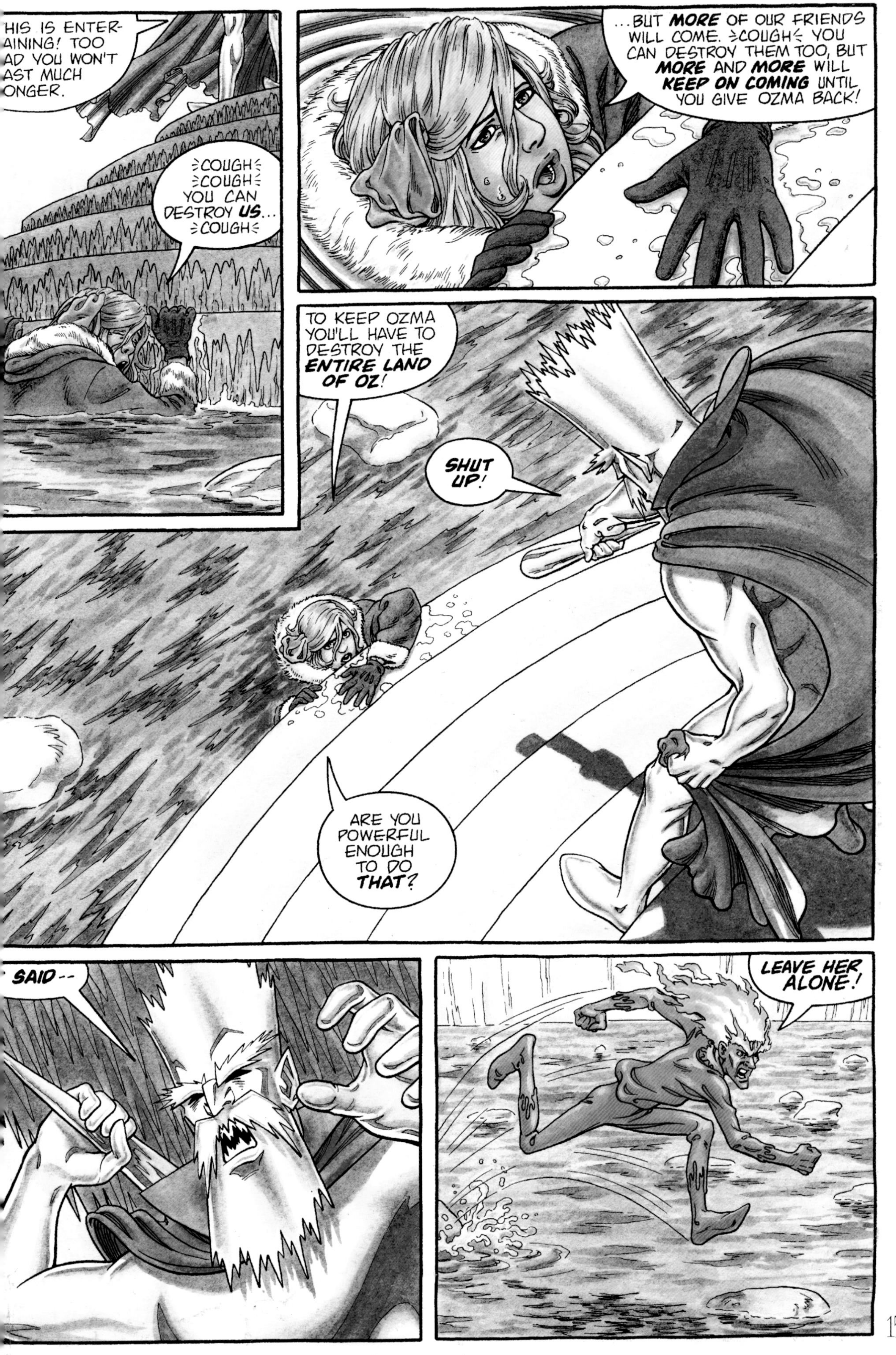
HIS IS ENTER-AINING! TOO AD YOU WON'T AST MUCH ONGER.
≥COUGH≤ ≥COUGH≤ YOU CAN DESTROY **US**... ≥COUGH≤
...BUT **MORE** OF OUR FRIENDS WILL COME. ≥COUGH≤ YOU CAN DESTROY THEM TOO, BUT **MORE** AND **MORE** WILL **KEEP ON COMING** UNTIL YOU GIVE OZMA BACK!
TO KEEP OZMA YOU'LL HAVE TO DESTROY THE **ENTIRE LAND OF OZ**!
SHUT UP!
ARE YOU POWERFUL ENOUGH TO DO **THAT**?
SAID--
LEAVE HER ALONE!

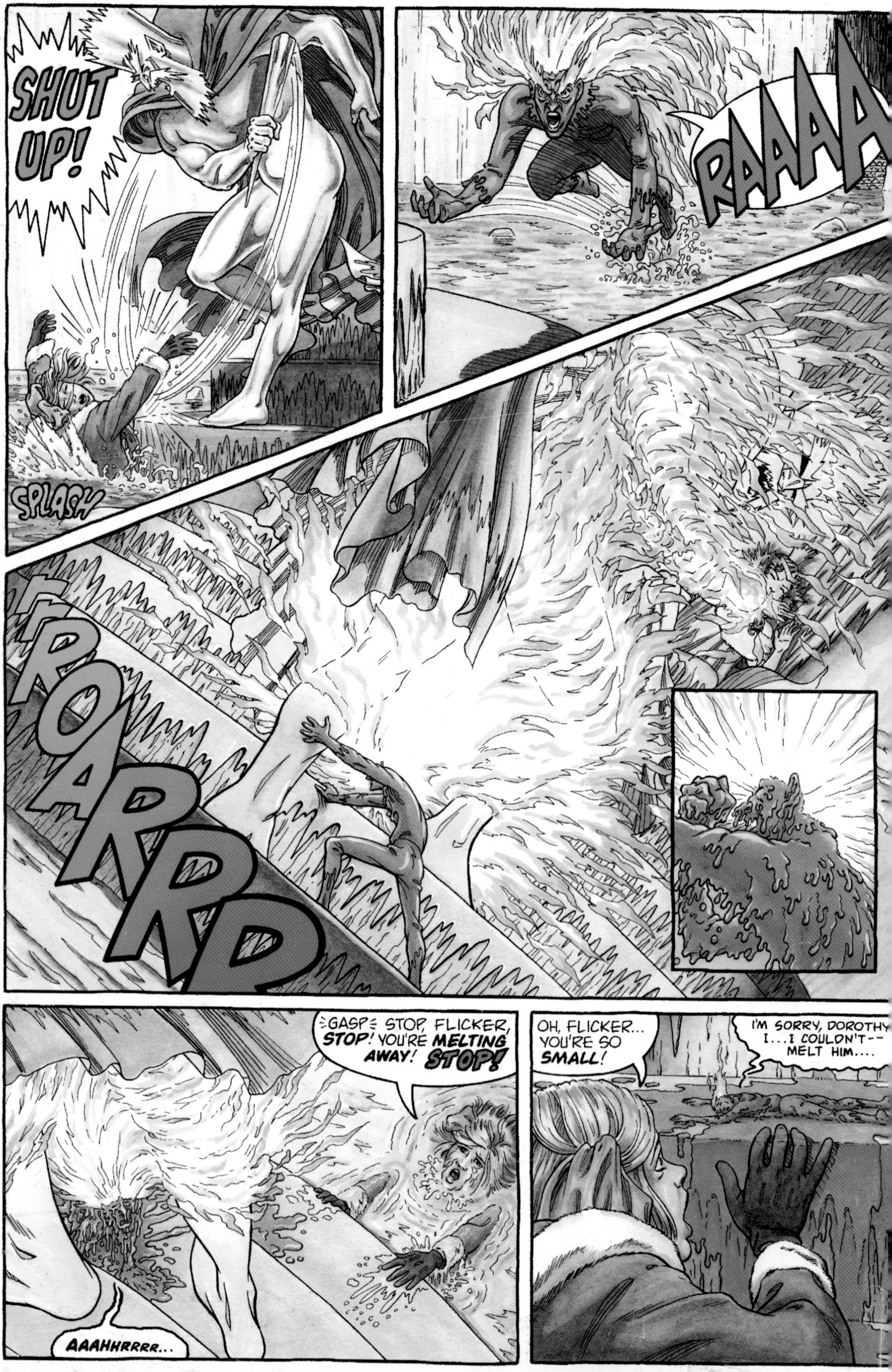
SHUT UP!
SPLASH
RAAAA
rrROARRRD
≡GASP≡ STOP, FLICKER, STOP! YOU'RE MELTING AWAY! STOP!
AAAHHRRRR...
OH, FLICKER... YOU'RE SO SMALL!
I'M SORRY, DOROTHY I... I COULDN'T-- MELT HIM....

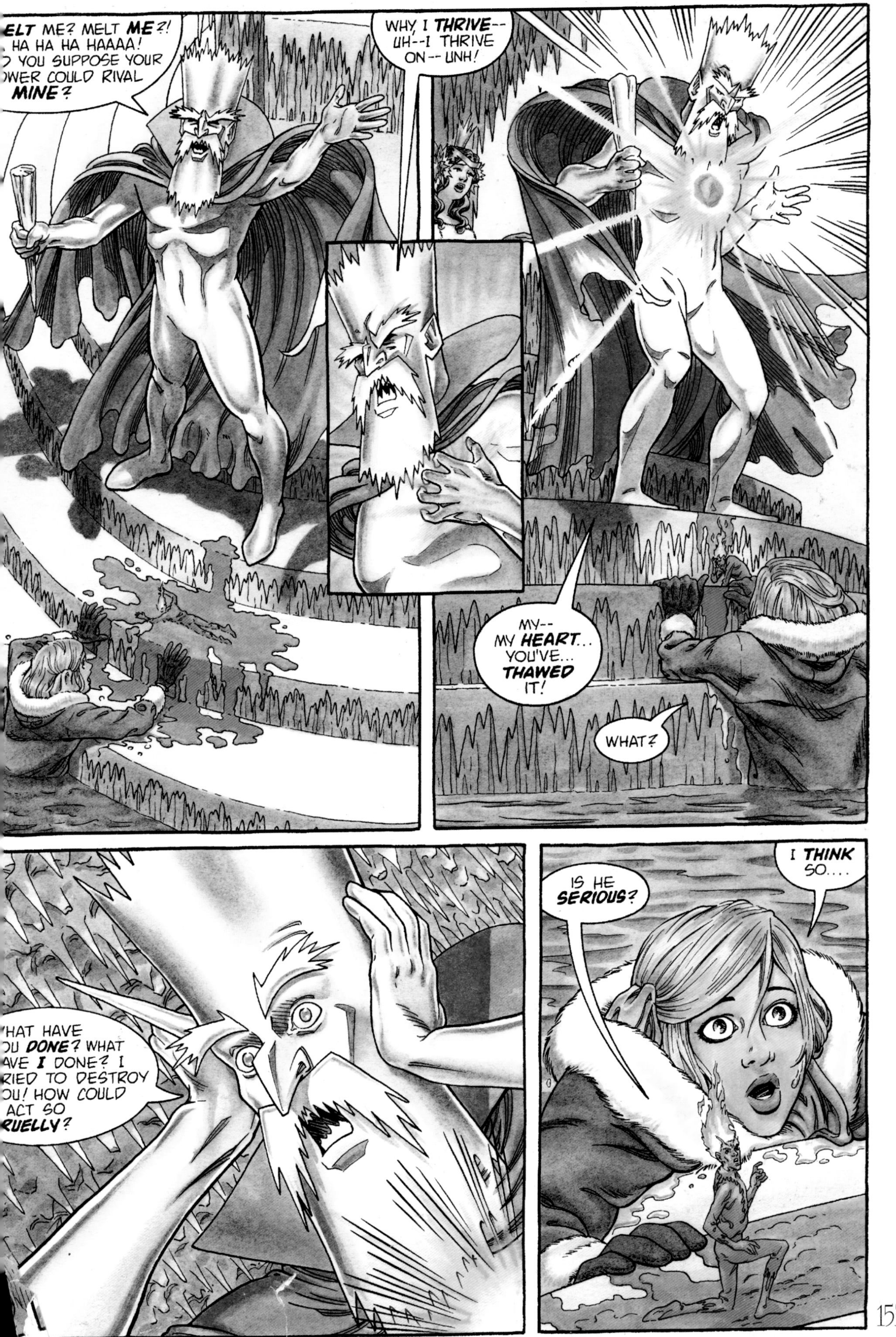
ELT ME? MELT ME?! HA HA HA HAAAA! D YOU SUPPOSE YOUR OWER COULD RIVAL MINE?
WHY, I THRIVE-- UH--I THRIVE ON--UNH!
MY-- MY HEART... YOU'VE... THAWED IT!
WHAT?
HAT HAVE OU DONE? WHAT AVE I DONE? I RIED TO DESTROY OU! HOW COULD ACT SO RUELLY?
IS HE SERIOUS?
I THINK SO....

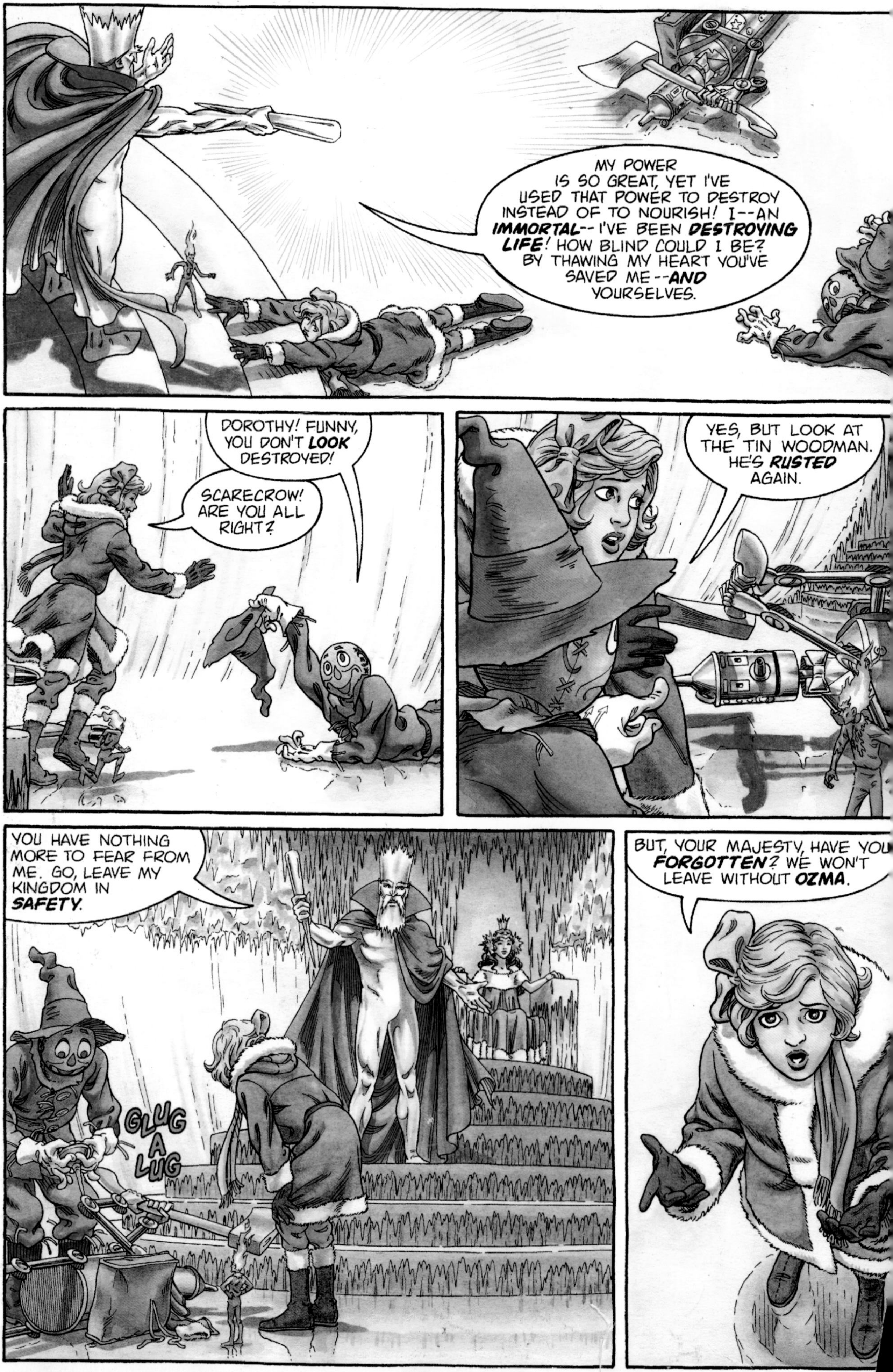
MY POWER IS SO GREAT, YET I'VE USED THAT POWER TO DESTROY INSTEAD OF TO NOURISH! I--AN **IMMORTAL**-- I'VE BEEN **DESTROYING LIFE**! HOW BLIND COULD I BE? BY THAWING MY HEART YOU'VE SAVED ME --**AND** YOURSELVES.
DOROTHY! FUNNY, YOU DON'T **LOOK** DESTROYED!
SCARECROW! ARE YOU ALL RIGHT?
YES, BUT LOOK AT THE TIN WOODMAN. HE'S **RUSTED** AGAIN.
YOU HAVE NOTHING MORE TO FEAR FROM ME. GO, LEAVE MY KINGDOM IN **SAFETY**.
GLUG A LUG
BUT, YOUR MAJESTY, HAVE YOU **FORGOTTEN**? WE WON'T LEAVE WITHOUT **OZMA**.

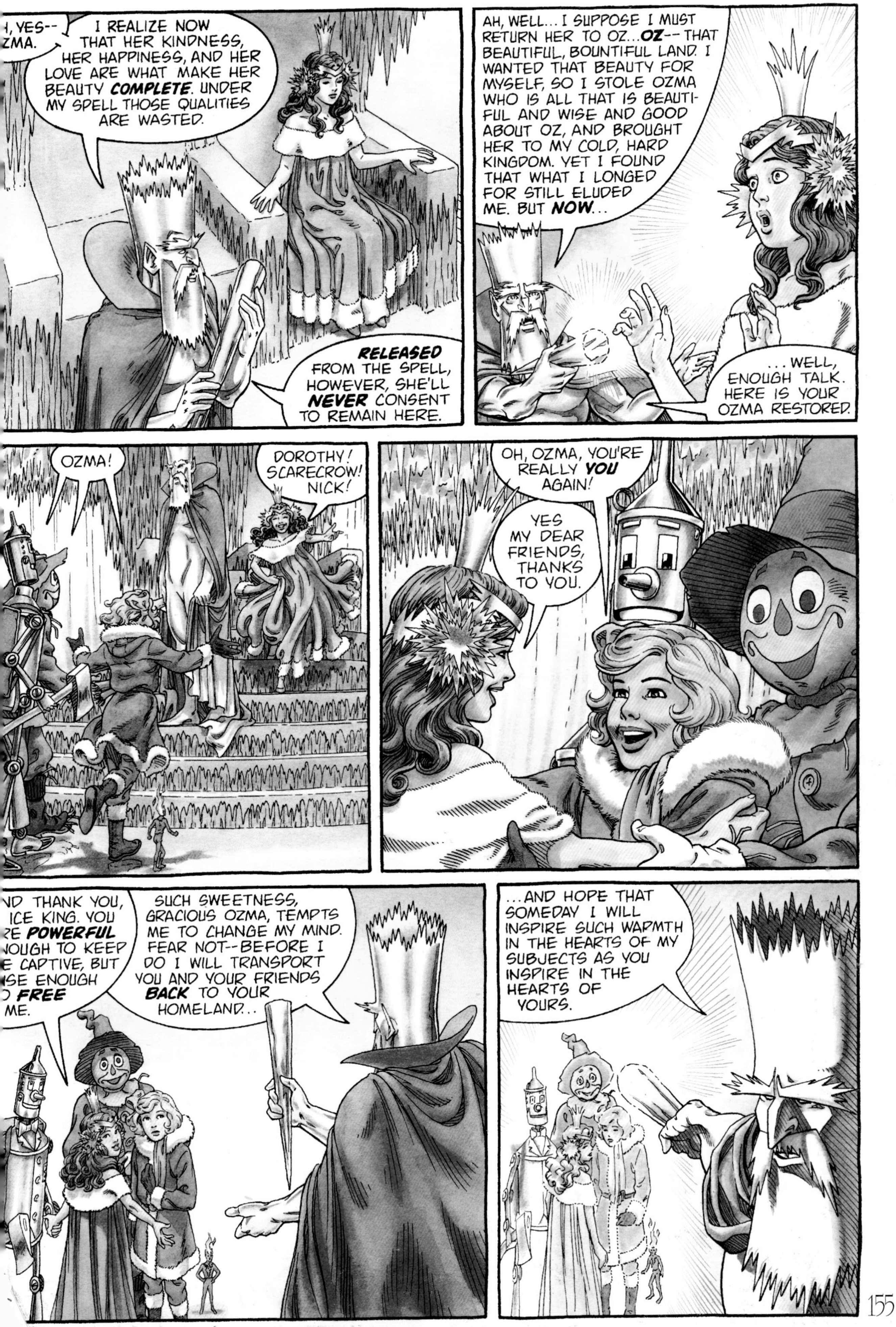

I, YES--
ZMA.
I REALIZE NOW THAT HER KINDNESS, HER HAPPINESS, AND HER LOVE ARE WHAT MAKE HER BEAUTY **COMPLETE**. UNDER MY SPELL THOSE QUALITIES ARE WASTED.
RELEASED FROM THE SPELL, HOWEVER, SHE'LL **NEVER** CONSENT TO REMAIN HERE.
AH, WELL... I SUPPOSE I MUST RETURN HER TO OZ...**OZ**-- THAT BEAUTIFUL, BOUNTIFUL LAND. I WANTED THAT BEAUTY FOR MYSELF, SO I STOLE OZMA WHO IS ALL THAT IS BEAUTIFUL AND WISE AND GOOD ABOUT OZ, AND BROUGHT HER TO MY COLD, HARD KINGDOM. YET I FOUND THAT WHAT I LONGED FOR STILL ELUDED ME. BUT **NOW**...
...WELL, ENOUGH TALK. HERE IS YOUR OZMA RESTORED.
OZMA!
DOROTHY! SCARECROW! NICK!
OH, OZMA, YOU'RE REALLY **YOU** AGAIN!
YES MY DEAR FRIENDS, THANKS TO YOU.
ND THANK YOU, ICE KING. YOU E **POWERFUL** NOUGH TO KEEP E CAPTIVE, BUT SE ENOUGH **FREE** ME.
SUCH SWEETNESS, GRACIOUS OZMA, TEMPTS ME TO CHANGE MY MIND. FEAR NOT--BEFORE I DO I WILL TRANSPORT YOU AND YOUR FRIENDS **BACK** TO YOUR HOMELAND...
...AND HOPE THAT SOMEDAY I WILL INSPIRE SUCH WARMTH IN THE HEARTS OF MY SUBJECTS AS YOU INSPIRE IN THE HEARTS OF YOURS.

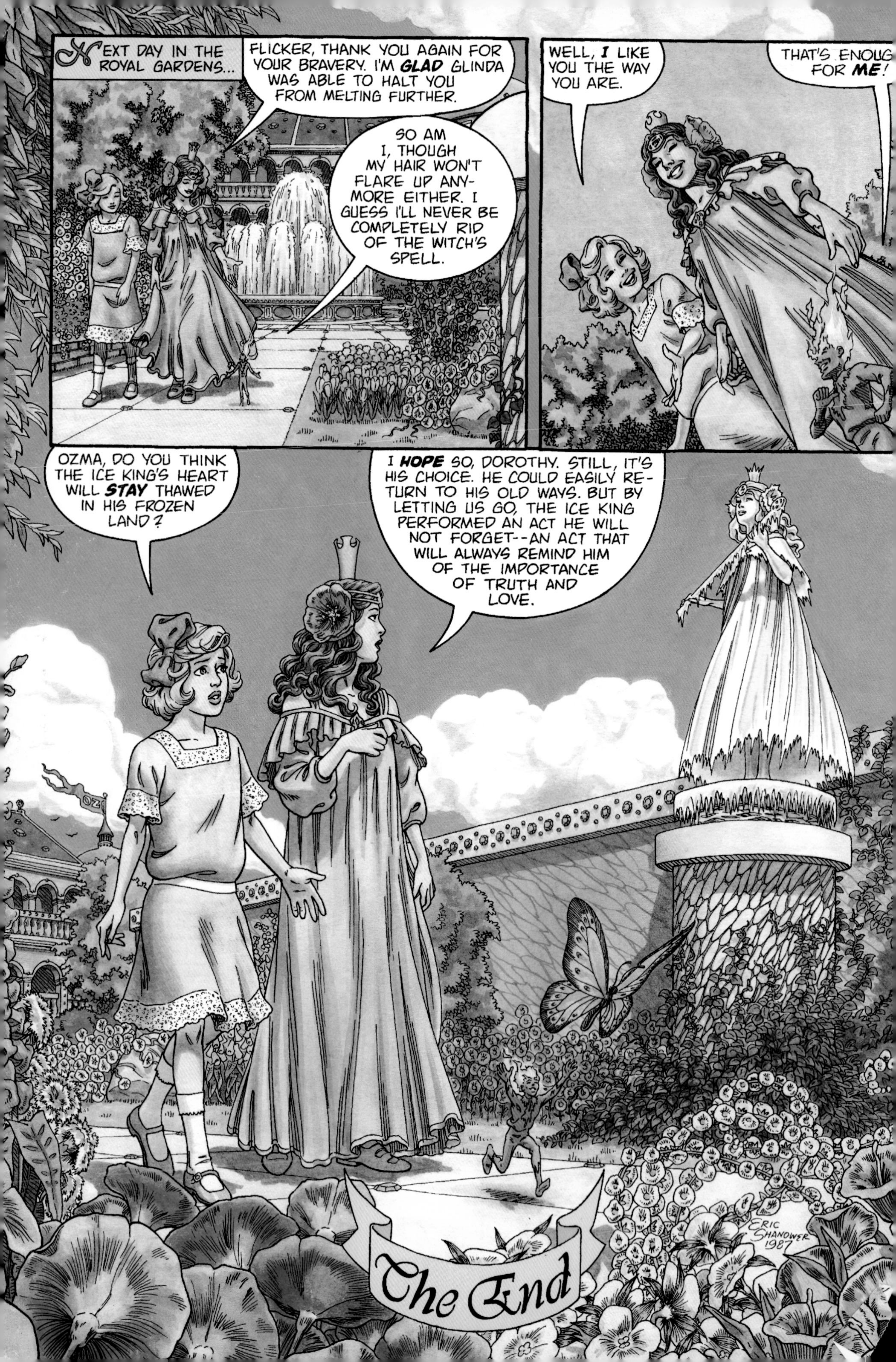
NEXT DAY IN THE ROYAL GARDENS...
FLICKER, THANK YOU AGAIN FOR YOUR BRAVERY. I'M GLAD GLINDA WAS ABLE TO HALT YOU FROM MELTING FURTHER.
SO AM I, THOUGH MY HAIR WON'T FLARE UP ANY-MORE EITHER. I GUESS I'LL NEVER BE COMPLETELY RID OF THE WITCH'S SPELL.
WELL, I LIKE YOU THE WAY YOU ARE.
THAT'S ENOUGH FOR ME!
OZMA, DO YOU THINK THE ICE KING'S HEART WILL STAY THAWED IN HIS FROZEN LAND?
I HOPE SO, DOROTHY. STILL, IT'S HIS CHOICE. HE COULD EASILY RE-TURN TO HIS OLD WAYS. BUT BY LETTING US GO, THE ICE KING PERFORMED AN ACT HE WILL NOT FORGET--AN ACT THAT WILL ALWAYS REMIND HIM OF THE IMPORTANCE OF TRUTH AND LOVE.
OZ
ERIC SHANOWER 1987
The End

Oz

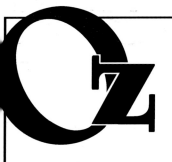

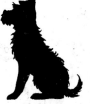

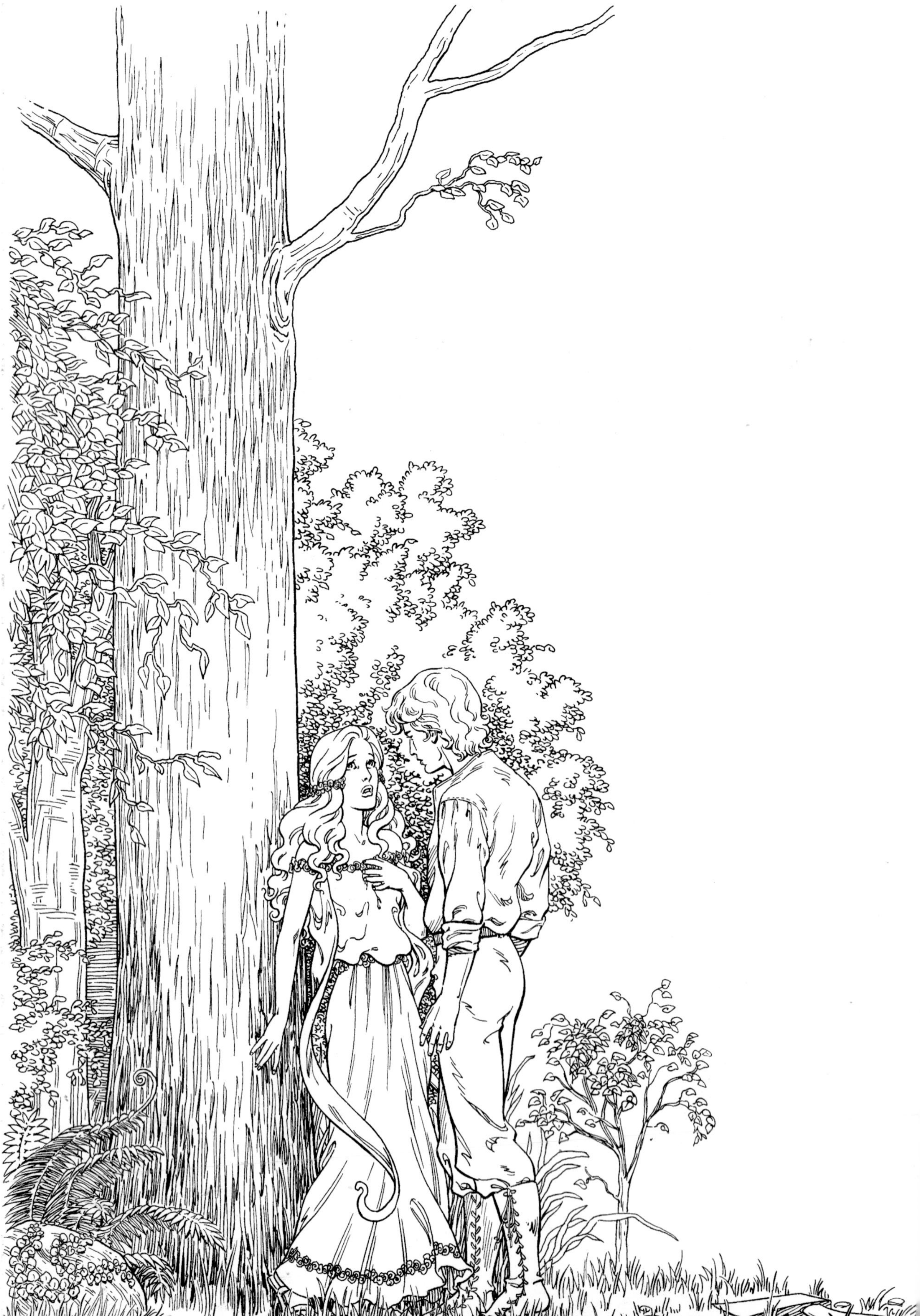
ES 88

The FORGOTTEN FOREST of Oz

For David

Chapter One — Out of Burzee

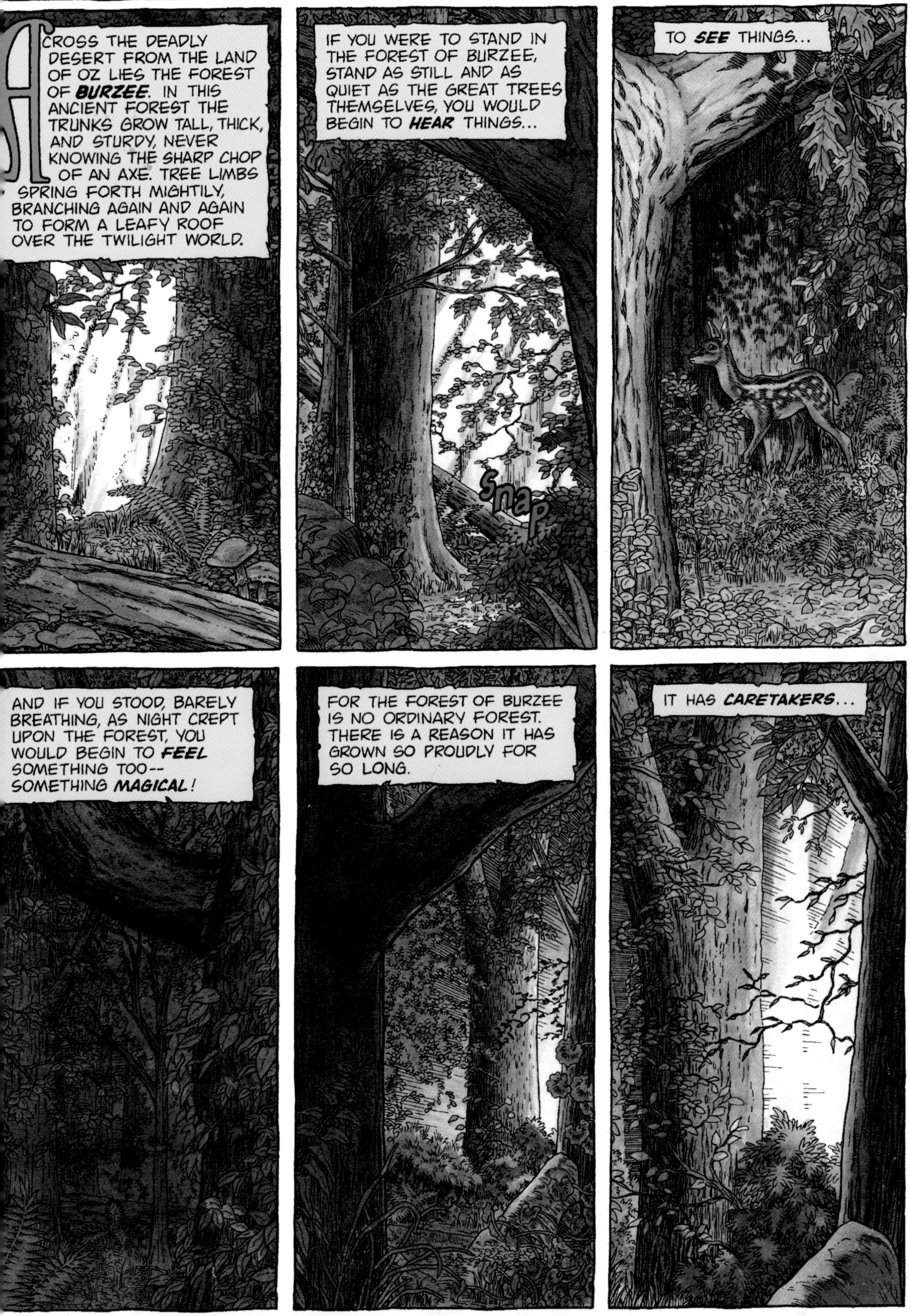
ACROSS THE DEADLY DESERT FROM THE LAND OF OZ LIES THE FOREST OF BURZEE. IN THIS ANCIENT FOREST THE TRUNKS GROW TALL, THICK, AND STURDY, NEVER KNOWING THE SHARP CHOP OF AN AXE. TREE LIMBS SPRING FORTH MIGHTILY, BRANCHING AGAIN AND AGAIN TO FORM A LEAFY ROOF OVER THE TWILIGHT WORLD.
IF YOU WERE TO STAND IN THE FOREST OF BURZEE, STAND AS STILL AND AS QUIET AS THE GREAT TREES THEMSELVES, YOU WOULD BEGIN TO HEAR THINGS...
SNAP
TO SEE THINGS...
AND IF YOU STOOD, BARELY BREATHING, AS NIGHT CREPT UPON THE FOREST, YOU WOULD BEGIN TO FEEL SOMETHING TOO-- SOMETHING MAGICAL!
FOR THE FOREST OF BURZEE IS NO ORDINARY FOREST. THERE IS A REASON IT HAS GROWN SO PROUDLY FOR SO LONG.
IT HAS CARETAKERS...

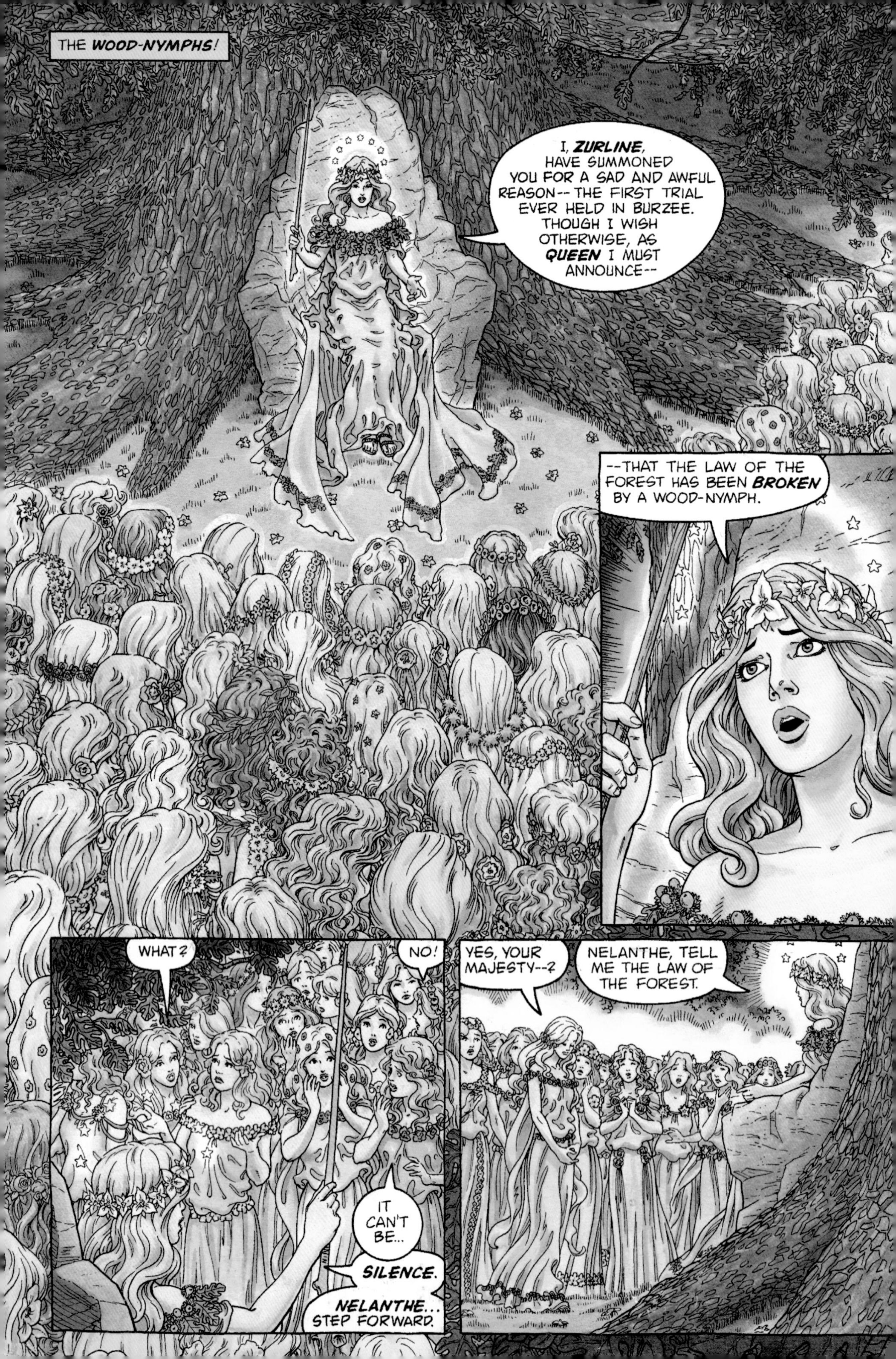
THE WOOD-NYMPHS!
I, ZURLINE, HAVE SUMMONED YOU FOR A SAD AND AWFUL REASON-- THE FIRST TRIAL EVER HELD IN BURZEE. THOUGH I WISH OTHERWISE, AS QUEEN I MUST ANNOUNCE--
--THAT THE LAW OF THE FOREST HAS BEEN BROKEN BY A WOOD-NYMPH.
WHAT?
NO!
IT CAN'T BE...
SILENCE.
NELANTHE... STEP FORWARD.
YES, YOUR MAJESTY--?
NELANTHE, TELL ME THE LAW OF THE FOREST.

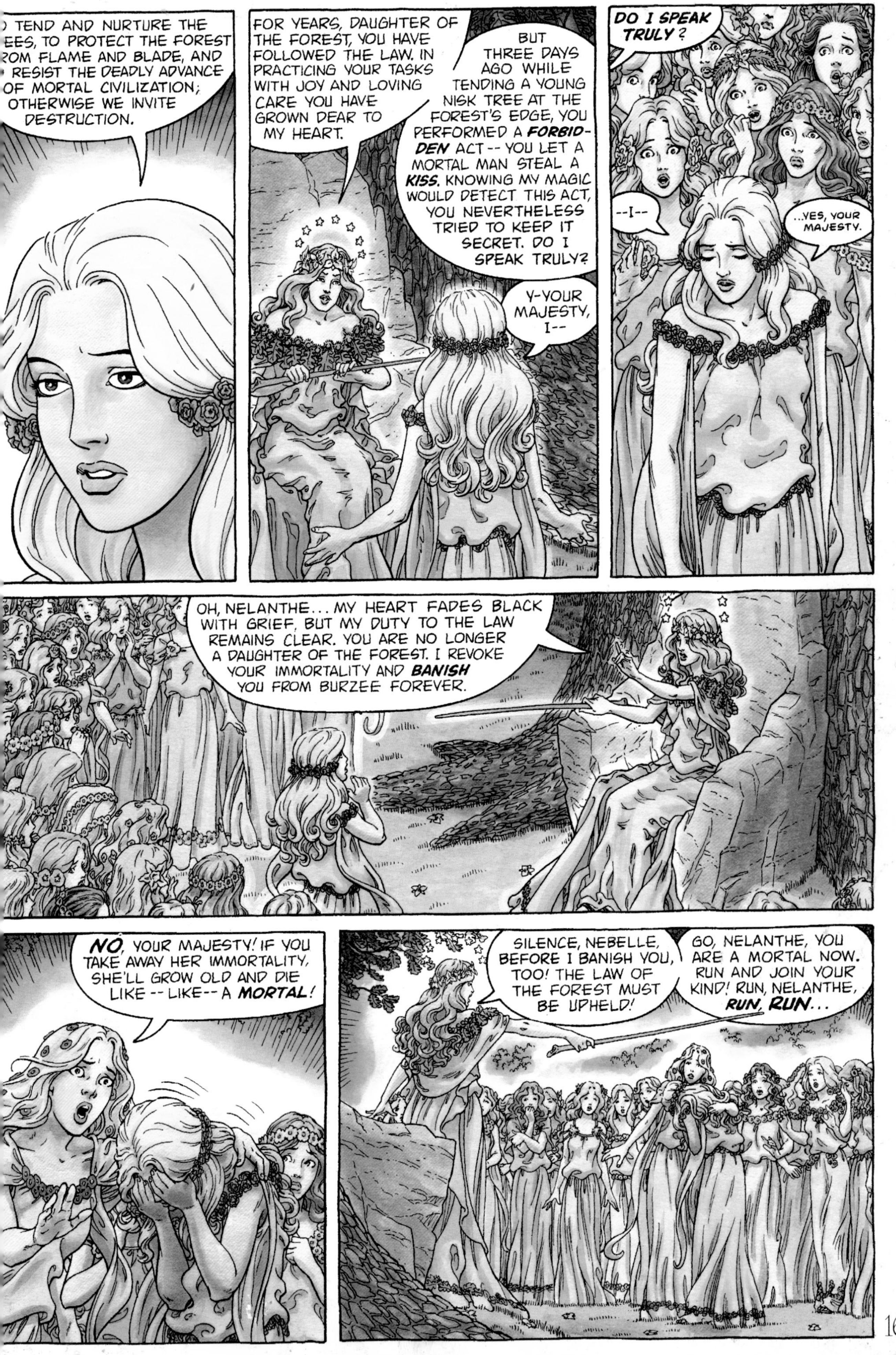

O TEND AND NURTURE THE
EES, TO PROTECT THE FOREST
ROM FLAME AND BLADE, AND
RESIST THE DEADLY ADVANCE
OF MORTAL CIVILIZATION;
OTHERWISE WE INVITE
DESTRUCTION.
FOR YEARS, DAUGHTER OF THE FOREST, YOU HAVE FOLLOWED THE LAW. IN PRACTICING YOUR TASKS WITH JOY AND LOVING CARE YOU HAVE GROWN DEAR TO MY HEART.
BUT THREE DAYS AGO WHILE TENDING A YOUNG NISK TREE AT THE FOREST'S EDGE, YOU PERFORMED A FORBIDDEN ACT -- YOU LET A MORTAL MAN STEAL A KISS. KNOWING MY MAGIC WOULD DETECT THIS ACT, YOU NEVERTHELESS TRIED TO KEEP IT SECRET. DO I SPEAK TRULY?
Y-YOUR MAJESTY, I--
DO I SPEAK TRULY?
--I--
...YES, YOUR MAJESTY.
OH, NELANTHE... MY HEART FADES BLACK WITH GRIEF, BUT MY DUTY TO THE LAW REMAINS CLEAR. YOU ARE NO LONGER A DAUGHTER OF THE FOREST. I REVOKE YOUR IMMORTALITY AND BANISH YOU FROM BURZEE FOREVER.
NO, YOUR MAJESTY! IF YOU TAKE AWAY HER IMMORTALITY, SHE'LL GROW OLD AND DIE LIKE -- LIKE -- A MORTAL!
SILENCE, NEBELLE, BEFORE I BANISH YOU, TOO! THE LAW OF THE FOREST MUST BE UPHELD!
GO, NELANTHE, YOU ARE A MORTAL NOW. RUN AND JOIN YOUR KIND! RUN, NELANTHE, RUN, RUN...

...RUN...

So NELANTHE RUNS, LEAVING BEHIND ALL THAT SHE LOVES...

LEAVING BEHIND THE LIFE SHE WAS MEANT TO LIVE...

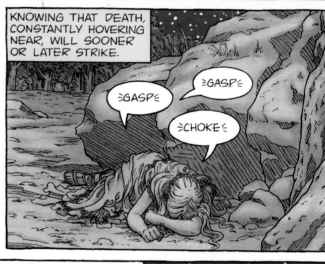

KNOWING THAT DEATH, CONSTANTLY HOVERING NEAR, WILL SOONER OR LATER STRIKE.

≶GASP≶

≶GASP≶

≶CHOKE≶

WHAT IS YOUR TROUBLE, PRETTY ONE?

WHO ARE YOU?!

DON'T BE AFRAID. I'M MERELY THE KING OF THE TROLLS, OUT FOR A MOONLIGHT STROLL. PLEASE...WHY DO YOU SPOIL YOUR LOVELI- NESS WITH TEARS, LITTLE WOOD- NYMPH?

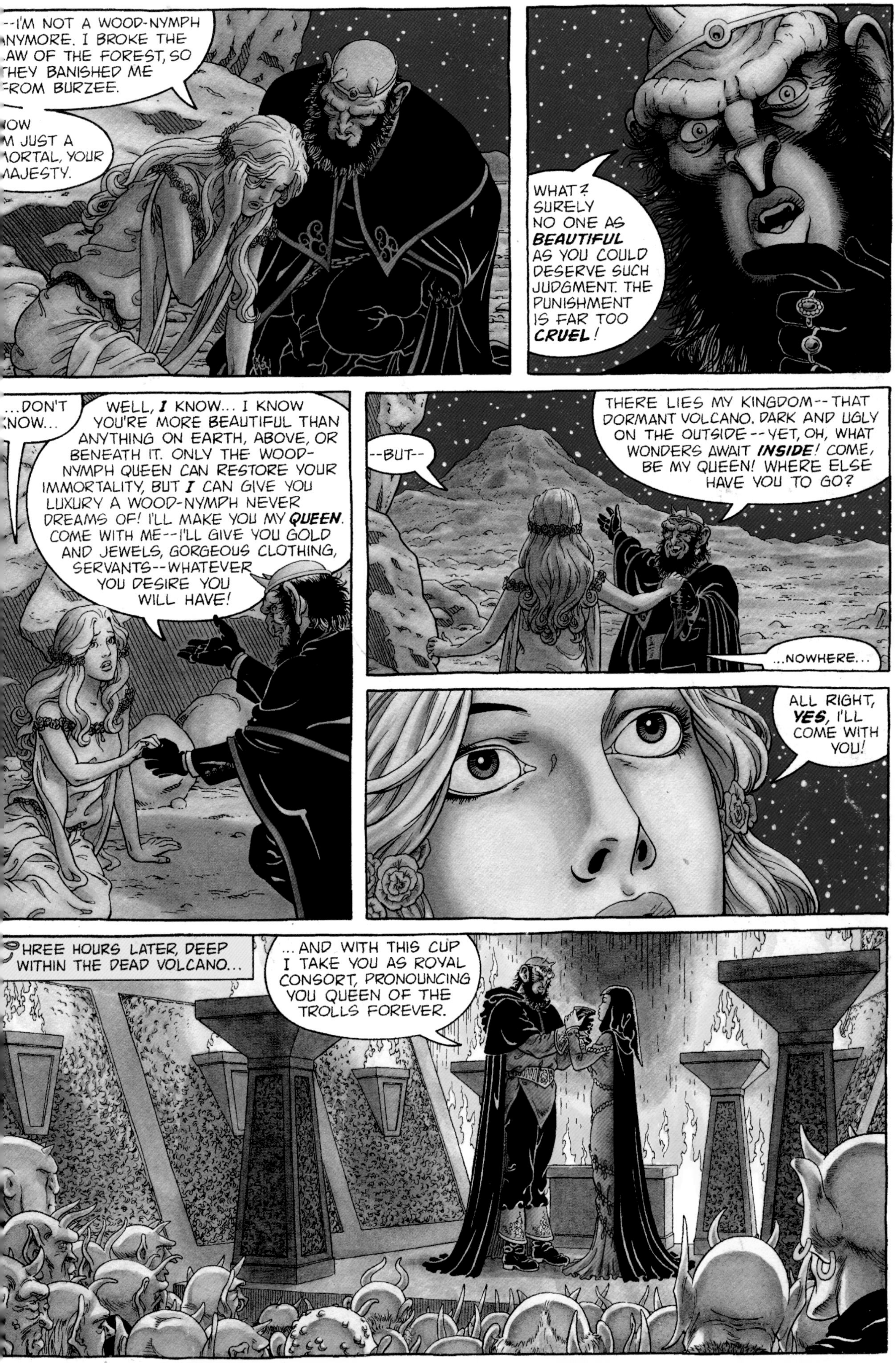
--I'M NOT A WOOD-NYMPH ANYMORE. I BROKE THE LAW OF THE FOREST, SO THEY BANISHED ME FROM BURZEE.
NOW I'M JUST A MORTAL, YOUR MAJESTY.
WHAT? SURELY NO ONE AS **BEAUTIFUL** AS YOU COULD DESERVE SUCH JUDGMENT. THE PUNISHMENT IS FAR TOO **CRUEL**!
...DON'T KNOW...
WELL, **I** KNOW... I KNOW YOU'RE MORE BEAUTIFUL THAN ANYTHING ON EARTH, ABOVE, OR BENEATH IT. ONLY THE WOOD-NYMPH QUEEN CAN RESTORE YOUR IMMORTALITY, BUT **I** CAN GIVE YOU LUXURY A WOOD-NYMPH NEVER DREAMS OF! I'LL MAKE YOU MY **QUEEN**. COME WITH ME--I'LL GIVE YOU GOLD AND JEWELS, GORGEOUS CLOTHING, SERVANTS--WHATEVER YOU DESIRE YOU WILL HAVE!
--BUT--
THERE LIES MY KINGDOM--THAT DORMANT VOLCANO. DARK AND UGLY ON THE OUTSIDE--YET, OH, WHAT WONDERS AWAIT **INSIDE**! COME, BE MY QUEEN! WHERE ELSE HAVE YOU TO GO?
...NOWHERE...
ALL RIGHT, **YES**, I'LL COME WITH YOU!
THREE HOURS LATER, DEEP WITHIN THE DEAD VOLCANO...
...AND WITH THIS CUP I TAKE YOU AS ROYAL CONSORT, PRONOUNCING YOU QUEEN OF THE TROLLS FOREVER.

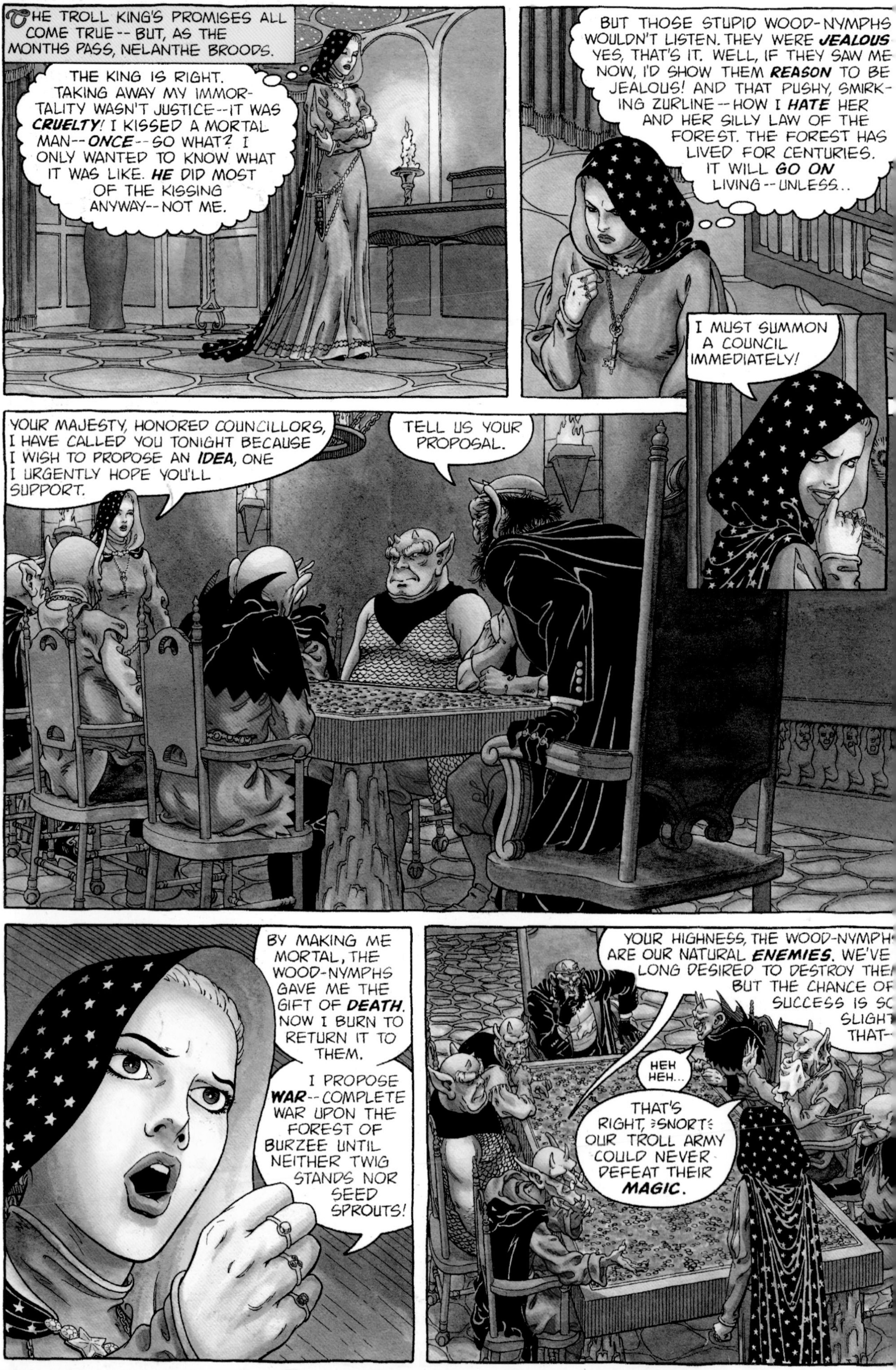
THE TROLL KING'S PROMISES ALL COME TRUE -- BUT, AS THE MONTHS PASS, NELANTHE BROODS.
THE KING IS RIGHT. TAKING AWAY MY IMMORTALITY WASN'T JUSTICE -- IT WAS CRUELTY! I KISSED A MORTAL MAN -- ONCE -- SO WHAT? I ONLY WANTED TO KNOW WHAT IT WAS LIKE. HE DID MOST OF THE KISSING ANYWAY -- NOT ME.
BUT THOSE STUPID WOOD-NYMPHS WOULDN'T LISTEN. THEY WERE JEALOUS YES, THAT'S IT. WELL, IF THEY SAW ME NOW, I'D SHOW THEM REASON TO BE JEALOUS! AND THAT PUSHY, SMIRKING ZURLINE -- HOW I HATE HER AND HER SILLY LAW OF THE FOREST. THE FOREST HAS LIVED FOR CENTURIES. IT WILL GO ON LIVING -- UNLESS...
I MUST SUMMON A COUNCIL IMMEDIATELY!
YOUR MAJESTY, HONORED COUNCILLORS, I HAVE CALLED YOU TONIGHT BECAUSE I WISH TO PROPOSE AN IDEA, ONE I URGENTLY HOPE YOU'LL SUPPORT.
TELL US YOUR PROPOSAL.
BY MAKING ME MORTAL, THE WOOD-NYMPHS GAVE ME THE GIFT OF DEATH. NOW I BURN TO RETURN IT TO THEM.
I PROPOSE WAR -- COMPLETE WAR UPON THE FOREST OF BURZEE UNTIL NEITHER TWIG STANDS NOR SEED SPROUTS!
YOUR HIGHNESS, THE WOOD-NYMPH ARE OUR NATURAL ENEMIES. WE'VE LONG DESIRED TO DESTROY THE BUT THE CHANCE OF SUCCESS IS SO SLIGHT THAT--
HEH HEH...
THAT'S RIGHT, ≥SNORT≤ OUR TROLL ARMY COULD NEVER DEFEAT THEIR MAGIC.

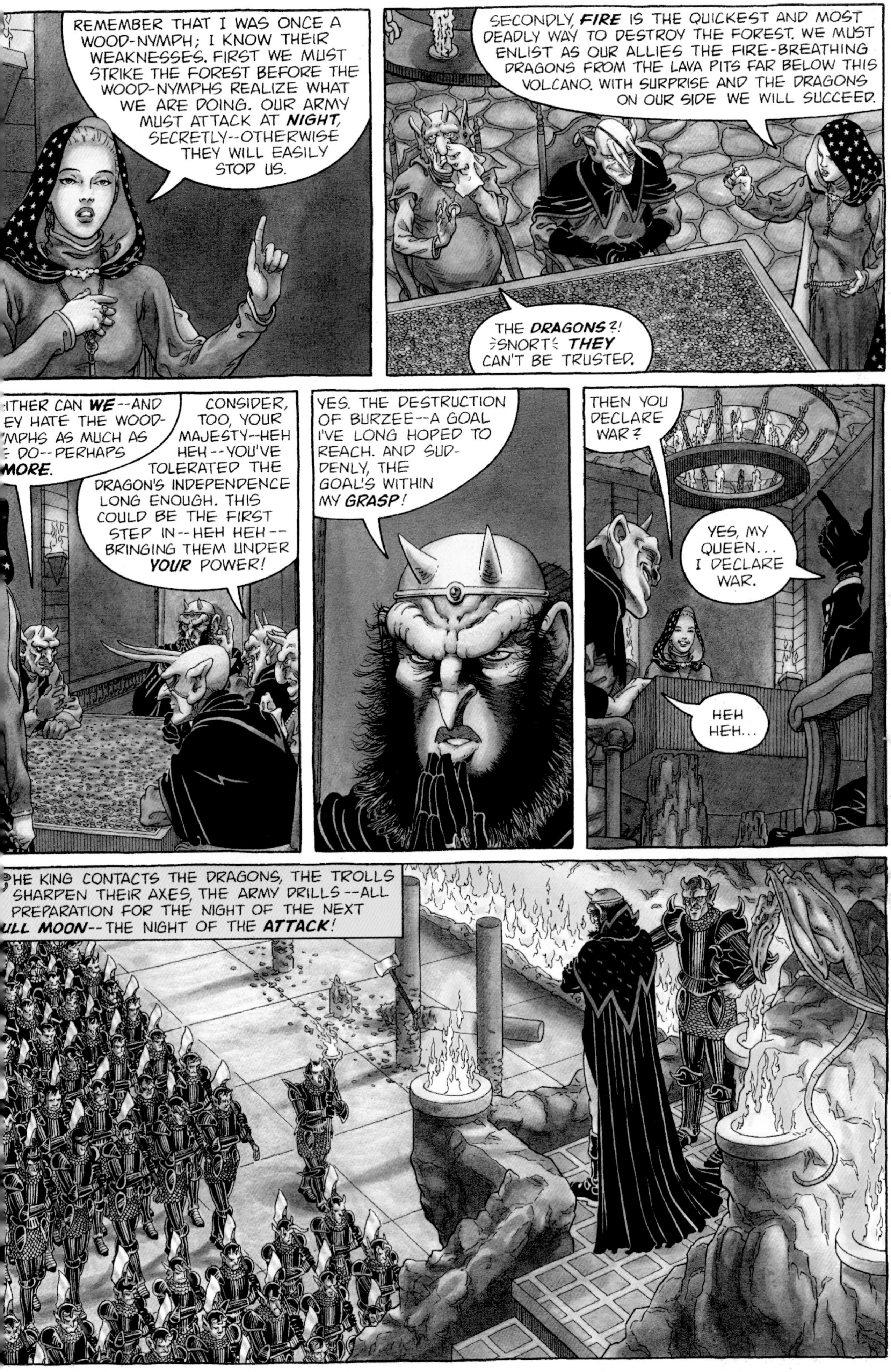
REMEMBER THAT I WAS ONCE A WOOD-NYMPH; I KNOW THEIR WEAKNESSES. FIRST WE MUST STRIKE THE FOREST BEFORE THE WOOD-NYMPHS REALIZE WHAT WE ARE DOING. OUR ARMY MUST ATTACK AT **NIGHT**, SECRETLY--OTHERWISE THEY WILL EASILY STOP US.
SECONDLY, **FIRE** IS THE QUICKEST AND MOST DEADLY WAY TO DESTROY THE FOREST. WE MUST ENLIST AS OUR ALLIES THE FIRE-BREATHING DRAGONS FROM THE LAVA PITS FAR BELOW THIS VOLCANO. WITH SURPRISE AND THE DRAGONS ON OUR SIDE WE WILL SUCCEED.
THE **DRAGONS**?! SNORT **THEY** CAN'T BE TRUSTED.
ITHER CAN **WE**--AND EY HATE THE WOOD-YMPHS AS MUCH AS DO--PERHAPS **MORE**.
CONSIDER, TOO, YOUR MAJESTY--HEH HEH--YOU'VE TOLERATED THE DRAGON'S INDEPENDENCE LONG ENOUGH. THIS COULD BE THE FIRST STEP IN--HEH HEH--BRINGING THEM UNDER **YOUR** POWER!
YES. THE DESTRUCTION OF BURZEE--A GOAL I'VE LONG HOPED TO REACH. AND SUDDENLY, THE GOAL'S WITHIN MY **GRASP**!
THEN YOU DECLARE WAR?
YES, MY QUEEN... I DECLARE WAR.
HEH HEH...
HE KING CONTACTS THE DRAGONS, THE TROLLS SHARPEN THEIR AXES, THE ARMY DRILLS--ALL PREPARATION FOR THE NIGHT OF THE NEXT **ULL MOON**--THE NIGHT OF THE **ATTACK**!

THE NIGHT ARRIVES.

OH, WHAT'S THE MATTER WITH ME? EVER SINCE THE KING DECLARED WAR, I'VE BEEN HAVING SECOND THOUGHTS.

WHY? WHY?

SOMETIMES I ALMOST WISH TO RETURN TO BURZEE. TO LAUGH WITH THE OTHER BY CRYSTAL SPRINGS.

...TO DANCE UPON THE SUNBEAMS THAT SPLIT THE LAYERS OF GLOWING LEAVES... AND, AH, TO TEND THE MAGNIFICENT TREES...

THE CURSED TREES. SLAVING OVER THEM DAY AFTER DAY-- AND FOR WHAT? USELESS, USELESS!

rrrip

YAAAA!

IF ONLY I COULD FORGET! I NEED TO FORGET! BUT HOW?

CRASH

HOW? I CAN'T GO-- OH!

WHAT'S THIS?

ENCYCLOPÆDIA of MAGIC

The Water of Oblivion

In the royal gardens of the Emerald City is the Forbidden Fountain containing the potent Water of Oblivion. This water is capable of completely erasing the memory of any being who drinks it. For this reason Ozma, ruler of Oz, has decreed the water forbidden to all.

Long ago Glinda, Good Sorceress of the South, placed the fountain in 1043

...nd of A-Ramose.
...owerful spell.
...f Velkemin
...lden Valley of
...Sea of Sighs
...race of wasps
...magical sting.
...sting of a wasp
...painful, though
...granted to the
...the stinger is
...he wasp dies.

hapter Two — Sounds in the Night

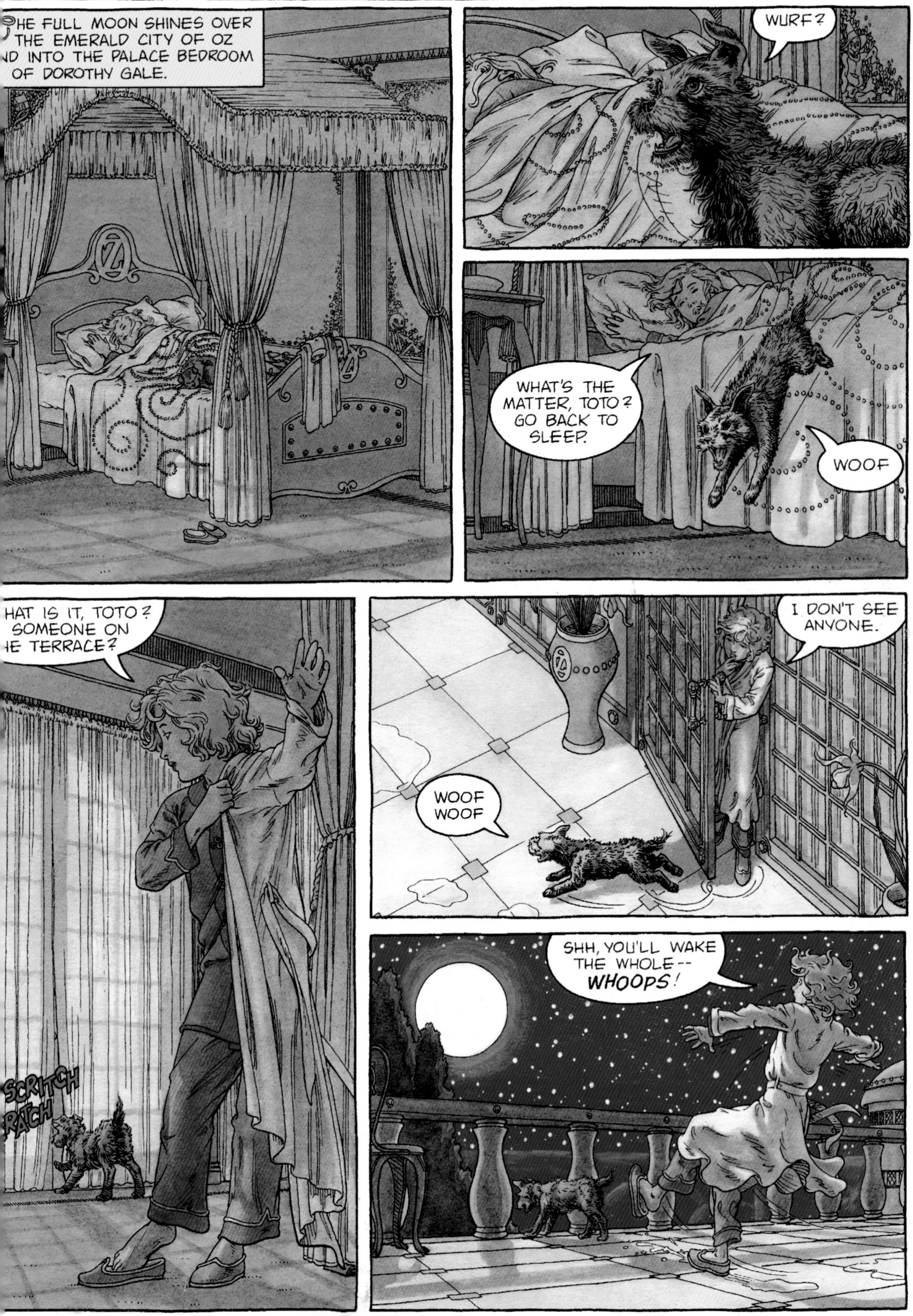
HE FULL MOON SHINES OVER THE EMERALD CITY OF OZ
ND INTO THE PALACE BEDROOM OF DOROTHY GALE.
WURF?
WHAT'S THE MATTER, TOTO? GO BACK TO SLEEP.
WOOF
HAT IS IT, TOTO? SOMEONE ON
IE TERRACE?
SCRITCH
RATCH
I DON'T SEE ANYONE.
WOOF WOOF
SHH, YOU'LL WAKE THE WHOLE-- WHOOPS!

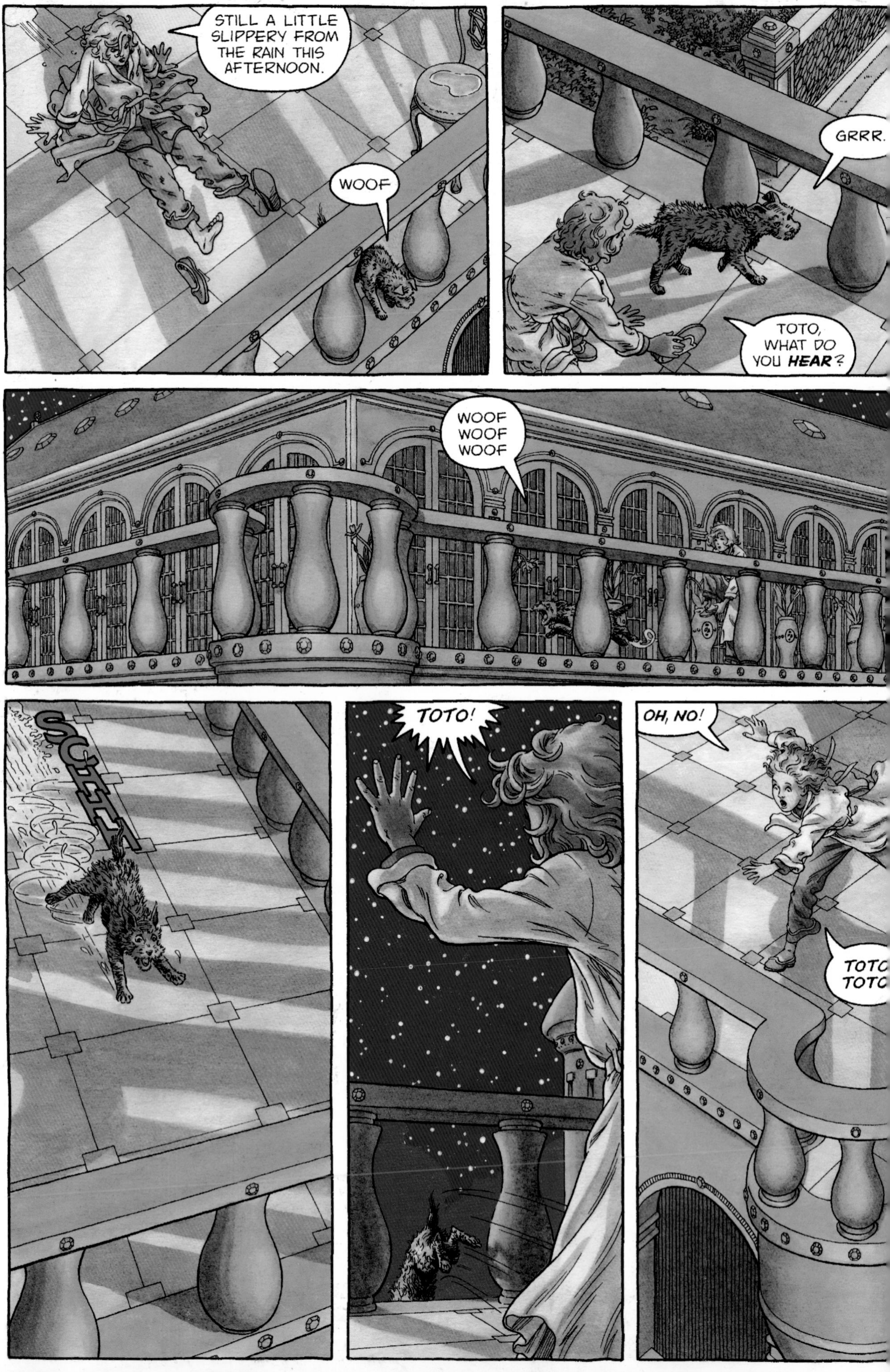
STILL A LITTLE SLIPPERY FROM THE RAIN THIS AFTERNOON.
WOOF
GRRR.
TOTO, WHAT DO YOU **HEAR**?
WOOF WOOF WOOF
TOTO!
OH, NO!

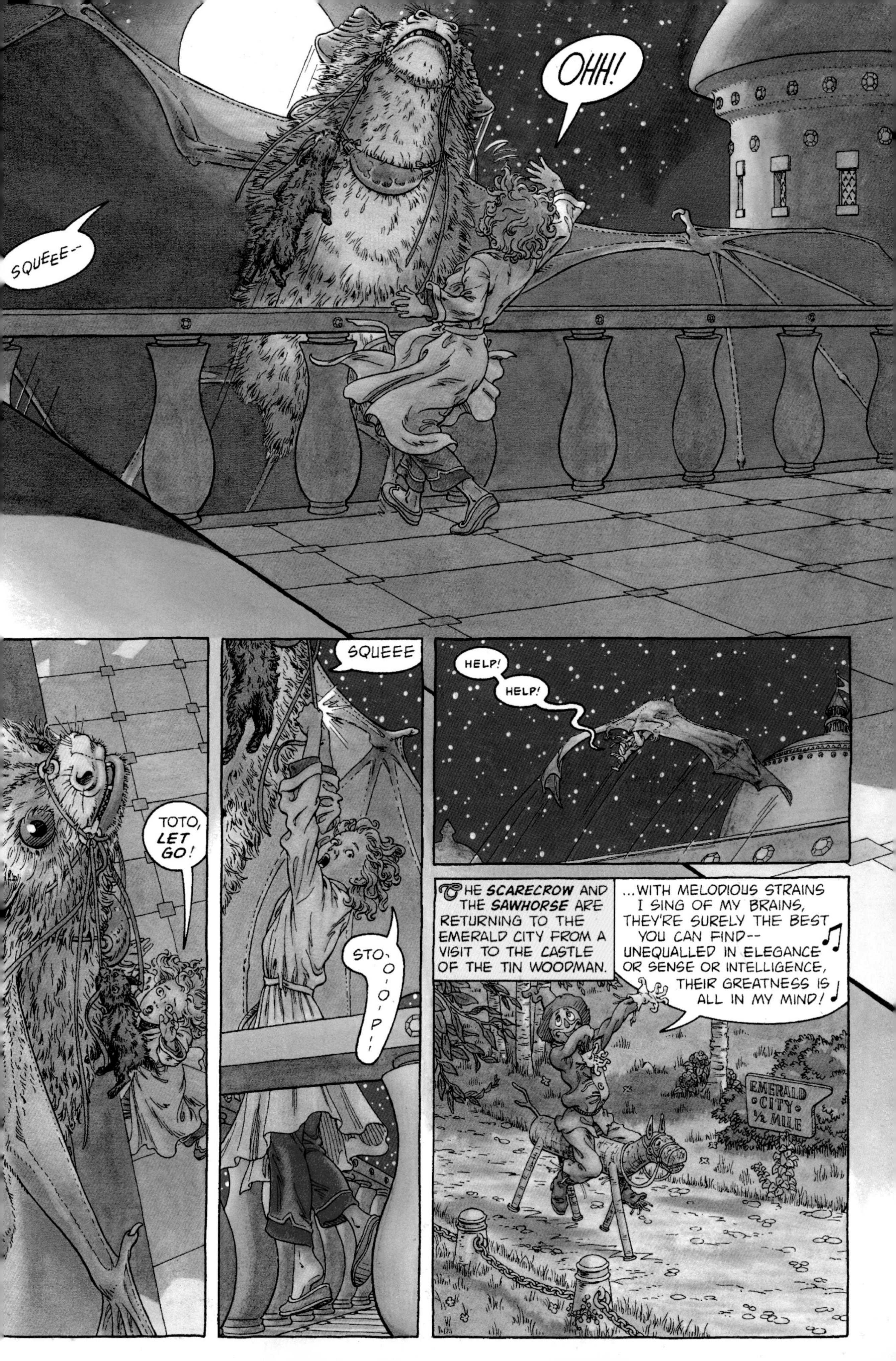

OHH!
SQUEEE--
TOTO, LET GO!
SQUEEE
STO-O-O-O-P!
HELP!
HELP!
THE SCARECROW AND THE SAWHORSE ARE RETURNING TO THE EMERALD CITY FROM A VISIT TO THE CASTLE OF THE TIN WOODMAN.
...WITH MELODIOUS STRAINS I SING OF MY BRAINS, THEY'RE SURELY THE BEST YOU CAN FIND-- UNEQUALLED IN ELEGANCE OR SENSE OR INTELLIGENCE, THEIR GREATNESS IS ALL IN MY MIND!
EMERALD CITY ½ MILE

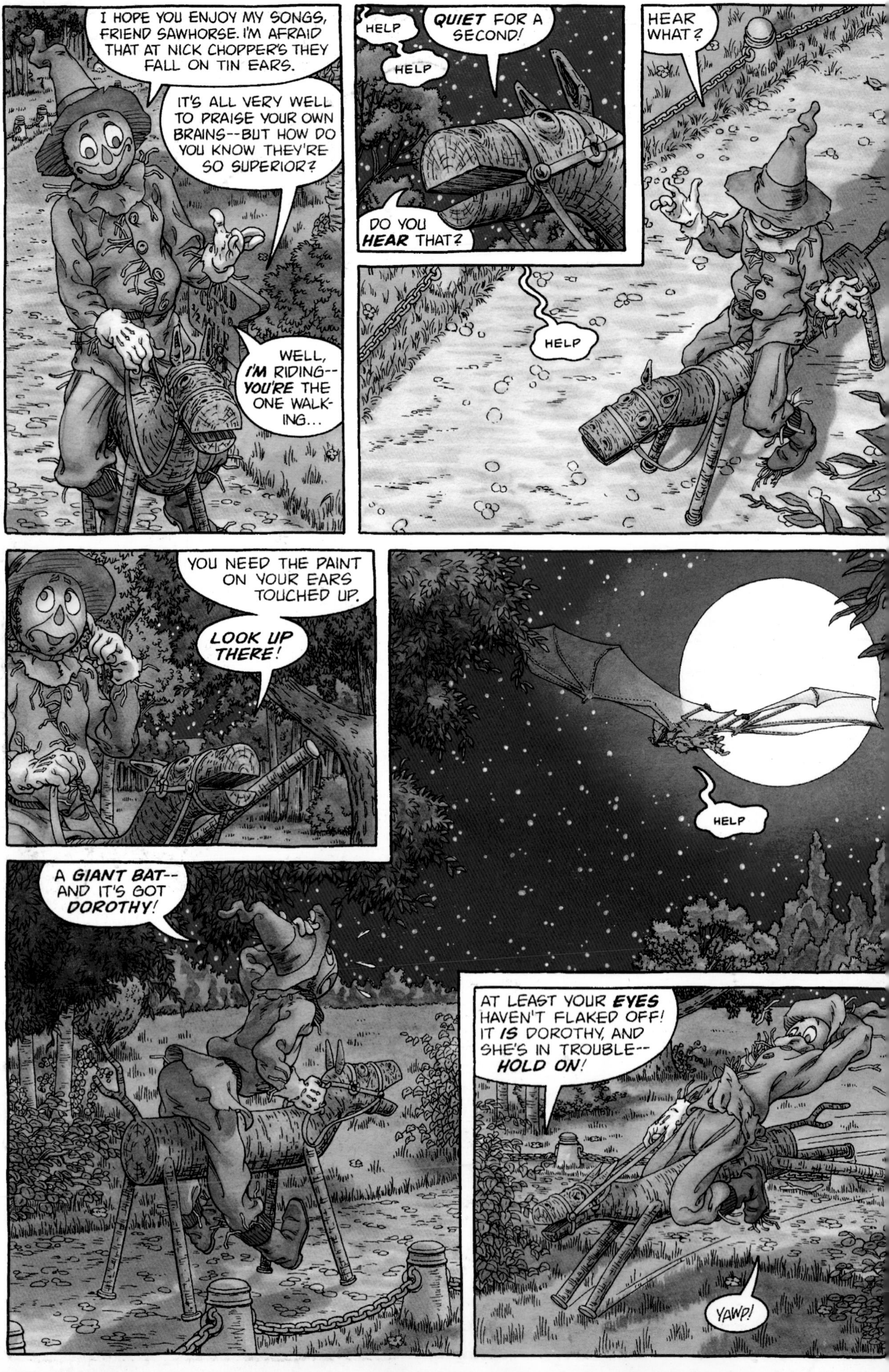
I HOPE YOU ENJOY MY SONGS, FRIEND SAWHORSE. I'M AFRAID THAT AT NICK CHOPPER'S THEY FALL ON TIN EARS.
IT'S ALL VERY WELL TO PRAISE YOUR OWN BRAINS--BUT HOW DO YOU KNOW THEY'RE SO SUPERIOR?
WELL, I'M RIDING--YOU'RE THE ONE WALKING...
HELP
HELP
QUIET FOR A SECOND!
DO YOU HEAR THAT?
HEAR WHAT?
HELP
YOU NEED THE PAINT ON YOUR EARS TOUCHED UP.
LOOK UP THERE!
HELP
A GIANT BAT--AND IT'S GOT DOROTHY!
AT LEAST YOUR EYES HAVEN'T FLAKED OFF! IT IS DOROTHY, AND SHE'S IN TROUBLE--HOLD ON!
YAWP!

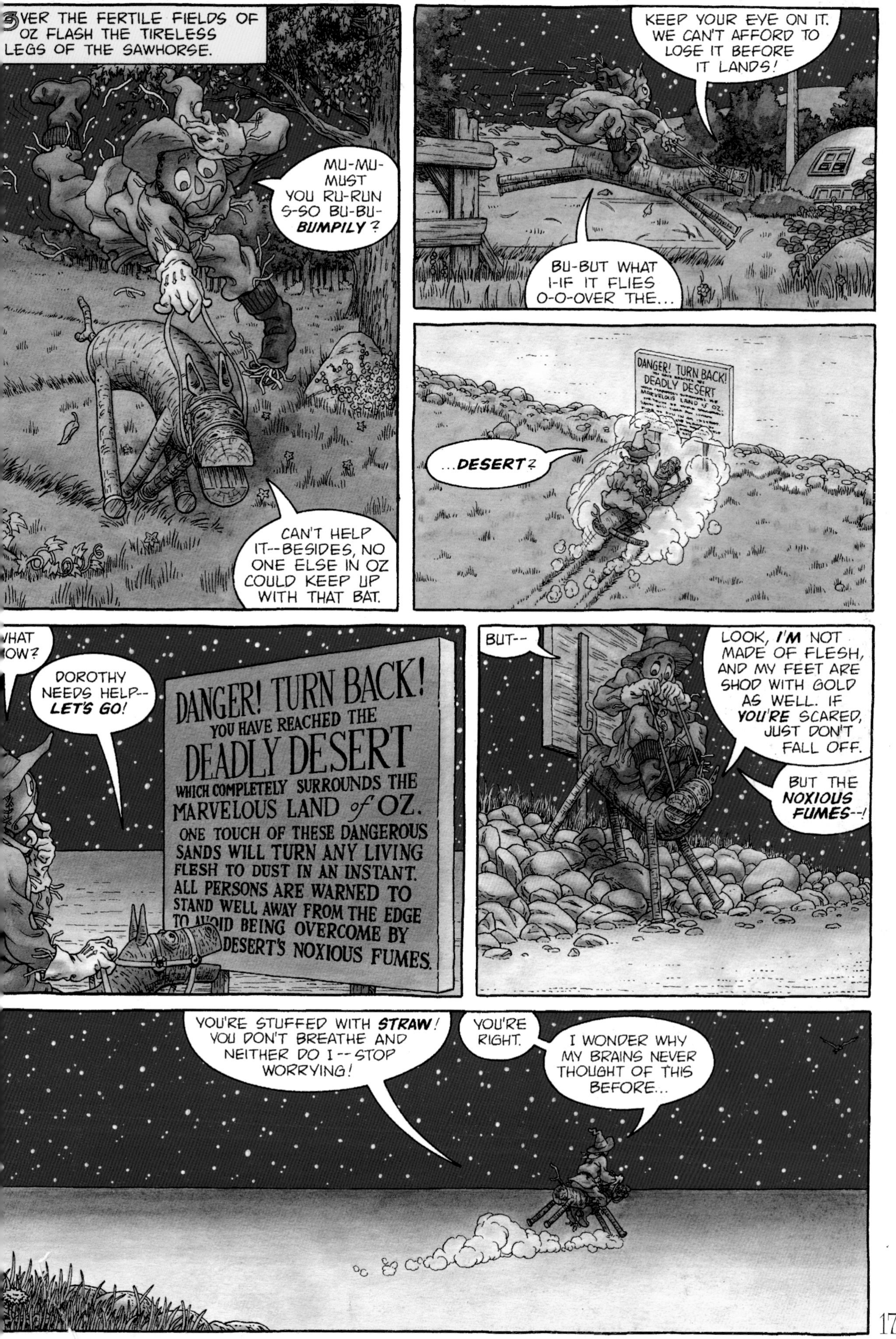

OVER THE FERTILE FIELDS OF OZ FLASH THE TIRELESS LEGS OF THE SAWHORSE.
MU-MU-MUST YOU RU-RUN S-SO BU-BU-BUMPILY?
CAN'T HELP IT--BESIDES, NO ONE ELSE IN OZ COULD KEEP UP WITH THAT BAT.
KEEP YOUR EYE ON IT. WE CAN'T AFFORD TO LOSE IT BEFORE IT LANDS!
BU-BUT WHAT I-IF IT FLIES O-O-OVER THE...
DANGER! TURN BACK! DEADLY DESERT
...DESERT?
WHAT NOW?
DOROTHY NEEDS HELP-- LET'S GO!
DANGER! TURN BACK! YOU HAVE REACHED THE DEADLY DESERT WHICH COMPLETELY SURROUNDS THE MARVELOUS LAND of OZ. ONE TOUCH OF THESE DANGEROUS SANDS WILL TURN ANY LIVING FLESH TO DUST IN AN INSTANT. ALL PERSONS ARE WARNED TO STAND WELL AWAY FROM THE EDGE TO AVOID BEING OVERCOME BY DESERT'S NOXIOUS FUMES.
BUT--
LOOK, I'M NOT MADE OF FLESH, AND MY FEET ARE SHOD WITH GOLD AS WELL. IF YOU'RE SCARED, JUST DON'T FALL OFF.
BUT THE NOXIOUS FUMES--!
YOU'RE STUFFED WITH STRAW! YOU DON'T BREATHE AND NEITHER DO I -- STOP WORRYING!
YOU'RE RIGHT.
I WONDER WHY MY BRAINS NEVER THOUGHT OF THIS BEFORE...

Chapter Three The Troll Queen

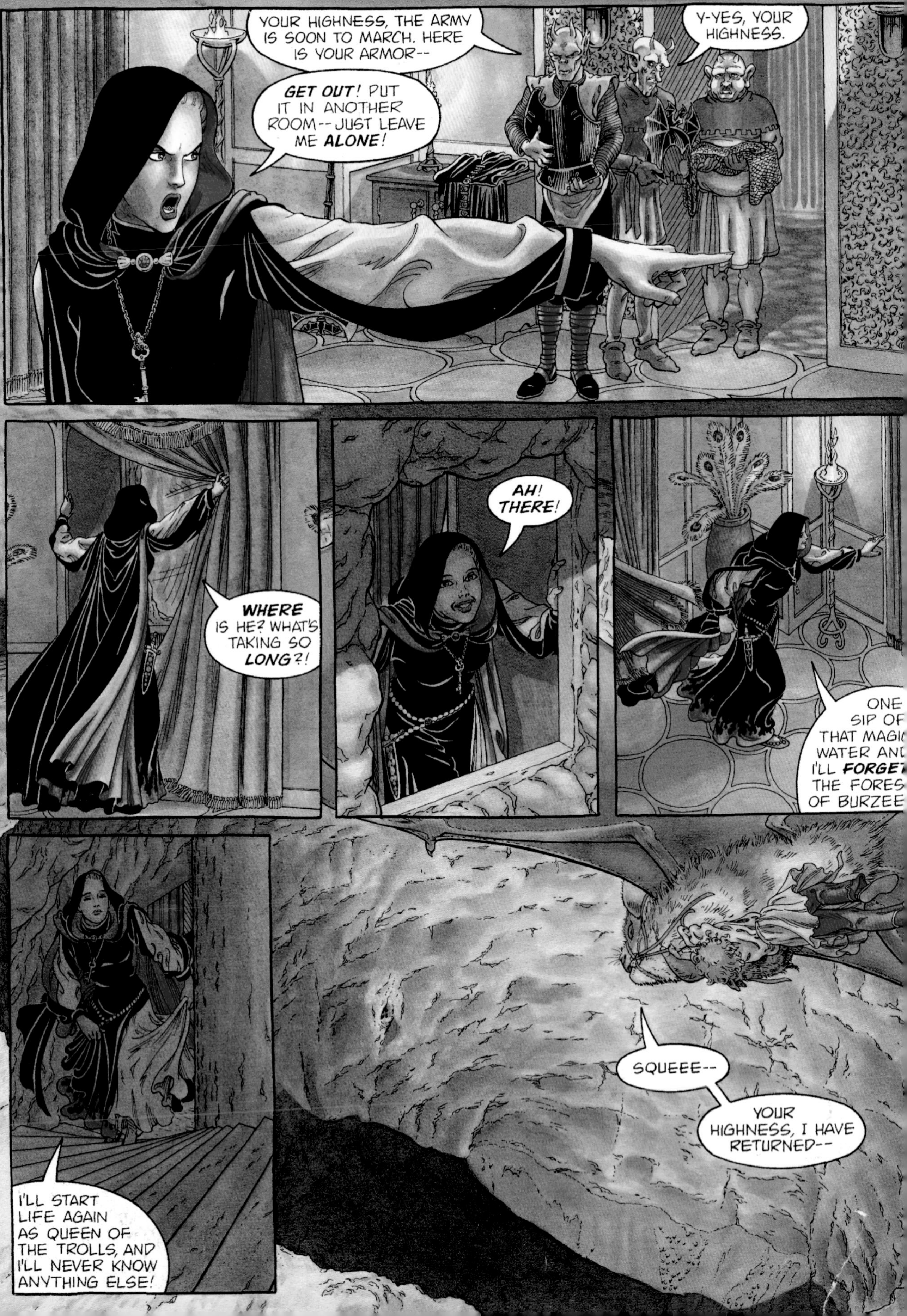
YOUR HIGHNESS, THE ARMY IS SOON TO MARCH. HERE IS YOUR ARMOR--
GET OUT! PUT IT IN ANOTHER ROOM--JUST LEAVE ME ALONE!
Y-YES, YOUR HIGHNESS.
WHERE IS HE? WHAT'S TAKING SO LONG?!
AH! THERE!
ONE SIP OF THAT MAGI WATER AN I'LL FORGE THE FORES OF BURZEE
I'LL START LIFE AGAIN AS QUEEN OF THE TROLLS, AND I'LL NEVER KNOW ANYTHING ELSE!
SQUEEE--
YOUR HIGHNESS, I HAVE RETURNED--

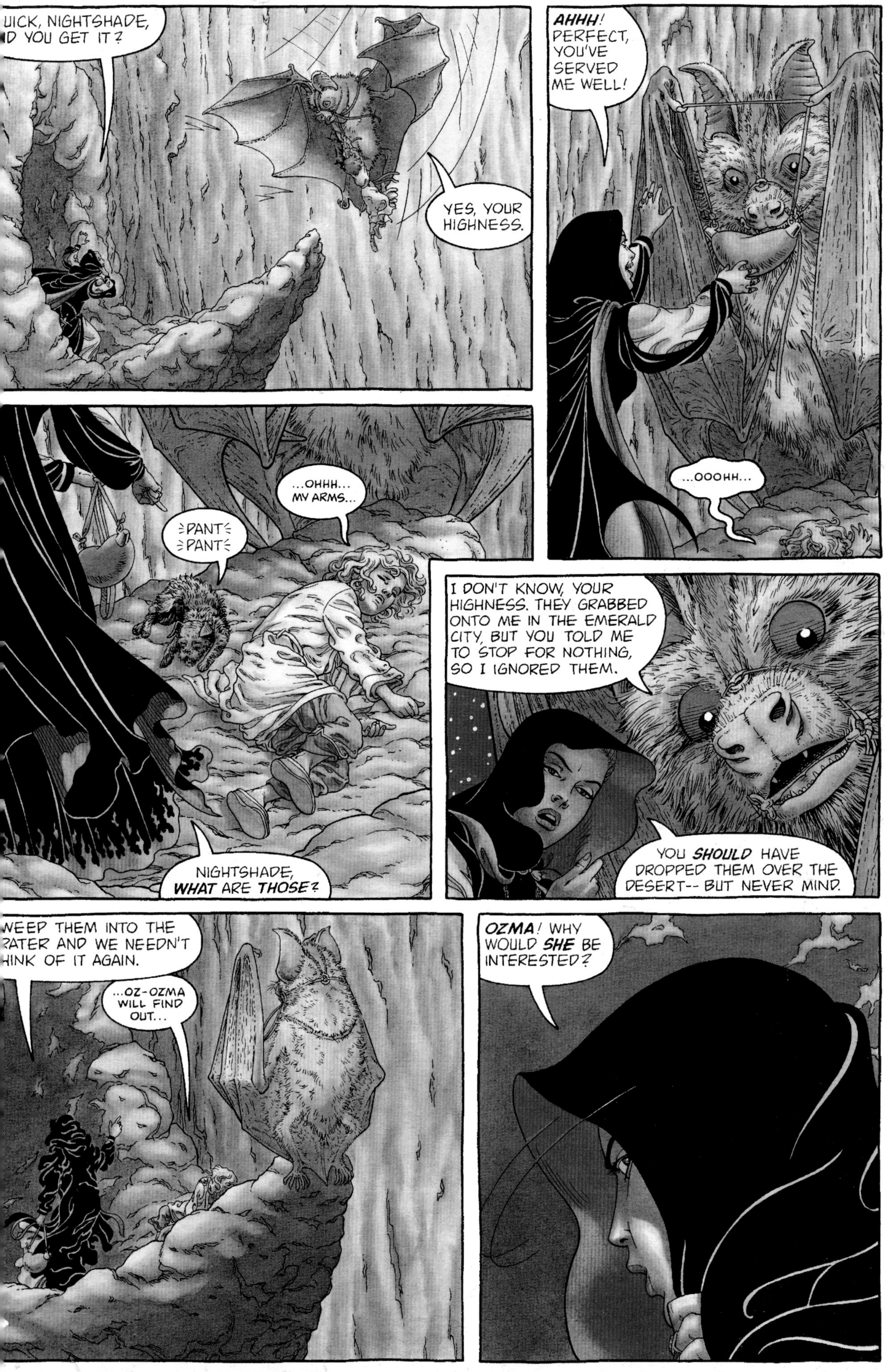
UICK, NIGHTSHADE,
D YOU GET IT?
YES, YOUR HIGHNESS.
AHHH! PERFECT, YOU'VE SERVED ME WELL!
...OOOHH...
...OHHH... MY ARMS...
PANT PANT
NIGHTSHADE, WHAT ARE THOSE?
I DON'T KNOW, YOUR HIGHNESS. THEY GRABBED ONTO ME IN THE EMERALD CITY, BUT YOU TOLD ME TO STOP FOR NOTHING, SO I IGNORED THEM.
YOU SHOULD HAVE DROPPED THEM OVER THE DESERT-- BUT NEVER MIND.
WEEP THEM INTO THE RATER AND WE NEEDN'T HINK OF IT AGAIN.
...OZ-OZMA WILL FIND OUT...
OZMA! WHY WOULD SHE BE INTERESTED?

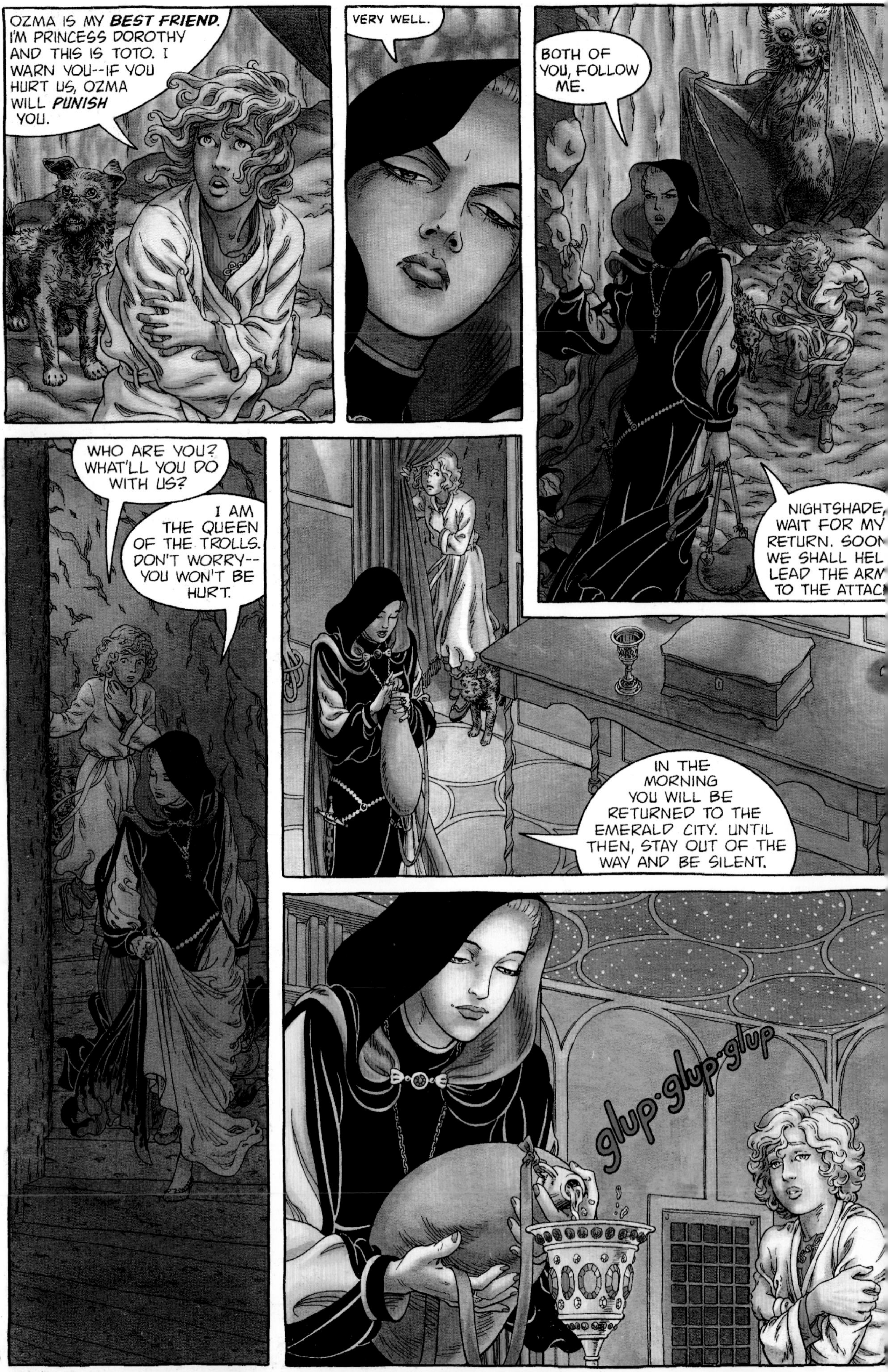
OZMA IS MY BEST FRIEND. I'M PRINCESS DOROTHY AND THIS IS TOTO. I WARN YOU--IF YOU HURT US, OZMA WILL PUNISH YOU.
VERY WELL.
BOTH OF YOU, FOLLOW ME.
NIGHTSHADE, WAIT FOR MY RETURN. SOON WE SHALL HEL LEAD THE ARM TO THE ATTAC
WHO ARE YOU? WHAT'LL YOU DO WITH US?
I AM THE QUEEN OF THE TROLLS. DON'T WORRY--YOU WON'T BE HURT.
IN THE MORNING YOU WILL BE RETURNED TO THE EMERALD CITY. UNTIL THEN, STAY OUT OF THE WAY AND BE SILENT.
glup-glup-glup

WHAT'S THAT... WATER?

WHY WOULD YOU GO ALL THE WAY TO THE *EMERALD CITY* TO STEAL-- *WATER*...?

I TOLD YOU TO BE *SILENT!*

--AHH-- THE *END* OF ALL MY TROUBLES...

STOP!

THAT'S THE *WATER OF OBLIVION!* ISN'T IT?

CURSE YOU!!

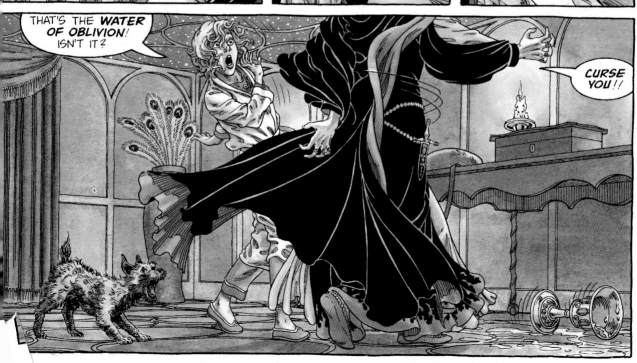

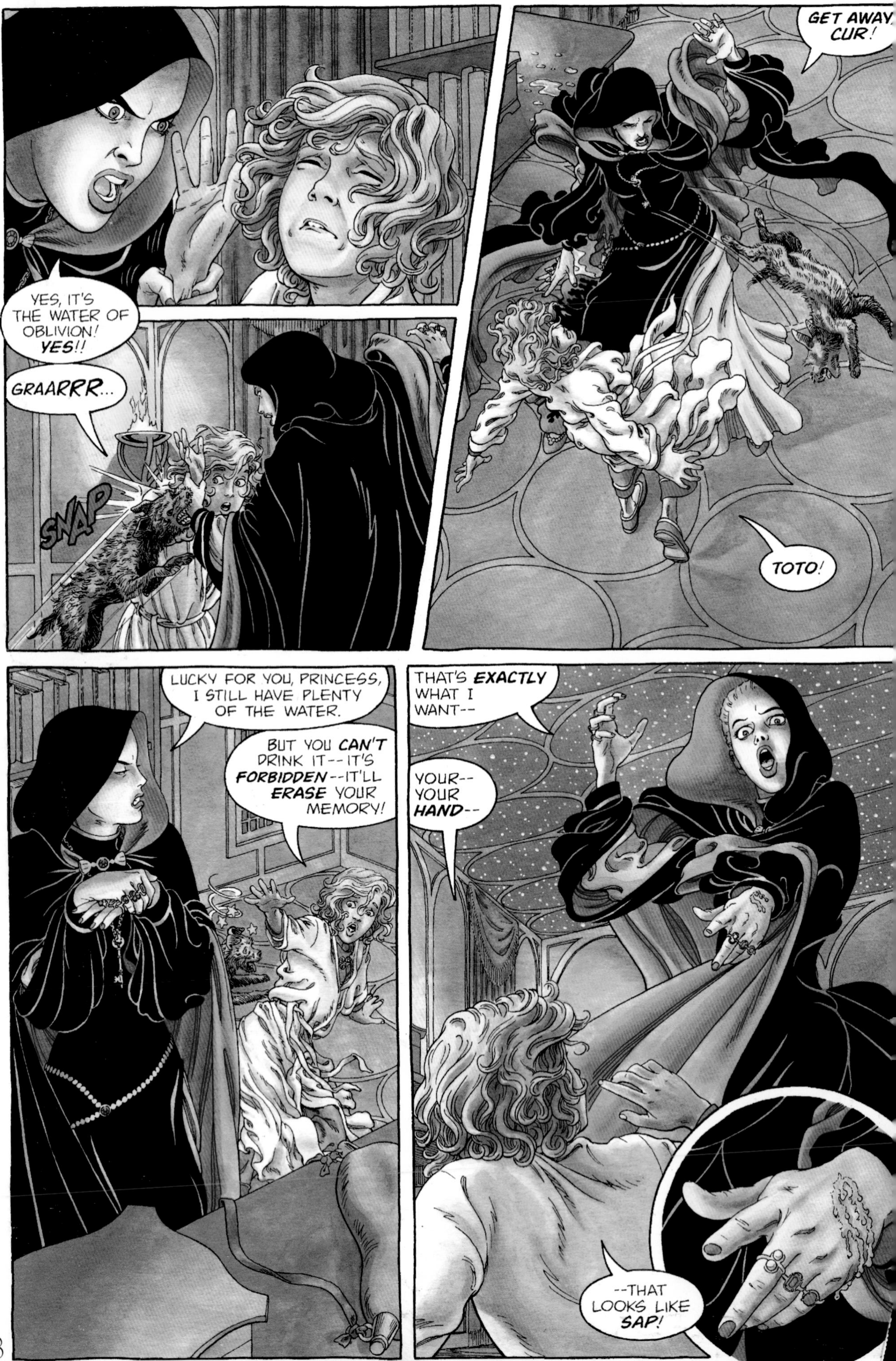

YES, IT'S THE WATER OF OBLIVION! YES!!
GRAARRR...
SNAP
GET AWAY, CUR!
TOTO!
LUCKY FOR YOU, PRINCESS, I STILL HAVE PLENTY OF THE WATER.
BUT YOU CAN'T DRINK IT--IT'S FORBIDDEN--IT'LL ERASE YOUR MEMORY!
THAT'S EXACTLY WHAT I WANT--
YOUR--YOUR HAND--
--THAT LOOKS LIKE SAP!

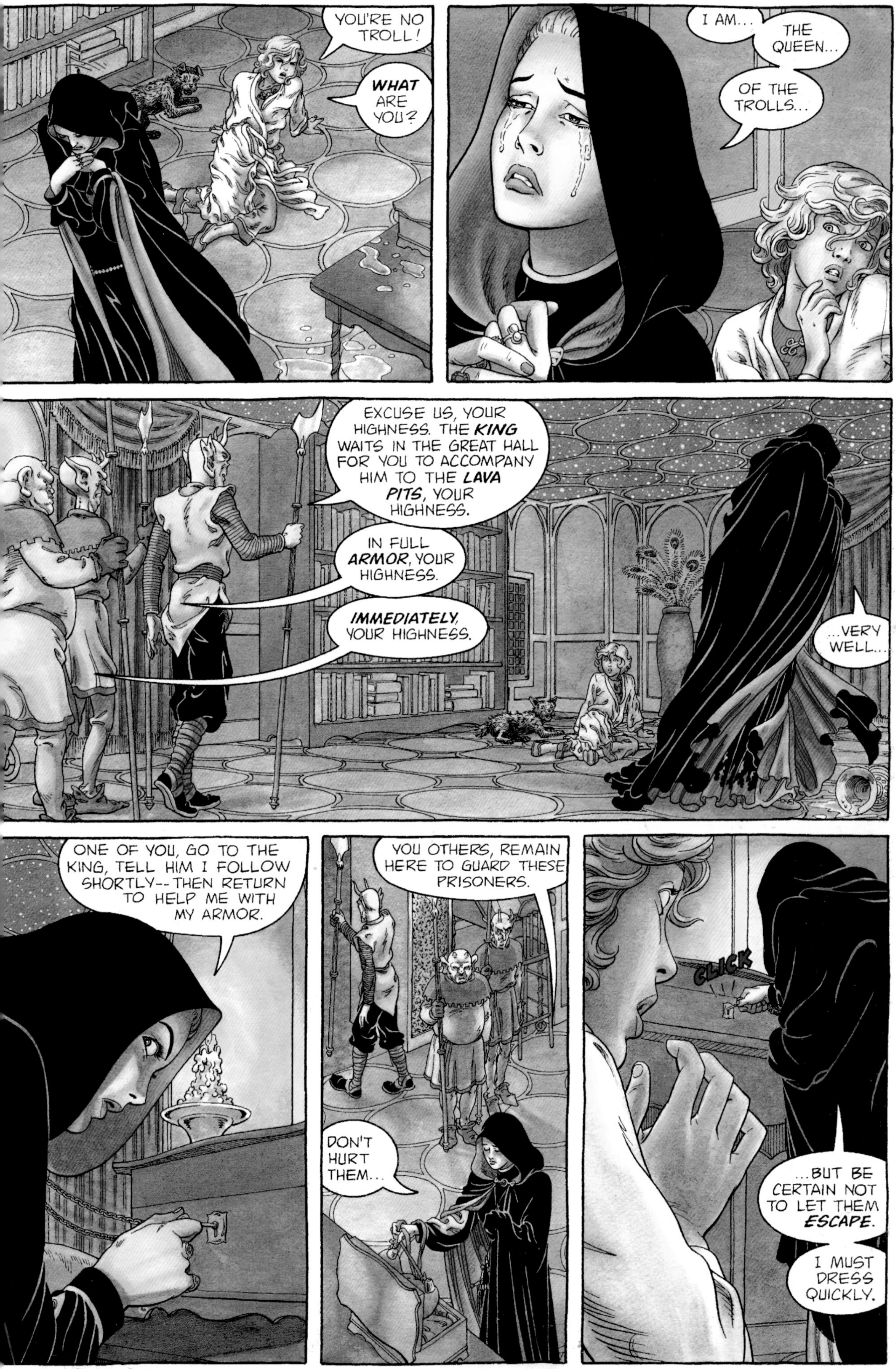
YOU'RE NO TROLL!
WHAT ARE YOU?
I AM...
THE QUEEN...
OF THE TROLLS...
EXCUSE US, YOUR HIGHNESS. THE KING WAITS IN THE GREAT HALL FOR YOU TO ACCOMPANY HIM TO THE LAVA PITS, YOUR HIGHNESS.
IN FULL ARMOR, YOUR HIGHNESS.
IMMEDIATELY, YOUR HIGHNESS.
...VERY WELL...
ONE OF YOU, GO TO THE KING, TELL HIM I FOLLOW SHORTLY--THEN RETURN TO HELP ME WITH MY ARMOR.
YOU OTHERS, REMAIN HERE TO GUARD THESE PRISONERS.
DON'T HURT THEM...
CLICK
...BUT BE CERTAIN NOT TO LET THEM ESCAPE.
I MUST DRESS QUICKLY.

Chapter Four In the Troll Tunne

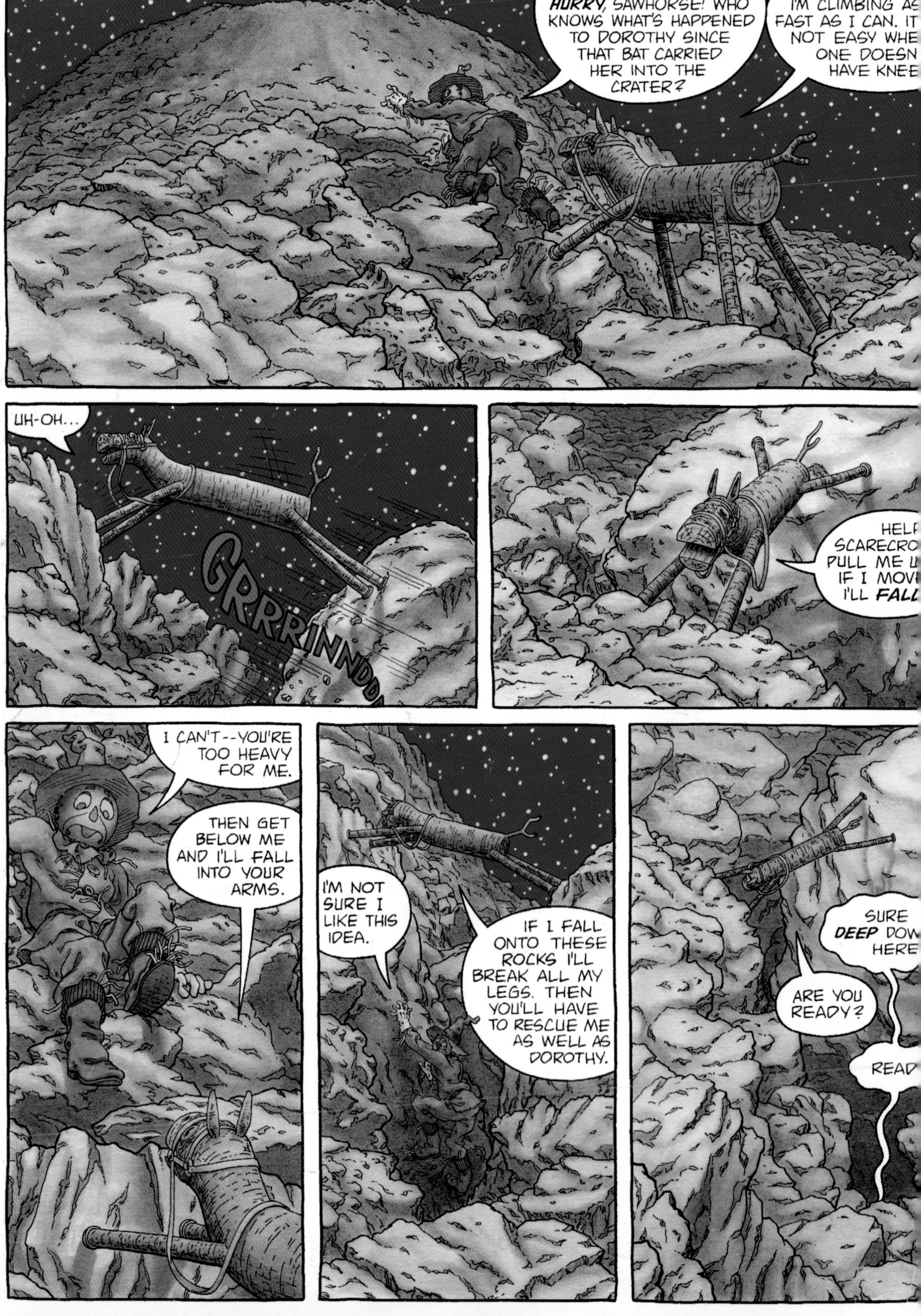

HURRY, SAWHORSE! WHO KNOWS WHAT'S HAPPENED TO DOROTHY SINCE THAT BAT CARRIED HER INTO THE CRATER?
I'M CLIMBING AS FAST AS I CAN. IT NOT EASY WHE ONE DOESN HAVE KNEE
UH-OH...
GRRRRINNNDD
HELP SCARECRO PULL ME U IF I MOVE I'LL FALL
I CAN'T--YOU'RE TOO HEAVY FOR ME.
THEN GET BELOW ME AND I'LL FALL INTO YOUR ARMS.
I'M NOT SURE I LIKE THIS IDEA.
IF I FALL ONTO THESE ROCKS I'LL BREAK ALL MY LEGS. THEN YOU'LL HAVE TO RESCUE ME AS WELL AS DOROTHY.
SURE DEEP DOW HERE
ARE YOU READY?
READ

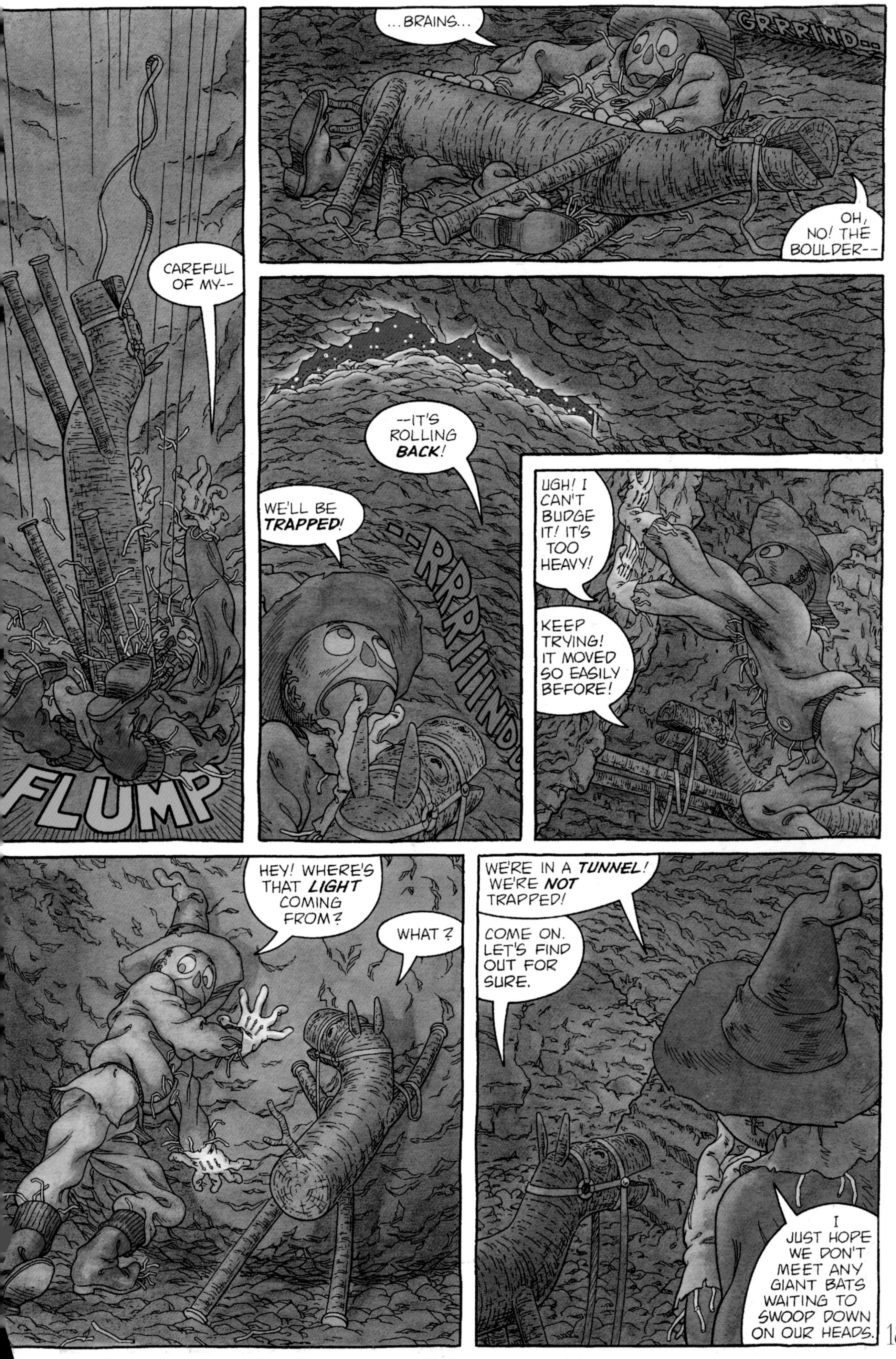
CAREFUL OF MY--
FLUMP
...BRAINS...
GRRRIND...
OH, NO! THE BOULDER--
--IT'S ROLLING BACK!
WE'LL BE TRAPPED!
--RRRIIINDD
UGH! I CAN'T BUDGE IT! IT'S TOO HEAVY!
KEEP TRYING! IT MOVED SO EASILY BEFORE!
HEY! WHERE'S THAT LIGHT COMING FROM?
WHAT?
WE'RE IN A TUNNEL! WE'RE NOT TRAPPED!
COME ON. LET'S FIND OUT FOR SURE.
I JUST HOPE WE DON'T MEET ANY GIANT BATS WAITING TO SWOOP DOWN ON OUR HEADS.

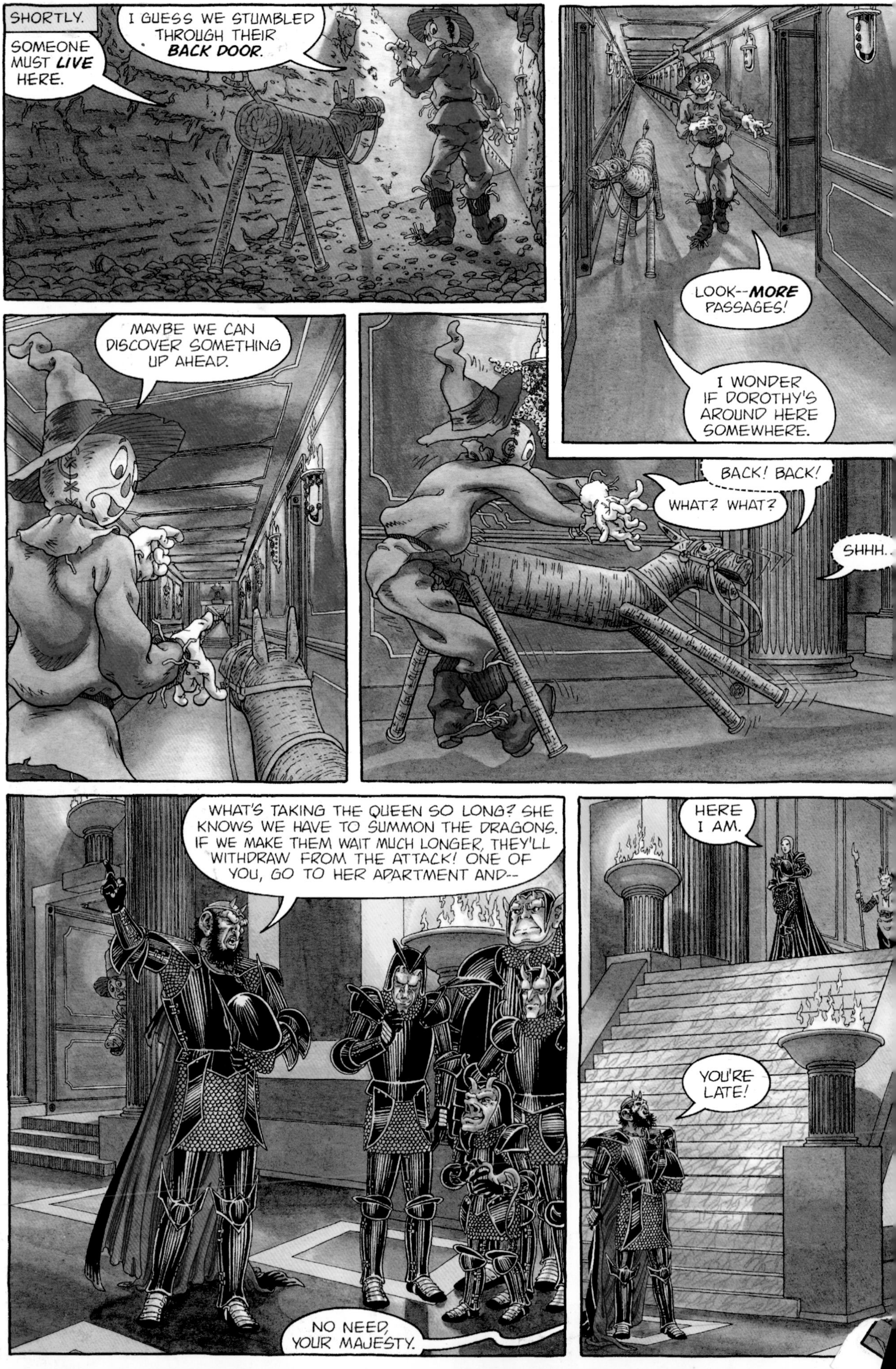
SHORTLY.
SOMEONE MUST LIVE HERE.
I GUESS WE STUMBLED THROUGH THEIR BACK DOOR.
LOOK--MORE PASSAGES!
I WONDER IF DOROTHY'S AROUND HERE SOMEWHERE.
MAYBE WE CAN DISCOVER SOMETHING UP AHEAD.
BACK! BACK!
WHAT? WHAT?
SHHH.
WHAT'S TAKING THE QUEEN SO LONG? SHE KNOWS WE HAVE TO SUMMON THE DRAGONS. IF WE MAKE THEM WAIT MUCH LONGER, THEY'LL WITHDRAW FROM THE ATTACK! ONE OF YOU, GO TO HER APARTMENT AND--
NO NEED, YOUR MAJESTY.
HERE I AM.
YOU'RE LATE!

FORGIVE ME, YOUR MAJESTY.

COME QUICKLY! DAWN DRAWS EVER NEARER, AND WE CANNOT SE-CRETLY ATTACK BURZEE *AFTER* SUNRISE.

THEY'RE COMING THIS WAY!

I WAS UNFORSEE-ABLY DELAYED.

HOW STRANGE THAT *TONIGHT* YOU MEET DELAY. YOU'RE NOT HAVING SECOND THOUGHTS I HOPE.

ECOND THOUGHTS, OUR MAJESTY? NOT *I*!

AT THIS MOMENT MY CONSUMING NEED IS TO *DESTROY* THAT FOREST AND WIPE THE WOOD-NYMPHS FROM MY MEMORY *FOREVER*!

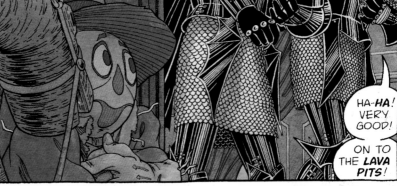

HA-*HA*! VERY GOOD!

ON TO THE *LAVA PITS*!

ARE THEY GONE?

YES, THEY TURNED DOWN ANOTHER HALLWAY.

AWP! WHAT'S THAT?

WOOOSH-SH

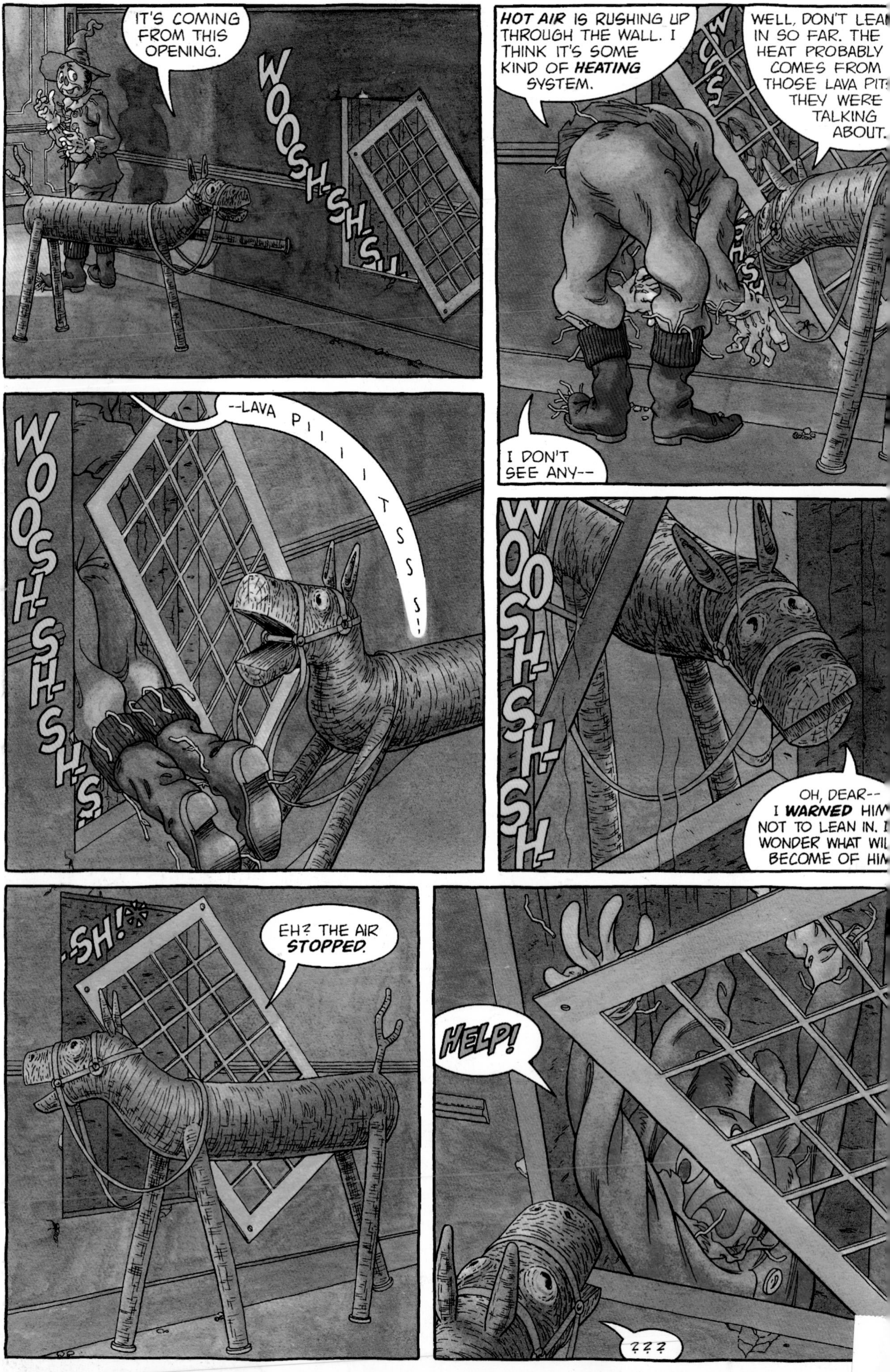
IT'S COMING FROM THIS OPENING.
WOOSH-SH-SH...
HOT AIR IS RUSHING UP THROUGH THE WALL. I THINK IT'S SOME KIND OF HEATING SYSTEM.
WELL, DON'T LEAN IN SO FAR. THE HEAT PROBABLY COMES FROM THOSE LAVA PITS THEY WERE TALKING ABOUT.
I DON'T SEE ANY--
--LAVA PIIIITSSSS!
WOOSH-SH-SH-SH-SH-SH
WOOSH-SH-SH-SH-
OH, DEAR-- I WARNED HIM NOT TO LEAN IN. I WONDER WHAT WILL BECOME OF HIM
-SH!
EH? THE AIR STOPPED.
HELP!
???

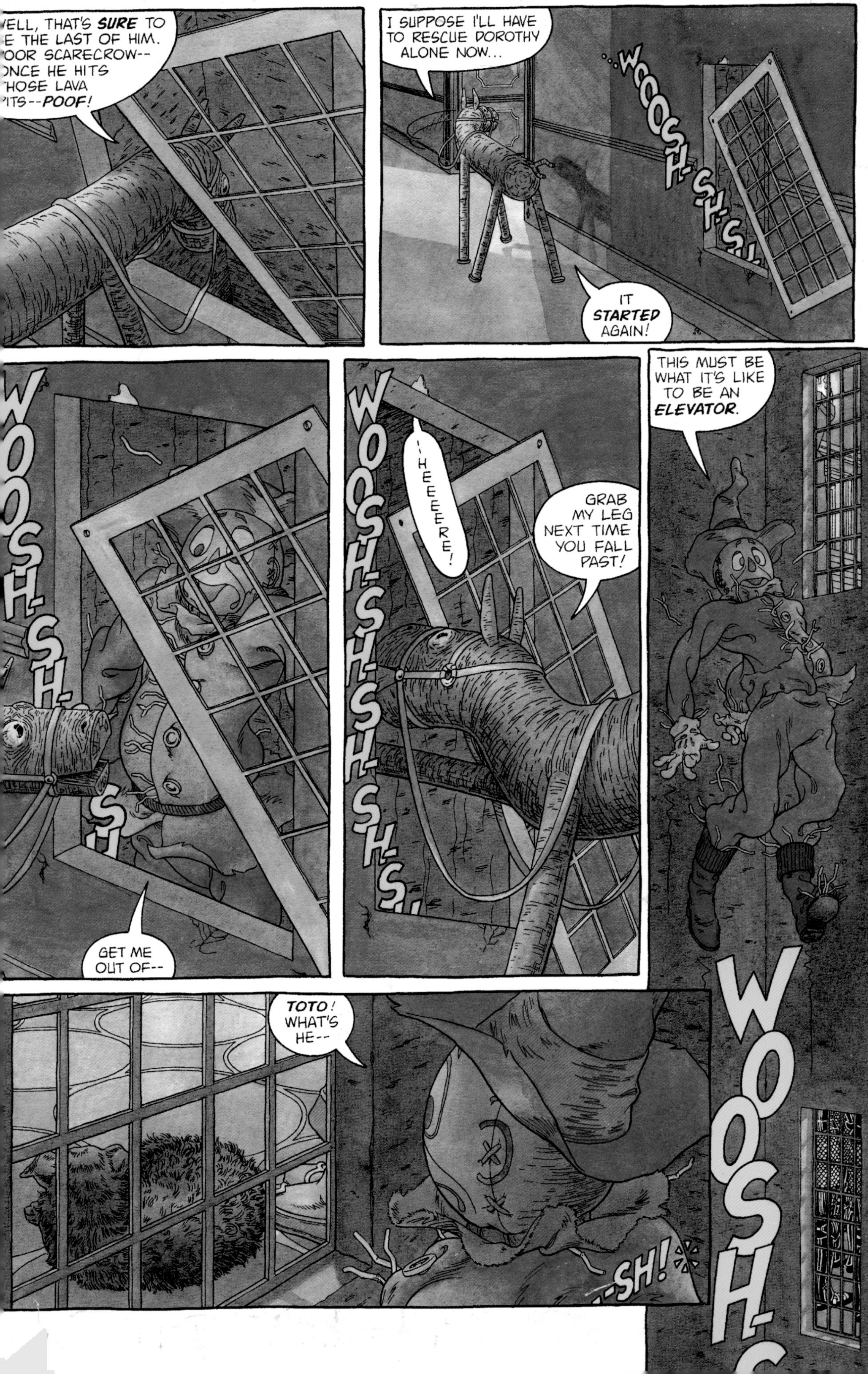

WELL, THAT'S SURE TO BE THE LAST OF HIM. POOR SCARECROW-- ONCE HE HITS THOSE LAVA PITS--POOF!
I SUPPOSE I'LL HAVE TO RESCUE DOROTHY ALONE NOW...
..WOOOSH-SH-SH..
IT STARTED AGAIN!
WOOSH-SH-SH-
GET ME OUT OF--
WOOSH-SH-SH-SH-SH-SH..
..HEEEERE!
GRAB MY LEG NEXT TIME YOU FALL PAST!
THIS MUST BE WHAT IT'S LIKE TO BE AN ELEVATOR.
WOOSH-
TOTO! WHAT'S HE--
-SH!

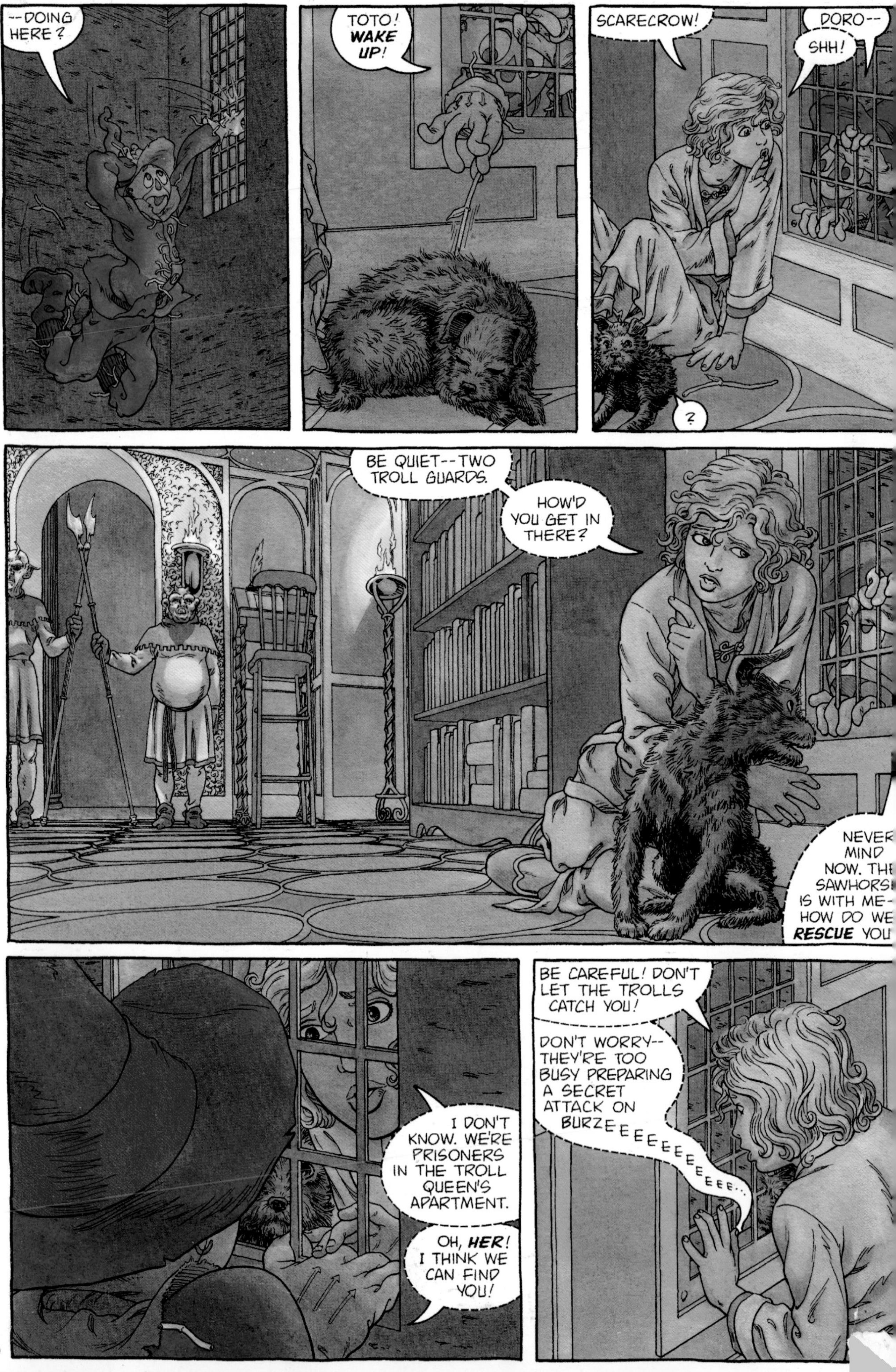
--DOING HERE?
TOTO! WAKE UP!
SCARECROW!
DORO--
SHH!
?
BE QUIET--TWO TROLL GUARDS.
HOW'D YOU GET IN THERE?
NEVER MIND NOW. THE SAWHORSE IS WITH ME-- HOW DO WE RESCUE YOU
I DON'T KNOW. WE'RE PRISONERS IN THE TROLL QUEEN'S APARTMENT.
OH, HER! I THINK WE CAN FIND YOU!
BE CAREFUL! DON'T LET THE TROLLS CATCH YOU!
DON'T WORRY-- THEY'RE TOO BUSY PREPARING A SECRET ATTACK ON BURZEEEEEEEEEEEE...

WHAT'S HAPPENED TO HIM? THE AIR CURRENT STOPPED AWHI--

SPLOP

WHO'RE YOU *TALKING* TO?

UH--MY *DOG*--

WELL, *DON'T!*

RZEE...? ISN'T HAT THE HUGE, LD FOREST FULL F MAGICAL EINGS I'VE EARD OZMA LK ABOUT? F THE ROLLS RE GOING O *ATTACK* THE FOREST...

DOROTHY! TOTO!

HUNH?

YII!

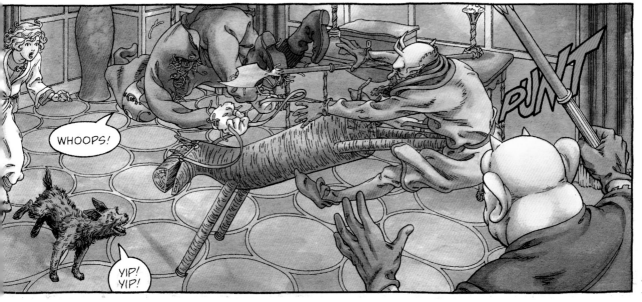

WHOOPS!

PUN!T

YIP! YIP!

187

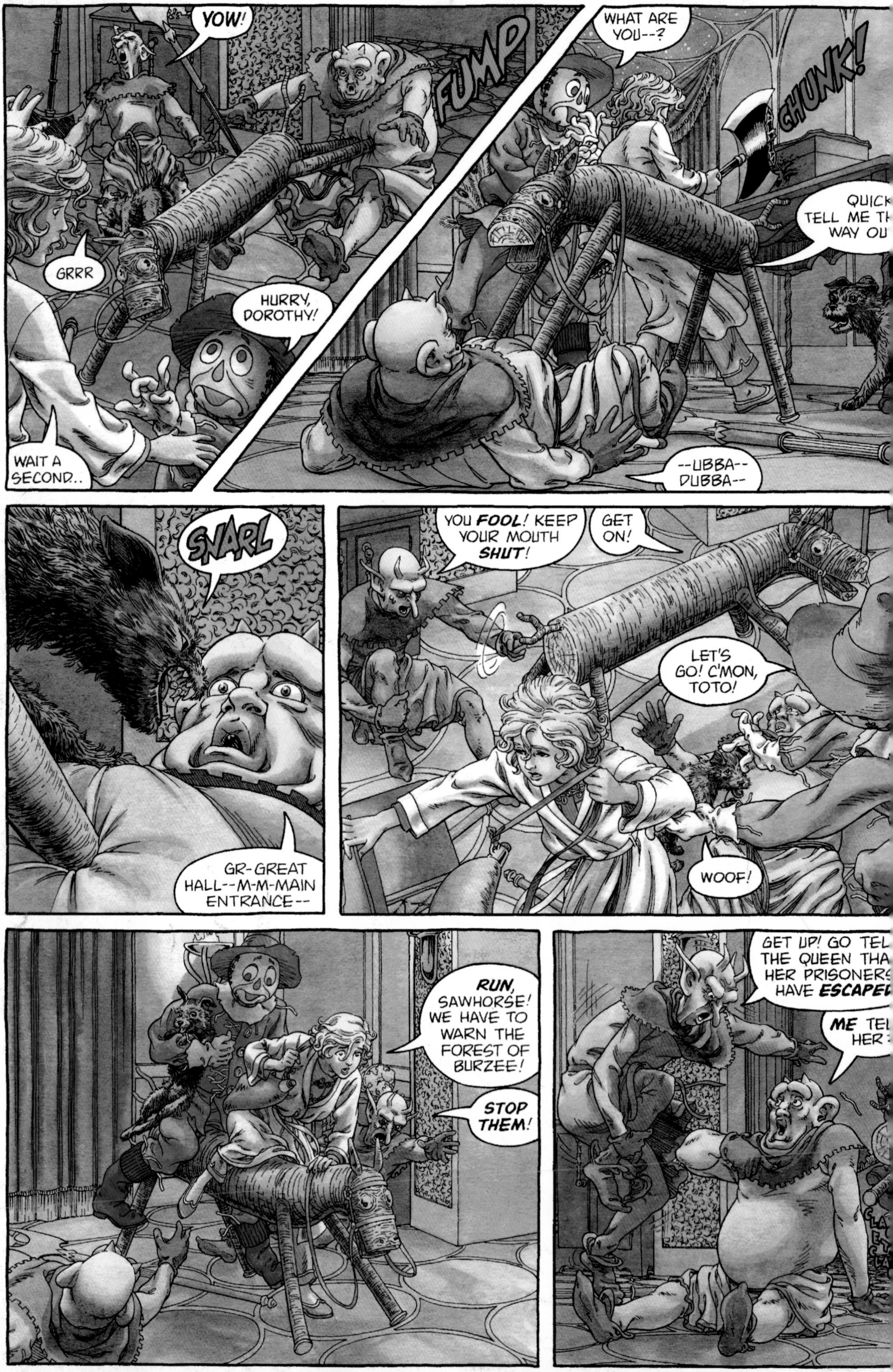
YOW!
FUMP
GRRR
HURRY, DOROTHY!
WAIT A SECOND..
WHAT ARE YOU--?
CHUNK!
QUICK TELL ME TH WAY OU
--UBBA-- DUBBA--
SNARL
GR-GREAT HALL--M-M-MAIN ENTRANCE--
YOU **FOOL**! KEEP YOUR MOUTH **SHUT**!
GET ON!
LET'S GO! C'MON, TOTO!
WOOF!
RUN, SAWHORSE! WE HAVE TO WARN THE FOREST OF BURZEE!
STOP THEM!
GET UP! GO TEL THE QUEEN THA HER PRISONERS HAVE **ESCAPED**
ME TEL HER

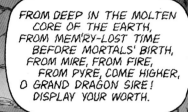

FROM DEEP IN THE MOLTEN CORE OF THE EARTH, FROM MEM'RY-LOST TIME BEFORE MORTALS' BIRTH, FROM MIRE, FROM FIRE, FROM PYRE, COME HIGHER, O GRAND DRAGON SIRE! DISPLAY YOUR WORTH.

THERE, THAT SHOULD DO IT.

YOU'RE *LATE*. I BEGAN TO THINK YOU'D CALLED OFF THE ATTACK.

BLORP BLORPLE BLUP

SHLORP

OF COURSE NOT--WE'VE *PLENTY* OF TIME BEFORE DAWN. I SIMPLY NEEDED TO CHECK MY PREPARA- TIONS...MUSTN'T BE TOO *HASTY*.

I UNDERSTAND--YOU TROLLS WANT TO BE CERTAIN OF *SUCCESS*-- CERTAIN THAT THE HATED WOOD-NYMPHS ARE *DESTROYED*.

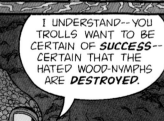

YES...THAT'S RIGHT...

THEN WHY DOES A WOOD-NYMPH STAND AMONG YOU?!

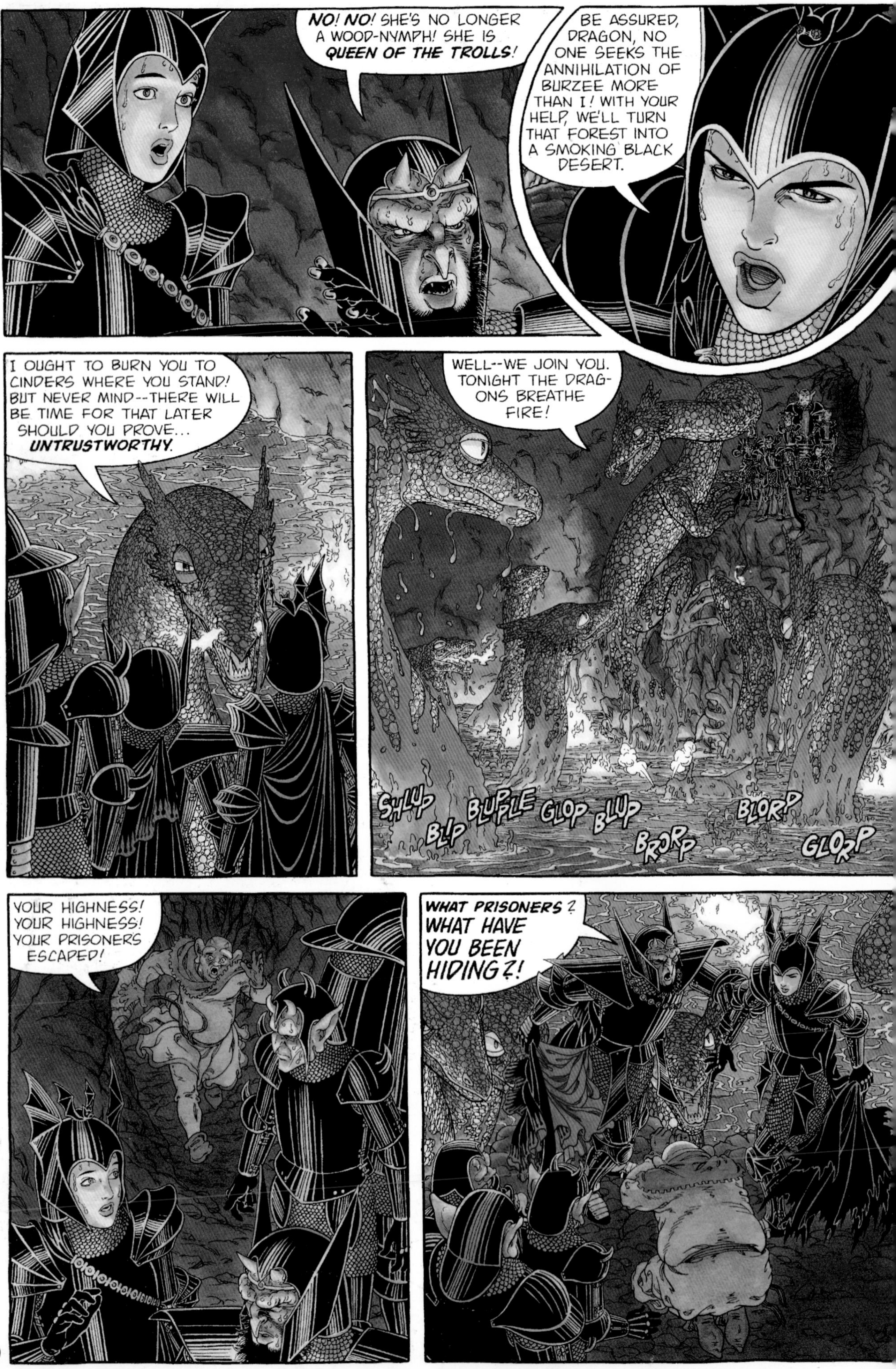
NO! NO! SHE'S NO LONGER A WOOD-NYMPH! SHE IS QUEEN OF THE TROLLS!
BE ASSURED, DRAGON, NO ONE SEEKS THE ANNIHILATION OF BURZEE MORE THAN I! WITH YOUR HELP, WE'LL TURN THAT FOREST INTO A SMOKING BLACK DESERT.
I OUGHT TO BURN YOU TO CINDERS WHERE YOU STAND! BUT NEVER MIND--THERE WILL BE TIME FOR THAT LATER SHOULD YOU PROVE... UNTRUSTWORTHY.
WELL--WE JOIN YOU. TONIGHT THE DRAGONS BREATHE FIRE!
SHLUP BLIP BLUPPLE GLOP BLUP BRORP BLORP GLORP
YOUR HIGHNESS! YOUR HIGHNESS! YOUR PRISONERS ESCAPED!
WHAT PRISONERS? WHAT HAVE YOU BEEN HIDING?!

...O-OZ PEOPLE-- I DIDN'T--

ELL ME.

OZ?! WHAT HAVE YOU DONE? IF OZMA KNOWS ABOUT THIS...! ARE YOU TRYING TO RUIN ALL MY PLANS--PLANS I'VE NURTURED SINCE THE DAY YOU KISSED ME AT THE EDGE OF THE FOREST!?!

WHAT...WHAT DO YOU MEAN...?

YOU HAVEN'T GUESSED? DO YOU THINK THAT WHAT'S HAPPENED TO YOU HAS BEEN BY CHANCE?

FOR YEARS I'VE BEEN TRYING TO LEARN THE WOOD-NYMPHS' SECRETS! WHO BETTER TO LEARN THEM FROM THAN A WOOD-NYMPH? LISTEN TO ME, MY QUEEN--I WAS THE ONE YOU KISSED--I, DISGUISED BY MAGIC! I WAS THAT MORTAL MAN!

OU--? THEN IT'S YOUR FAULT-- MY BANISHMENT--MY MORTALITY--ALL BECAUSE OF YOU!

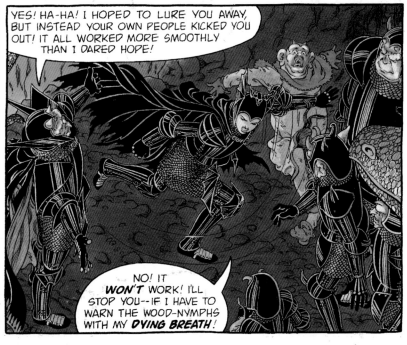

YES! HA-HA! I HOPED TO LURE YOU AWAY, BUT INSTEAD YOUR OWN PEOPLE KICKED YOU OUT! IT ALL WORKED MORE SMOOTHLY THAN I DARED HOPE!

NO! IT WON'T WORK! I'LL STOP YOU--IF I HAVE TO WARN THE WOOD-NYMPHS WITH MY DYING BREATH!

191

STOP HER!

YOU REALLY SHOULD HAVE LET ME BURN HER....

FORGET HER -- MY OFFICERS WILL TAKE CARE OF HER. ALL THAT MATTERS NOW IS THAT WE DESTROY THE FOREST. WE MARCH AT ONCE!

VERY GOOD. IF I DON'T BURN SOMETHING SOON I'LL EXPLODE!

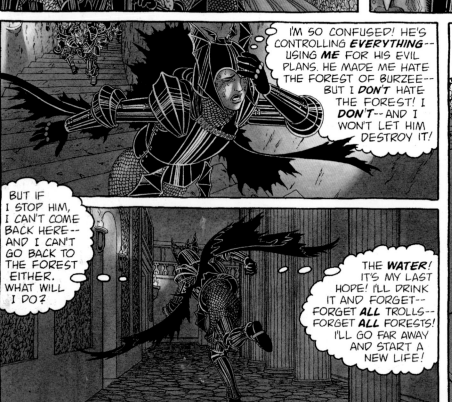

I'M SO CONFUSED! HE'S CONTROLLING EVERYTHING -- USING ME FOR HIS EVIL PLANS. HE MADE ME HATE THE FOREST OF BURZEE -- BUT I DON'T HATE THE FOREST! I DON'T -- AND I WON'T LET HIM DESTROY IT!

BUT IF I STOP HIM, I CAN'T COME BACK HERE -- AND I CAN'T GO BACK TO THE FOREST EITHER. WHAT WILL I DO?

THE WATER! IT'S MY LAST HOPE! I'LL DRINK IT AND FORGET -- FORGET ALL TROLLS -- FORGET ALL FORESTS! I'LL GO FAR AWAY AND START A NEW LIFE!

THE WATER! AT LEAST I HAVE THE WA--

NO!!

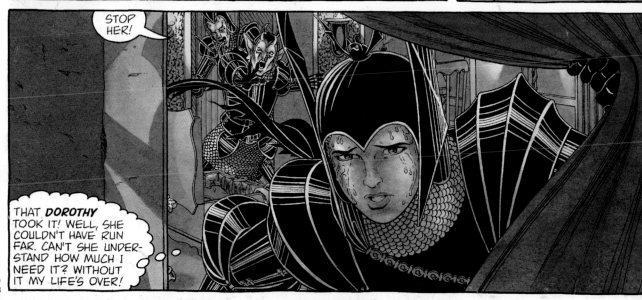

STOP HER!

THAT DOROTHY TOOK IT! WELL, SHE COULDN'T HAVE RUN FAR. CAN'T SHE UNDERSTAND HOW MUCH I NEED IT? WITHOUT IT MY LIFE'S OVER!

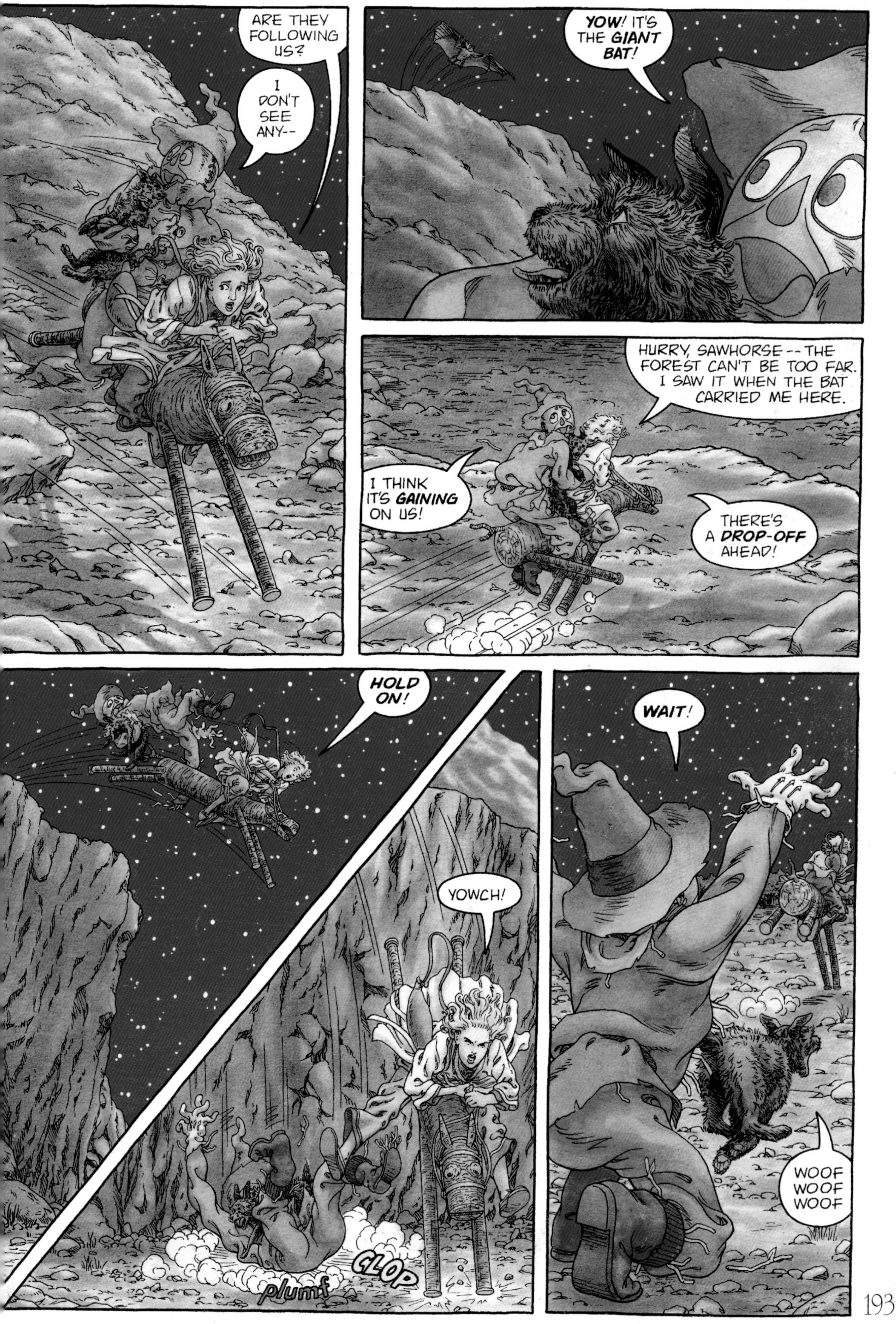
ARE THEY FOLLOWING US?
I DON'T SEE ANY--
YOW! IT'S THE GIANT BAT!
HURRY, SAWHORSE -- THE FOREST CAN'T BE TOO FAR. I SAW IT WHEN THE BAT CARRIED ME HERE.
I THINK IT'S GAINING ON US!
THERE'S A DROP-OFF AHEAD!
HOLD ON!
YOWCH!
CLOP
plumf
WAIT!
WOOF WOOF WOOF

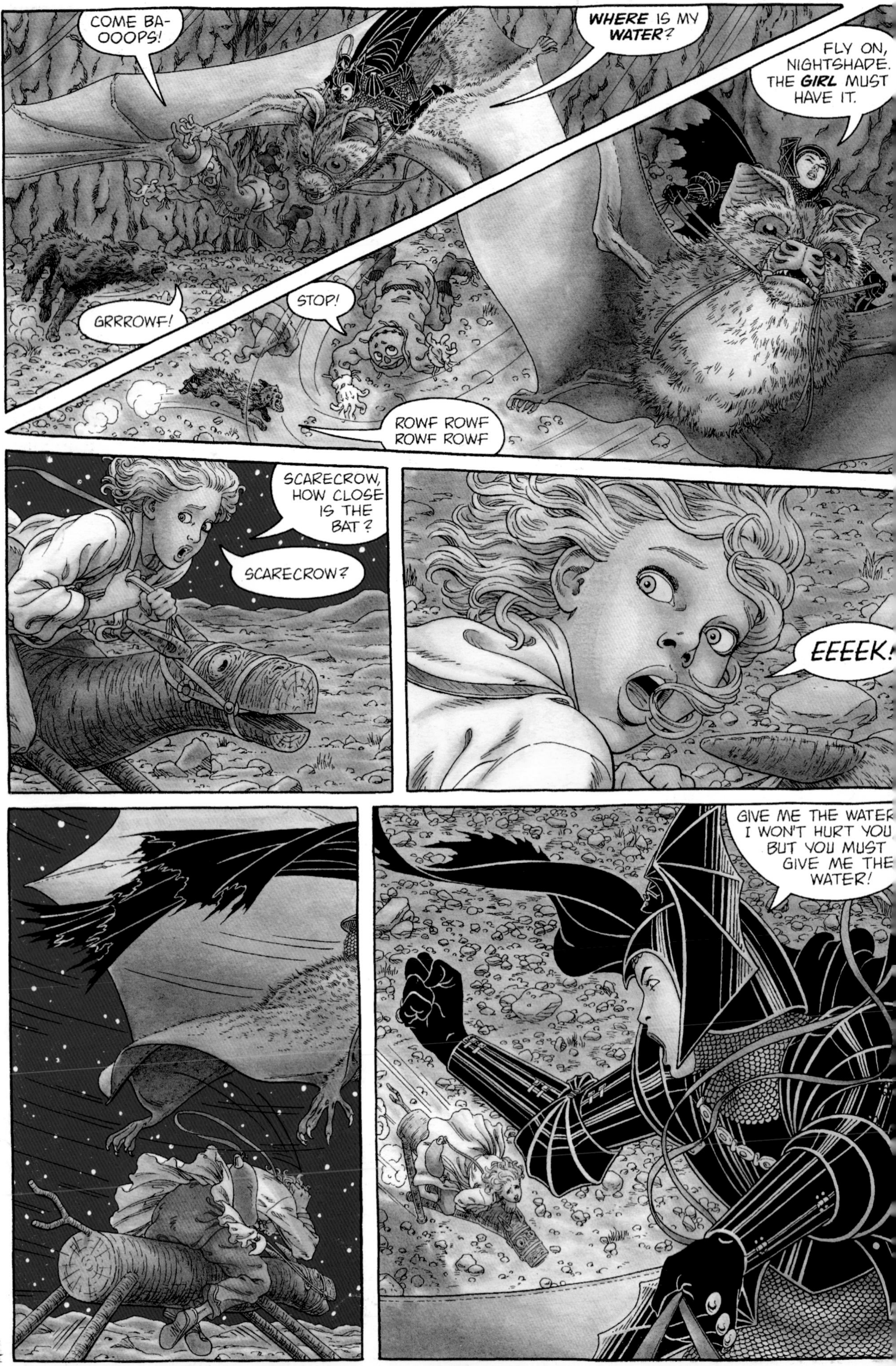
COME BA-
OOOPS!
WHERE IS MY
WATER?
FLY ON,
NIGHTSHADE.
THE GIRL MUST
HAVE IT.
GRRROWF!
STOP!
ROWF ROWF
ROWF ROWF
SCARECROW,
HOW CLOSE
IS THE
BAT?
SCARECROW?
EEEEK!
GIVE ME THE WATER
I WON'T HURT YOU
BUT YOU MUST
GIVE ME THE
WATER!

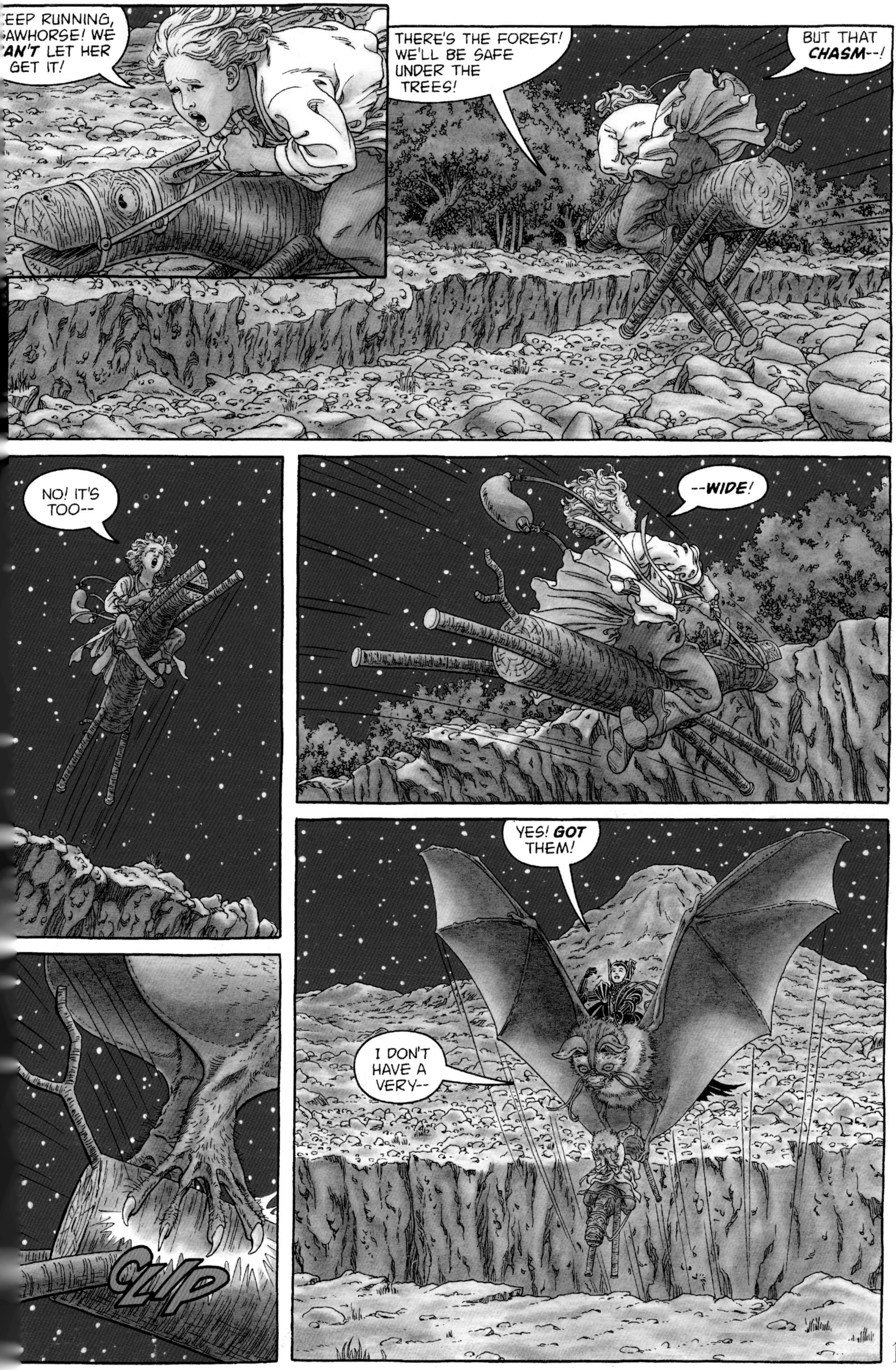

EEP RUNNING, AWHORSE! WE AN'T LET HER GET IT!
THERE'S THE FOREST! WE'LL BE SAFE UNDER THE TREES!
BUT THAT **CHASM**--!
NO! IT'S TOO--
--**WIDE**!
YES! **GOT** THEM!
I DON'T HAVE A VERY--
CLIP

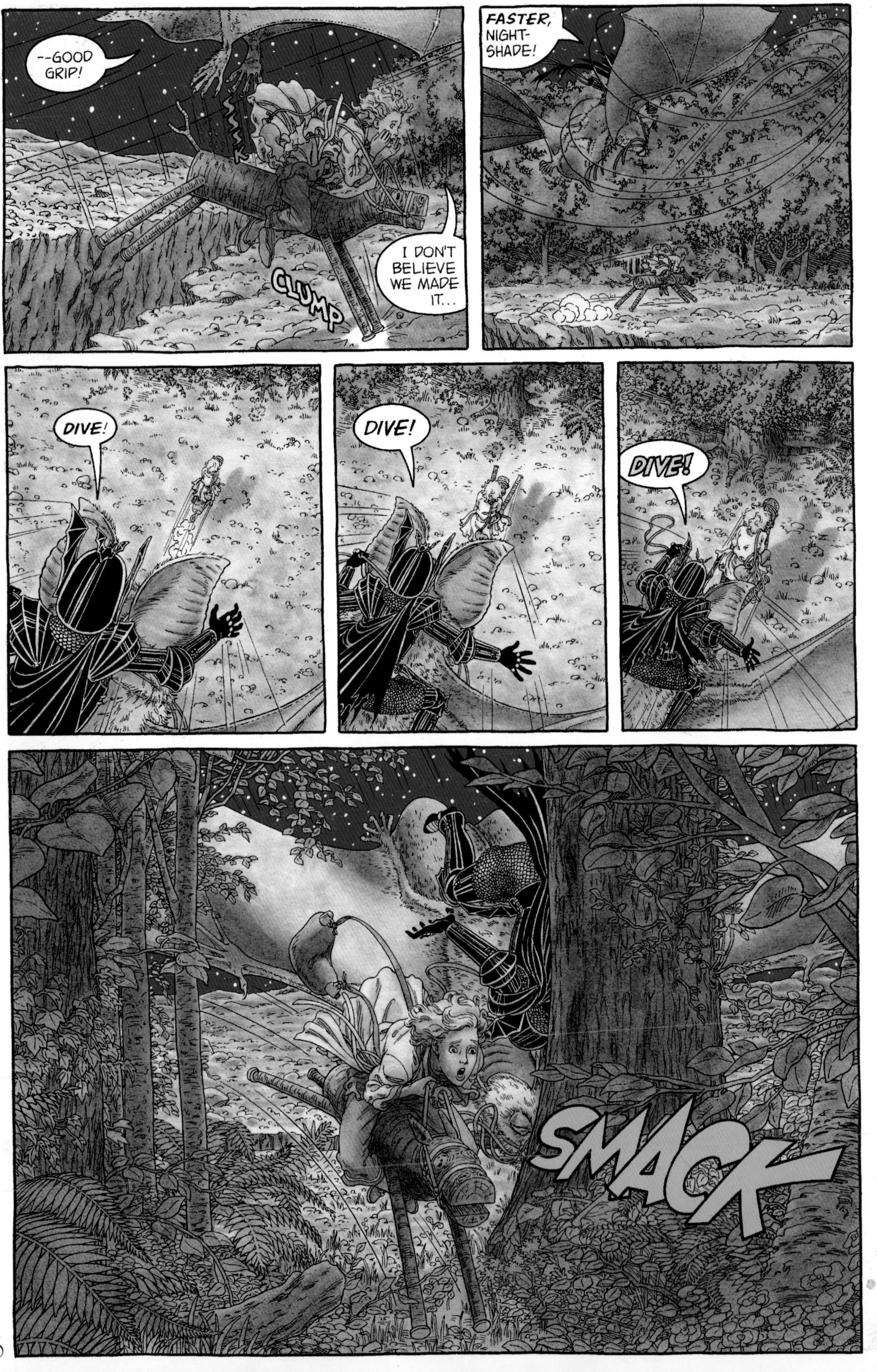
--GOOD GRIP!
SSSK
I DON'T BELIEVE WE MADE IT...
CLUMP
FASTER, NIGHT-SHADE!
DIVE!
DIVE!
DIVE!
SMACK

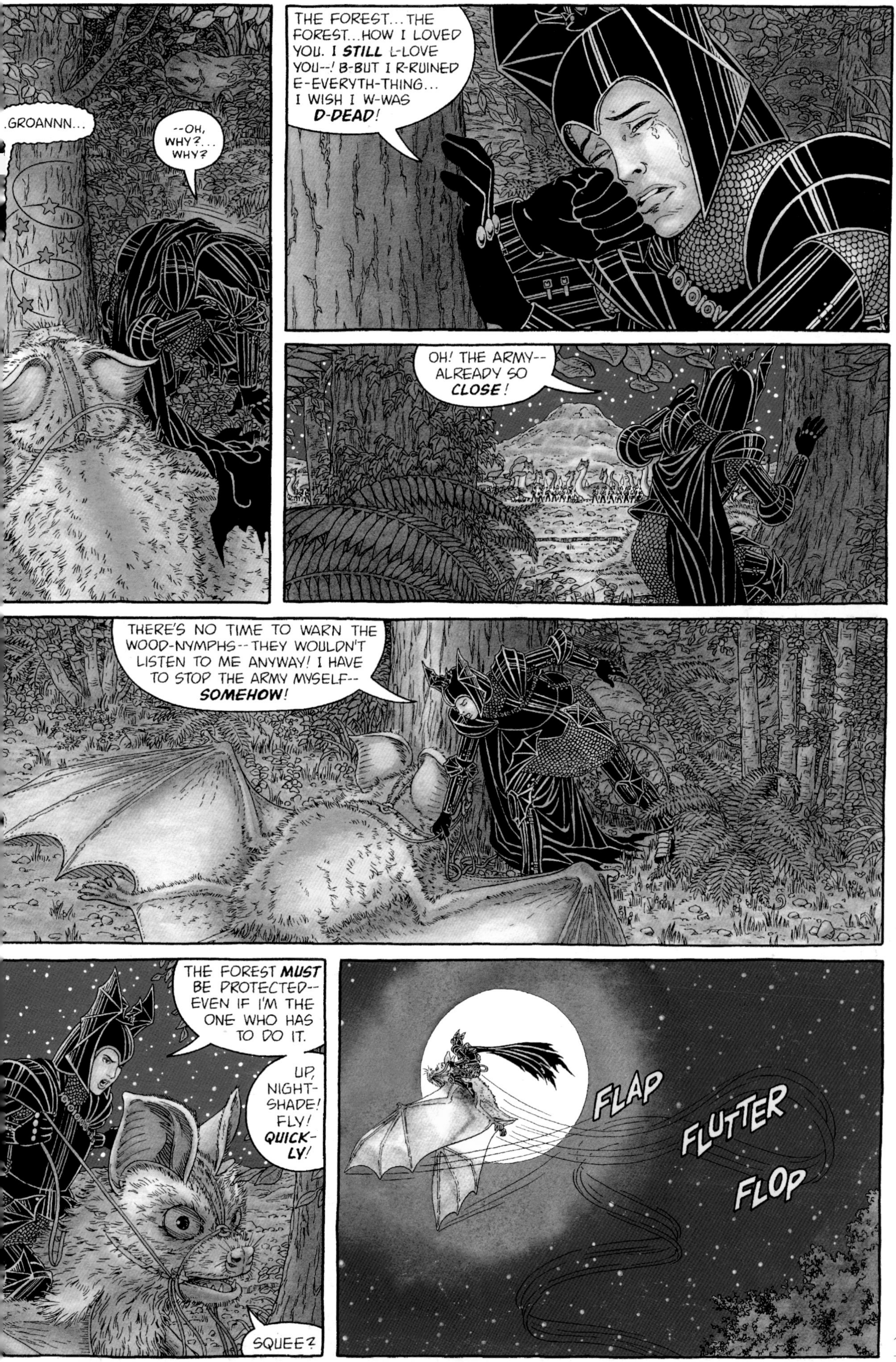
..GROANNN...
--OH, WHY?... WHY?
THE FOREST... THE FOREST... HOW I LOVED YOU. I STILL L-LOVE YOU--! B-BUT I R-RUINED E-EVERYTH-THING... I WISH I W-WAS D-DEAD!
OH! THE ARMY-- ALREADY SO CLOSE!
THERE'S NO TIME TO WARN THE WOOD-NYMPHS--THEY WOULDN'T LISTEN TO ME ANYWAY! I HAVE TO STOP THE ARMY MYSELF-- SOMEHOW!
THE FOREST MUST BE PROTECTED-- EVEN IF I'M THE ONE WHO HAS TO DO IT.
UP, NIGHT-SHADE! FLY! QUICK-LY!
SQUEE?
FLAP
FLUTTER
FLOP

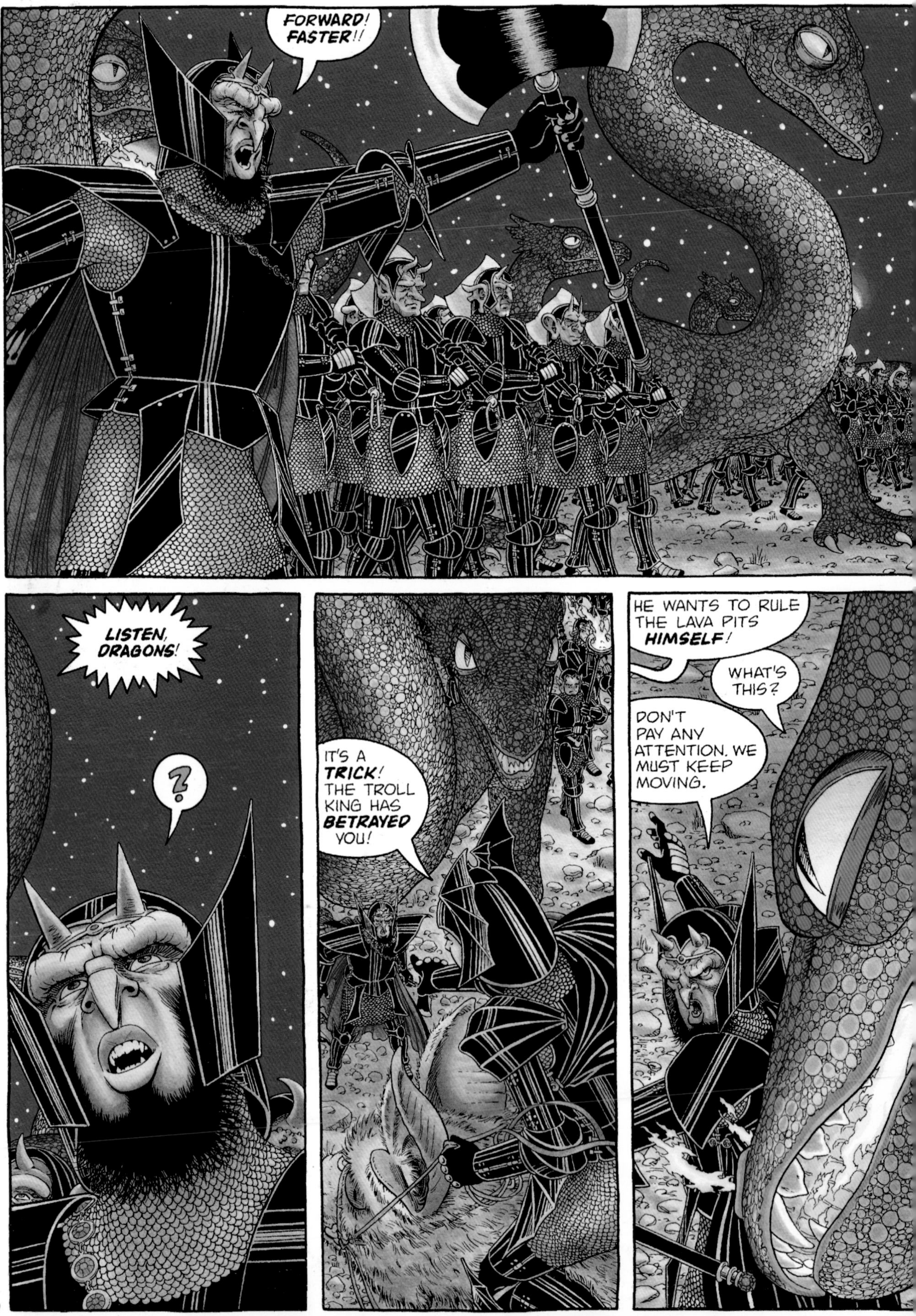
FORWARD! FASTER!!
LISTEN, DRAGONS!
?
IT'S A TRICK! THE TROLL KING HAS BETRAYED YOU!
HE WANTS TO RULE THE LAVA PITS HIMSELF!
WHAT'S THIS?
DON'T PAY ANY ATTENTION. WE MUST KEEP MOVING.

HE'S **LURING** YOU TO BURZEE TO BE **DESTROYED** BY THE WOOD-NYMPHS!

THAT'S NON-SENSE!

THE WOOD-NYMPHS DO HAVE POWERFUL MAGIC, DON'T THEY?

I MAY BE MISTAKEN-- YOU ALL LOOK THE SAME TO ME-- BUT ISN'T THAT THE QUEEN OF THE TROLLS?

ES--SHE **WAS**. UT SHE'S GONE RAZY! **YOU** EARD HER ACK IN THE AVERN.

EEP OW--DAWN'S OT FAR OFF.

WAIT A MOMENT, YOU SEEM A LITTLE TOO **EAGER**...

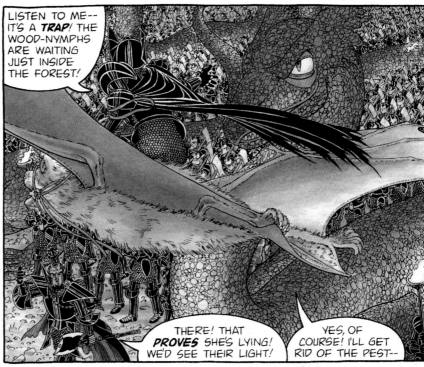

LISTEN TO ME-- IT'S A **TRAP**! THE WOOD-NYMPHS ARE WAITING JUST INSIDE THE FOREST!

THERE! THAT **PROVES** SHE'S LYING! WE'D SEE THEIR LIGHT!

YES, OF COURSE! I'LL GET RID OF THE PEST--

WOOOSH

SQUEEE-

OH, NIGHT-SHADE, NIGHT-SHADE, WHAT CAN I DO? THEY'RE STILL ADVANCING.

199

THAT FELT GOOD!

WHAT'S THAT GLOW?

IT CAN'T BE DAWN YET--

THERE THEY ARE, YOUR MAJESTY.

THE WOOD-NYMPHS!

IT **IS** A TRAP! **TRAITOR**

NO!

FWOOM

Krakle

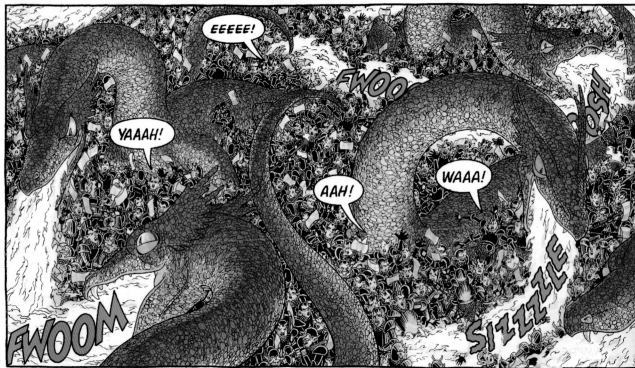

EEEEE!

YAAAH!

AAH!

WAAA!

FWOO

OSH

FWOOM

SIZZZZLE

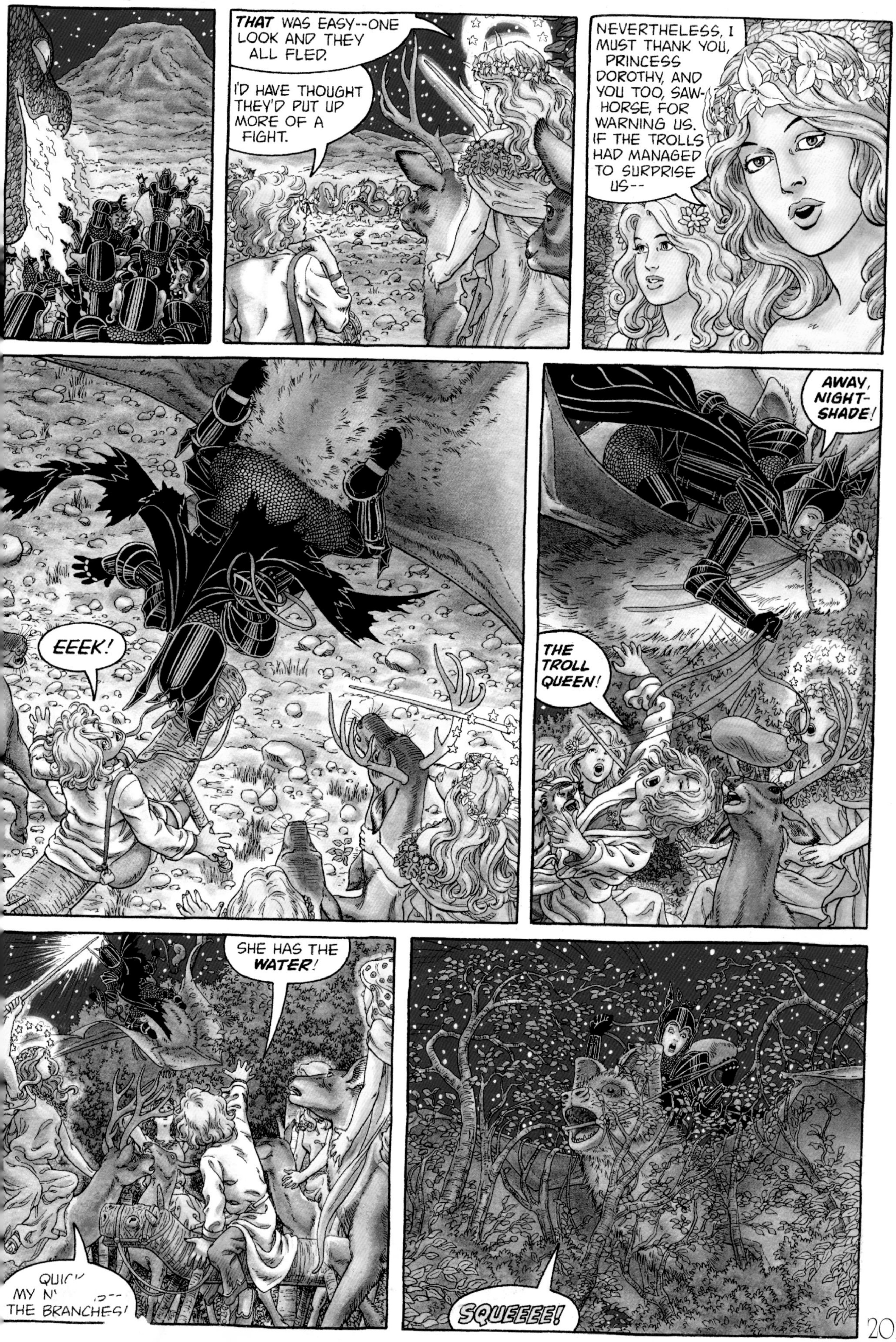

THAT WAS EASY--ONE LOOK AND THEY ALL FLED.
I'D HAVE THOUGHT THEY'D PUT UP MORE OF A FIGHT.
NEVERTHELESS, I MUST THANK YOU, PRINCESS DOROTHY, AND YOU TOO, SAW-HORSE, FOR WARNING US. IF THE TROLLS HAD MANAGED TO SURPRISE US--
EEEK!
AWAY, NIGHT-SHADE!
THE TROLL QUEEN!
SHE HAS THE WATER!
MY
THE BRANCHES!
SQUEEEEE!

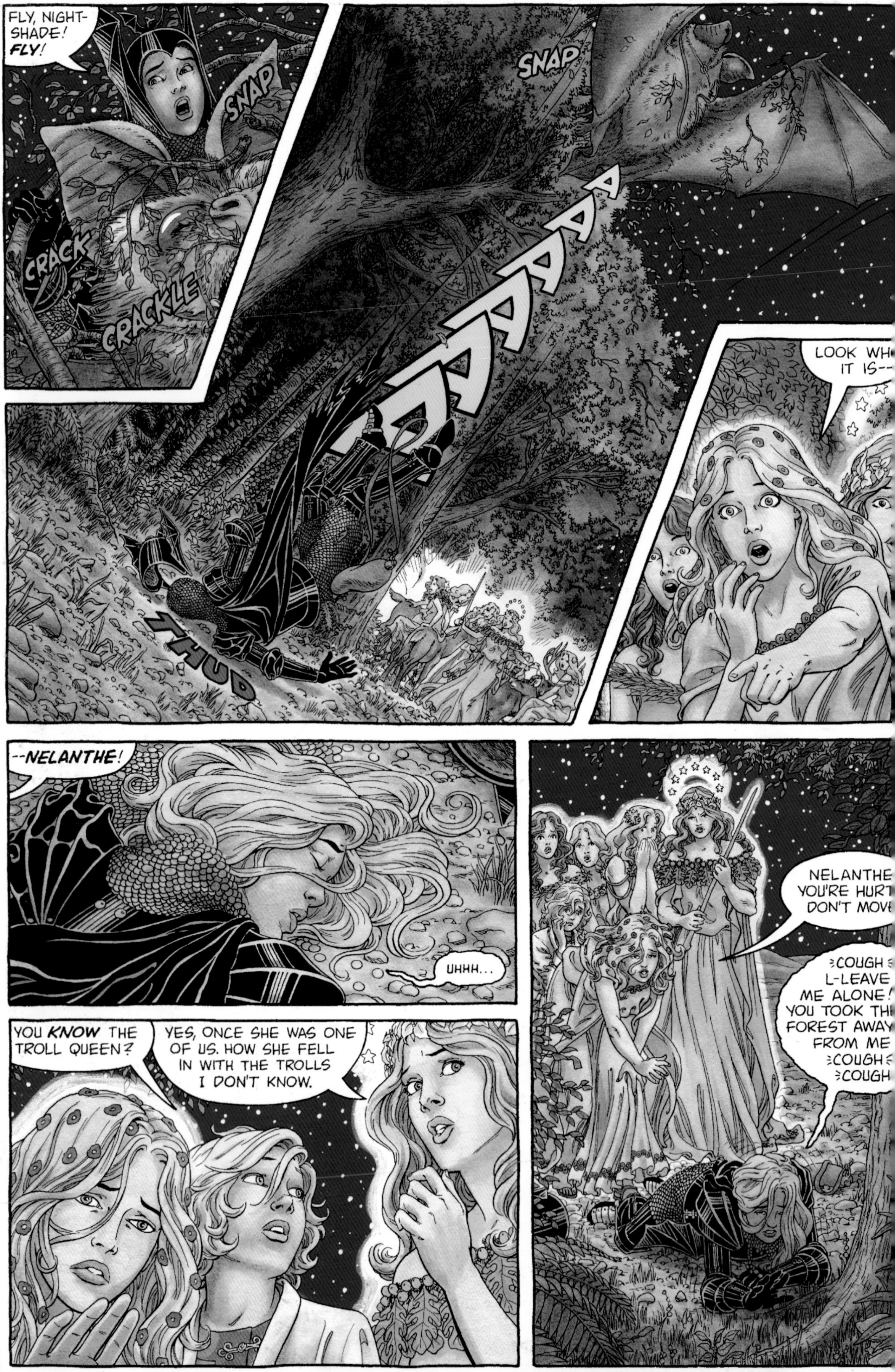

FLY, NIGHT-SHADE! **FLY**!
SNAP
CRACK
CRACKLE
SNAP
AAAAAA
THUD
LOOK WH
IT IS--
--**NELANTHE**!
UHHH...
NELANTHE
YOU'RE HURT
DON'T MOVE
COUGH
L-LEAVE ME ALONE!
YOU TOOK TH
FOREST AWAY
FROM ME
COUGH
COUGH
YOU **KNOW** THE TROLL QUEEN?
YES, ONCE SHE WAS ONE OF US. HOW SHE FELL IN WITH THE TROLLS I DON'T KNOW.

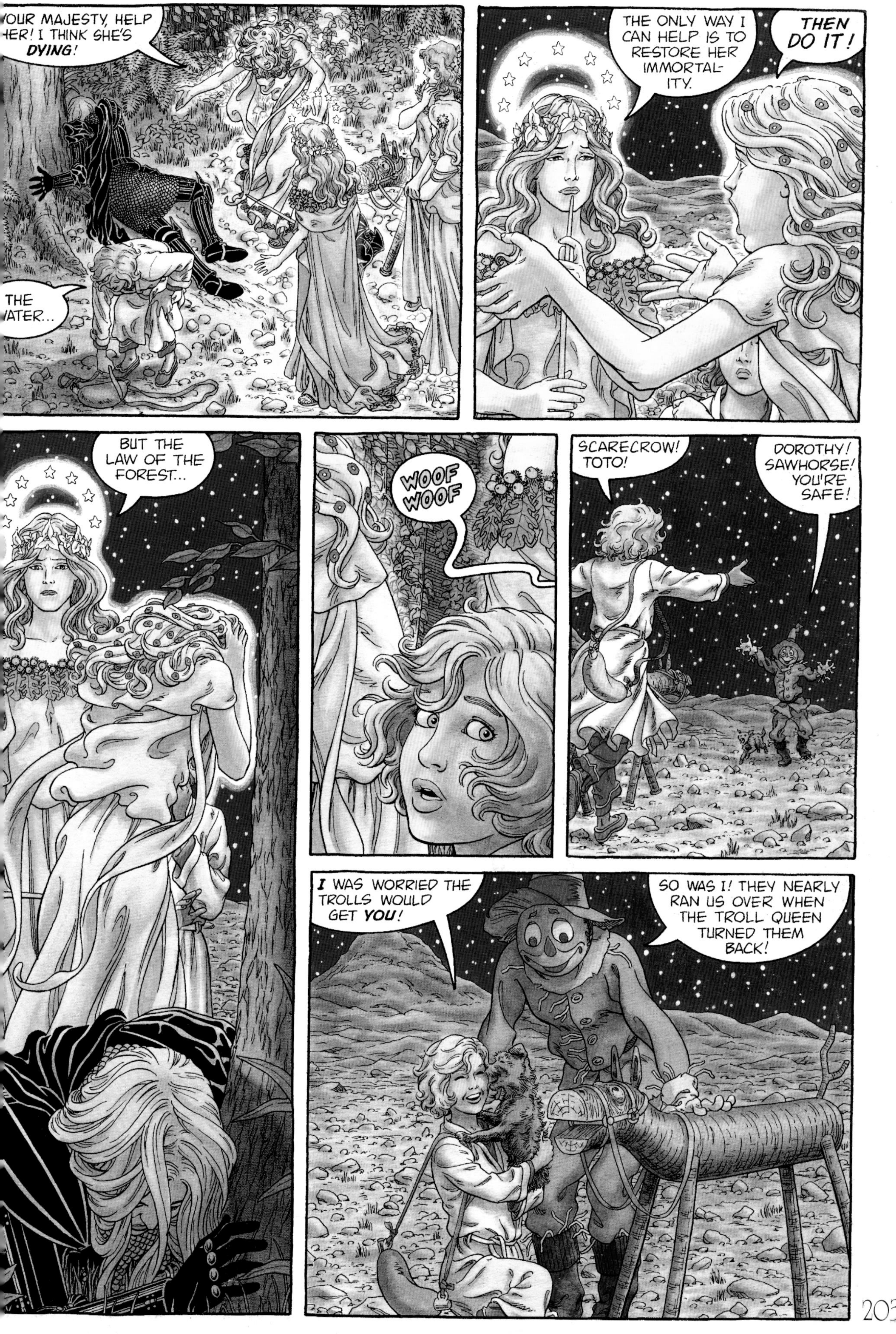

YOUR MAJESTY, HELP HER! I THINK SHE'S **DYING**!
THE WATER...
THE ONLY WAY I CAN HELP IS TO RESTORE HER IMMORTAL-ITY.
THEN DO IT!
BUT THE LAW OF THE FOREST...
WOOF WOOF
SCARECROW! TOTO!
DOROTHY! SAWHORSE! YOU'RE SAFE!
I WAS WORRIED THE TROLLS WOULD GET ***YOU***!
SO WAS I! THEY NEARLY RAN US OVER WHEN THE TROLL QUEEN TURNED THEM BACK!

TROLL QUEEN? YOU MUST MEAN THE **WOOD-NYMPH** QUEEN.

NO, THE **TROLL** QUEEN TRICKED THE DRAGONS INTO ATTACKING THE TROLLS...

WHAT?

BUT THAT MEANS SHE TURNED AGAINST THE TROLLS TO SAVE THE FOREST! THEN SHE HAS **NOTHING LEFT** --EXCEPT...

...EXCEPT THE WATER OF OBLIVION.

BUT I--I **CAN'T** GIVE IT TO HER. OZMA'S FORBIDDEN IT.

CAN IT HELP HER?

I DON'T KNOW, BUT--

AHHHHHHHH

OH, **SO WHAT** IF IT'S FORBIDDEN! I'LL BE IN DEEP TROUBLE WHEN I GET BACK TO THE EMERALD CITY, BUT I DON'T CARE ANYMORE

POP

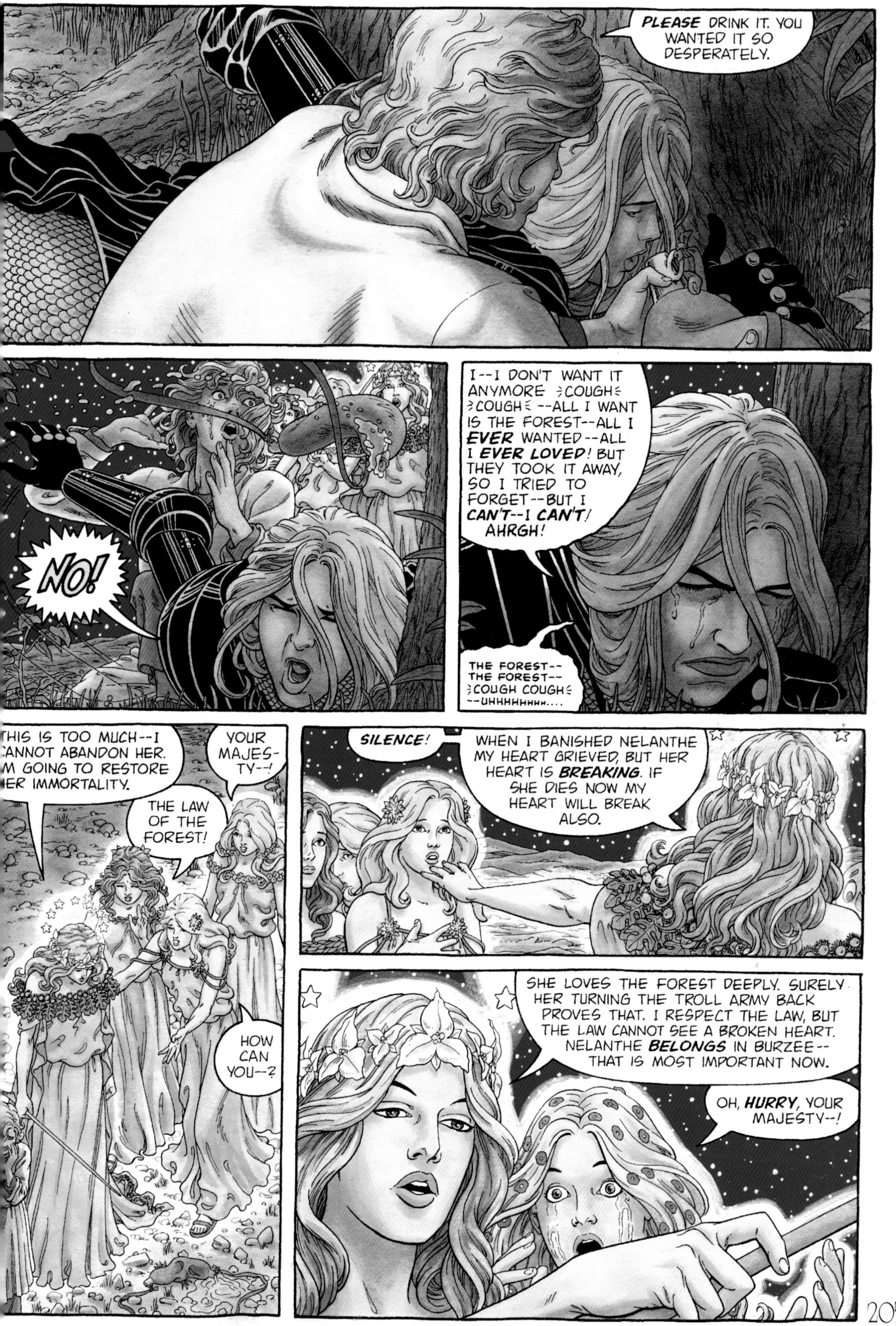
PLEASE DRINK IT. YOU WANTED IT SO DESPERATELY.
I--I DON'T WANT IT ANYMORE ⋛COUGH⋚ ⋛COUGH⋚ --ALL I WANT IS THE FOREST--ALL I EVER WANTED--ALL I EVER LOVED! BUT THEY TOOK IT AWAY, SO I TRIED TO FORGET--BUT I CAN'T--I CAN'T! AHRGH!
NO!
THE FOREST-- THE FOREST-- ⋛COUGH COUGH⋚ --UHHHHHHHH....
THIS IS TOO MUCH--I CANNOT ABANDON HER. I'M GOING TO RESTORE HER IMMORTALITY.
YOUR MAJESTY--!
THE LAW OF THE FOREST!
HOW CAN YOU--?
SILENCE!
WHEN I BANISHED NELANTHE MY HEART GRIEVED, BUT HER HEART IS BREAKING. IF SHE DIES NOW MY HEART WILL BREAK ALSO.
SHE LOVES THE FOREST DEEPLY. SURELY HER TURNING THE TROLL ARMY BACK PROVES THAT. I RESPECT THE LAW, BUT THE LAW CANNOT SEE A BROKEN HEART. NELANTHE BELONGS IN BURZEE-- THAT IS MOST IMPORTANT NOW.
OH, HURRY, YOUR MAJESTY--!

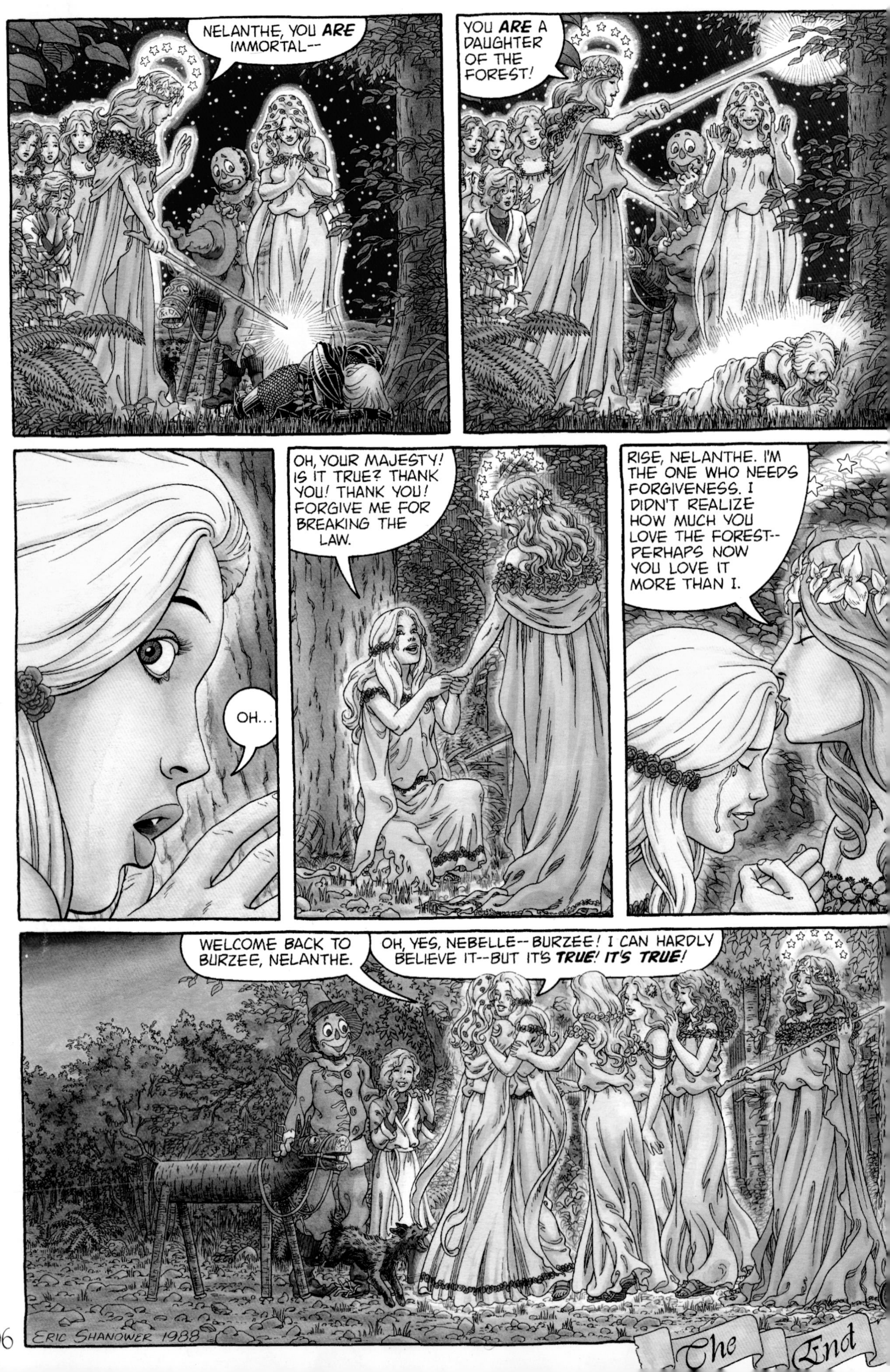
NELANTHE, YOU **ARE** IMMORTAL--
YOU **ARE** A DAUGHTER OF THE FOREST!
OH...
OH, YOUR MAJESTY! IS IT TRUE? THANK YOU! THANK YOU! FORGIVE ME FOR BREAKING THE LAW.
RISE, NELANTHE. I'M THE ONE WHO NEEDS FORGIVENESS. I DIDN'T REALIZE HOW MUCH YOU LOVE THE FOREST-- PERHAPS NOW YOU LOVE IT MORE THAN I.
WELCOME BACK TO BURZEE, NELANTHE.
OH, YES, NEBELLE-- BURZEE! I CAN HARDLY BELIEVE IT--BUT IT'S ***TRUE! IT'S TRUE!***
ERIC SHANOWER 1988
The End

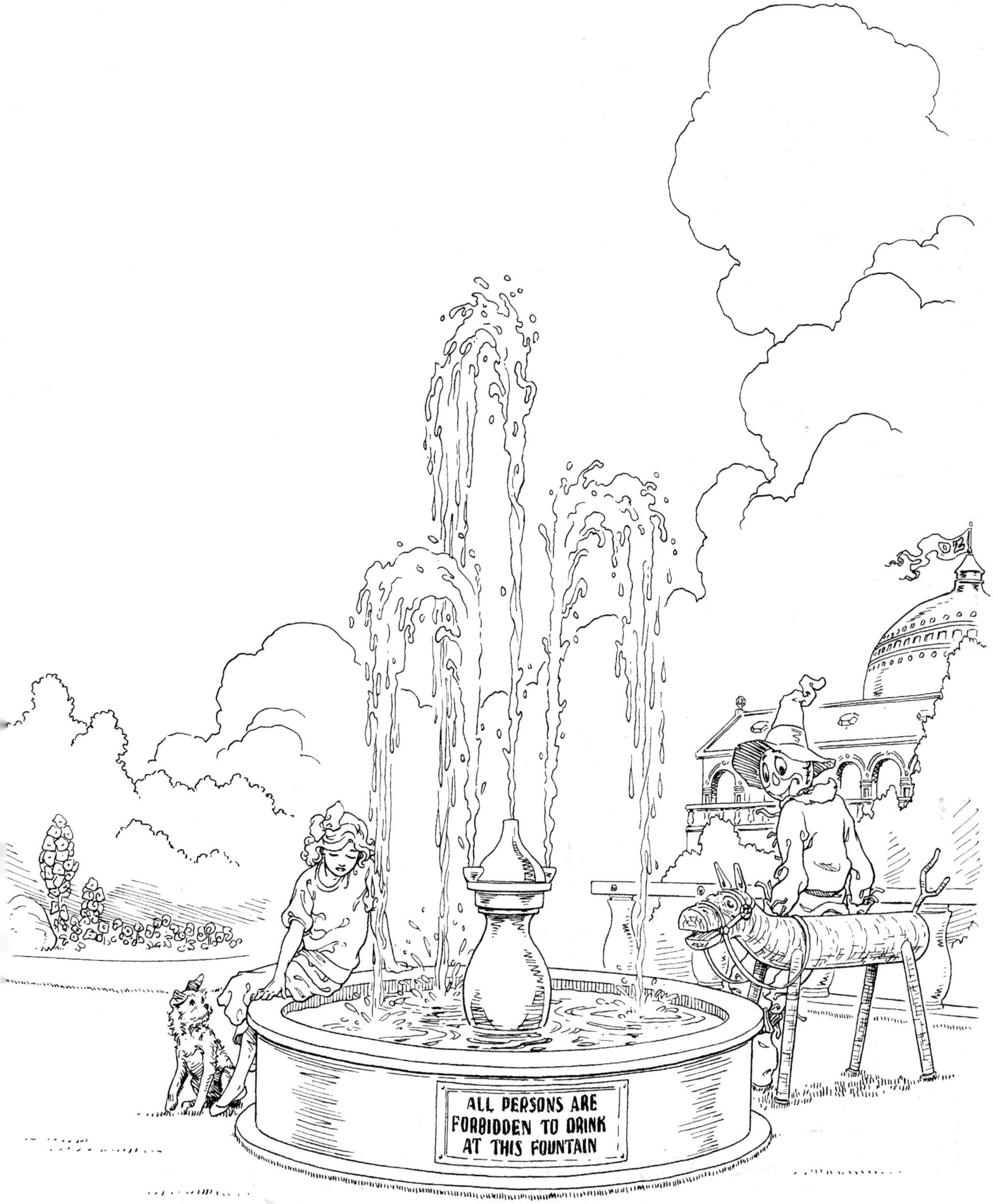
ALL PERSONS ARE
FORBIDDEN TO DRINK
AT THIS FOUNTAIN
OZ

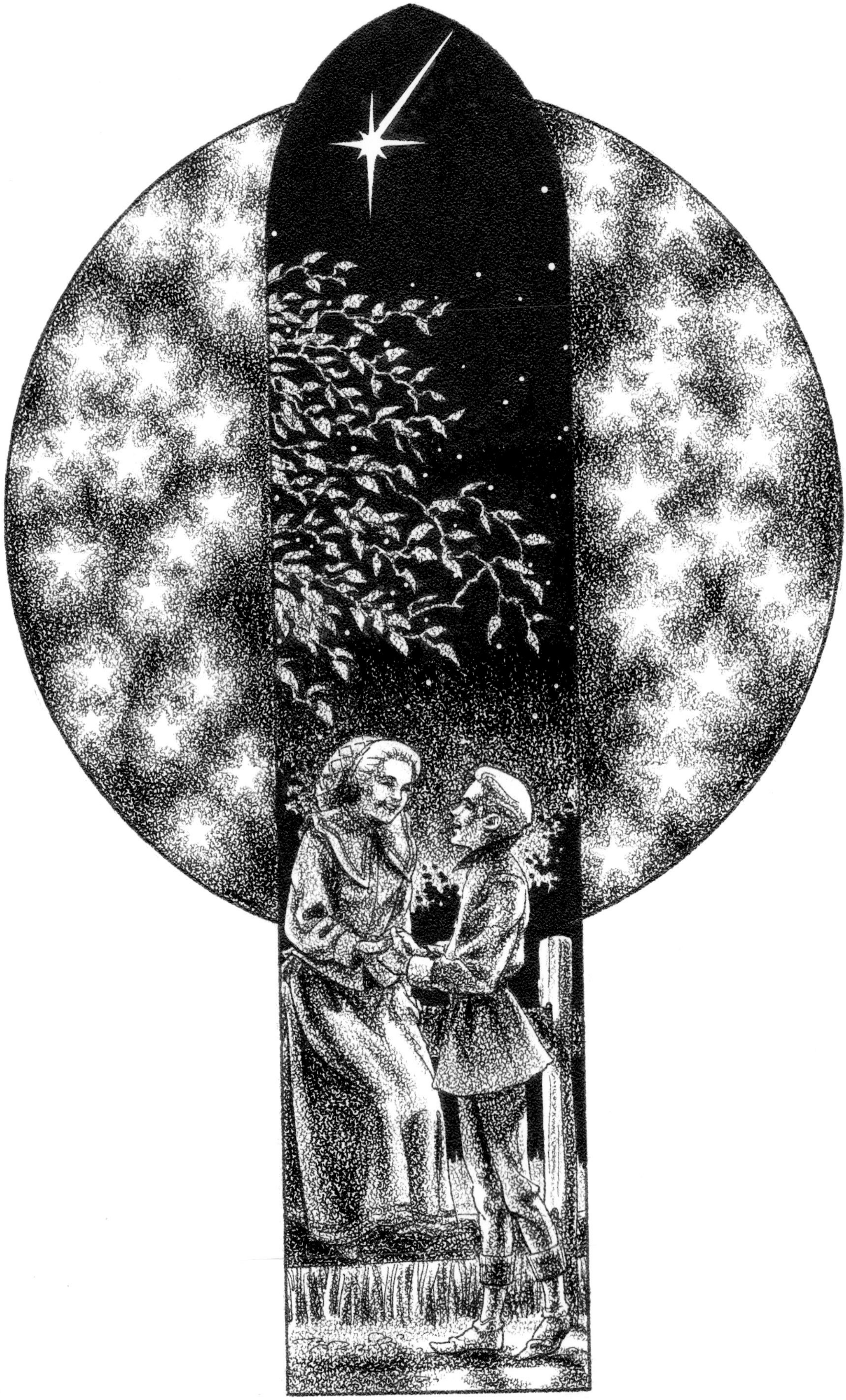

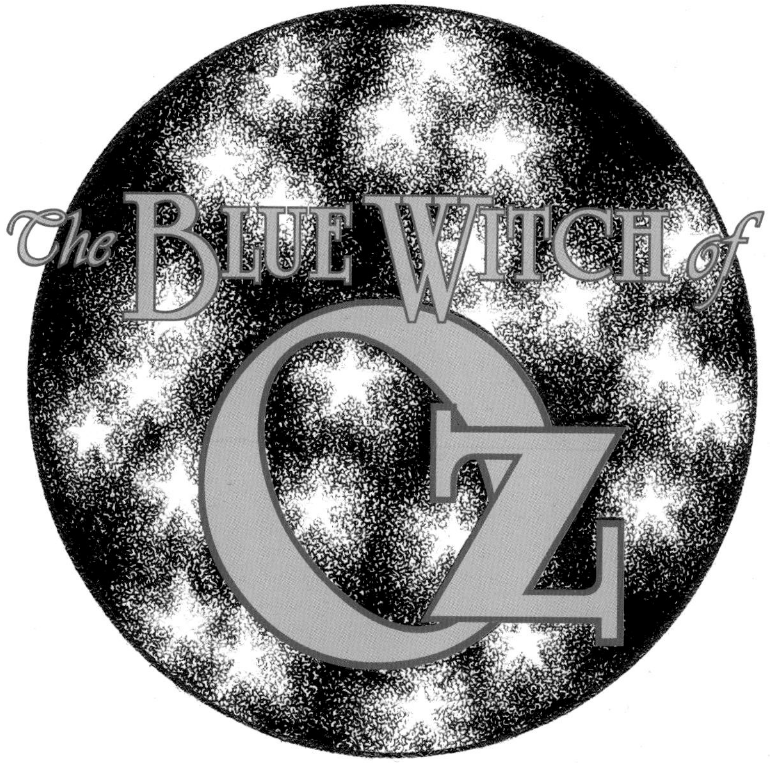
The Blue Witch of Oz

At last,
Elizabeth,
here's one
for you.

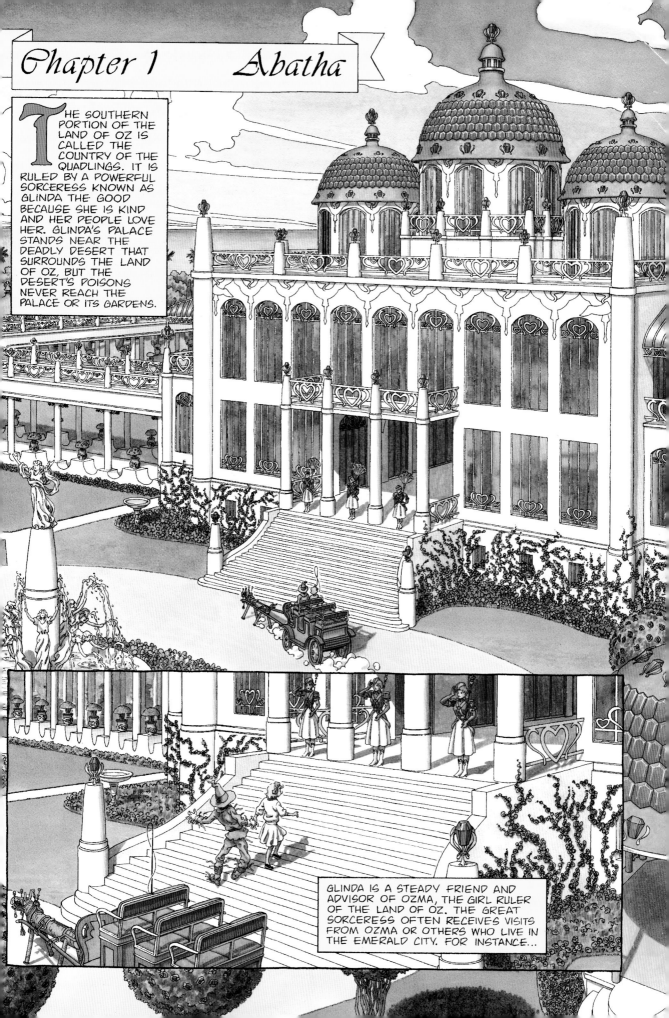

Chapter 1   Abatha

THE SOUTHERN PORTION OF THE LAND OF OZ IS CALLED THE COUNTRY OF THE QUADLINGS. IT IS RULED BY A POWERFUL SORCERESS KNOWN AS GLINDA THE GOOD BECAUSE SHE IS KIND AND HER PEOPLE LOVE HER. GLINDA'S PALACE STANDS NEAR THE DEADLY DESERT THAT SURROUNDS THE LAND OF OZ, BUT THE DESERT'S POISONS NEVER REACH THE PALACE OR ITS GARDENS.

GLINDA IS A STEADY FRIEND AND ADVISOR OF OZMA, THE GIRL RULER OF THE LAND OF OZ. THE GREAT SORCERESS OFTEN RECEIVES VISITS FROM OZMA OR OTHERS WHO LIVE IN THE EMERALD CITY. FOR INSTANCE...

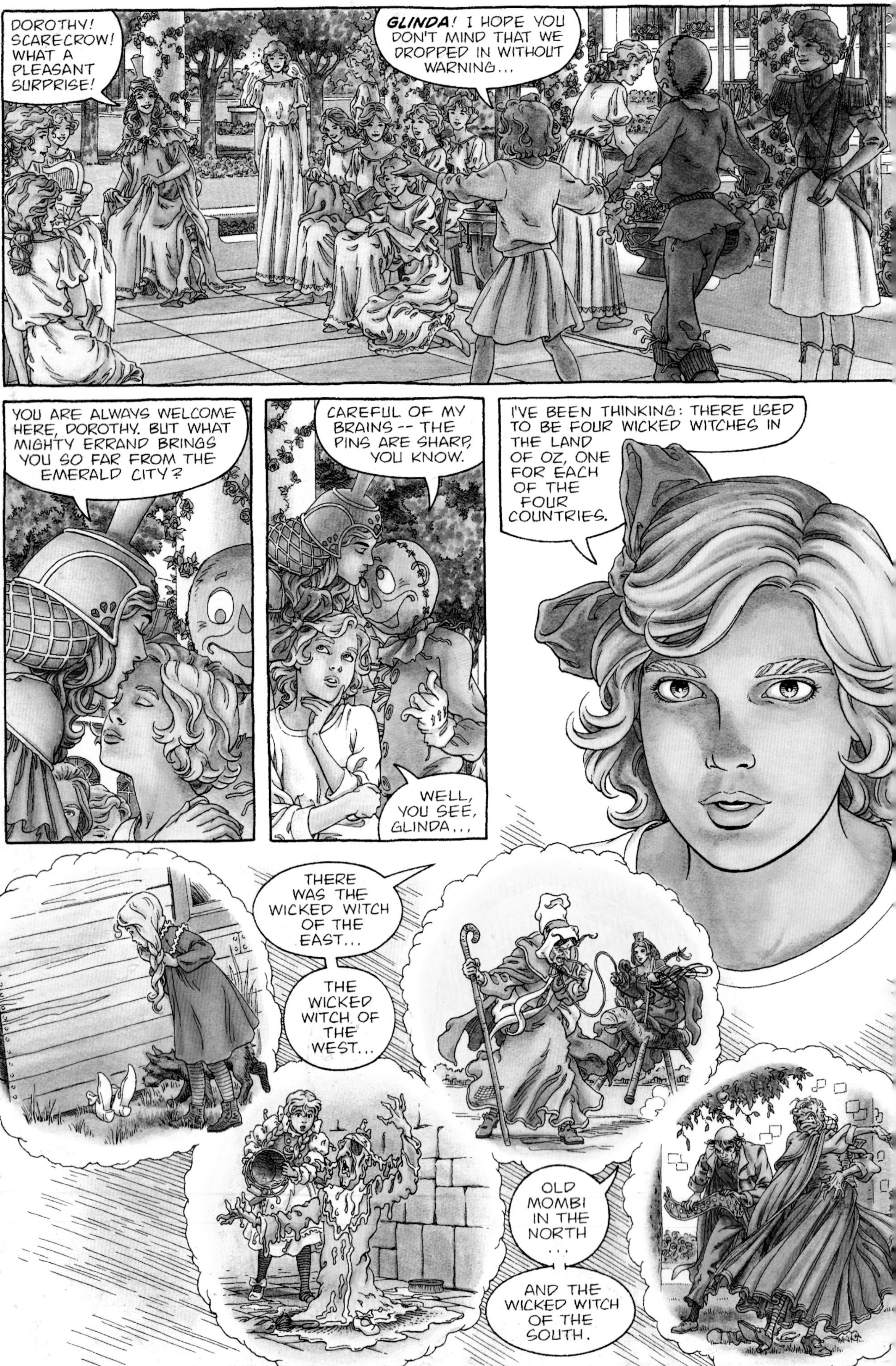
DOROTHY! SCARECROW! WHAT A PLEASANT SURPRISE!
GLINDA! I HOPE YOU DON'T MIND THAT WE DROPPED IN WITHOUT WARNING...
YOU ARE ALWAYS WELCOME HERE, DOROTHY. BUT WHAT MIGHTY ERRAND BRINGS YOU SO FAR FROM THE EMERALD CITY?
CAREFUL OF MY BRAINS -- THE PINS ARE SHARP, YOU KNOW.
WELL, YOU SEE, GLINDA...
I'VE BEEN THINKING: THERE USED TO BE FOUR WICKED WITCHES IN THE LAND OF OZ, ONE FOR EACH OF THE FOUR COUNTRIES.
THERE WAS THE WICKED WITCH OF THE EAST...
THE WICKED WITCH OF THE WEST...
OLD MOMBI IN THE NORTH...
AND THE WICKED WITCH OF THE SOUTH.

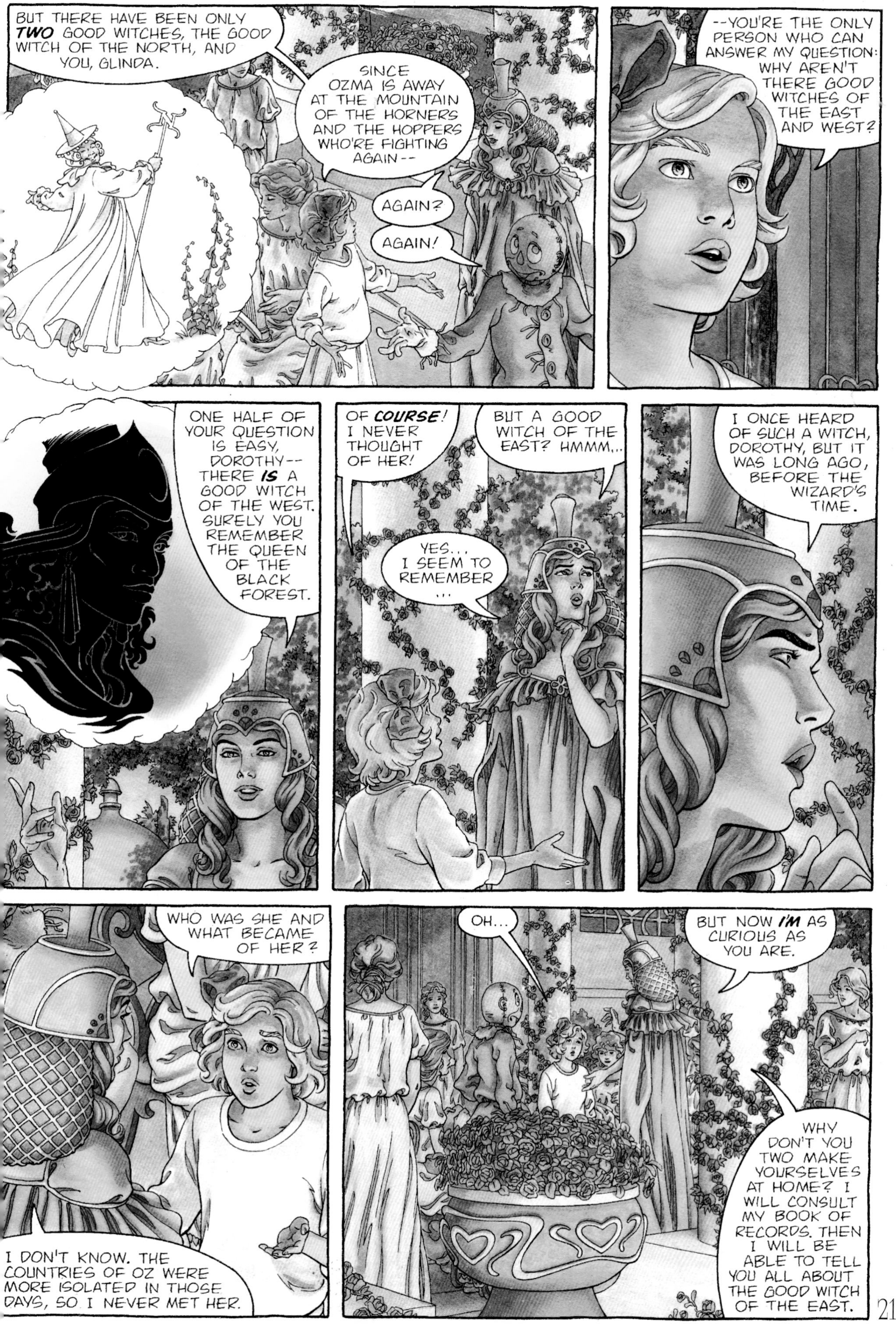

BUT THERE HAVE BEEN ONLY **TWO** GOOD WITCHES, THE GOOD WITCH OF THE NORTH, AND YOU, GLINDA.
SINCE OZMA IS AWAY AT THE MOUNTAIN OF THE HORNERS AND THE HOPPERS WHO'RE FIGHTING AGAIN--
AGAIN?
AGAIN!
--YOU'RE THE ONLY PERSON WHO CAN ANSWER MY QUESTION: WHY AREN'T THERE GOOD WITCHES OF THE EAST AND WEST?
ONE HALF OF YOUR QUESTION IS EASY, DOROTHY-- THERE **IS** A GOOD WITCH OF THE WEST. SURELY YOU REMEMBER THE QUEEN OF THE BLACK FOREST.
OF **COURSE**! I NEVER THOUGHT OF HER!
BUT A GOOD WITCH OF THE EAST? HMMM...
YES... I SEEM TO REMEMBER ...
I ONCE HEARD OF SUCH A WITCH, DOROTHY, BUT IT WAS LONG AGO, BEFORE THE WIZARD'S TIME.
WHO WAS SHE AND WHAT BECAME OF HER?
I DON'T KNOW. THE COUNTRIES OF OZ WERE MORE ISOLATED IN THOSE DAYS, SO I NEVER MET HER.
OH...
BUT NOW **I'M** AS CURIOUS AS YOU ARE.
WHY DON'T YOU TWO MAKE YOURSELVES AT HOME? I WILL CONSULT MY BOOK OF RECORDS. THEN I WILL BE ABLE TO TELL YOU ALL ABOUT THE GOOD WITCH OF THE EAST.

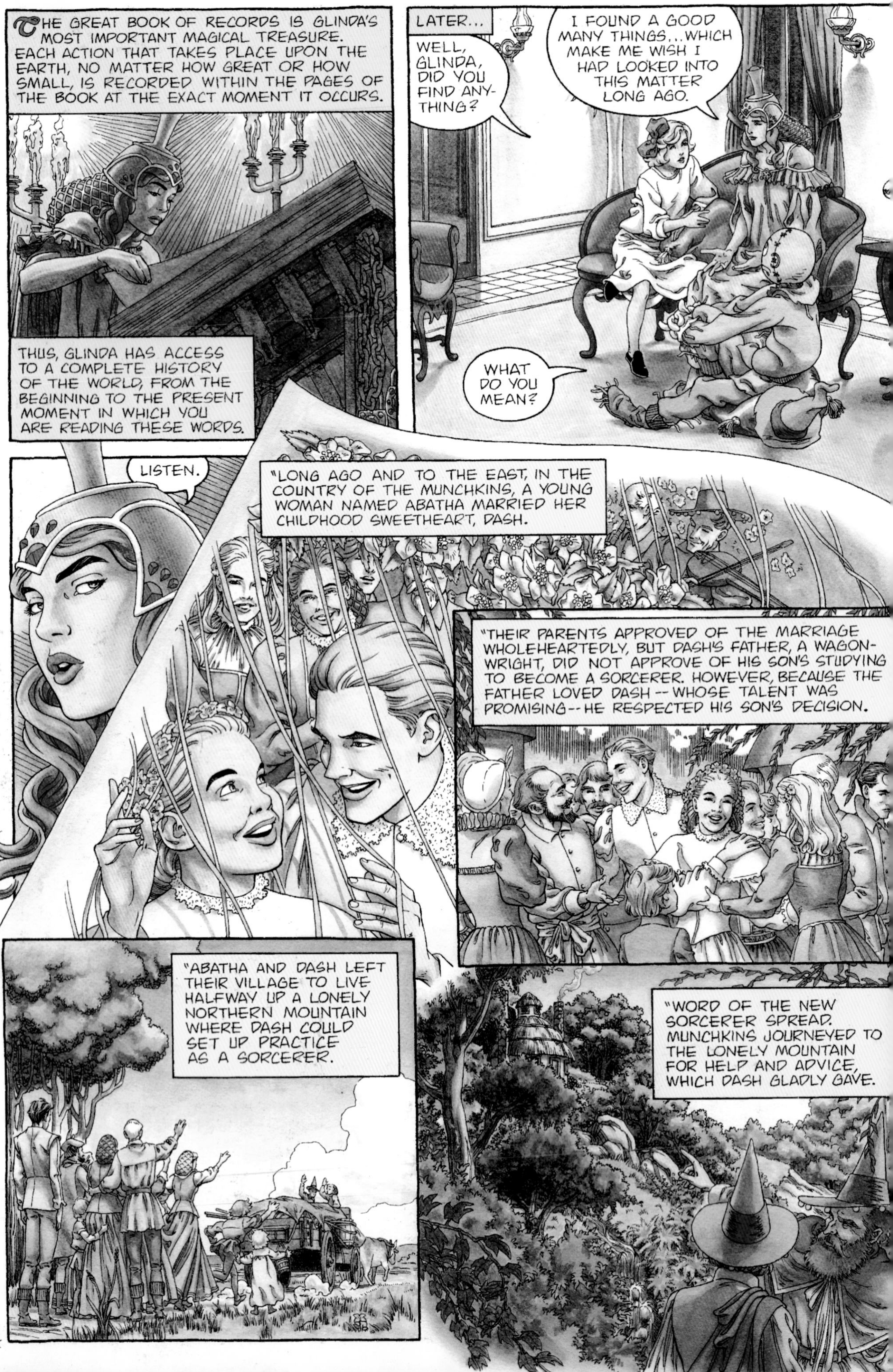
THE GREAT BOOK OF RECORDS IS GLINDA'S MOST IMPORTANT MAGICAL TREASURE. EACH ACTION THAT TAKES PLACE UPON THE EARTH, NO MATTER HOW GREAT OR HOW SMALL, IS RECORDED WITHIN THE PAGES OF THE BOOK AT THE EXACT MOMENT IT OCCURS.
THUS, GLINDA HAS ACCESS TO A COMPLETE HISTORY OF THE WORLD, FROM THE BEGINNING TO THE PRESENT MOMENT IN WHICH YOU ARE READING THESE WORDS.
LATER...
WELL, GLINDA, DID YOU FIND ANYTHING?
I FOUND A GOOD MANY THINGS...WHICH MAKE ME WISH I HAD LOOKED INTO THIS MATTER LONG AGO.
WHAT DO YOU MEAN?
LISTEN.
"LONG AGO AND TO THE EAST, IN THE COUNTRY OF THE MUNCHKINS, A YOUNG WOMAN NAMED ABATHA MARRIED HER CHILDHOOD SWEETHEART, DASH.
"THEIR PARENTS APPROVED OF THE MARRIAGE WHOLEHEARTEDLY, BUT DASH'S FATHER, A WAGON-WRIGHT, DID NOT APPROVE OF HIS SON'S STUDYING TO BECOME A SORCERER. HOWEVER, BECAUSE THE FATHER LOVED DASH -- WHOSE TALENT WAS PROMISING -- HE RESPECTED HIS SON'S DECISION.
"ABATHA AND DASH LEFT THEIR VILLAGE TO LIVE HALFWAY UP A LONELY NORTHERN MOUNTAIN WHERE DASH COULD SET UP PRACTICE AS A SORCERER.
"WORD OF THE NEW SORCERER SPREAD. MUNCHKINS JOURNEYED TO THE LONELY MOUNTAIN FOR HELP AND ADVICE, WHICH DASH GLADLY GAVE.

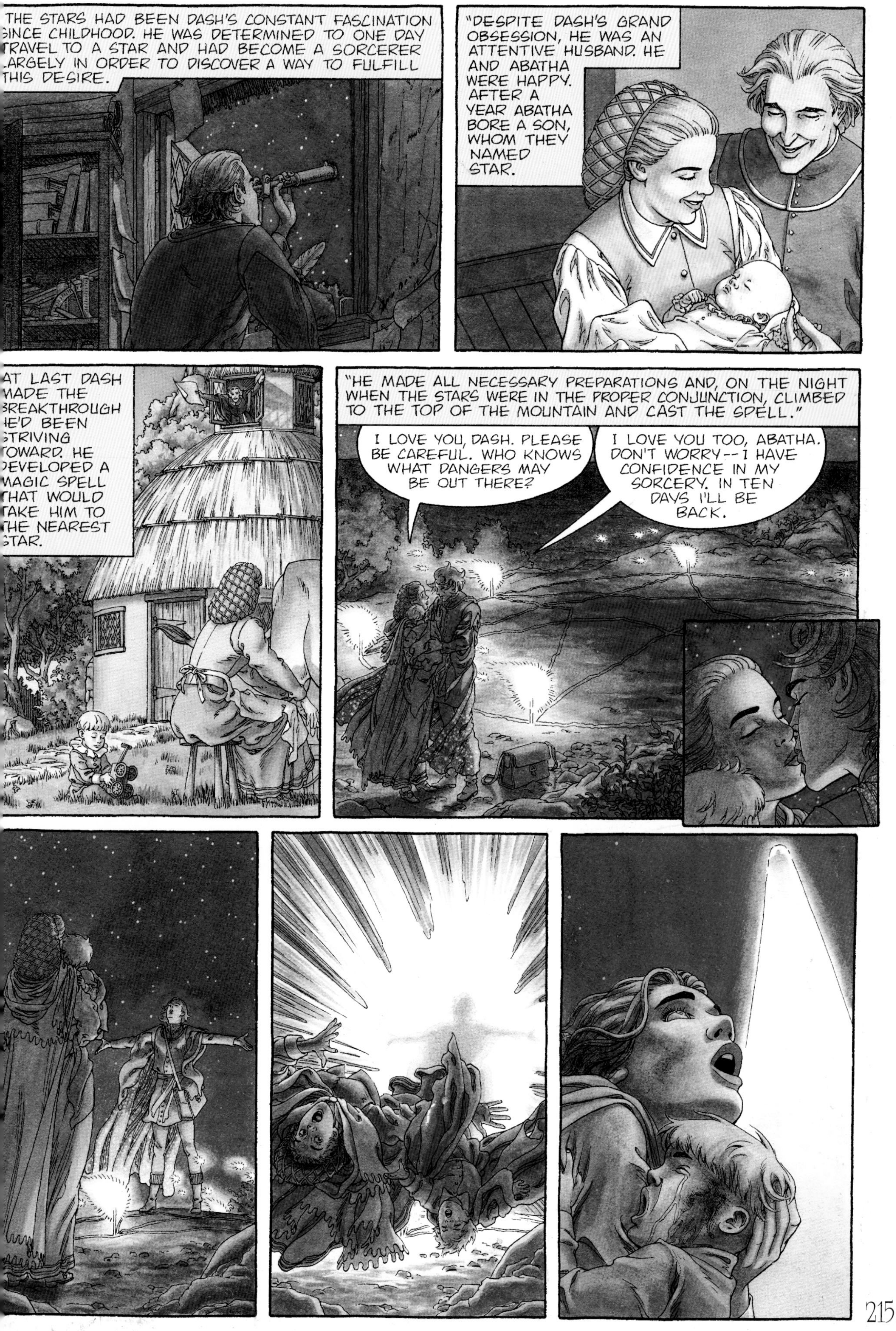
THE STARS HAD BEEN DASH'S CONSTANT FASCINATION SINCE CHILDHOOD. HE WAS DETERMINED TO ONE DAY TRAVEL TO A STAR AND HAD BECOME A SORCERER LARGELY IN ORDER TO DISCOVER A WAY TO FULFILL THIS DESIRE.
"DESPITE DASH'S GRAND OBSESSION, HE WAS AN ATTENTIVE HUSBAND. HE AND ABATHA WERE HAPPY. AFTER A YEAR ABATHA BORE A SON, WHOM THEY NAMED STAR.
AT LAST DASH MADE THE BREAKTHROUGH HE'D BEEN STRIVING TOWARD. HE DEVELOPED A MAGIC SPELL THAT WOULD TAKE HIM TO THE NEAREST STAR.
"HE MADE ALL NECESSARY PREPARATIONS AND, ON THE NIGHT WHEN THE STARS WERE IN THE PROPER CONJUNCTION, CLIMBED TO THE TOP OF THE MOUNTAIN AND CAST THE SPELL."
I LOVE YOU, DASH. PLEASE BE CAREFUL. WHO KNOWS WHAT DANGERS MAY BE OUT THERE?
I LOVE YOU TOO, ABATHA. DON'T WORRY-- I HAVE CONFIDENCE IN MY SORCERY. IN TEN DAYS I'LL BE BACK.

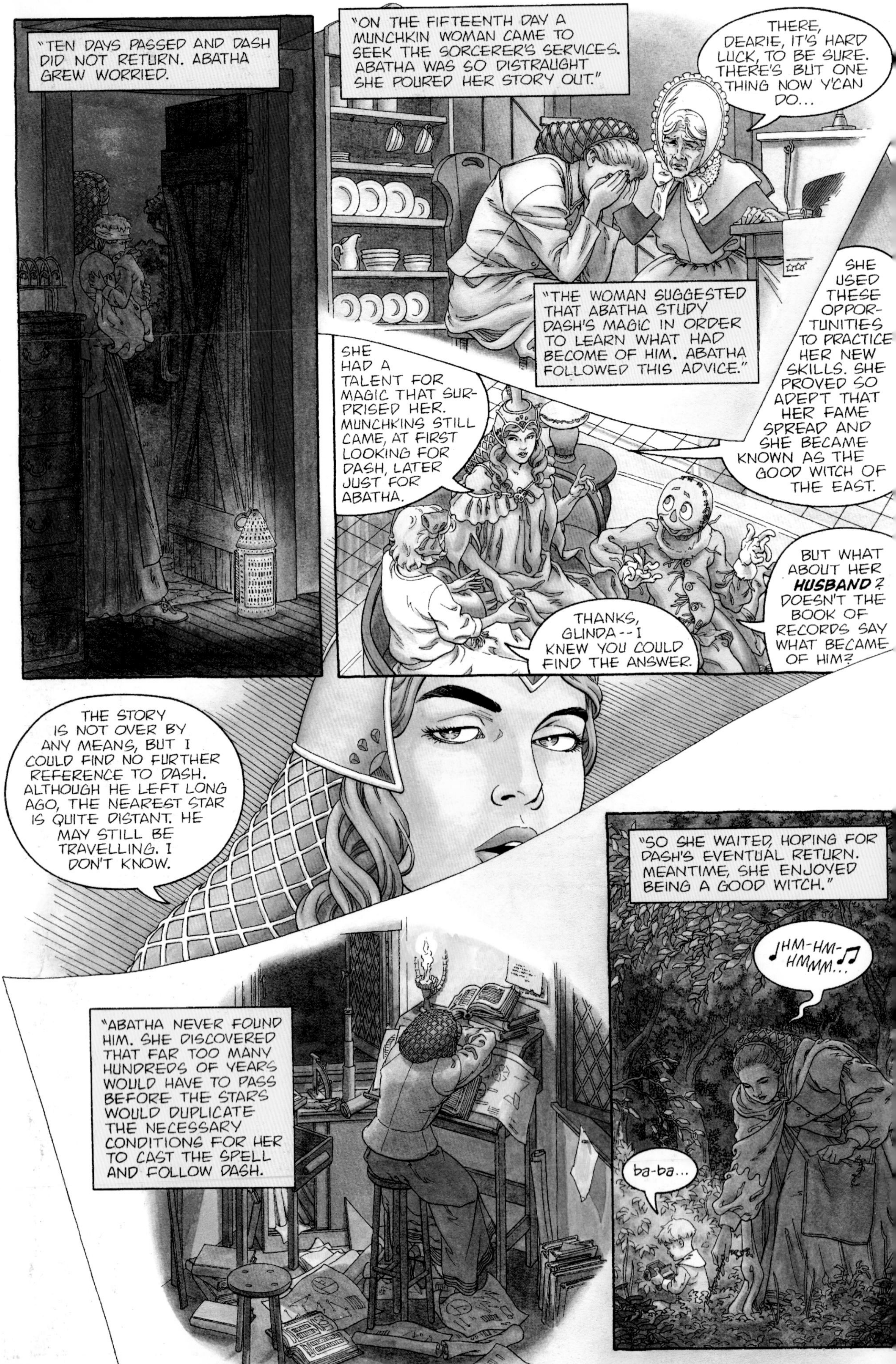
"TEN DAYS PASSED AND DASH DID NOT RETURN. ABATHA GREW WORRIED.
"ON THE FIFTEENTH DAY A MUNCHKIN WOMAN CAME TO SEEK THE SORCERER'S SERVICES. ABATHA WAS SO DISTRAUGHT SHE POURED HER STORY OUT."
THERE, DEARIE, IT'S HARD LUCK, TO BE SURE. THERE'S BUT ONE THING NOW Y'CAN DO...
"THE WOMAN SUGGESTED THAT ABATHA STUDY DASH'S MAGIC IN ORDER TO LEARN WHAT HAD BECOME OF HIM. ABATHA FOLLOWED THIS ADVICE."
SHE HAD A TALENT FOR MAGIC THAT SURPRISED HER. MUNCHKINS STILL CAME, AT FIRST LOOKING FOR DASH, LATER JUST FOR ABATHA.
SHE USED THESE OPPORTUNITIES TO PRACTICE HER NEW SKILLS. SHE PROVED SO ADEPT THAT HER FAME SPREAD AND SHE BECAME KNOWN AS THE GOOD WITCH OF THE EAST.
THANKS, GLINDA--I KNEW YOU COULD FIND THE ANSWER.
BUT WHAT ABOUT HER **HUSBAND**? DOESN'T THE BOOK OF RECORDS SAY WHAT BECAME OF HIM?
THE STORY IS NOT OVER BY ANY MEANS, BUT I COULD FIND NO FURTHER REFERENCE TO DASH. ALTHOUGH HE LEFT LONG AGO, THE NEAREST STAR IS QUITE DISTANT. HE MAY STILL BE TRAVELLING. I DON'T KNOW.
"ABATHA NEVER FOUND HIM. SHE DISCOVERED THAT FAR TOO MANY HUNDREDS OF YEARS WOULD HAVE TO PASS BEFORE THE STARS WOULD DUPLICATE THE NECESSARY CONDITIONS FOR HER TO CAST THE SPELL AND FOLLOW DASH.
"SO SHE WAITED, HOPING FOR DASH'S EVENTUAL RETURN. MEANTIME, SHE ENJOYED BEING A GOOD WITCH."
♪HM-HM-HMMM...♫
ba-ba...

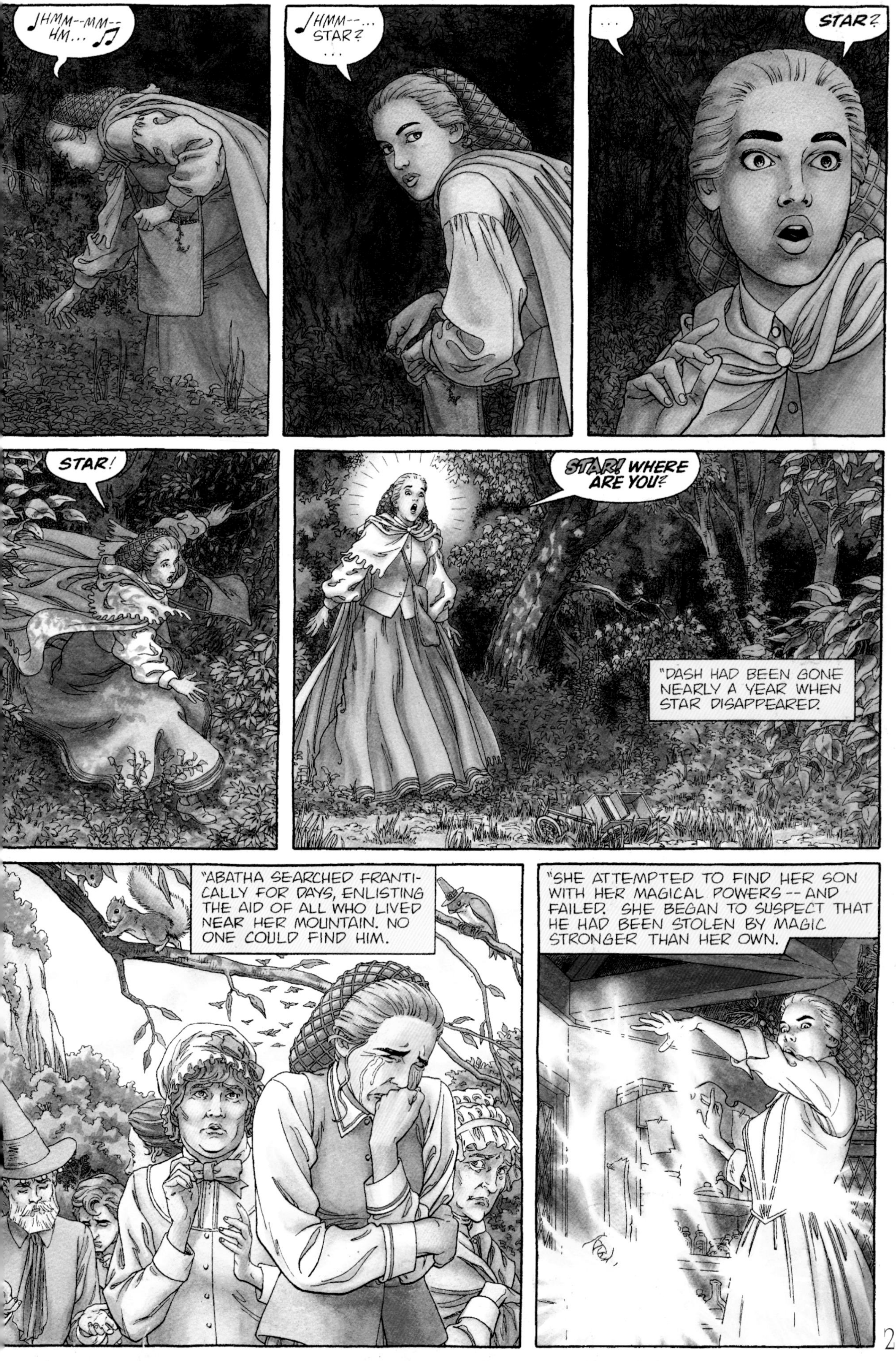
♩HMM--MM--HM... ♫
♩HMM--... STAR? ...
...
STAR?
STAR!
STAR! WHERE ARE YOU?
"DASH HAD BEEN GONE NEARLY A YEAR WHEN STAR DISAPPEARED.
"ABATHA SEARCHED FRANTICALLY FOR DAYS, ENLISTING THE AID OF ALL WHO LIVED NEAR HER MOUNTAIN. NO ONE COULD FIND HIM.
"SHE ATTEMPTED TO FIND HER SON WITH HER MAGICAL POWERS -- AND FAILED. SHE BEGAN TO SUSPECT THAT HE HAD BEEN STOLEN BY MAGIC STRONGER THAN HER OWN.

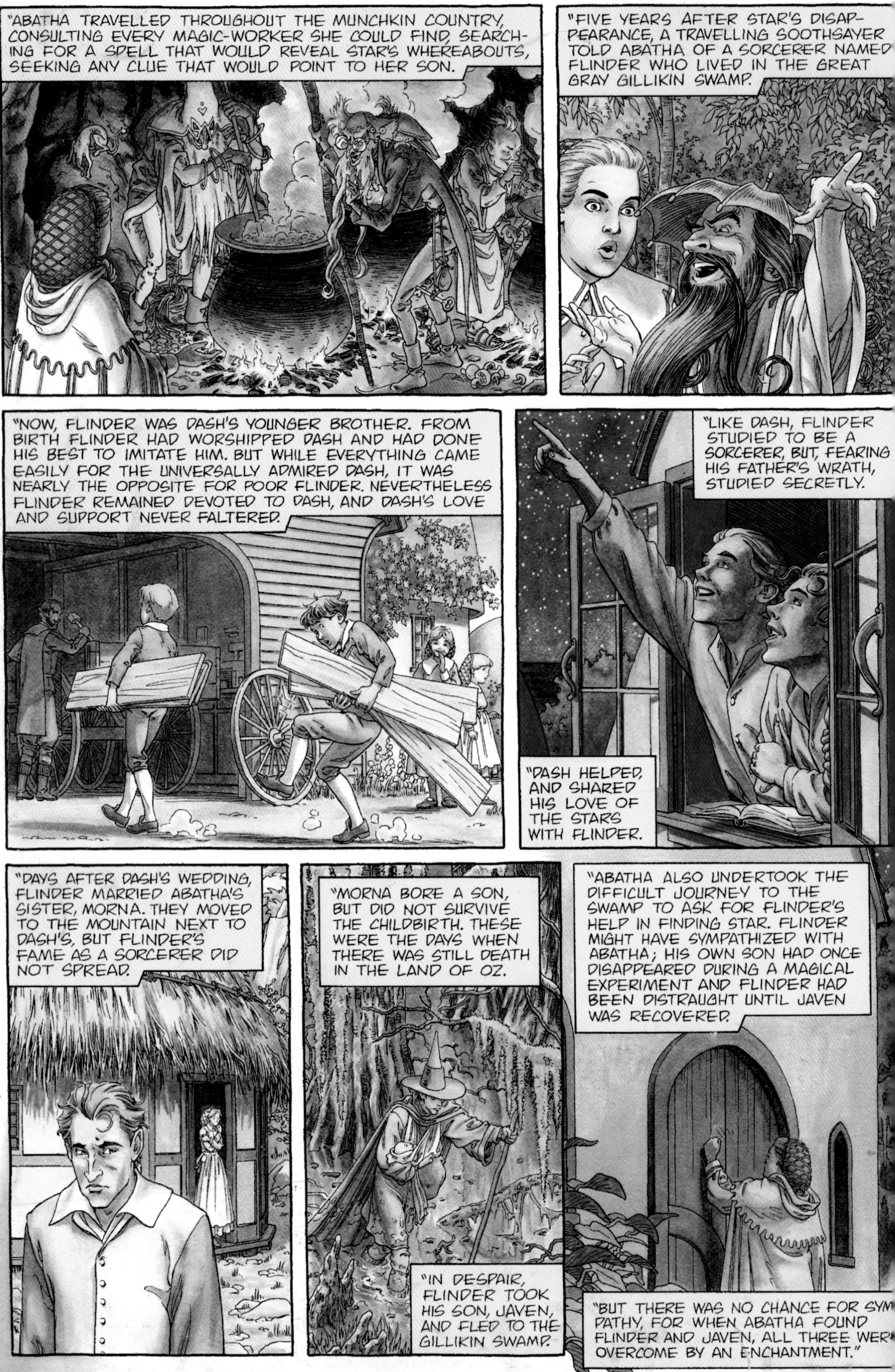
"ABATHA TRAVELLED THROUGHOUT THE MUNCHKIN COUNTRY, CONSULTING EVERY MAGIC-WORKER SHE COULD FIND, SEARCHING FOR A SPELL THAT WOULD REVEAL STAR'S WHEREABOUTS, SEEKING ANY CLUE THAT WOULD POINT TO HER SON.
"FIVE YEARS AFTER STAR'S DISAPPEARANCE, A TRAVELLING SOOTHSAYER TOLD ABATHA OF A SORCERER NAMED FLINDER WHO LIVED IN THE GREAT GRAY GILLIKIN SWAMP.
"NOW, FLINDER WAS DASH'S YOUNGER BROTHER. FROM BIRTH FLINDER HAD WORSHIPPED DASH AND HAD DONE HIS BEST TO IMITATE HIM. BUT WHILE EVERYTHING CAME EASILY FOR THE UNIVERSALLY ADMIRED DASH, IT WAS NEARLY THE OPPOSITE FOR POOR FLINDER. NEVERTHELESS FLINDER REMAINED DEVOTED TO DASH, AND DASH'S LOVE AND SUPPORT NEVER FALTERED.
"LIKE DASH, FLINDER STUDIED TO BE A SORCERER, BUT, FEARING HIS FATHER'S WRATH, STUDIED SECRETLY.
"DASH HELPED, AND SHARED HIS LOVE OF THE STARS WITH FLINDER.
"DAYS AFTER DASH'S WEDDING, FLINDER MARRIED ABATHA'S SISTER, MORNA. THEY MOVED TO THE MOUNTAIN NEXT TO DASH'S, BUT FLINDER'S FAME AS A SORCERER DID NOT SPREAD.
"MORNA BORE A SON, BUT DID NOT SURVIVE THE CHILDBIRTH. THESE WERE THE DAYS WHEN THERE WAS STILL DEATH IN THE LAND OF OZ.
"IN DESPAIR, FLINDER TOOK HIS SON, JAVEN, AND FLED TO THE GILLIKIN SWAMP.
"ABATHA ALSO UNDERTOOK THE DIFFICULT JOURNEY TO THE SWAMP TO ASK FOR FLINDER'S HELP IN FINDING STAR. FLINDER MIGHT HAVE SYMPATHIZED WITH ABATHA; HIS OWN SON HAD ONCE DISAPPEARED DURING A MAGICAL EXPERIMENT AND FLINDER HAD BEEN DISTRAUGHT UNTIL JAVEN WAS RECOVERED.
"BUT THERE WAS NO CHANCE FOR SYMPATHY, FOR WHEN ABATHA FOUND FLINDER AND JAVEN, ALL THREE WERE OVERCOME BY AN ENCHANTMENT."

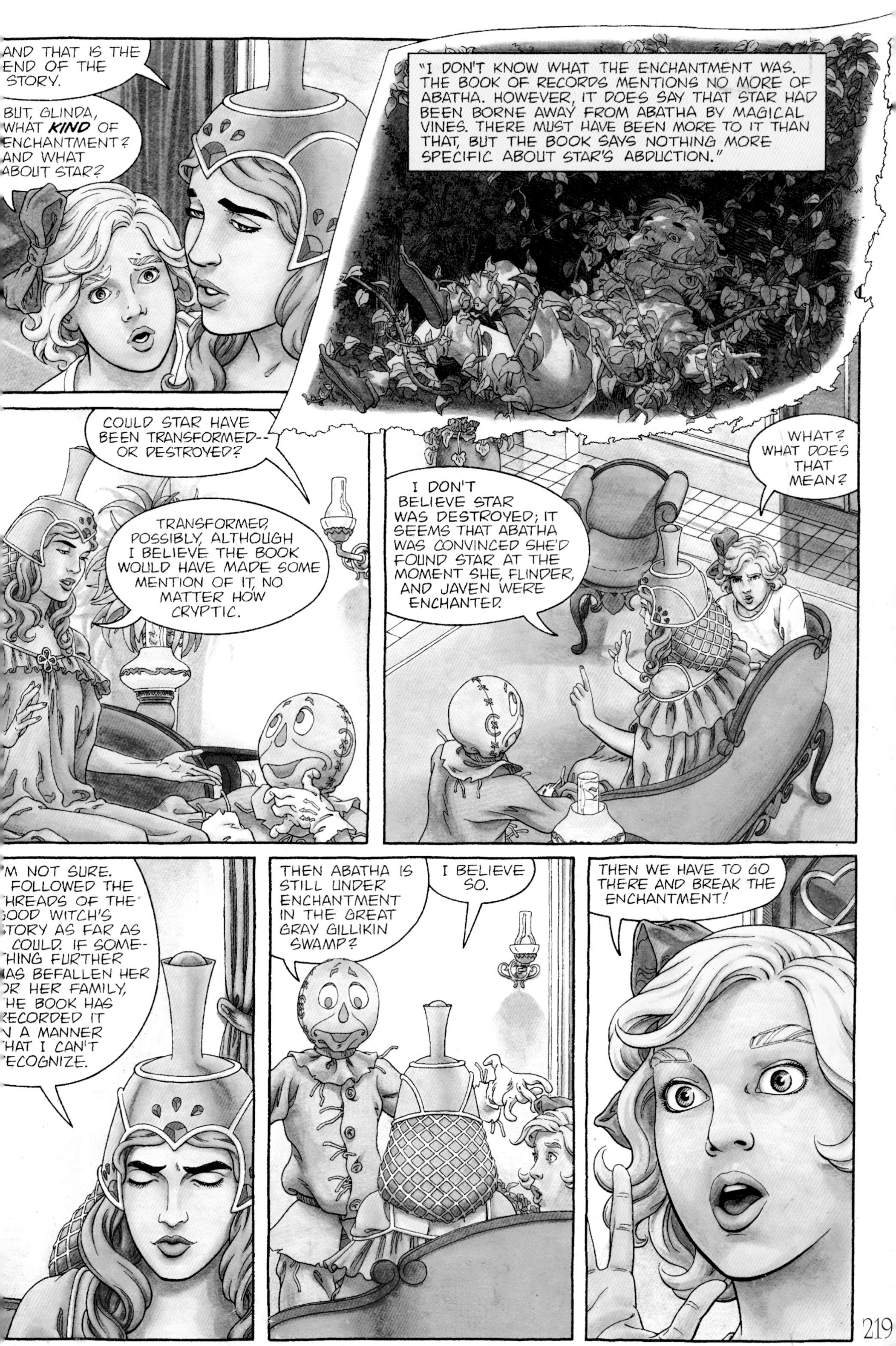
AND THAT IS THE END OF THE STORY.
BUT, GLINDA, WHAT KIND OF ENCHANTMENT? AND WHAT ABOUT STAR?
"I DON'T KNOW WHAT THE ENCHANTMENT WAS. THE BOOK OF RECORDS MENTIONS NO MORE OF ABATHA. HOWEVER, IT DOES SAY THAT STAR HAD BEEN BORNE AWAY FROM ABATHA BY MAGICAL VINES. THERE MUST HAVE BEEN MORE TO IT THAN THAT, BUT THE BOOK SAYS NOTHING MORE SPECIFIC ABOUT STAR'S ABDUCTION."
COULD STAR HAVE BEEN TRANSFORMED-- OR DESTROYED?
TRANSFORMED, POSSIBLY, ALTHOUGH I BELIEVE THE BOOK WOULD HAVE MADE SOME MENTION OF IT, NO MATTER HOW CRYPTIC.
I DON'T BELIEVE STAR WAS DESTROYED; IT SEEMS THAT ABATHA WAS CONVINCED SHE'D FOUND STAR AT THE MOMENT SHE, FLINDER, AND JAVEN WERE ENCHANTED.
WHAT? WHAT DOES THAT MEAN?
I'M NOT SURE. I FOLLOWED THE THREADS OF THE GOOD WITCH'S STORY AS FAR AS I COULD. IF SOMETHING FURTHER HAS BEFALLEN HER OR HER FAMILY, THE BOOK HAS RECORDED IT IN A MANNER THAT I CAN'T RECOGNIZE.
THEN ABATHA IS STILL UNDER ENCHANTMENT IN THE GREAT GRAY GILLIKIN SWAMP?
I BELIEVE SO.
THEN WE HAVE TO GO THERE AND BREAK THE ENCHANTMENT!

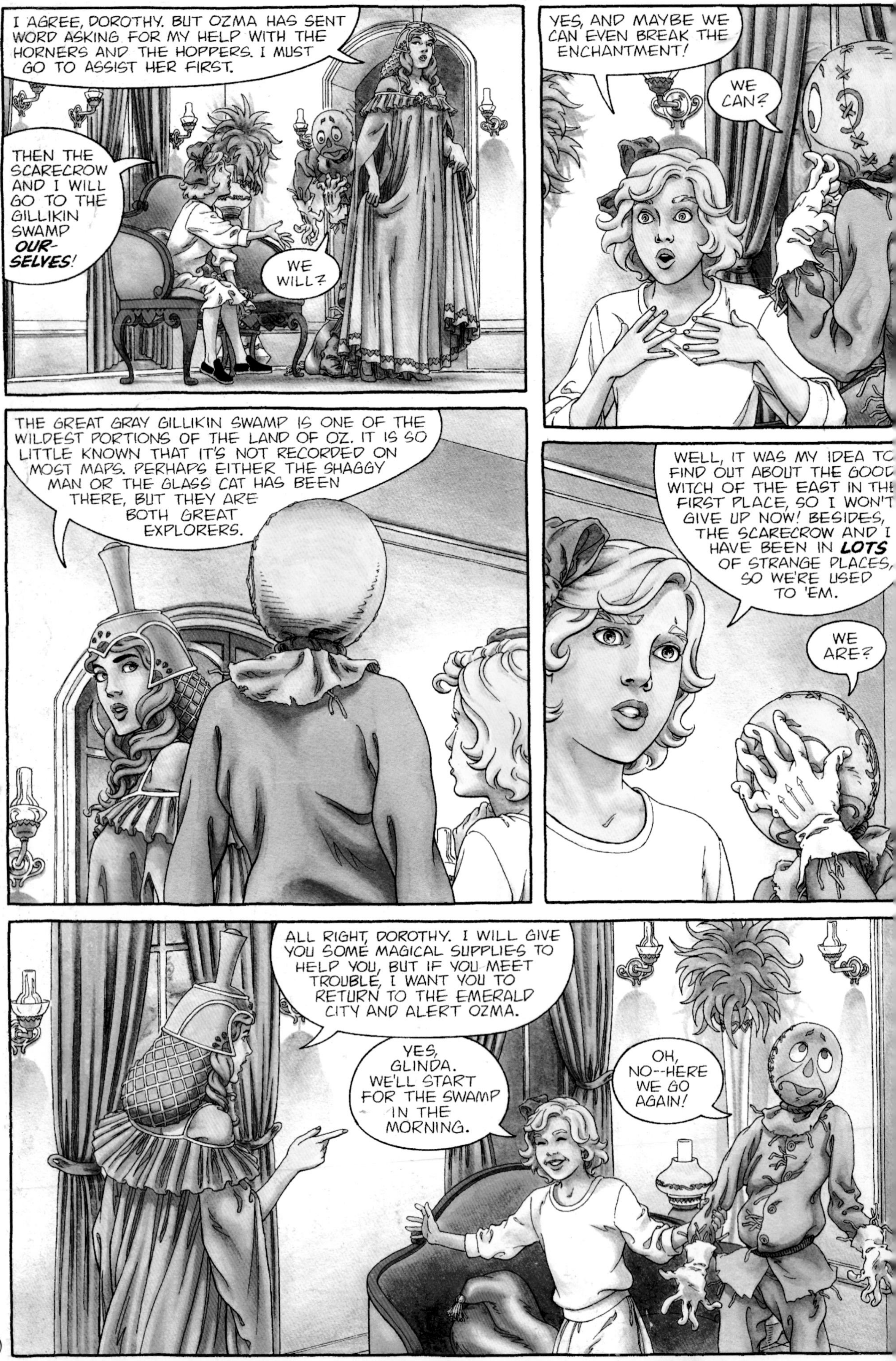
I AGREE, DOROTHY. BUT OZMA HAS SENT WORD ASKING FOR MY HELP WITH THE HORNERS AND THE HOPPERS. I MUST GO TO ASSIST HER FIRST.
THEN THE SCARECROW AND I WILL GO TO THE GILLIKIN SWAMP **OUR-SELVES**!
WE WILL?
YES, AND MAYBE WE CAN EVEN BREAK THE ENCHANTMENT!
WE CAN?
THE GREAT GRAY GILLIKIN SWAMP IS ONE OF THE WILDEST PORTIONS OF THE LAND OF OZ. IT IS SO LITTLE KNOWN THAT IT'S NOT RECORDED ON MOST MAPS. PERHAPS EITHER THE SHAGGY MAN OR THE GLASS CAT HAS BEEN THERE, BUT THEY ARE BOTH GREAT EXPLORERS.
WELL, IT WAS MY IDEA TO FIND OUT ABOUT THE GOOD WITCH OF THE EAST IN THE FIRST PLACE, SO I WON'T GIVE UP NOW! BESIDES, THE SCARECROW AND I HAVE BEEN IN **LOTS** OF STRANGE PLACES, SO WE'RE USED TO 'EM.
WE ARE?
ALL RIGHT, DOROTHY. I WILL GIVE YOU SOME MAGICAL SUPPLIES TO HELP YOU, BUT IF YOU MEET TROUBLE, I WANT YOU TO RETURN TO THE EMERALD CITY AND ALERT OZMA.
YES, GLINDA. WE'LL START FOR THE SWAMP IN THE MORNING.
OH, NO--HERE WE GO AGAIN!

Chapter 2 The Swamp

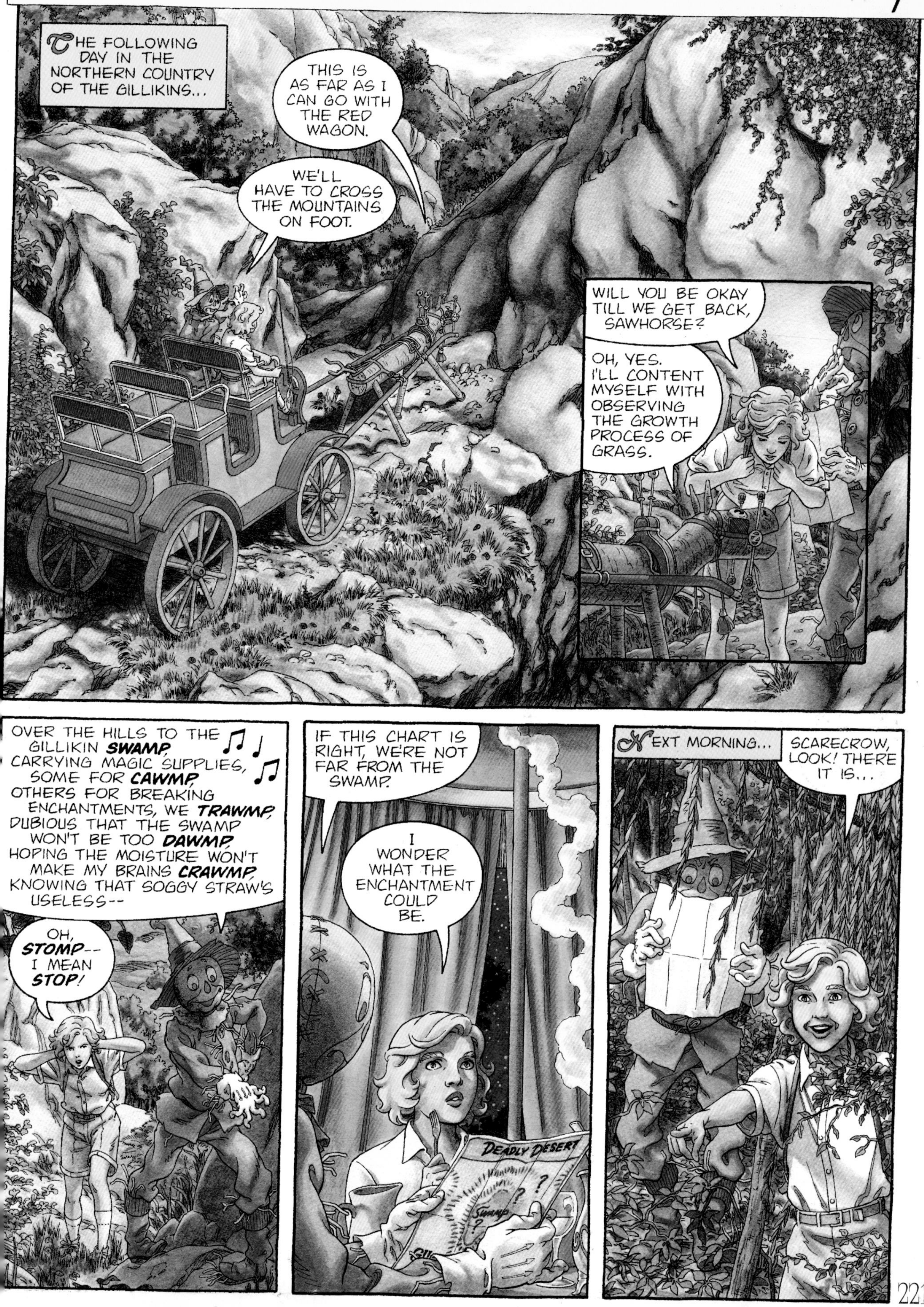

THE FOLLOWING DAY IN THE NORTHERN COUNTRY OF THE GILLIKINS...
THIS IS AS FAR AS I CAN GO WITH THE RED WAGON.
WE'LL HAVE TO CROSS THE MOUNTAINS ON FOOT.
WILL YOU BE OKAY TILL WE GET BACK, SAWHORSE?
OH, YES. I'LL CONTENT MYSELF WITH OBSERVING THE GROWTH PROCESS OF GRASS.
OVER THE HILLS TO THE GILLIKIN SWAMP, CARRYING MAGIC SUPPLIES, SOME FOR CAWMP, OTHERS FOR BREAKING ENCHANTMENTS, WE TRAWMP, DUBIOUS THAT THE SWAMP WON'T BE TOO DAWMP, HOPING THE MOISTURE WON'T MAKE MY BRAINS CRAWMP, KNOWING THAT SOGGY STRAW'S USELESS--
OH, STOMP-- I MEAN STOP!
IF THIS CHART IS RIGHT, WE'RE NOT FAR FROM THE SWAMP.
I WONDER WHAT THE ENCHANTMENT COULD BE.
DEADLY DESERT
SWAMP
NEXT MORNING...
SCARECROW, LOOK! THERE IT IS...

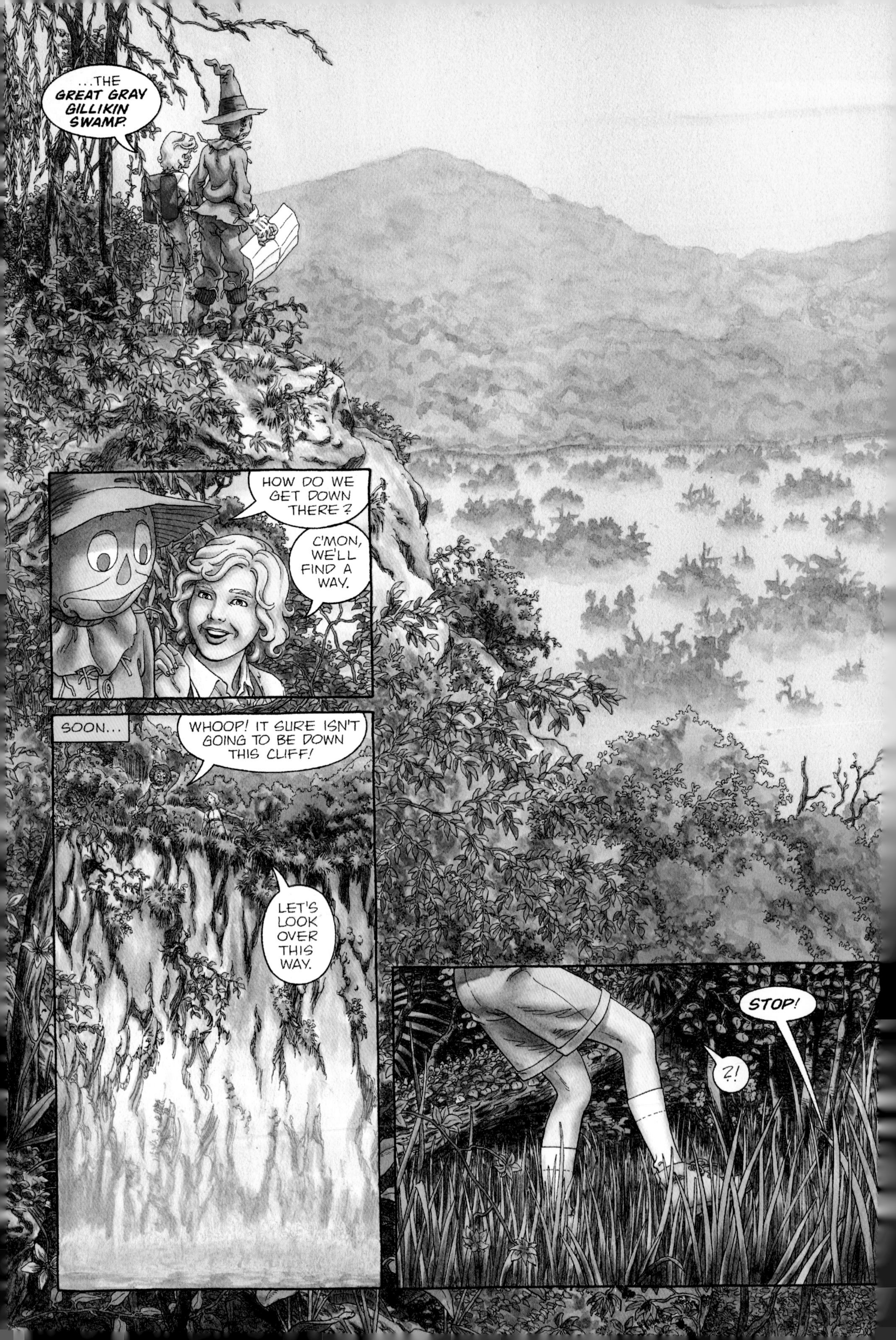
...THE GREAT GRAY GILLIKIN SWAMP.
HOW DO WE GET DOWN THERE?
C'MON, WE'LL FIND A WAY.
SOON...
WHOOP! IT SURE ISN'T GOING TO BE DOWN THIS CLIFF!
LET'S LOOK OVER THIS WAY.
STOP!
?!

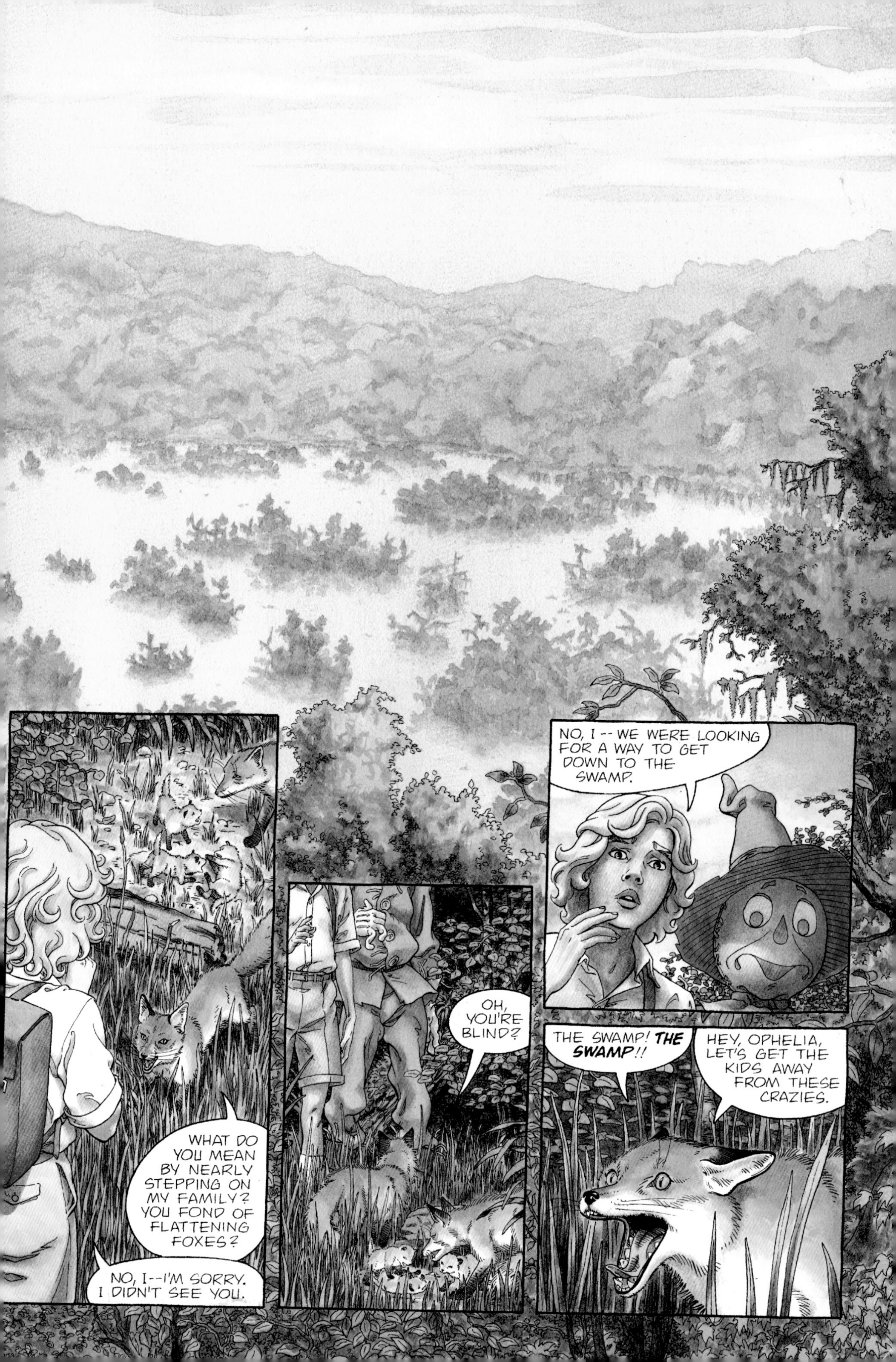
WHAT DO YOU MEAN BY NEARLY STEPPING ON MY FAMILY? YOU FOND OF FLATTENING FOXES?
NO, I--I'M SORRY. I DIDN'T SEE YOU.
OH, YOU'RE BLIND?
NO, I -- WE WERE LOOKING FOR A WAY TO GET DOWN TO THE SWAMP.
THE SWAMP! THE SWAMP!!
HEY, OPHELIA, LET'S GET THE KIDS AWAY FROM THESE CRAZIES.

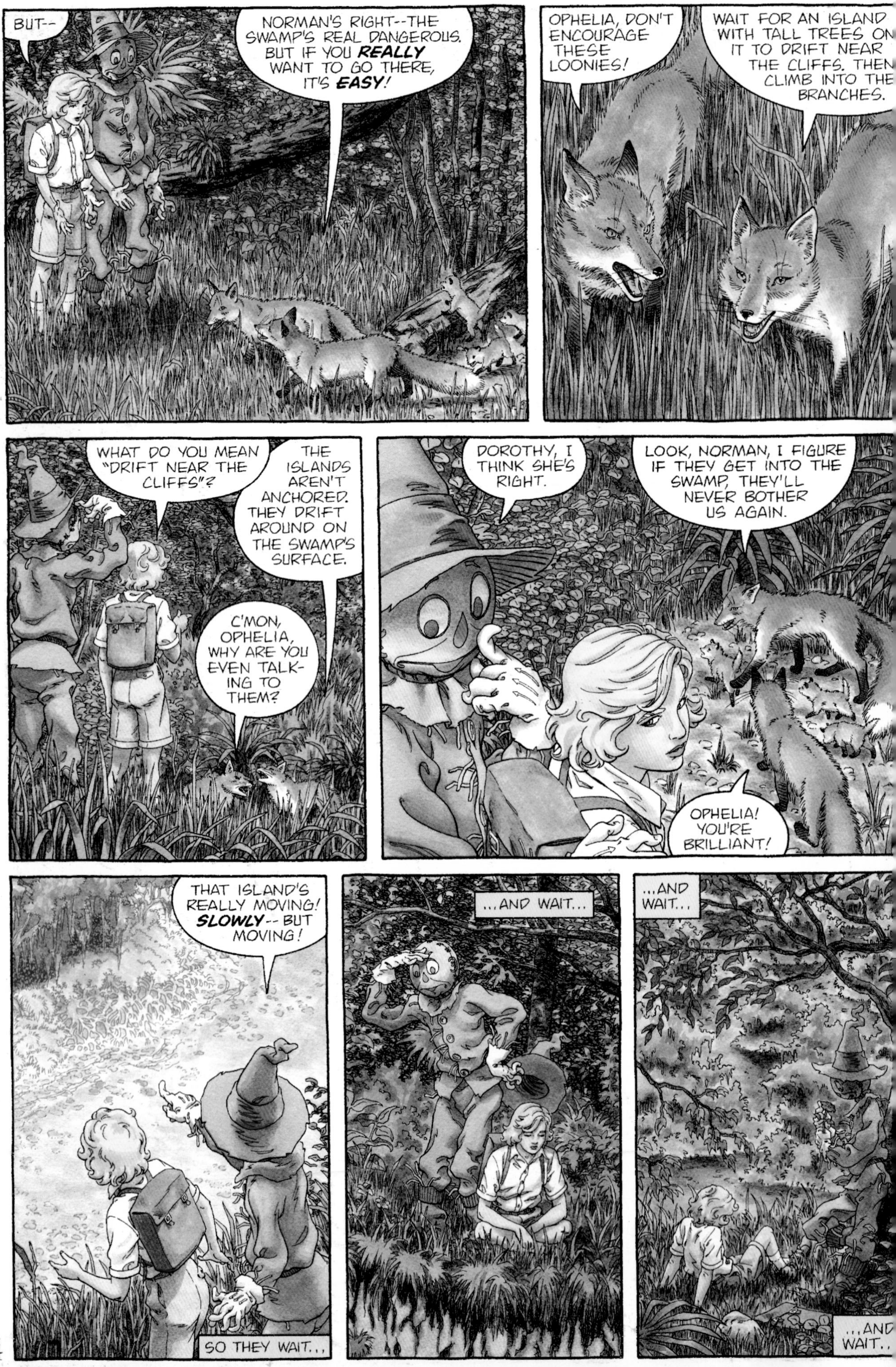
BUT--
NORMAN'S RIGHT--THE SWAMP'S REAL DANGEROUS. BUT IF YOU REALLY WANT TO GO THERE, IT'S EASY!
OPHELIA, DON'T ENCOURAGE THESE LOONIES!
WAIT FOR AN ISLAND WITH TALL TREES ON IT TO DRIFT NEAR THE CLIFFS. THEN CLIMB INTO THE BRANCHES.
WHAT DO YOU MEAN "DRIFT NEAR THE CLIFFS"?
THE ISLANDS AREN'T ANCHORED. THEY DRIFT AROUND ON THE SWAMP'S SURFACE.
C'MON, OPHELIA, WHY ARE YOU EVEN TALKING TO THEM?
DOROTHY, I THINK SHE'S RIGHT.
LOOK, NORMAN, I FIGURE IF THEY GET INTO THE SWAMP, THEY'LL NEVER BOTHER US AGAIN.
OPHELIA! YOU'RE BRILLIANT!
THAT ISLAND'S REALLY MOVING! SLOWLY-- BUT MOVING!
SO THEY WAIT...
...AND WAIT...
...AND WAIT...
...AND WAIT...

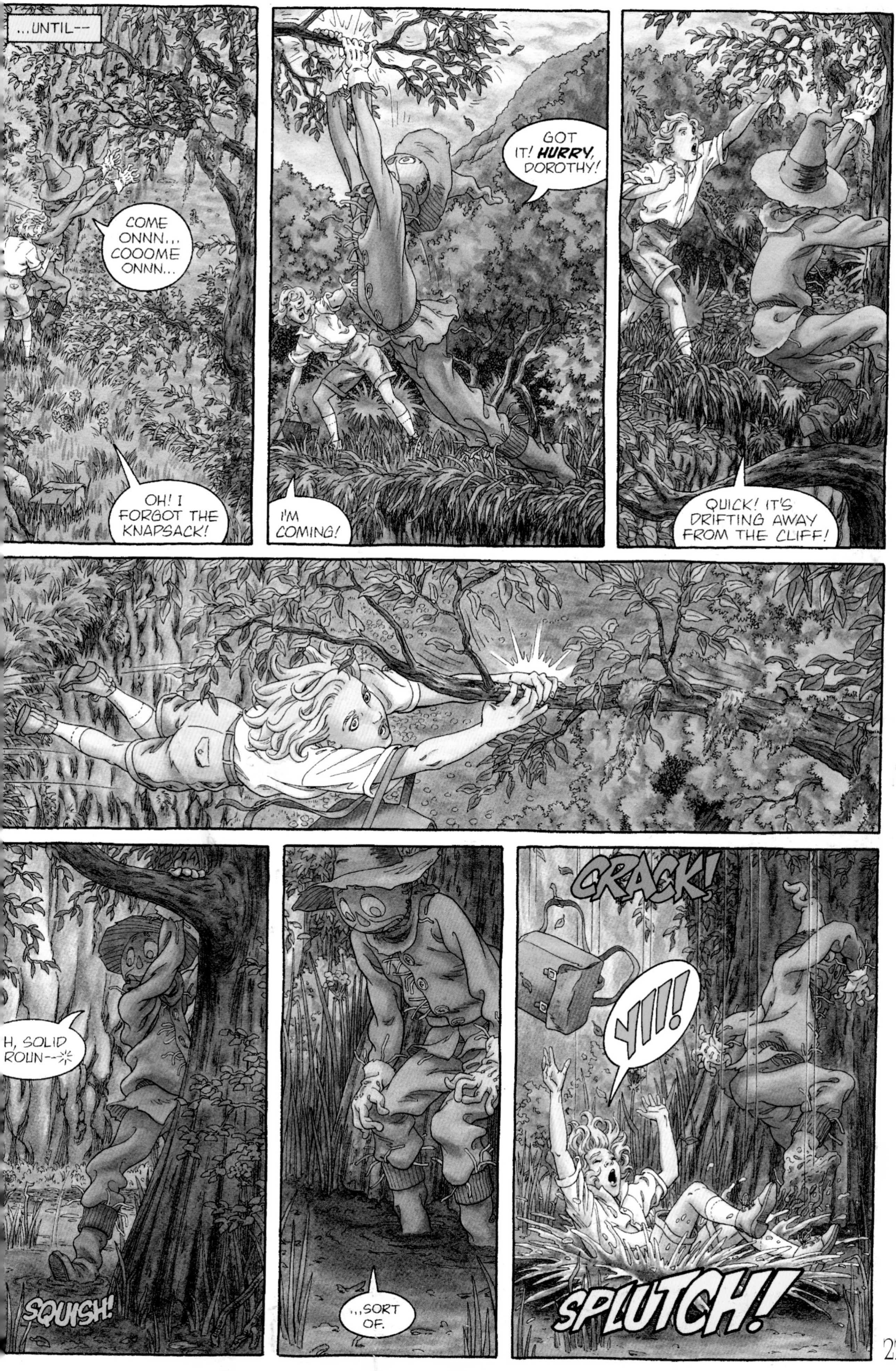
...UNTIL--
COME ONNN... COOOME ONNN...
OH! I FORGOT THE KNAPSACK!
GOT IT! HURRY, DOROTHY!
I'M COMING!
QUICK! IT'S DRIFTING AWAY FROM THE CLIFF!
H, SOLID ROUN--
SQUISH!
...SORT OF.
CRACK!
YII!
SPLUTCH!

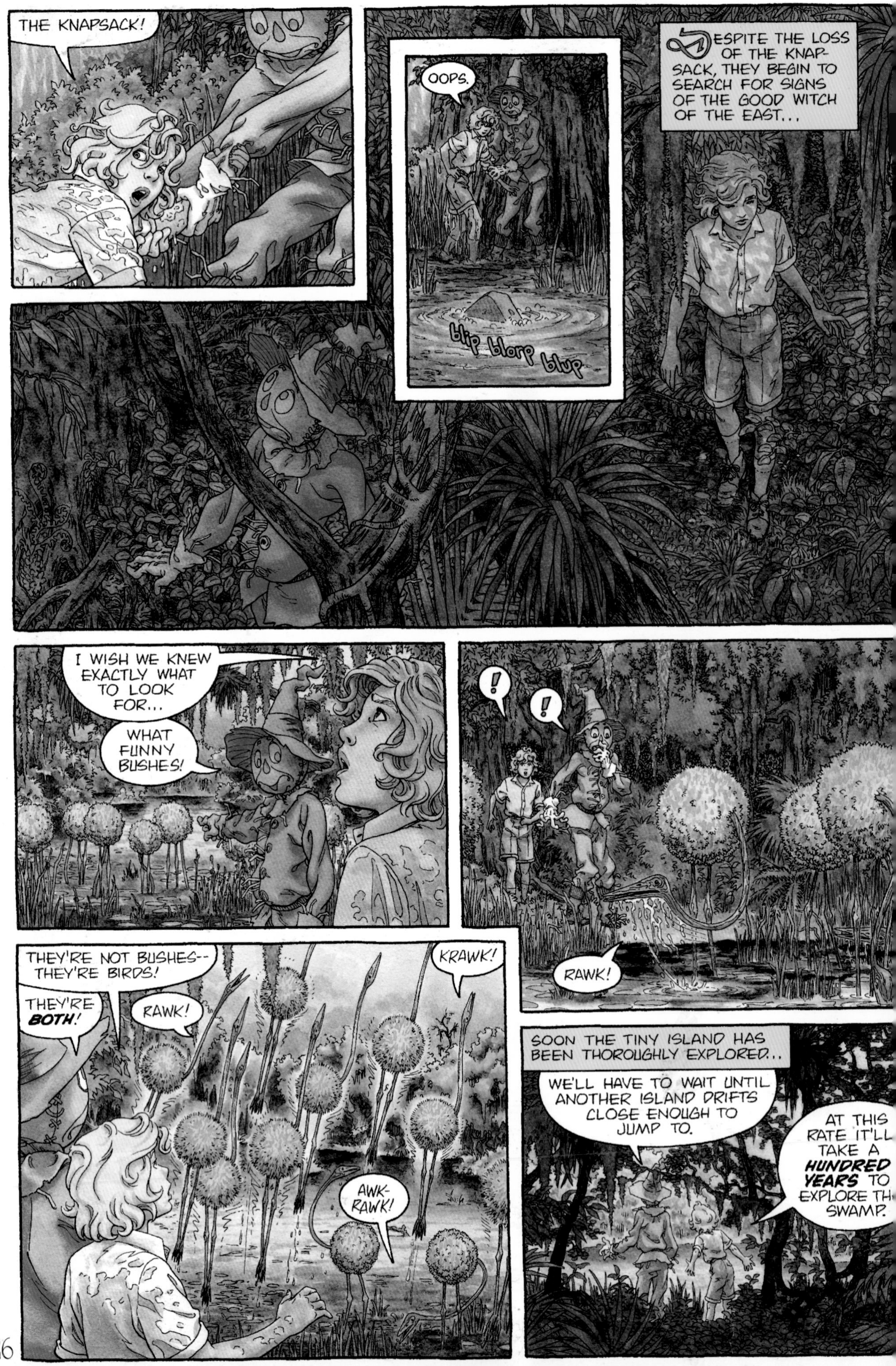
THE KNAPSACK!
OOPS.
blip blorp blup
DESPITE THE LOSS OF THE KNAPSACK, THEY BEGIN TO SEARCH FOR SIGNS OF THE GOOD WITCH OF THE EAST...
I WISH WE KNEW EXACTLY WHAT TO LOOK FOR...
WHAT FUNNY BUSHES!
!
!
RAWK!
THEY'RE NOT BUSHES-- THEY'RE BIRDS!
THEY'RE **BOTH**!
RAWK!
KRAWK!
AWK-RAWK!
SOON THE TINY ISLAND HAS BEEN THOROUGHLY EXPLORED...
WE'LL HAVE TO WAIT UNTIL ANOTHER ISLAND DRIFTS CLOSE ENOUGH TO JUMP TO.
AT THIS RATE IT'LL TAKE A **HUNDRED YEARS** TO EXPLORE TH SWAMP.

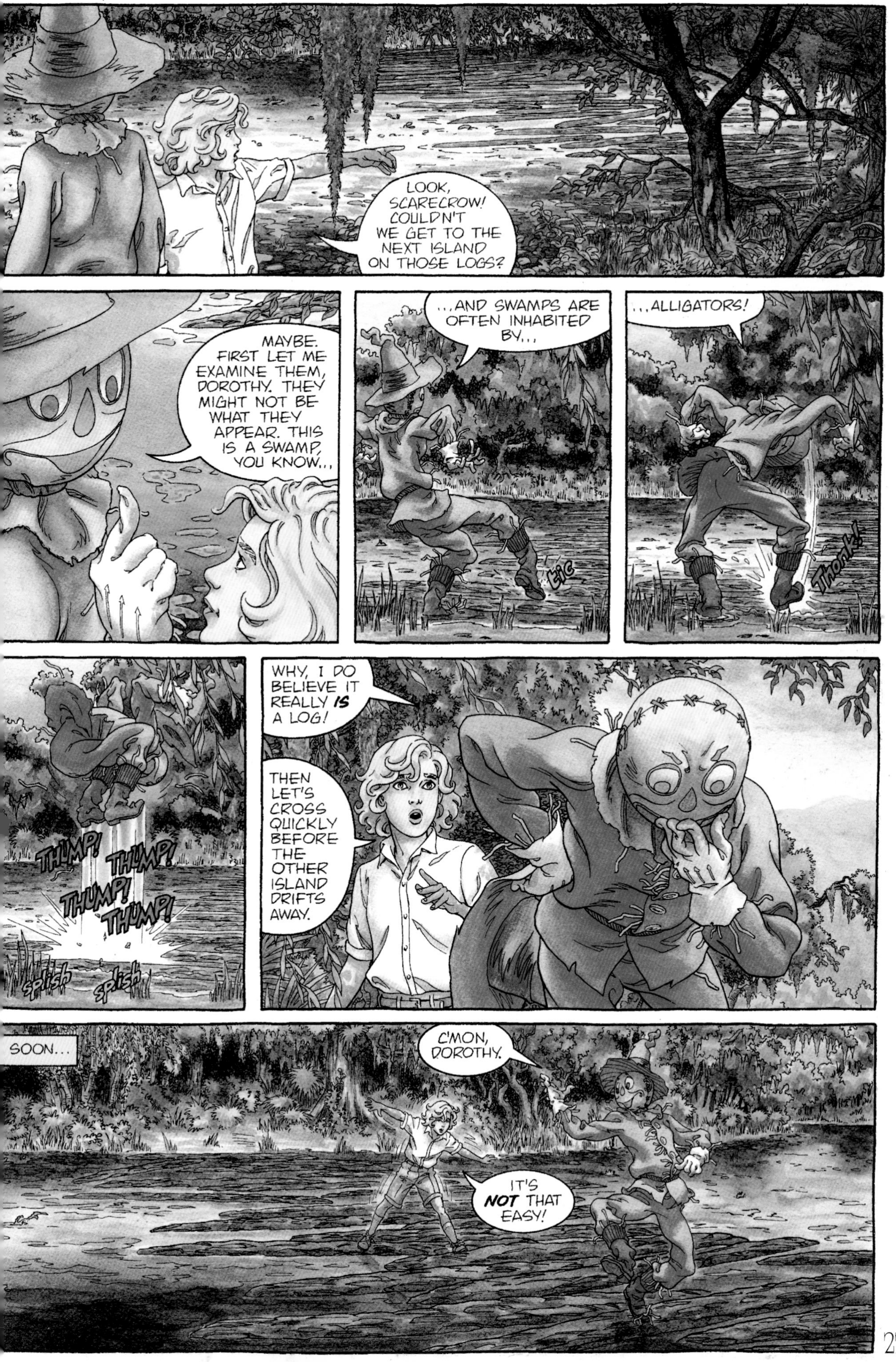
LOOK, SCARECROW! COULDN'T WE GET TO THE NEXT ISLAND ON THOSE LOGS?
MAYBE. FIRST LET ME EXAMINE THEM, DOROTHY. THEY MIGHT NOT BE WHAT THEY APPEAR. THIS IS A SWAMP, YOU KNOW...
...AND SWAMPS ARE OFTEN INHABITED BY...
tic
...ALLIGATORS!
Thonk!
THUMP! THUMP! THUMP! THUMP!
splish splish
WHY, I DO BELIEVE IT REALLY **IS** A LOG!
THEN LET'S CROSS QUICKLY BEFORE THE OTHER ISLAND DRIFTS AWAY.
SOON...
C'MON, DOROTHY.
IT'S **NOT** THAT EASY!

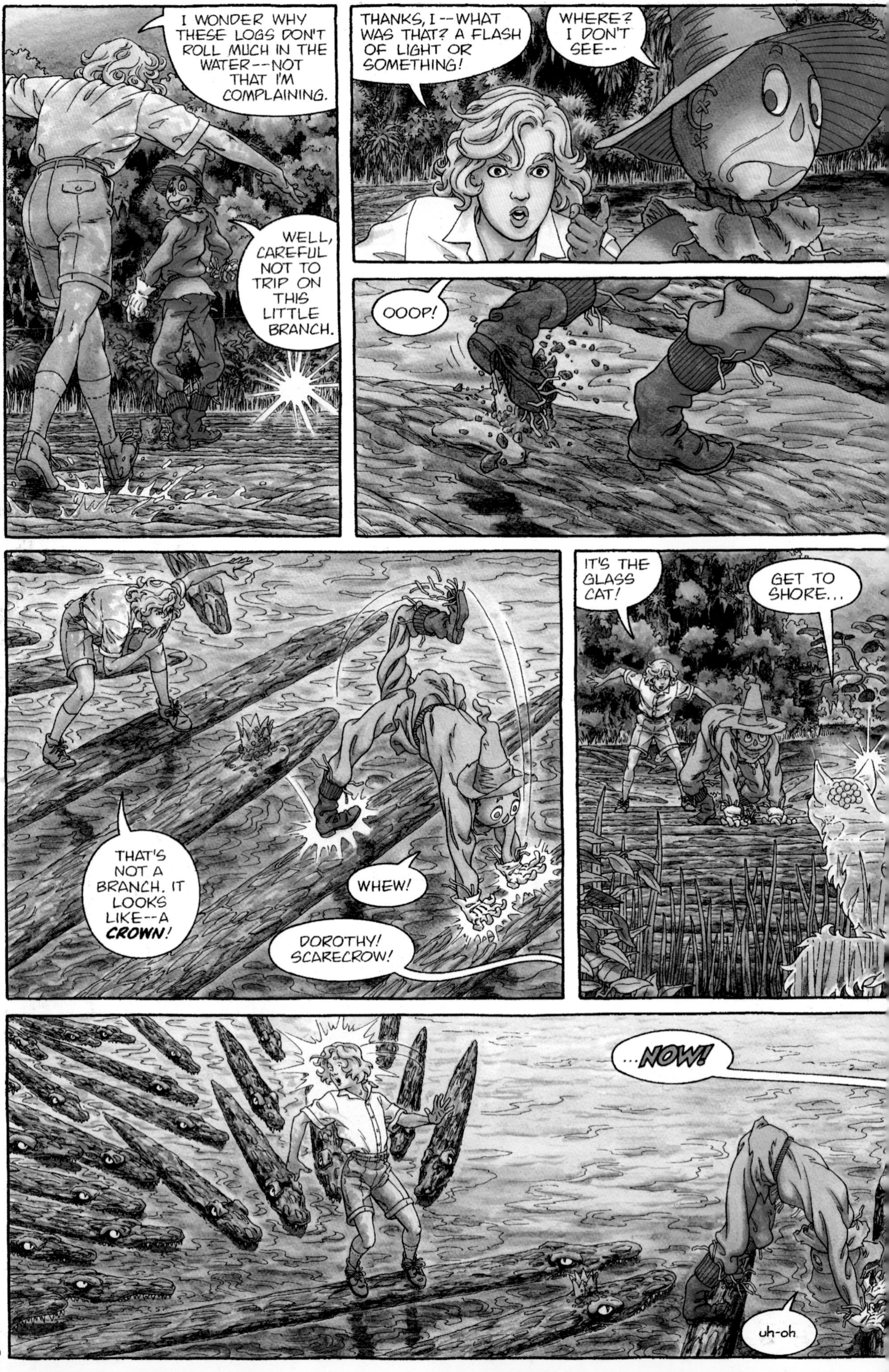
I WONDER WHY THESE LOGS DON'T ROLL MUCH IN THE WATER--NOT THAT I'M COMPLAINING.
WELL, CAREFUL NOT TO TRIP ON THIS LITTLE BRANCH.
THANKS, I--WHAT WAS THAT? A FLASH OF LIGHT OR SOMETHING!
WHERE? I DON'T SEE--
OOOP!
THAT'S NOT A BRANCH. IT LOOKS LIKE--A CROWN!
WHEW!
DOROTHY! SCARECROW!
IT'S THE GLASS CAT!
GET TO SHORE...
...NOW!
uh-oh

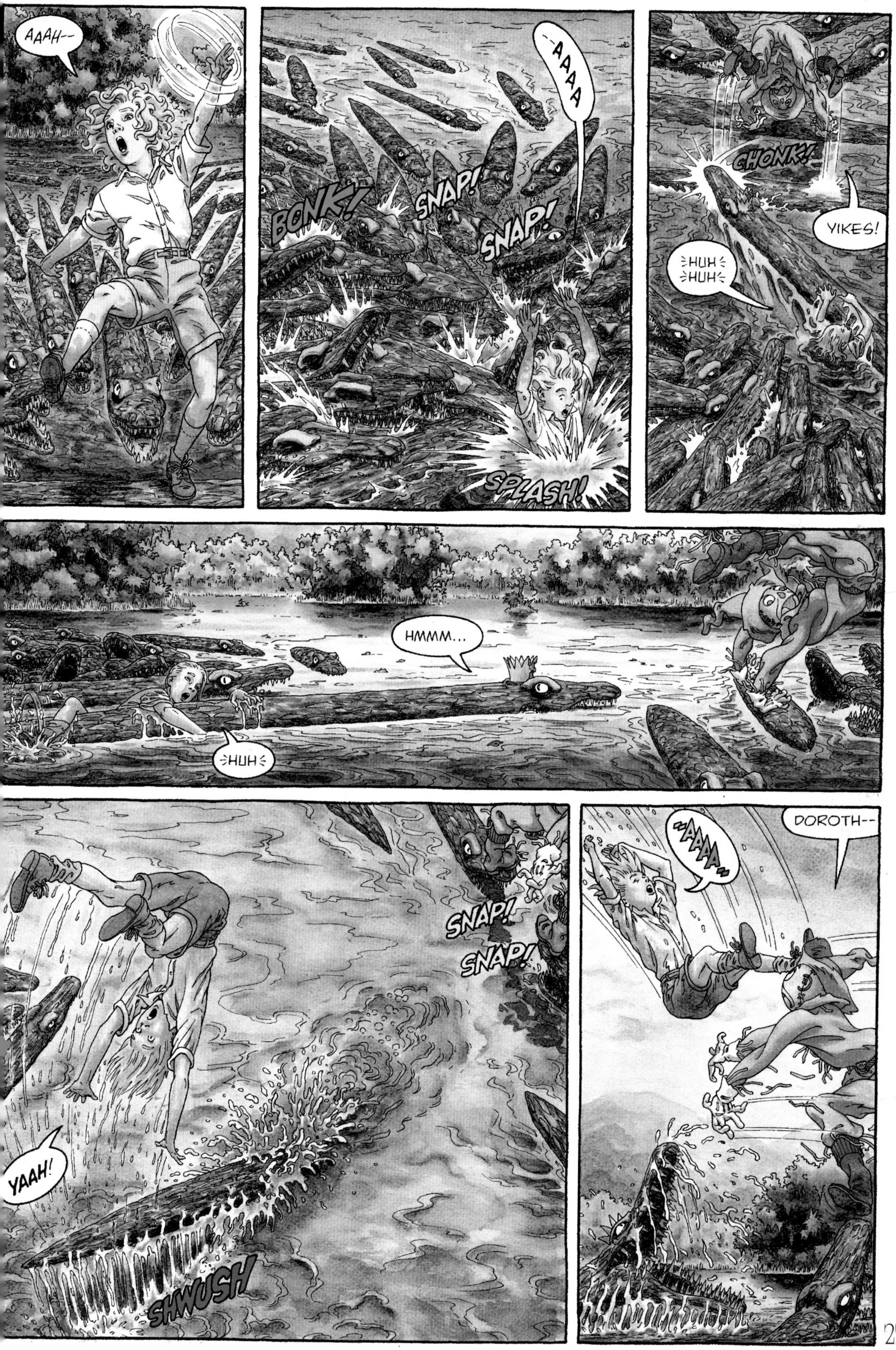
AAAH--
--AAAA
BONK!
SNAP!
SNAP!
SPLASH!
CHONK!
YIKES!
HUH HUH
HMMM...
HUH
SNAP!
SNAP!
YAAH!
SHWUSH
AAAA
DOROTH--

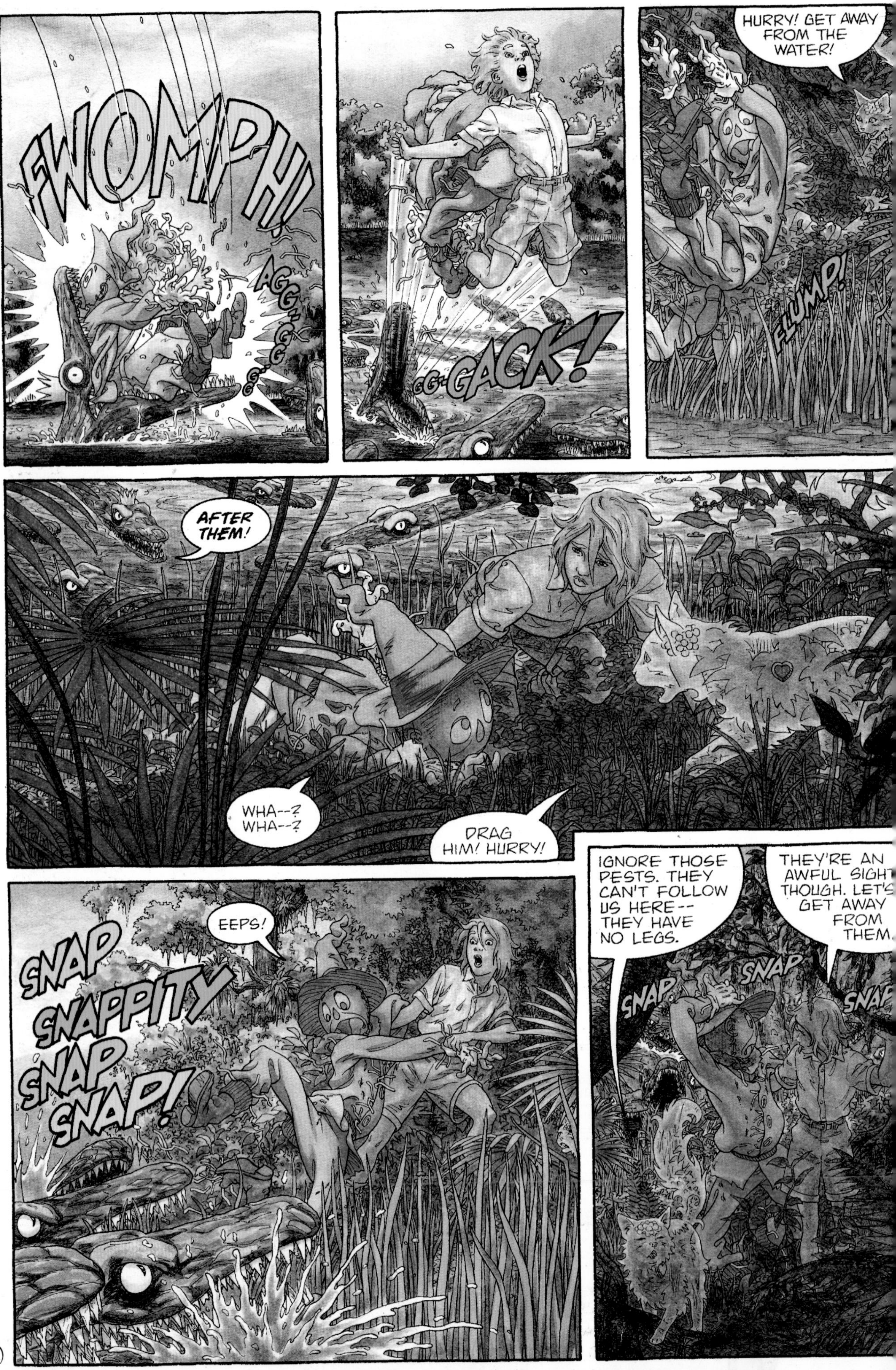

FWOMPH!
AGG-G-G-G-
GG-GACK!
HURRY! GET AWAY FROM THE WATER!
FLUMP!
AFTER THEM!
WHA--? WHA--?
DRAG HIM! HURRY!
SNAP SNAPPITY SNAP SNAP!
EEPS!
IGNORE THOSE PESTS. THEY CAN'T FOLLOW US HERE-- THEY HAVE NO LEGS.
THEY'RE AN AWFUL SIGHT THOUGH. LET'S GET AWAY FROM THEM.
SNAP
SNAP
SNAP

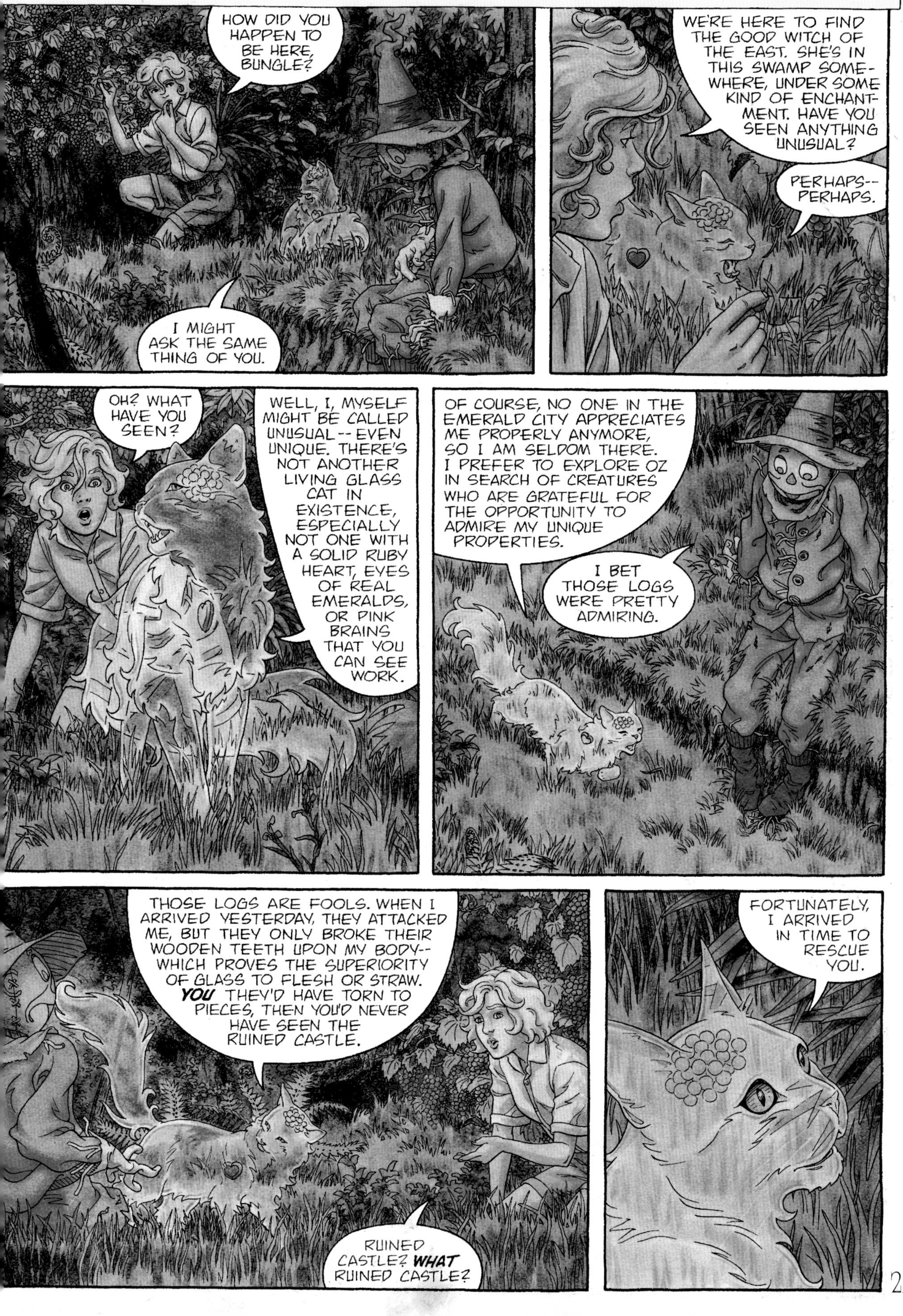
HOW DID YOU HAPPEN TO BE HERE, BUNGLE?
I MIGHT ASK THE SAME THING OF YOU.
WE'RE HERE TO FIND THE GOOD WITCH OF THE EAST. SHE'S IN THIS SWAMP SOMEWHERE, UNDER SOME KIND OF ENCHANTMENT. HAVE YOU SEEN ANYTHING UNUSUAL?
PERHAPS-- PERHAPS.
OH? WHAT HAVE YOU SEEN?
WELL, I, MYSELF MIGHT BE CALLED UNUSUAL -- EVEN UNIQUE. THERE'S NOT ANOTHER LIVING GLASS CAT IN EXISTENCE, ESPECIALLY NOT ONE WITH A SOLID RUBY HEART, EYES OF REAL EMERALDS, OR PINK BRAINS THAT YOU CAN SEE WORK.
OF COURSE, NO ONE IN THE EMERALD CITY APPRECIATES ME PROPERLY ANYMORE, SO I AM SELDOM THERE. I PREFER TO EXPLORE OZ IN SEARCH OF CREATURES WHO ARE GRATEFUL FOR THE OPPORTUNITY TO ADMIRE MY UNIQUE PROPERTIES.
I BET THOSE LOGS WERE PRETTY ADMIRING.
THOSE LOGS ARE FOOLS. WHEN I ARRIVED YESTERDAY, THEY ATTACKED ME, BUT THEY ONLY BROKE THEIR WOODEN TEETH UPON MY BODY-- WHICH PROVES THE SUPERIORITY OF GLASS TO FLESH OR STRAW. YOU THEY'D HAVE TORN TO PIECES, THEN YOU'D NEVER HAVE SEEN THE RUINED CASTLE.
RUINED CASTLE? WHAT RUINED CASTLE?
FORTUNATELY, I ARRIVED IN TIME TO RESCUE YOU.

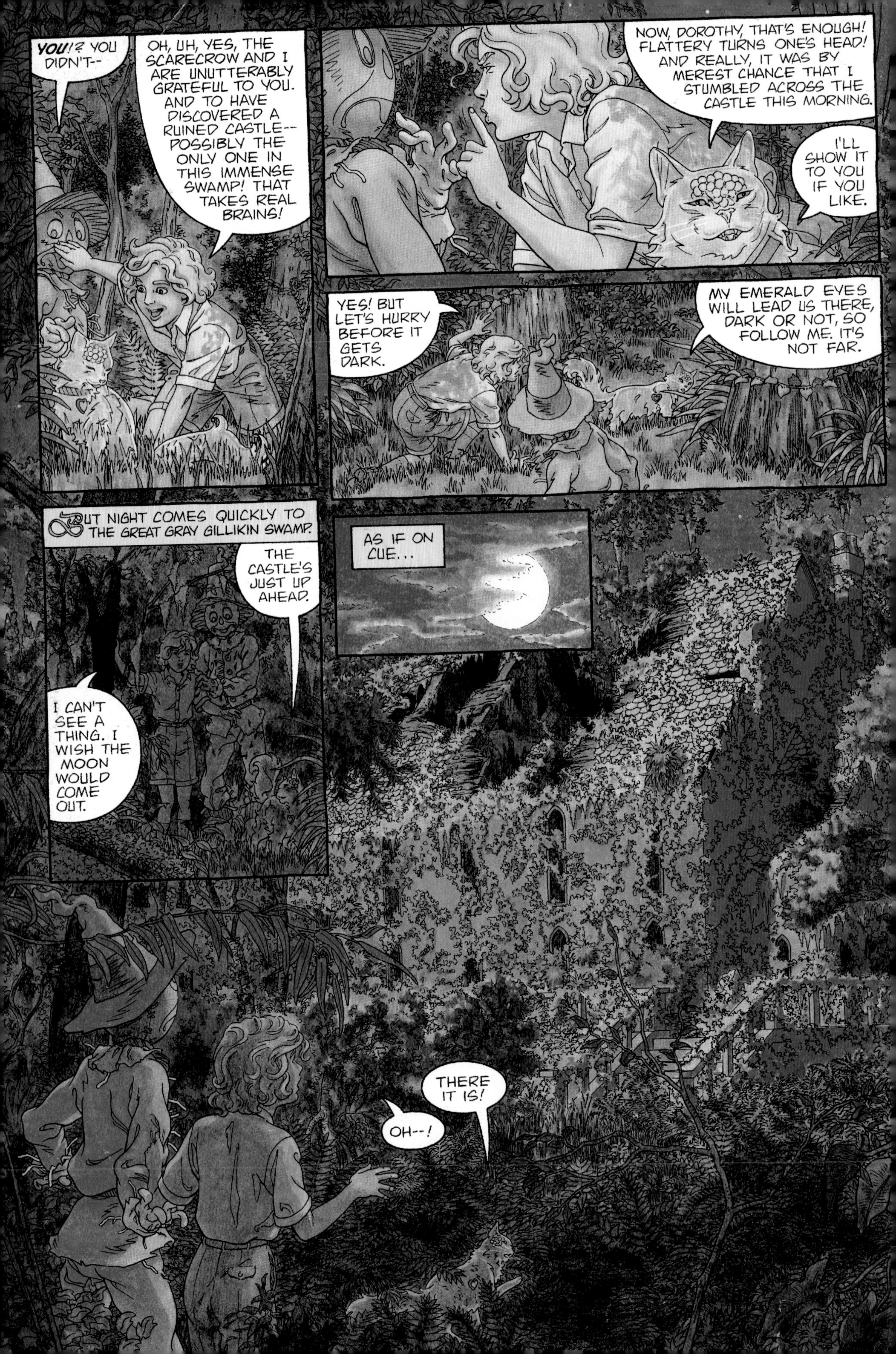
YOU!? YOU DIDN'T--
OH, UH, YES, THE SCARECROW AND I ARE UNUTTERABLY GRATEFUL TO YOU. AND TO HAVE DISCOVERED A RUINED CASTLE-- POSSIBLY THE ONLY ONE IN THIS IMMENSE SWAMP! THAT TAKES REAL BRAINS!
NOW, DOROTHY, THAT'S ENOUGH! FLATTERY TURNS ONE'S HEAD! AND REALLY, IT WAS BY MEREST CHANCE THAT I STUMBLED ACROSS THE CASTLE THIS MORNING.
I'LL SHOW IT TO YOU IF YOU LIKE.
YES! BUT LET'S HURRY BEFORE IT GETS DARK.
MY EMERALD EYES WILL LEAD US THERE, DARK OR NOT, SO FOLLOW ME. IT'S NOT FAR.
BUT NIGHT COMES QUICKLY TO THE GREAT GRAY GILLIKIN SWAMP.
THE CASTLE'S JUST UP AHEAD.
I CAN'T SEE A THING. I WISH THE MOON WOULD COME OUT.
AS IF ON CUE...
THERE IT IS!
OH--!

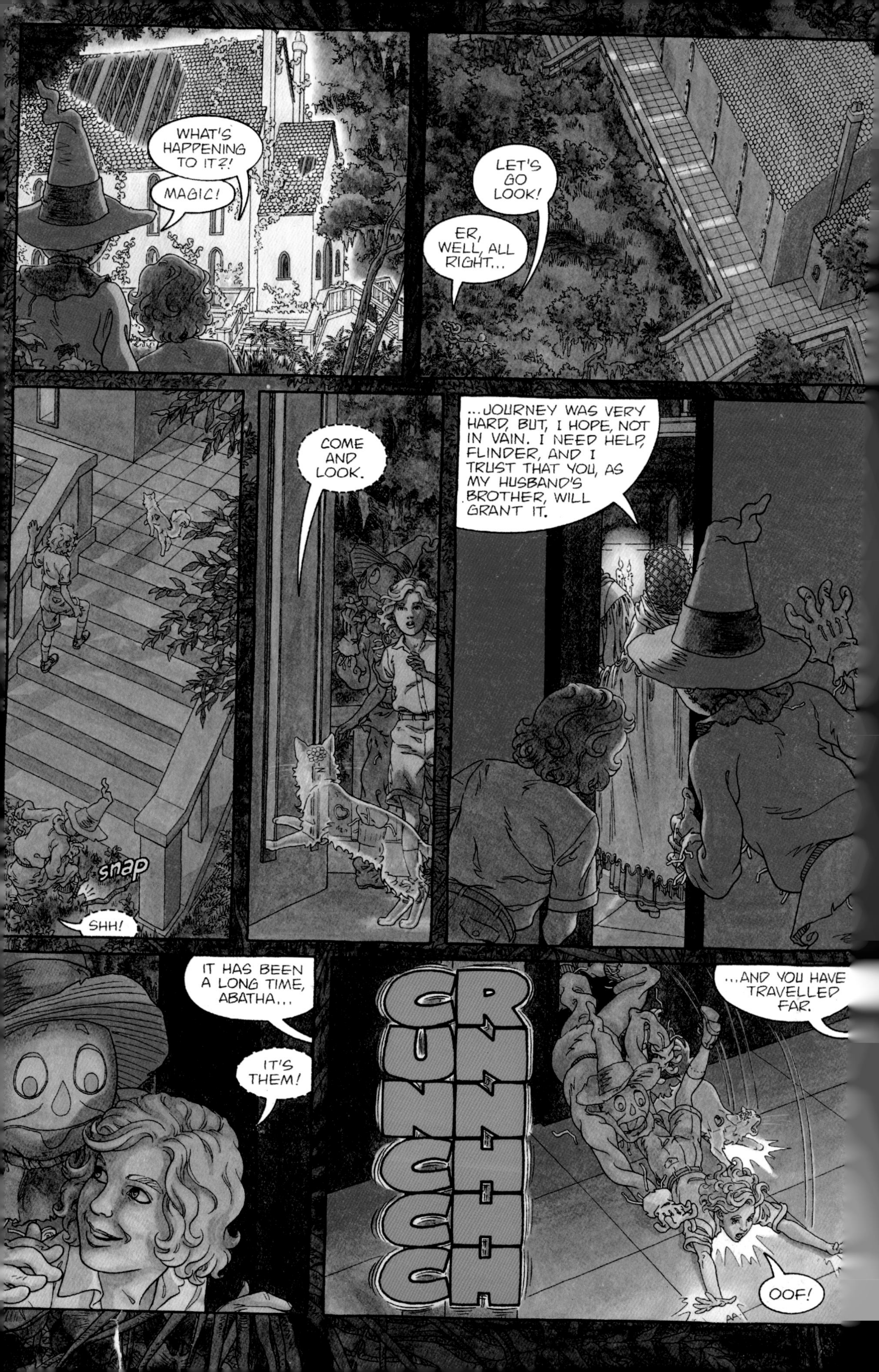
WHAT'S HAPPENING TO IT?!
MAGIC!
LET'S GO LOOK!
ER, WELL, ALL RIGHT...
snap
SHH!
COME AND LOOK.
...JOURNEY WAS VERY HARD, BUT, I HOPE, NOT IN VAIN. I NEED HELP, FLINDER, AND I TRUST THAT YOU, AS MY HUSBAND'S BROTHER, WILL GRANT IT.
IT HAS BEEN A LONG TIME, ABATHA...
IT'S THEM!
CRUNCH
CRUNCH
...AND YOU HAVE TRAVELLED FAR.
OOF!

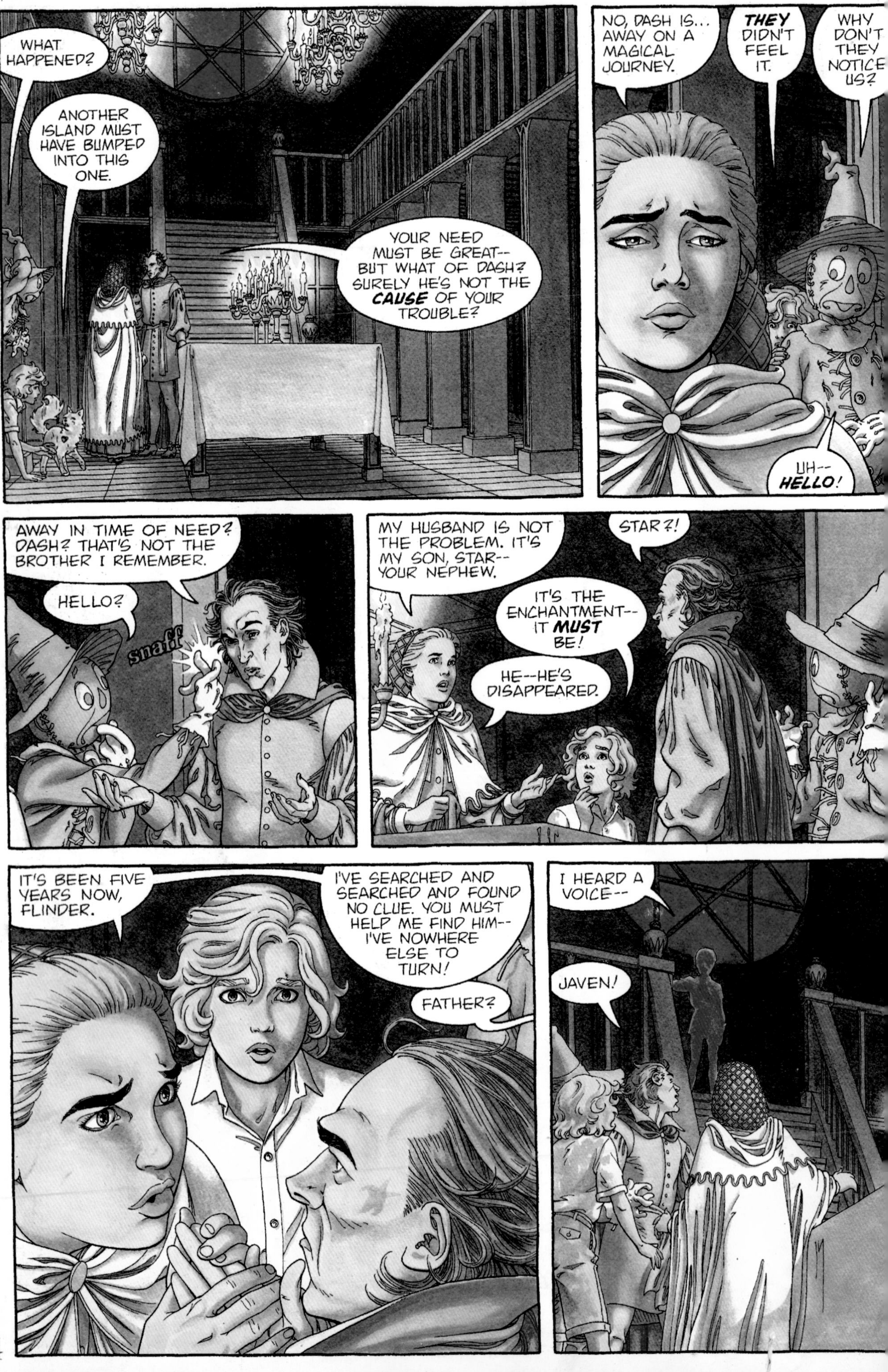

WHAT HAPPENED?
ANOTHER ISLAND MUST HAVE BUMPED INTO THIS ONE.
YOUR NEED MUST BE GREAT-- BUT WHAT OF DASH? SURELY HE'S NOT THE **CAUSE** OF YOUR TROUBLE?
NO, DASH IS... AWAY ON A MAGICAL JOURNEY.
THEY DIDN'T FEEL IT.
WHY DON'T THEY NOTICE US?
UH-- **HELLO!**
AWAY IN TIME OF NEED? DASH? THAT'S NOT THE BROTHER I REMEMBER.
HELLO?
snaff
MY HUSBAND IS NOT THE PROBLEM. IT'S MY SON, STAR-- YOUR NEPHEW.
STAR?!
IT'S THE ENCHANTMENT-- IT **MUST** BE!
HE--HE'S DISAPPEARED.
IT'S BEEN FIVE YEARS NOW, FLINDER.
I'VE SEARCHED AND SEARCHED AND FOUND NO CLUE. YOU MUST HELP ME FIND HIM-- I'VE NOWHERE ELSE TO TURN!
FATHER?
I HEARD A VOICE--
JAVEN!

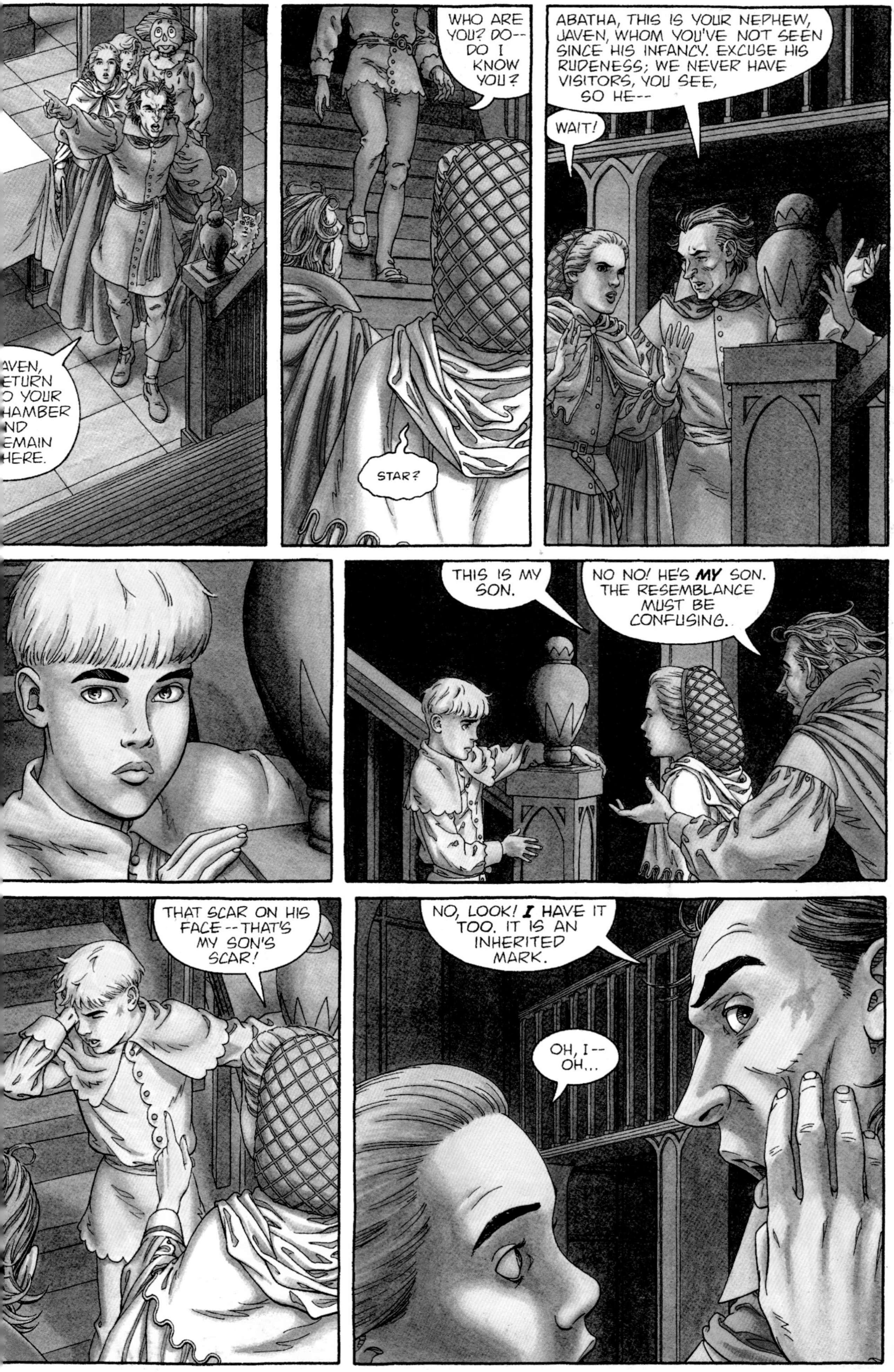
AVEN, ETURN O YOUR HAMBER ND EMAIN HERE.
WHO ARE YOU? DO-- DO I KNOW YOU?
STAR?
ABATHA, THIS IS YOUR NEPHEW, JAVEN, WHOM YOU'VE NOT SEEN SINCE HIS INFANCY. EXCUSE HIS RUDENESS; WE NEVER HAVE VISITORS, YOU SEE, SO HE--
WAIT!
THIS IS MY SON.
NO NO! HE'S MY SON. THE RESEMBLANCE MUST BE CONFUSING.
THAT SCAR ON HIS FACE--THAT'S MY SON'S SCAR!
NO, LOOK! I HAVE IT TOO. IT IS AN INHERITED MARK.
OH, I-- OH...

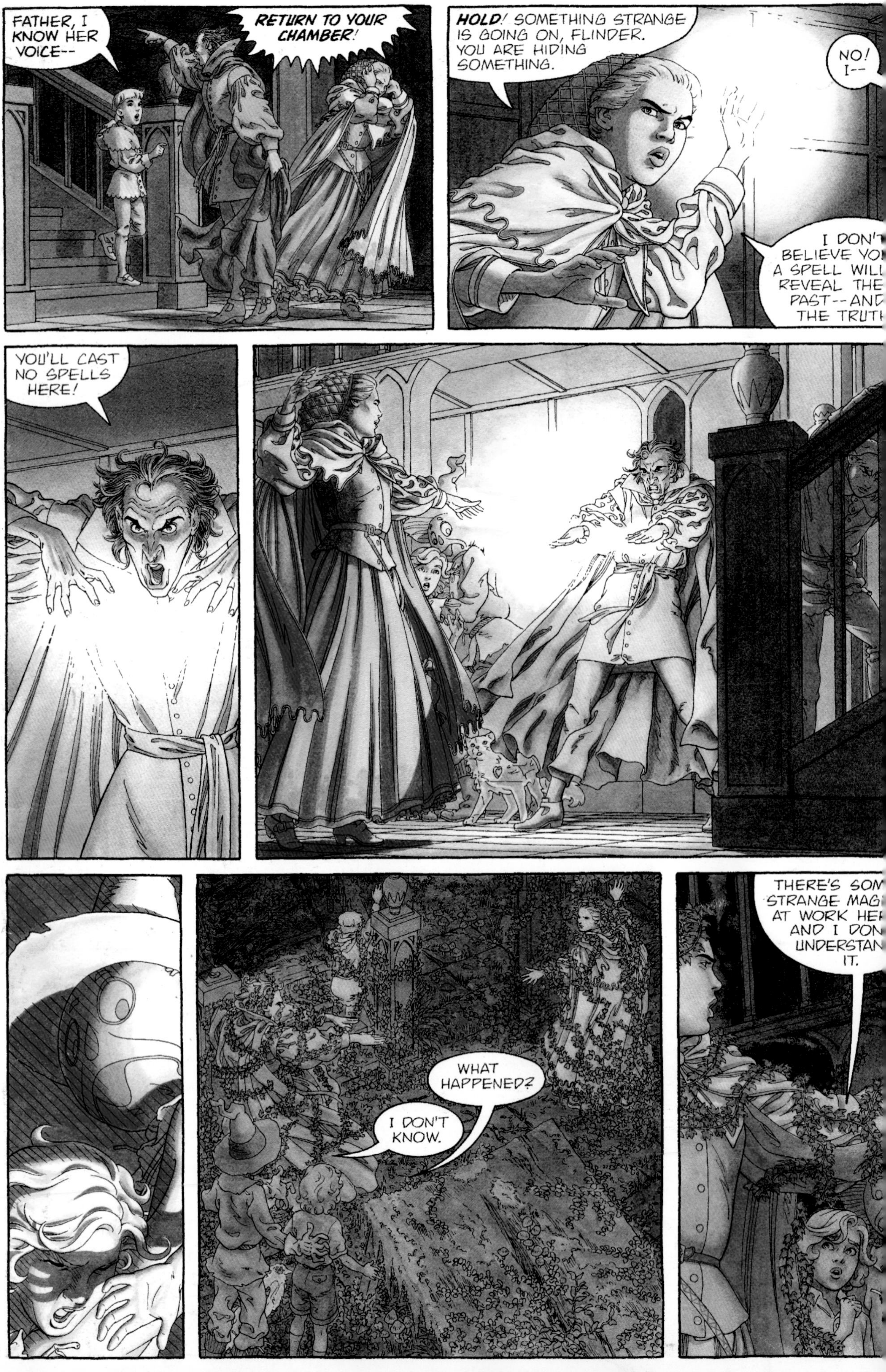
FATHER, I KNOW HER VOICE--
RETURN TO YOUR CHAMBER!
HOLD! SOMETHING STRANGE IS GOING ON, FLINDER. YOU ARE HIDING SOMETHING.
NO! I--
I DON'T BELIEVE YO A SPELL WIL REVEAL THE PAST--AN THE TRUT
YOU'LL CAST NO SPELLS HERE!
WHAT HAPPENED?
I DON'T KNOW.
THERE'S SOM STRANGE MAG AT WORK HER AND I DON UNDERSTAN IT.

EXT MORNING...

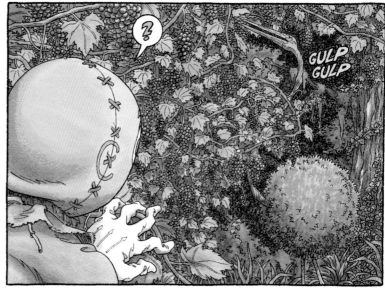

?

GULP GULP

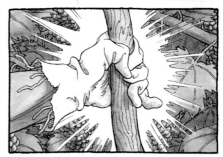

SKRAWWWK!!

YOWP! DOWN! DOWN!

PLEASE, PLEASE, **PLEASE** DON'T HURT ME, GOOD GHOST! LET ME GO AND I'LL NEVER COME TO YOUR ISLAND AGAIN!

I'M NOT GOING TO HURT YOU. I JUST HOPE YOU CAN GIVE ME SOME INFORMATION.

YES, YOUR GHOSTLINESS! WHATEVER YOU WANT, SIR GHOST!

STOP CALLING ME THAT.

237

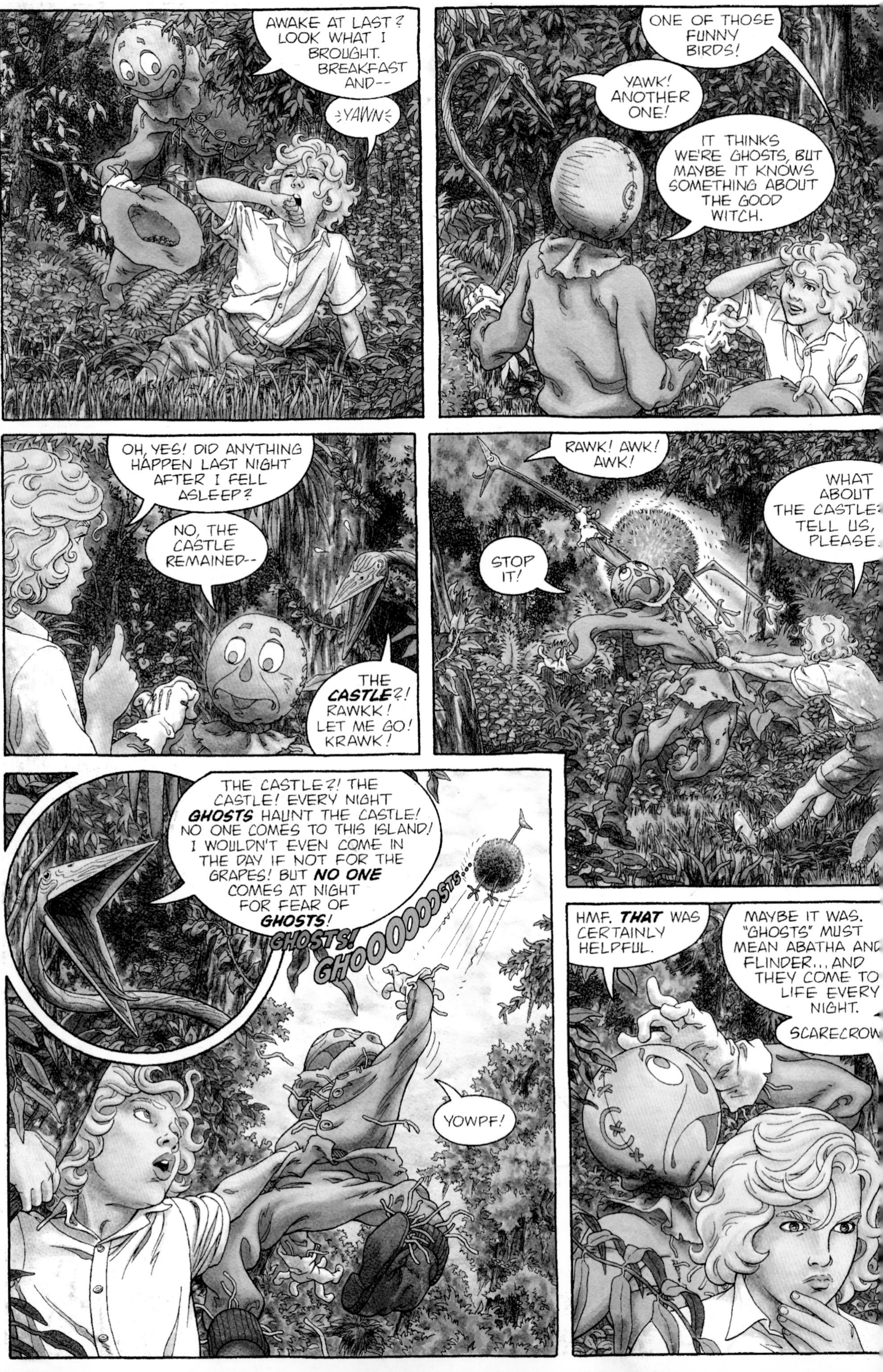
AWAKE AT LAST? LOOK WHAT I BROUGHT. BREAKFAST AND--
YAWN
ONE OF THOSE FUNNY BIRDS!
YAWK! ANOTHER ONE!
IT THINKS WE'RE GHOSTS, BUT MAYBE IT KNOWS SOMETHING ABOUT THE GOOD WITCH.
OH, YES! DID ANYTHING HAPPEN LAST NIGHT AFTER I FELL ASLEEP?
NO, THE CASTLE REMAINED--
THE **CASTLE**?! RAWKK! LET ME GO! KRAWK!
RAWK! AWK! AWK!
STOP IT!
WHAT ABOUT THE CASTLE? TELL US, PLEASE.
THE CASTLE?! THE CASTLE! EVERY NIGHT **GHOSTS** HAUNT THE CASTLE! NO ONE COMES TO THIS ISLAND! I WOULDN'T EVEN COME IN THE DAY IF NOT FOR THE GRAPES! BUT **NO ONE** COMES AT NIGHT FOR FEAR OF **GHOSTS**!
GHOSTS! GHOOOOOOSTS...
YOWPF!
HMF. **THAT** WAS CERTAINLY HELPFUL.
MAYBE IT WAS. "GHOSTS" MUST MEAN ABATHA AND FLINDER... AND THEY COME TO LIFE EVERY NIGHT.
SCARECROW

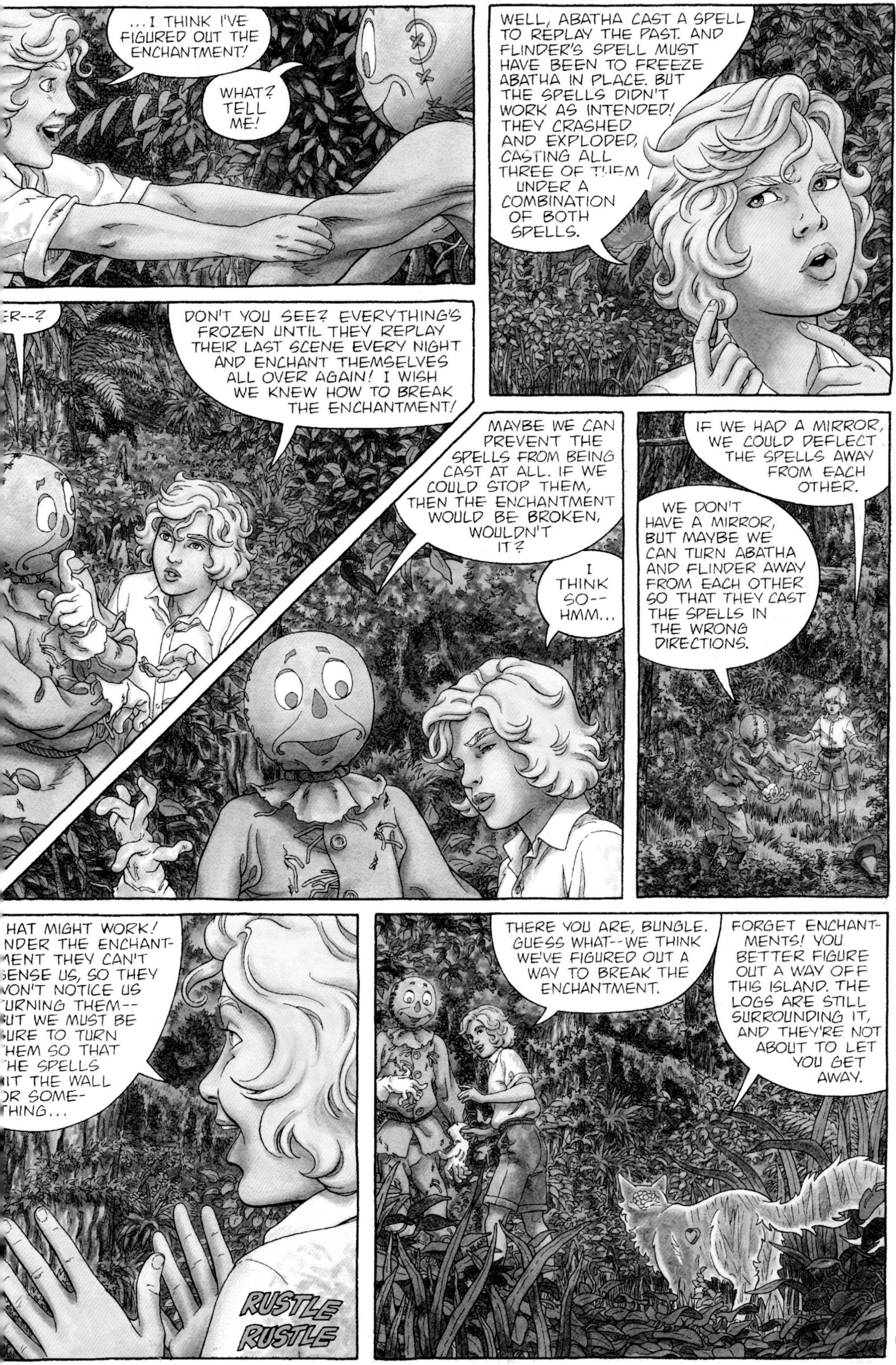
...I THINK I'VE FIGURED OUT THE ENCHANTMENT!
WHAT? TELL ME!
WELL, ABATHA CAST A SPELL TO REPLAY THE PAST. AND FLINDER'S SPELL MUST HAVE BEEN TO FREEZE ABATHA IN PLACE. BUT THE SPELLS DIDN'T WORK AS INTENDED! THEY CRASHED AND EXPLODED, CASTING ALL THREE OF THEM UNDER A COMBINATION OF BOTH SPELLS.
ER--?
DON'T YOU SEE? EVERYTHING'S FROZEN UNTIL THEY REPLAY THEIR LAST SCENE EVERY NIGHT AND ENCHANT THEMSELVES ALL OVER AGAIN! I WISH WE KNEW HOW TO BREAK THE ENCHANTMENT!
MAYBE WE CAN PREVENT THE SPELLS FROM BEING CAST AT ALL. IF WE COULD STOP THEM, THEN THE ENCHANTMENT WOULD BE BROKEN, WOULDN'T IT?
I THINK SO-- HMM...
IF WE HAD A MIRROR, WE COULD DEFLECT THE SPELLS AWAY FROM EACH OTHER.
WE DON'T HAVE A MIRROR, BUT MAYBE WE CAN TURN ABATHA AND FLINDER AWAY FROM EACH OTHER SO THAT THEY CAST THE SPELLS IN THE WRONG DIRECTIONS.
HAT MIGHT WORK! NDER THE ENCHANT-MENT THEY CAN'T SENSE US, SO THEY VON'T NOTICE US TURNING THEM-- UT WE MUST BE URE TO TURN THEM SO THAT HE SPELLS IT THE WALL OR SOME-THING...
RUSTLE RUSTLE
THERE YOU ARE, BUNGLE. GUESS WHAT--WE THINK WE'VE FIGURED OUT A WAY TO BREAK THE ENCHANTMENT.
FORGET ENCHANT-MENTS! YOU BETTER FIGURE OUT A WAY OFF THIS ISLAND. THE LOGS ARE STILL SURROUNDING IT, AND THEY'RE NOT ABOUT TO LET YOU GET AWAY.

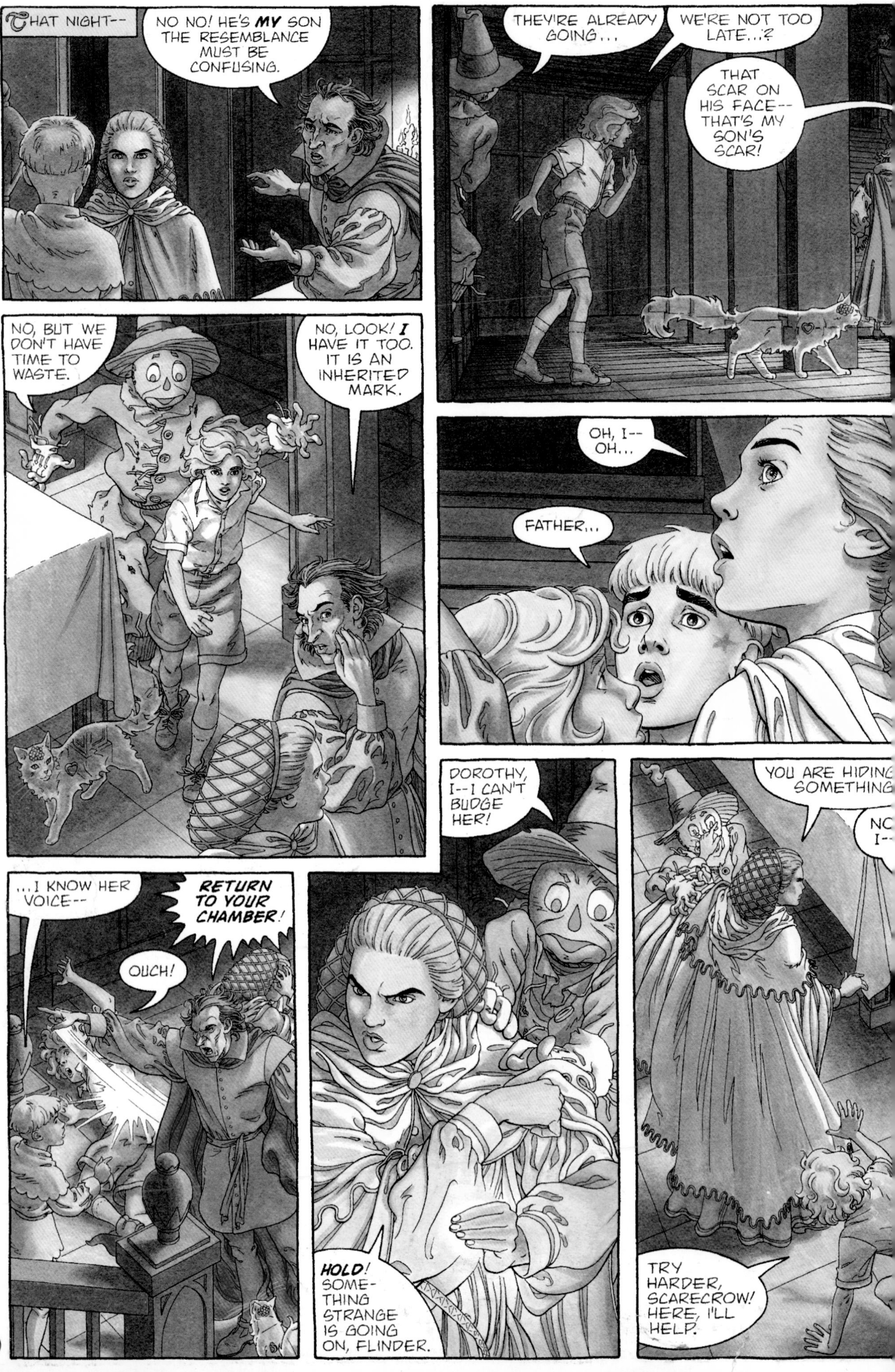
THAT NIGHT--
NO NO! HE'S MY SON THE RESEMBLANCE MUST BE CONFUSING.
THEY'RE ALREADY GOING...
WE'RE NOT TOO LATE...?
THAT SCAR ON HIS FACE-- THAT'S MY SON'S SCAR!
NO, BUT WE DON'T HAVE TIME TO WASTE.
NO, LOOK! I HAVE IT TOO. IT IS AN INHERITED MARK.
OH, I-- OH...
FATHER...
DOROTHY, I--I CAN'T BUDGE HER!
YOU ARE HIDING SOMETHING
NO I--
...I KNOW HER VOICE--
RETURN TO YOUR CHAMBER!
OUCH!
HOLD! SOMETHING STRANGE IS GOING ON, FLINDER.
TRY HARDER, SCARECROW! HERE, I'LL HELP.

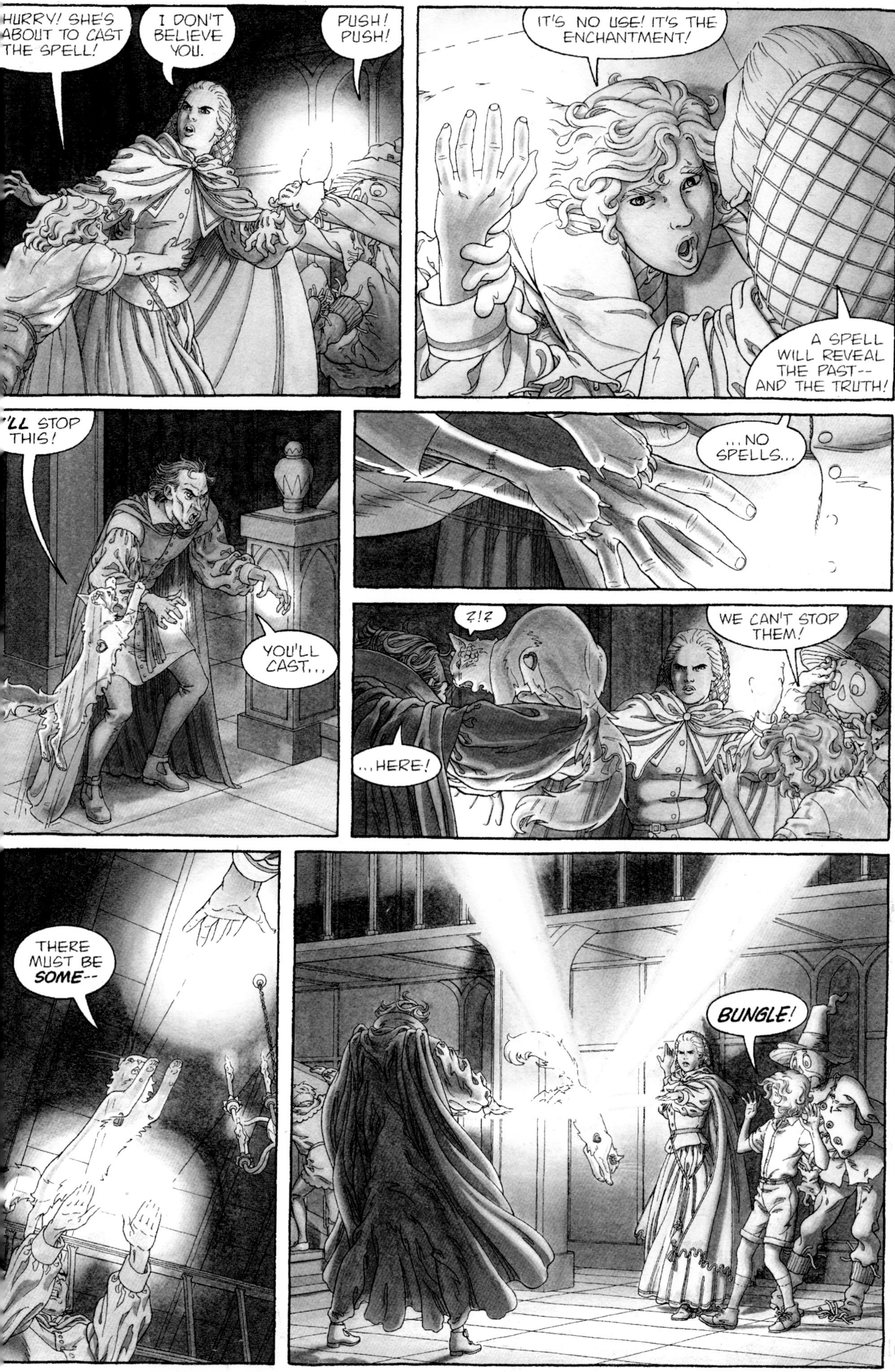
HURRY! SHE'S ABOUT TO CAST THE SPELL!
I DON'T BELIEVE YOU.
PUSH! PUSH!
IT'S NO USE! IT'S THE ENCHANTMENT!
A SPELL WILL REVEAL THE PAST-- AND THE TRUTH!
'LL STOP THIS!
YOU'LL CAST...
...NO SPELLS...
?!?
WE CAN'T STOP THEM!
...HERE!
THERE MUST BE SOME--
BUNGLE!

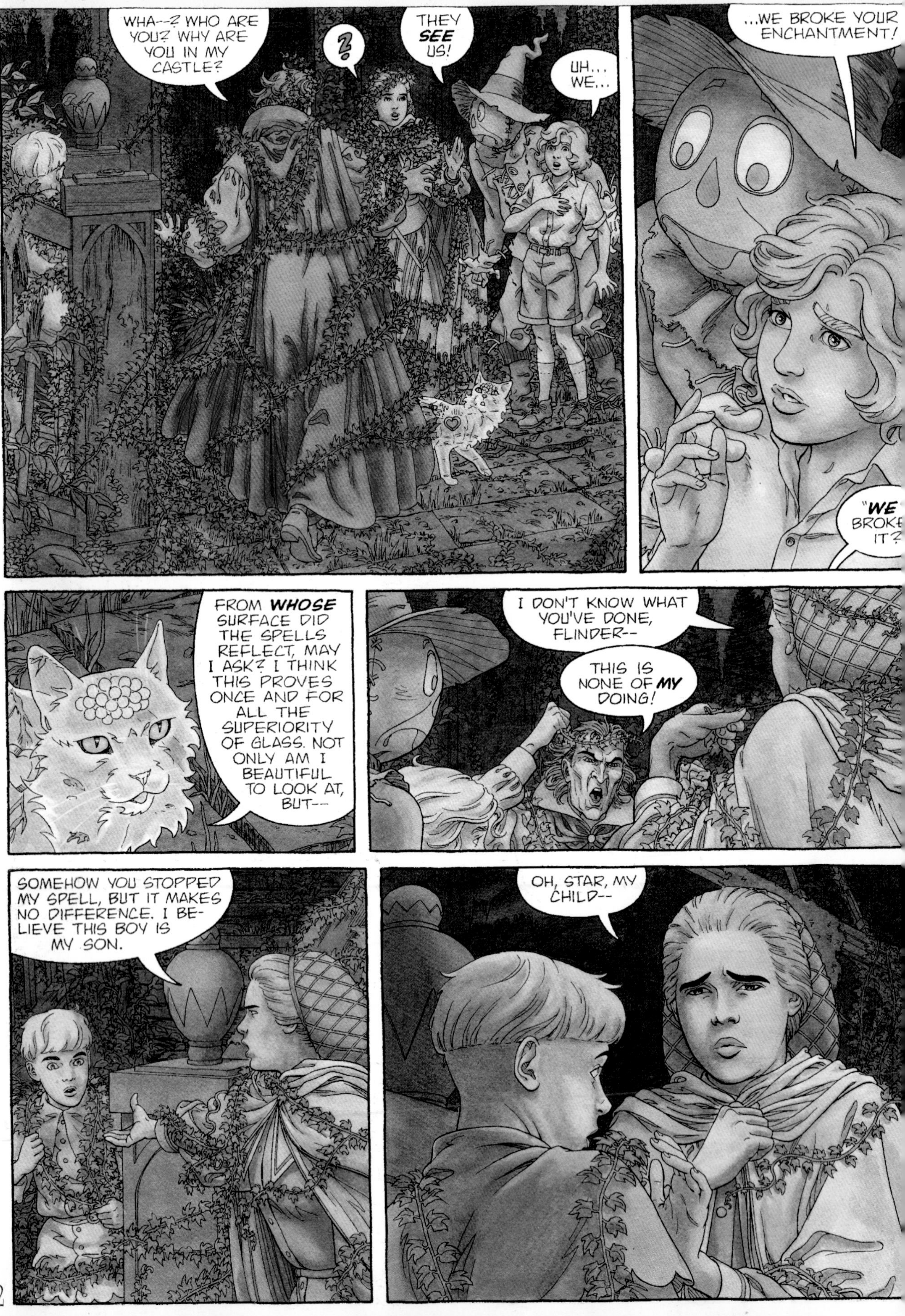
WHA--? WHO ARE YOU? WHY ARE YOU IN MY CASTLE?
?
THEY SEE US!
UH... WE...
...WE BROKE YOUR ENCHANTMENT!
"WE" BROKE IT?
FROM WHOSE SURFACE DID THE SPELLS REFLECT, MAY I ASK? I THINK THIS PROVES ONCE AND FOR ALL THE SUPERIORITY OF GLASS. NOT ONLY AM I BEAUTIFUL TO LOOK AT, BUT--
I DON'T KNOW WHAT YOU'VE DONE, FLINDER--
THIS IS NONE OF MY DOING!
SOMEHOW YOU STOPPED MY SPELL, BUT IT MAKES NO DIFFERENCE. I BELIEVE THIS BOY IS MY SON.
OH, STAR, MY CHILD--

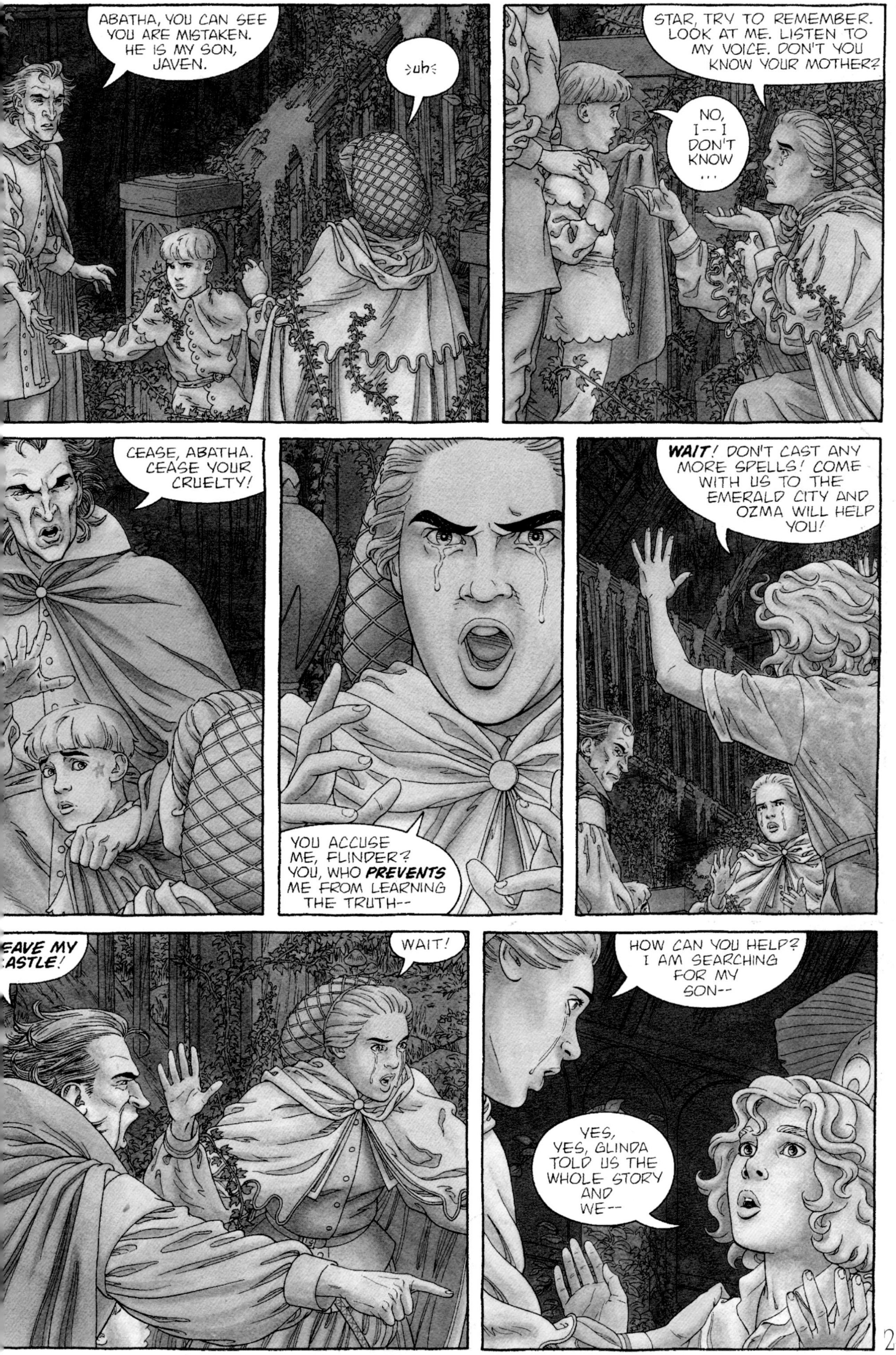
ABATHA, YOU CAN SEE YOU ARE MISTAKEN. HE IS MY SON, JAVEN.
uh
STAR, TRY TO REMEMBER. LOOK AT ME. LISTEN TO MY VOICE. DON'T YOU KNOW YOUR MOTHER?
NO, I -- I DON'T KNOW . . .
CEASE, ABATHA. CEASE YOUR CRUELTY!
YOU ACCUSE ME, FLINDER? YOU, WHO **PREVENTS** ME FROM LEARNING THE TRUTH--
WAIT! DON'T CAST ANY MORE SPELLS! COME WITH US TO THE EMERALD CITY AND OZMA WILL HELP YOU!
EAVE MY ASTLE!
WAIT!
HOW CAN YOU HELP? I AM SEARCHING FOR MY SON--
YES, YES, GLINDA TOLD US THE WHOLE STORY AND WE--

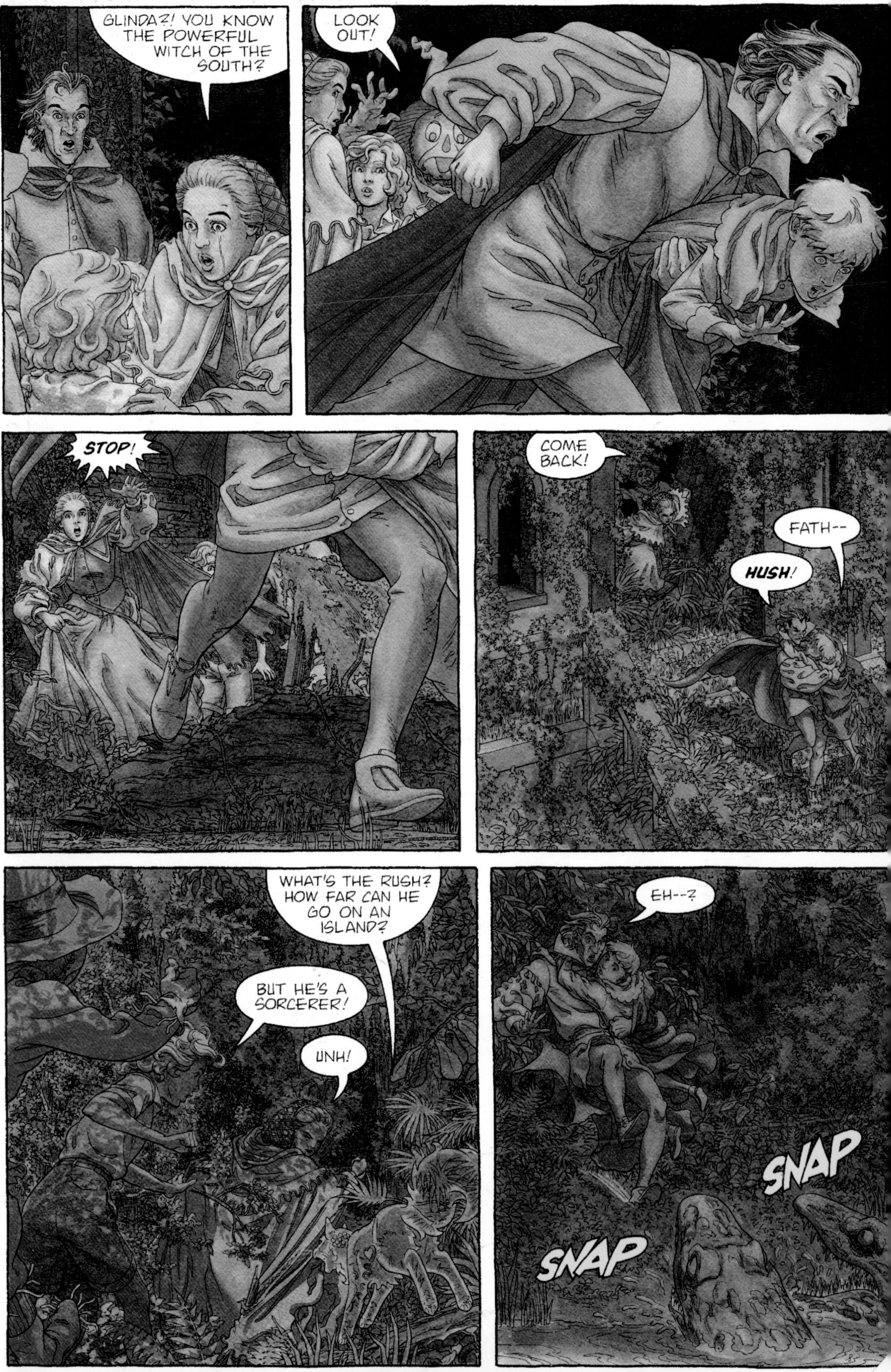
GLINDA?! YOU KNOW THE POWERFUL WITCH OF THE SOUTH?
LOOK OUT!
STOP!
COME BACK!
FATH--
HUSH!
WHAT'S THE RUSH? HOW FAR CAN HE GO ON AN ISLAND?
BUT HE'S A SORCERER!
UNH!
EH--?
SNAP
SNAP

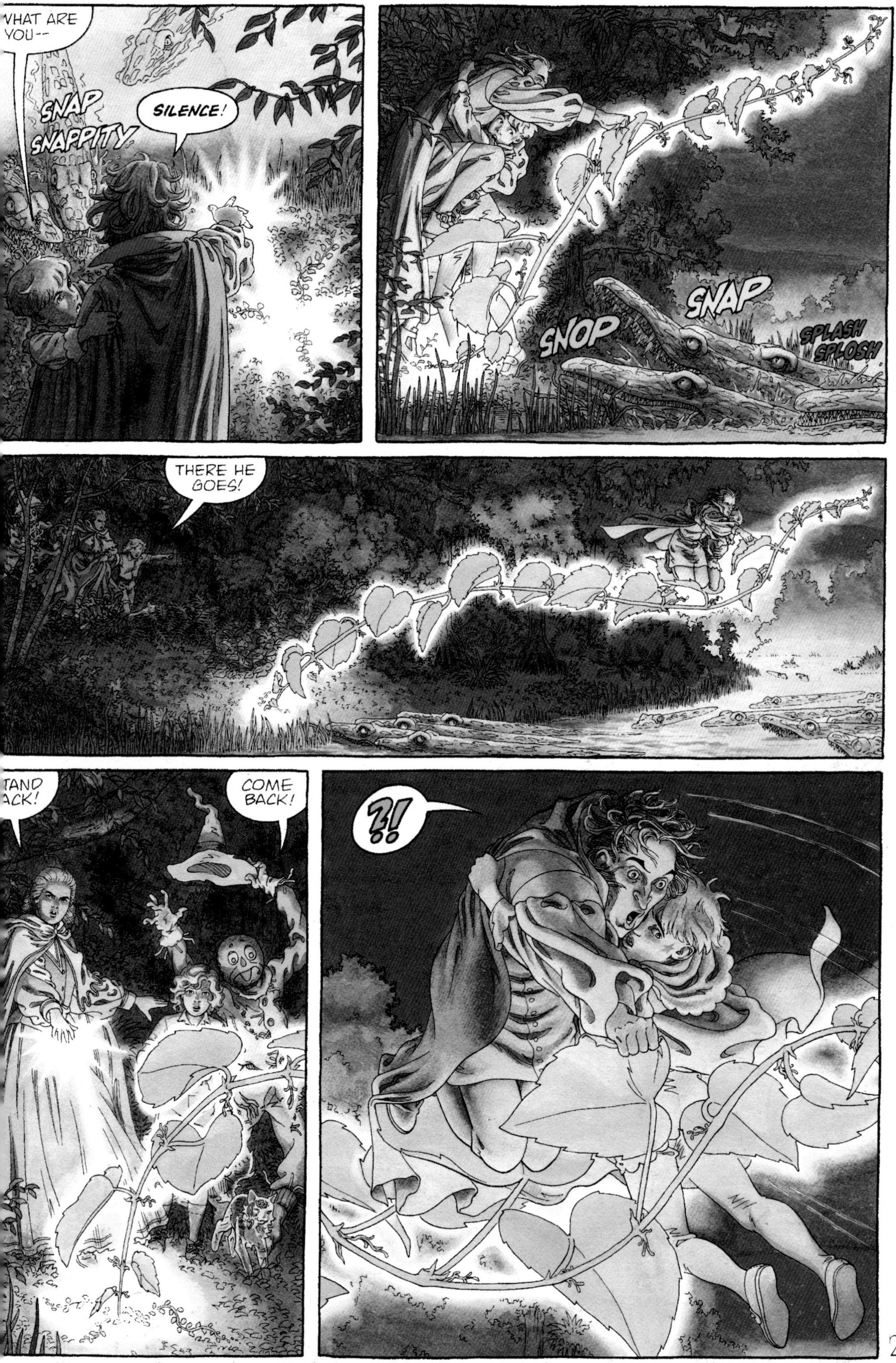
WHAT ARE YOU--
SNAP SNAPPITY
SILENCE!
SNOP
SNAP
SPLASH SPLOSH
THERE HE GOES!
TAND ACK!
COME BACK!
?!

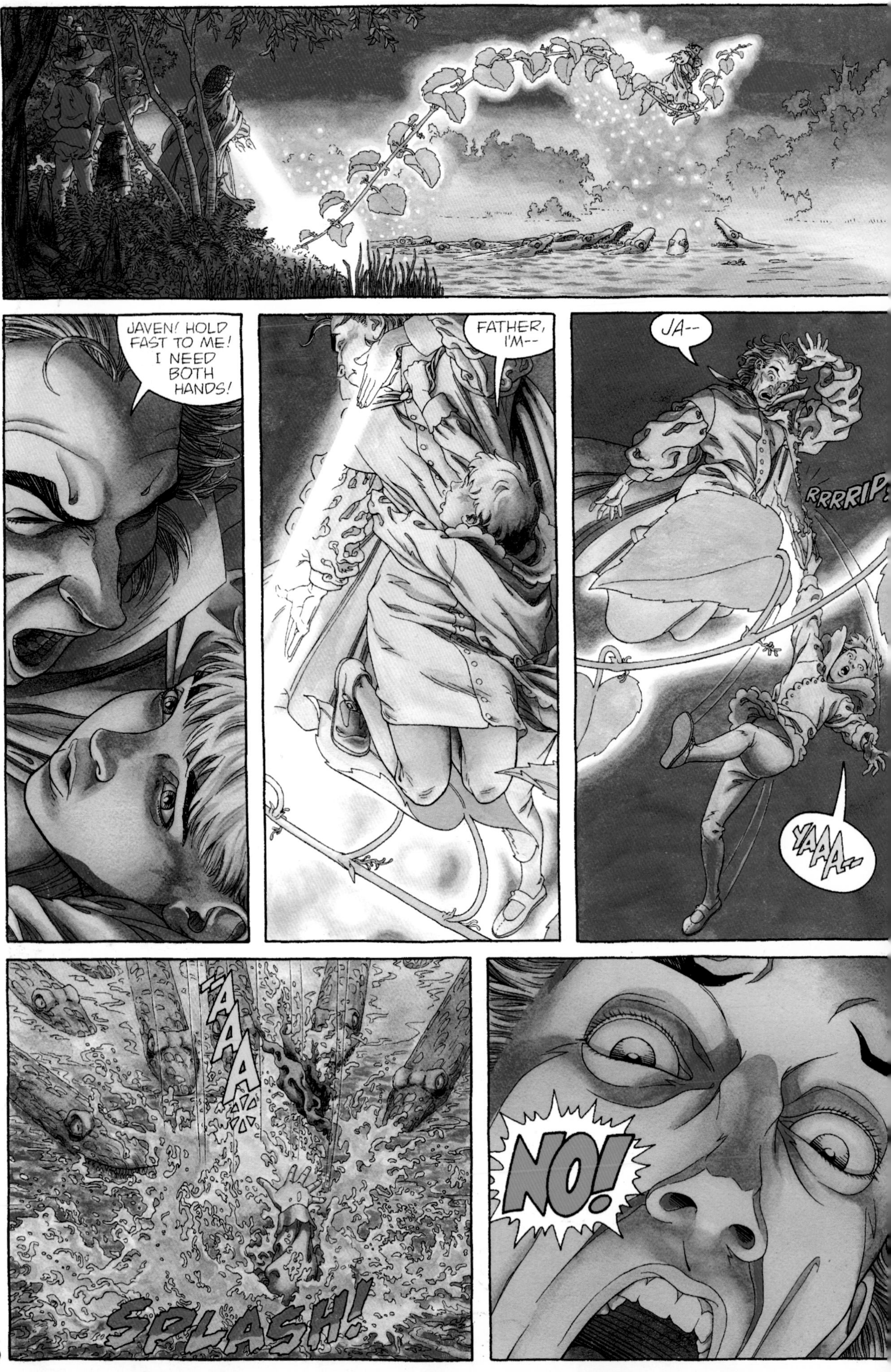

JAVEN! HOLD FAST TO ME! I NEED BOTH HANDS!
FATHER, I'M--
JA--
RRRRIP!
YAAA--
AAAA
SPLASH!
NO!

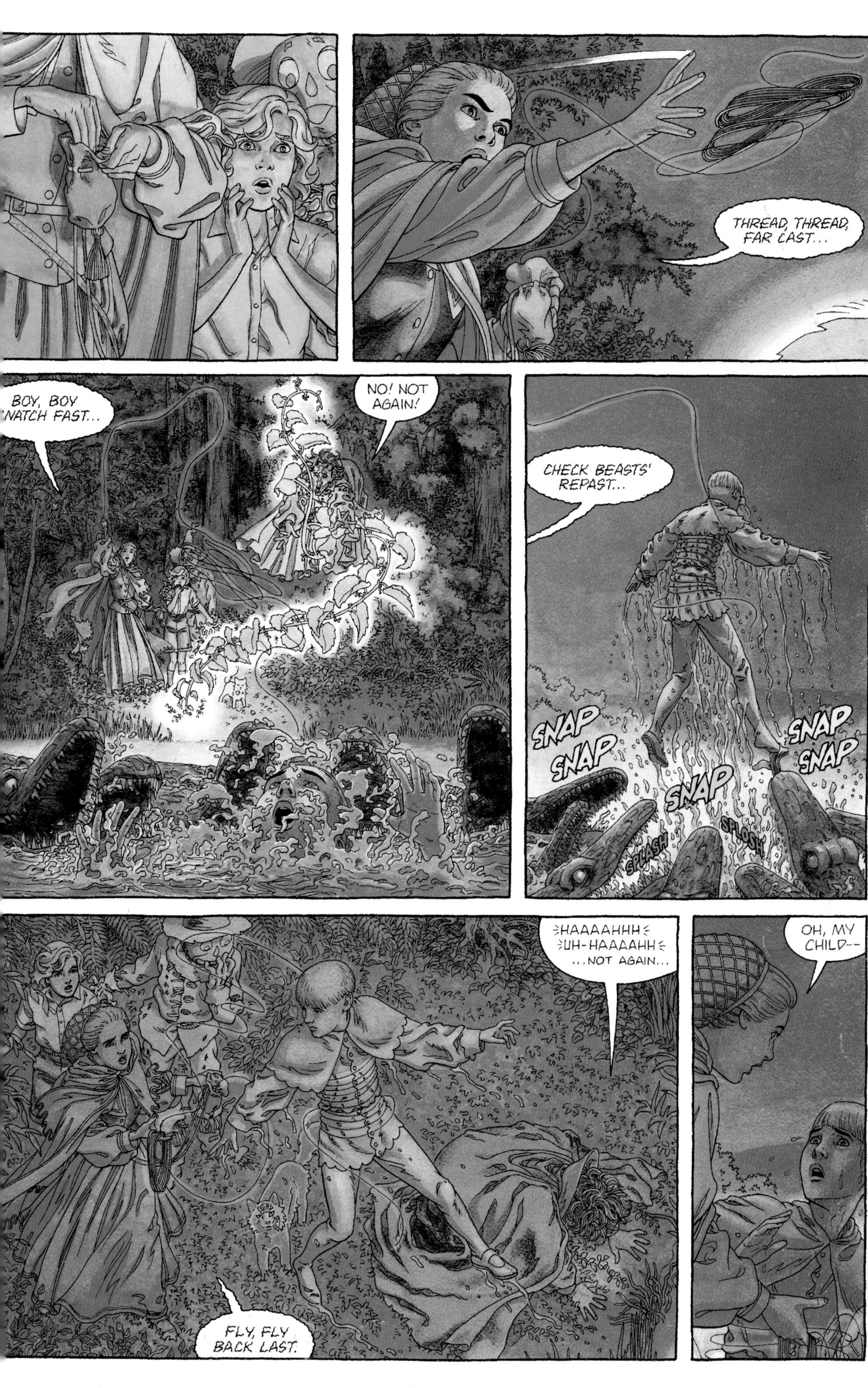
THREAD, THREAD, FAR CAST...
BOY, BOY WATCH FAST...
NO! NOT AGAIN!
CHECK BEASTS' REPAST...
SNAP SNAP
SNAP
SNAP SNAP
SPLASH
SPLOSH
HAAAAHHH UH-HAAAAHH ...NOT AGAIN...
OH, MY CHILD--
FLY, FLY BACK LAST.

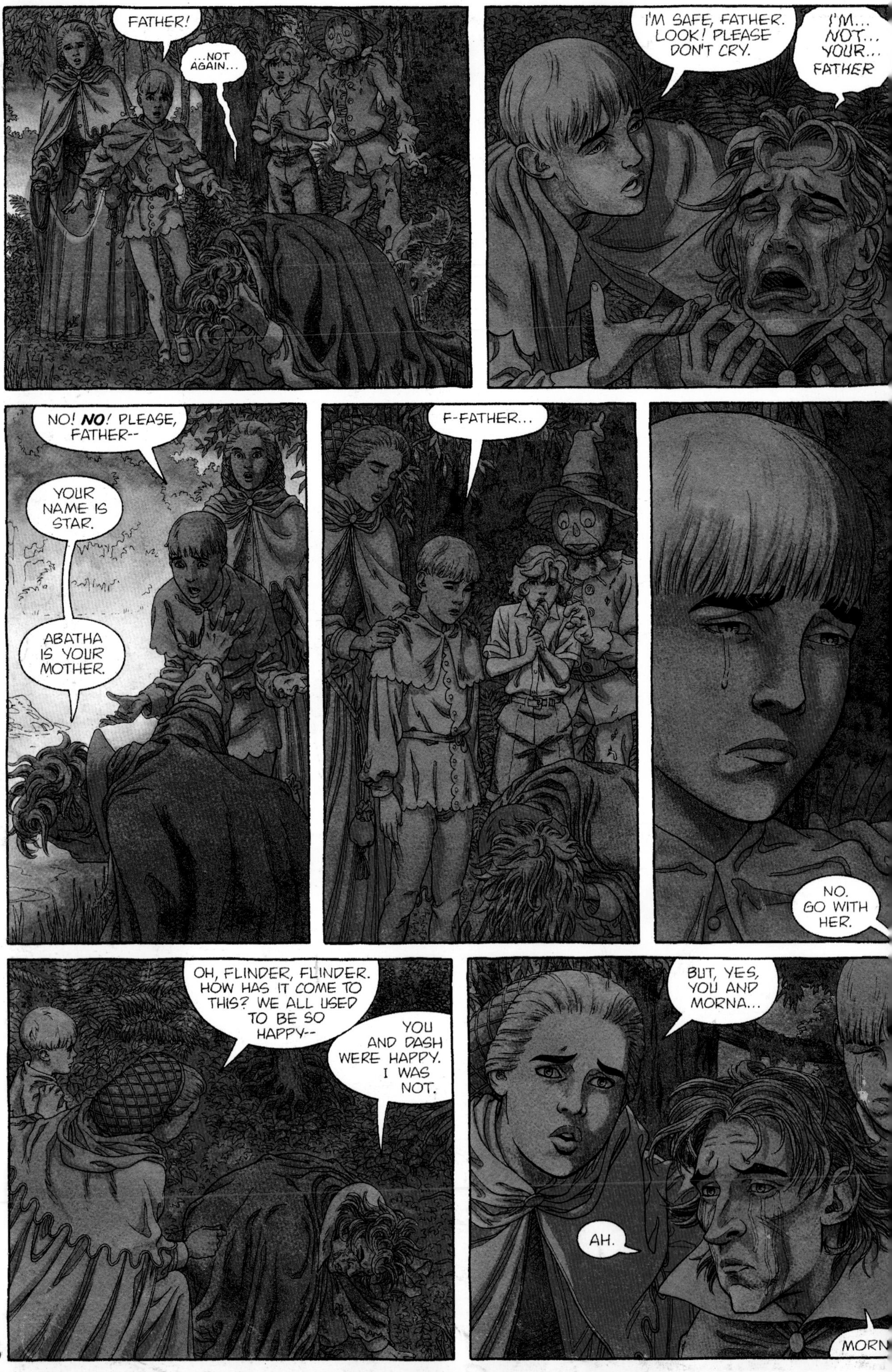
FATHER!
...NOT AGAIN...
I'M SAFE, FATHER. LOOK! PLEASE DON'T CRY.
I'M... NOT... YOUR... FATHER
NO! NO! PLEASE, FATHER--
YOUR NAME IS STAR.
ABATHA IS YOUR MOTHER.
F-FATHER...
NO. GO WITH HER.
OH, FLINDER, FLINDER. HOW HAS IT COME TO THIS? WE ALL USED TO BE SO HAPPY--
YOU AND DASH WERE HAPPY. I WAS NOT.
BUT, YES, YOU AND MORNA...
AH.
MORN

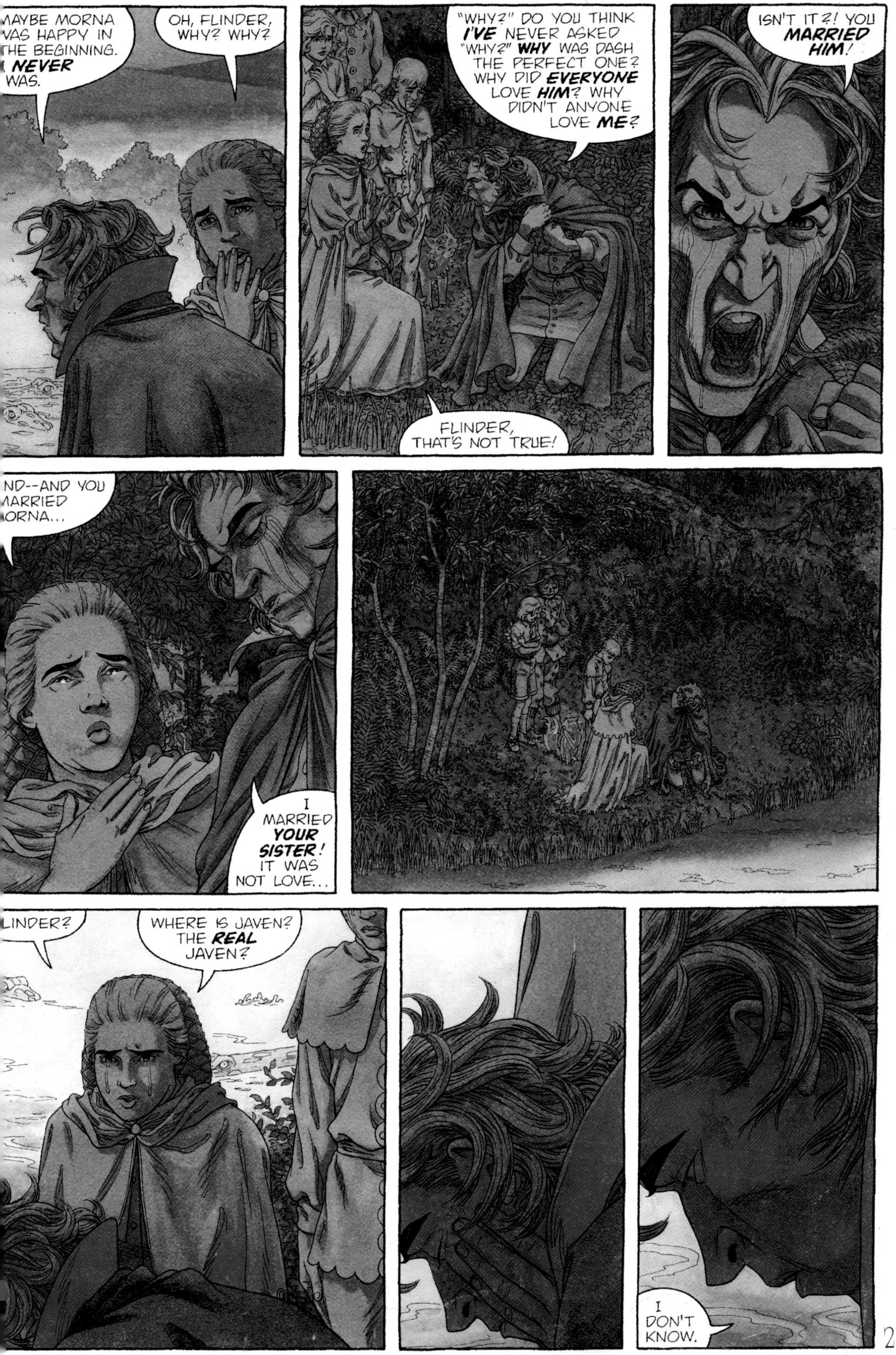
MAYBE MORNA WAS HAPPY IN THE BEGINNING. I NEVER WAS.
OH, FLINDER, WHY? WHY?
"WHY?" DO YOU THINK I'VE NEVER ASKED "WHY?" WHY WAS DASH THE PERFECT ONE? WHY DID EVERYONE LOVE HIM? WHY DIDN'T ANYONE LOVE ME?
FLINDER, THAT'S NOT TRUE!
ISN'T IT?! YOU MARRIED HIM!
AND--AND YOU MARRIED MORNA...
I MARRIED YOUR SISTER! IT WAS NOT LOVE...
FLINDER?
WHERE IS JAVEN? THE REAL JAVEN?
I DON'T KNOW.

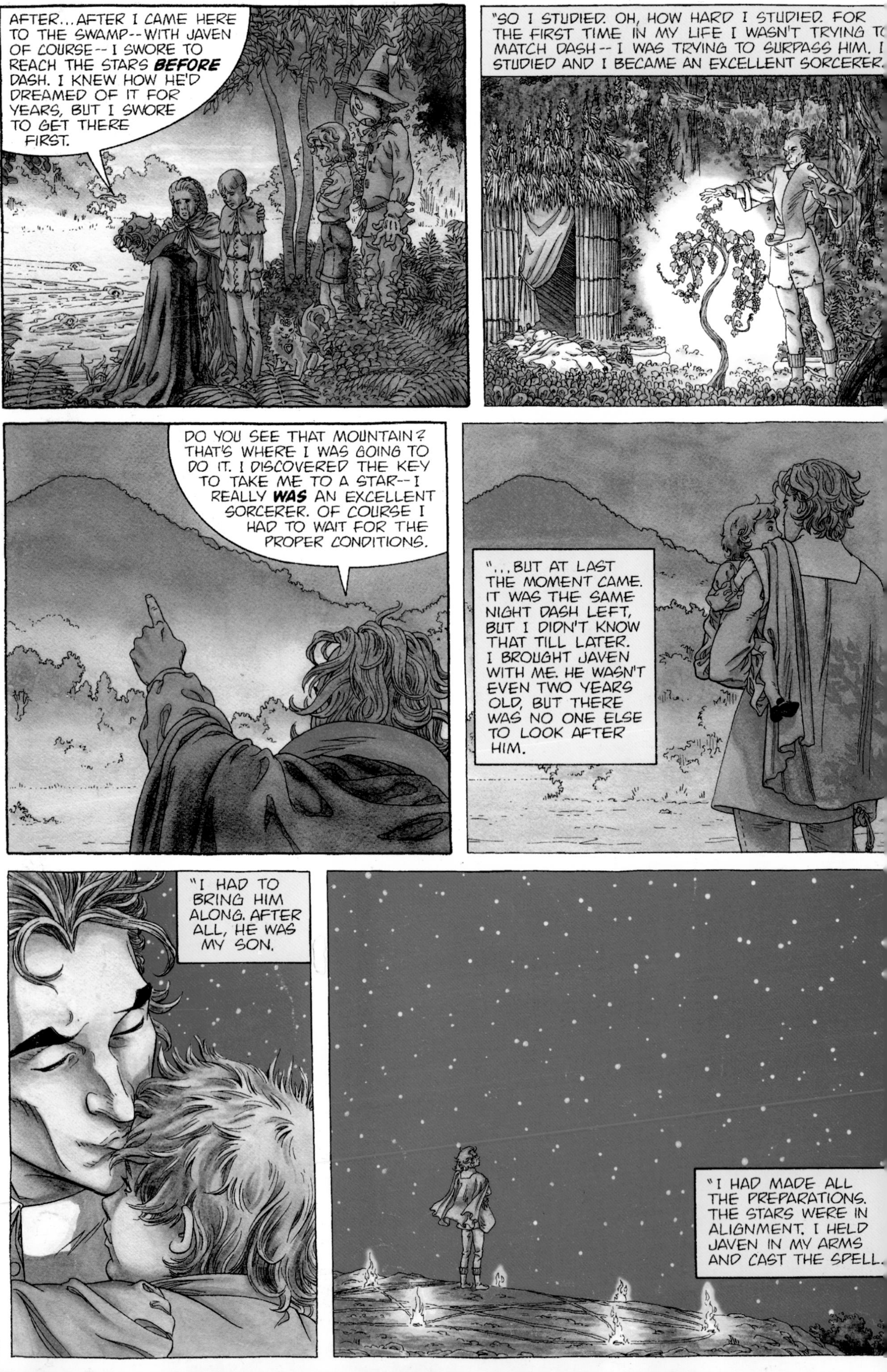
AFTER... AFTER I CAME HERE TO THE SWAMP--WITH JAVEN OF COURSE--I SWORE TO REACH THE STARS **BEFORE** DASH. I KNEW HOW HE'D DREAMED OF IT FOR YEARS, BUT I SWORE TO GET THERE FIRST.
"SO I STUDIED. OH, HOW HARD I STUDIED. FOR THE FIRST TIME IN MY LIFE I WASN'T TRYING T MATCH DASH -- I WAS TRYING TO SURPASS HIM. I STUDIED AND I BECAME AN EXCELLENT SORCERER.
DO YOU SEE THAT MOUNTAIN? THAT'S WHERE I WAS GOING TO DO IT. I DISCOVERED THE KEY TO TAKE ME TO A STAR--I REALLY **WAS** AN EXCELLENT SORCERER. OF COURSE I HAD TO WAIT FOR THE PROPER CONDITIONS.
"...BUT AT LAST THE MOMENT CAME. IT WAS THE SAME NIGHT DASH LEFT, BUT I DIDN'T KNOW THAT TILL LATER. I BROUGHT JAVEN WITH ME. HE WASN'T EVEN TWO YEARS OLD, BUT THERE WAS NO ONE ELSE TO LOOK AFTER HIM.
"I HAD TO BRING HIM ALONG. AFTER ALL, HE WAS MY SON.
"I HAD MADE ALL THE PREPARATIONS. THE STARS WERE IN ALIGNMENT. I HELD JAVEN IN MY ARMS AND CAST THE SPELL.

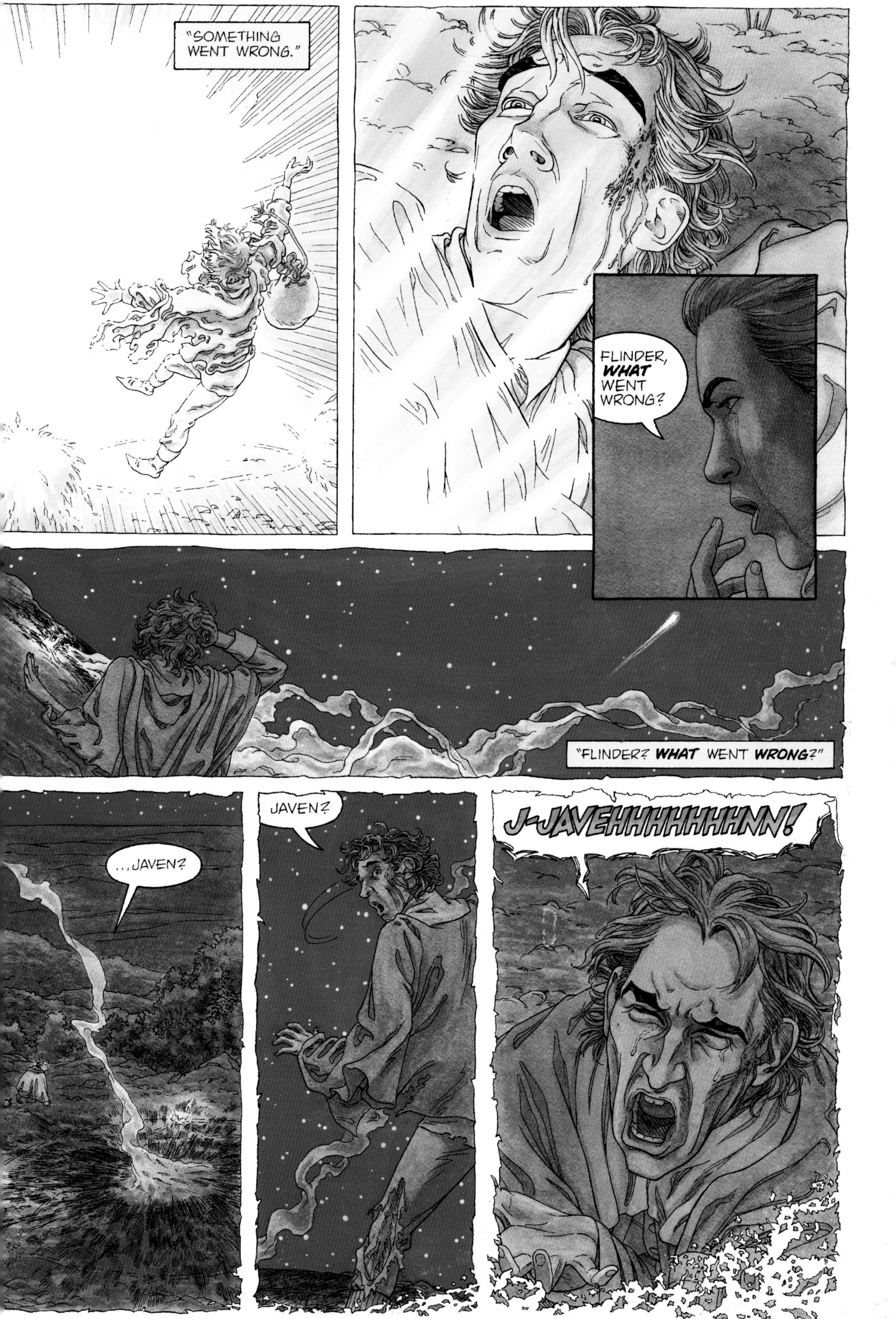
"SOMETHING WENT WRONG."
FLINDER, WHAT WENT WRONG?
"FLINDER? WHAT WENT WRONG?"
...JAVEN?
JAVEN?
J-JAVEHHHHHHHNN!

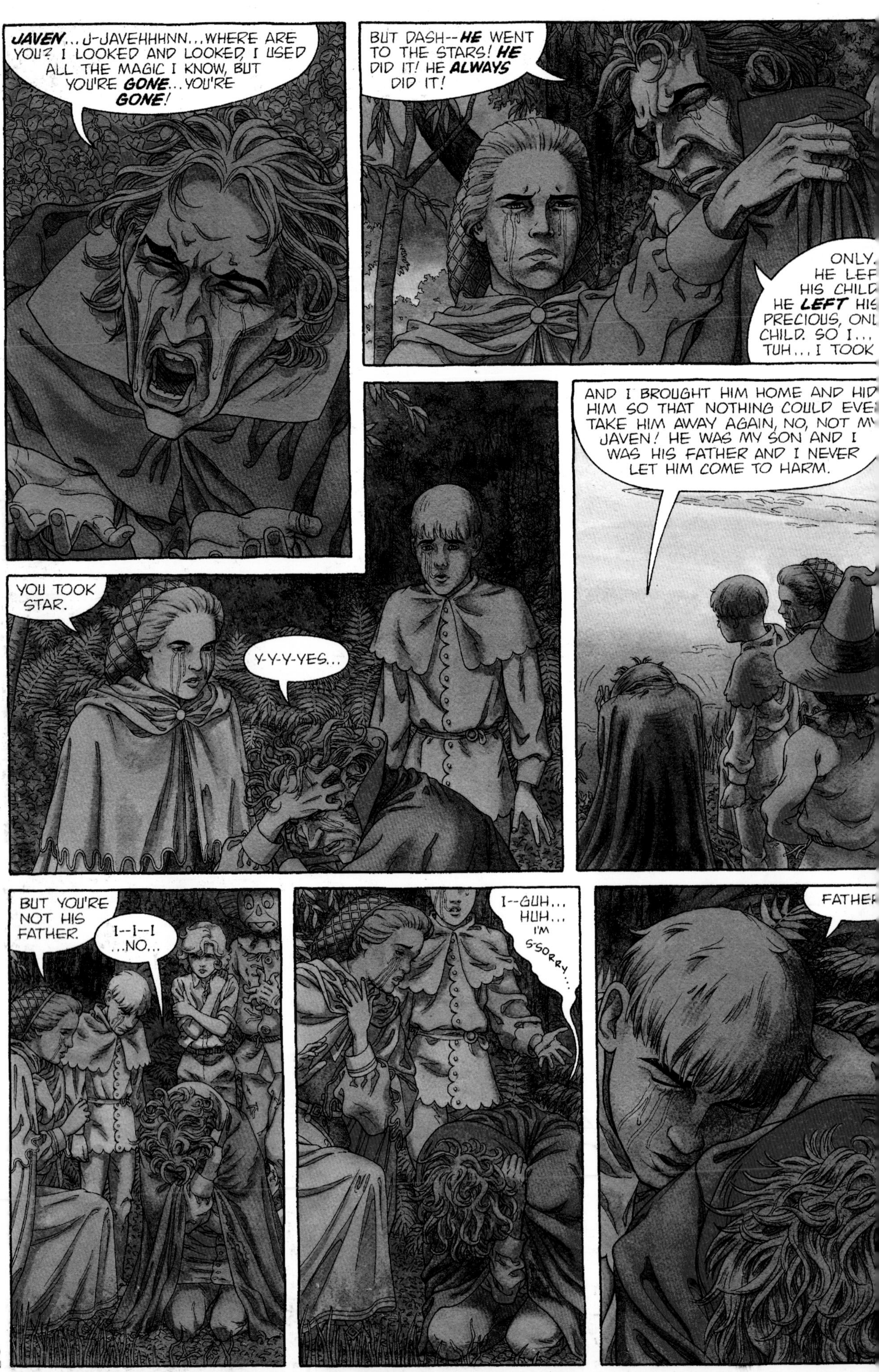
JAVEN... J-JAVEHHHNN... WHERE ARE YOU? I LOOKED AND LOOKED, I USED ALL THE MAGIC I KNOW, BUT YOU'RE GONE... YOU'RE GONE!
BUT DASH--HE WENT TO THE STARS! HE DID IT! HE ALWAYS DID IT!
ONLY... HE LEF HIS CHILD HE LEFT HIS PRECIOUS, ONL CHILD. SO I... TUH... I TOOK
AND I BROUGHT HIM HOME AND HID HIM SO THAT NOTHING COULD EVE TAKE HIM AWAY AGAIN, NO, NOT MY JAVEN! HE WAS MY SON AND I WAS HIS FATHER AND I NEVER LET HIM COME TO HARM.
YOU TOOK STAR.
Y-Y-Y-YES...
BUT YOU'RE NOT HIS FATHER.
I--I--I ...NO...
I--GUH... HUH... I'M S-SORRY...
FATHER

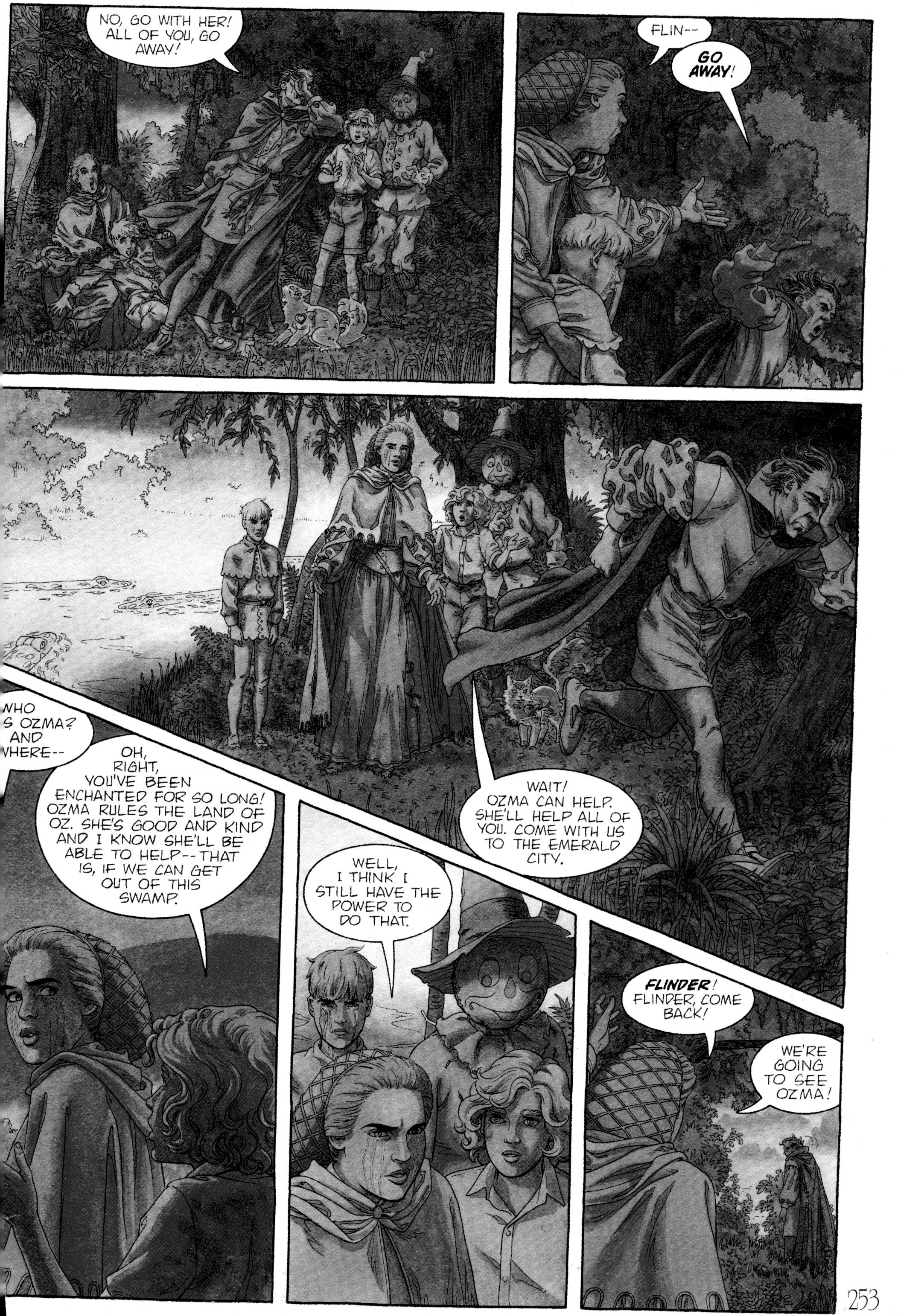
NO, GO WITH HER! ALL OF YOU, GO AWAY!
FLIN--
GO AWAY!
WAIT! OZMA CAN HELP. SHE'LL HELP ALL OF YOU. COME WITH US TO THE EMERALD CITY.
WHO S OZMA? AND WHERE--
OH, RIGHT, YOU'VE BEEN ENCHANTED FOR SO LONG! OZMA RULES THE LAND OF OZ. SHE'S GOOD AND KIND AND I KNOW SHE'LL BE ABLE TO HELP--THAT IS, IF WE CAN GET OUT OF THIS SWAMP.
WELL, I THINK I STILL HAVE THE POWER TO DO THAT.
FLINDER! FLINDER, COME BACK!
WE'RE GOING TO SEE OZMA!

Chapter 5 Decisions

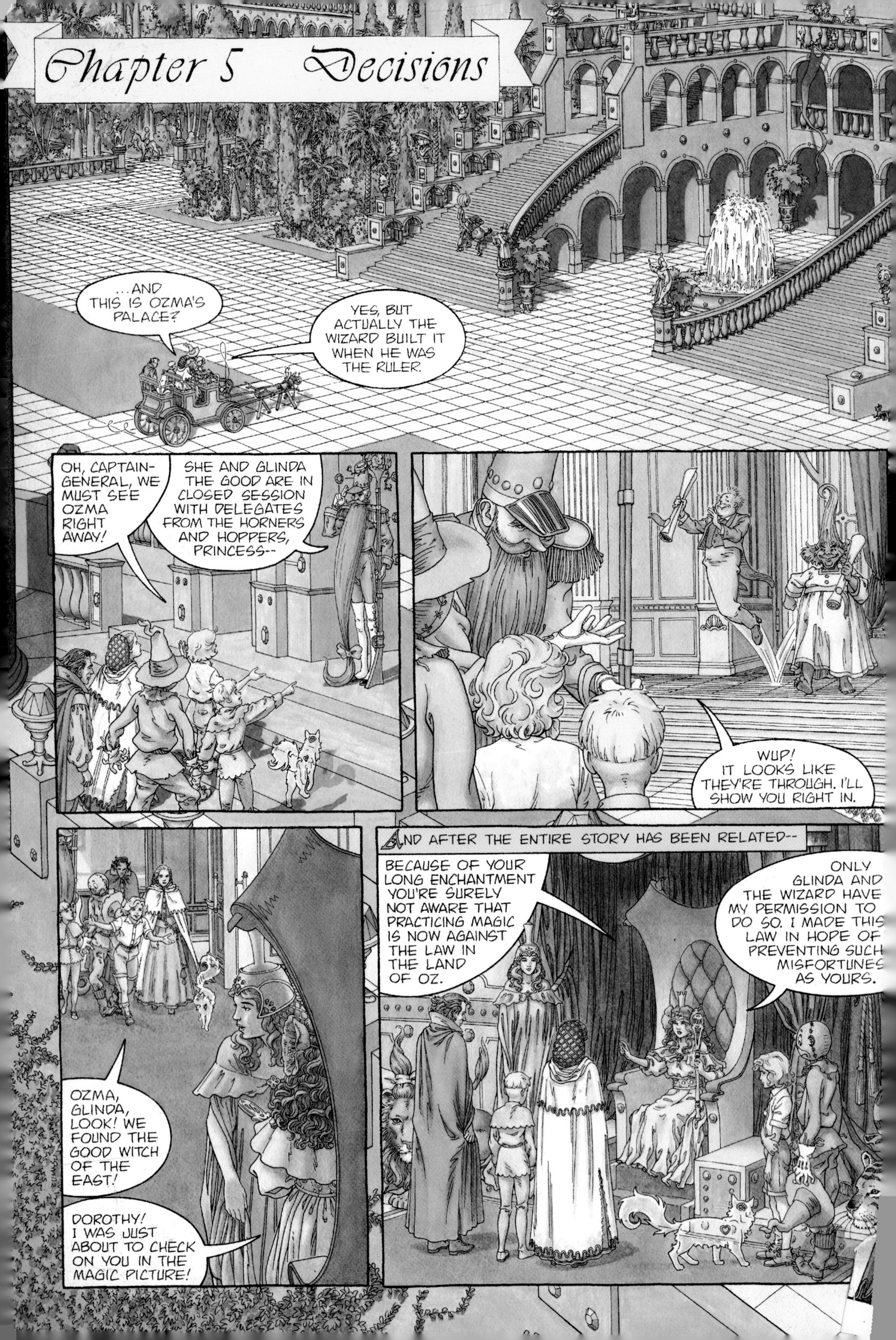
...AND THIS IS OZMA'S PALACE?
YES, BUT ACTUALLY THE WIZARD BUILT IT WHEN HE WAS THE RULER.
OH, CAPTAIN-GENERAL, WE MUST SEE OZMA RIGHT AWAY!
SHE AND GLINDA THE GOOD ARE IN CLOSED SESSION WITH DELEGATES FROM THE HORNERS AND HOPPERS, PRINCESS--
WUP! IT LOOKS LIKE THEY'RE THROUGH. I'LL SHOW YOU RIGHT IN.
OZMA, GLINDA, LOOK! WE FOUND THE GOOD WITCH OF THE EAST!
DOROTHY! I WAS JUST ABOUT TO CHECK ON YOU IN THE MAGIC PICTURE!
AND AFTER THE ENTIRE STORY HAS BEEN RELATED--
BECAUSE OF YOUR LONG ENCHANTMENT YOU'RE SURELY NOT AWARE THAT PRACTICING MAGIC IS NOW AGAINST THE LAW IN THE LAND OF OZ.
ONLY GLINDA AND THE WIZARD HAVE MY PERMISSION TO DO SO. I MADE THIS LAW IN HOPE OF PREVENTING SUCH MISFORTUNES AS YOURS.

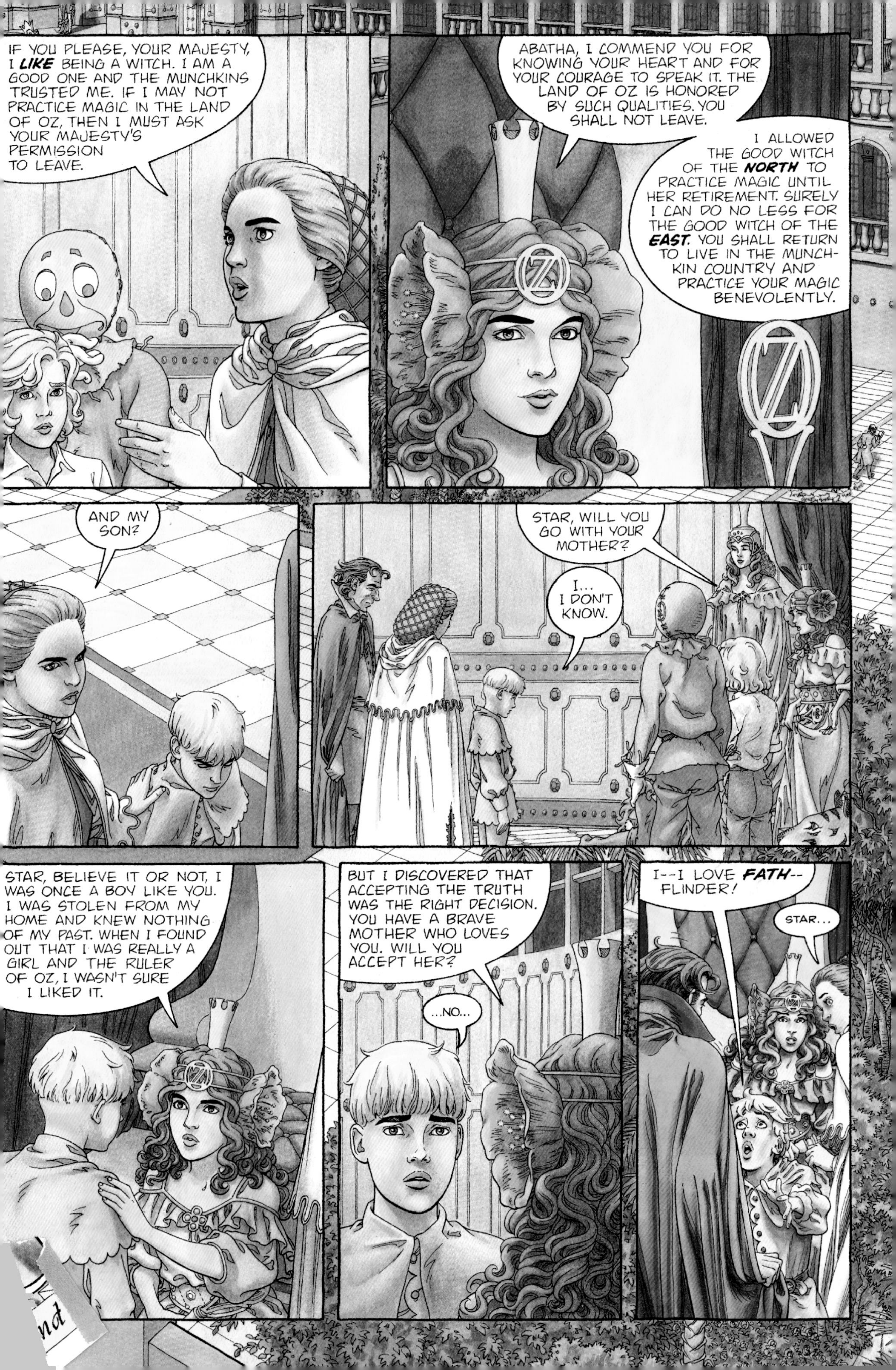
IF YOU PLEASE, YOUR MAJESTY, I LIKE BEING A WITCH. I AM A GOOD ONE AND THE MUNCHKINS TRUSTED ME. IF I MAY NOT PRACTICE MAGIC IN THE LAND OF OZ, THEN I MUST ASK YOUR MAJESTY'S PERMISSION TO LEAVE.
ABATHA, I COMMEND YOU FOR KNOWING YOUR HEART AND FOR YOUR COURAGE TO SPEAK IT. THE LAND OF OZ IS HONORED BY SUCH QUALITIES. YOU SHALL NOT LEAVE.
I ALLOWED THE GOOD WITCH OF THE NORTH TO PRACTICE MAGIC UNTIL HER RETIREMENT. SURELY I CAN DO NO LESS FOR THE GOOD WITCH OF THE EAST. YOU SHALL RETURN TO LIVE IN THE MUNCHKIN COUNTRY AND PRACTICE YOUR MAGIC BENEVOLENTLY.
AND MY SON?
STAR, WILL YOU GO WITH YOUR MOTHER?
I... I DON'T KNOW.
STAR, BELIEVE IT OR NOT, I WAS ONCE A BOY LIKE YOU. I WAS STOLEN FROM MY HOME AND KNEW NOTHING OF MY PAST. WHEN I FOUND OUT THAT I WAS REALLY A GIRL AND THE RULER OF OZ, I WASN'T SURE I LIKED IT.
BUT I DISCOVERED THAT ACCEPTING THE TRUTH WAS THE RIGHT DECISION. YOU HAVE A BRAVE MOTHER WHO LOVES YOU. WILL YOU ACCEPT HER?
...NO...
I--I LOVE FATH-- FLINDER!
STAR...

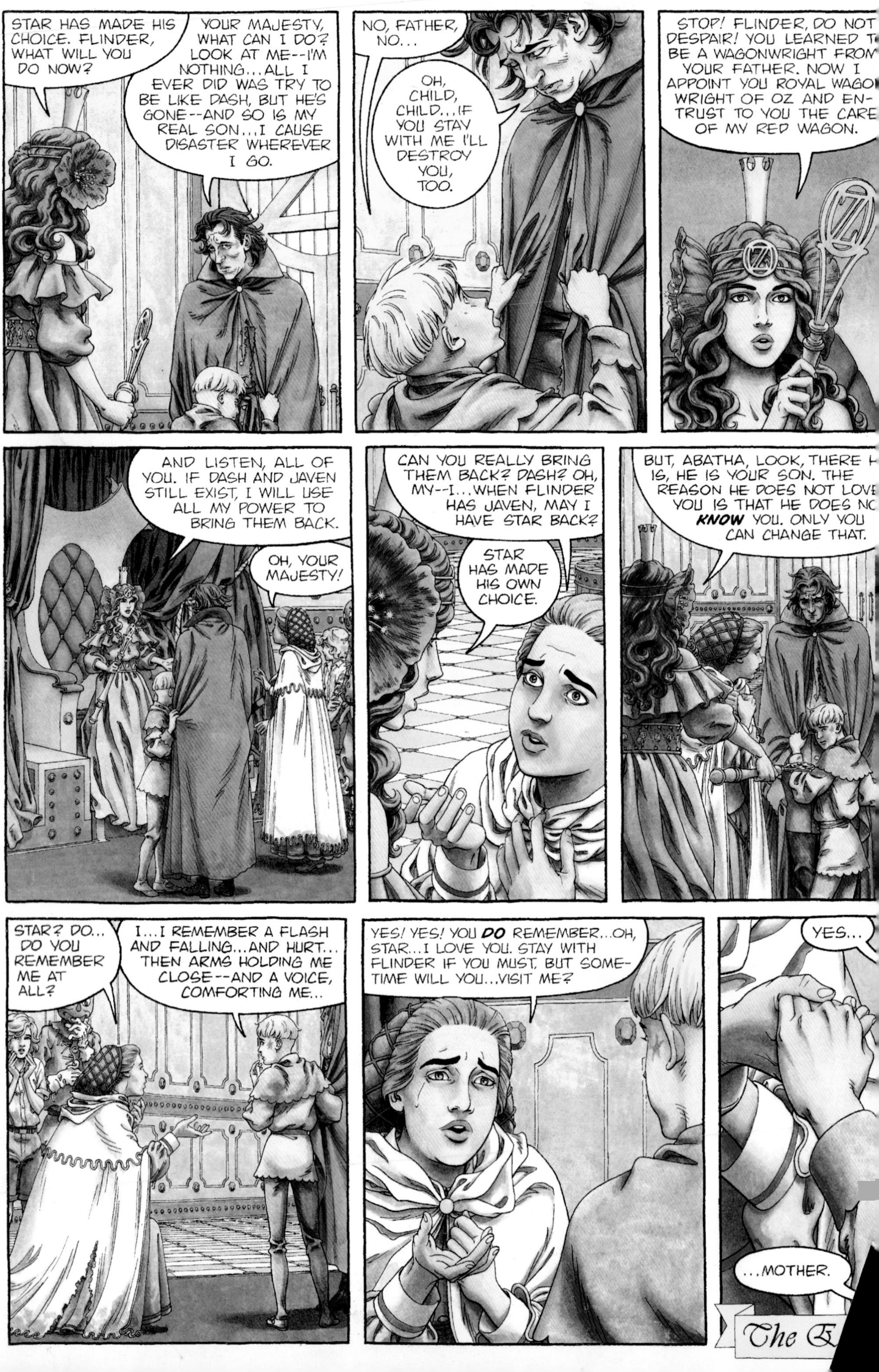
STAR HAS MADE HIS CHOICE. FLINDER, WHAT WILL YOU DO NOW?
YOUR MAJESTY, WHAT CAN I DO? LOOK AT ME--I'M NOTHING...ALL I EVER DID WAS TRY TO BE LIKE DASH, BUT HE'S GONE--AND SO IS MY REAL SON...I CAUSE DISASTER WHEREVER I GO.
NO, FATHER, NO...
OH, CHILD, CHILD...IF YOU STAY WITH ME I'LL DESTROY YOU, TOO.
STOP! FLINDER, DO NOT DESPAIR! YOU LEARNED T BE A WAGONWRIGHT FROM YOUR FATHER. NOW I APPOINT YOU ROYAL WAGO WRIGHT OF OZ AND EN- TRUST TO YOU THE CARE OF MY RED WAGON.
AND LISTEN, ALL OF YOU. IF DASH AND JAVEN STILL EXIST, I WILL USE ALL MY POWER TO BRING THEM BACK.
OH, YOUR MAJESTY!
CAN YOU REALLY BRING THEM BACK? DASH? OH, MY--I...WHEN FLINDER HAS JAVEN, MAY I HAVE STAR BACK?
STAR HAS MADE HIS OWN CHOICE.
BUT, ABATHA, LOOK, THERE H IS, HE IS YOUR SON. THE REASON HE DOES NOT LOVE YOU IS THAT HE DOES NO **KNOW** YOU. ONLY YOU CAN CHANGE THAT.
STAR? DO... DO YOU REMEMBER ME AT ALL?
I...I REMEMBER A FLASH AND FALLING...AND HURT... THEN ARMS HOLDING ME CLOSE--AND A VOICE, COMFORTING ME...
YES! YES! YOU **DO** REMEMBER...OH, STAR...I LOVE YOU. STAY WITH FLINDER IF YOU MUST, BUT SOME- TIME WILL YOU...VISIT ME?
YES...
...MOTHER.
The E

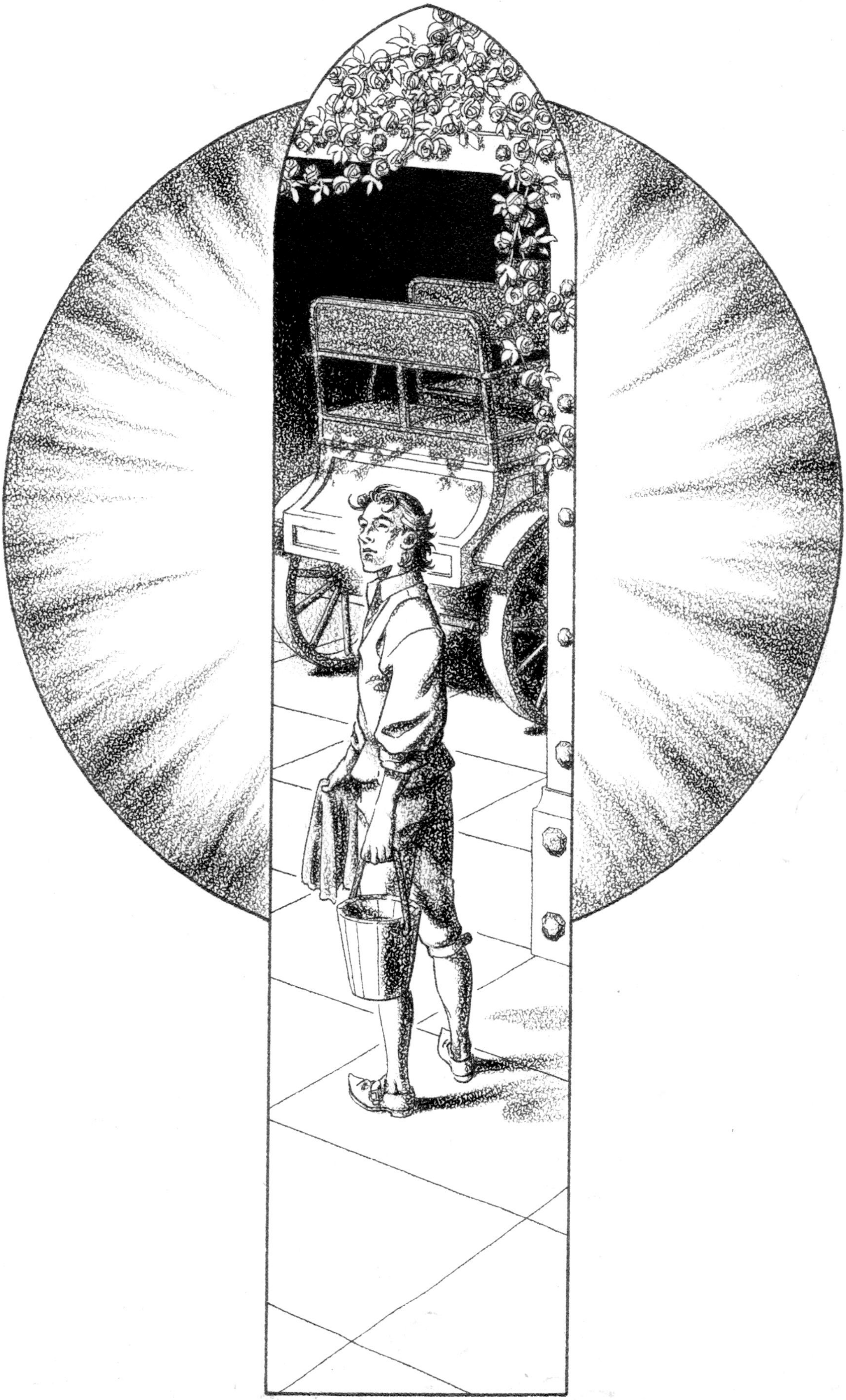

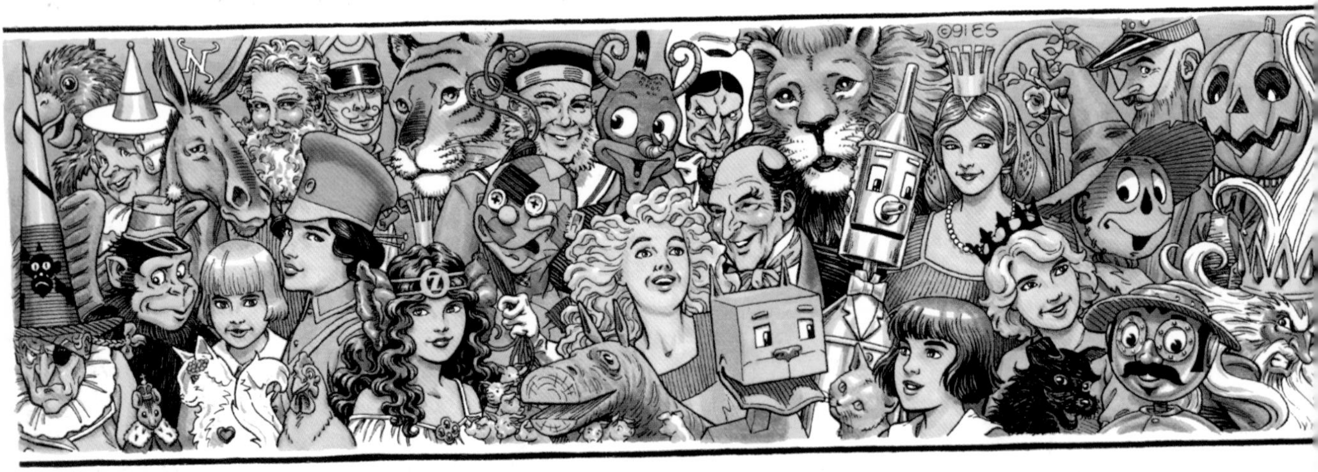
©91ES

MORE ADVENTURES IN OZ
THE OZ GRAPHIC NOVELS AND BEYOND
by Eric Shanower

WAS SIX YEARS OLD when I discovered the Oz books by L. Frank Baum. Previously I'd seen the movie of *The Wizard of Oz*—the 1939 MGM version starring Judy Garland—on a black-and-white TV, and in the bookmobile, I'd found an abridgement of *The Wizard of Oz* illustrated by Anton Loeb. Then, one afternoon, my parents took my sister and me to a bookstore and allowed each of us to choose one book. I chose *The Road to Oz.*

My parents read us a chapter a night, and for me, that was it. I was hooked on Oz books, no turning back. I started to draw Oz pictures and I organized my sister and our friends into playing our own Oz adventures. In the front of each Oz book was a long list of the forty titles in the series. I saw that many authors had written Oz books following series creator L. Frank Baum, so I decided that I would grow up to write and illustrate Oz stories, too.

For my first Oz manuscript, I cobbled together a title from two titles in the official Oz series. I called it *The Magical Mimics Vally [sic] of Oz.* I'd read neither *The Magical Mimics in Oz* nor *The Hidden Valley of Oz,* but that minor detail wasn't going to stop me. My story started strong, but lost momentum halfway through and wandered about aimlessly through eighty pages of illustrated manuscript—pages with extremely generous margins by the time I reached the final page.

Throughout elementary school I came up with all sorts of original ideas for books, Oz and otherwise, and covered countless sheets of paper with text and illustrations. Titles included *The Guinea [Pig?] of Oz, The Lost Children of Oz, Mr. [Wizard?] and the City of Noodles,* and others. Many of these remain incomplete.

At eleven years old, I submitted a short Oz story to *Oziana,* the annual fiction magazine of The International Wizard of Oz Club. My story appeared in the 1976 issue of *Oziana.* It was heavily rewritten by the editor. Nevertheless, I was thrilled—my name was in print on an Oz story!

After graduating high school, I attended The Joe Kubert School of Cartoon and Graphic Art in order to acquire the skills to become a professional cartoonist. For the assignment just prior to graduation, Joe Kubert explained that if a student was to create a war comic story of at least minimal professional quality, Joe would consider publishing it in *Sgt. Rock,* a comic book he edited for DC Comics. My eager attempt resulted in "General Jinjur of Oz." This story was never finished. Part One is complete, but Part Two consists primarily of rough sketches and a synopsis.

Even though I'd made several attempts at Oz comics as a child, it took a classmate at the Kubert School to suggest that I sell the idea for an Oz comic book to a publisher. So I began work on a proposal for an Oz comic book series that would star Trot and Cap'n Bill from Baum's Oz books. I called their first adventure "The Forbidden Fruit of Oz."

The scarcrow was taking a walk

This page: pencil and crayon illustration for the manuscript of *The Magical Mimics Hidden Vally [sic] of Oz,* 1971.

Next two pages: student assignment, 1982.

Following four pages: "General Jinjur of Oz" Part One, 1984.

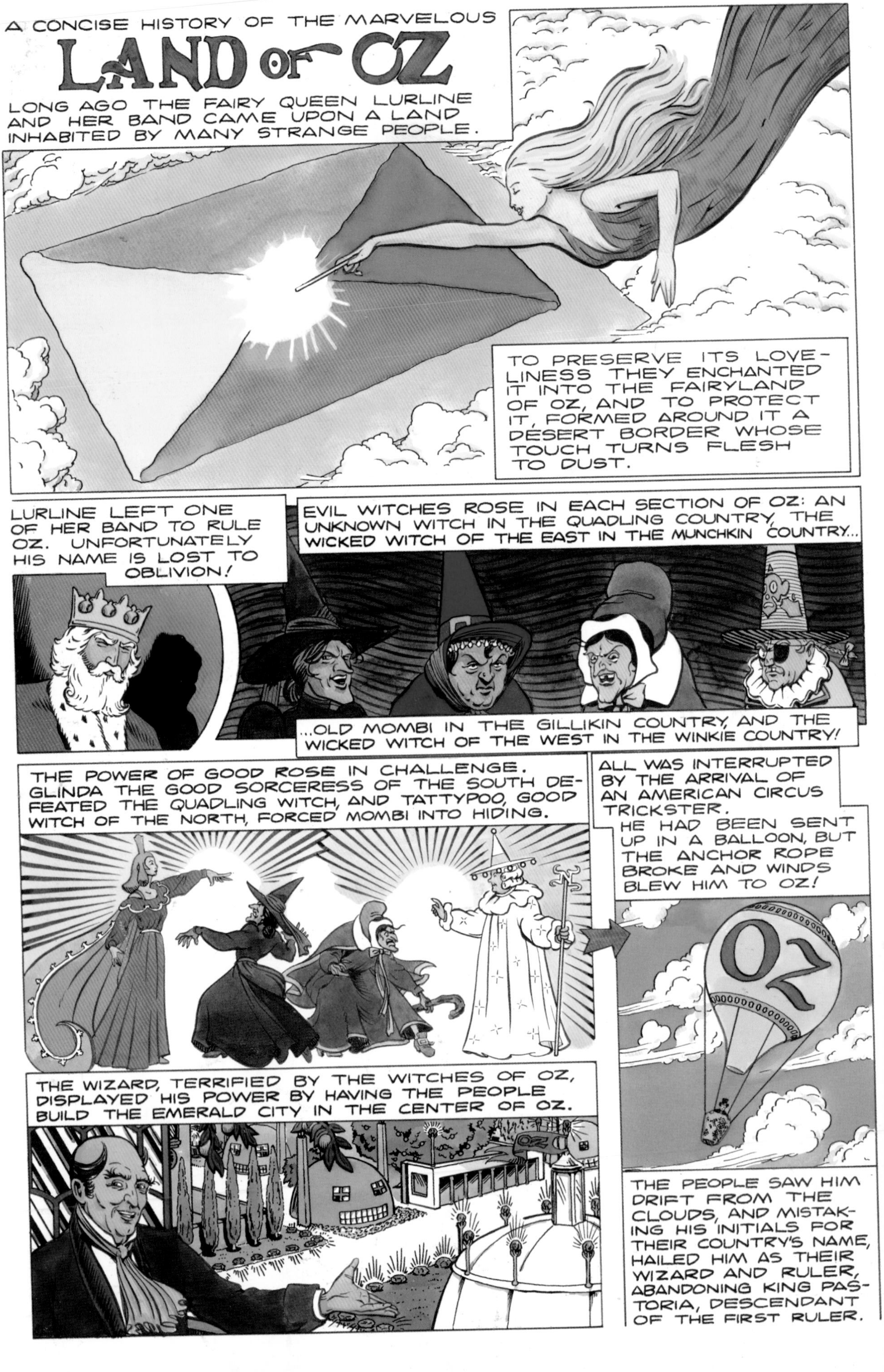
A CONCISE HISTORY OF THE MARVELOUS
LAND OF OZ
LONG AGO THE FAIRY QUEEN LURLINE AND HER BAND CAME UPON A LAND INHABITED BY MANY STRANGE PEOPLE.
TO PRESERVE ITS LOVELINESS THEY ENCHANTED IT INTO THE FAIRYLAND OF OZ, AND TO PROTECT IT, FORMED AROUND IT A DESERT BORDER WHOSE TOUCH TURNS FLESH TO DUST.
LURLINE LEFT ONE OF HER BAND TO RULE OZ. UNFORTUNATELY HIS NAME IS LOST TO OBLIVION!
EVIL WITCHES ROSE IN EACH SECTION OF OZ: AN UNKNOWN WITCH IN THE QUADLING COUNTRY, THE WICKED WITCH OF THE EAST IN THE MUNCHKIN COUNTRY...
...OLD MOMBI IN THE GILLIKIN COUNTRY, AND THE WICKED WITCH OF THE WEST IN THE WINKIE COUNTRY!
THE POWER OF GOOD ROSE IN CHALLENGE. GLINDA THE GOOD SORCERESS OF THE SOUTH DEFEATED THE QUADLING WITCH, AND TATTYPOO, GOOD WITCH OF THE NORTH, FORCED MOMBI INTO HIDING.
ALL WAS INTERRUPTED BY THE ARRIVAL OF AN AMERICAN CIRCUS TRICKSTER.
HE HAD BEEN SENT UP IN A BALLOON, BUT THE ANCHOR ROPE BROKE AND WINDS BLEW HIM TO OZ!
OZ
THE WIZARD, TERRIFIED BY THE WITCHES OF OZ, DISPLAYED HIS POWER BY HAVING THE PEOPLE BUILD THE EMERALD CITY IN THE CENTER OF OZ.
THE PEOPLE SAW HIM DRIFT FROM THE CLOUDS, AND MISTAKING HIS INITIALS FOR THEIR COUNTRY'S NAME, HAILED HIM AS THEIR WIZARD AND RULER, ABANDONING KING PASTORIA, DESCENDANT OF THE FIRST RULER.

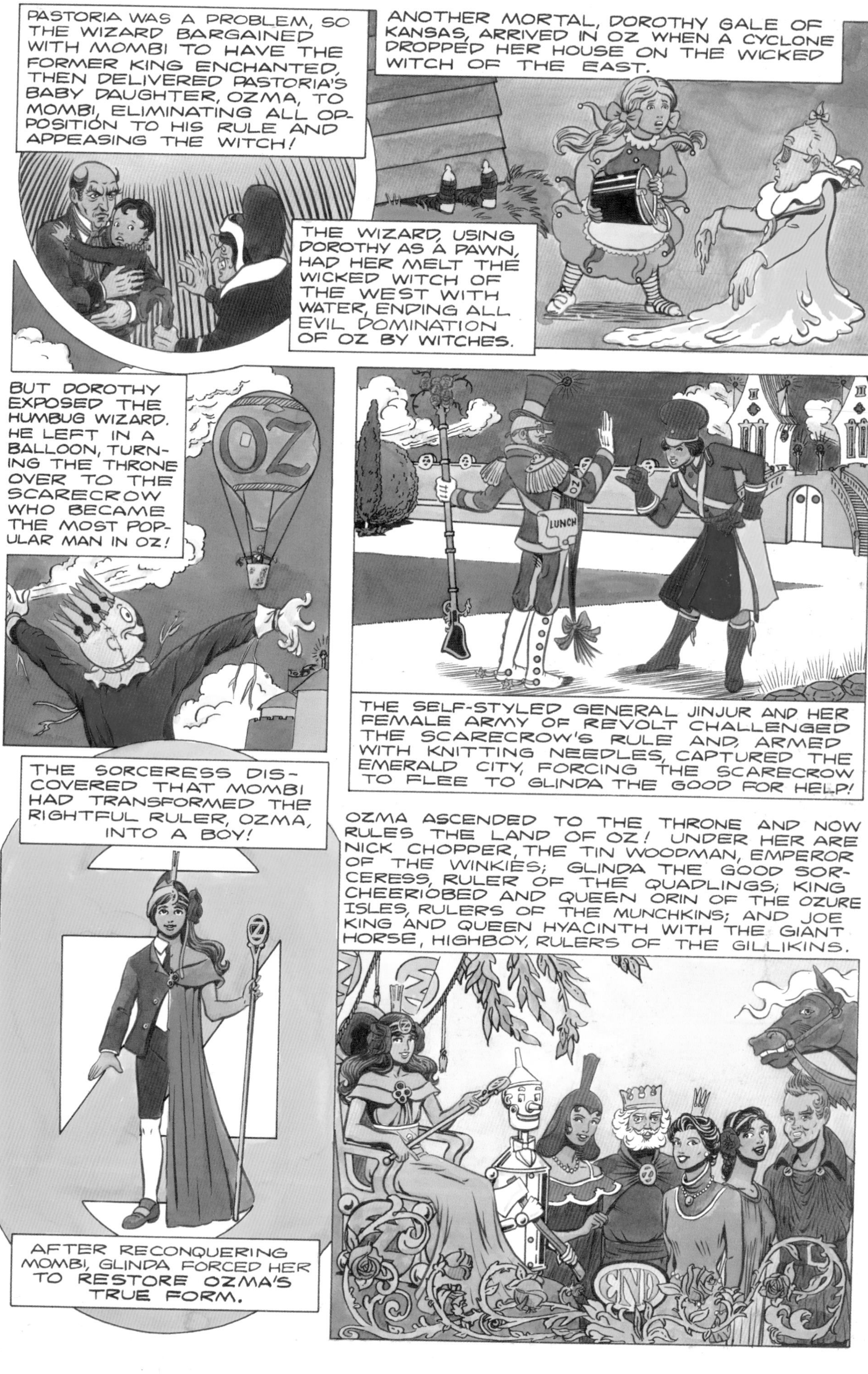
PASTORIA WAS A PROBLEM, SO THE WIZARD BARGAINED WITH MOMBI TO HAVE THE FORMER KING ENCHANTED, THEN DELIVERED PASTORIA'S BABY DAUGHTER, OZMA, TO MOMBI, ELIMINATING ALL OPPOSITION TO HIS RULE AND APPEASING THE WITCH!
ANOTHER MORTAL, DOROTHY GALE OF KANSAS, ARRIVED IN OZ WHEN A CYCLONE DROPPED HER HOUSE ON THE WICKED WITCH OF THE EAST.
THE WIZARD, USING DOROTHY AS A PAWN, HAD HER MELT THE WICKED WITCH OF THE WEST WITH WATER, ENDING ALL EVIL DOMINATION OF OZ BY WITCHES.
BUT DOROTHY EXPOSED THE HUMBUG WIZARD. HE LEFT IN A BALLOON, TURNING THE THRONE OVER TO THE SCARECROW WHO BECAME THE MOST POPULAR MAN IN OZ!
OZ
LUNCH
THE SELF-STYLED GENERAL JINJUR AND HER FEMALE ARMY OF REVOLT CHALLENGED THE SCARECROW'S RULE AND, ARMED WITH KNITTING NEEDLES, CAPTURED THE EMERALD CITY, FORCING THE SCARECROW TO FLEE TO GLINDA THE GOOD FOR HELP!
THE SORCERESS DISCOVERED THAT MOMBI HAD TRANSFORMED THE RIGHTFUL RULER, OZMA, INTO A BOY!
OZMA ASCENDED TO THE THRONE AND NOW RULES THE LAND OF OZ! UNDER HER ARE NICK CHOPPER, THE TIN WOODMAN, EMPEROR OF THE WINKIES; GLINDA THE GOOD SORCERESS, RULER OF THE QUADLINGS; KING CHEERIOBED AND QUEEN ORIN OF THE OZURE ISLES, RULERS OF THE MUNCHKINS; AND JOE KING AND QUEEN HYACINTH WITH THE GIANT HORSE, HIGHBOY, RULERS OF THE GILLIKINS.
AFTER RECONQUERING MOMBI, GLINDA FORCED HER TO RESTORE OZMA'S TRUE FORM.

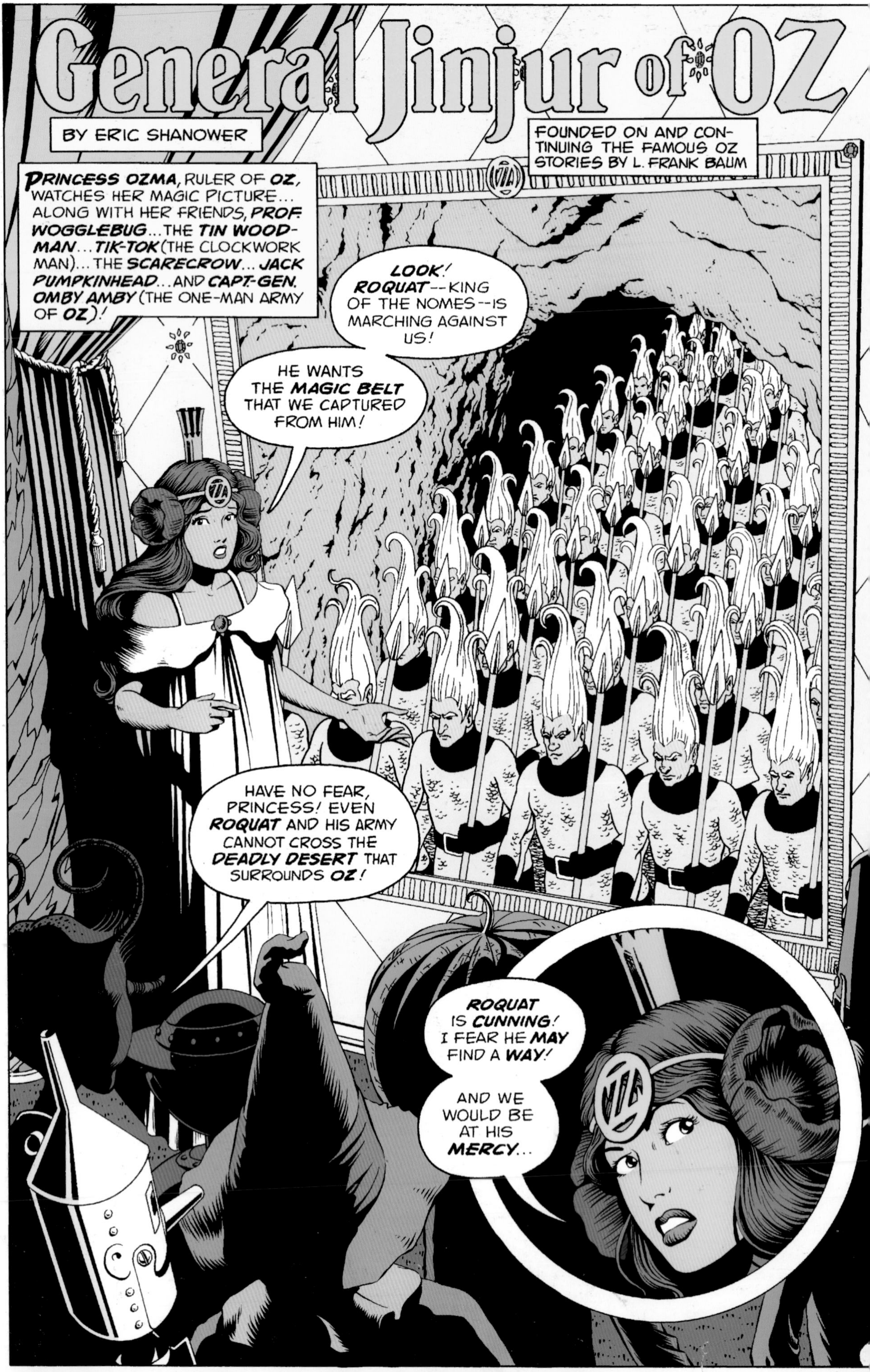

General Jinjur of OZ
BY ERIC SHANOWER
FOUNDED ON AND CONTINUING THE FAMOUS OZ STORIES BY L. FRANK BAUM
PRINCESS OZMA, RULER OF OZ, WATCHES HER MAGIC PICTURE... ALONG WITH HER FRIENDS, PROF. WOGGLEBUG... THE TIN WOODMAN... TIK-TOK (THE CLOCKWORK MAN)... THE SCARECROW... JACK PUMPKINHEAD... AND CAPT-GEN. OMBY AMBY (THE ONE-MAN ARMY OF OZ)!
LOOK! ROQUAT--KING OF THE NOMES--IS MARCHING AGAINST US!
HE WANTS THE MAGIC BELT THAT WE CAPTURED FROM HIM!
HAVE NO FEAR, PRINCESS! EVEN ROQUAT AND HIS ARMY CANNOT CROSS THE DEADLY DESERT THAT SURROUNDS OZ!
ROQUAT IS CUNNING! I FEAR HE MAY FIND A WAY!
AND WE WOULD BE AT HIS MERCY...

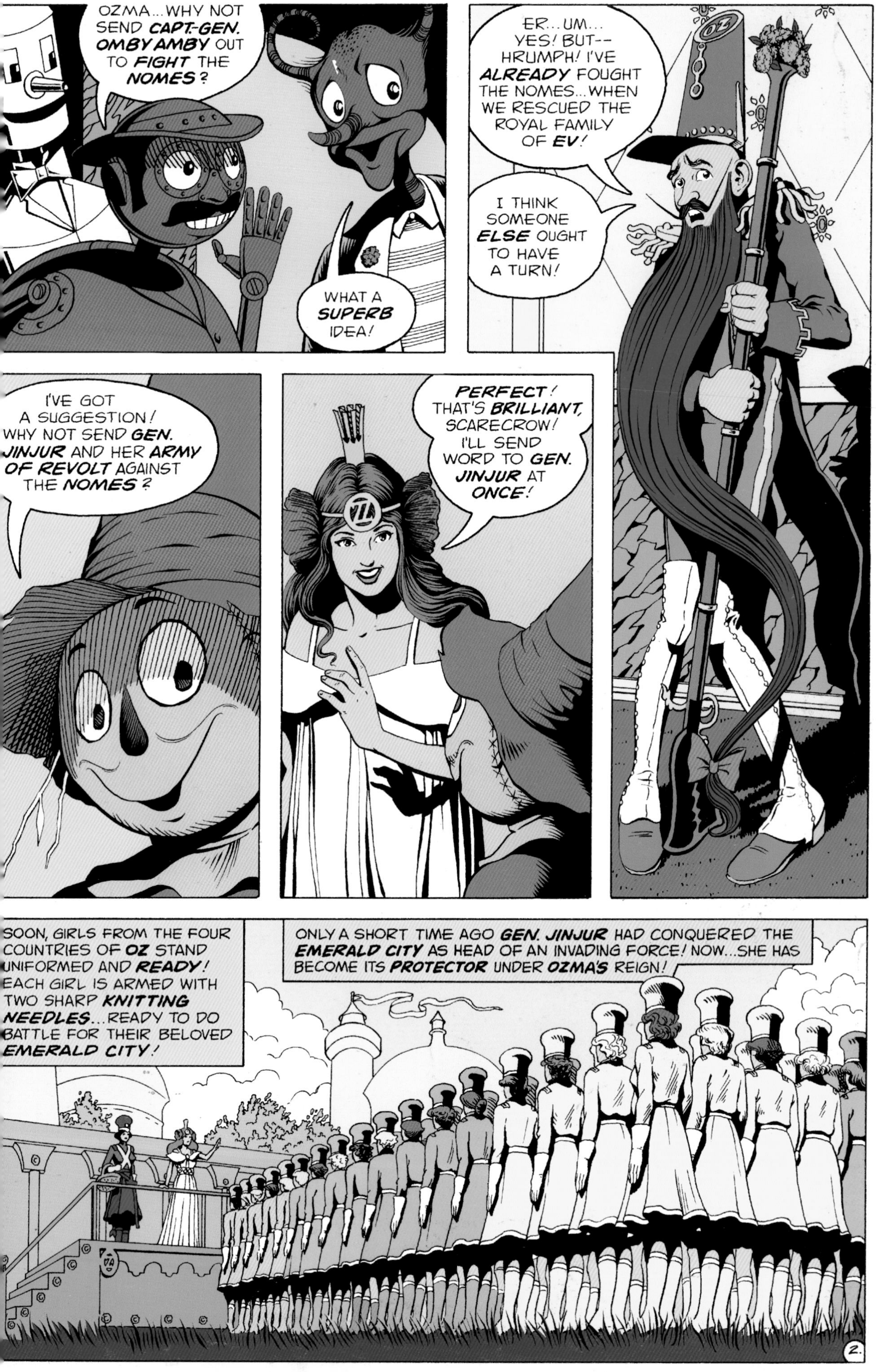

OZMA...WHY NOT SEND **CAPT.-GEN. OMBY AMBY** OUT TO **FIGHT** THE **NOMES**?
WHAT A **SUPERB** IDEA!
ER...UM... YES! BUT-- HRUMPH! I'VE **ALREADY** FOUGHT THE NOMES...WHEN WE RESCUED THE ROYAL FAMILY OF **EV**!
I THINK SOMEONE **ELSE** OUGHT TO HAVE A TURN!
I'VE GOT A SUGGESTION! WHY NOT SEND **GEN. JINJUR** AND HER **ARMY OF REVOLT** AGAINST THE **NOMES**?
PERFECT! THAT'S **BRILLIANT**, SCARECROW! I'LL SEND WORD TO **GEN. JINJUR** AT **ONCE**!
SOON, GIRLS FROM THE FOUR COUNTRIES OF **OZ** STAND UNIFORMED AND **READY**! EACH GIRL IS ARMED WITH TWO SHARP **KNITTING NEEDLES**...READY TO DO BATTLE FOR THEIR BELOVED **EMERALD CITY**!
ONLY A SHORT TIME AGO **GEN. JINJUR** HAD CONQUERED THE **EMERALD CITY** AS HEAD OF AN INVADING FORCE! NOW...SHE HAS BECOME ITS **PROTECTOR** UNDER **OZMA'S** REIGN!

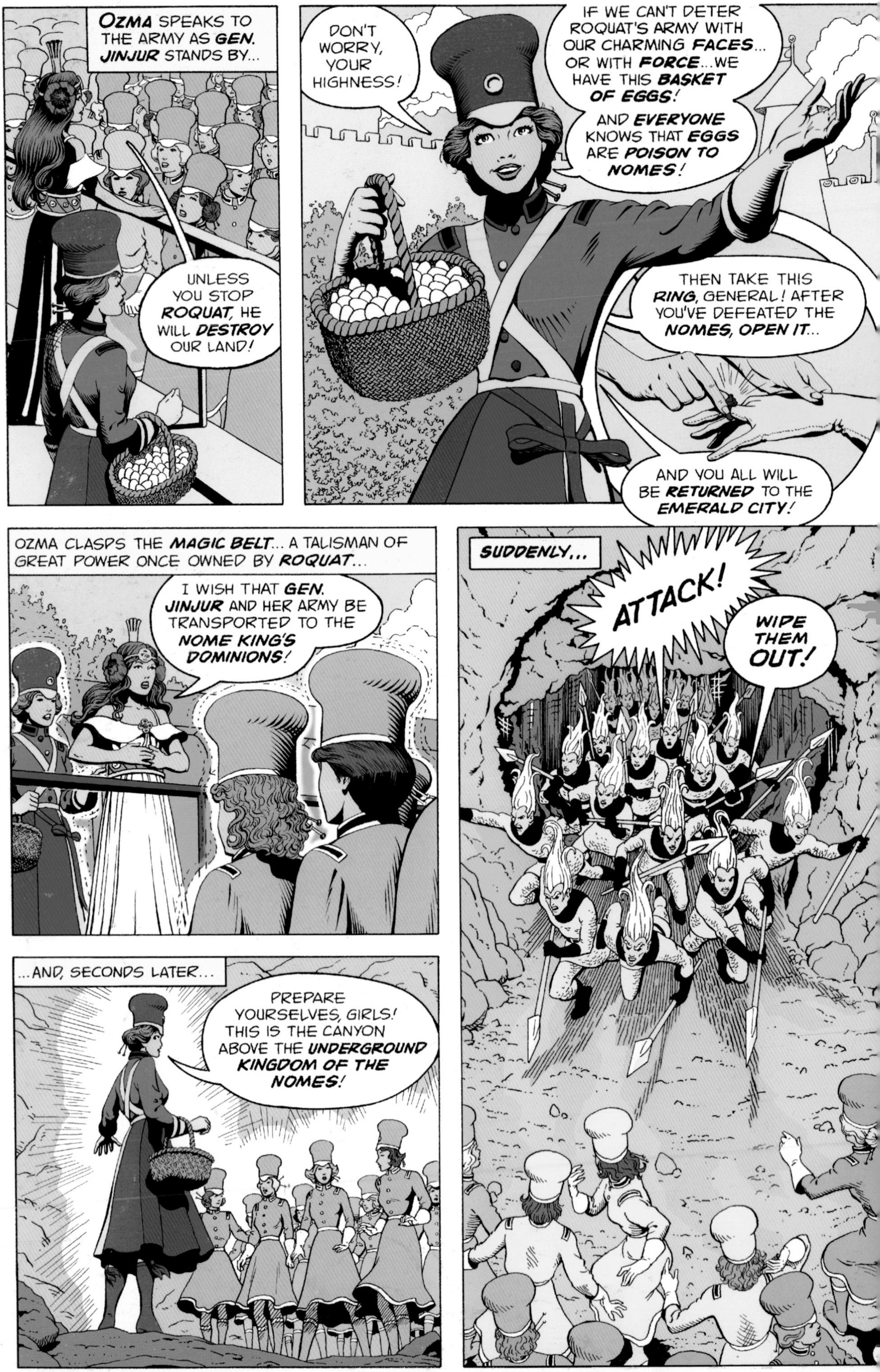

OZMA SPEAKS TO THE ARMY AS GEN. JINJUR STANDS BY...
UNLESS YOU STOP ROQUAT, HE WILL DESTROY OUR LAND!
DON'T WORRY, YOUR HIGHNESS!
IF WE CAN'T DETER ROQUAT'S ARMY WITH OUR CHARMING FACES... OR WITH FORCE...WE HAVE THIS BASKET OF EGGS!
AND EVERYONE KNOWS THAT EGGS ARE POISON TO NOMES!
THEN TAKE THIS RING, GENERAL! AFTER YOU'VE DEFEATED THE NOMES, OPEN IT...
AND YOU ALL WILL BE RETURNED TO THE EMERALD CITY!
OZMA CLASPS THE MAGIC BELT... A TALISMAN OF GREAT POWER ONCE OWNED BY ROQUAT...
I WISH THAT GEN. JINJUR AND HER ARMY BE TRANSPORTED TO THE NOME KING'S DOMINIONS!
...AND, SECONDS LATER...
PREPARE YOURSELVES, GIRLS! THIS IS THE CANYON ABOVE THE UNDERGROUND KINGDOM OF THE NOMES!
SUDDENLY...
ATTACK!
WIPE THEM OUT!

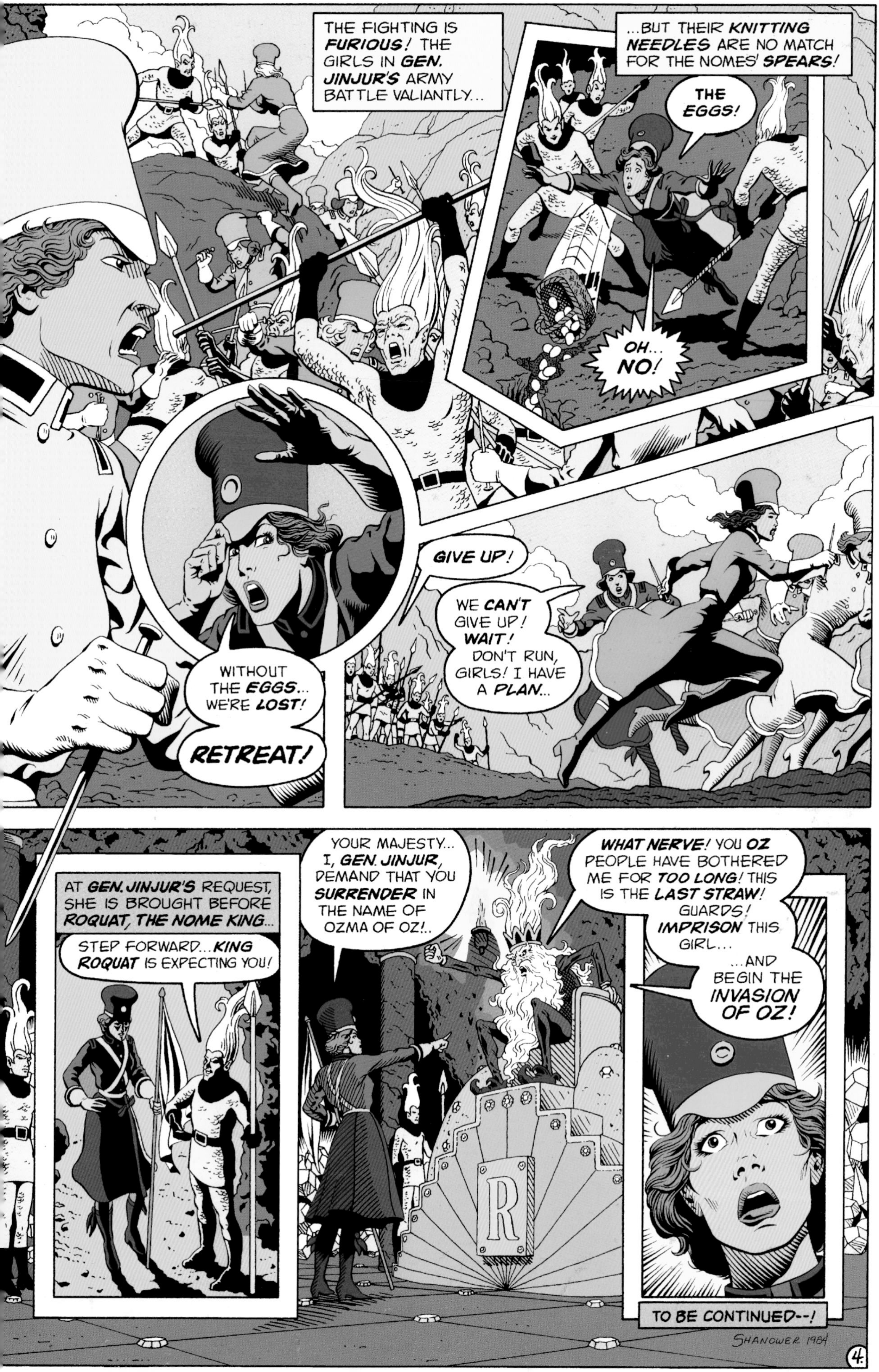
THE FIGHTING IS FURIOUS! THE GIRLS IN GEN. JINJUR'S ARMY BATTLE VALIANTLY...
...BUT THEIR KNITTING NEEDLES ARE NO MATCH FOR THE NOMES' SPEARS!
THE EGGS!
OH... NO!
WITHOUT THE EGGS... WE'RE LOST!
RETREAT!
GIVE UP!
WE CAN'T GIVE UP! WAIT! DON'T RUN, GIRLS! I HAVE A PLAN...
AT GEN. JINJUR'S REQUEST, SHE IS BROUGHT BEFORE ROQUAT, THE NOME KING...
STEP FORWARD... KING ROQUAT IS EXPECTING YOU!
YOUR MAJESTY... I, GEN. JINJUR, DEMAND THAT YOU SURRENDER IN THE NAME OF OZMA OF OZ!..
R
WHAT NERVE! YOU OZ PEOPLE HAVE BOTHERED ME FOR TOO LONG! THIS IS THE LAST STRAW! GUARDS! IMPRISON THIS GIRL...
...AND BEGIN THE INVASION OF OZ!
TO BE CONTINUED--!
SHANOWER 1984

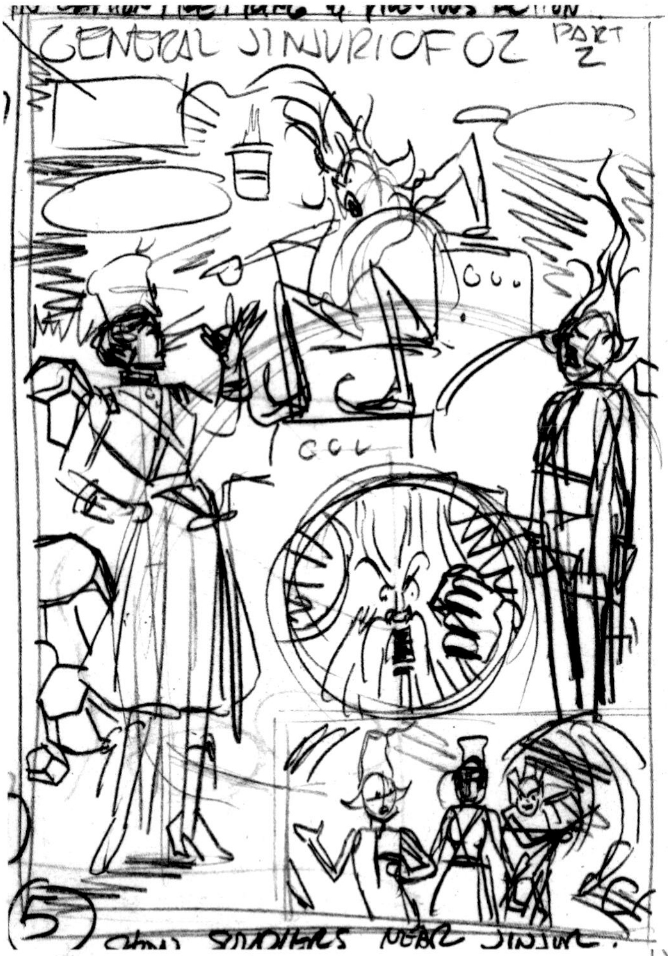
GENERAL JINJUR OF OZ
PART 2

Page 5

Panel 1 *(Jinjur, undaunted, steps up to throne, shakin her finger at Roquat who stares down gleefully.)*

JINJUR: I shall be obliged to <u>box</u> your ears!

ROQUAT: <u>Oho!</u> You seem quite determined to do m <u>harm</u>, I who have never hurt <u>you</u>, but only se retribution for what was <u>stolen</u> from <u>me</u>! Wel go ahead!

Panel 2 *(Jinjur climbs the steps to the throne and trie hit the king, but can not touch him. He laughs. Sh is surprised.)*

ROQUAT: Hee hee hee! Although you Oz people st my Magic Belt, I still have a bit of magic left protect me!

Synopsis

He says she has broken their truce by attempting violence.

He orders Kaliko, his steward, to take her to prisc

Kaliko and a guard escort her through the cavern Kaliko tells her that she'll see the transport tc Oz around the next corner.

Page 6

They enter a huge cavern and see a giant, fiercely hot lava lizard.

Kaliko tells Jinjur how some nomes were mining a vein of molten gold when they came upon the lava lizard near the earth's core. The nomes managed to imprison it and bring it to Roquat's domain.

They only need to wait for it to fully cool. Then the nome army will climb onto the expansive back and ride it safely over the desert. The lava lizard is impervious to the desert's harm.

Jinjur notices something about the lizard. Also it is very sad because of its imprisonment. Jinjur asks Kaliko if she may try to cheer it up.

Kaliko, who is actually kind-hearted, gives in.

Jinjur speaks to the lava lizard and Kaliko notices that the lizard actually becomes a little happier. He doesn't like the way Roquat has it imprisoned.

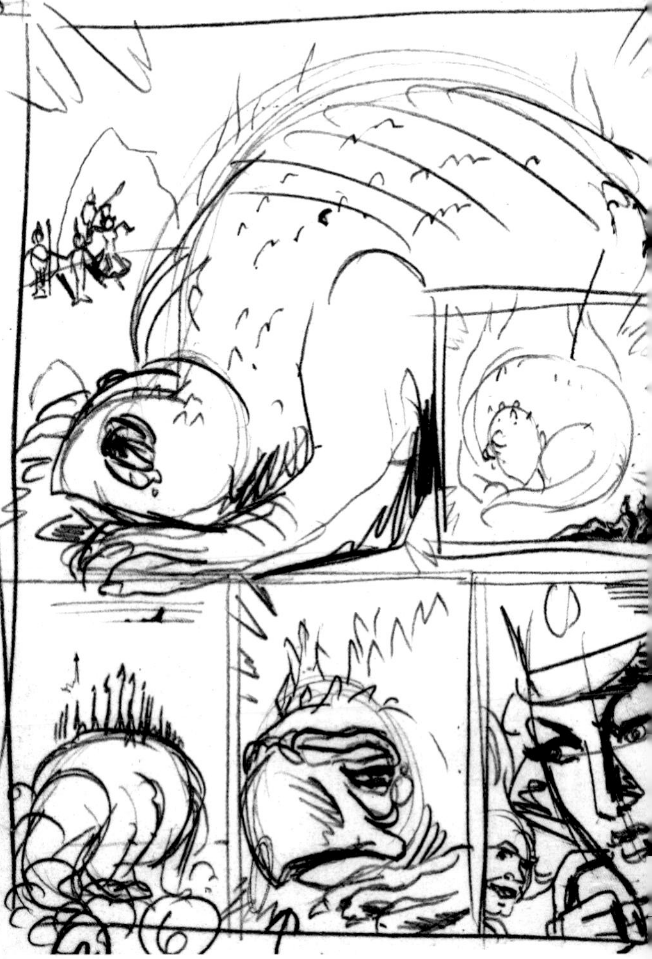

Page 7

Kaliko calls Jinjur back to prison.
At last the day comes when the lava lizard has
  cooled. Roquat is directing his army to go to
  war.
The nome army begins to mount the lizard.
She begins to lay her eggs.
The nomes panic.

ge 8

ey all flee.
ur presses the magic ring (now that the nomes
  have been defeated) to signal Ozma.
e Army of Revolt returns to Oz amid a cheering
  populace.
ma thanks Jinjur who replies, "I'm glad to serve
  you, your highness, but I'm getting awfully
  tired of this war business. Hopefully, I'll never
  need this uniform again and can live my life in
  peace."

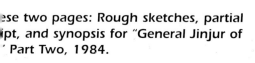
ese two pages: Rough sketches, partial
pt, and synopsis for "General Jinjur of
Part Two, 1984.

DC Comics never published "General Jinjur of Oz," but during the summer of 1984, editor Nic Cuti saw the pages for Part One at the publisher's office in New York City. Nic liked "General Jinjur" and asked me to put together an Oz comic book proposal for a new line of children's comic books DC Comics was planning. Since I'd already been working on a proposal, it didn't take me long.

For the finished proposal, I made some changes to my original concept. Because they were still under copyright, Trot and Cap'n Bill were out. Dorothy and the Scarecrow were in. But by the autumn of 1984, it seemed evident that a children's line of DC Comics wasn't going to materialize.

I took the Oz proposal elsewhere, eventually signing a publishing agreement with First Comics in Chicago in 1985. Publisher Rick Obadiah at First Comics was interested in turning my idea into a series of graphic novels instead of an ongoing series of comic books. At first I was disappointed by the graphic novel idea, but I wanted the project published, so I acquiesced and was soon glad I did. In April 1986, *The Enchanted Apples of Oz* was published. I was thrilled.

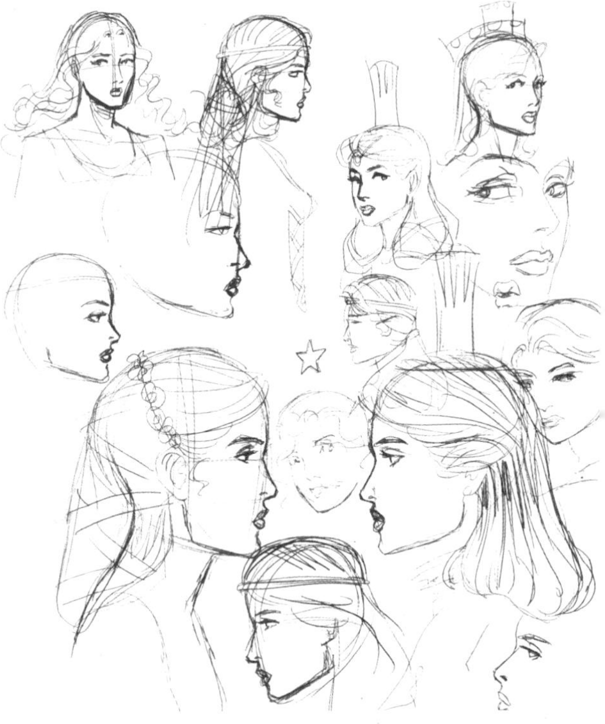

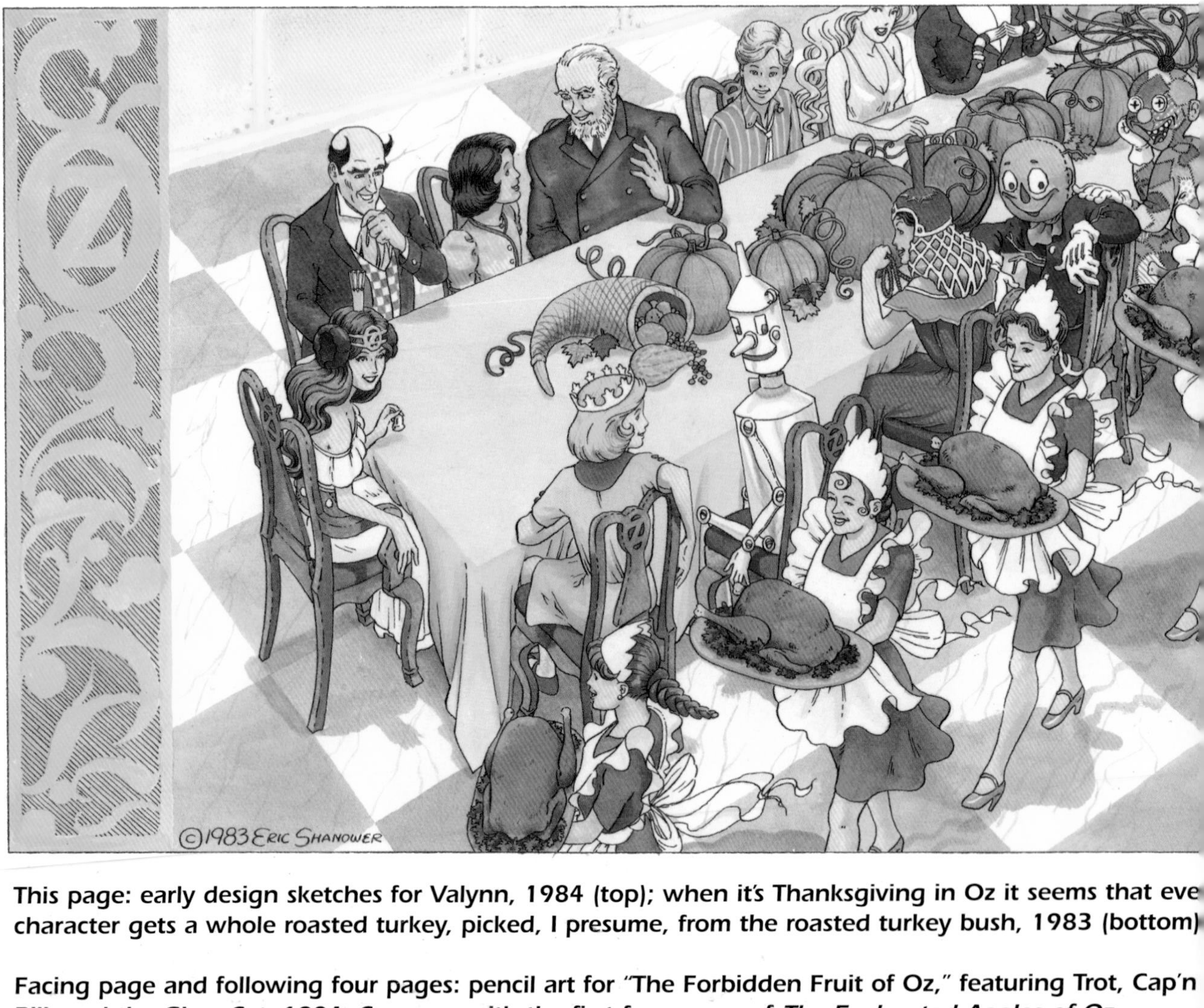
©1983 ERIC SHANOWER

This page: early design sketches for Valynn, 1984 (top); when it's Thanksgiving in Oz it seems that eve character gets a whole roasted turkey, picked, I presume, from the roasted turkey bush, 1983 (bottom)

Facing page and following four pages: pencil art for "The Forbidden Fruit of Oz," featuring Trot, Cap'n Bill, and the Glass Cat, 1984. Compare with the first few pages of *The Enchanted Apples of Oz*.

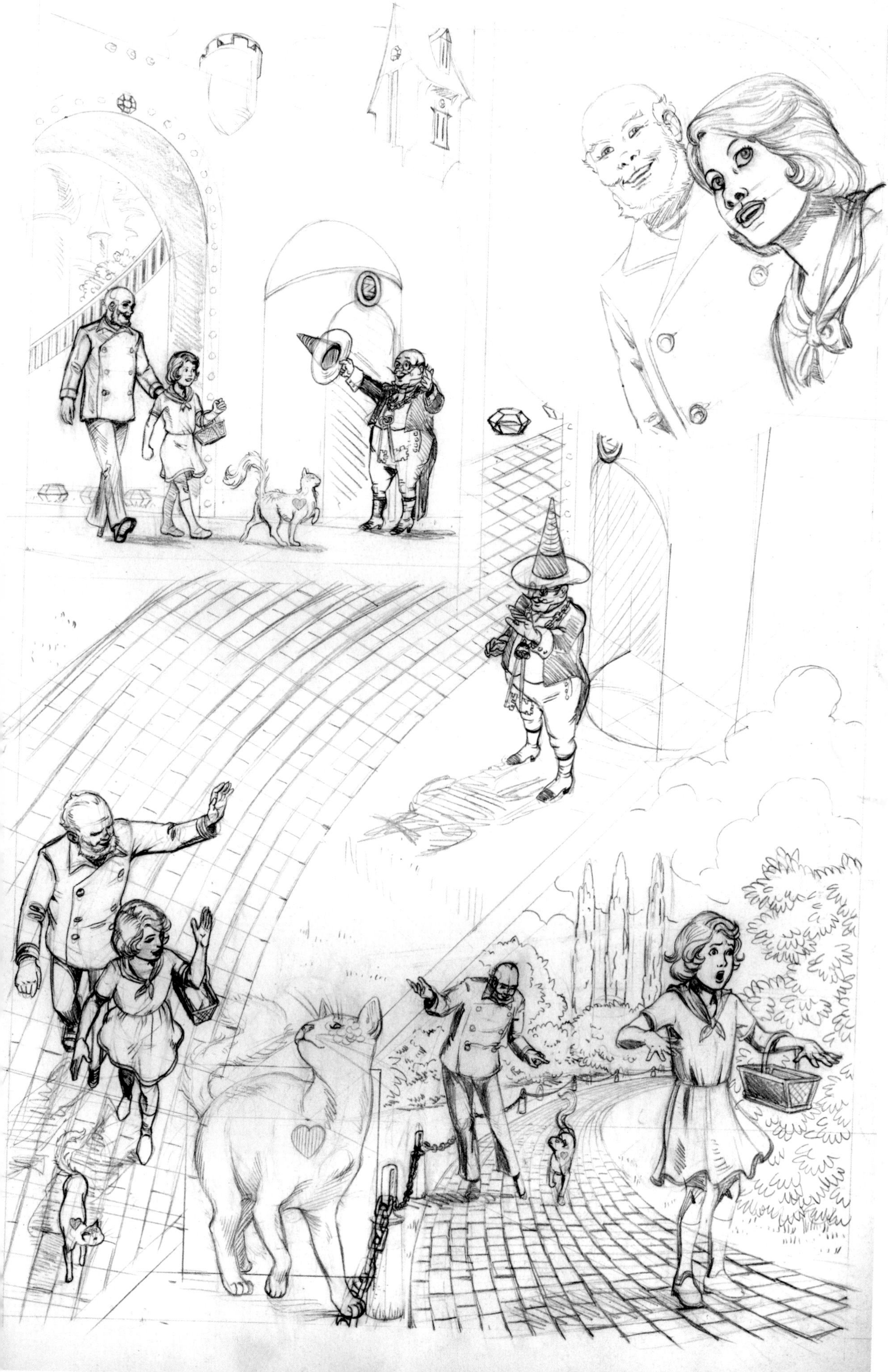

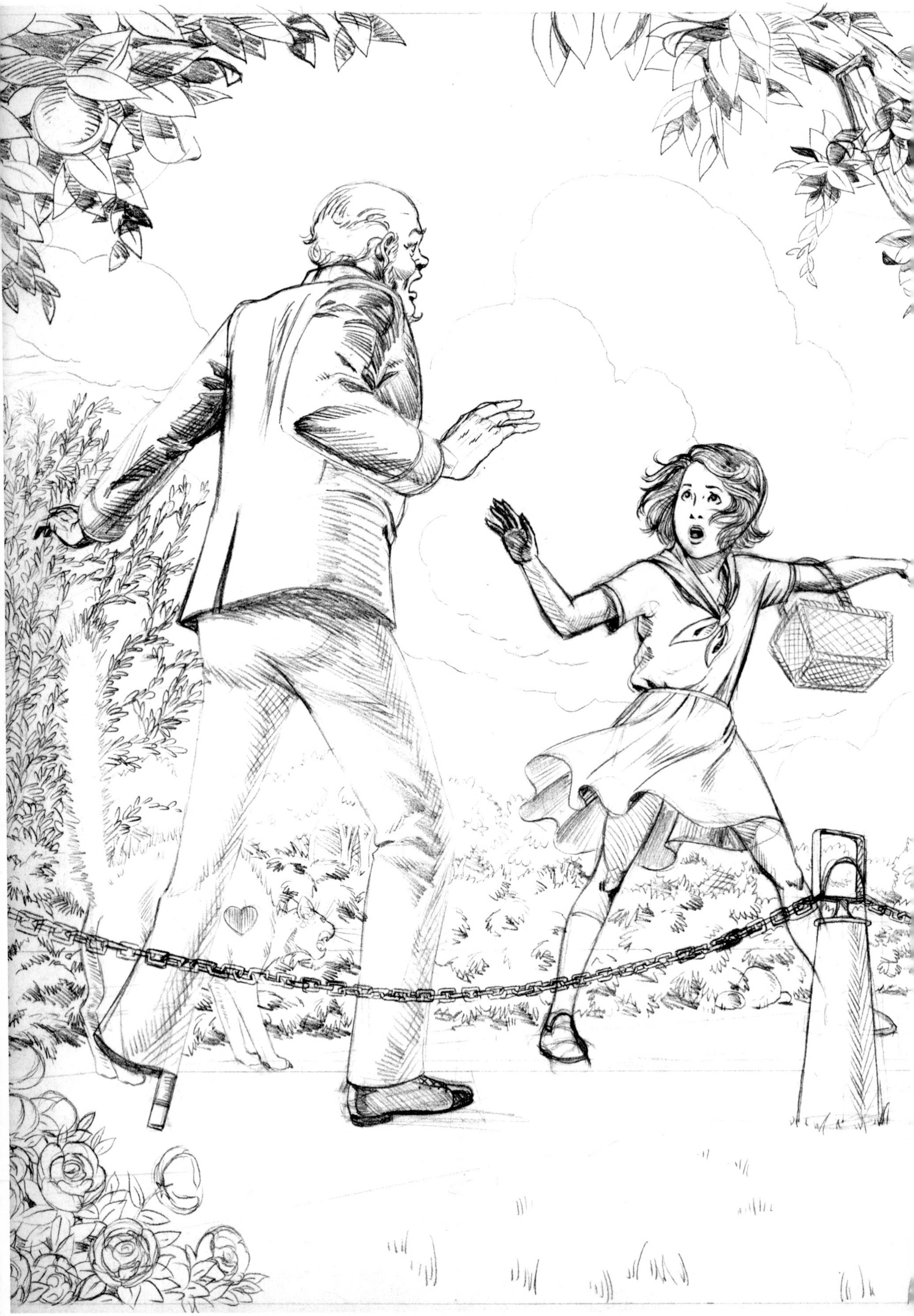

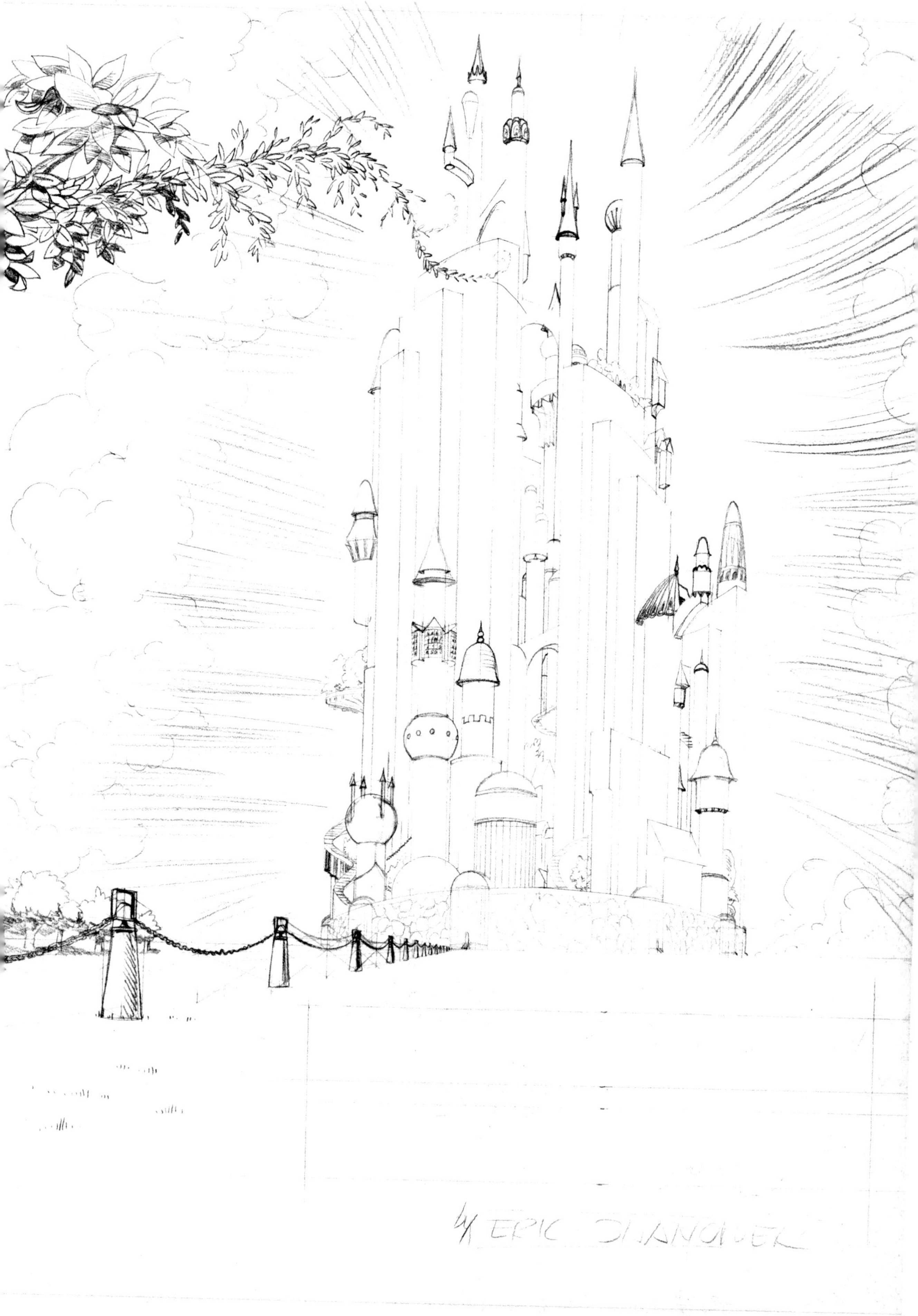
ERIC SHANOWER

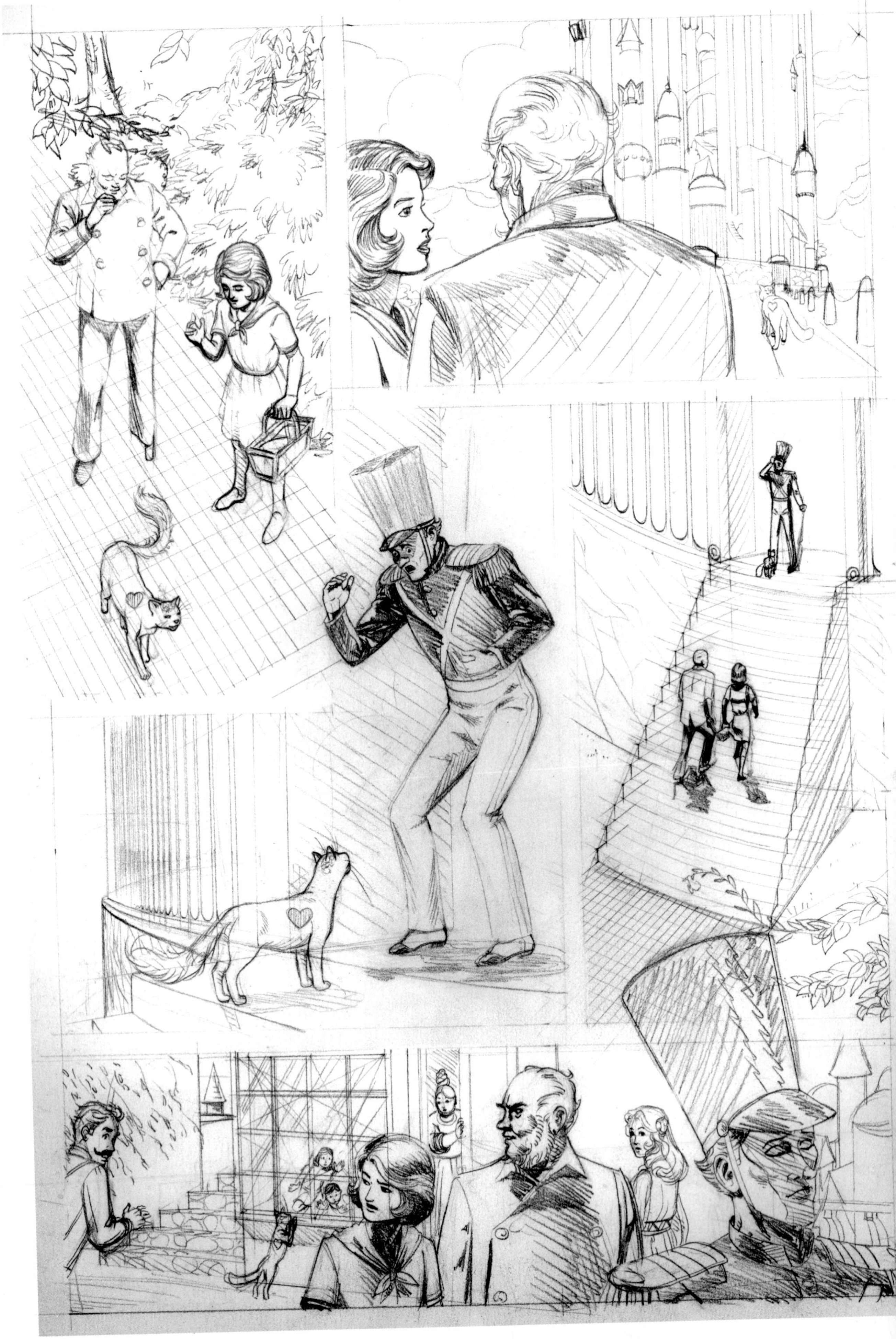

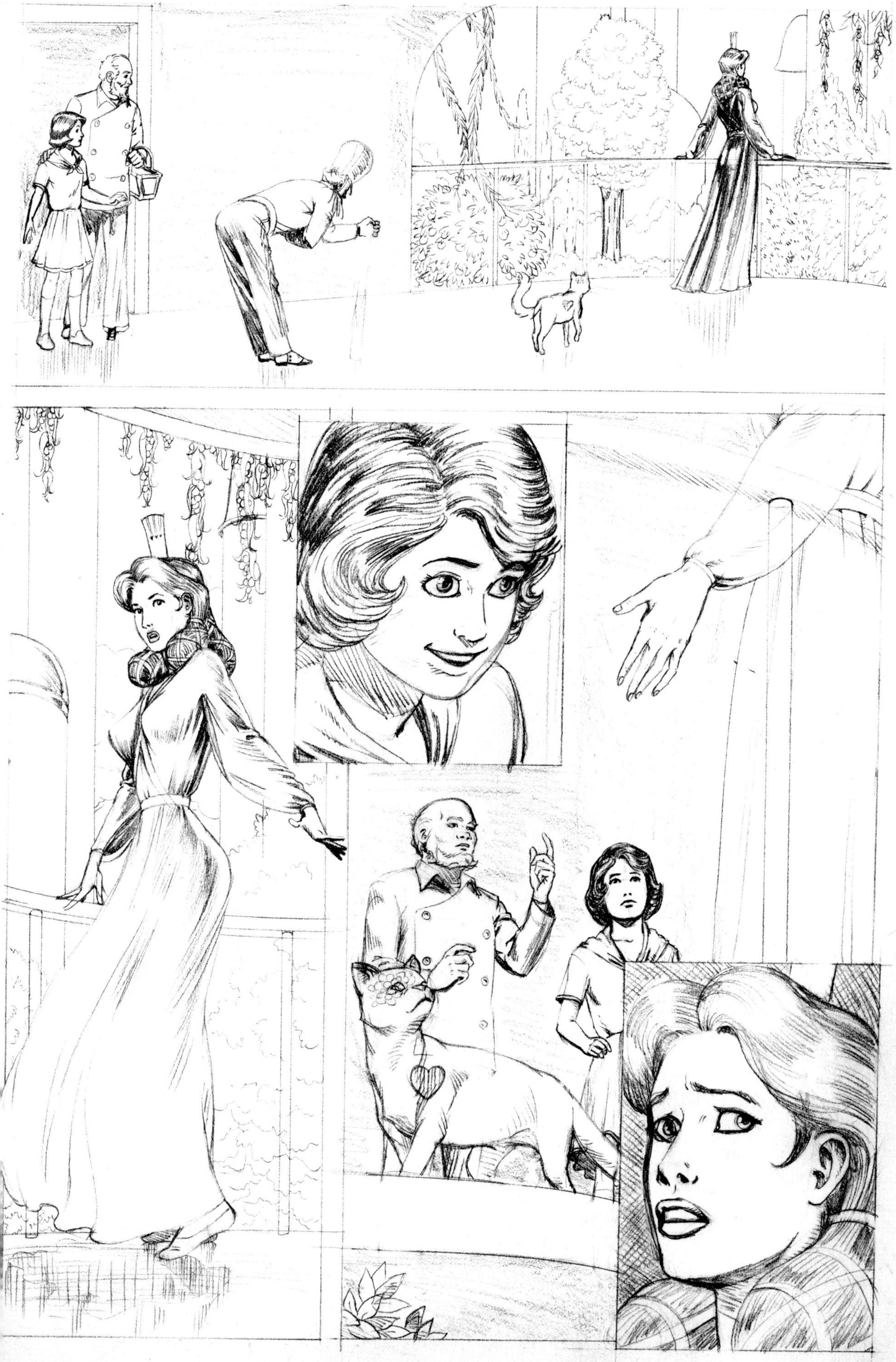

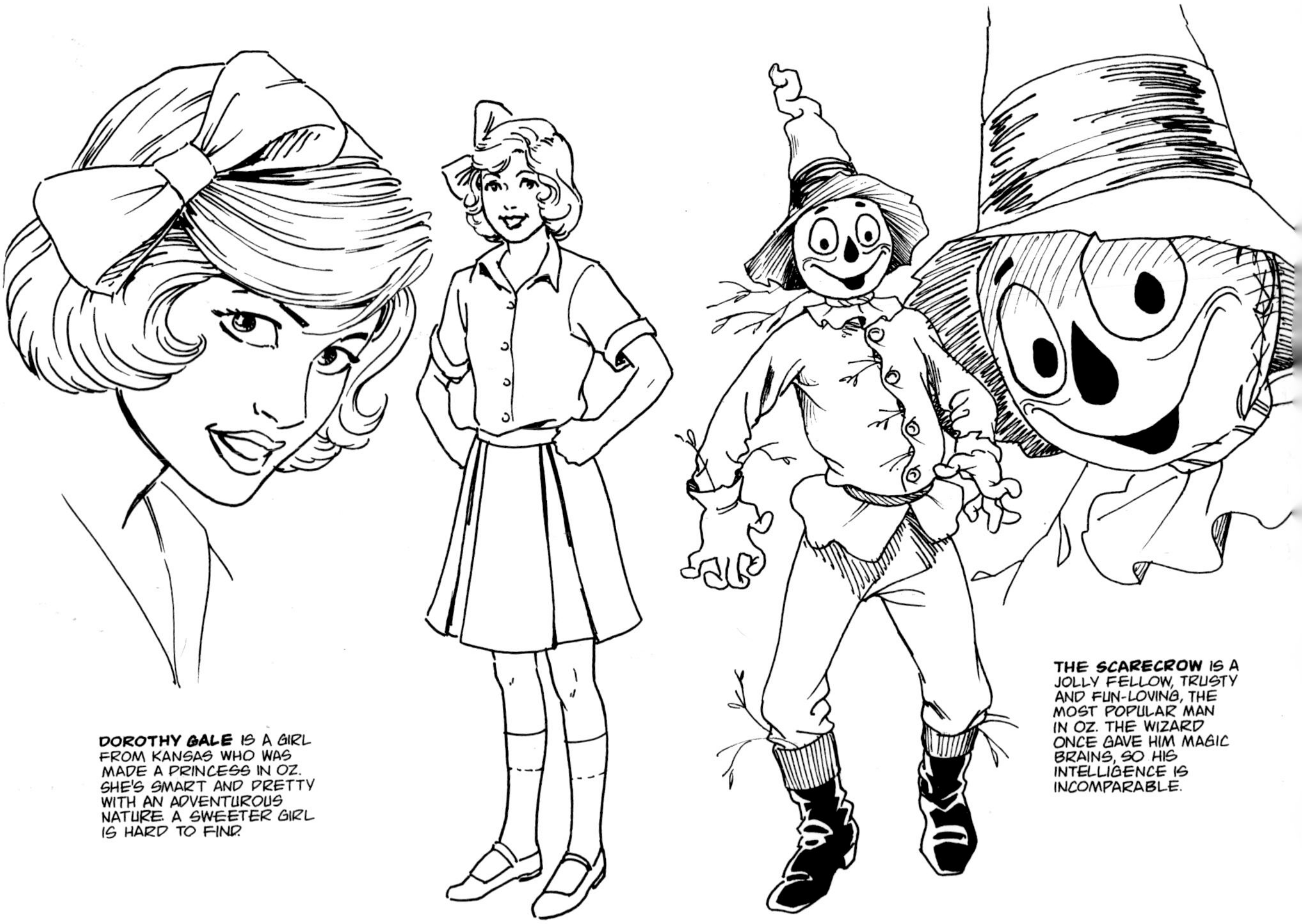
DOROTHY GALE IS A GIRL FROM KANSAS WHO WAS MADE A PRINCESS IN OZ. SHE'S SMART AND PRETTY WITH AN ADVENTUROUS NATURE. A SWEETER GIRL IS HARD TO FIND.
THE SCARECROW IS A JOLLY FELLOW, TRUSTY AND FUN-LOVING, THE MOST POPULAR MAN IN OZ. THE WIZARD ONCE GAVE HIM MAGIC BRAINS, SO HIS INTELLIGENCE IS INCOMPARABLE.

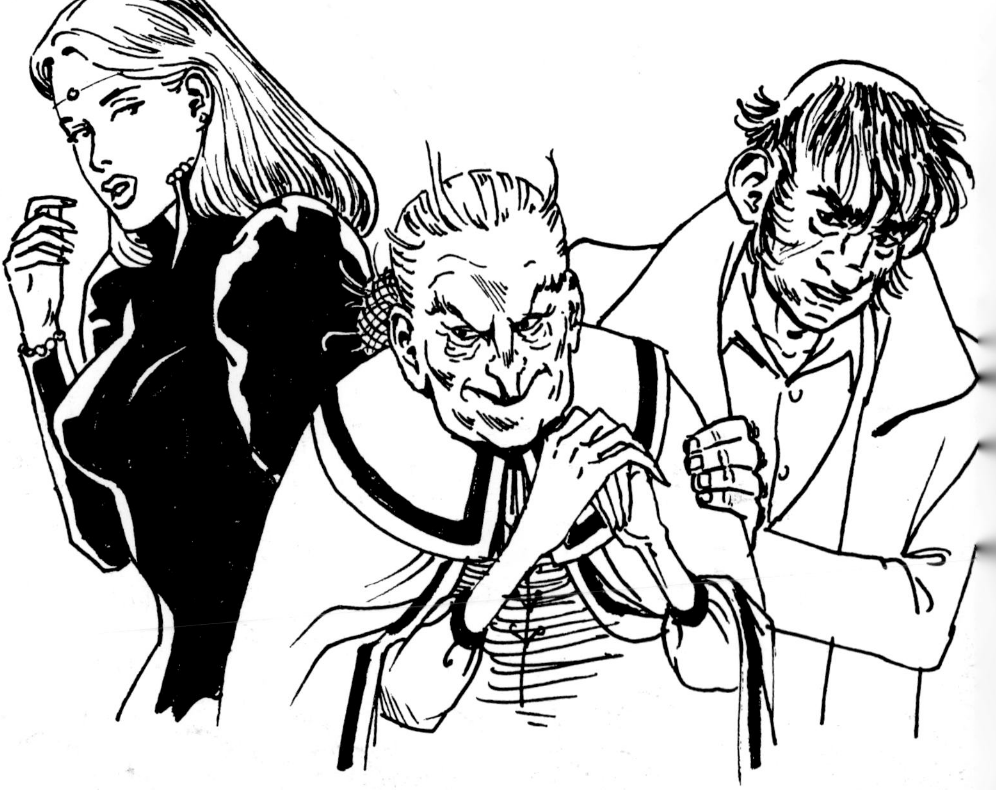

This page: sketches of characters from the proposal for an Oz comic book series. Dorothy (top left); the Scarecrow (top right); and Valynn, the Wicked Witch of the South, and Bortag (bottom), 1984.

Facing page: sketch of Drox from the proposal, 1984 (top); color study for the cover of *The Enchanted Apples of Oz*, 1986 (bottom).

Following two pages: cover of *The Enchanted Apples of Oz*, 1986.

DROX THE FLYING SWORDFISH FLEW ACROSS THE DESERT TO OZ FROM HIS HOME IN THE OCEAN. EXTENDED PERIODS WITHOUT WATER WEAKEN HIM AND SINCE THERE ARE NO OCEANS IN OZ, HE'LL NEVER BE STRONG ENOUGH TO FLY HOME. BORTAG SAVED DROX'S LIFE, SO DROX SERVES BORTAG.

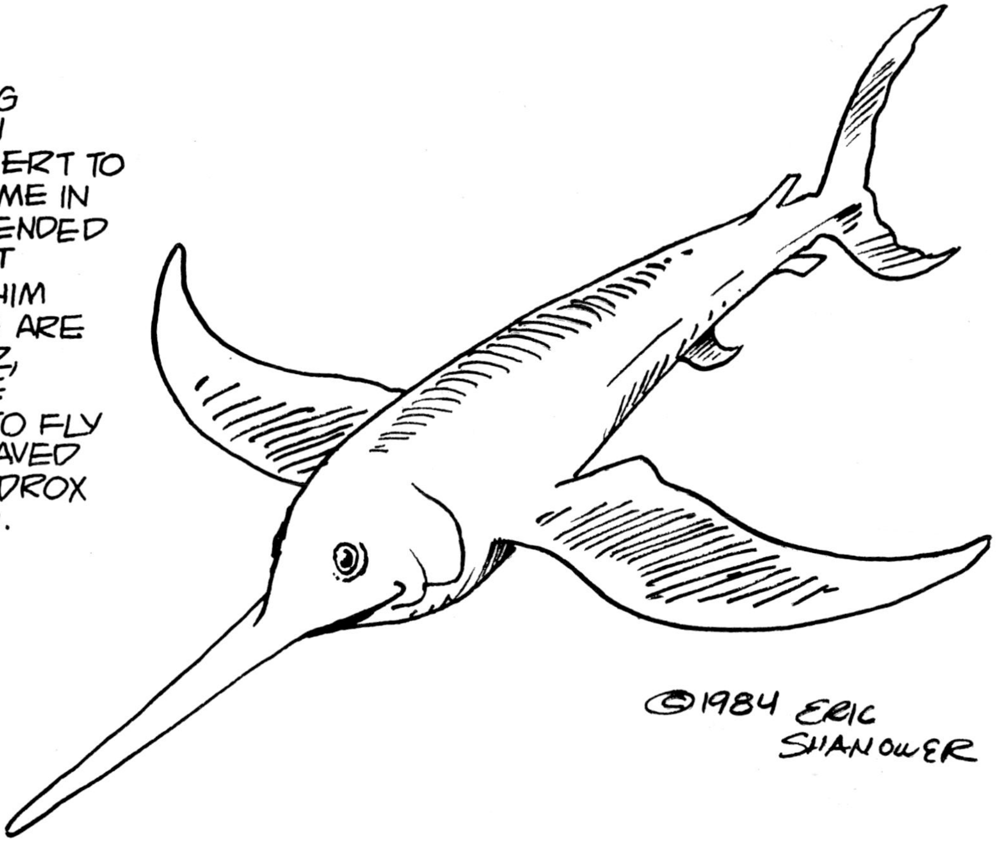
©1984 ERIC SHANOWER

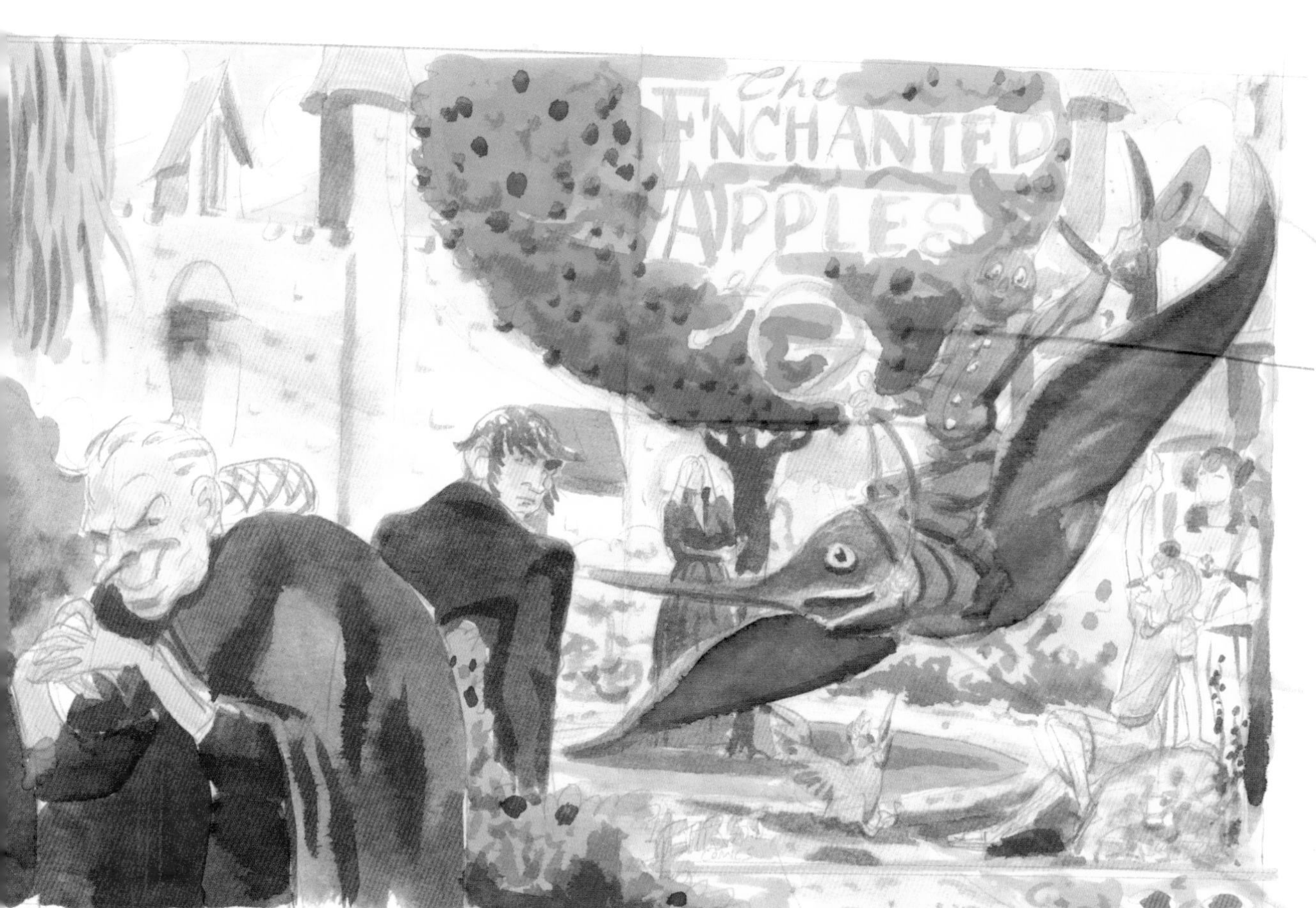
The
ENCHANTED APPLES

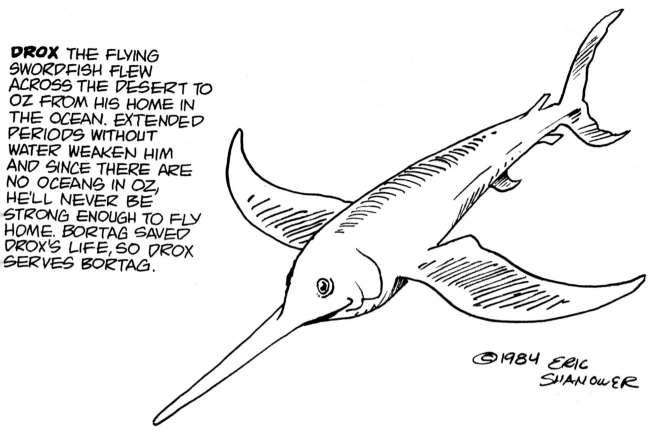

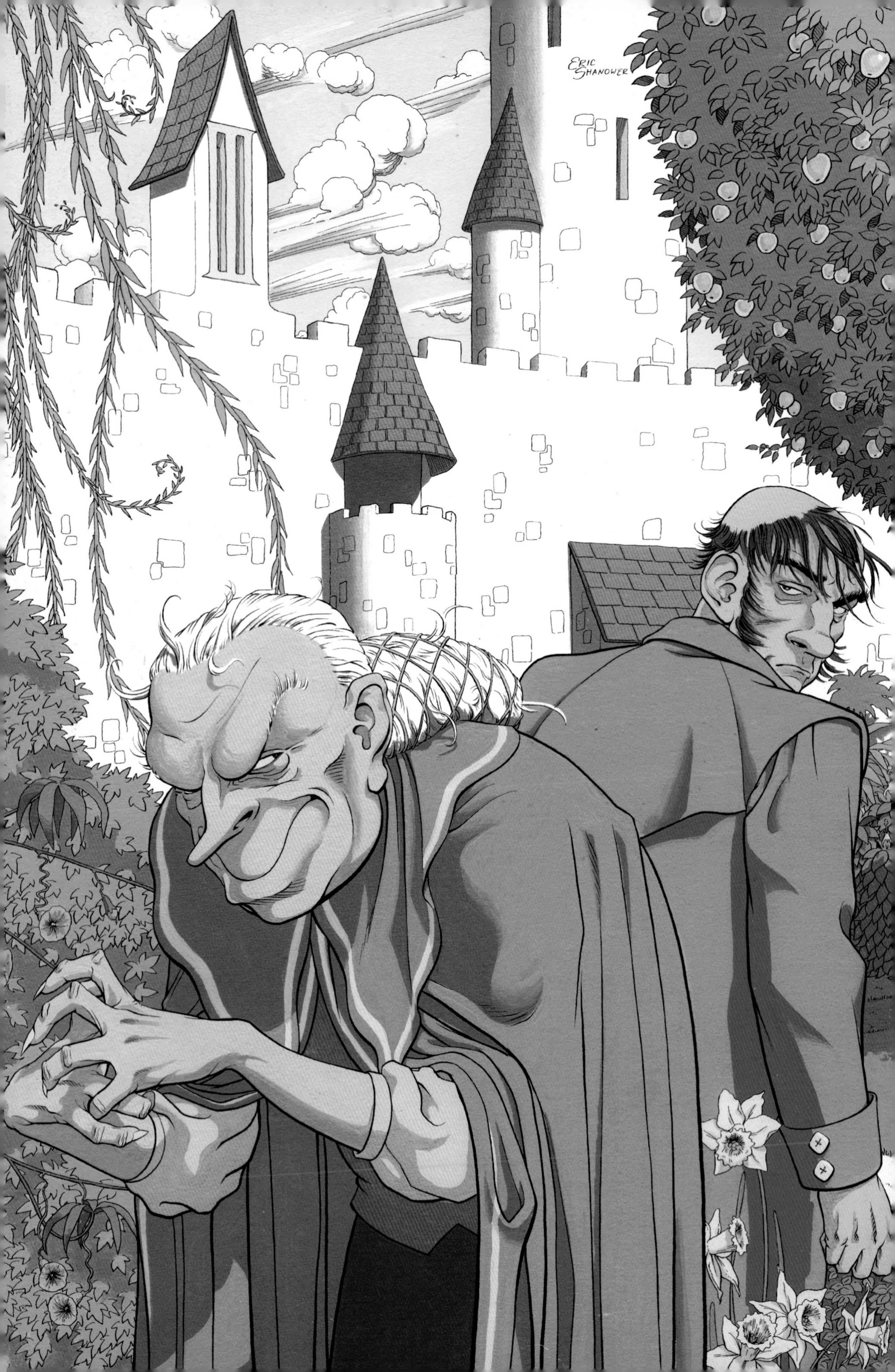
ERIC SHANOWER

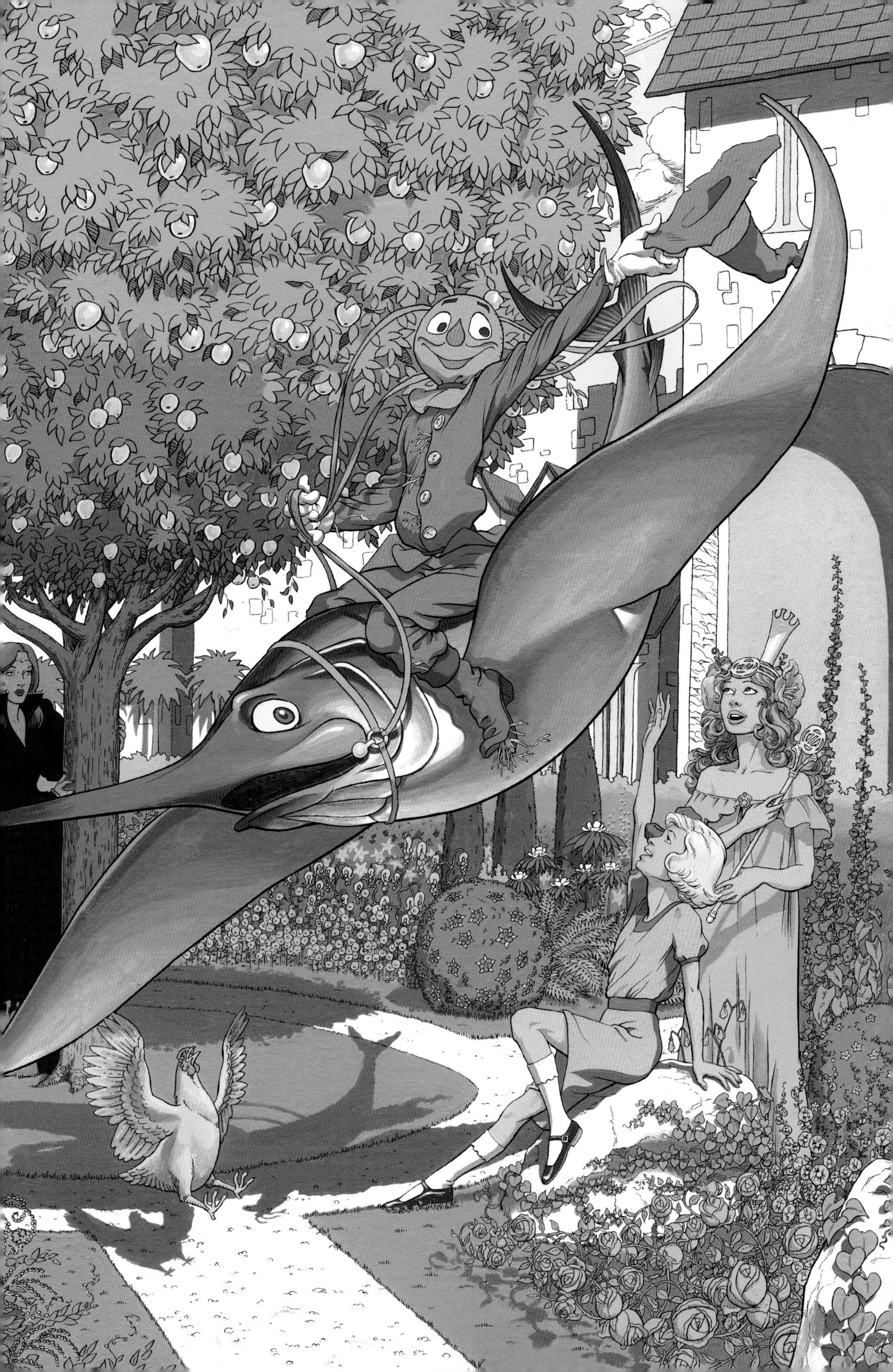

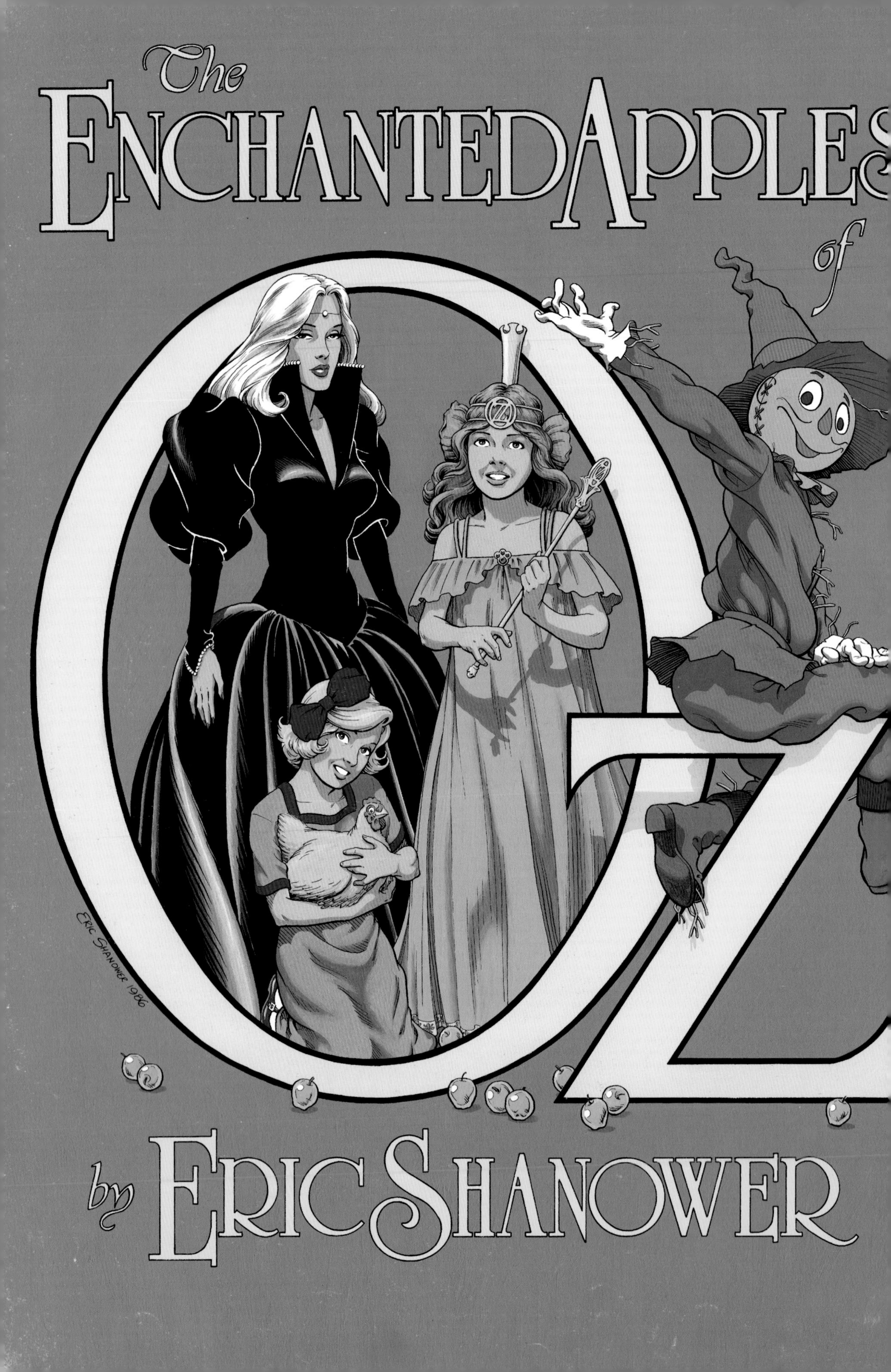
The Enchanted Apples of Oz
by Eric Shanower
Eric Shanower 1986

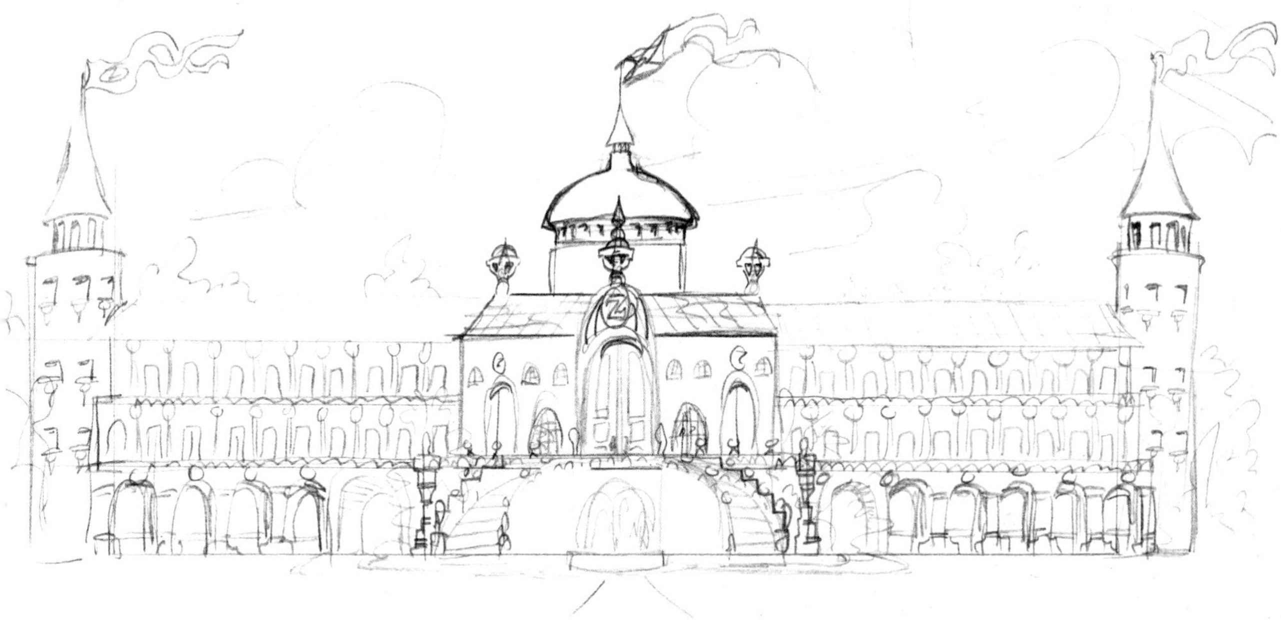

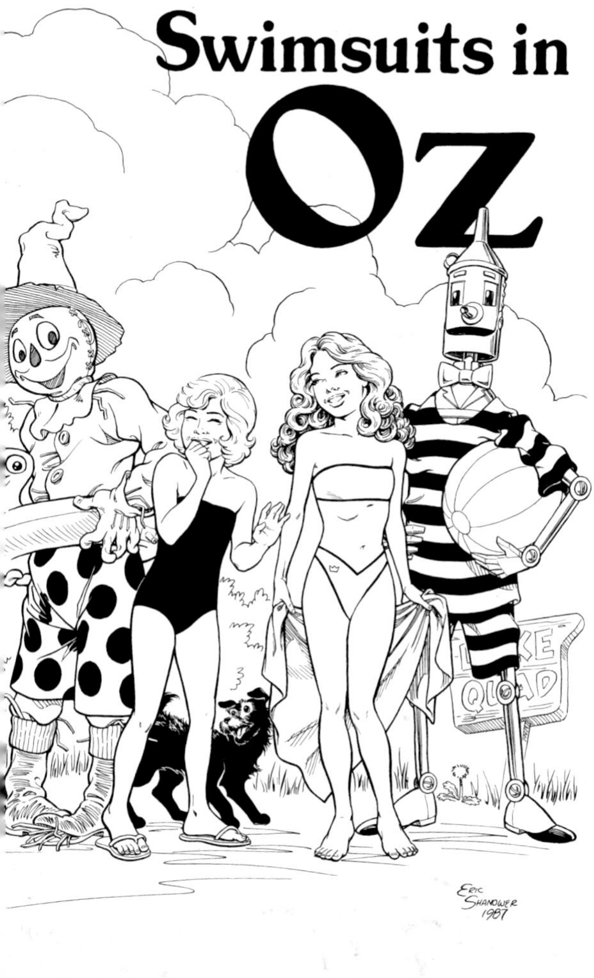
Swimsuits in Oz
Eric Shanower 1987

As soon as *Enchanted Apples* was published, I began work on the next volume in the series. Originally, it was titled *The Mysterious Mountain of Oz,* but people seemed to have difficulty remembering that, so I changed it to *The Secret Island of Oz.*

I intended *Secret Island* to have the feel of a Carl Barks *Uncle Scrooge* extravaganza with a dash of Milton Caniff's *Terry and the Pirates.* But the schedule for finishing the project was tight. First Comics brought in Willie Schubert for the lettering, and I hired Tom McCraw to help paint the color. Tom mixed Eureka's pink and painted the mushrooms, his most visible contributions. Despite this assistance, my work was rushed. The story never quite gelled and my drawings of Dorothy are almost all ugly. (I've made minor revisions to Dorothy for this edition.) *The Secret Island of Oz,* published in November 1986, remains my least-favorite Oz graphic novel. Here's a little rhyme I made up about it:

Secret Island, what a story!
Action! Thrills! Suspense and glory!
They're all here, but as for plot
And clarity—whoops! I forgot . . .

Facing page: advertising poster for The Enchanted Apples of Oz, 1986.

This page: sketch of Ozma's palace in the Emerald City, 1985 (top); pin-up from the "swimsuit" issue of the magazine Amazing Heroes, #115, 1987 (bottom).

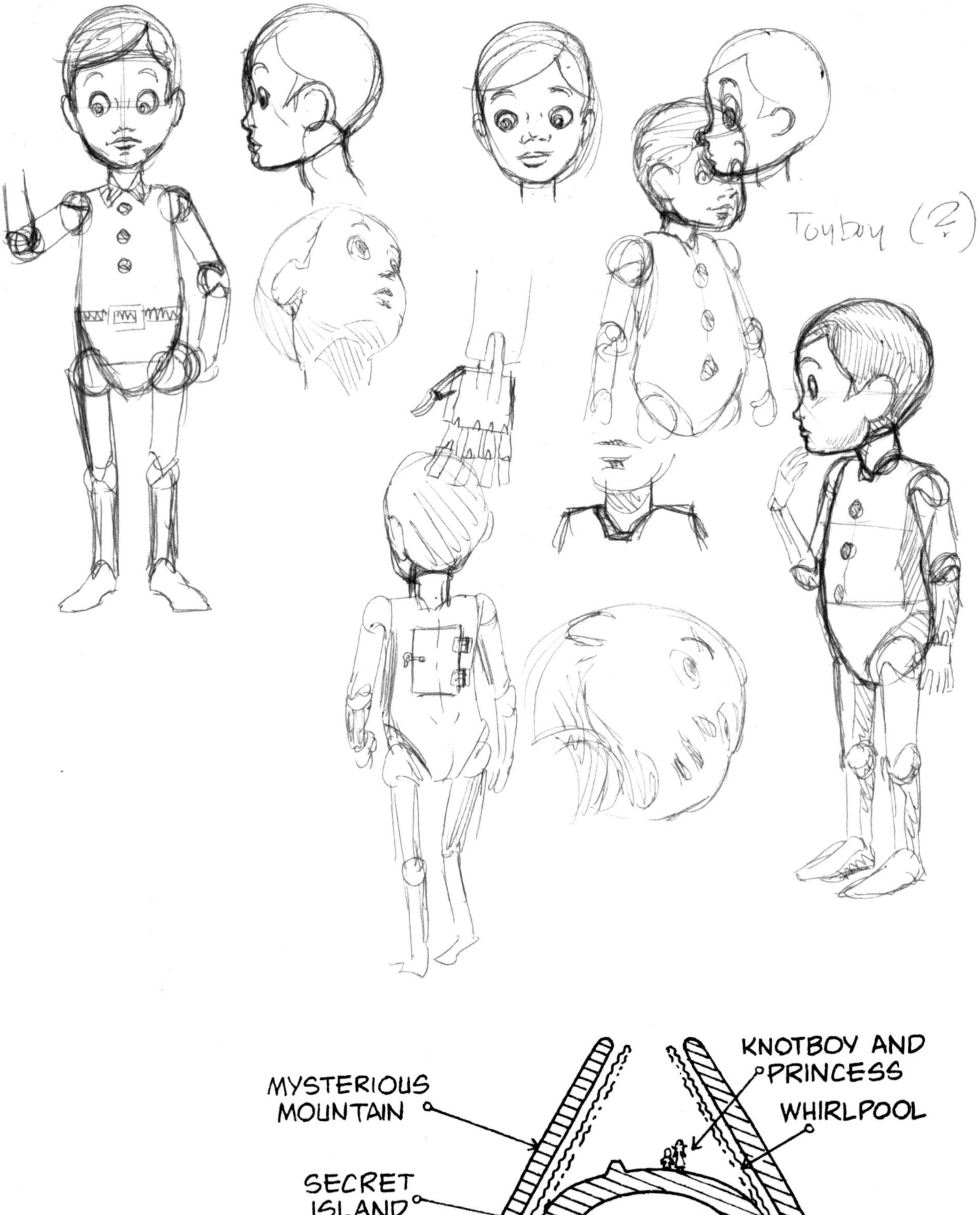
Toyboy (?)

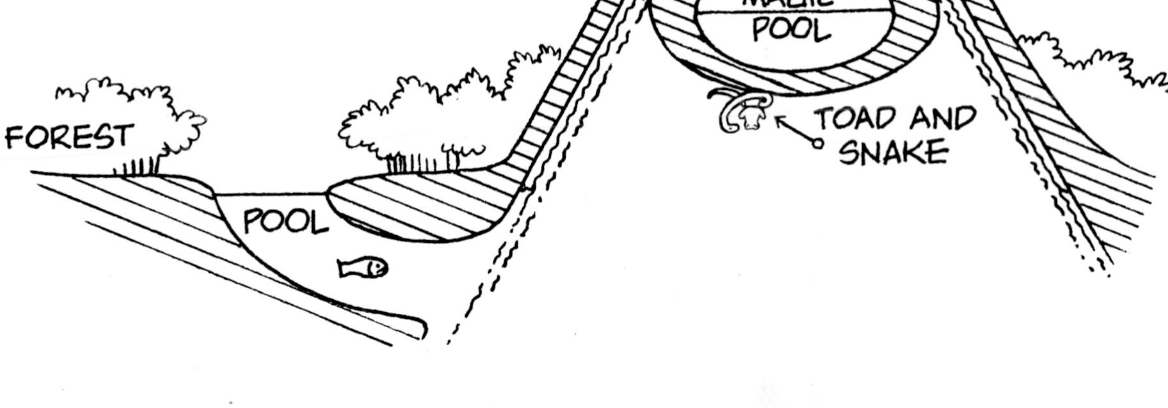
MYSTERIOUS
MOUNTAIN
KNOTBOY AND
PRINCESS
WHIRLPOOL
SECRET
ISLAND
MAGIC
POOL
FOREST
POOL
TOAD AND
SNAKE

:ing page: design
·tches for the
racter Knotboy,
ginally called
·boy, 1986 (top);
gram showing
ations of the main
ion of *The Secret*
nd of Oz, 1986
ttom).

s page: design
tches for the
racter of Princess
karinkarina, 1986
·ht); diagram
wing the
centric circles of
plot of *The Secret*
nd of Oz, 1986
low).

lowing two pages:
ign for a
paround cover for
Secret Island of
1986, featuring
original title for
book.

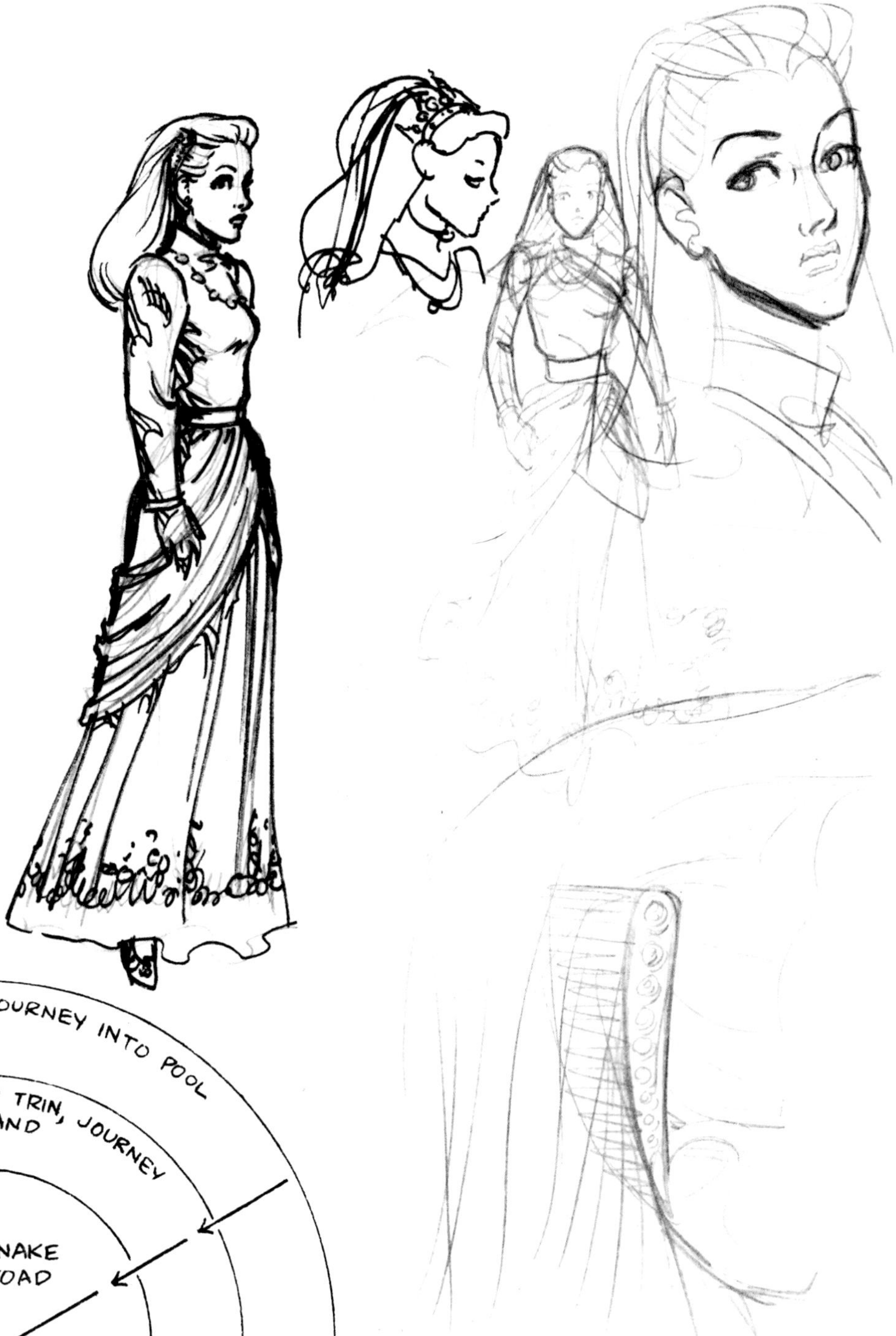

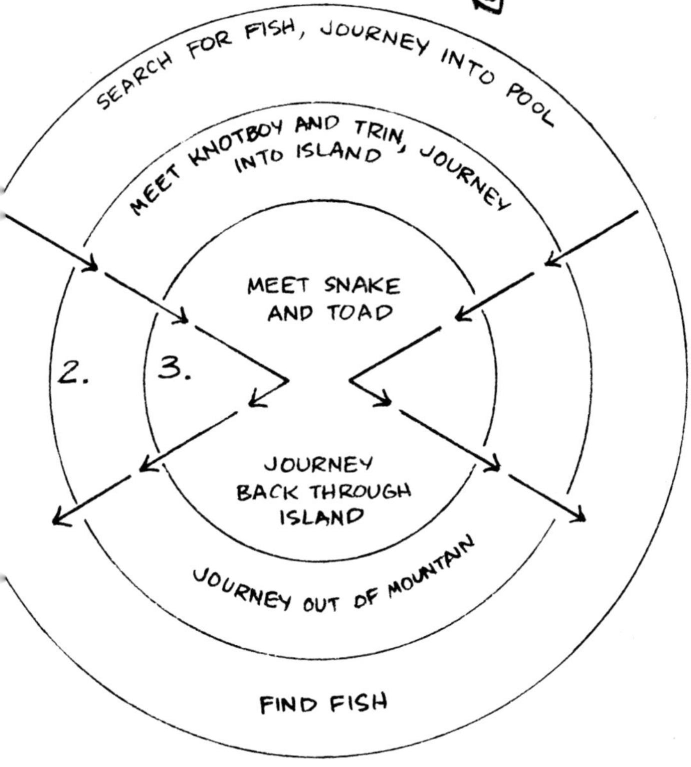
SEARCH FOR FISH, JOURNEY INTO POOL
MEET KNOTBOY AND TRIN, JOURNEY INTO ISLAND
MEET SNAKE AND TOAD
2.
3.
JOURNEY BACK THROUGH ISLAND
JOURNEY OUT OF MOUNTAIN
FIND FISH

PLOT DIAGRAM FOR SECRET ISLAND

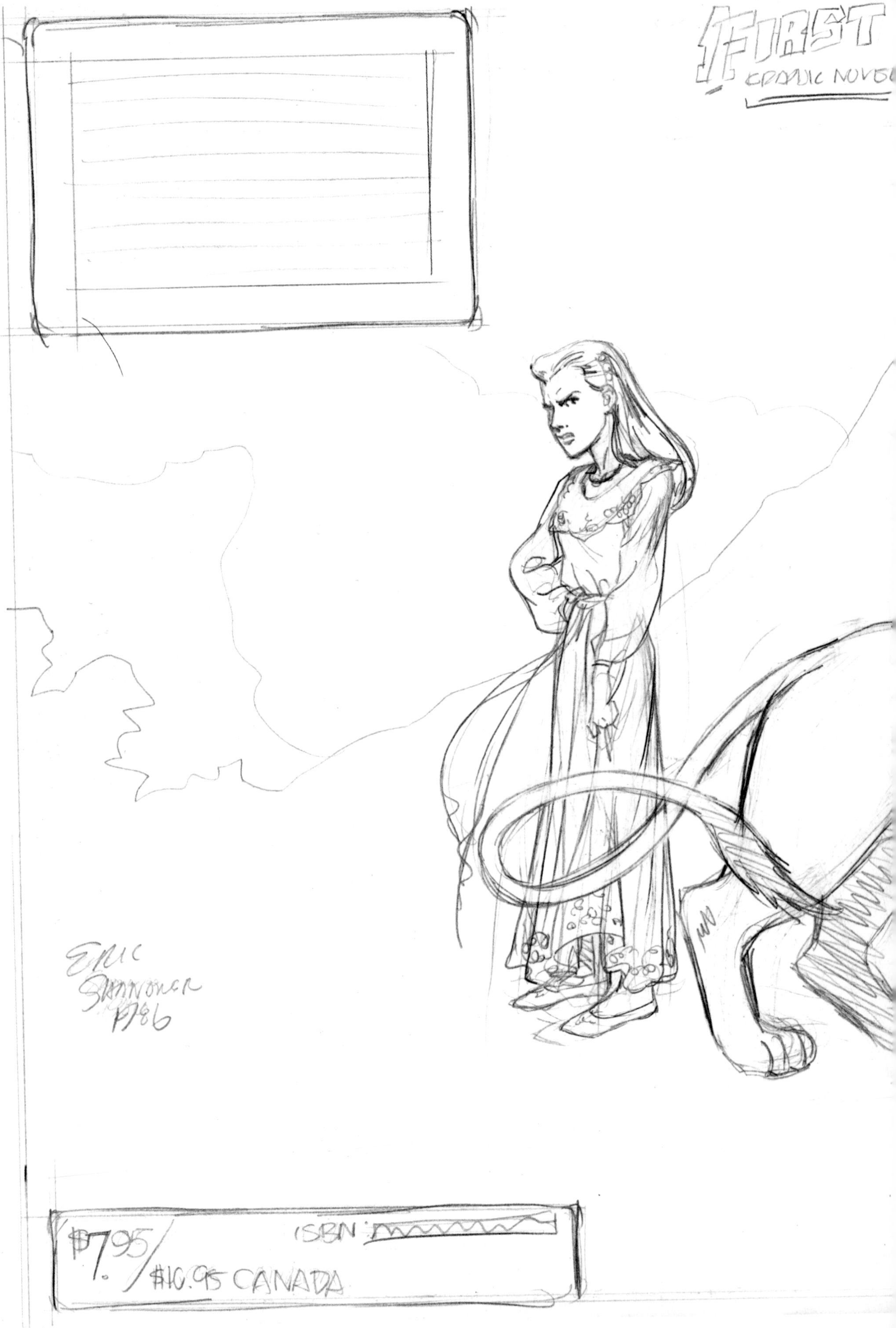
FIRST
GRAPHIC NOVEL
ERIC SHANOWER 1986
$7.95 / $10.95 CANADA
ISBN

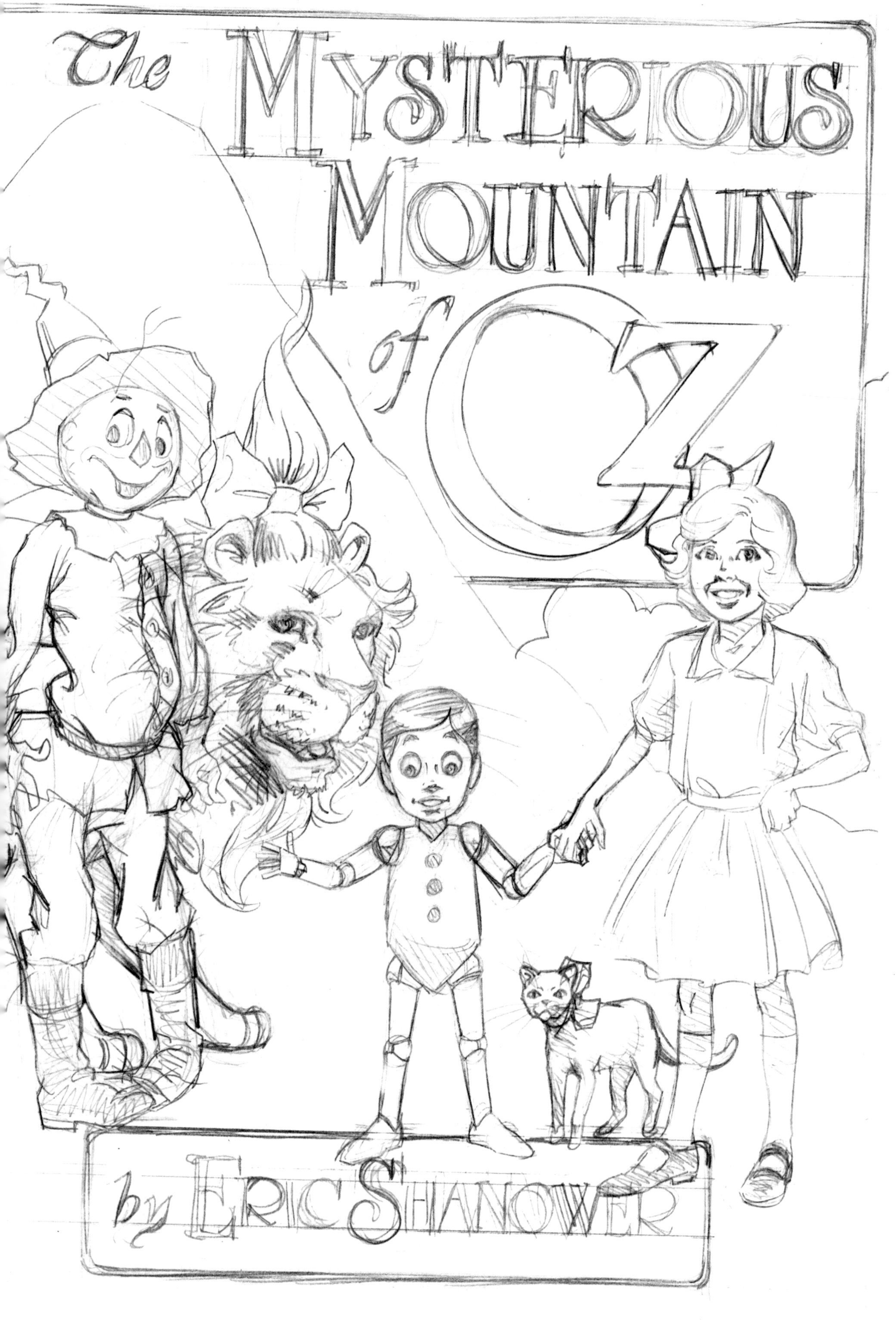
The Mysterious Mountain of Oz
by Eric Shanower

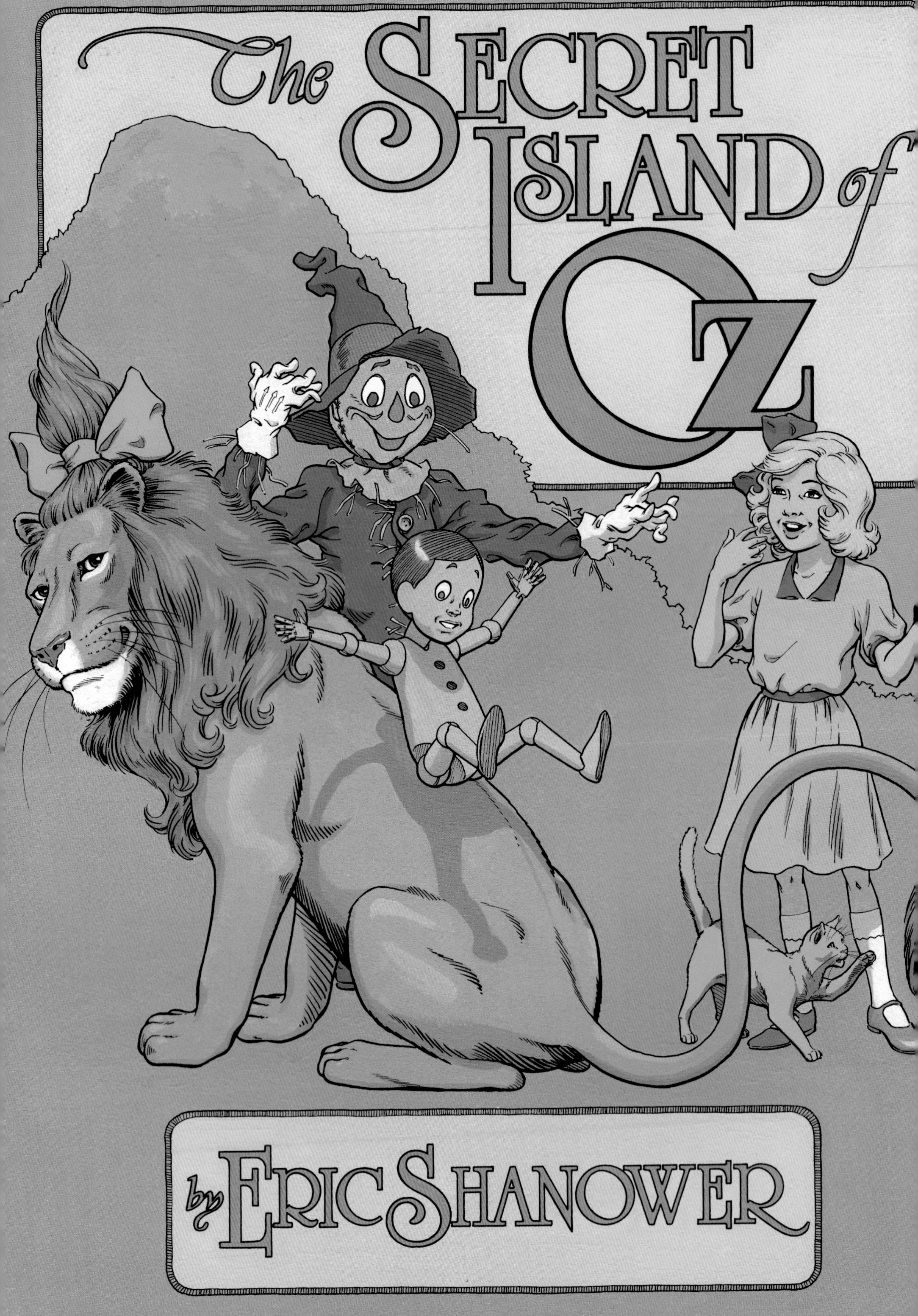
The Secret Island of Oz
by Eric Shanower

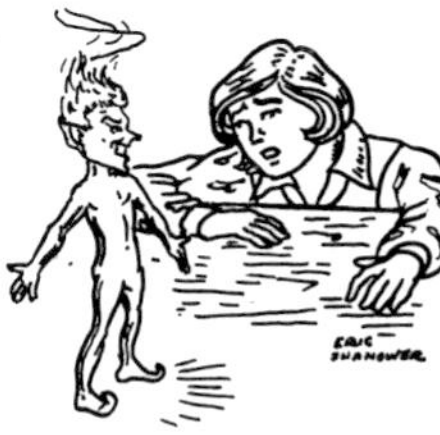

Facing page: cover of *The Secret Island of Oz,* 1986.

This page: illustrations for the first version of "The Ice King" from *Spindrift Fever,* a high school literary magazine, 1979.

Following two pages: art school version of *The Ice King,* 1982.

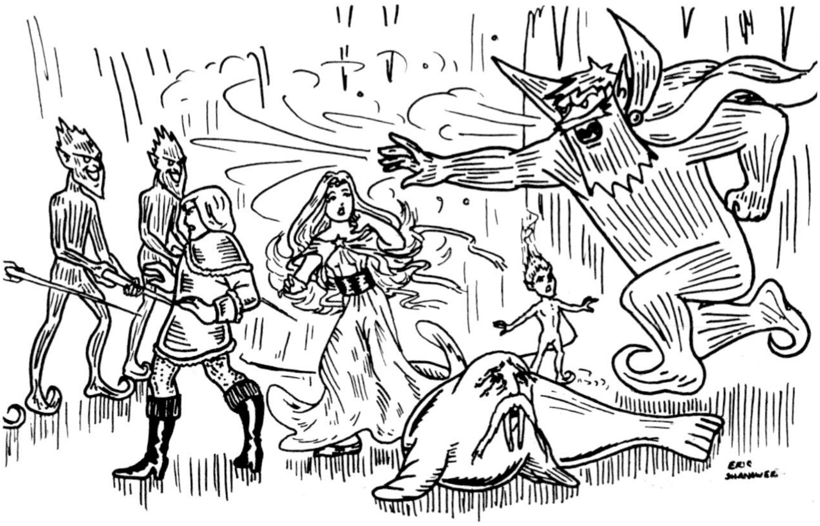

My third Oz graphic novel, *The Ice g of Oz,* was a good experience. Back 978, I'd first conceived the idea as an story, but the first version of "The Ice g" was actually a non-Oz story lished with my illustrations in my gh school's literary magazine. I'd altered the Oz elements, so, for instance, Polychrome, daughter of the rainbow, became Aurora, daughter of the Northern Lights. Flicker was part of the story from the start, though at that point he was named Reddy.

In 1979, I developed "The Ice King" into an overblown plot for an Oz book involving almost every known Oz character. That summer, I set a timetable to finish the manuscript, planning to publish the book myself, but when school began in the fall, *The Ice King of Oz* fell by the wayside.

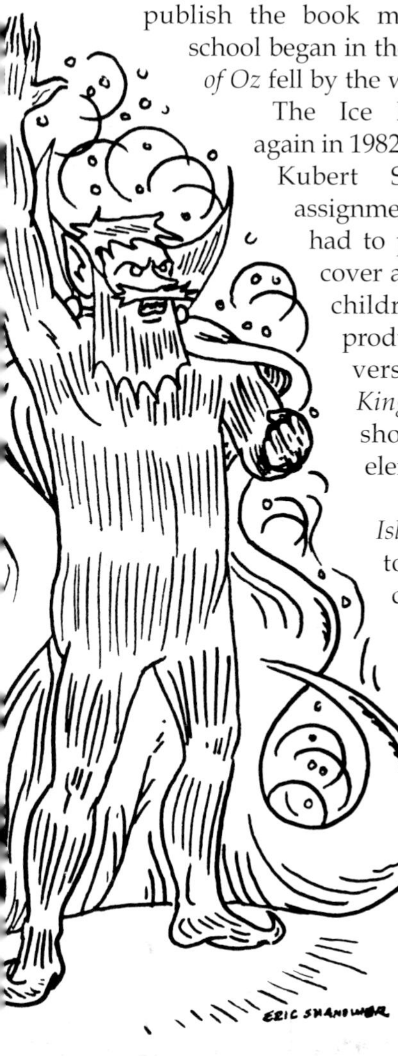

The Ice King resurfaced again in 1982 in a project at the Kubert School. As an assignment, each student had to prepare a sample cover and first page of a children's book. I produced yet another version of *The Ice King,* once again shorn of Oz elements.

After *Secret Island* had proved to be such a disappointment, I dusted off the Ice King idea. Since it had lasted through several versions, I figured that it had some strength to it. I turned it back into an Oz story and cut away the fat. Aurora, daughter of the Northern Lights, turned back into Polychrome, daughter of the rainbow, then at editor Rick Oliver's suggestion was promptly cut as well. *The Ice King of Oz* was published in November 1987.

For *Enchanted Apples* and *Secret Island* I'd used acrylic paint for the coloring. First, the black lines I'd drawn for the artwork were printed in blue on illustration board. After these "bluelines" were painted, they were scanned and combined with the black line art for publication. The chemical process of printing the early "bluelines" roughened the surface of the board, but by the time of *Ice King,* the process had been somewhat refined. Rather than hardy plastic acrylics, I was able to paint with more delicate watercolor dyes, and the results were far more pleasing.

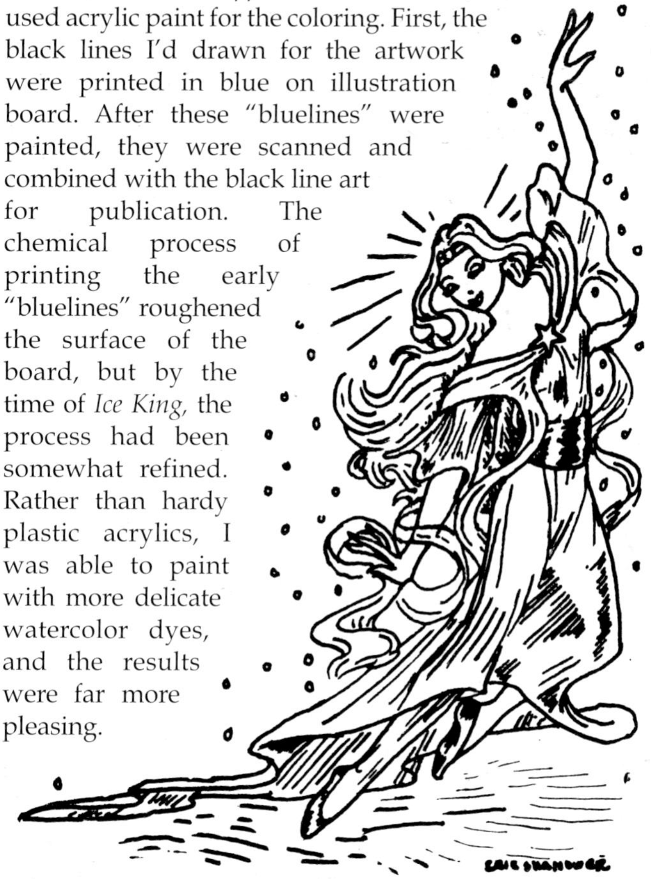

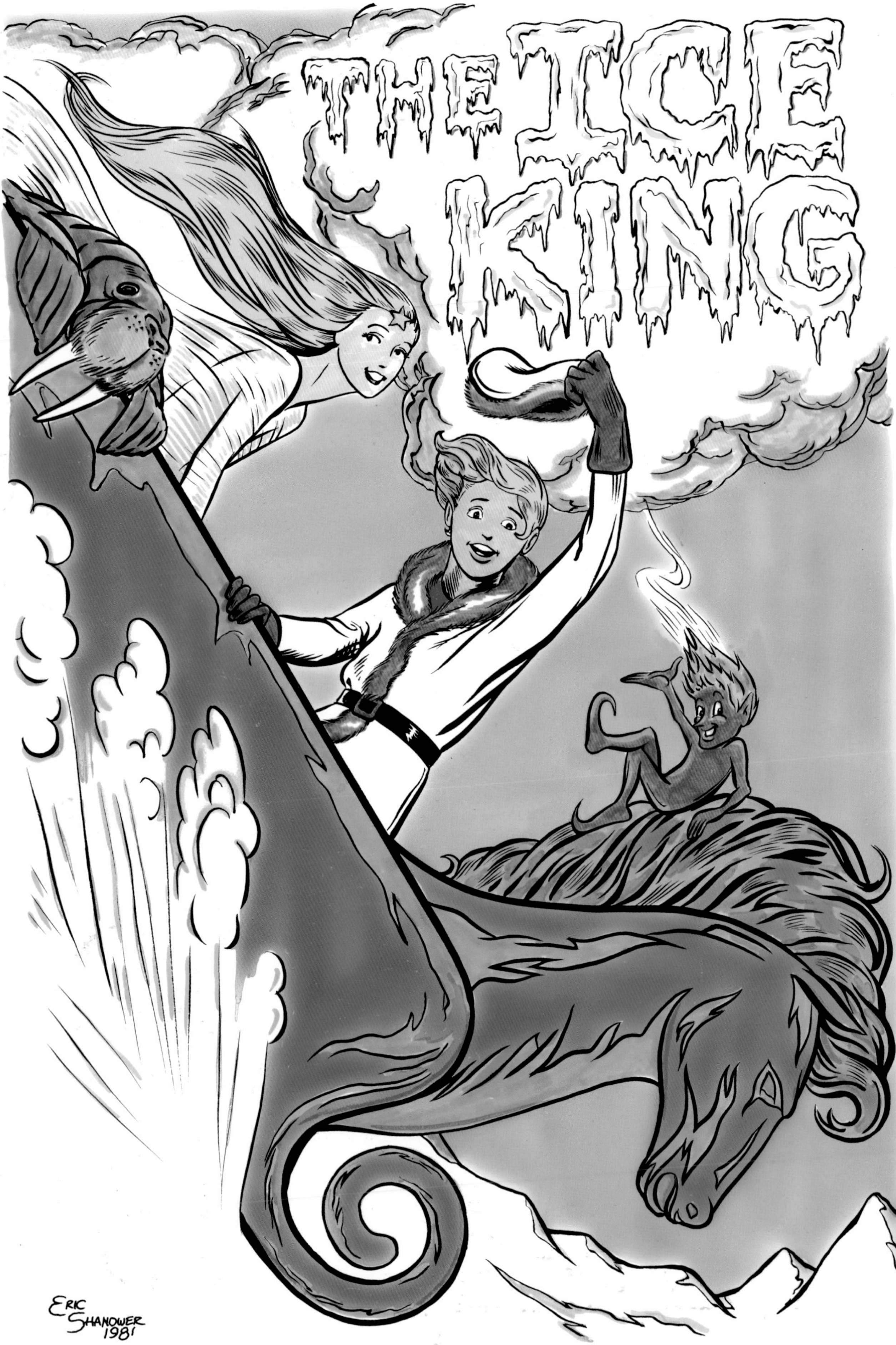
THE ICE KING
ERIC SHANOWER 1981

1 ✶ The Ice King's Palace

AR, far, far to the north a great, white mass of ice and snow lay sprawled across the waters of the frigid seas. Snowstorms played over it and wind spirits howled loudly and long as they chased after one another. Aurora Borealis and her little daughters, the Northern Lights, danced frequently in the skies above the frozen continent, bringing the only radiance and beauty known to this barren polar region. The sun never shone here and even the polar bears deliberately stayed away. Every living thing was afraid of the evil being who lived deep within the snow-strewn mountains, the Ice King.

The Ice King was a terrible tyrant who commanded a thousand hard-hearted little sprites called ice-imps. He himself had no heart for he was ice through and through, and so ruled savagely, forcing the ice-imps to carry out his every whim.

In the center of the highest ice mountain the Ice King had forced the imps to build a palace. So grand and lovely was the palace that it would make you gasp with wonder and delight if ever you had a chance to see its great halls and sparkling, snowflake fountains. The Ice King was very proud of his palace, though he had not done a bit of the work that went into building it.

In the giant, domed throne room of the ice palace was the carved-ice seat of the Ice King. The room's arched cieling was covered thickly with weird, glowing icicles, shedding light on the floor and walls which were polished like mirrors so that they reflected every ray, giving the effect of illumination from each facet of the room's huge length. The Ice King often sat here to look over his many ice-imps and gleefully sent one off to be punished after it had collapsed from the strain of standing for many hours.

Today the Ice King was seated at his throne, but instead of inspecting his throng of ice-imps, he had summoned his Lord High Advisor and all around go-getter, Popsicle. Soon the roly-poly little ice-imp came rushing through a side door to the throne room.

"You're late," growled the Ice King, "as usual." He wrinkled his frosty eyebrows and stared from the throne coldly.

"I'm very sorry, Your Iciness," cried Popsicle, bowing furiously before the throne. "I was just finishing my breakfast of cold cakes and snow syrup."

"Well, next time see that you're here when I send for you," the king

1

This page: design sketches for the character Flicker, 1987 (left); color studies for Nick Chopper, the Tin Woodman, 1987 (right and below).

Facing page: cover of *The Ice King of Oz,* 1987.

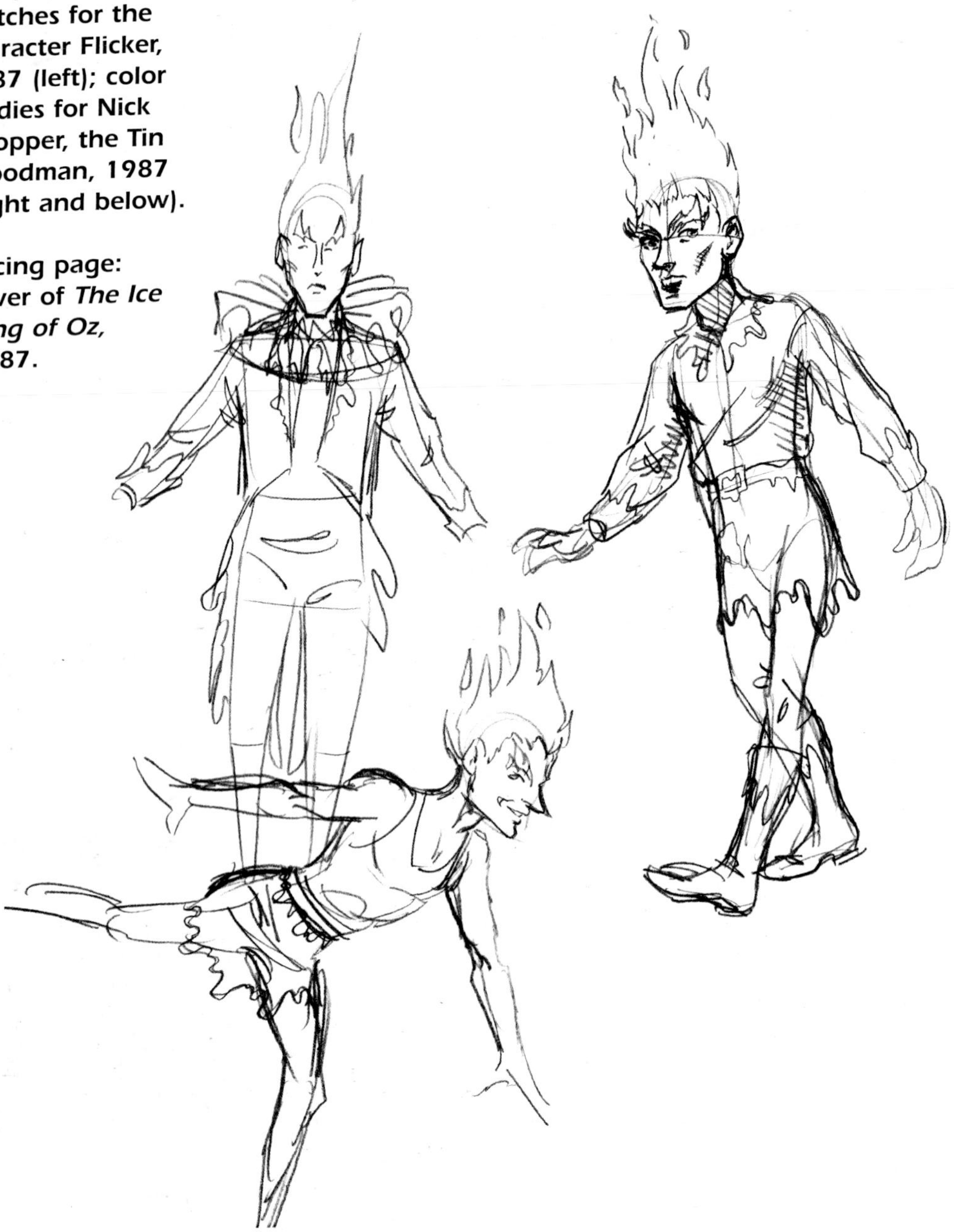

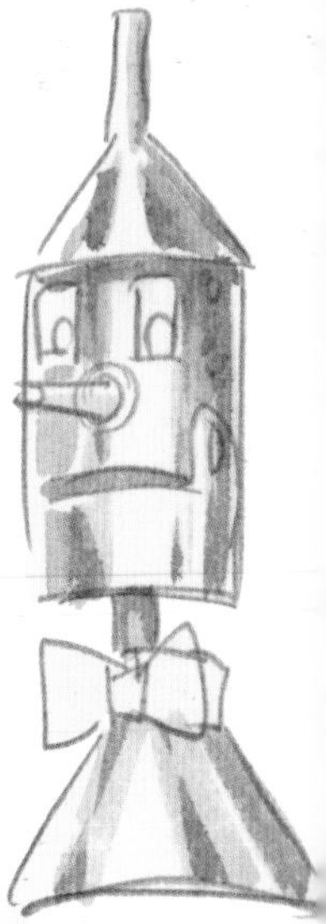

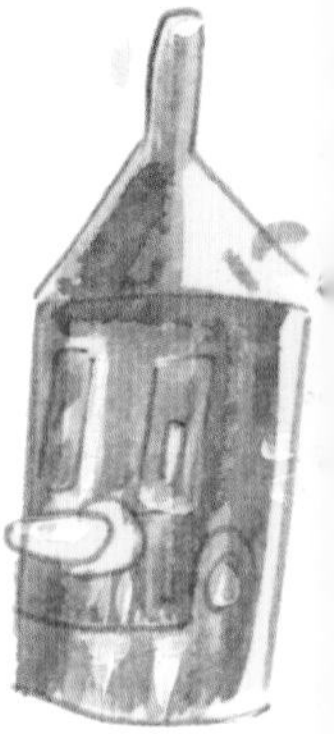

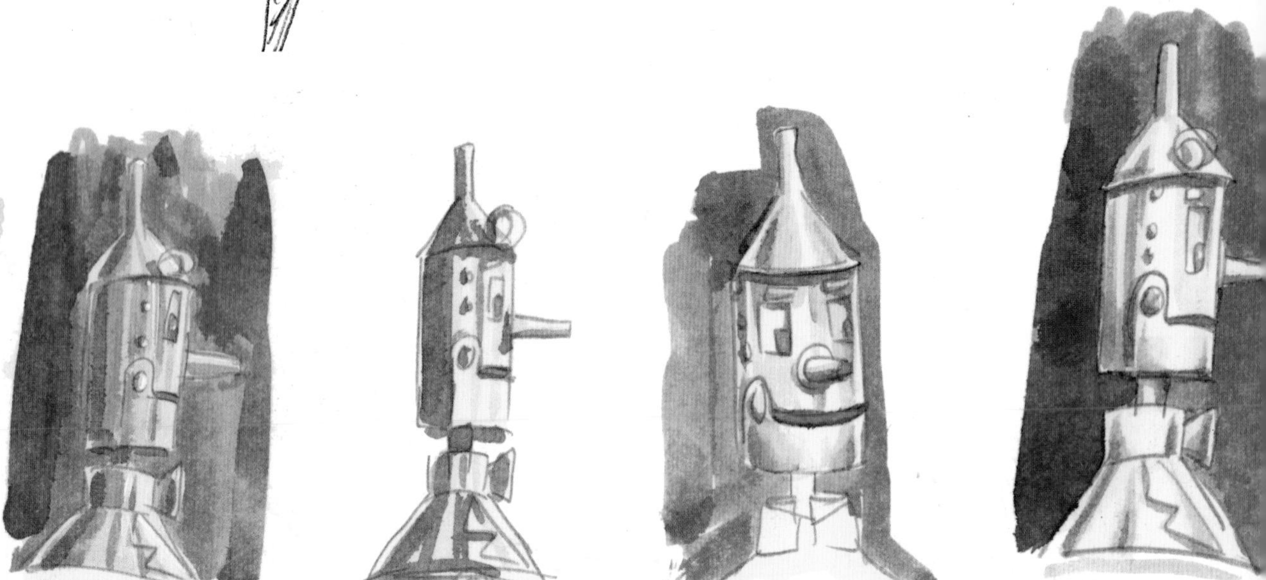

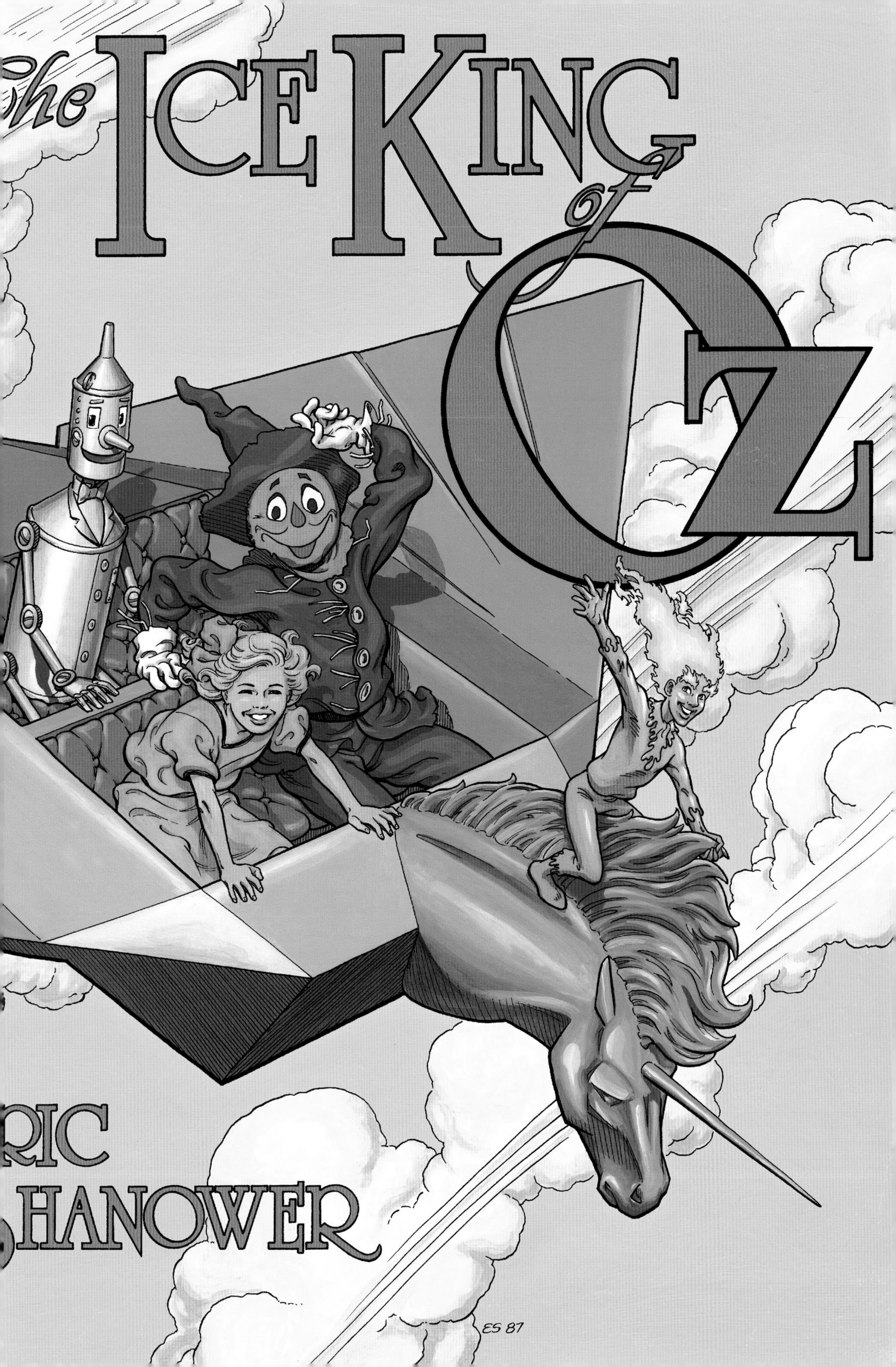
The Ice King of Oz
Eric Shanower
ES 87

The fourth graphic novel in the series, *The Forg[otten]* *Forest of Oz,* remains my favorite. It originated i[n an] uncompleted short comics story I began durin[g] school. "The Story of Nebelle" isn't an Oz story, b[ut] incorporates concepts such as the Forest of Burzee an[d] Council of Fairies from L. Frank Baum's 1902 book *Life and Adventures of Santa Claus.* In early 1988, I p[ulled] out "The Story of Nebelle" and expanded it into a[n] graphic novel. Some of the names were altered [or] switched, and the ending of the story was jettisoned[, but] even now I'm surprised by how similar some of the p[age] compositions remained.

The Forgotten Forest of Oz went through many cha[nges] before it was published in November 1988. The ori[ginal] title was *The Magic Water of Oz,* which even I didn't [like.] At first the story concluded with Nelanthe drinking [the] Water of Oblivion. But as I approached drawing the [last] few pages, that ending made me uneasy and I revise[d it.] I'm still pleased by and proud of the result.

The Story of Nebelle

Page 1

Panel 1
CAPTION: Deep within the forest is a clearing, illuminated by the magical glow of the fairy people! The people have assembled tonight for the Council of Fairies! The powerful Queen of Fairyland sits upon her throne, attended by the four Lords of the Earth! Before the council stands the accused, despairing, yet valiant!
QUEEN: Nebelle, my daughter, you have been charged with a great crime against fairykind: you have dared to fall in love with a human! The penalty for this crime is very great! How do you plead?
NEBELLE: Guilty, your majesty!

Panel 2
CAPTION: A pause, then—
QUEEN: By your own admission you have pronounced yourself guilty! Though it saddens me, I must now strip you of all your fairy powers and cast you out into the world! Go, Nebelle, you are now human and can never become fairy again!

Page 2

Panel 1
NELANTH: Please, your majesty! Don't! She didn't mean—
NEBELLE: No, Nelanth!

Panel 2
QUEEN: Silence, Nelanth! Let your sister go, lest yo[u be] forced to share her fate! Go, Nebelle!

Panel 3
CAPTION: Into the cold, dark forest flees Nebelle, tr[uly] alone for the first time in her life!

Panel 4
CAPTION: Where she once found warmth there is o[nly] hostility! Now subject to human fear she runs panicking through the darkness, hopelessly lo[st!]

Panel 5
CAPTION: At last she huddles weeping and exhaust[ed] in a small, rocky cave, and falls asleep!

Panel 6
SOUND EFFECT: Click

Panel 7
NEBELLE: Who's there?
CHUNGASH: Don't be afraid! I won't harm you!

This page: Dorothy and the Cowardly Lion on the Yellow Brick Road, 1987. This is one of several sample pieces I prepared when approached to illustrate the book *Dorothy of Oz* by Roger S. Baum. I ended up turning the job down.

Facing page and following three pages: pencil art for "The Story of Nebelle," 1984. Compare with the first few pages of *The Forgotten Forest of Oz*.

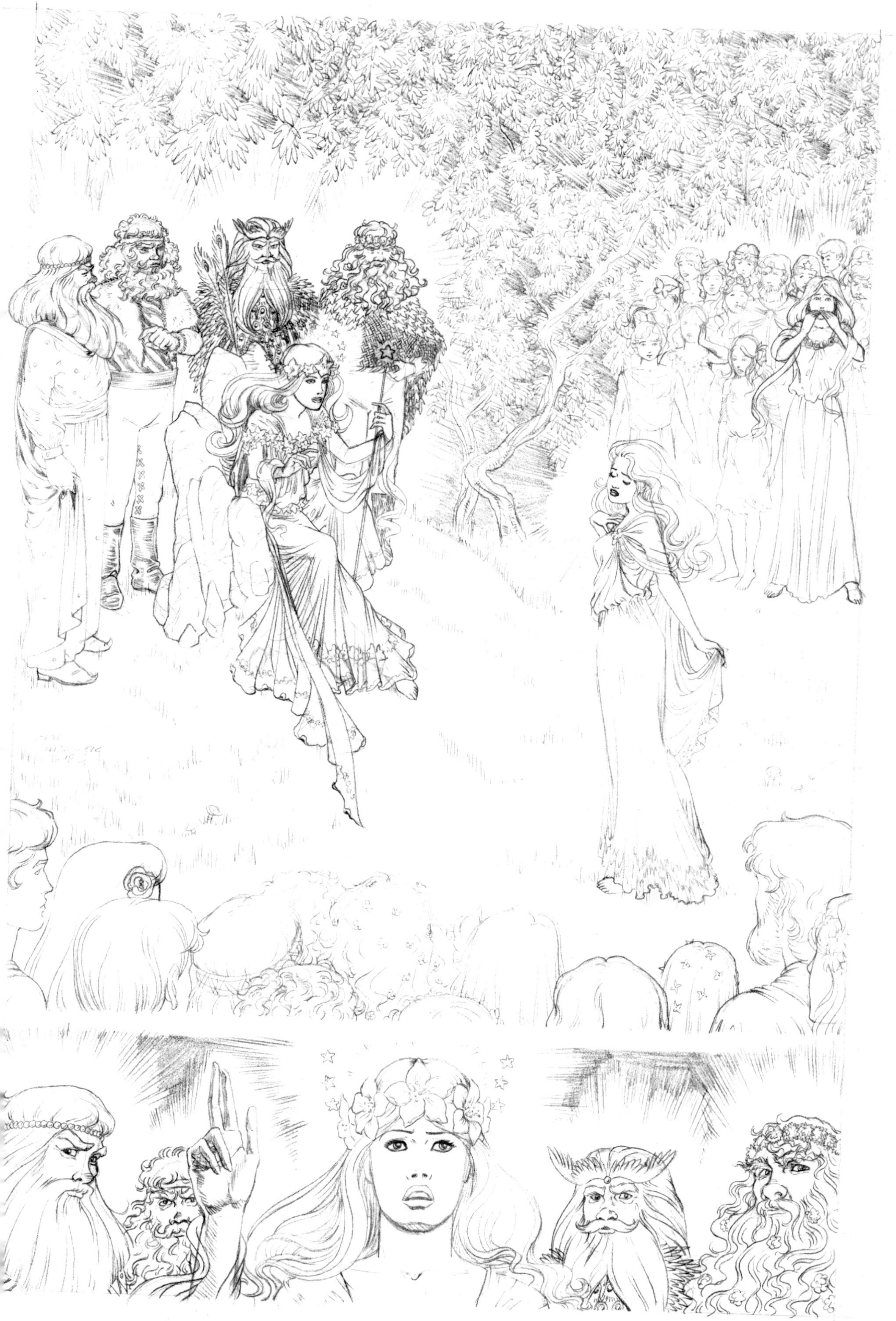

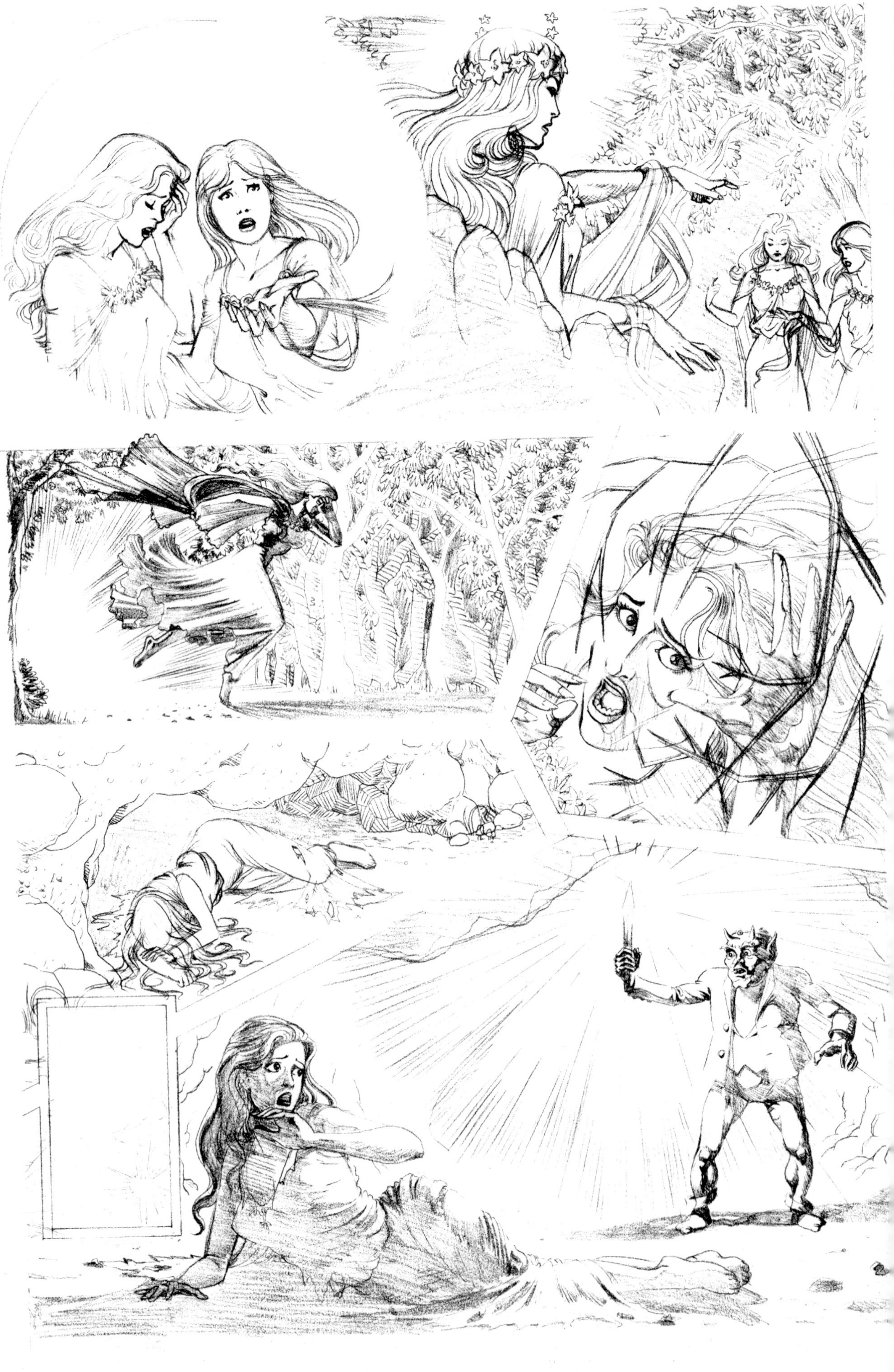

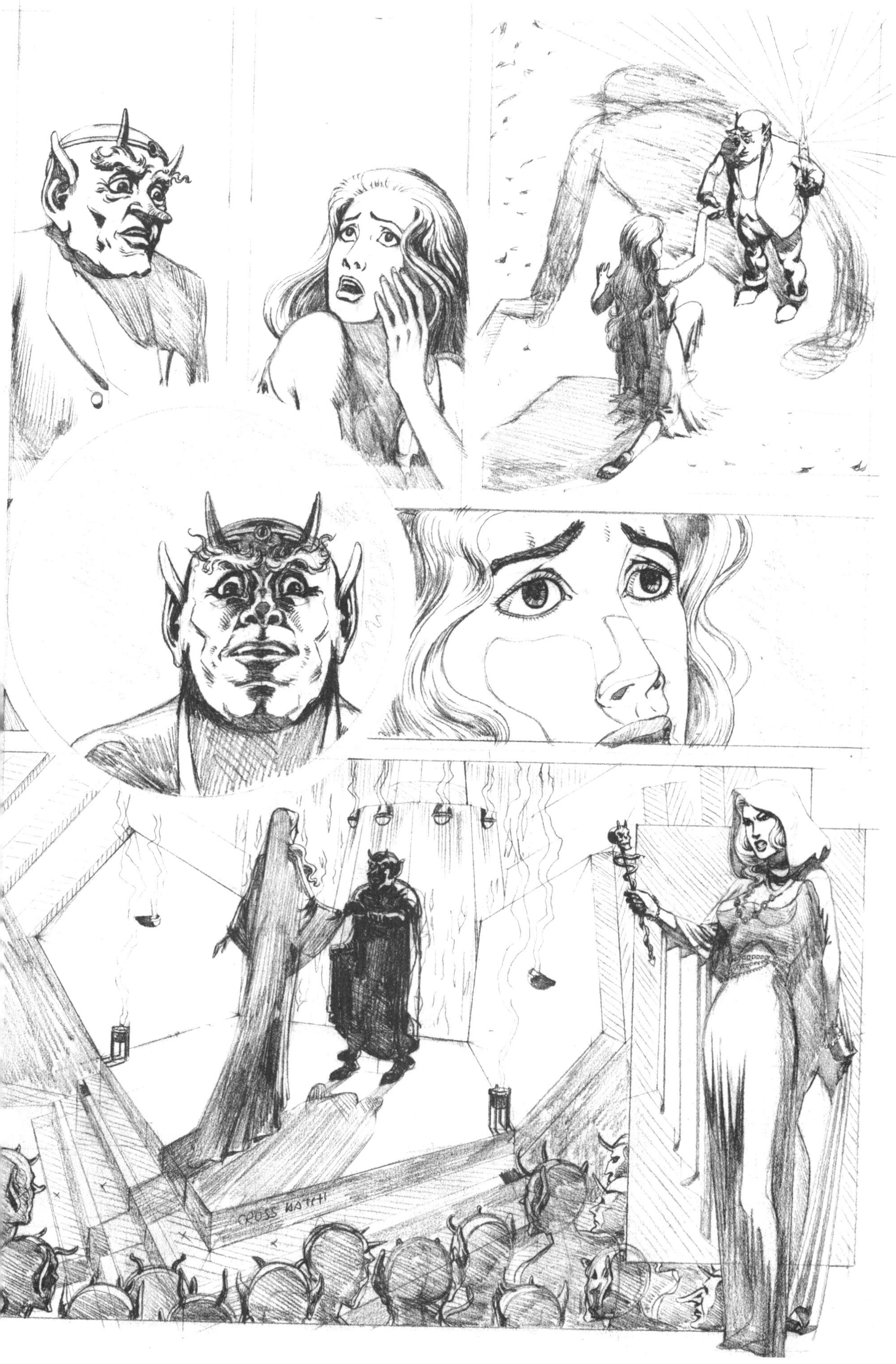
CROSS HATCH

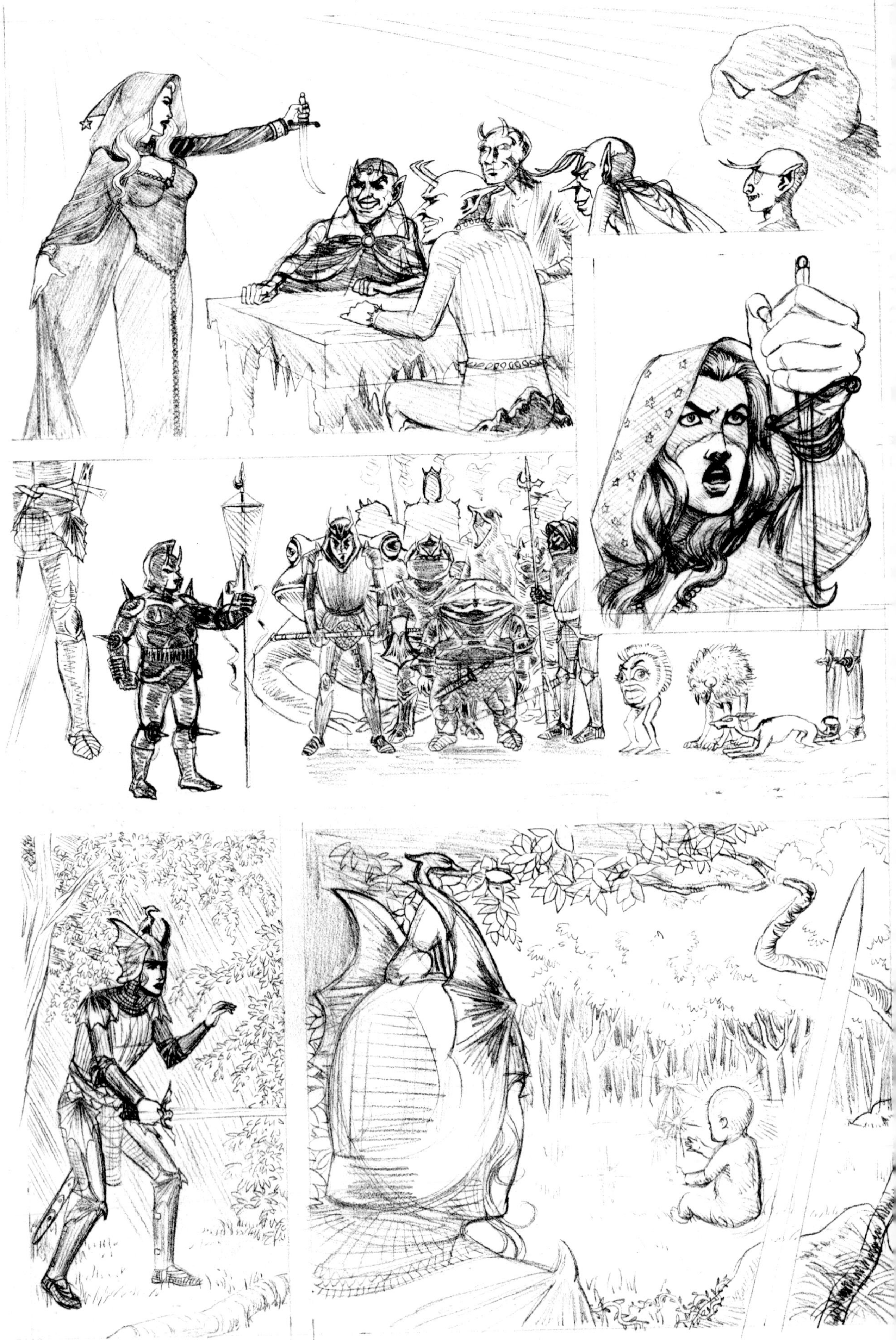

Page 3

Panel 1
CHUNGASH: I see you are a fairy! What are you doing here in this dark cave?

Panel 2
NEBELLE: You're mistaken! I am no longer a fairy, for I dared to fall in love with a mortal! But I'd do anything to regain my powers! I'm so cold and alone!

Panel 3
CHUNGASH: You'd do anything?

NEBELLE: Yes! But can you help me?

CHUNGASH: I can, for I am Chungash, King of the Demons and Lord of the Underworld! I can give you power in return for one favor!

NEBELLE: What favor?

Panel 4
CHUNGASH: Marry me! It will not be as difficult as you might think! You are already in love with me, for that human was I, disguised!

Panel 5
NEBELLE: I—I can no longer bear the cold and loneliness! Yes, I will marry you!

Panel 6
CAPTION: Thus did circumstances culminate in the marriage of Nebelle to Chungash! With her restored power came the acceptance of her role as Queen of the Demons!

Panel 7
CAPTION: Nebelle's heart became as hard as the stone beneath which she lived! A more cruel and evil demon queen had never lived!

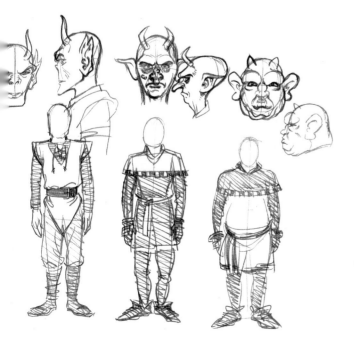

Page 4

Panel 1
CAPTION: Her heart, now vengeful, filled with hatred of her former race! At the Council of Demons she presented a daring plan!

NEBELLE: I propose a war on the fairy nation. The fairies are our natural enemies, and so should be exterminated!

DEMON: Have we any chance of winning such a war?

Panel 2
NEBELLE: Against our demon hordes the peaceful fairies have no hope of defense! We cannot lose! The fairies will die!

Panel 3
CAPTION: So war was declared! From the bowels of the earth came the most hideous demon-creatures to do battle! Thousands of evil phantasms rallied for the first sneak attack!

Panel 4
CAPTION: At last the night of the attack came! Queen Nebelle is among the first wave of warriors sweeping the woods on approach to fairyland!

Panel 5
NEBELLE: At last I shall have my revenge! Cast me out as a human, would they? I'll drive this sword ri—

ASH SWITCH

LIGHT BROWN (ACORN) HAIR

GREEN OAK LEAVES

—DRESS SLIGHTLY LIGHTER SHADE OF GREEN

QUEEN ZURLINE

SANDALS, THO' NOT SHOWN HERE

THIS IS MY CHANCE! I MUST KILL THIS FAIRY CHILD!
BUT-- I CAN'T! I--
NO!
EEEE!
NEBELLE? IS IT YOU?

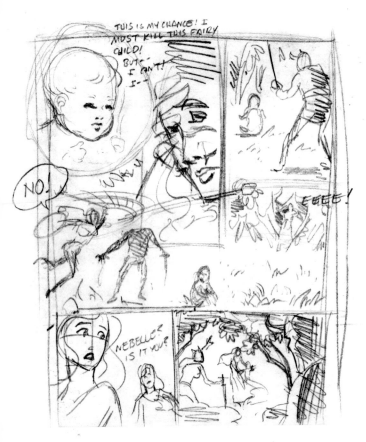

Page 5

Panel 1 *(Close-up of the baby fairy.)*
NEBELLE: This is my chance! I must kill this fairy child!

Panel 2 *(Close-up of Nebelle, troubled.)*
NEBELLE: But—I can't! I—

Panel 3 *(A demon steps from the forest to threaten the baby.)*
NEBELLE: No! Another demon sees the child!

Panel 4 *(Nebelle beheads the demon as Nelanth watches from the forest.)*
NEBELLE: NO!
NELANTH: EEEE!

Panel 5 *(Nebelle and Nelanth recognize each other.)*
NEBELLE: Nelanth!
NELANTH: Nebelle? Is it you?

Panel 6 *(Chungash watches Nebelle urge Nelanth to flee.)*
NEBELLE: Nelanth! Flee! Warn the Queen! The demon are coming to kill you all!
CHUNGASH: So—my dear Nebelle!

Page 6

Panel 1 *(Chungash shoots an arrow.)*
CHUNGASH: I see your loyalties have shifted again! You are no longer one of us!

Panel 2 *(Nebelle is struck.)*
NEBELLE: Run! Uk!
NELANTH: Nebelle?

Panel 3 *(Nebelle falls.)*
NEBELLE: Warn—the—Queen . . .

Panel 4 *(Nebelle dies.)*
CAPTION: Having renounced her demonic ways in her last moments, Nebelle dies a human.

Panel 5 *(Nebelle's body lies on a sepulchre surrounded by fairies, including Nelanth and the Queen.)*

RUN! UK!

Previous page: design sketch for three trolls, 1988 (left); design sketch for Zurline, Queen of the Wood-nymphs, 1988 (right).

This page: rough sketches for the two final pages of "The Story of Nebelle," 1983.

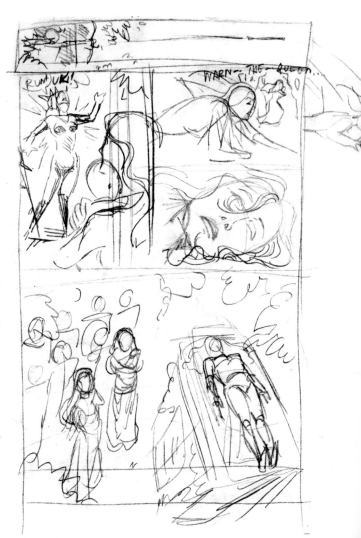

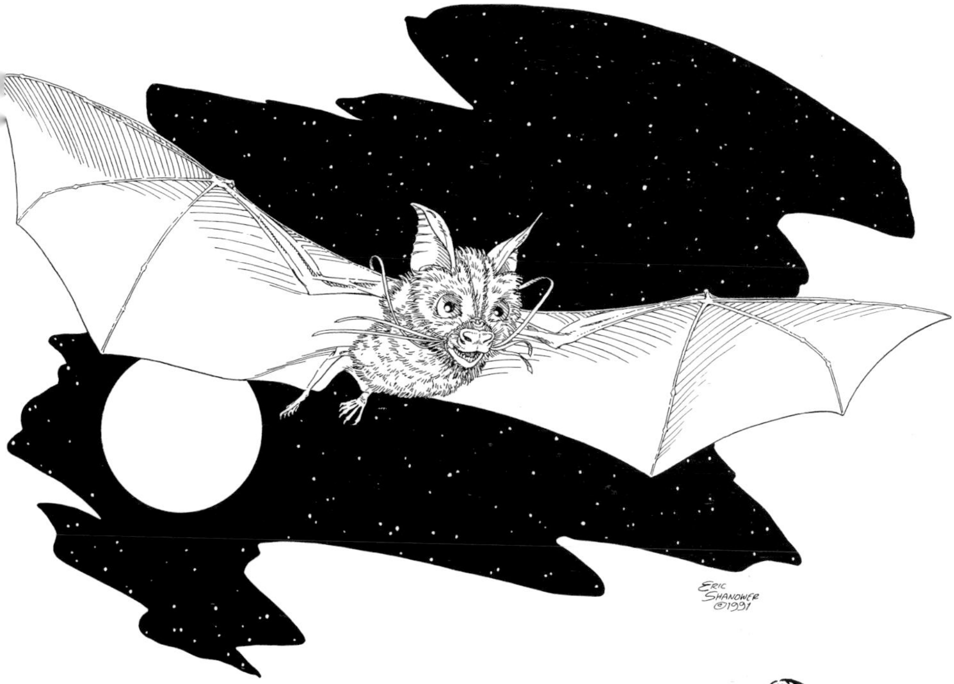
ERIC
SHANOWER
©1991

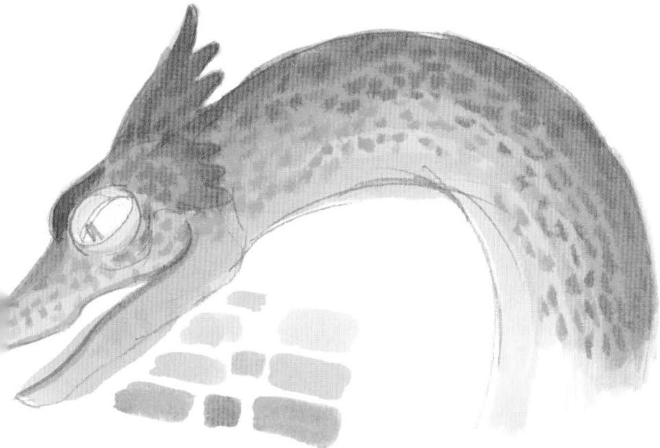

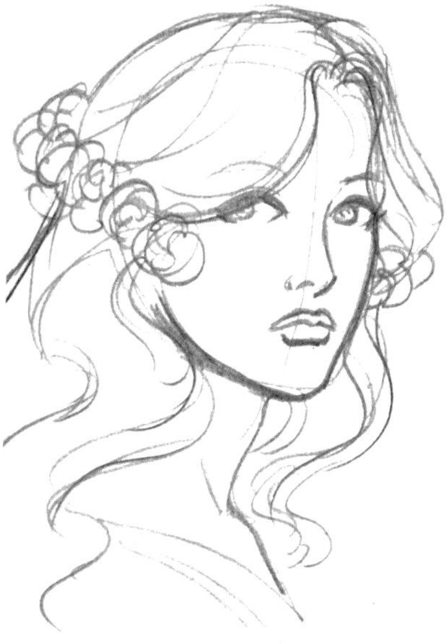

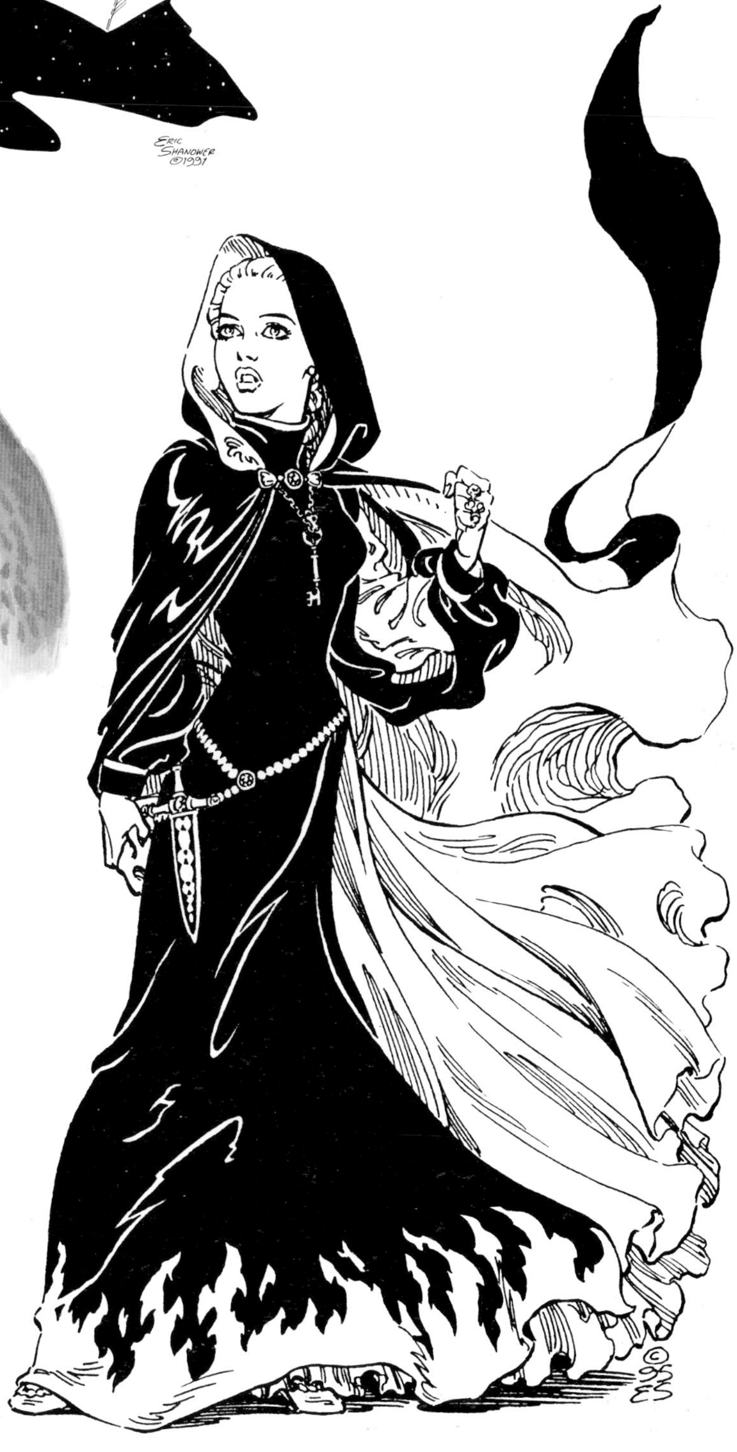
© 95
ES

Commissioned drawing of Nightshade, 1991 (top); color study for a dragon, 1988 (middle left); design sketch for Nelanthe, 1988 (bottom left); publicity art of Nelanthe as the Troll Queen, 1995 (bottom right).

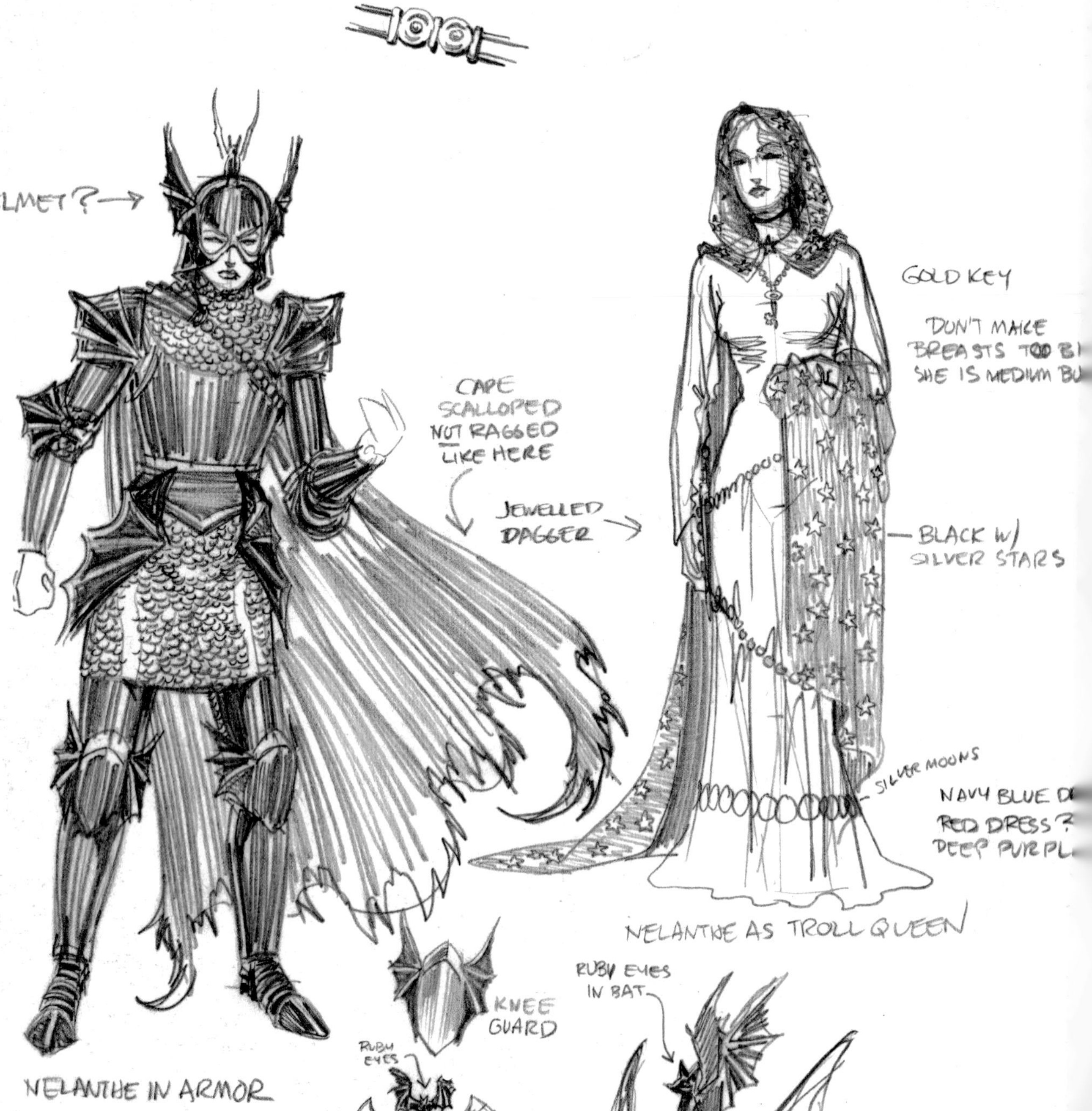
HELMET?
CAPE SCALLOPED NOT RAGGED LIKE HERE
JEWELLED DAGGER
GOLD KEY
DON'T MAKE BREASTS TOO BI
SHE IS MEDIUM BU
BLACK W/ SILVER STARS
SILVER MOONS
NAVY BLUE D
RED DRESS?
DEEP PURPL
NELANTHE AS TROLL QUEEN
NELANTHE IN ARMOR
KNEE GUARD

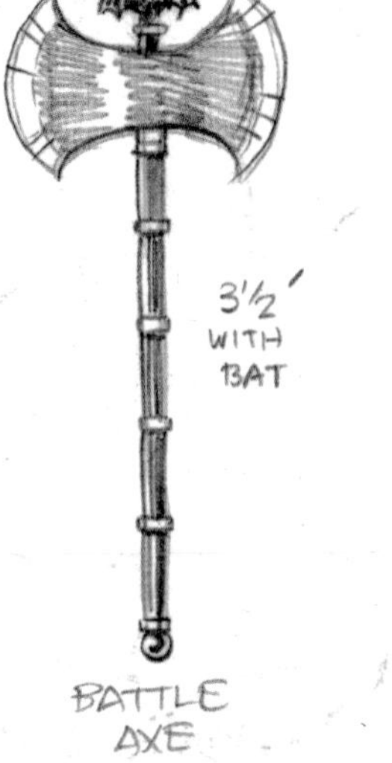
RUBY EYES
3½' WITH BAT
BATTLE AXE

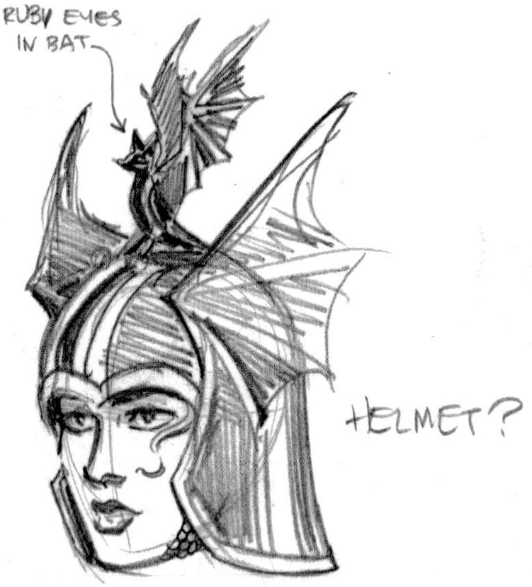
RUBY EYES IN BAT
HELMET?

This page: design sketches for Nelanthe as the Troll Queen, 1988.

Facing page: painting done for the San Diego Comic Con Art Auction, 1989.

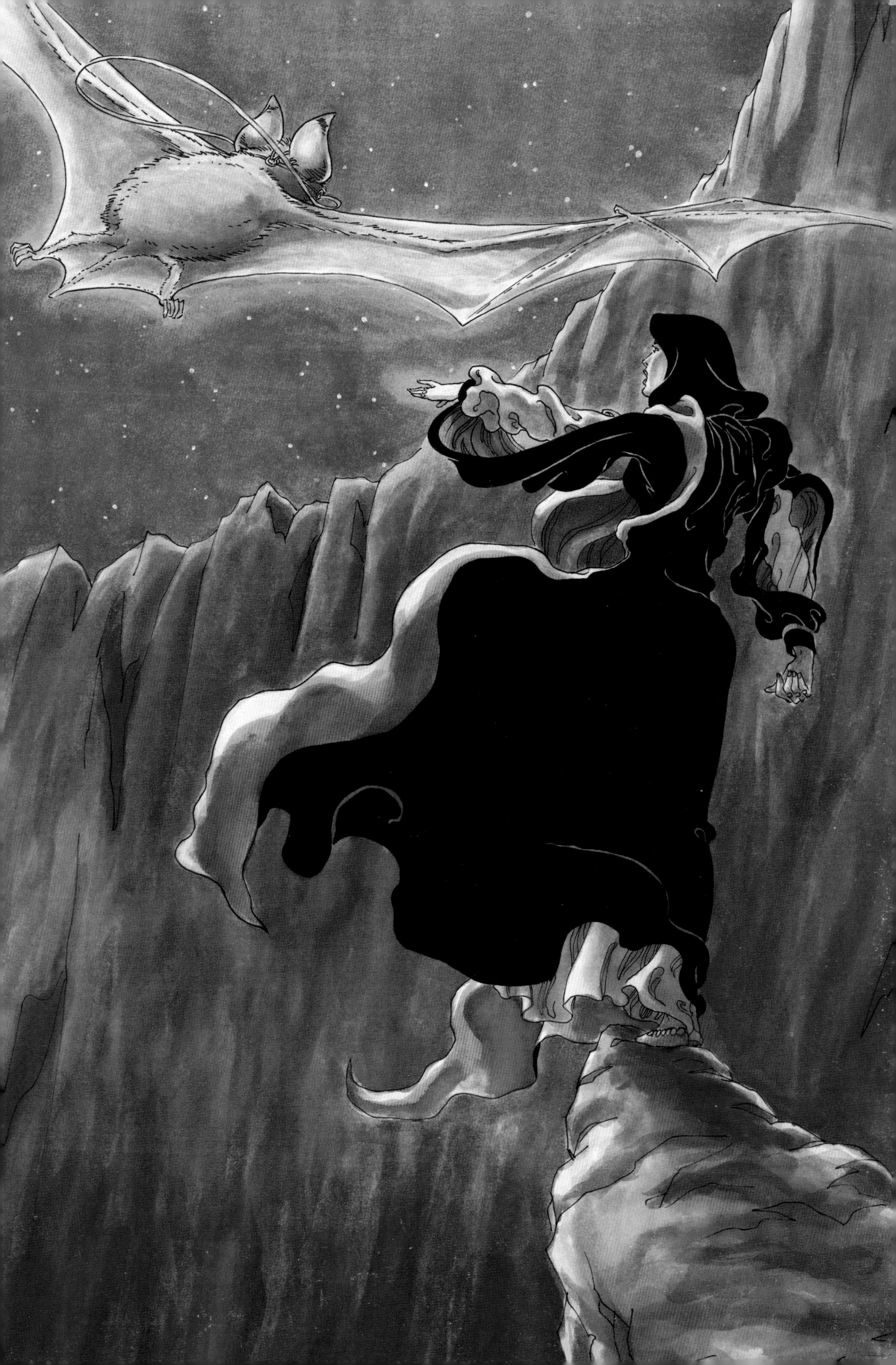

This page: publicity art drawn for the cover of *The Westfield Newsletter,* October 1988 issue.

Facing page: design sketches for Nightshade, 1988 (top left); design sketch for the Troll King, 1988 (top right); color studies for Nightshade 1988 (bottom)

Following page: cover of *The Forgotten Forest of Oz,* 1988

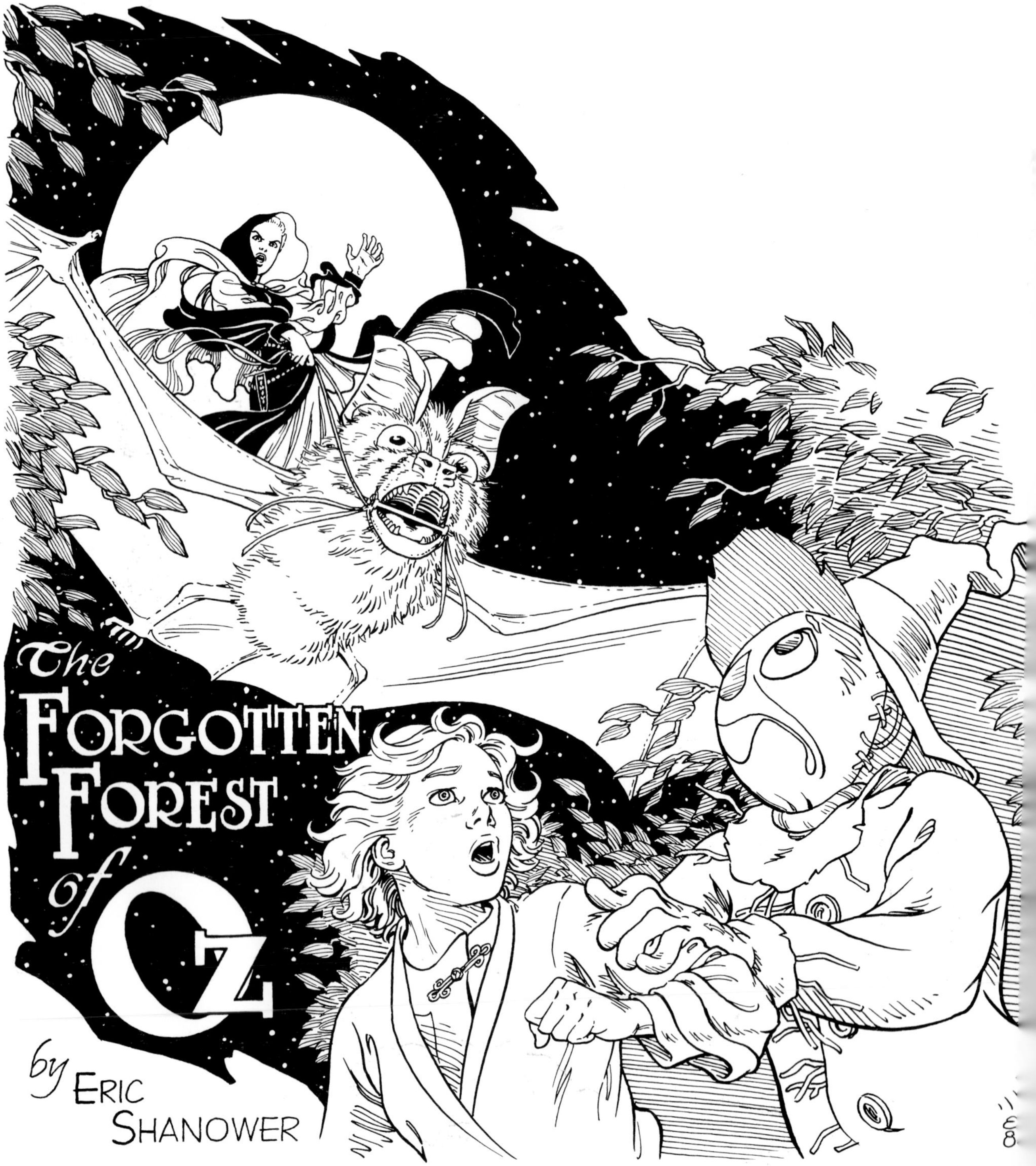
The
FORGOTTEN
FOREST
of
OZ
by ERIC
SHANOWER

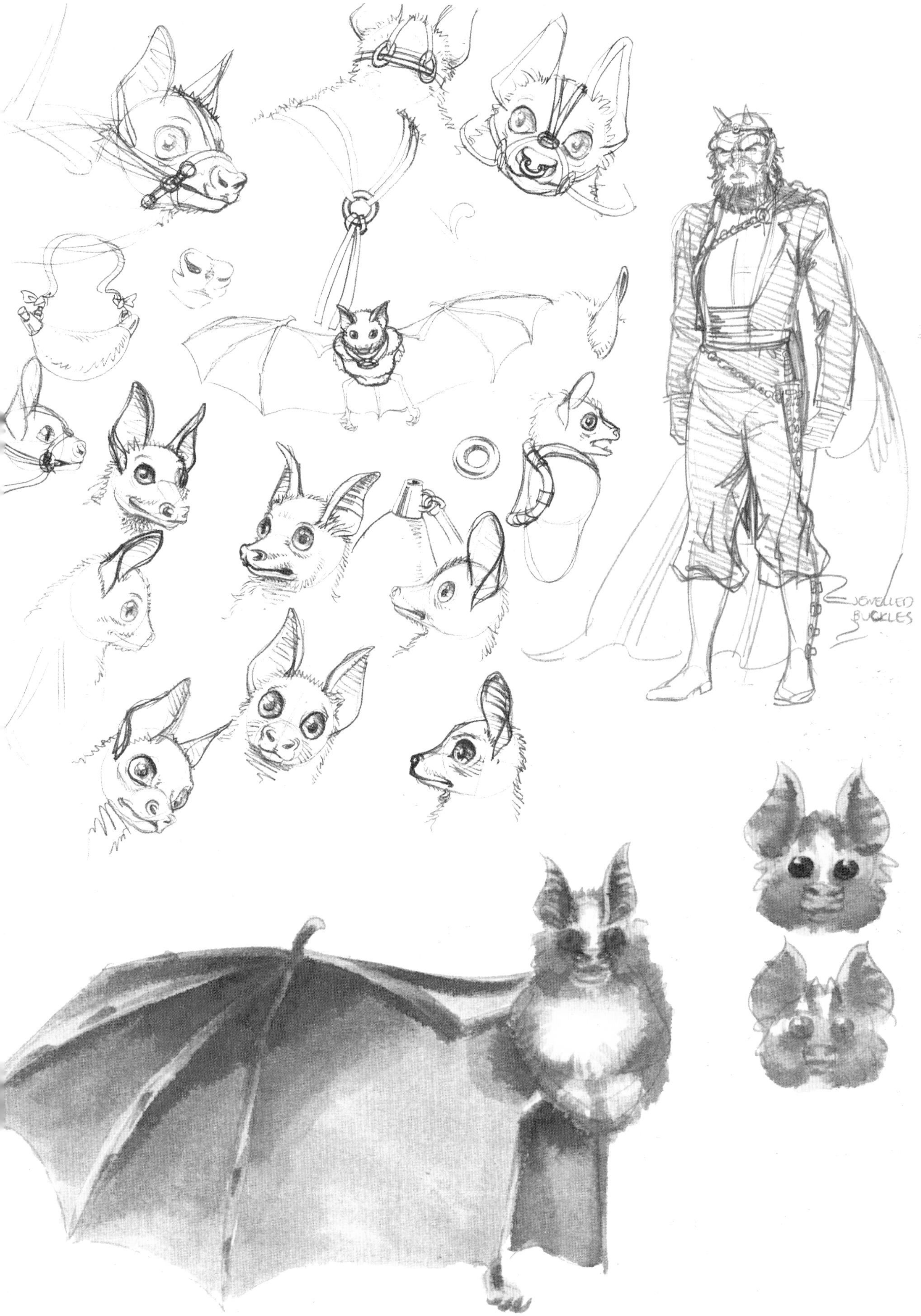
JEWELLED BUCKLES

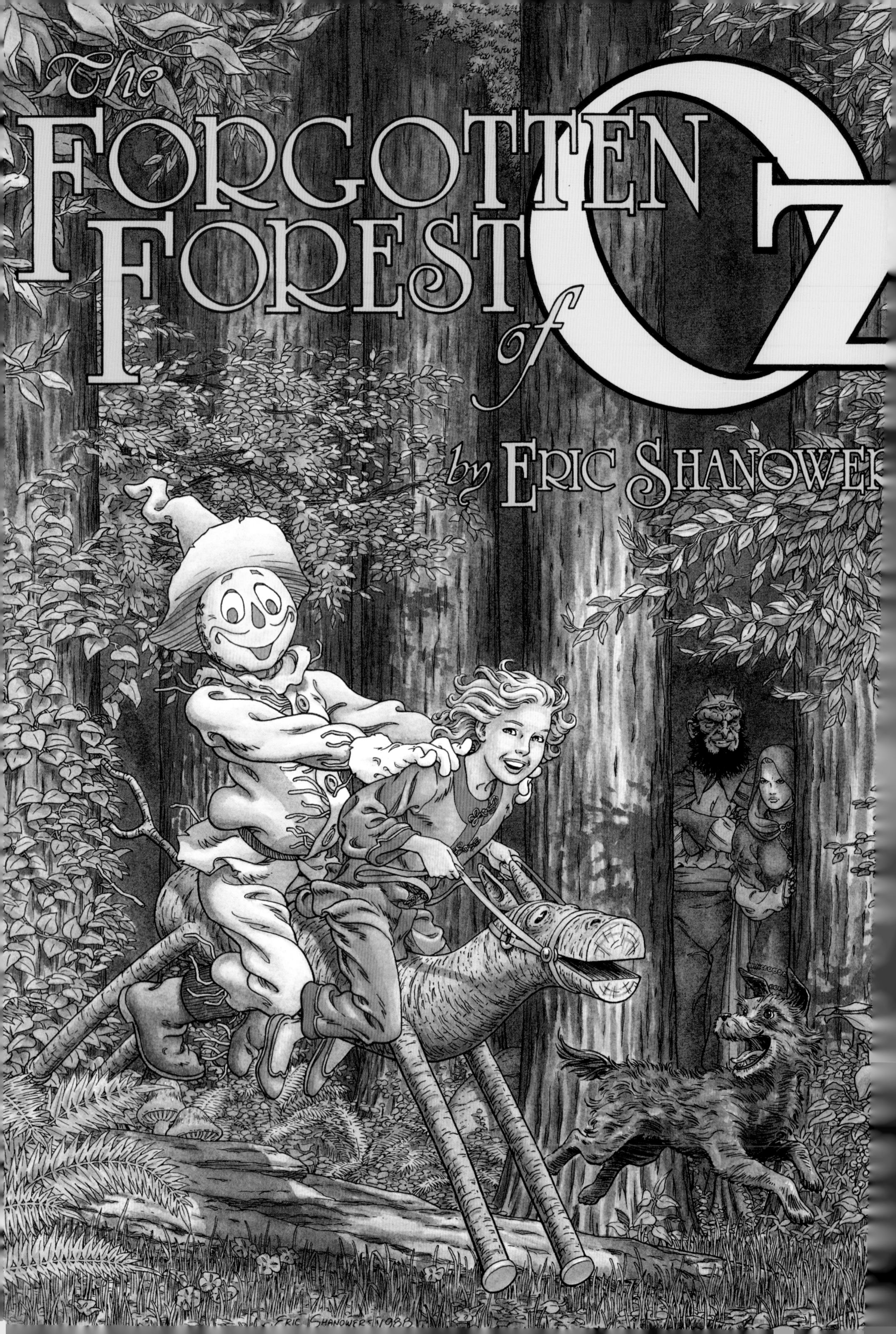
The
FORGOTTEN
FOREST
of OZ
by ERIC SHANOWER
ERIC SHANOWER 1988

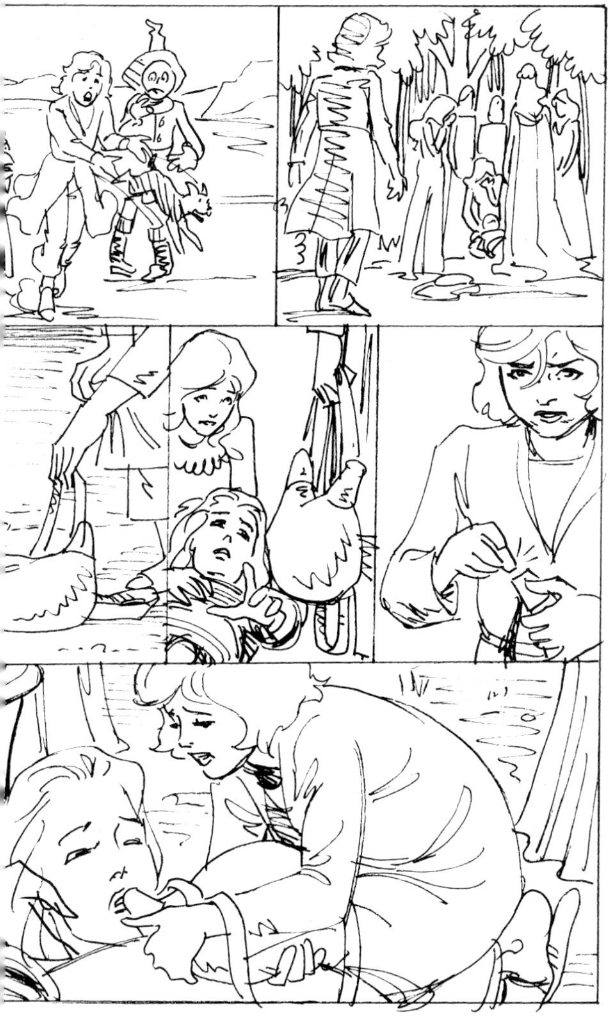

Page 44

Panel 1

DOROTHY: Now I understand! She really does have nothing left! Not the wood-nymphs . . . not the trolls . . .

Panel 2

DOROTHY: . . . only . . .

Panel 3

DOROTHY: . . . the Water of Oblivion. *(small letters)*

Panel 4

NELANTHE: . . . the water . . . the waterrr . . . *(small letters, wavery balloon)*

Panel 5

DOROTHY: I don't care anymore—so what if it's forbidden?

SOUND EFFECT: pop

Panel 6

DOROTHY: She wanted it so badly and it's all she has left. And maybe, just maybe, it'll help make death not so bad.

SOUND EFFECT: sssip

e 45

el 1

LINE: What has she drunk?

OTHY: The Water of Oblivion . . .

el 2

OTHY: . . . now her memory is gone forever.

ANTHE *(off-panel):* —oh, what a weight is lifted from my soul—

el 3

LINE: Forever?

OTHY: . . . yes.

ANTHE: Why . . . I can't even remember what troubled me.

el 4

ANTHE 1): Where am I?

2) Who are you?

3) Who am I?

el 5

LINE: You are the wood-nymph Nelanthe, you are mmortal—

el 6

LINE: —and this, the Forest of Burzee, is your nome.

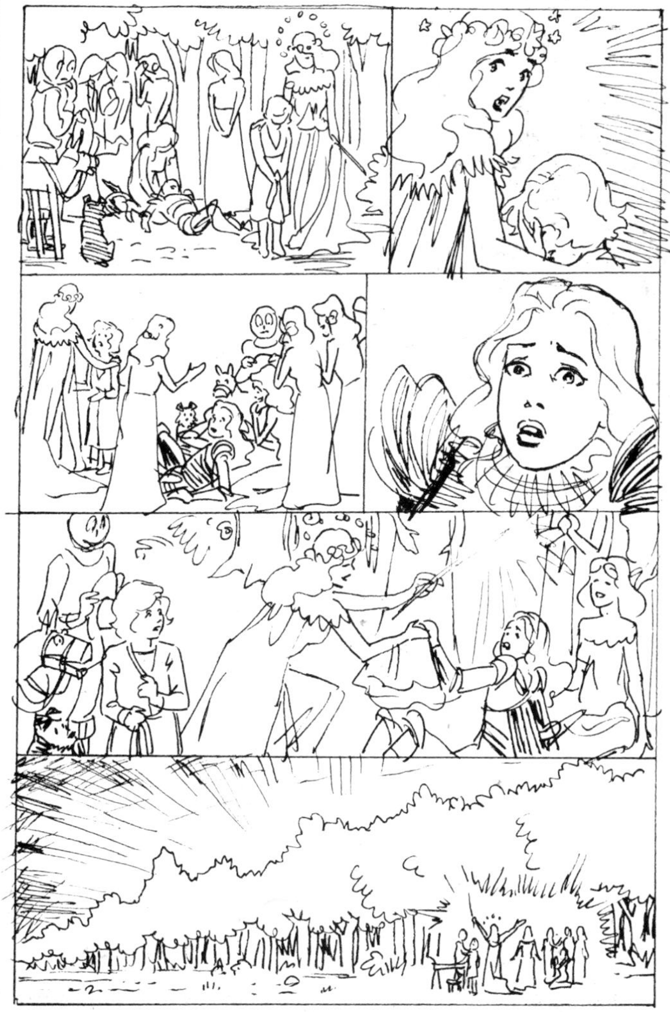

After *The Forgotten Forest of Oz,* I took a break from Oz graphic novels to work on other projects. I returned to the series in early 1990 and submitted a plot for a story titled *Ruggedo in Oz,* featuring the primary villain of the Oz books, Ruggedo, the former Nome King.

The publisher, First Comics, had undergone some changes. Rick Oliver, editor of the first four Oz graphic novels, had left to write Hardy Boys books. The new editor, Bob Garcia, rejected my new plot and even suggested that First Comics might continue the Oz graphic novels without me. I wasn't particularly sad when I learned that Bob had been replaced as editor by Byron Erickson. Byron accepted the next plot I submitted, which I intended as the final book in the series, *The Blue Witch of Oz*. In *Forgotten Forest,* I'd dealt with some heavy themes, such as love and revenge, but I'd integrated them successfully with the characters and atmosphere of Oz. In *Blue Witch,* however, the mature ideas of love, loss, and child custody developed not quite comfortably within the concept of the children's fantasyland of Oz. I was chafing to get out of the Oz sandbox. It was clearly time for me to move on to other projects.

I completed *The Blue Witch of Oz* in April 1991, the same month First Comics ceased operations. My final Oz graphic novel sat in limbo until Bob Schreck, an editor at Dark Horse Comics, convinced Dark Horse publisher Mike Richardson to rescue the project. Anina Bennett was assigned as editor in mid-1992.

In the meantime, I'd grown dissatisfied with my original ending for *Blue Witch.* It just didn't seem genuine to me anymore. The first thing I asked Anina was whether I could change the end. She agreed. *The Blue Witch of Oz* was published in December 1992, although it wasn't generally released to the comic book market until early 1993 and then with scant fanfare. By that time, I'd turned my attention to other projects, although I've still never managed to get out of Oz altogether. I don't think I ever will.

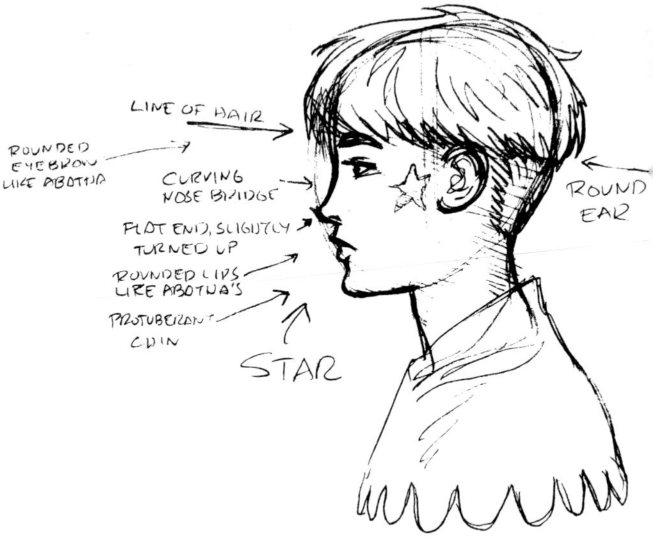
LINE OF HAIR
CURVING NOSE BRIDGE
FLAT END, SLIGHTLY TURNED UP
PROTUBERANT CHIN
STAR
ROUND EAR

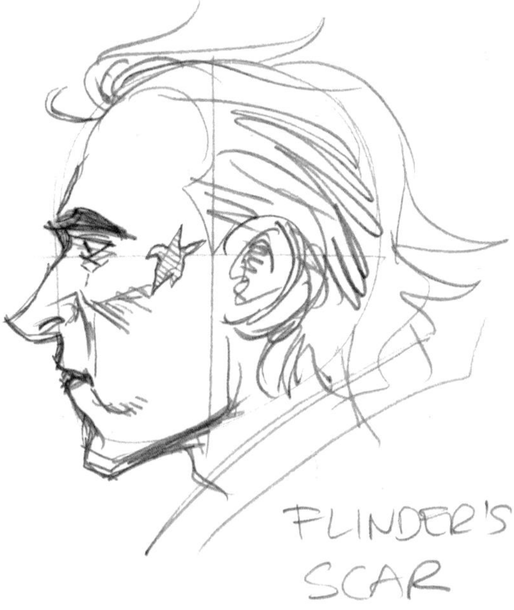
FLINDER'S SCAR

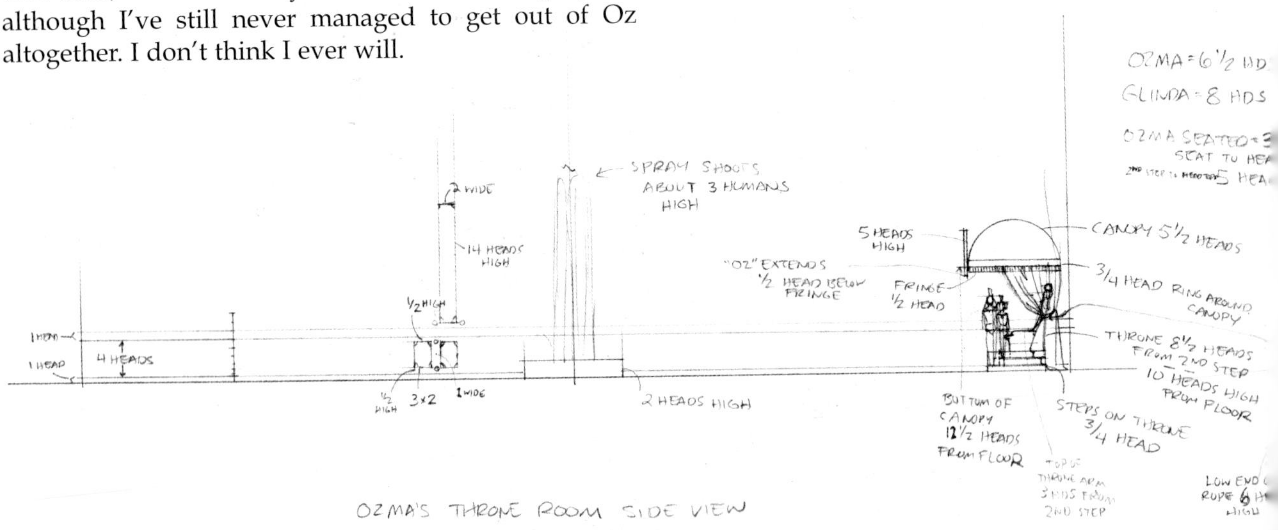
OZMA = 6 1/2 HDS
GLINDA = 8 HDS
SPRAY SHOOTS ABOUT 3 HUMANS HIGH
14 HEADS HIGH
4 HEADS
3x2
2 HEADS HIGH
5 HEADS HIGH
CANOPY 5 1/2 HEADS
"OZ" EXTENDS 1/2 HEAD BELOW FRINGE
FRINGE 1/2 HEAD
3/4 HEAD RING AROUND CANOPY
THRONE 8 1/2 HEADS FROM 2ND STEP
10 HEADS HIGH FROM FLOOR
STEPS ON THRONE 3/4 HEAD
BOTTOM OF CANOPY 12 1/2 HEADS FROM FLOOR
OZMA'S THRONE ROOM SIDE VIEW

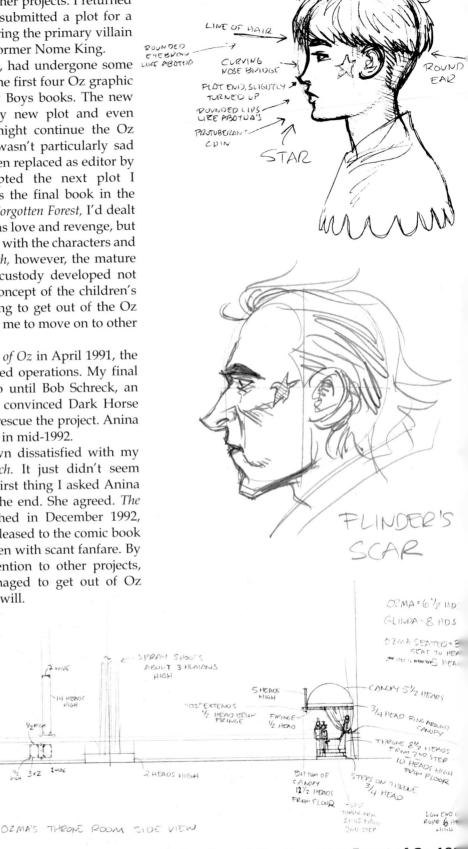

Previous page: rough sketches and script for a discarded ending of *The Forgotten Forest of Oz,* 19

This page: design sketch of Javen/Star, 1990 (top); Sketch showing Flinder's scar, 1990 (middle); section of Ozma's throne room, 1990 (bottom).

:olor study for the sky and
Deadly Desert beyond
Glinda's palace, 1991.

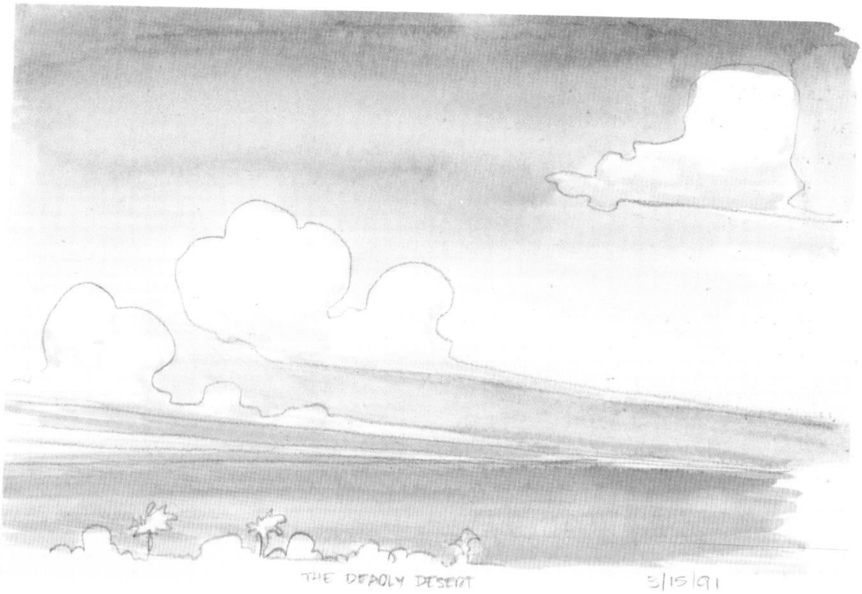
THE DEADLY DESERT
3/15/91

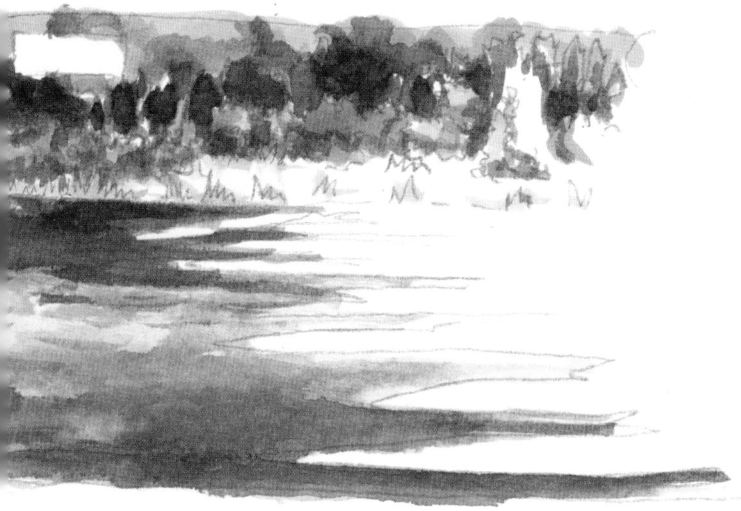

Color study for the Great Gray
Gillikin Swamp by day, 1991.

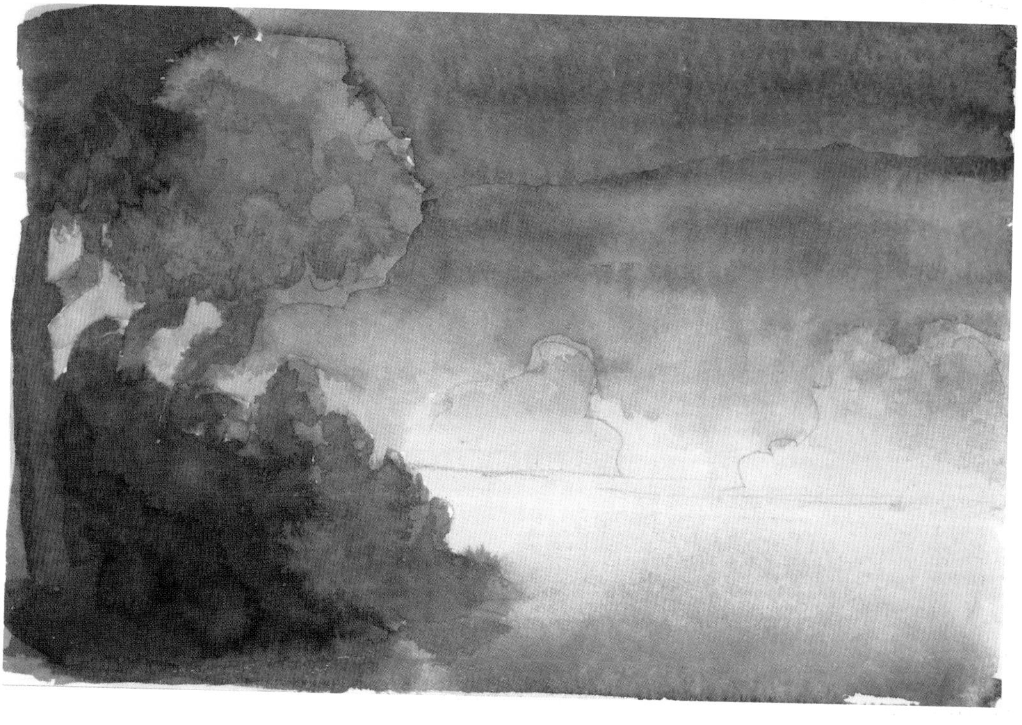

or study for
Great Gray
kin Swamp
ight, 1991.

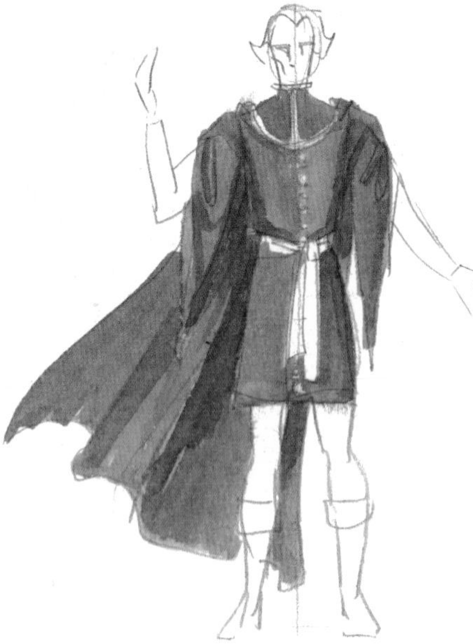

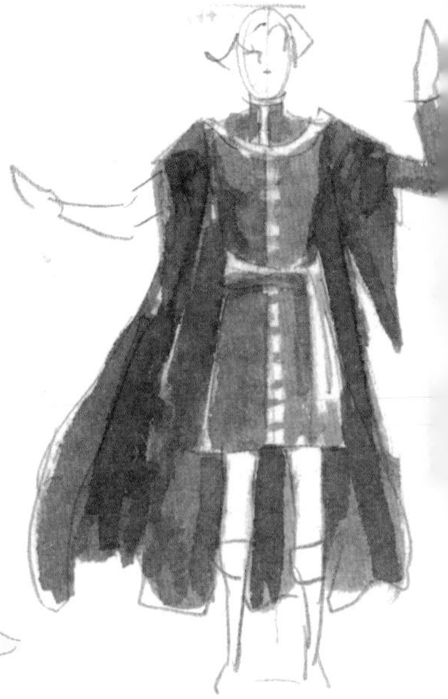

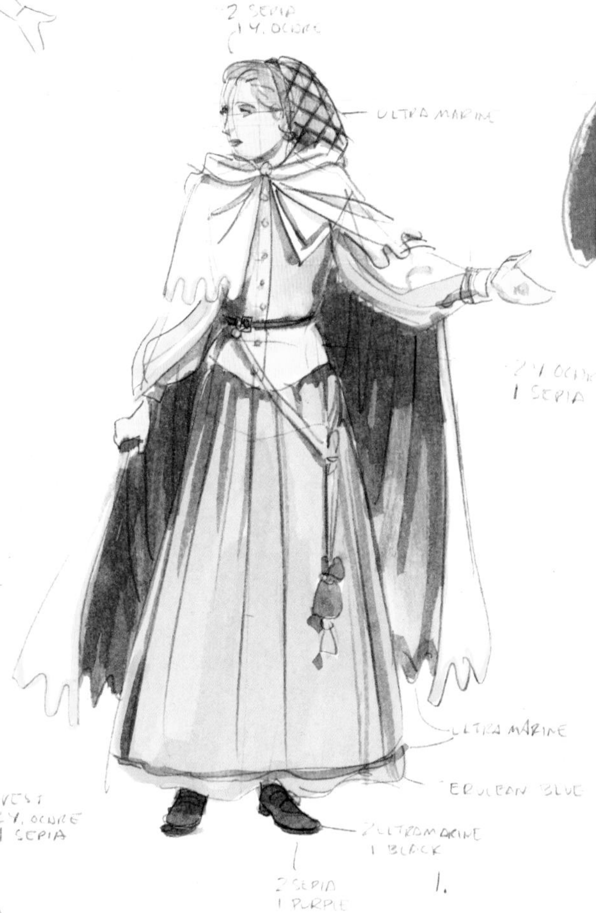
2 SEPIA
1 Y. OCHRE
ULTRA MARINE
2 Y. OCHRE
1 SEPIA
ULTRA MARINE
CERULEAN BLUE
2 ULTRAMARINE
1 BLACK
2 SEPIA
1 PURPLE
1.

This page: color studi
for Dash, 1990 (top le
top right); color studi
for Abatha, 19
(center, bottom le
color study for Bung
the Glass Cat, 19
(belov

Facing page: co
studies for Dorot
1990 (top two tie
color studies
Javen/Star, 19
(bottom le
color studies
Javen/Star and Abat
1990 (bottom rig

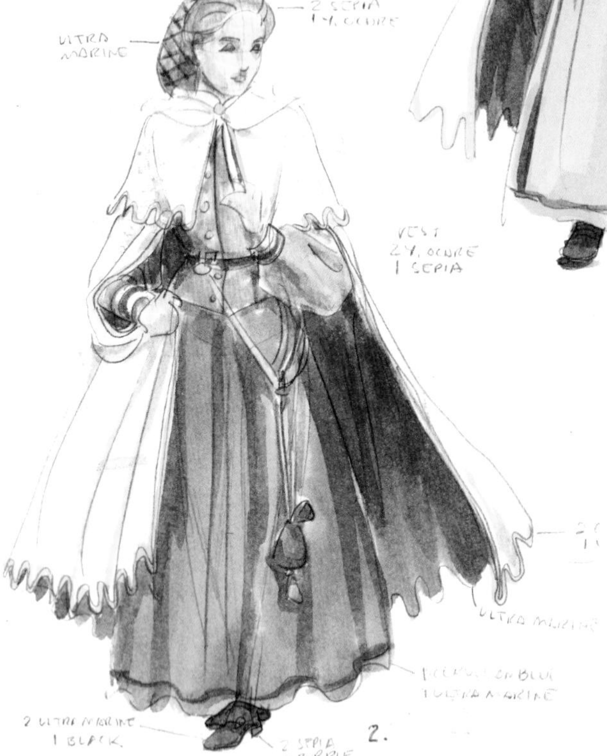
ULTRA MARINE
2 SEPIA
1 Y. OCHRE
VEST
2 Y. OCHRE
1 SEPIA
ULTRA MARINE
2 ULTRAMARINE
1 BLACK
2 SEPIA
1 PURPLE
2.

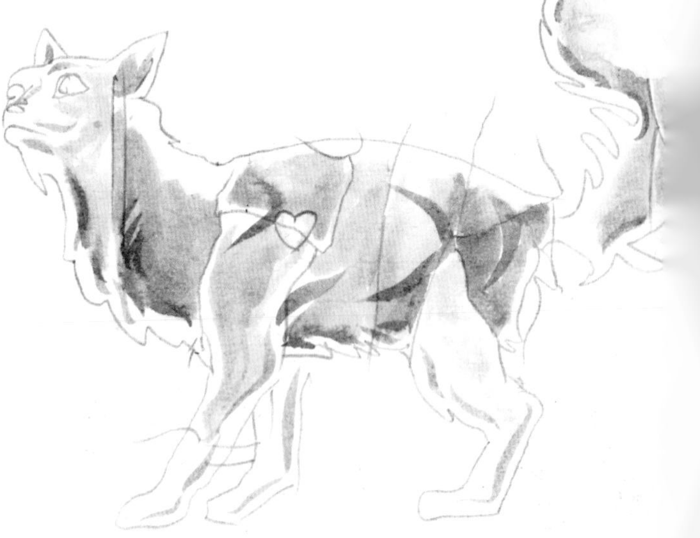

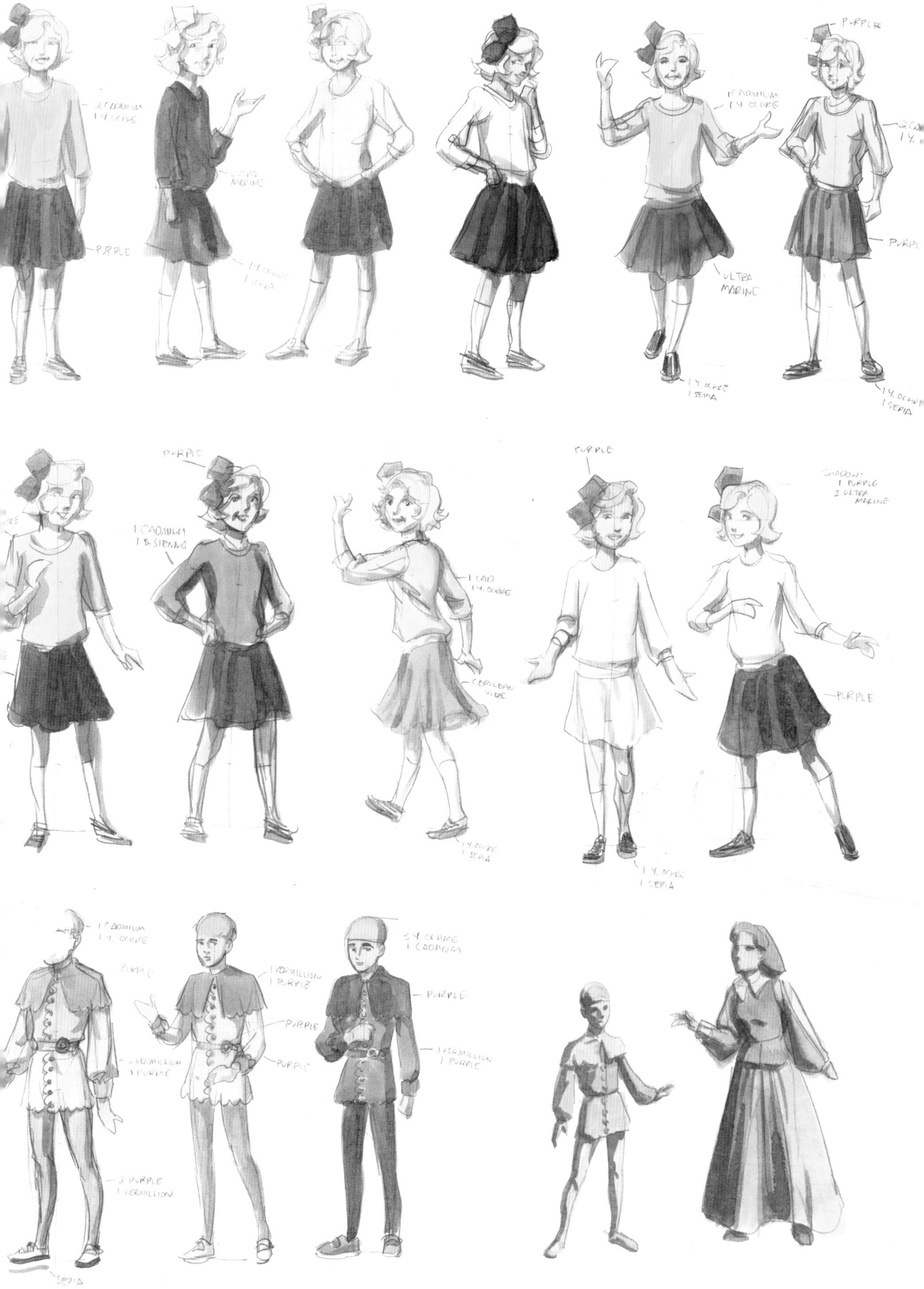
PURPLE
1 CADMIUM
1 Y. OCHRE
ULTRA MARINE
1 Y. OCHRE
1 SEPIA
1 CADMIUM
1 B. SIENNA
1 CAD
1 Y. OCHRE
CERULEAN BLUE
SHADOWS:
1 PURPLE
2 ULTRA MARINE
1 VERMILLION
1 PURPLE
3 Y. OCHRE
1 CADMIUM
2 PURPLE
1 VERMILLION
SEPIA

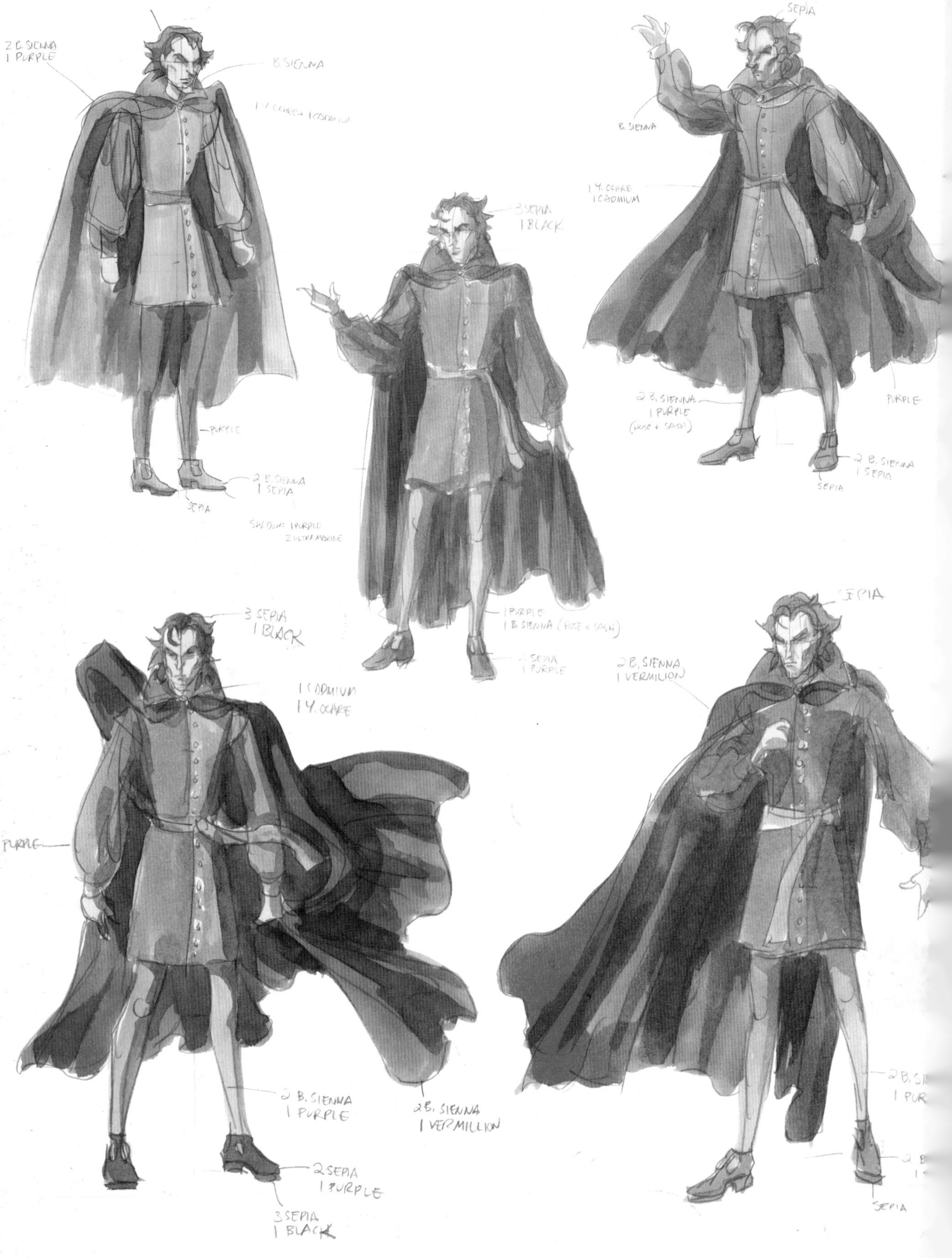
2 B. SIENNA
1 PURPLE
B. SIENNA
PURPLE
2 B. SIENNA
1 SEPIA
SEPIA
3 SEPIA
1 BLACK
1 PURPLE
1 B. SIENNA (HOSE + SASH)
2 SEPIA
1 PURPLE
SEPIA
B. SIENNA
1 Y. OCHRE
1 CADMIUM
2 B. SIENNA
1 PURPLE
(HOSE + SASH)
PURPLE
2 B. SIENNA
1 SEPIA
SEPIA
3 SEPIA
1 BLACK
1 CADMIUM
1 Y. OCHRE
PURPLE
2 B. SIENNA
1 PURPLE
2 B. SIENNA
1 VERMILLION
2 SEPIA
1 PURPLE
3 SEPIA
1 BLACK
SEPIA
2 B. SIENNA
1 VERMILION
SEPIA

This page: color studies for Flinder, 1991.

Facing page: cover of *The Blue Witch of Oz,* 1990.

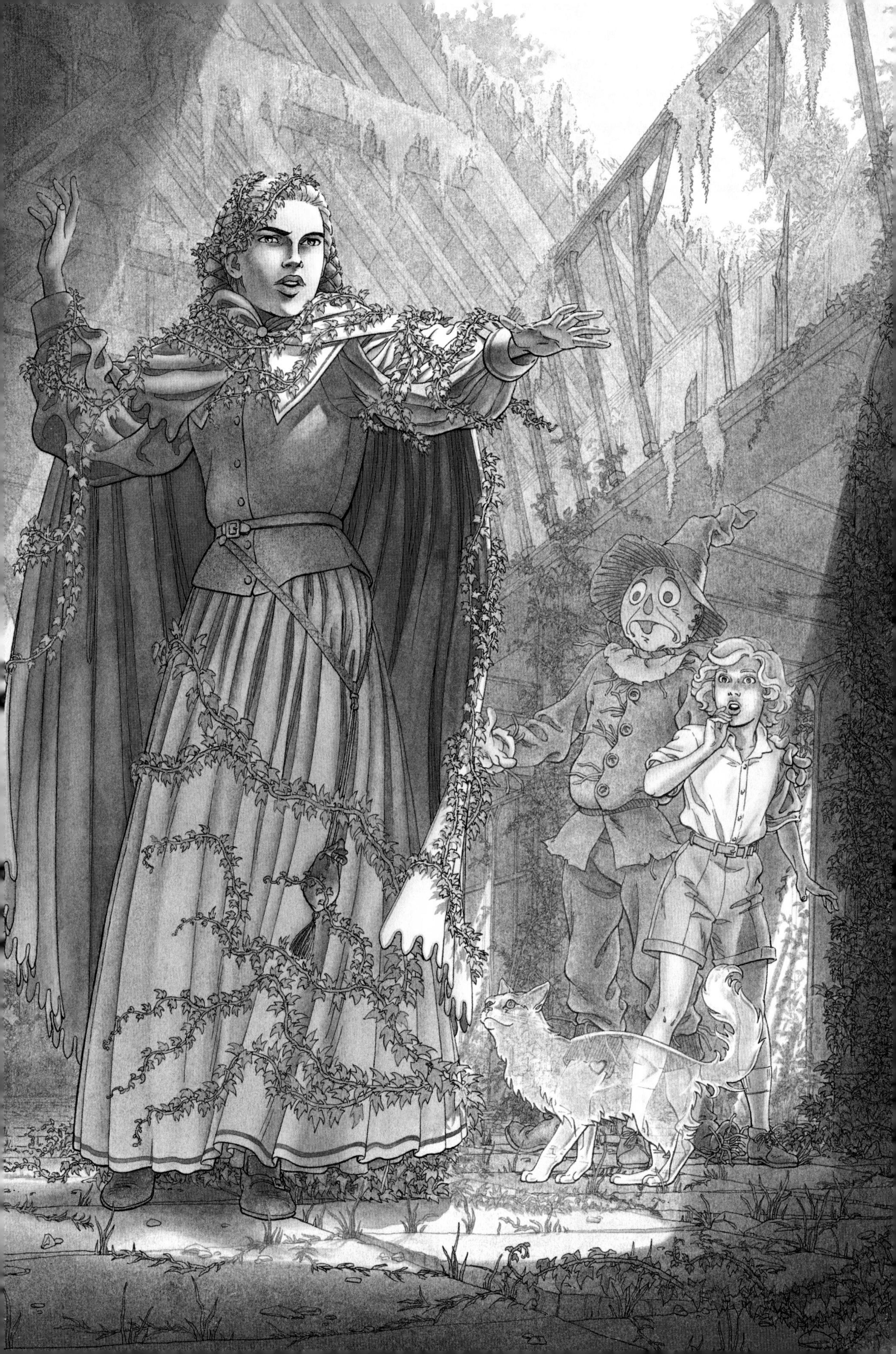

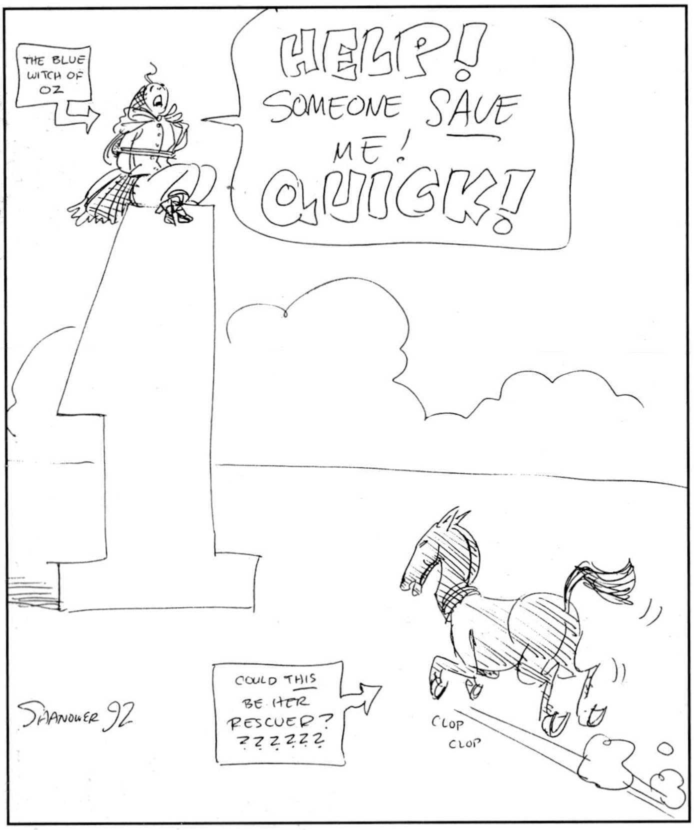
THE BLUE WITCH OF OZ
HELP! SOMEONE SAVE ME! QUICK!
COULD THIS BE HER RESCUER? ??????
CLOP CLOP
SHANOWER 92

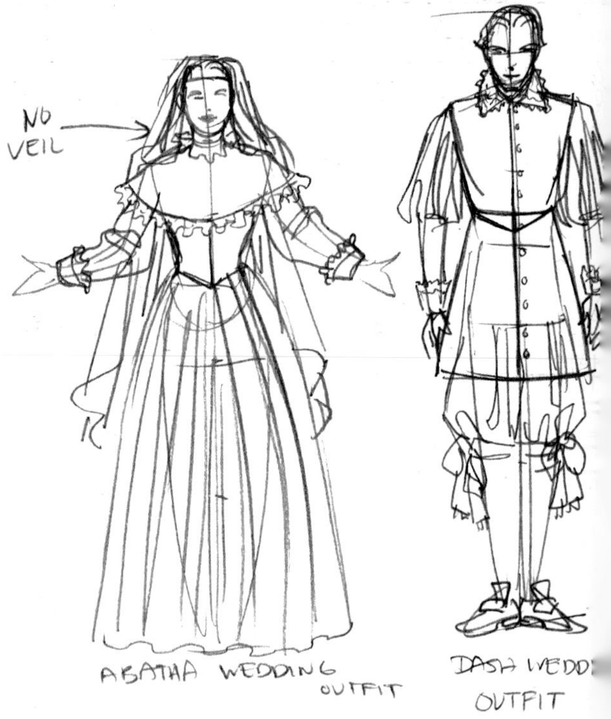
NO VEIL
ABATHA WEDDING OUTFIT
DASH WEDD
OUTFIT

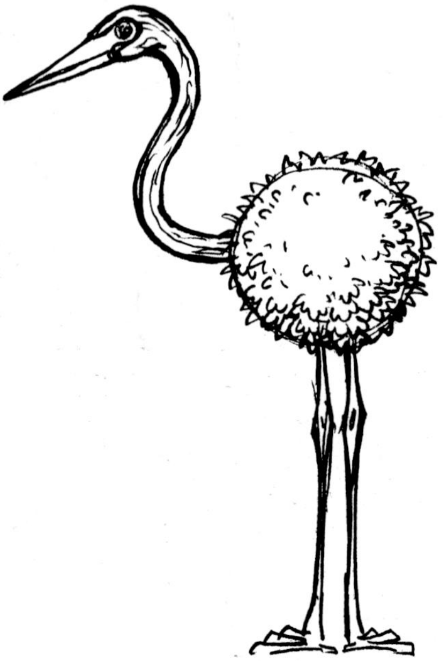

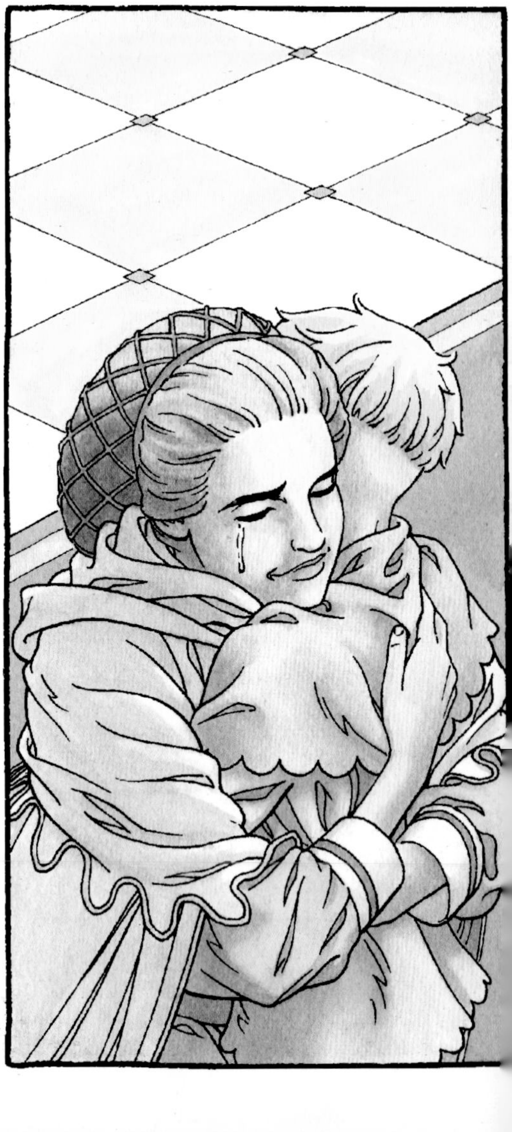

This page: after First Comics ceased operations, I sent this cartoon to Dark Horse Comics publisher Mike Richardson, showing Dark Horse's logo hurrying to rescue the Blue Witch stranded on First Comics's logo, 1992 (top left); design sketches for Abatha and Dash in wedding clothes, 1990 (top right); design sketch for a bush bird, 1990 (bottom left); discarded final panel for page 45 of *The Blue Witch of Oz,* 1990 (right).

Facing page: discarded final page of *The Blue Witch of Oz,* 1990.

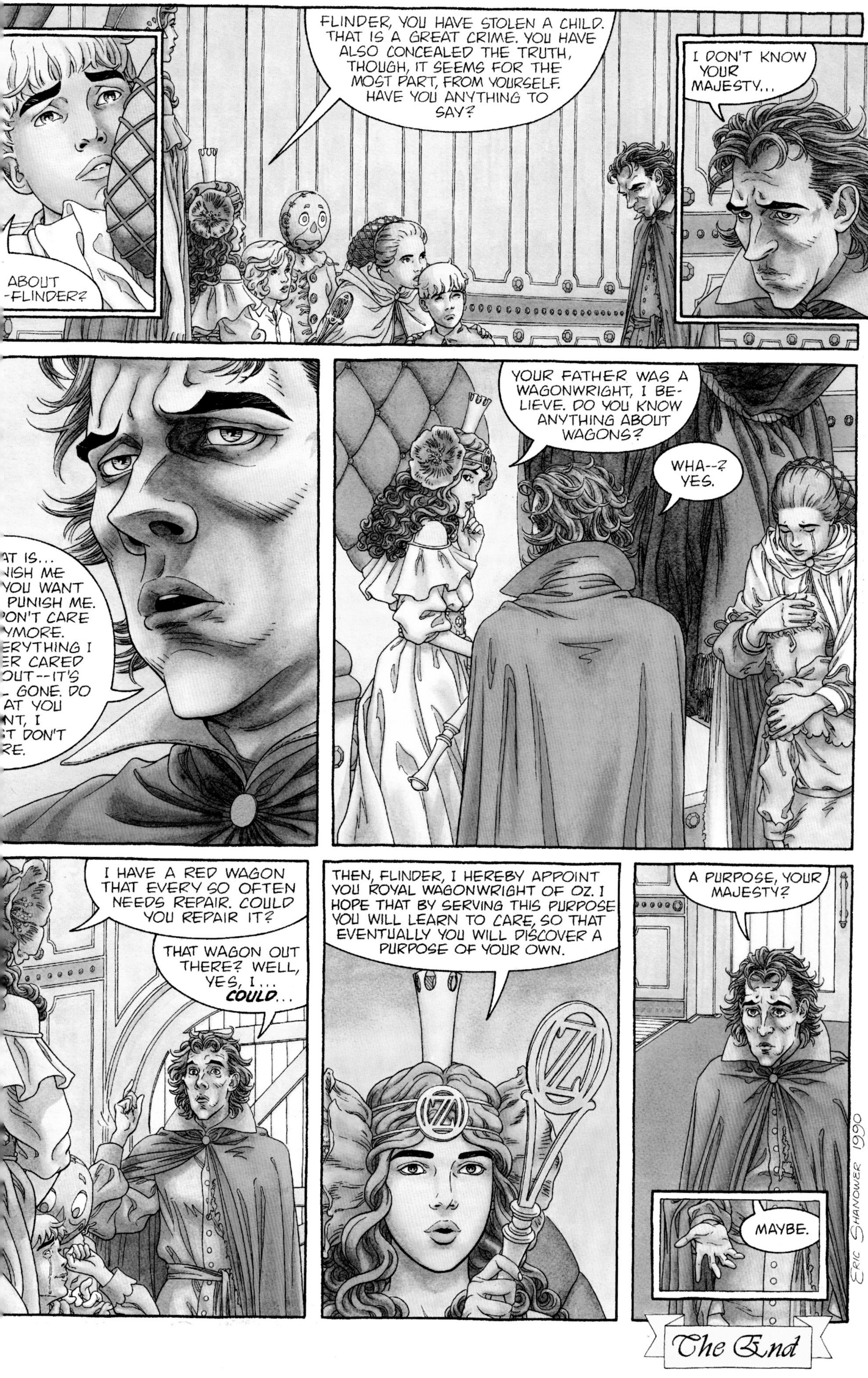
ABOUT
-FLINDER?
FLINDER, YOU HAVE STOLEN A CHILD. THAT IS A GREAT CRIME. YOU HAVE ALSO CONCEALED THE TRUTH, THOUGH, IT SEEMS FOR THE MOST PART, FROM YOURSELF. HAVE YOU ANYTHING TO SAY?
I DON'T KNOW YOUR MAJESTY...
AT IS... NISH ME YOU WANT PUNISH ME. PON'T CARE YMORE. ERYTHING I ER CARED OUT--IT'S GONE. DO AT YOU NT, I T DON'T RE.
YOUR FATHER WAS A WAGONWRIGHT, I BE-LIEVE. DO YOU KNOW ANYTHING ABOUT WAGONS?
WHA--? YES.
I HAVE A RED WAGON THAT EVERY SO OFTEN NEEDS REPAIR. COULD YOU REPAIR IT?
THAT WAGON OUT THERE? WELL, YES, I... COULD...
THEN, FLINDER, I HEREBY APPOINT YOU ROYAL WAGONWRIGHT OF OZ. I HOPE THAT BY SERVING THIS PURPOSE YOU WILL LEARN TO CARE, SO THAT EVENTUALLY YOU WILL DISCOVER A PURPOSE OF YOUR OWN.
A PURPOSE, YOUR MAJESTY?
MAYBE.
ERIC SHANOWER 1990
The End

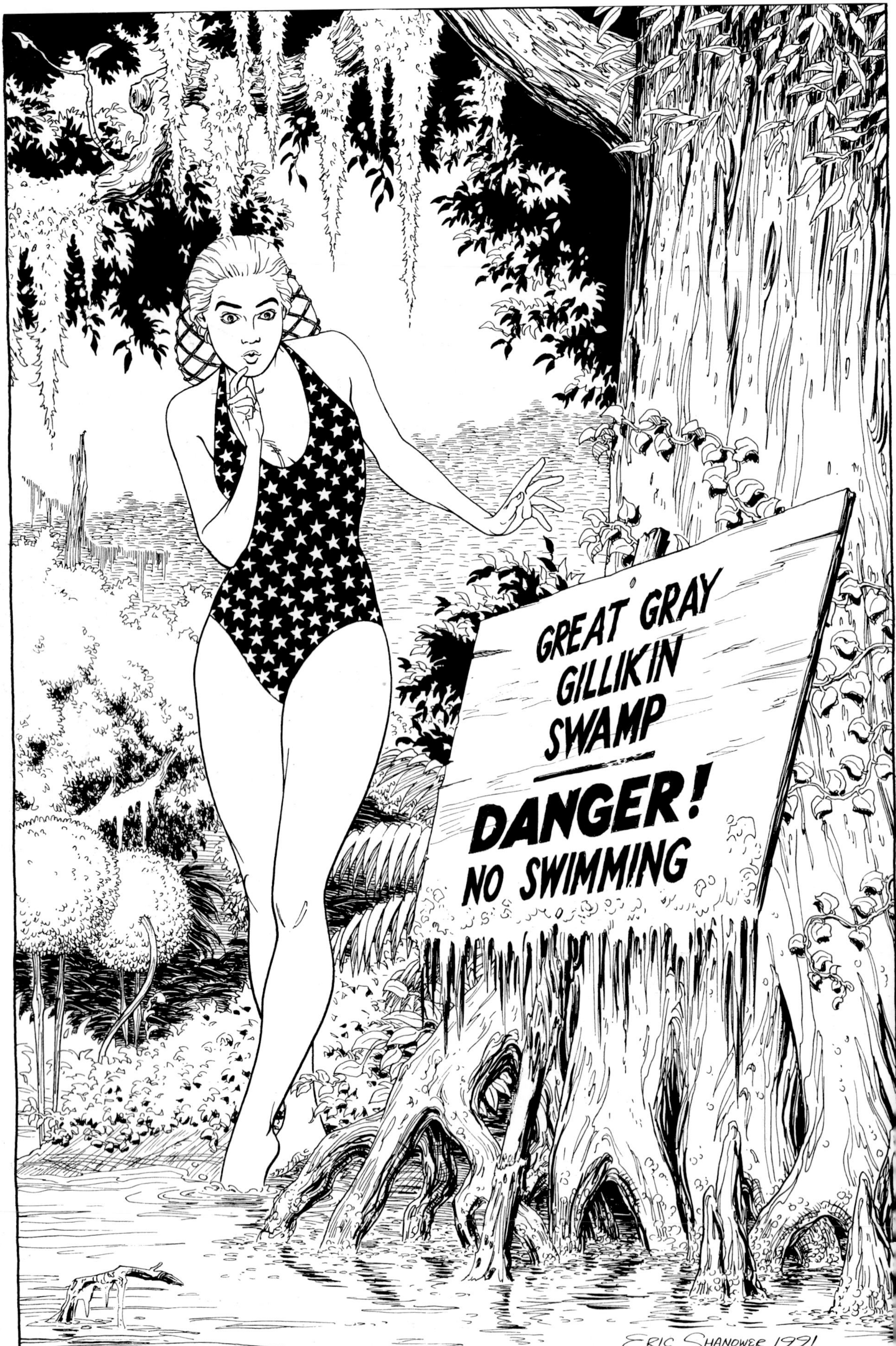
GREAT GRAY
GILLIKIN
SWAMP
DANGER!
NO SWIMMING
ERIC SHANOWER 1991

Facing page: pin-up for the magazine *Amazing Heroes Swimsuit Special* #2, 1991.

This page: Christmas card for 1987 featuring Flicker (top left); Christmas card for 1988 featuring characters from L. Frank Baum's *The Life and Adventures of Santa Claus*—Queen Zurline, Santa Claus, and Necile—with Nelanthe and Nebelle from *The Forgotten Forest of Oz* (middle right); Christmas card for 1990 featuring Abatha, Star, and, perhaps, Dash (bottom).

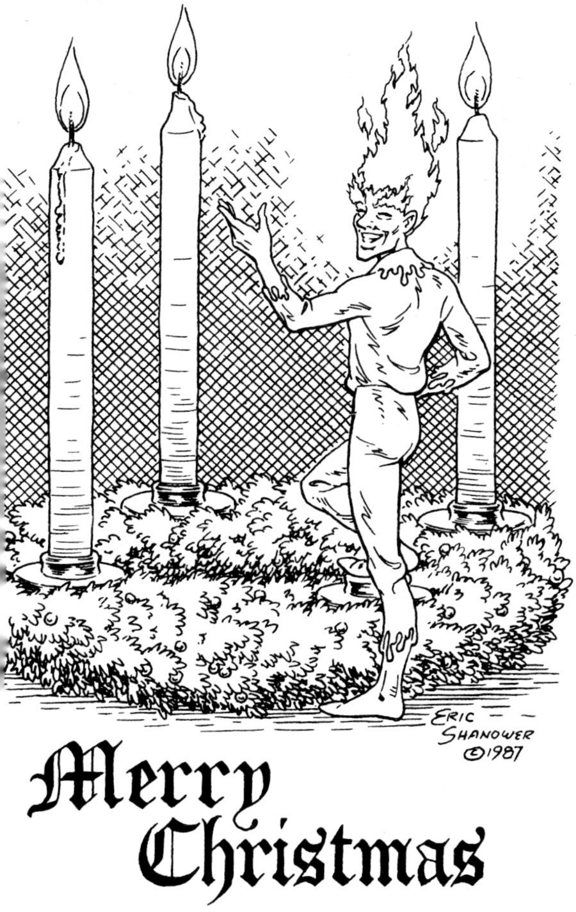
Eric Shanower ©1987
Merry Christmas

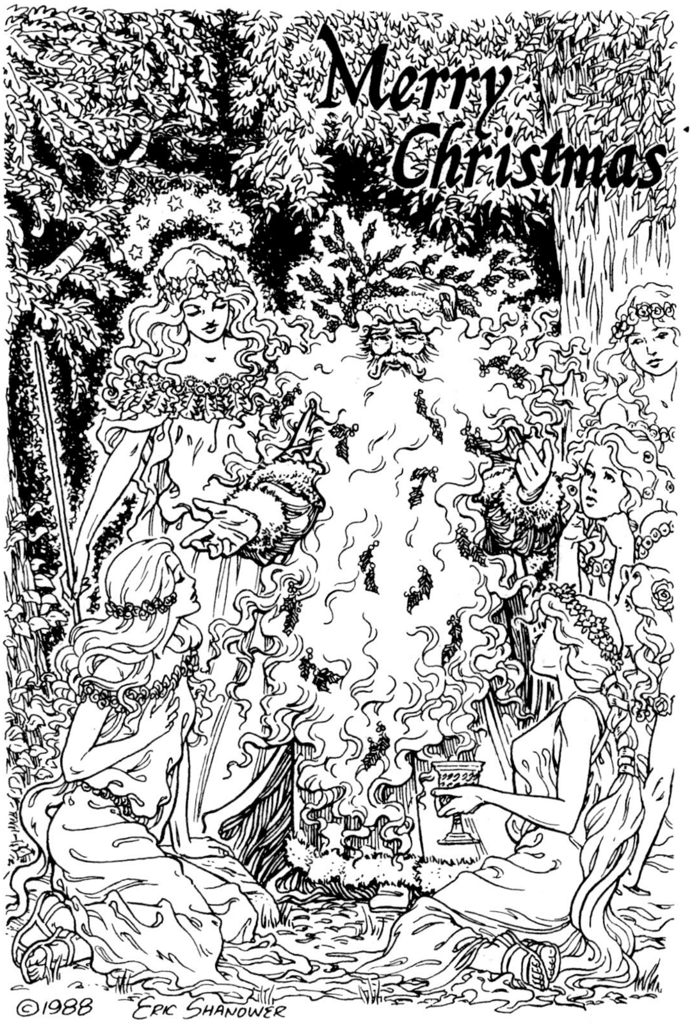
Merry Christmas
©1988 Eric Shanower

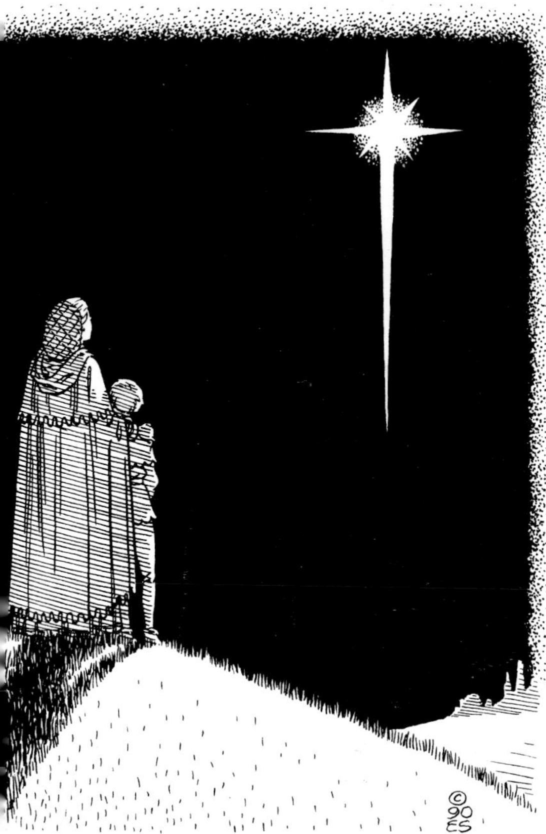
© 90 ES
May those you love be near.
Merry Christmas.

Since completing *The Blue Witch of Oz,* I've worked on a host of Oz projects—books, magazines, calendars, T-shirts, convention programs, and more. I was even interviewed for a documentary included on the 2005 DVD release of the 1939 MGM *Wizard of Oz* motion picture. Oz has led me to interesting places and introduced me to fascinating people. In 1994, I co-founded the publishing company Hungry Tiger Press, in part to issue Oz books and stories, both old and new. My partner, David Maxine, has since taken over the company, but I still draw Oz illustrations for Hungry Tiger Press, as well as for other publishers and projects. The following pages will give just a taste of that work.

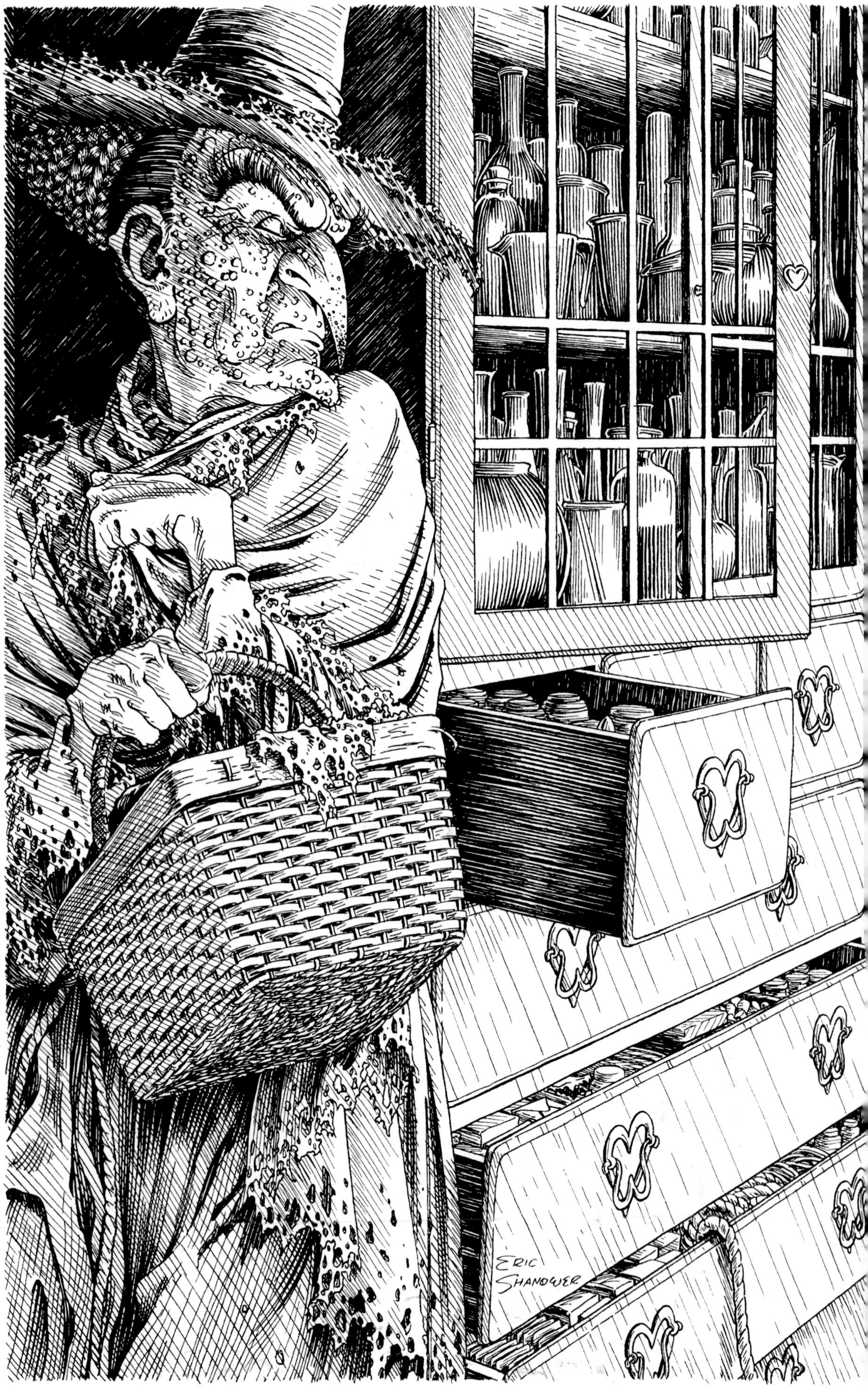
ERIC
SHANOWER

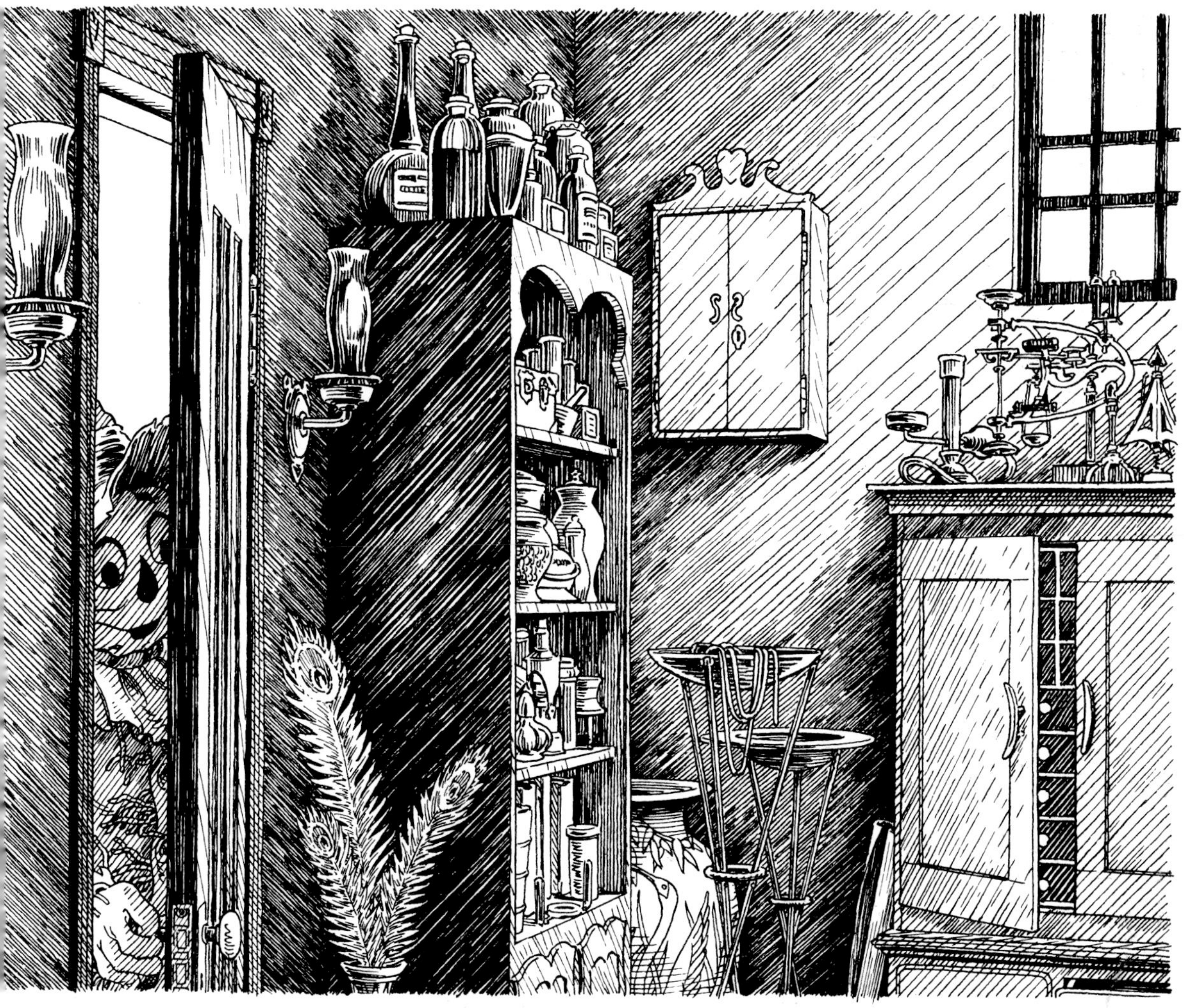

ng page
top of this
e:
tration for
book *The
ked Witch
Dz* by Rachel
grove Payes,
2. Singra
es in Glinda's
gic
kroom.

om of this
e: limited
ion color
es for *The
ked Witch
Dz*, 1993.
othy and
y meet
n the Neon
; Dorothy
ed into a
ue (right).

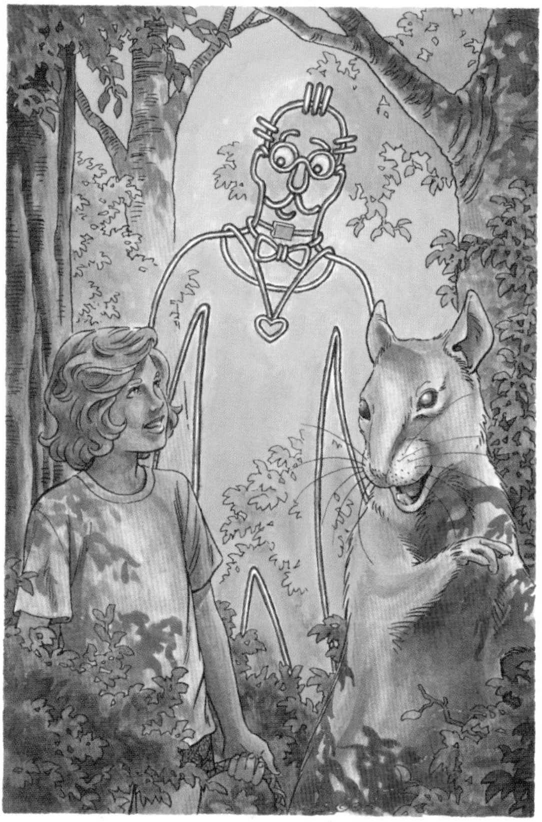

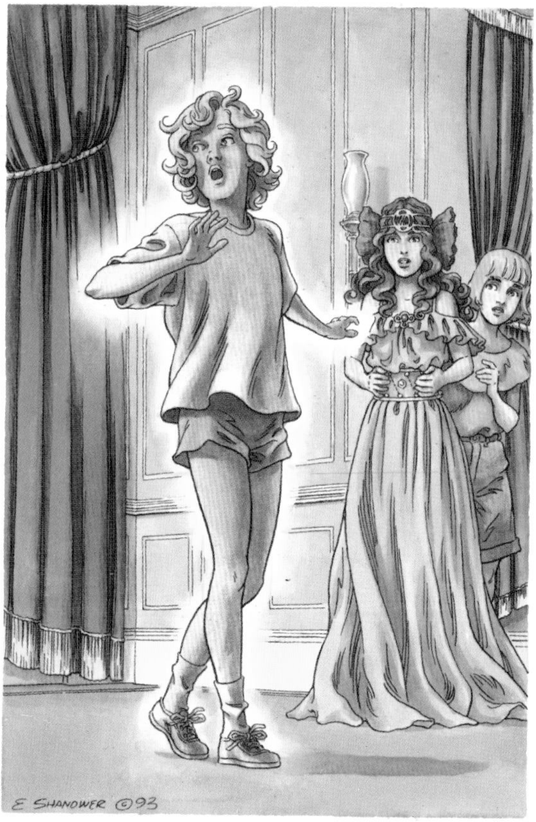
E SHANOWER ©93

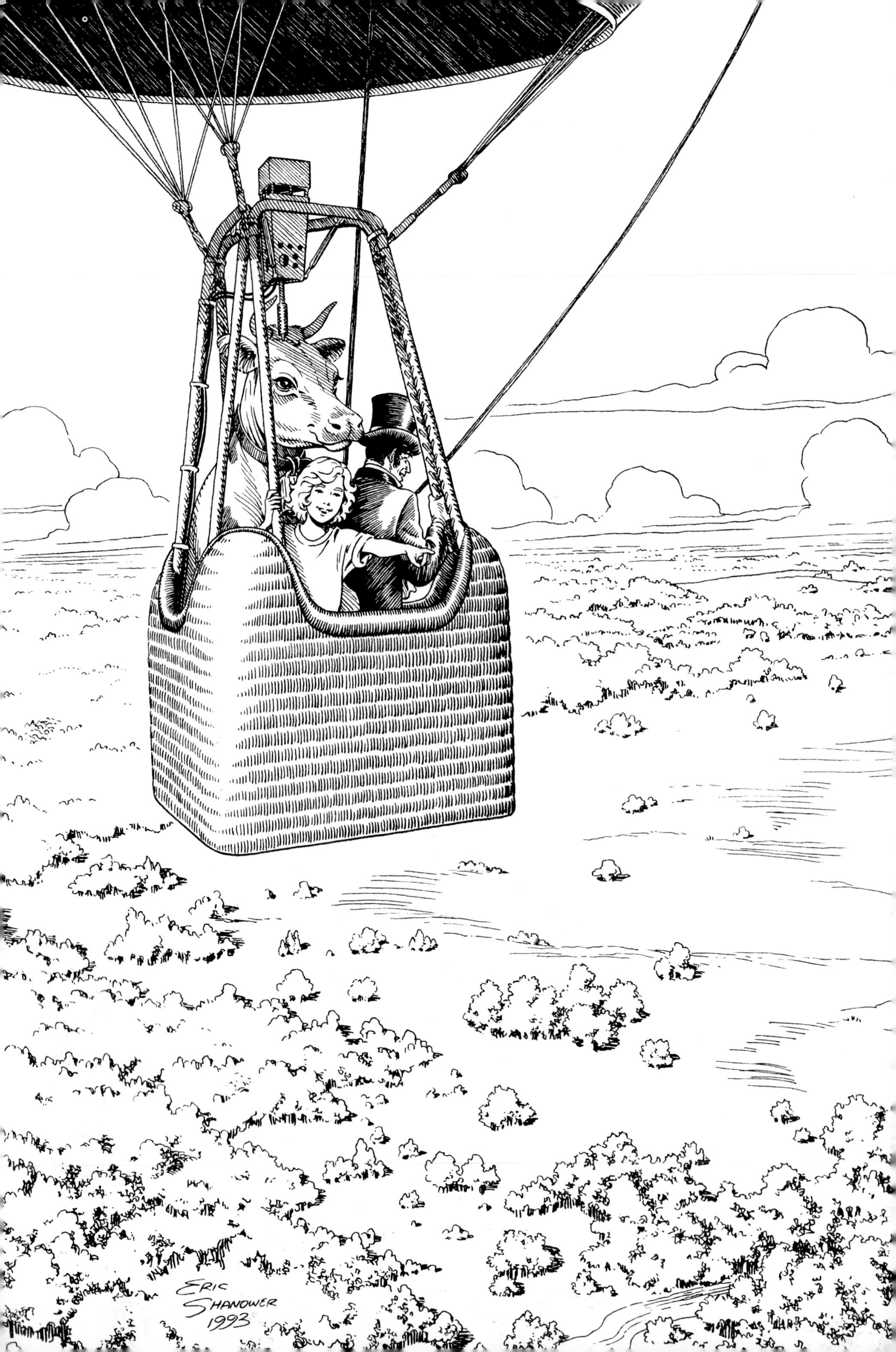
ERIC
SHANOWER
1993

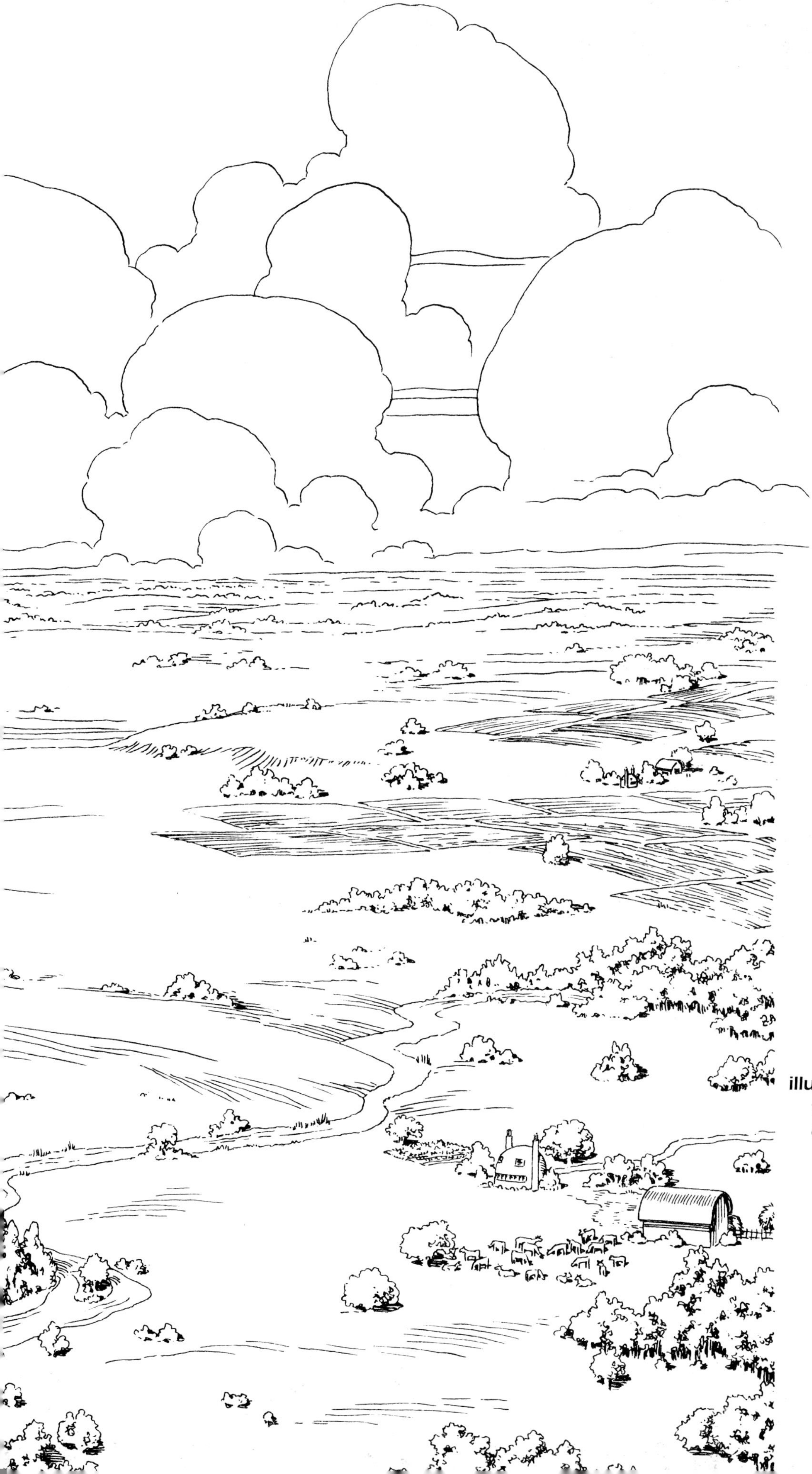

These two pages: endpaper illustration from the book *The Giant Garden of Oz* by Eric Shanower, 1993. Dorothy, the Wizard, and Imogene the cow float above the Munchkin Country.

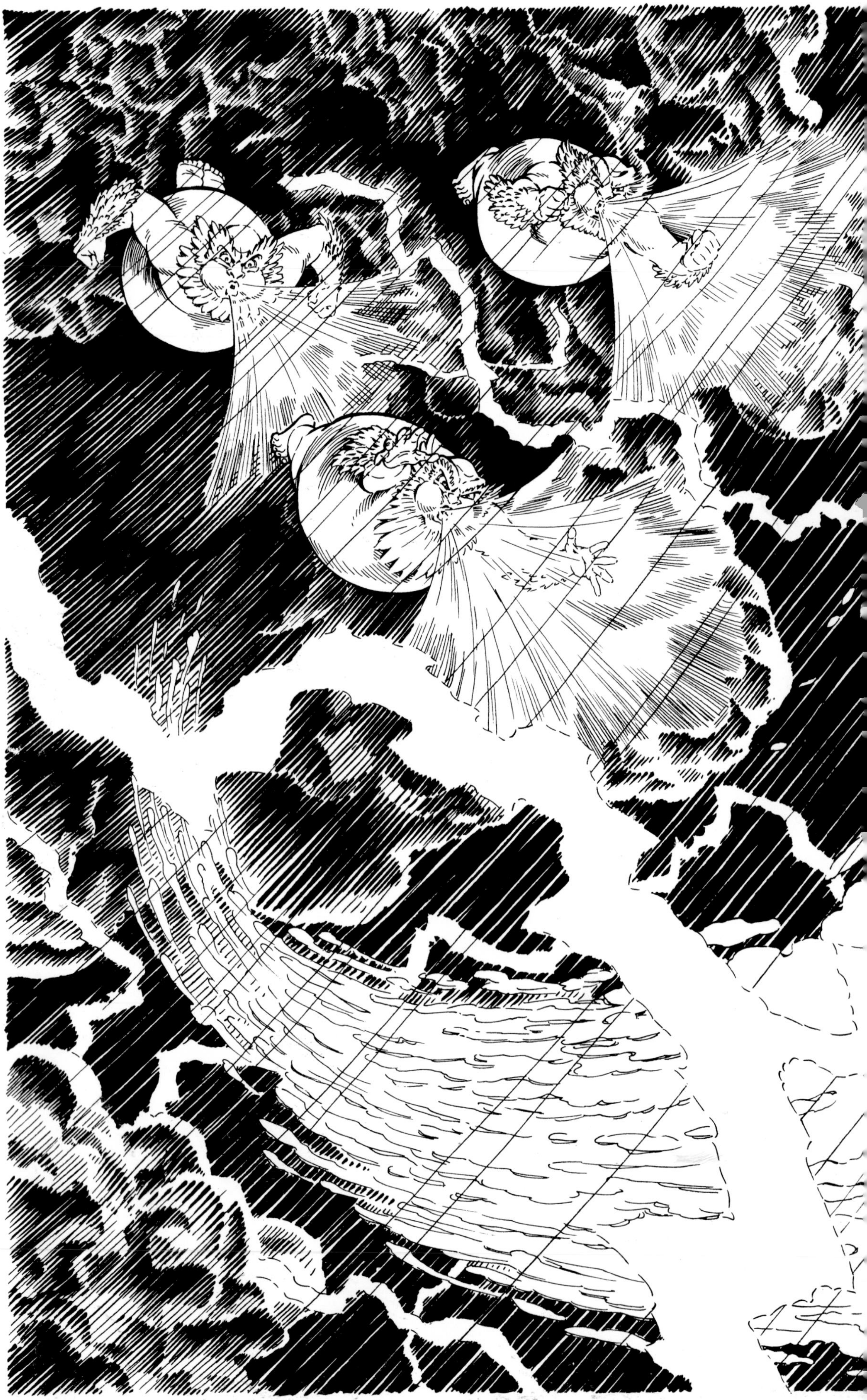

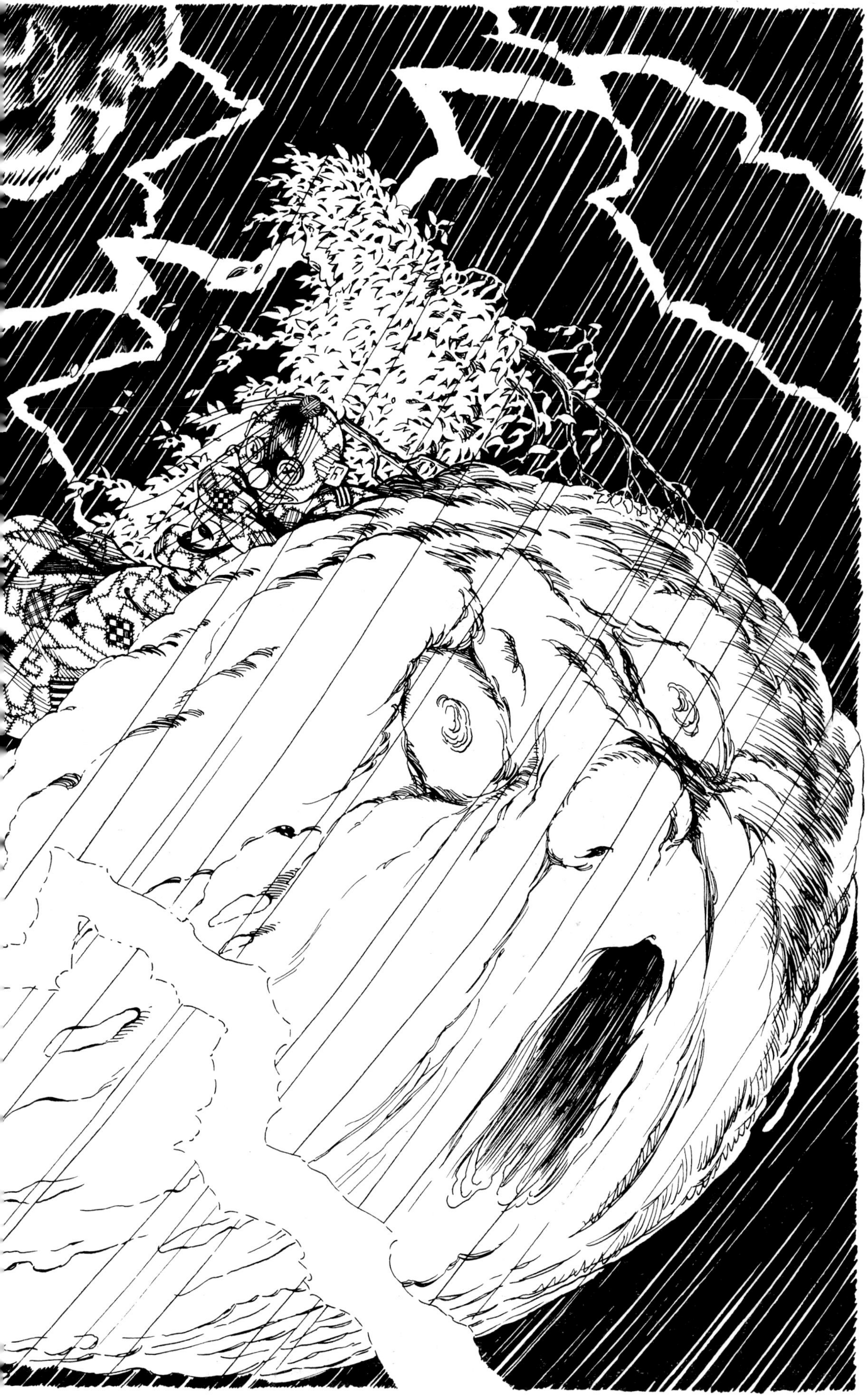

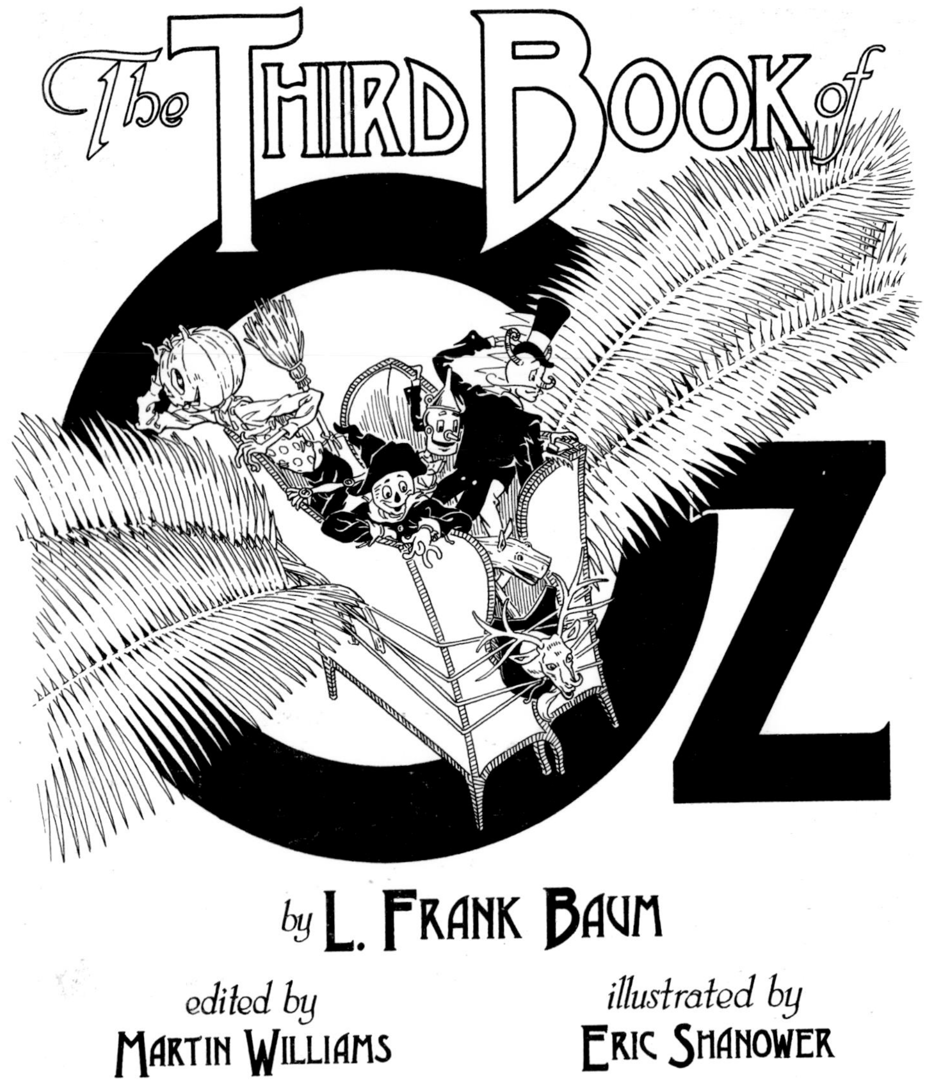
The Third Book of Oz
by L. Frank Baum
edited by
Martin Williams
illustrated by
Eric Shanower

Previous two pages: illustra
for the book *The Runaway in*
by John R. Neill, 1995. Scr
and Popla ride a fleeing cl
to escape the cloud-push

This page: cover for the sec
edition of *The Third Book o*
by L. Frank Baum, 1989 (l
illustration of Ozma, 2
(below); illustration for the s
"Trot of Oz" by Glenn Inge
and Eric Shanower f
Oz-story 6, 2000 (bottom of
page and bottom of fa
page). Trot and Cap'n Bill fir
reach the public dom

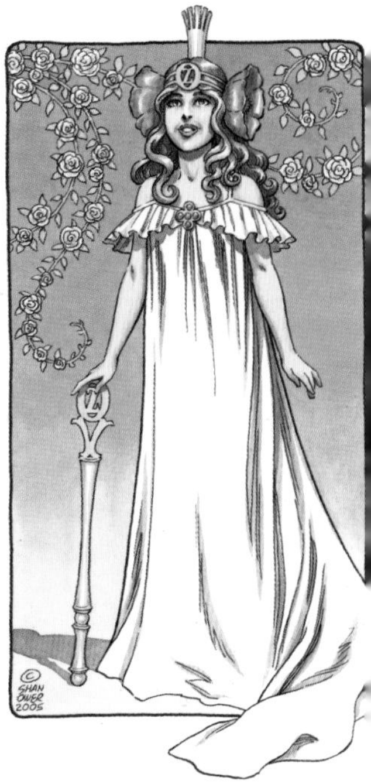
©
SHAN
OWER
2005

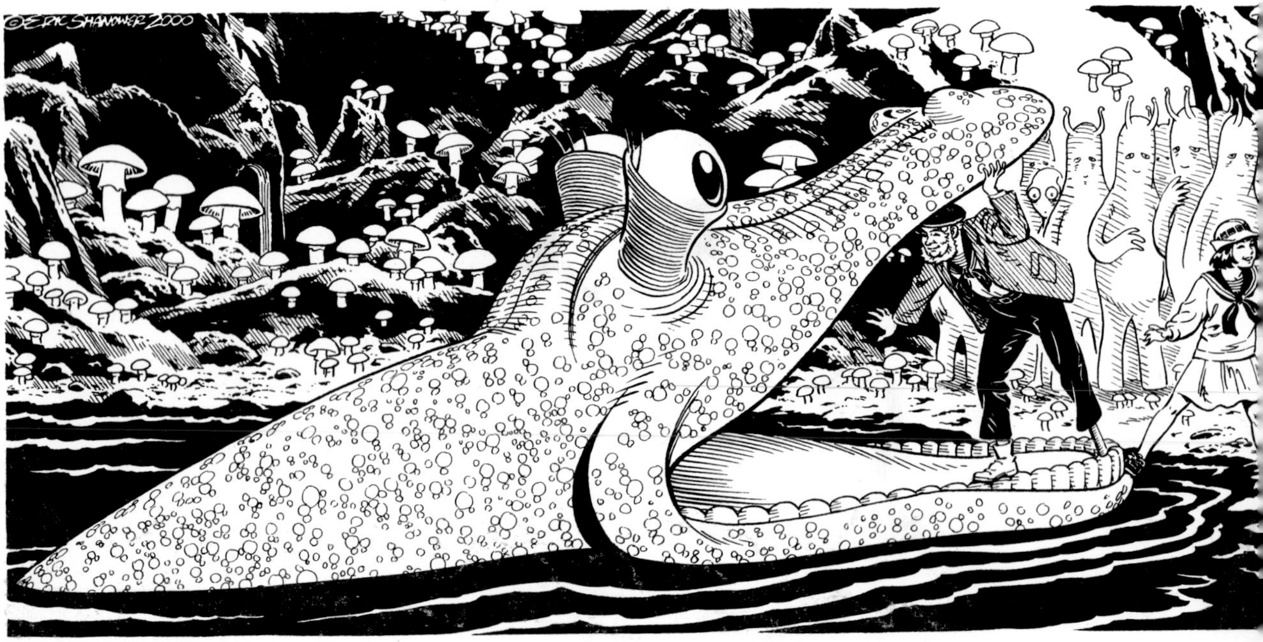
©ERIC SHANOWER 2000

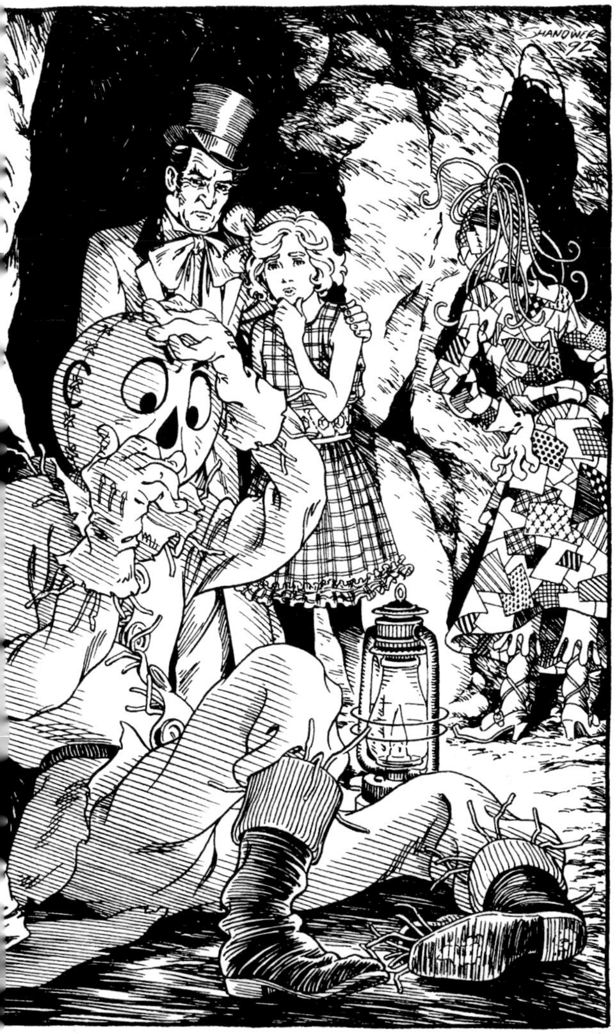
SHANOWER '92

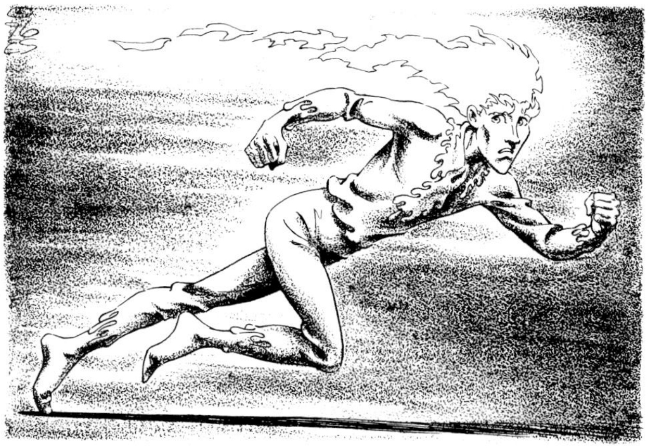

This page: illustration for the book *Invisible Inzi of Oz* by Virginia and Robert Wauchope, 1992 (left); illustration for the story "Dorothy and the Mushroom Queen" from the book *The Salt Sorcerer of Oz and Other Stories* by Eric Shanower, 1996 (above). The further adventures of Flicker.

Following two pages: illustration for the book *Paradox in Oz* by Edward Einhorn, 1999. Ozma plunges through the Ozziverse, past countless alternate visions of Oz.

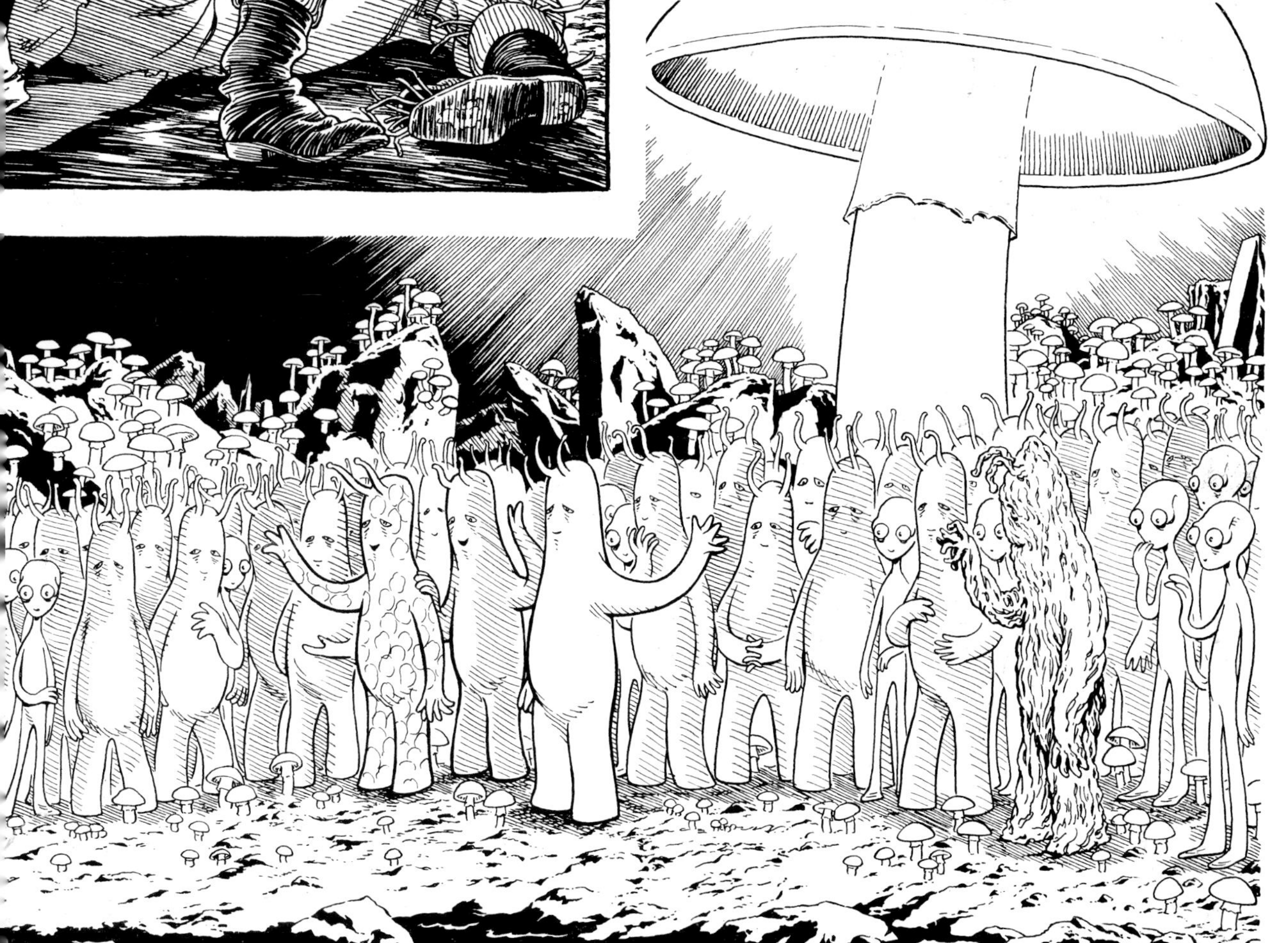

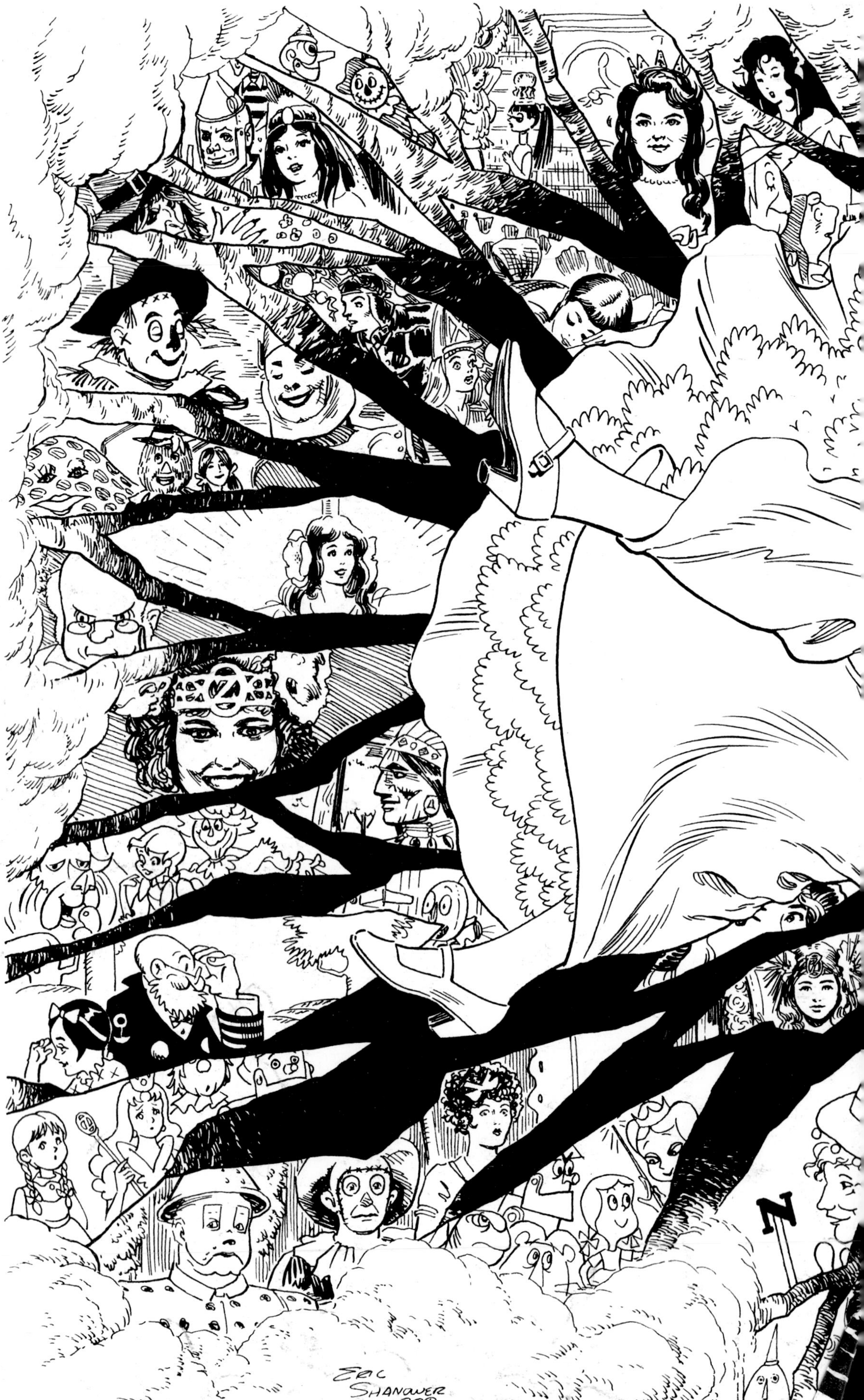
N
ERIC
SHANOWER
1999

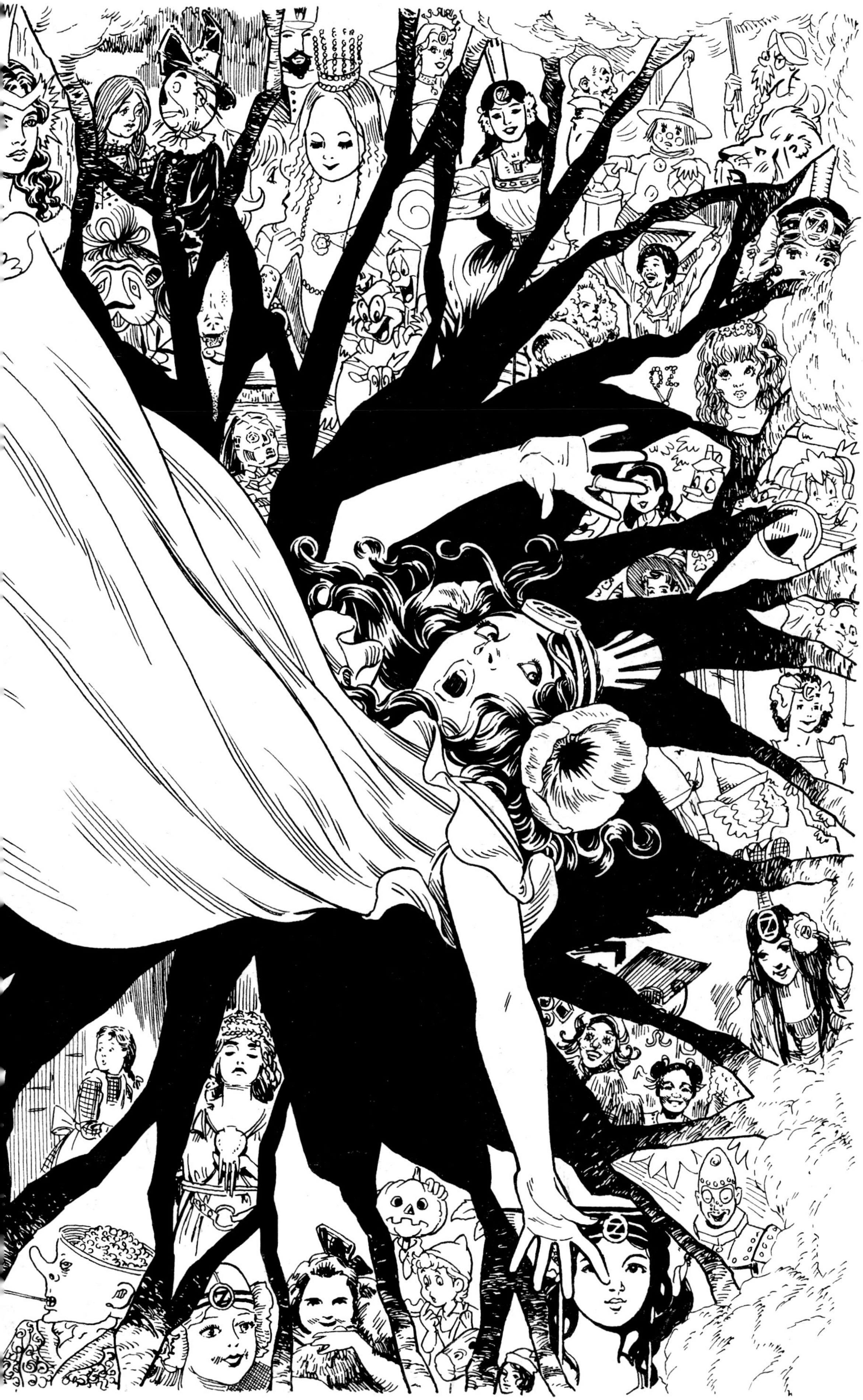

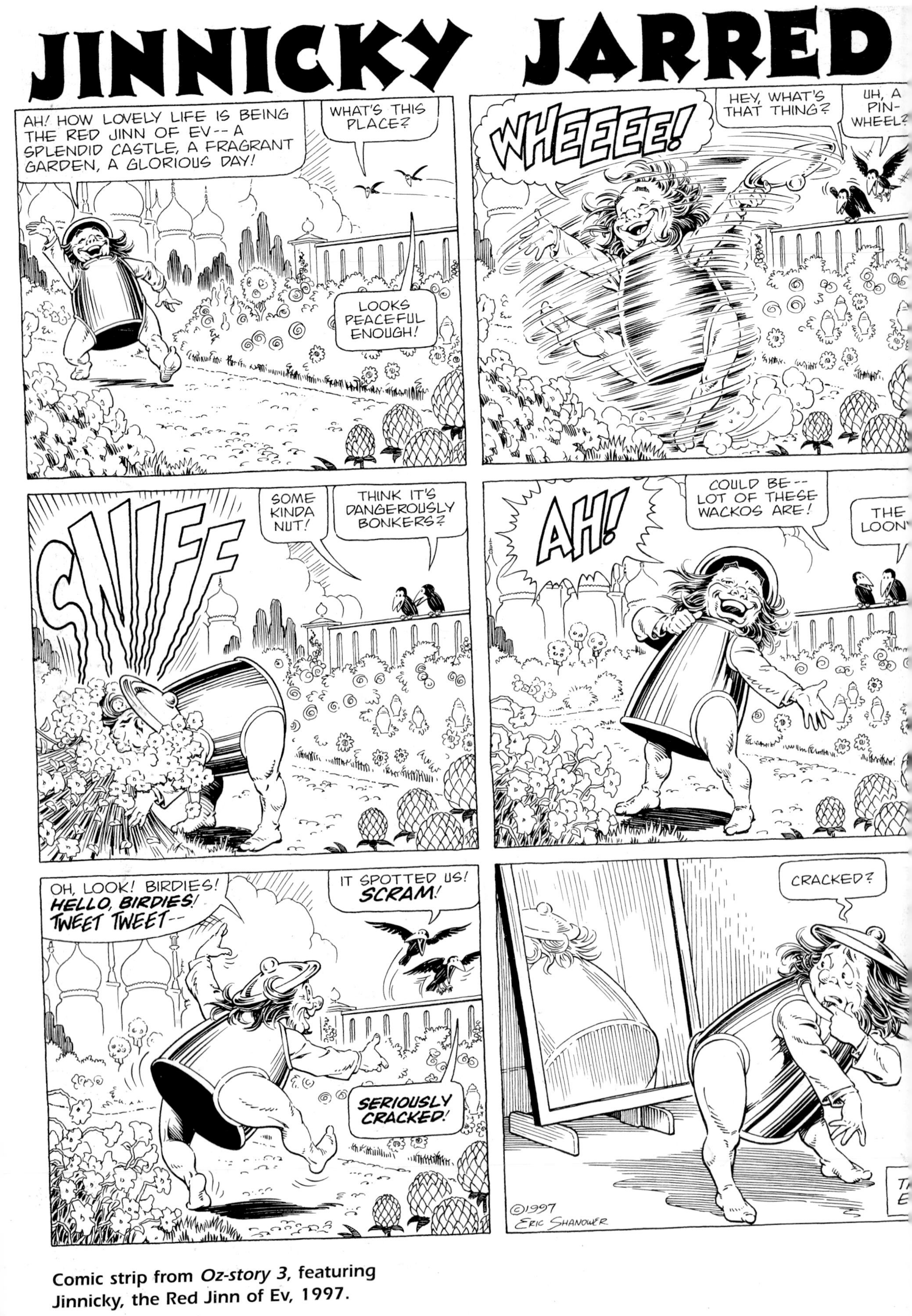
JINNICKY JARRED
AH! HOW LOVELY LIFE IS BEING THE RED JINN OF EV-- A SPLENDID CASTLE, A FRAGRANT GARDEN, A GLORIOUS DAY!
WHAT'S THIS PLACE?
LOOKS PEACEFUL ENOUGH!
WHEEEEE!
HEY, WHAT'S THAT THING?
UH, A PIN-WHEEL?
SNIFF
SOME KINDA NUT!
THINK IT'S DANGEROUSLY BONKERS?
AH!
COULD BE-- LOT OF THESE WACKOS ARE!
OH, LOOK! BIRDIES! HELLO, BIRDIES! TWEET TWEET--
IT SPOTTED US! SCRAM!
SERIOUSLY CRACKED!
CRACKED?
©1997 ERIC SHANOWER

Comic strip from *Oz-story 3*, featuring Jinnicky, the Red Jinn of Ev, 1997.

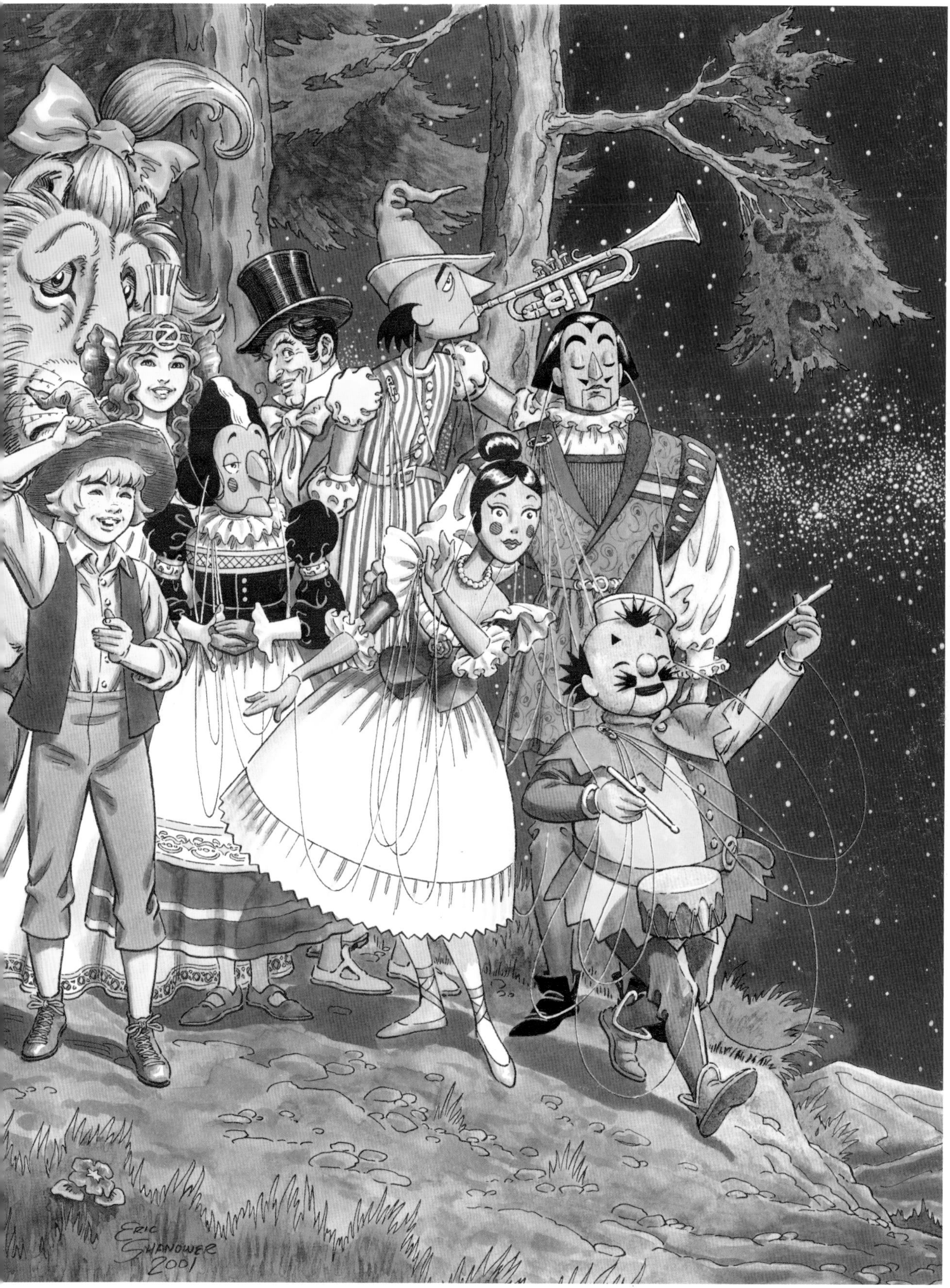
ERIC SHANOWER 2001

Rear dust-jacket panel for the book *The Rundelstone of Oz* by Eloise McGraw, 2001. Oz characters old and new.

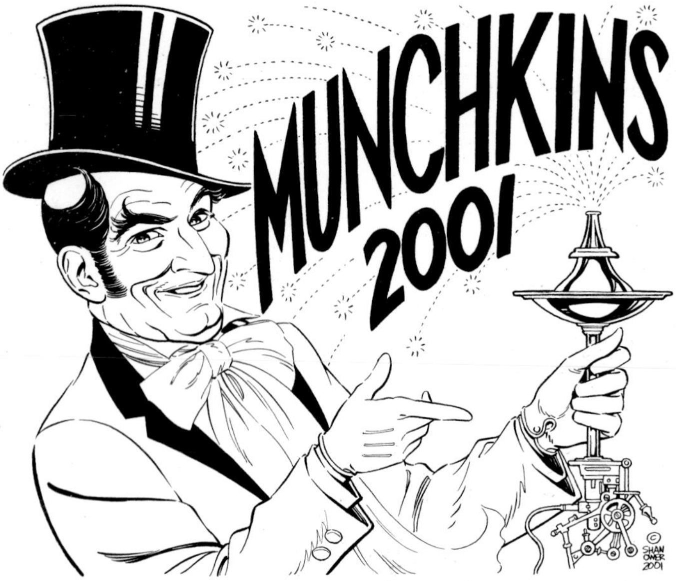
MUNCHKINS
2001

This page: T-shirt illustration for the an
Munchkin Convention of The Internati
Wizard of Oz Club, 2001 (

Bottom of this page and top of facing p
illustration for the book *The Living Hou*
Oz by Edward Einhorn, 2004, featu
several characters from the Oz gra
novels, including Flicker, Va
and Ab

Bottom of facing page: T-shirt illustratic
characters from the book *The Land of C*
L. Frank Baum for the annual W
Convention of The International Wizard c
Club, 2004 (left); illustration for Fred Me
annual Christmas card, 2002 (right). Wh
Betsy, Dorothy, and Trot each had a
book of Oz adventu

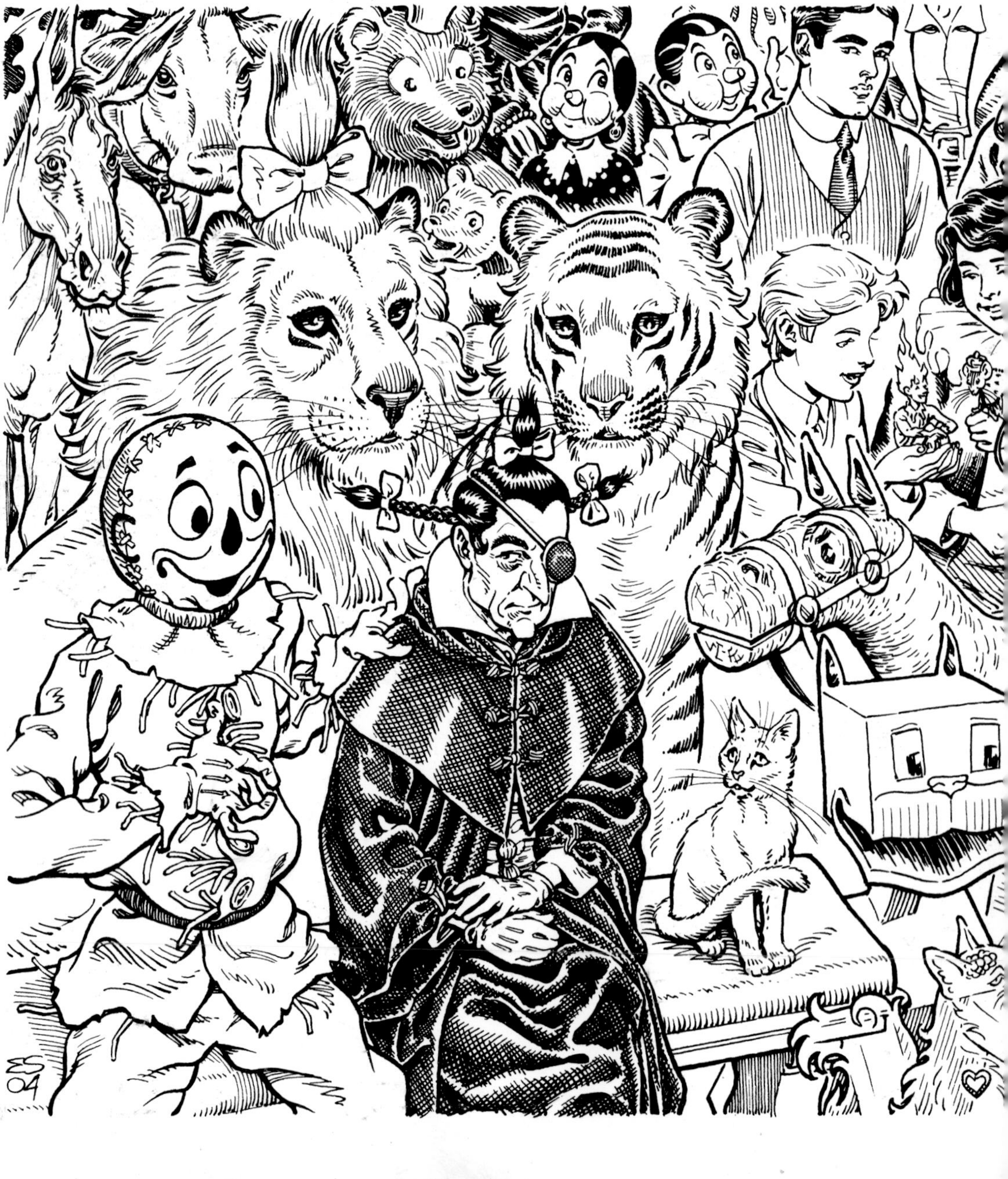

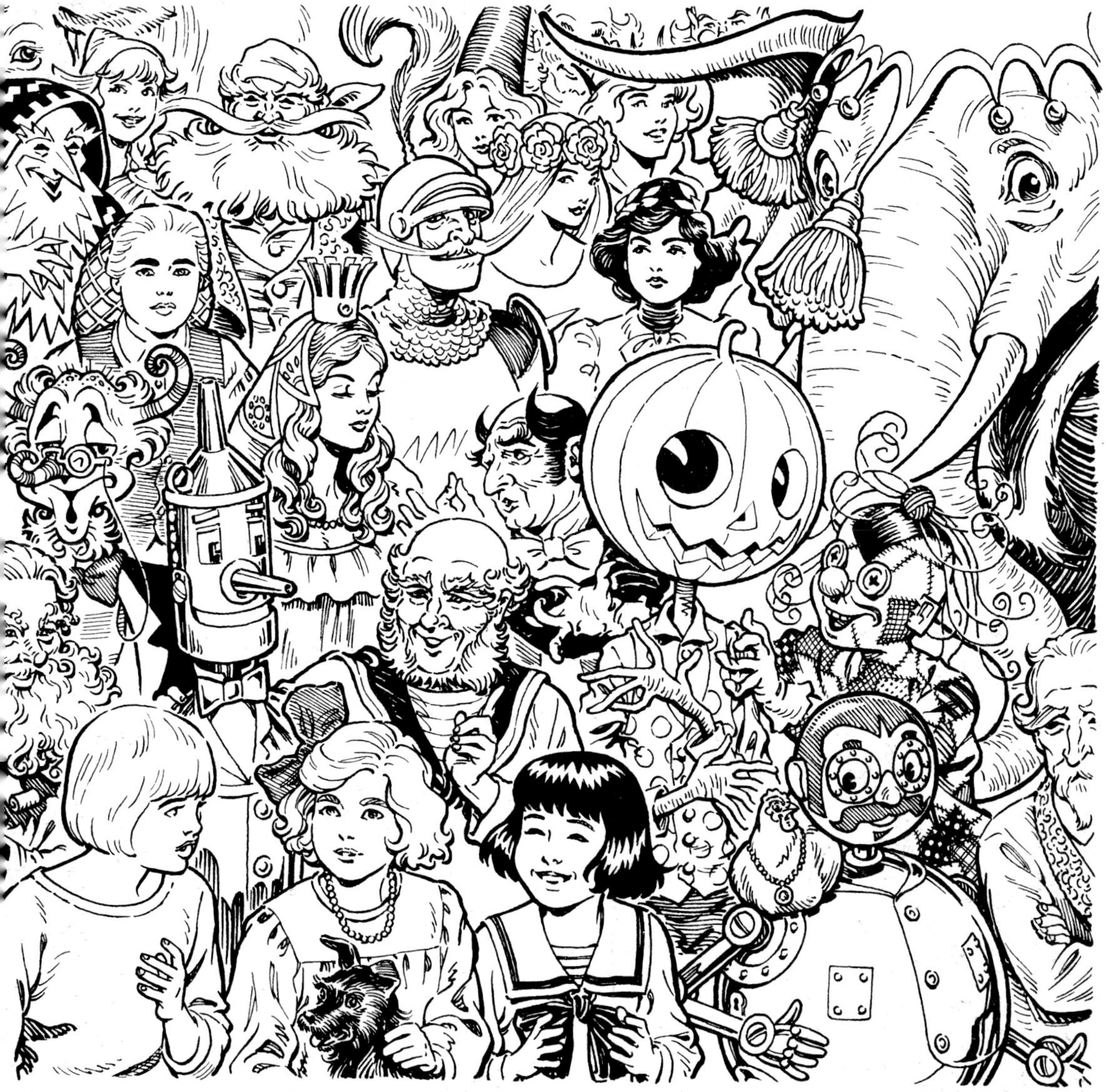

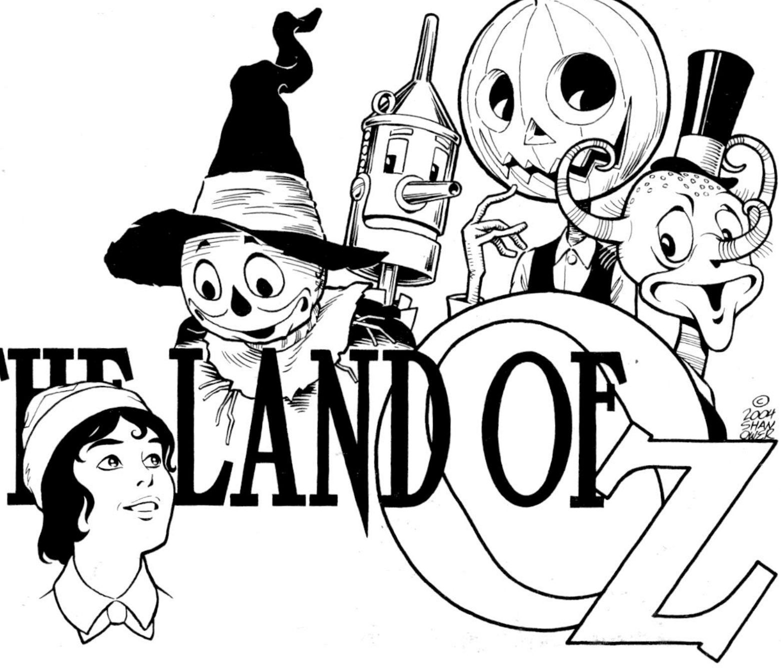
THE LAND OF OZ
© 2004 SHANOWER

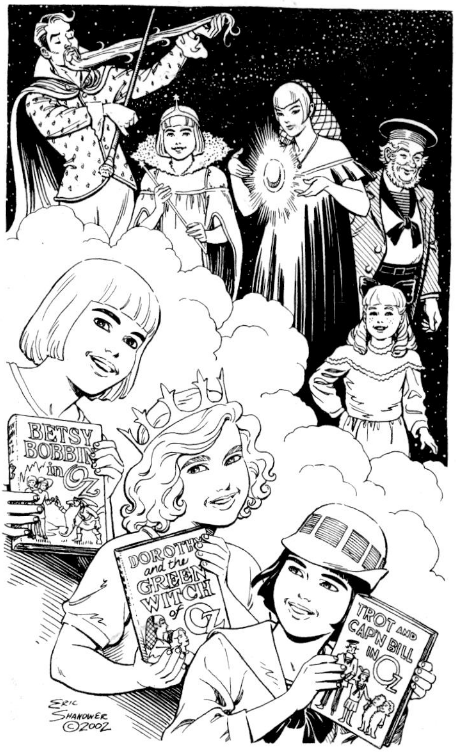
BETSY BOBBIN in OZ
DOROTHY and the GREEN WITCH of OZ
TROT AND CAP'N BILL IN OZ
ERIC SHANOWER ©2002

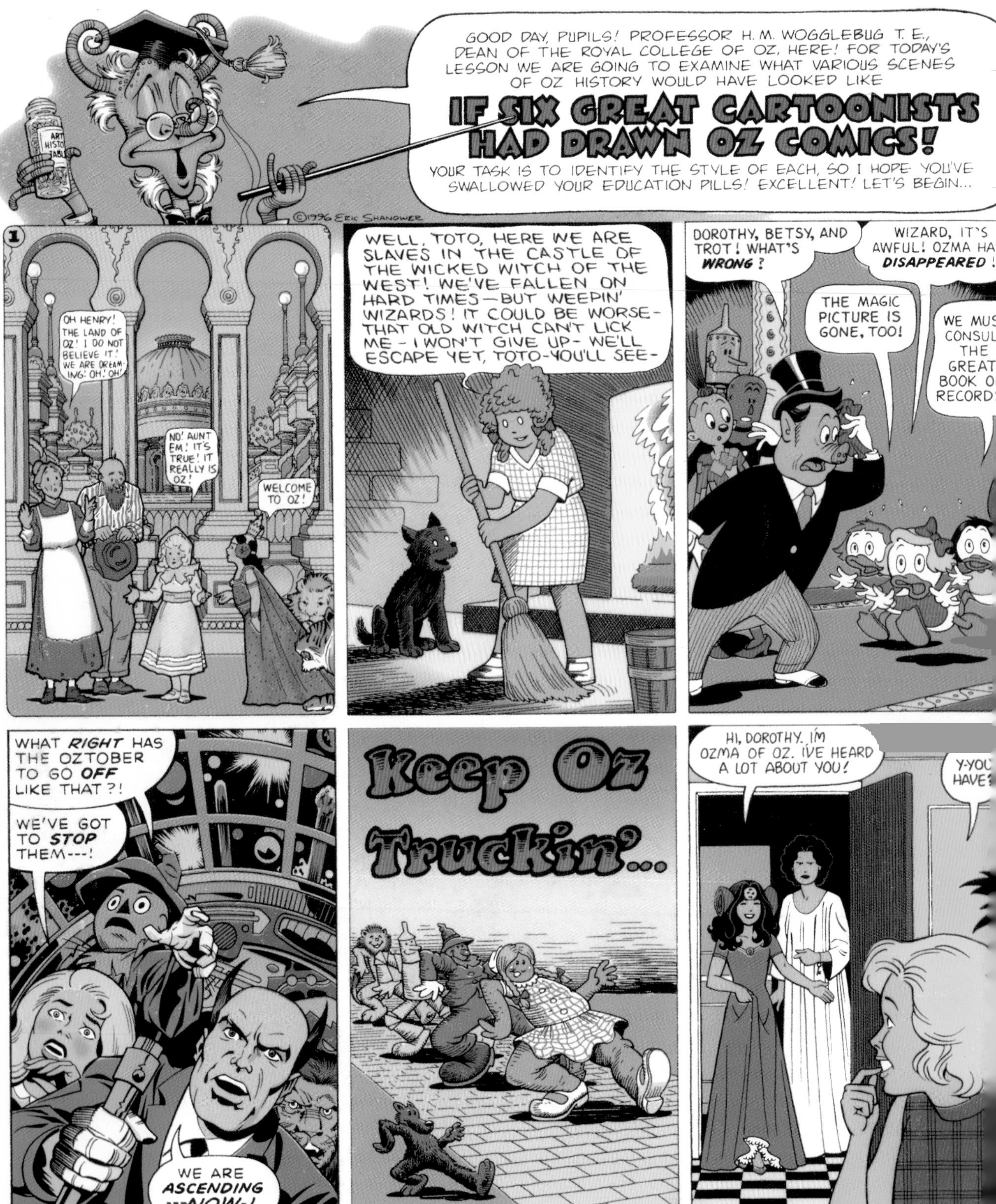
GOOD DAY, PUPILS! PROFESSOR H. M. WOGGLEBUG T. E., DEAN OF THE ROYAL COLLEGE OF OZ, HERE! FOR TODAY'S LESSON WE ARE GOING TO EXAMINE WHAT VARIOUS SCENES OF OZ HISTORY WOULD HAVE LOOKED LIKE
IF SIX GREAT CARTOONISTS HAD DRAWN OZ COMICS!
YOUR TASK IS TO IDENTIFY THE STYLE OF EACH, SO I HOPE YOU'VE SWALLOWED YOUR EDUCATION PILLS! EXCELLENT! LET'S BEGIN...
©1996 ERIC SHANOWER
1
OH HENRY! THE LAND OF OZ! I DO NOT BELIEVE IT! WE ARE DREAMING! OH! OH!
NO! AUNT EM! IT'S TRUE! IT REALLY IS OZ!
WELCOME TO OZ!
WELL, TOTO, HERE WE ARE SLAVES IN THE CASTLE OF THE WICKED WITCH OF THE WEST! WE'VE FALLEN ON HARD TIMES—BUT WEEPIN' WIZARDS! IT COULD BE WORSE-THAT OLD WITCH CAN'T LICK ME - I WON'T GIVE UP- WE'LL ESCAPE YET, TOTO-YOU'LL SEE-
DOROTHY, BETSY, AND TROT! WHAT'S WRONG?
WIZARD, IT'S AWFUL! OZMA HA DISAPPEARED!
THE MAGIC PICTURE IS GONE, TOO!
WE MUS CONSUL THE GREAT BOOK O RECORD
WHAT RIGHT HAS THE OZTOBER TO GO OFF LIKE THAT?!
WE'VE GOT TO STOP THEM---!
WE ARE ASCENDING ---NOW-!
Keep Oz Truckin'...
HI, DOROTHY. I'M OZMA OF OZ. I'VE HEARD A LOT ABOUT YOU!
Y-YOU HAVE?

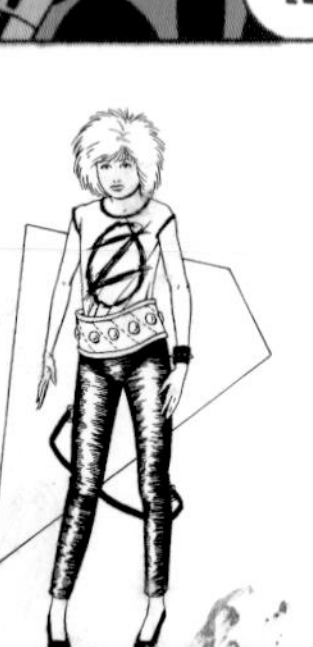

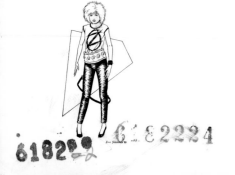

Contest in the form of a comics page originally printed on back cover of *Oz-story 2,* 1996 (above). The contest is over. The answers are: Winsor McCay, Harold Gray, Carl B. Jack Kirby, Robert Crumb, and Jaime Hernan
Punk Dorothy, 1983 (ri